CW01649901

The Fateful Years

Douglas Smith

New Millennium
292 Kennington Road, London SE11 4LD

By the same author:

The Winds of Destiny New Millennium 1997

The Fateful Years

by

Douglas Smith

British Library Cataloguing in Publication Data.
A catalogue record for this book is obtainable
from the British Library.

Printed and bound by Watkiss Studios Ltd.
Biggleswade, Beds.
Issued by New Millennium*

ISBN 1 85845 230 9
*An imprint of The Professional Authors' & Publishers' Association

Dedication

To the memory of my wife, Alice, whose encouragement and help was a great inspiration in the writing of this book.

Introductory Note

The Fateful Years (Book 2) is a sequel to *The Winds of Destiny* (Book 1) published in 1997.

A few incidents in Book 2 relate to past events in Book 1. These are marked with an asterisk in the text and have a related footnote.

Main Characters

Homefield Hall (Suffolk)

* Sir Roger Douglass – Lady Anne Douglas
(1762-1824) (1765-1824)

Andrew
(1790-)

Sebastian (Seb) – Maisie (Payne)
(1792-1815) (1794-)

Jonathan (Jon)
(1816-)
(Andrew's child)

Alison – Josh (Kennard)
(1793-) (1789)

Jane
(1815-)

Emily
(1820)
Died at birth

William
(1824-)

Gail
(1829-)

* Lady Amelia Wyngate – Lord Wyngate
(1753-1823) (1750-1790)
(Sir Roger's sister)

Staff

Gamekeeper: Bailey (James). Butler: Bates (John). Blacksmith: Holland (Joe). Housekeeper: Howard (Mrs). Coachman: Sharpe (Ben), after his retirement, Lambert (Joe). Doctor: Wallace, after his retirement, Scott (Len).

Homefield Rectory

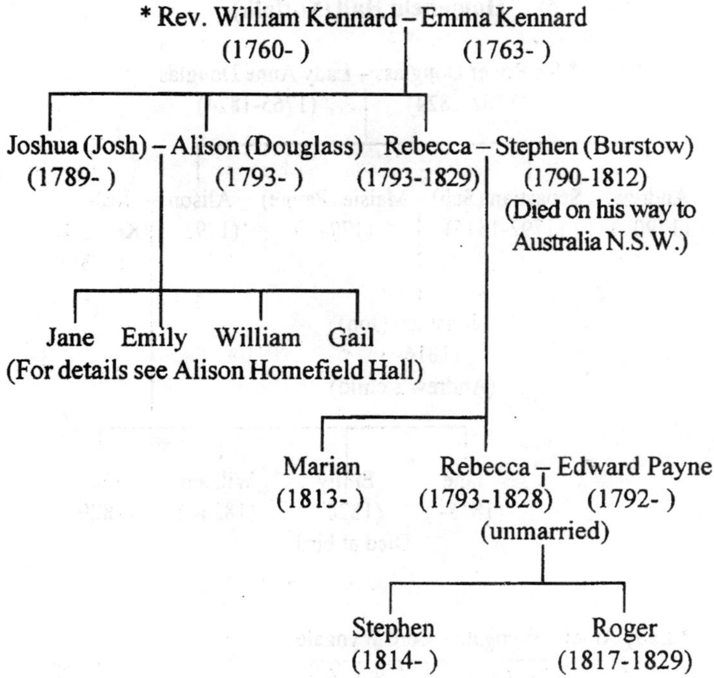

* Edgar Kennedy (William Kennard's brother)
(1755-1810)

Staff

Butler: Barton (Godfrey). Housekeeper: Foster (Elizabeth).
Housemain: Dalton (Freda). Upper maid: Green (May).

Foxleigh Hall

Colonel Grenville Markham – Dora Markham née Douglass
(1758-1828) (1760-1814)

Julie
(1793-1830)

George
(1812-)
(Edward Payne's child)

Staff

Butler: Jameson (Walter). Housekeeper: Thorpe (Helen). Coachman: Jenkins (Harold). Physician: Dr. Bamford, retired 1823, then Dr. Fenton. Rector: Parson Jameson and his sister: Agnes. After Parson Jameson: Darvell (Robin). Gamekeeper: Watson (James).

Gt. Yarmouth. Fisherman's Cottage

John (Tiger) Payne – Marian née Ambrose
(1763-1808) (1769-1805)

Edward – Rebecca Burton née Kennedy
(1792-) For details see Rebecca (Homefield Rectory)

Maisie – Sebastian (Douglass)
(1794-) (1792-1815)

Jonathan (Jon)
(1816-)
(Andrews child)

Staff

Blacksmith: Payne (Ben) (John Payne's brother). Ben's wife: Sara (1768-1809). Ben's second wife: Nelly née Cook.

Peterson Family. Portsmouth

Frank Peterson:	Ships chandler (1769-1810)
Joan Peterson:	Frank's wife (1772-1831)
Emma Peterson:	Daughter (1796-)
James (Jim) Peterson:	Son (1798-)

Prologue

'Ahoy there below!' The lookout's warning shout suddenly disturbed the early morning calm. Surprised glances became focused on the crow's nest. 'Small boat ahead!' Pointing a few degrees to starboard, the seaman indicated his sighting that was barely visible from the ship's deck.

'Check on the situation, Mr. Warner.' Captain Wallace turned to a young officer standing beside him.

'Aye aye, sir' Telescope in one hand, he clambered part way up the shrouds to focus on a small boat drifting almost ahead of them. 'Looks like a small dinghy, sir', he called down his observation.

'Any one in the boat?'

'No... I don't think so, sir.' There was a touch of uncertainty in his voice. Again, he trained his telescope on the small boat.

'Sir! I believe... there are people in the...'

'Well, make sure, dammit. That's why I sent you aloft.'

'Yes, sir.' Hurt by the captain's reprimand, the young officer concentrated his gaze for a few moments on the boat and its occupants.

'There appears to be... three bodies, sir.' James Warner hesitated, not wanting to bring further wrath upon his head.

'Bodies?'

'Aye, captain. There's no movement.' Again, he turned his telescope towards the small craft that was now clearly visible. He wanted one more look before scrambling down to the deck.

'Dear, God!' he gasped. 'A woman and...' Excitedly he turned towards the captain. 'There's movement. Someone feebly raised a hand and... one of the occupants is a woman.'

'Prepare to take in sail, boson. Make ready the starboard dinghy for bringing the survivors on board.' There was a burst of activity as the crew prepared to bring the transport, Cynthia to a stop and launch the dinghy.

'What is causing so much hustle, Robert?' The young woman had just emerged on the upper deck to stand beside her husband.

'A boat, my dear,' he pointed ahead, thoughtfully. 'containing it would seem survivors from some shipping disaster. They appear to be in a very weak condition... close to death.'

'Oh, Robert. Will your services be required...?'

'Yes, Beth,' He anticipated her anxious enquiry. 'As a surgeon it is my duty to assist those poor souls.'

'No need to worry, my love...' he gave her a reassuring smile, '... I shall not be away for long.' Before hurrying to join the dinghy's crew, he placed an affectionate kiss upon her lips.

Beth watched apprehensively as the Cynthia's small boat pulled alongside the survivor's stained and battered one. Robert was the first to cross over. With trepidation, she noticed her husband bend over to comfort and examine the two lying close together.

After a few minutes, Elizabeth noticed her husband and three of the seamen gently carry one of the survivors across to the waiting dingy. She became deeply concerned on realising that the person was a young woman. Her companion tried to follow but staggered and almost collapsed. Carefully the seamen helped him across. Eagerly he tried to reach the woman's side, only to fall prostrate as faintness overcame him. There was no movement from the third survivor, but after examining him, Beth noticed her husband indicate that he also should be taken back to the transport. It seemed an age to her as she waited for the dinghy to be rowed back alongside.

Gently, willing hands helped in the delicate operation of getting the three survivors safely on board the Cynthia. Once on the ship, they were soon being cared for.

'Beth, I shall need your help. I'm concerned for the young woman... She will need careful nursing. Just before she was overcome with faintness, she informed me that she is nearly seven months pregnant.'

'Pregnant!' Beth shot her husband a dismayed glance. 'Poor woman... is there... any chance?'

'I sincerely believe so. She will need skilled and careful nursing though.' He hesitated a moment as he watched his wife. 'I was hoping that you would care for her.'

'Me? But I'm not a nurse, Robert.' He noticed the colour drain from his wife's face. 'I... don't know if I could...' Seeing the expectant look on her husband's face, Beth offered her services. 'I shall be glad to give what help is required, Robert. I shall need your guidance. Now you must introduce me to your patient.'

'In here, Beth.' She followed her husband into the cabin that had been kindly evacuated by its previous occupants. She glanced over his shoulder, anxious to see what condition the expectant mother was in. 'It... it... can't possibly be!' Robert turned at his wife's startled words. Her face registered shocked disbelief as she stared at the exhausted young women's sunburnt face on the pillow.

'What troubles you so, Beth?' He followed her uncertain gaze, noticing the long fair hair, matted and tangled around the blotched and salt crusted features of the female survivor. Despite her bedraggled appearance and near comatose state, there was an aura of courtliness about the young woman.

'I believe,... no... I'm certain that I know this young woman.' For a few moments Elizabeth tried to recall where they had met. 'Yes... I remember. Newland's Academy. We were there together. I... once did her an... injustice.'

'Are you sure, Beth?' Robert looked at Beth, wondering what trouble could have been perpetrated by his lovely and pleasant natured wife.

'Yes. I'm sure her name is... Rebecca.' She called the name softly. There was a momentary response as the survivor's eyes flickered open. Beth noticed that they were the same dark brown eyes that had once stared so dispassionately into hers in silent condemnation. A moan of anguish escaped the young woman's lips as she struggled to orientate her thoughts.

Beth rushed to the bunk, eager to hold Rebecca in her caring arms. 'I shall help her undress, Robert. Prepare her for...' A commotion outside the cabin door caused her to hesitate.

'How are the survivors, Mr. Morrison?' Captain Wallace peered into the cabin. He glanced anxiously towards Beth who was comforting her charge in a gently embrace.

'Very ill, captain. Yes...' he anticipated the captain's question, '... I shall concentrate on saving this young woman and her baby.' His voice sounded uncertain as his gaze lingered on the woman being comforted by his wife. 'As regards the man...' he shook his head sadly, '... he is very weak, quite poorly.'

'Her husband,' the Captain stepping into the cabin. 'I checked his documents. They were found on his person along with their considerable savings.' He paused for their reactions before continuing.

'Who are they, captain?' Beth was eager to see if her supposition was correct.

'According to their official papers, they are Stephen Edward and Rebecca Burstow,' He hesitated as he noticed the look of cognisance that passed between his listeners. 'They... were on passage to New South Wales. It would appear that the Badger on which they were taking passage went down in a storm.'

'Is it known why they were sailing to the new colony, captain?'

'Settlers, ma'am! Their documents indicate that they own two farms near Sydney. A considerable screage.'

'What wonderful news!' Elizabeth could not contain her excitement. 'I know Rebecca, captain.' She inclined her head towards the young woman lying in her arms. 'We were at school together. I'm hoping...' She gave her husband a pleading look, '... to renew acquaintance should... when her situation improves. My wish is that Rebecca has forgiven my impetuous actions at Newlands. My indiscretion caused her great distress,' Elisabeth's face saddened as she recalled the incident that had shattered the authoritarian routine of the Academy.*

'I'm sure your nursing will compensate for any school girl's misdemeanours, Beth and ensure an affectionate responses from, er... Rebecca.'

'Oh, I do hope so, Robert.' Already she was removing her patient's dress. 'She was such a pleasant girl.'

'Now we must leave you, my dear. I to see how the husband is and the captain to arrange for the dead seaman's burial. Unfortunately, we do not know his name, perhaps we never shall.'

*Book I The Winds of Destiny

Part One (1813-1819)
The Settlers

Chapter One

'So you are leaving for Newacres in a couple of days Edward?' Robert Morrison glanced anxiously at the young man beside him. He was still concerned about his companion's health. Although it was nearly two months since he had found Edward and Rebecca near to death in an open dinghy. He still felt responsible for their well-being.

'Yes I feel well enough to visit the farm, but I appreciate your concern, Robert. After all, had it not been for your medical skill, it is doubtful whether Rebecca or myself, would be here today. We certainly owe you our lives.' He gave the young doctor a look of gratitude as they strolled towards the harbour.

'My er ... wife and I ...' Edward was finding it difficult in taking on the role of Rebecca's husband, but it was necessary for him to continue the masquerade, '*... are deeply indebted to you and Elizabeth for your wonderful hospitality.'

'You will not be taking Rebecca and your baby daughter with you for the time being? I would suggest that ... you ...' Robert hesitated, to follow Edward's gaze across Sydney Cove to where a frigate having waited for a change of wind off Port Jackson was now sailing towards the harbour.

'No I shall take your advice Robert. Rebecca and Marian will follow as soon as I have made arrangements for their welfare at Newacres.' He placed a friendly arm across his companion's shoulders. 'I realise your concern for the three of us is as our doctor ...'

'And friend!' Robert's smile was cordial as he turned to face Edward. 'It's been wonderful having you and Becky as our guests ... not forgetting the baby of course. My relief was considerable when I delivered your wife of a healthy daughter ... especially after what she had suffered before being rescued. Thankfully mother and baby ... and indeed yourself, are now recovered and enjoying excellent health.

'Elizabeth was overjoyed when she recognised your wife. They were at school together. An unpleasant incident caused

* In Book I The Winds of Destiny

some agitation between them during that period.'* A frown momentarily creased his brow as he waited to see if Edward was able to elucidate the matter. Edward remained silent indicating with a shake of his head that he was unaware of any untoward happening. Robert, aware that his companion had no idea of what had transpired, referred to the recent conversation with his wife regarding their incongruous actions at school. 'Elizabeth did promise to enlighten me but Rebecca suggested to her that the incident should be forgotten. Your wife ...' he paused noticing Edward's interest in the frigate now approaching its anchorage, '... was kind enough to forget their altercation, insisting that it was nothing more than a schoolgirl's impulsive prank that got ... out of hand.'

'In that case Robert, I suggest we respect Becky's wishes and forget the incident.' He waited for the young doctor's nod of agreement. 'What pleases me greatly, is that Elizabeth and my er ... wife, are now such good friends. Being new arrivals to the colony, they will appreciate each others companionship amidst strange surroundings.'

'Yes I agree. Your decision to leave Becky behind until you have Newacres organised is a prudent one. She will be safe with us while you are away. We had not expected you to leave quite so soon, but I fully understand your urgency. Remember though ...' he gave Edward and anxious look, '... you are still not fully fit!'

Edward had another more impending reason for wanting to depart for Newacres as soon as possible. He had fully concurred with Robert's medical advice that Rebecca must be nursed by Elizabeth during the final weeks of her pregnancy. It had given him the excuse to sleep apart from Becky as their hosts, thinking they were man and wife would have expected them to share the same bedroom. Becky's pregnancy and the grievous state of their health following their rescue, had been a natural justification for them being apart initially.

Since Marian's birth the situation had changed. Over the past two weeks there had been no plausible reason for them to sleep apart. To have done otherwise would have aroused their new

*Book I The Winds of Destiny

friend's suspicions as to their unnatural behaviour. Edward was recalling the situation as he watched the frigate prepared to drop anchor.

Rebecca had shared in their embarrassing situation. Had they been out on the farm, they could have used separate sleeping quarters but living temporarily with their friends they had naturally been expected to share the same bed. Secretly they had solved the embarrassing problem by Rebecca and the baby sleeping in the bed, while Edward had slept fitfully on the floor.

'We shall miss you and Becky, when you are out at Newacres,' Robert's words startled Edward from his mediation. He became alert as his friend continued his discourse. 'If you will permit a word of warning ...' Robert paused to give his companion an astute look, '... you should take things easy to start with. Remember both yourself and Becky were near to death when rescued.'

'Have no fear on that score dear friend. I shall bear your concern in mind.' Edward bestowed a benign look on a serious faced Robert before conveying his undying gratitude. 'Becky and I will forever be indebted to Elizabeth and yourself for the care and friendship you have extended to us. We shall look forward to returning that hospitality when we have settled in at Newacres.'

'Let us hope it will be soon. I'm longing to visit this farm of yours.' For a few minutes the two friends watched in silence as the frigate's crew prepared to wear ship. Shouted orders drifted over the cove, bringing immediate action from the man out on the yards. Nostalgic moments for Edward. There was something about the ship that deepened his frown of concentration.

'Tops' sheets!' As the sails were furled the ship was fast losing way. 'Helm a'lee!' While the quarter-master was pulling on the wheel to swing the frigate's bows into the wind, a startled gasp escaped Edward's lips. Suddenly as the boat glided silently towards her anchorage, he had noticed the name. Edward stared in disbelief as the anchor splashed into the clear water. It was the Saracen, the frigate on which he had served as a press-gang victim. Four years previously he had deserted the ship in Portsmouth harbour.*

* In Book I The Winds of Destiny

'What is it Edward? You look surprised.' Robert was watching the conflicting emotions on his companion's face as the frigate came to anchor.

'Nothing!' he shook his head vigorously. 'Nothing. I er, thought for a moment that I recognised the frigate.' Edward fighting to suppress his alarm, nodded towards the naval ship. It's appearance induced a feeling of uncertainty. A moment of foreboding. Anxious to be away from its vision, he turned and started to walk back towards the town. 'A mistaken observation,' he informed Robert as they retraced their steps.

Edward's reaction on recognising the frigate, had however troubled his friend. Robert was sure that the startled response had connotations not covered by Edward's explanation. Perhaps the frigate's appearance had induced a shocked reminder of his recent ordeal in the dinghy. Believing that this was the explanation for his friend's disquieting behaviour, Robert refrained from further discourse on the activities in the harbour. He spoke of Newacres in an attempt to divert Edward's thoughts.

'When do you expect Becky and the baby to join you on the farm?' Edward was barely aware of his friend's question. He had been worriedly considering the possibility of being recognised by a member of the Saracen's crew who had served with him.

Since his rescue, Edward had retained his full beard. With its trimmed and groomed appearance, he was hopeful that he would not be recognised as the clean shaven youth who had once sailed on the ship. Nevertheless, he would have to remain vigilant Identification would be catastrophic for him as a convict and naval deserter. He suddenly became aware that Robert was observing him very intently.

'I'm sorry, Robert! My thoughts were momentarily distracted.'

'I was speaking of your move to Newacres. Enquiring when you expected your family to join you there.'

'Until I have seen what accommodation is suitable, their arrival must remain uncertain. I intend to use the best of the farm houses as our permanent home. When I have the buildings in reasonable condition I shall then come for Becky and her, er ... Marian.'

'Have you received any news from the farm? From the young

man you said remained behind to continue running the farm after his parents had returned to England?'

'Henry ... you mean. Their son!' They were just crossing the bridge over the Tank Stream before turning into Bridge Street. 'Yes. He paid me a visit last weekend to give me a full report on the situation. Understandably, he is anxious for me to take up residence on the farm as soon as possible. It would appear that he is experiencing some trouble from an adjacent farmer.'

'What of the other farm? The one willed to Becky by her uncle.'

'All is well it would appear, but the family who have been caretakers on the farm are very anxious to be away. Their passage has been provisionally reserved on the Sentinel. Not a fast ship, but it should be sailing the week after next.

Because of their mother's poor health, the family are urgently desirous of sailing without delay. They have kindly agreed to carry out mail and ensure it is safely delivered to our families when they reach England.

'A long journey and one that I don't envy them!' Robert spoke as he opened the door to his house and waited for his friend to enter.

It was dusk on the following day as Edward walked from Government House. He had just received final authorisation and confirmation to take over the two farms and amalgamate them.

'Good luck ... to your enterprise, Burstow.' Edward hesitated as Stephen's name was used. Something he would have to get used to. 'It is to be hoped that your charming wife will soon be well enough to join you.' Colonel Lachlan Macquarie's austere features as he spoke were momentarily softened by a smile.

'Thank you, Governor!' Edwards was about to make his departure when Governor Macquarie referred to the Badger's loss.*

'Your statement ...' he indicated some documents lying on his desk, '... validates that there were no other survivors other than those in the boat with you.' The Governor's hair had a red tinge in the candlelight as he sadly shook his head.

'That is so. Apart from the seaman who died immediately after being rescued, there were three others who perished while

* In Book I The Winds of Destiny

in the dinghy. An officer, another seaman and one other … a … convict.'

'You are unable to name those that died?'

'Only the officer.' He pointed to Roger's name as confirmation. As the Governor checked the young officer's name, Edward wondered why he was so interested.

'Ah well!' he sighed. 'Most unfortunate. We must now assume, that apart from Mrs. Burstow and yourself, everyone else on the Badger perished.'

'That would appear to be so, Governor.'

'Thank you. It must have been a very distressing experience for you and Mrs. Burstow.' With a sympathetic gesture he accompanied Edward to the door.

As he walked away from Government House, Edward reflected on the conversation he had just shared with Governor Macquarie. Had it any connection with the Saracen's arrival, he wondered. He was never to know just how much the frigate's arrival did affect himself. Sailing direct from England, it had carried official mail for the Governor. Among his correspondence had been Edward's pardon. Assuming that the convict Edward Payne was one of those lost when the Badger went down, Governor Macquarie had filed the documents in Government House where they were to remain forgotten until several years later.

Unaware of his pardon, Edward walked back through the evening crowds. He was in a pensive mood as he reached a street junction and failed to notice the two naval officers approaching. Having brushed against one of the men, he turned to apologise only to find that they were officers from the Saracen. They accepted his expressions of regret good naturedly, but he realised that one of the men was observing him closely.

'Excuse me, Sir,' the officer gave him an uncertain look. 'I have a feeling that we at sometime in the past, have been acquainted.' Edward's heart skipped a beat as he noticed the officer's frown of concentration. As he returned the enquirer's gaze he recognised the young officer who had been in charge of the captain's barge on the occasion of his desertion at Portsmouth.

'Not unless you have er … farming connections in East Anglia, sir. That was my home before I came out to settle in the new colony.'

'In that case the mistake is mine. I'm sorry to have detained you.' Edward walked away, relieved but deeply worried. There had been something about the young officer's look that warned him that further enquiries might arise about his past.

Next morning as dawn was spreading its pale light over the town, Edward rode his horse in a gently canter along George Street. He was anxious to be away from Sydney and the possibility of being recognised again. Having bid Rebecca and his hosts a temporary farewell, he now tried to concentrate his thoughts on what his plans should be when he reached Newacres.

Once clear of the town he settled his horse into a steady trot. Early sunlight gave the eucalyptus trees a hazy sheen where they edged the roadside. Timbered areas interspersed with bushland, gradually gave way to lush green pastures. Isolated weatherboard houses came into view as Edward continued his journey along the turnpike road towards Parramatta. These whitewashed buildings, surrounded by open pastures stood against a backdrop of timbered hills. Edward's apprehension deepened as he realised the enormous responsibility involved in farming such large areas.

Suddenly, ahead of him he noticed a strange animal with large hind limbs that it used for leaping. Fascinated by its appearance, Edward watched as it bounded along ahead of him. After a short distance, the creature left the road to disappear into the bushes and trees.

A profusion of blossoms displayed their vivid colours all around him, filling the air with an aromatic scent. It was not the colourful flora that attracted Edward's attention, his interest was centred on the gaily hued parakeets that rose in alarm from the branches at his approach. He had never seen such beautiful creatures. As he rode along, Edward was continually dazzled by the bright plumage of the avifauna that used the roadside trees and bushes as their habitat.

On the summit of a low hill, he paused to look down upon the small town of Parramatta. Edward had planned to rest there before riding on towards Newacres, where he had planned to arrive later that afternoon, or early evening.

Outside the single story building that served as Government House, Edward became aware of being the centre of attention as he handed his horse to a hostelry. He noticed that one of the observers had detached himself from a small group and was heading towards him.

'Expect you'll be wantin' t'see me ... sir?' He hesitated, unsure what degree of protocol he should extend to the new arrival.

'That depends...' Edward looked down at the man, ... who you are.'

'Name's Watson! James Watson at yer service, sir.' He had noticed the official pouch that Edward had been requested to deliver by Governor Macquarie. Assuming that Edward was an official representative, he had decided on a more diplomatic approach.

'My names ... Burstow!' Edward handed over the pouch. 'I'm on my way to Newacres ... my farm. Originally it consisted of two farms, but now ...'

'Yes ... yes. I'm familiar with the situation ... Mr. Burstow.' Edward nodded, smiling inwardly at the man's instinctive reassessment of his status. A farmer only merited the normal prefix before his name. At the man's invitation, Edward followed him into the Government building.

'You'll be having official documents as to the boundaries regarding your land?'

'Of course!' Edward patted his coat pocket. 'All have been checked and the plans certified in Government House before I left Sydney.

'Could I see them, Mr Burstow?' Edward gave the official a questioning look before laying them out for perusal. 'Ah yes! Paul Harrison, your neighbour, is claiming these acres as his property.' Watson tapped his index finger on the sheets near Newacres outer boundaries.

'Well, he'd better disclaim it! See for yourself…' Edward in turn pointed to the map showing his farm's borders, '… it's officially mine.'

'Yes er … quite, but I'm not sure if Harrison will agree.'

'He has no option … look!' Once again Edward's finger traced his farm's official boundaries.

'Yes!' Watson nodded agreement. 'Seems plain enough ter me.' He hesitated a moment before imparting final words on the matter. 'I'll er, leaver yer t' define y'area when you see Harrison.' There was a note of relief in his voice as he shifted the onus onto Edward.

'I most certainly will, should the need ever arise.' It most certainly will, thought Watson, but he remained silent.

Even he could not have realised just how soon the matter would be contested and Edward called upon to display his strength of character – and courage. Now, after refreshments with the Governor's representative, Edward spoke of his plans and hopes for the future of Newacres, unaware of the pending confrontation awaiting him.

'It's good land, Mr. Burstow. Hope yer find everything to your satisfaction. and er, good luck.' Edward was mounting his horse so he did not notice Watson's worried frown, but he did detect the troubled undertones in the official's voice. He gave the matter little thought as he rode out of Parramatta in a westerly direction along a rough and dusty road towards his farm – Newacres.

Chapter Two

As Edward continued his journey, he passed isolated farms and settlements where the inquisitive inhabitants were anxious to exchange greetings and enquire of any outside news. 'Where yer from, young fella?' The question usually followed the settlers initial salutations. Having ascertained that he had just come from Sydney, the would then press for any information regarding the town.

What ships had arrive? What prices were the livestock fetching? What stores had arrived? The isolated and hard working settlers were desirous for any news that might affect their living. Their working days, normally from early morning until sundown, precluded any chance of them leaving their farms. A few, if they were within a couple of hours journey to the church, did attend the occasional service, but mostly it was the case of work as usual. Stock had to be tended whatever the day.

After a few miles, Edward glimpsed the farm that had been bequeathed to Becky. Pulling his horse to a stop on a slight rise, he spent a few anxious minutes surveying the gently undulating pastures that surrounded the farm buildings. Cattle and sheep grazed contentedly on the lush grass, while distant labourers were busy on the arable scree. Their activities were indicative of good husbandry by the farmer who had been caretaker on the farm.

Edward experienced a feeling of being under close observation as he approached the white weather-board farmhouse. His keen scrutiny noticed that the outbuildings, like the farmhouse, were in fairly good condition. A minimum of time would be necessary to make the buildings habitable for Becky and the baby should they decided to reside here. A decision that he would have to make after he had seen the other farm.

'You'll be lookin' for pa, I reckon?' Edward, his concentration on the buildings, had failed to notice the young girl standing in the shade of a tree.

'You reckoned correctly, young lady!' His surprised look soon turned into a friendly smile as he noticed her inquisitive surveillance. 'Any idea where your pa might be?'

'Right a'hind yer, young man!' Edward turned to find a middle aged man watching him closely. He noticed that the ruddy features were almost obliterated by a fair, grey-flecked beard. His build was willowy and his gait as he walked forward with outstretched hand was that of a man who had spent a lifetime on the land. A plodding, resolute stride of someone used to battling against the elements and adversity.

'Names, Porter ... Matthew Porter! What can I do f'yer?'

'Edward P... er, Burstow!' Edward was till having difficulties in remembering to use Stephen's surname. 'I'm the owner ...' he nodded towards the farmhouse, '... come to take up residence.'

'Aaah ... yes!' Relief showed on his troubled features. 'You and Mrs. Burstow are t'take ...'

'My er ... wife has just had a baby. She is hoping to join me as soon as her health permits.'

Oh! I thought ...' Edward noticed the concern on his face. Realising the cause, he soon eased the farmer's disappointment.

'I've come on ahead so that you and your family can leave as soon as possible. Everything is arranged. You can take passage on the Sentinal, or any other ship of your choice.'

' 'tis good news yer bring us ... Edward!' Mathew turned to his daughter. 'Run an' tell your Ma, that Mr. Burstow has arrived t'take over the farm'.

Above the hills the sun, a glowing crimson orb, was nearing the end of its descent. The day that had been a busy one for Edward was rapidly closing. Soon the long shadows of himself and his companion would be lost as sunlight faded into dusk. Edward, although dusty and tired after a long day in the saddle, had found it a rewarding one. Mainly because of the expert advice that had been willingly imparted to him.

'Thanks for your help, Matthew!' Edward gave his companion a grateful look. 'Your company ... and advice has been very helpful.'

'Yer more'an welcome. Thought it best yer met t'labourers and viewed the work situation.' Matthew reflected a moment as they rode towards the farm. 'If yer wants t'change labourers, or need additional help, yer'll hev t'git in touch with'em at Sydney.'

Don't anticipate any changes for the moment, Matthew. You and James appear to have trained them well.' Edward nodded his satisfaction. 'I'm very pleased that James is staying on. His help will be invaluable.'

'Yes. Making him your foreman was a wise decision, Edward. I've known James for many years. A man yer c'n trust and one who is respected by the convict labourers.' Matthew reflected a moment, unsure about imparting further information about his friend. Eventually he decided in the affirmative. 'James be hopin' t' wed, Maggy, one of the servants, when she receives her pardon in about …' he frowned in concentration, '… three months time. I believe they're hopin' yer'll ask'em to stay on.'

'Thank you for that piece of information, Matthew. I'll confirm with them, that they will be most welcome.' Edward turned his attention to Matthew as they neared the farm. 'What about yourselves? What plans have you for your return to England?'

'Don't rightly know as yet.' He gave Edward an uncertain look. 'Main thing is t'git wife well again …' His hesitation reflected the uncertainty regarding her health. '… then we'll see what's available. Farmin' again I shouldn't wonder!'

Edward's gaze moved furtively round the table. The evening meal was a fairly silent occasion, each member of the Porter family was in a reflective mood as they reflected on their departure in the morning. His surreptitious observation of the family around him, revealed each ones personal emotions as anxiously they anticipated the long sea voyage ahead of them.

He could appreciate their troubled thoughts as they prepared themselves for a departure that would surely induce feelings of remorse. Regret, at leaving familiar surroundings for the uncertainty of a future that awaited them on their return to England.

Matthew continued chewing meditatively as he kept casting anxious glances towards his wife. Anne aware of his concern, returned his looks with a quiet reassuring smile. Williams, the eldest of the three children had wanted to remain and continue working on the farm, but his father had insisted that he return with them.

Disappointment kept William in a quiet mood throughout the meal. He was a strong, eighteen year old lad and already an experienced herdsman. A natural affinity drew Edward towards the lad, but aware of Matthew's wishes, he had not tried to dissuade Will from leaving with his parents.

Jenny, pretty and vivacious girl of fourteen, was already planning her future and looking forward to living in England again. A country she remembered only from her parents hearsay, as she had been only two when they left to farm in the new colony. Tom, the youngest at eleven, was the quiet one of the family, accepting their departure with a stoicism that reflected his imperturbable character.

Edward turned to James Masters, the man sitting beside him. A long standing friend of the family and an experienced farmer who had twice suffered disaster when nature had dealt him catastrophic blows.

'I understand that you lost most of your cattle and crops in the Hawkesbury floods, James?'

'Aye!' James nodded his head reflectively. 'A terrible disaster to us all!'

'Many settlers lost stored crops and livestock.' Matthew, anxious to join the conversation spoke up. 'A few lives were lost as the flood waters raged across t'land.'

'Happened 'bout six years ago.' James' face took on a forlorn look as he referred to the floods. 'I lost almost everything. Had t'start from scratch on m'farm.' He paused as if the loss was still fresh in his memory. 'Governor Blight, as was then, done his best t'help us over our problems. Understandin' our predicament, he offered us practical help.'

'Aye, he did!' Matthew took up the story. 'Governor offered to replace some of our lost breeding stock from the Government herds, as well as building material to restore our damaged buildings.'

'Such terrible storms.' Anne Porter joined the conversation for the first time. In a weak voice she detailed the risks they experienced as the raging floods swept across the area. She spoke emotionally of those traumatic days as the river rose by several feet before flooding the surrounding farms. 'We was more fortunate than James. Our losses were fortunately lighter.'

'The crops produced poor yields the following season...' James shook his head sadly as he turned toward Edward. 'Suffered a rust infection. Many of m'sheep sustained foot-rot. We survived eventually and after another season, or two, t'farm was almost back to normal. Then ...' he shrugged his shoulders as distressing memories were recalled. 'Never take things for granted out her, Mr. Burstow. That's where I went wrong. Dropped me guard so t'speak.'

'What happened?' Edward had noticed the sadness reflected in his eyes as he spoke.

'Fire!'

'Fire?' Edward frowned his surprise.

'Aye. Swept through m'crops .. destroying everything. Farm buildings 'n all.'

'Have you an idea how the fire started?' There was an anxious note to Edward's question. A conflagration was one hazard that he had not considered.

'Probably the natives.' James appeared to accept the possible cause stoically. 'Sometimes they deliberately start bush fires to drive out game. Often these small fires are harmless, but occasionally the fires git out o'hand. This time the fire was started too close t'my crops, sparks are believed to have driven on t'the tinder dry corn. It was unintentional ... arid conditions and a fresh breeze soon had the fire out o'control. We didn't hev much chance agin it.'

'By the time I'd gathered the labourers and hurried over,' Matthew cast a rueful glance around the table, noticing the sympathetic nods of his family, 'James' crops, most of his cattle were lost and his farm lay in smouldering ruins. It were a heartbreakin' sight.' Matthew reached over and clasped his friend's arm in commiseration.

'I had no heart to'continue. Matthew ...' he nodded towards his friend, '... encouraged me to stay on an' help him.'

'Poor Mrs. Master's...' Anne gave James a kindly look, '... tried to save the house, but unfortunately she became... trapped.'

She paused to wipe the tears from her cheeks. 'Never had a chance ... poor soul.' James sat silently at the table, his head bowed as he relived those moments of horror on that calamitous day. The meal was concluded in a slightly sombre mood.

Early next morning, Edward watched as the Porters departed for Sydney, where they were expected to board the transports ship, Sentinal en route for England. Matthew's face reflected his concern as he helped his wife into the cart that Edward had placed at their disposal. At Parramatta he had arranged for a more comfortable carriage to convey the family along the turnpike road to Sydney.

A ribbon of dust drifted behind the cart as the family set off on their long journey home. Its presence partly obliterated the Porter's progress from Edward as he observed their departure. For several moments he remained watching as the dust settled upon the now deserted track. He was thinking of his letter to Julie, that he had entrusted to Matthew. What would she make of its contents, he wondered.

He had stressed the importance of both his and Becky's letter to Matthew, when handing them over that morning. 'Take great care of them, Matthew. My er, wife ...' Edward still hesitated when referring to Becky as his spouse, '... sent her letter so that you could carry our correspondence together. We trust you to deliver the letters to the solicitors in London. Their address is on the back.'

'I'll deliver 'em m'self. The solicitors are familiar to us as since Mr. Kennard's death, we've had reg lar letters from 'em.'

'Yes, of course.' Edward remembered the connection. 'They were the solicitors who dealt with my ... wife's late uncle, Edgar Kennard's estate.' He had watched as Matthew tucked the two letters into a well worn pouch. 'The solicitors are holding a small sum of money for you.' Edward had confided this information to Matthew just before the family's departure. 'Compensation for your efforts and help towards what enterprise you may consider when you reach England.'

'That be right kind o'yer, Edward an' God Bless to yer self an' Mrs. Burstow.' With a final handshake he had turned and clambered into the waiting cart.

Edward continued to reflect on his letter to Julie as he stared vacantly at the empty track. He recalled his warning message word for word.

He had informed her of his survival and that contrary to what she might eventually hear, he was alive and well. A mutual friend, he had mentioned in his letter, was a survivor also and was sending a letter to her parents explaining her circumstances and begging an answer if like her, forgiveness was in their hearts.

Edward turned his gaze to a flock of sheep grazing on distant pastures while he contemplated further on what he had mentioned in his letter. Julie, he was sure would recognise Rebecca as their mutual friend. He could not be more specific as names could be traced if the letter should fall into the wrong hands. Yes, he was sure his letter had contained sufficient information to comfort Julie in the knowledge that he was alive.

Once more he concentrated his thoughts on the letter, wondering if he had made Julie aware of his precarious situation. He had stressed that he could not in the foreseeable future divulge his whereabouts as his freedom – perhaps his life, might be in danger. A sadness tugged at his heart as he remembered his final words to his love. He had offered her release from their betrothal as he was uncertain if they would ever see each other again.

Later, he had regretted not sending a letter to his sister, Maisie. He had intended to write, but there had been so much activity in taking over the farm, that time had permitted him little chance. It was only with great difficulty that he had managed a few lines to Julie. He was sure that she would reassure Maisie that he was well despite his covert actions.

He heaved a deep emotional sigh before turning to enter the house. As he did so, he noticed the two convict servants standing with tear filled eyes in the doorway. One of them spoke softly as he neared them. 'The poor mistress. I doubt if she'll survive the journey, sir.' Shaking her head sadly she looked up into Edward's troubled features.

'We must hope for the best, Maggy. Perhaps the sea air will aid her recovery.' Fate, however, was to ordain otherwise. Not only was the ailing mistress destined for a watery grave, but also her family and all those who sailed on the stricken Cybele.

Matthew was anxious to reach England as soon as possible because of his wife's failing health, had taken passage on the Cybele. As her departure was scheduled several days before the Sentinal, he had decided at the last minute to sail on her. It was to prove a fateful decision, as driven south by hurricane force winds and squalls, the Cybele eventually went down in heavy seas in the Southern Atlantic.

*Letters from Edward and Rebecca explaining their circumstances were never to reach the ones they loved. Thinking that the Porter's had sailed on the Sentinal as planned, they both assumed the letter explaining their survival had safely reached their destination.

Consequently, when the Badger's loss was eventually published in the press, Edward Payne, a convict en route for New South Wales, was listed among the names of those lost at sea. Conformation of that tragic event,, together with that of the Cybele's sinking was still a few months away as Edward walked thoughtfully into the farmhouse. All was now quiet and peaceful after the hustle of the past few days.

Edward glanced up as his farm foreman joined him. 'What of your plans, James? Will you be moving on now your friends have departed?'

'If 'tis yer wish, Mr. Burstow ... stayin' on here 'ould do me fine.'

'Good! I would certainly appreciate your help ... and it would please me if you would call be Edward.' He gave the stocky built foreman a musing look, hoping he would accept his sincere offer of friendship.

'Suits me fine Mr ... er ... Edward.' Mutual chuckles emanated from them as James momentarily hesitated over the appellation.

'I understand that you and Maggy hope to marry on her becoming emancipated?' A frown wrinkled the corners of James' hazel eyes. He lifted the front of his hat to scratch his head in an embarrassing gesture before a broad grin spread over his hirsute countenance.

* In Book I The Winds of Destiny

'Aye! That were our intentions …' he gave Edward a sheepish look, '… we were hopin' tar marry come June.'

'In that case, how would you and Maggy like to set up home here?' Edward swept his arm around the farm buildings. 'As my manager, you would work more efficiently from here, while my wife and I can control overall operations from Newacres itself.' The full implications of Edward's words took a few moments to sink in. James' look of astonishment gradually changed to one of beaming pleasure.

'That be right kind of yer, Edward, Yer'll never regret it – ever.'

'Of that I feel sure, James.' He nodded his head assuredly. 'Now, I must ride over and view the other half of Newacres… especially the farm buildings. With all the hustle here, I've not had a chance to visit Henry.' He noticed the worried expression on his companion's face as he prepared to leave.

'Like me t'ride with yer, Edward, I c'n check on the labourers while Henry gives you details of the farm. He's a good lad. Since his parents sailed for England, he's had trouble from Harrison. He's your neighbour, an ugly customer!'

'Yes … I was forewarned about some altercation regarding boundaries.' Edward waited to see what information James had regarding the matter.

'He is trying to claim some of your land that borders his. Yer'll need t'watch him. He's evil … at least his chargeman is.'

They rode across the vast areas of arable and grazing land that with the joining of the two farms were to be known as Newacres. Edward was surprised at the size of the farms, they were much larger than he had expected. According to James, the combined farm covered around four thousand acres. The magnitude of his task filled him with apprehension.

With his limited knowledge of farming, Edward wondered if he would be able to cope with the situation. It was a daunting prospect… a challenge, but one that he was determined to overcome for Becky and Stephen's sake. Thankfully, he would have the support of James and hopefully that of the young man they were riding to meet.

'Looks like a fire!' Edward's keen eyesight had spotted the small cloud of smoke just beyond a hillock.

'It's... close to the farm!' James frowned as his gaze concentrated on the smoke spiralling into the cloudless sky. 'Best if we hurry, Edward.' There was a troubled look on his face as he turned to his companion. 'Don't like the look o'it.' Already he was urging his horse into a gallop. Edward, alert to potential danger, quickly followed James' action. At full stretch they urged their horses towards the fire.

'It's the outbuilding ... the barn.' James pointed to a blazing structure that stood a short distance from the house. A few labourers were already attempting to extinguish the flames with buckets of water. As the two riders reined in their mounts on reaching the blaze, one of the men, his face ashen with fright, stepped forward.

'It's the young master ... sir! He's inside!' choking and gasping from the smoke, he looked up at Edward as he pointed towards the blazing barn. His features were rigid with horror.

'Where abouts?' Edward shouted above hubbub. Flames were already licking the eaves as he leapt from his horse.

'We glimpsed him lying by the window.' His anxious gaze was directed towards the window where the flames were just beginning to take hold. 'We were unable t'reach 'im a'fore the smoke drove us back ...' He found himself talking to Edward's back.

'No, Edward! Wait!' James was shocked as he realised his companion's intentions. 'It's ... too ... dangerous!' Edward ignored the warning, he was determined to try and rescue Henry, trapped in the blazing barn. He grabbed a bucket of water and tipped the contents over himself. Without stopping he dashed into the barn and was soon engulfed in the thick acrid smoke. Eyes smarting and gasping for air, he scrambled forwards on hands and knees, gradually feeling his way across the smoke filled barn.

As he crawled his way over unseen obstacles, Edward continually reached out, feeling for a touch of the young man lying somewhere in the darkness. Perhaps he was already dead, but Edward had to be sure. He could hear his heart pounding as conditions rapidly deteriorated.

Gagging and choking and with his eyes screwed up against the stinging smoke, Edward realised that he must get out of the blazing inferno as soon as possible, else he might become trapped himself. He decided to make one last attempt before retreating. Taking his wet kerchief from around his neck, he pulled it up over his mouth and nostrils before making his final effort to find Henry.

Flames, now leaping up the side of the barn, showered him with sparks as he forced himself ever forward. He gasped in agony from the excruciating pain induced by the heat and smoke. Cursing from frustration because his rescue attempt had failed, Edward made a last despairing sweep with his hands. In the darkness his hand touched something soft. Clothing … an arm … a body. His excited cry was lost against the background of roaring flames as he began to drag the seemingly lifeless body towards the barn door.

Gasping … Crawling … Dragging. Slowly and painfully he was edging to safety. He was beginning to wonder if he would make the barn entrance. His clothes were smouldering and his lungs ached from the inhaled smoke. Suddenly, there was a crush. Flames and sparks leapt up from the burning beam that now lay between them and the door. Edward realised with horror that they were trapped behind the blazing timber. As he hesitated, the whirling smoke cleared momentarily revealing the doorway. So near and yet … Edward refused to be beaten.

Gathering his remaining strength, Edward hoisted Henry up onto his shoulders and made a concerted dash for safety. There were startled shouts of relief as Edward staggered from the conflagration with Henry lying across his shoulders. James dashed to their assistance, easing Henry gently down to the ground. He splashed water over the smouldering clothes of both men as Edward, panting from exhaustion gradually recovered from his ordeal.

'Keep those buckets going!' James shouted to the labourers who had formed a human chain to pass the buckets of water from a tank to the raging fire. Eventually, their efforts, combined with the isolated position of the barn, helped to confine the blaze to the one building that was left a smouldering ruin.

Anxious eyes continually glanced to where Edward and James were carefully assessing Henry's condition. 'I ... believe ... he's dead.' Edward shaking his head looked up from the limp body lying beside him. 'I can feel no heartbeat.'

'Dead!' A shocked James gasped in a harsh, croaking whisper.

'Yes. Murdered I believe.' Edward pointed out the severe bruise marks around the young lad's face and throat. 'No fires was responsible for those.'

'Murdered?' James shook his head in disbelief. 'How? Why?' He was stunned ... bemused.

'Beaten up. Look at his facial and scalp injuries.' Edward gently touched Henry's bruised and battered face as he looked up at a shocked James standing close beside him. 'After the beating, his attackers made certain he would not talk by leaving him unconscious in the barn.'

'And. tried to make it look as if he was burnt ter death in the fire ... that they deliberately started.' James spoke emotionally through gritted teeth. 'The bastards ... I'll settle ...' both men turned as a young woman raced from the house.

Her ashen face glistened with tears as she hurried towards them. She paused for a moment as she noticed the still form of Henry stretched out on the grass. Then sobbing uncontrollably and near to hysterics, she flung herself across the incumbent form. 'On no ... no Henry ...' she moaned. '... don't leave me. Please ... please don't die.' She looked up with tear filled eyes as Edward gently placed his arm around her shoulders. 'He won't ... die, will 'e sir?'

Edward was about to confirm her worst fears when he noticed Henry's eyes momentary flicker open. Gently he eased the girl aside and peered closely at the bruised and blood stained face. Perhaps he imagined the movement? He could detect no further signs of life. 'Henry!' he called softly. 'Can you hear me?' In the ensuing silence he hear the girl's muffled sobbing as she watched with anguish emotions.

Once again Edward attempted to feel for a pulse. He could feel nothing… but if only he could be sure. 'Henry! Oh, Henry!' As the girl sobbed his name, Edward noticed the eyelids flicker briefly. He reacted immediately by sending a rider to Parramatta for the doctor that James confirmed was in residence there. Gently easing the young woman to her feet he dispatched her to the farmhouse.

'Have plenty of hot water ready and a bed made up for the patient.'

'Yes… yes, sir.' She curtsied briefly before hurrying away with her skirts billowing and her auburn hair streaming from under her bonnet. At the door she was met by a younger girl, where after a brief animated conversation, they both disappeared rapidly inside the house.

'We must get him inside…' Edward looked round, but James was already organising some labourers to carry Henry inside. Gently they lifted the comatose victim and made their way slowly and carefully to the house. He had been brutally attacked and Edward intended to fully investigate the circumstances when Henry was better and able to talk. He sincerely hoped that the lad would recover, but his appearance as they awaited the doctor's arrival did not appear to encourage such a possibility.

* * * * *

'Feeling better?' Edward walked along the veranda towards the vacant chair beside the recuperating Henry.

'Yes… thanks…' he gave Edward a mischievous grin, '… but I am being spoilt as you can see.' Henry's warm glance went toward the young woman approaching them with a jug of fresh water in her hand. Edward gave his companion an understanding wink when he noticed that it was the girl who had been so distressed at Henry's condition after he had been rescued from the fire. In the month since that happening, he had learnt that Linda, a convict servant at the farm, and Henry were deeply attached to each other. The warm smiles exchanged as she filled Henry's glass was a manifestation that their amorous emotions were serious.

'Mr. Burstow?' She hesitated with the jug poised over an empty glass.

'Er... no thanks, Linda. Not just now,' he smiled his refusal and then watched her retreat into the house. After Linda has disappeared inside, he turned to his companion. 'Feel well enough for a talk, Henry?' There was an anxious look on his face as he made the enquiry.

Henry nodded silently before commenting. 'Time I done something. Makes me feel guilty sitting here with so much activity going on around me.' He indicated the builders that were nearing the end of their renovation work on the farm building. Convict labourers under the directions of an emancipated builder from Sydney had succeeded in changing Newacres into a soundly constructed brick building. A small house had also been erected on the site of the burnt out barn. It was an afterthought of Edward's, induced by an idea that he might soon have inhabitants for it.

Edward was pleased with what the workers had achieved in such a short period. He felt sure that his generous contributions to the men's welfare, had encouraged their friendly and energetic response. It had been worth the extra cost as Newacres was almost ready for Becky and the baby, Marian, to join him.

'What's your opinion of Newacres, now, Henry?'

'A big improvement. Very... imposing.' He cast an appreciative glance over the renovated house that he had shared with his family before their return to England. 'However, I doubt if it's the building work you've come to discuss, Edward. You're wondering about my decision?' A questioning look crossed his face as he turned for confirmation.

'A correct presumption on your part, Henry.' He nodded reflectively before requesting an answer. 'Have you considered my proposition?'

'I have indeed...' There was an exciting look in his eyes as he hesitated.

'And...?' Edward waited expectantly.

'In brief... Yes. Your offer for me to remain as your foreman was most generous, as was your proposition that I should live in the new building.' Henry looked towards the small house standing on the site of the burnt out barn.

'I thought the three rooms and kitchen space would be suitable for a man and... his family.' Edward chuckled inwardly as he noticed the surprised look on Henry's face. 'Think Linda will approve?'

'You don't miss much, do you?' A happy grin spread over his pallid features as he posed the question.

'Not where my staff are concerned.' Shared laughter expressed their developing friendship. 'Their welfare remains my main concern.'

Henry extended his hand. 'You just got yourself a new foreman, Edward.' Both felt the strong grip of each others hand shake.

'When do you expect to fetch your family out to Newacres?'

'As soon as this building work is finished.' Edward glanced round at the builders putting the finishing touches to the renovated farmhouse. 'Next week, if all goes well.' On noticing the conglomeration of the building material strewn around, he wondered if his estimate was biased on the optimistic side. He was certainly looking forward to having Becky and Marian with him at Newacres.

Thinking of Becky's arrival had reminded him of the uncertainty over their sleeping arrangements. It was causing him moments of anxiety whenever he considered their unusual circumstances. It would be very difficult to use separate bedrooms without the two house servants becoming aware of their nocturnal arrangements. Any talk by the staff might lead to questions being asked of their unusual relationship. They must at all costs avoid gossip that might in some way arouse suspicion, but...

'You were unable to identify your assailants, Henry?' Edward forced his domestic problems to the back of his mind as he reopened the subject of his foreman's attackers.

'Unfortunately, no. They set upon me as I entered the barn. My eyes never readjusted to the gloom inside before I was attacked.'

'Three of them, I believe you thought at the time?'

'Yes! Each had a kerchief tied over the lower half of their face.'

'You... noticed nothing familiar about any of the assailants?'

'I'm not sure. One of them was large... a great hulking brute.'

'Like someone you recognised?'

'Yes...' he shook his head uncertainly, '... but I can't say for sure.;

'Who was the man you thought you recognised? A local person?' Edward was pressing for a clue as to why the attack had been carried out and who might be responsible.

'Aye... Grant Medler! Harrison's foreman!' Edward gave his companion a surprised look.'

'Why would he... they, want to kill you?'

'Medler drove sheep on to my, err... your land, Edward. The section that Harrison wrongfully claimed as his. Myself and a few of our labourers rode over there at dawn two mornings later and surprised his men. After a brief confrontation we drove them and their sheep back onto Harrison's farm, White Gables.'

'You done the right thing, but made an enemy, it would seem. If what I hear about Harrison is true, he was bound to seek revenge.'

'Oh, yes... I was expecting some kind of retaliation – but murder? That's what it would have been... had you not arrived when you did, Edward.' Reaching across he slapped his companion gently on the shoulder. 'Thanks again... for saving my life.'

'If Harrison makes another attempt to claim that section, I'll deal with the man myself.'

'Oh, he'll try again. Call your bluff.' he gave Edward a word of warning. 'when they do... take care.' Edward nodded silently in acknowledgement of Henry's concern. He had to wait four months before his safety... his life was threatened. A confrontation that necessitate some positive action on Edward's part.

Rebecca, with the six month old Marian in her arms, watched as Edward and his young foreman rode away to view the East

Pastures, the section of Newacres that his disreputable neighbour, Harrison, was claiming as his land.

'I intend to settle the boundary dispute once and for all, Henry.' Edward tapped the official land documents in his saddle bag. 'These should prove to Harrison that his claims are without foundation.' He failed to notice the look of concern that crossed his companion's face.

An apprehension that was well founded as the previous owner of the farm, Gordon McDonald, a heavy drinker and gambler had borrowed heavily from Harrison. It was these debts that had generated the acrimonious dispute over the East Pastures, a three hundred acre section of lush pastures adjacent to White Gables.

Henry was thinking about that neighbour as he and Edward rode across the bushland towards these pastures. The two riders skirted the area of woodland that partially sheltered these lush grazing acres, before emerging onto the open scrub-land. Edward guided his horse onto a long narrow ridge that stretched out into the centre of the lower section of the East Pastures. From their slightly elevated position on top of the ridge they could view the surrounding controversial pastures.

Paul Harrison, a retired colonel from the infamous Rum Corps, or New South Wales Corps as they were officially known, was an unscrupulous character. He was one of the leading instigators in the unethical rum trade. In collaboration with some of his fellow officers he had imported rum during the early years of the new colony's existence and then sold, or bartered it, at least for four times its import cost. Until promissory notes were issued rum had been the main source of payments, bringing lucrative deals and wealth to the unprincipled dealers.

From these nefarious transactions, Paul Harrison had made himself a prosperous landowner, by buying out small settlers at rock bottom prices when they were unable to foreclose on loans. He had taken unfair advantage of the struggling farmers and pressured them into settling their loans or, as was most often the case, selling their property to him cheaply. They were left with no choice but to sell.

His allegations that the three hundred acres of Newacre's lush grazing area had been transferred to him in lieu of gambling debts, had never been substantiated. With McDonald dead and his widow now in England, there were no means of verifying Harrison's declaration.

No proof existed that his claims were genuine. Despite the Governor's ruling to the contrary, Harrison had been endeavouring by intimidation and attempted murder, if Henry's intuition was correct, to obtain the acres under dispute.

As they approached the acres in question, Henry was reminded of the pressure and intimidation exerted by the owner of White Gables on to his parents while they were caretakers of Edward's farm. Eventually the aggravation had become too much for his quiet natured parents, forcing them to return earlier than they intended for England.

Aggressive actions and terrorising by Harrison and his men had deeply distressed his family, especially his mother. Anxiety had eventually caused a deterioration in her health. Reluctantly his father had given his consent for Henry, his eldest son to remain behind until the new owners arrived. 'After that it'll be up t'yerself, son.' A wistful smile touched Henry's troubled face as he remembered his father's parting words. He hoped that by now his parents were safely home and that his ma's health was improved.

'What in damnation's going on?' They had just crested the ridge and were looking across a large area of lush pastures. Edward pulled his horse to a stop as he noticed the three distant riders driving a herd of cattle across a dried gully that his map confirmed was Newacres boundary. In an act of defiance, Harrison had ordered his foreman and two convicts to drive some of his cattle onto the disputed pasture. He was calling Edward's bluff. An act of intimidation.

'That's Grant Medler and a couple of his labourers.' Henry shaded his eyes against the sun as he watched the distant activities. He waited anxiously, wondering what Edward's reaction would be.

'In that case I'll tell him to take his cattle and get to hell off our land.' With that he urged his horse towards the trespassers. A very apprehensive Henry was soon riding behind the man who had nearly died to save his life... his true friend.

Chapter Three

Edward was comforted by Henry's presence as they headed for the inevitable confrontation. It gave him trusted support as he rode to challenge the men from White Gables. 'Beware... Edward!' Henry whispered a harsh warning as they waited for their horses to settle. 'Medler's a vicious devil!' There was an uneasy silence as the three interlopers found their way barred.

'You're trespassing on my land.' Edward addressed the burly rider who he guessed to be Grant Medler, the churlish foreman from White Gables.

' 'Yer land, be damned,' snorted Medler. 'Since when 'ave yer owned these pastures?' He glared menacingly into Edward's grim features.

'Since I purchased the farm. These documents prove my ownership and define the boundaries.'

'Don't prove nothin' t'me.' He snarled sardonically at Edward ...

'Well, it had better. Either you drive your cattle back across the gully, or...'

'... Or what, mister?' The brutish foreman was leaning forward in his saddle, a leer on his evil face as he taunted Edward.

'Unless you get your cattle off my land, I shall claim them... as... as compensation for my barn that your burnt down.' Edward had mentioned the barn as an involuntary afterthought, watching for Medler's reaction. It was a guilty one. His shifty look in Henry's direction and the momentary loss of his aggressiveness, confirmed he was responsible for the savage attack on Henry. 'Attempted murder – and arson, are serious crimes, Medler.'

The foreman's sudden moved took Edward by surprise. Before he could move, Medler had urged his horse closer and lashed out with his stock whip. Caught off guard, Edward grimace as the vicious blow landed on his shoulders. He reflex action had saved his face from the stinging lash, but his movement to defend himself and the force of the blow had partially unbalanced him.

Before he could recover, his horse, nervous at the action of the lashing whip had reared and thrown him. With lightning reflexes Edward regain his feet ready for the sneering foreman's next aggressive move. He did not have long to wait. 'The cattle stay where they are!' Medler snarled the statement as he gripped his whip tighter. 'This is White Gables property far as we're concerned.' Leaning forward he took another vicious swing with his whip.

Edward had glimpsed the sadistic look in his assailants eyes and was anticipating the next attack. Since his ordeal in the boat, Edward had gradually regained his strength and was not fit and fully recovered. In the brief moment before Medler's attack, Edward wondered if his speed and strength would be sufficient against the giant of a man now preparing to lash him once more with his whip.

As his attacker raised his whip, Edward noticed that it had a leather loop on the end through which Medler had inserted his wrist. This ensured that the whip never slipped from his grasp, accidentally or otherwise and was always at hand as was the case now. Edward's observation alerted him to a means of protecting himself, but it would entail precise timing and speed of action.

As Medler, cursing with rage lashed out with his whip, Edward waited until the last moment before swerving with lightning reflexes from its path. He felt the brush of the wind as the thong whistled past his face. With a speed that took his attacker by surprise, Edward leapt in close and grabbed the whip before Medler could recover his balance. Exerting all his strength he gave a sharp pull that completely unbalanced his antagonist. Even though Medler released his hold of the whip in an attempt to regain his balance, he was unsuccessful. The loop still attached to his wrist aided Edward in hauling him from his horse.

The bulky foreman landed with a bone-shaking crash at Edward's feet. Bellowing like a bull he scrambled to his feet ready to launch an all out attack on the man who had just humiliated him. Eyes blazing and roaring with rage he advanced menacingly towards Edward.

'I'll kill... yer f'that!' With a sadistic snarl he lunged at the man who had affronted him. No one made a fool of Grant Medler and survived without punishment. Muttering obnoxious threats he rushed forward, determined to put this interfering newcomer in his rightful place, an obsequious subordinate.

Calmly, Edward waited for his opponent's opening move, alert for any cunning manoeuvre. His old prize fighting temperament induced a feeling of excited calmness and vigilance. He was prepared for Medler's powerful onrush when it came. Dancing aside at the last minute, he easily avoided the blows, then sent two mighty punches into his adversary's face. Blood poured from the enraged Medler's nose while his left eye was battered and cut.

The punches angered Medler and spurred him into violent action. His fury erupted at such painful treatment and throwing caution to the wind he came swinging powerful punches at random. Edward was almost caught off guard by his attacker's savage onslaught. He just managed to evade the wildly aimed punches before he counter attacked. Even so, he was unable to prevent Medler from landing two crushing blows to his ribs. Edward was driven backwards by their force and his opponents momentum. He held on in an endeavour to regain his breath, but found himself being forced onto the defensive as Medler threw a flurry of punches, most of which he managed to evade.

'Not s'fancy nah... huh, mister!' Medler snarled as he came in close. Spittle splashed on Edward's face as the obnoxious foreman tried to show his contempt. It was a repulsive act that produced an immediate reaction. Dancing backwards on his feet, Edward feinted as if continuing on the retreat, hoping it would induce his opponent to rush forward. A ruse that was to prove very effective.

Medler lunged forward expecting to land some savage blows, but instead received two crushing blows onto his chin. Edward had deftly side-stepped and delivered the two powerful punches, one of which broke his adversary's jaw. Bemused and in pain, his shattered opponent was in no position to protect himself as Edward smashed in a series of painful punches. As the last, an extra powerful one landed, Medler's legs were already collapsing. With a resounding crash he hit the grass and remained still.

Edward indicated to the two convict labourers that they should depart with their unconscious foreman. They had been watching the fight in shocked amazement and disbelief as the new owner of Newacres had knocked their brutish overseer senseless. There were no pangs of remorse as they stepped forward, only ones of elation.

'Strewth guv… yer an 'ero.' The older one glanced round to make certain that his foreman was still unconscious before continuing. 'Dun this old 'eart o'mine a power o'good'. He was still shaking his head in disbelief. 'Sure was a joy seeing' the bastard git 'is deserts.' He spat in the direction of the senseless Medler. 'You're right 'bout the fire…' he spoke softly to Edward, '… 'twas 'im.' In little more than a whisper he gave more details. 'Made us 'old the young lad…' he nodded towards Henry, '… while he punched 'im. Threatened us with a lashin'… if we didn't. But honest guv… we 'ad no part wi' t'fire. It were 'is doing''

'Here's Harrison now!' Henry, stunned into silence at what he had just witnessed, spoke for the first time. 'He'll not be pleased with your welcome, Edward.' There was a chuckle in his voice as he anticipated the imminent confrontation between his young boss and the rogue Harrison.

'You can collect your scum…' Edward pointed to the dazed, semiconscious Medler, '… and inform him when he recovers to keep off my land in future.' Harrison, glaring with anger and disbelief at his charge-hand was about to protest, when he was stopped by Edward's pronouncement. 'That also applies to you, Harrison. As for… your cattle…' he indicated the grazing herd that had been driven onto Newacres pastures, '… I'm keeping them as compensation for my barn that was burn down by your overseer and for his murderous attack on my foreman.'

'You'll… you'll… live to regret this day… damn you.' Harrison's face was contorted with rage. 'Who in damnation are you, anyway?'

'This is Mr. Burstow. The new owner of… Newacres!' It was Henry who made the conventional introduction to the raging owner of White Gables.

'You'll regret setting foot in this country. Damned... interloper.' After directing his two labourers to assist their dazed foreman, Harrison turned and rode off, but not before uttering a final threat. 'You'll not remain on the farm for long... Burstow.' Bitterness gave his face an evil look – a grotesque mask of hate.

'I'll see to the cattle, Edward.' Henry glanced at the departing group, now on the far side of the gully, as if expecting some retaliatory action. There was no response from the subdued transgressors – for the time being.

As they herded the cattle deeper into the confines of Newacres safer pastures, Henry paused to face his companion. 'You ever done any prize fighting, Edward?'*

The question caught Edward unawares. Startling him momentarily. Wanting time to consider his reply, he feigned puzzlement as he returned his questioner's steady gaze.

'Prize fighting? What ever gave you that idea, Henry?'

'No particular reason.' He shook his head. 'It's just that...' a reflective frown creased his brow, '... just the way you handled that brute Medler.'

'A, er... hereditary part of my character perhaps, or as is more likely, an act of preservation.' Edward grinned at his companion. 'Farmers as you should very well know, Henry, have little time for indulging in such pugilistic activities.'

'That's true!' Henry nodded vigorously. 'One thing I am certain of though...' he gave Edward a roguish look, '... I'm thankful to be your friend – not your enemy.'

As they neared an area where timbered slopes edged the trail, Edward's hand went quickly to his knife. A dark creature had suddenly emerged from the trees and shrubs just ahead of them. It was his first encounter with the natives. White paste-like substance marked his face and near naked body. Holding a long spear in a neutral manner he waited for them to draw near.

'It's "Gicky"!' Henry called softly as he turned towards Edward. 'He's my friend!' At the sound of his name, the young native smiled and uttered a series of strange click-like sounds. Seeing his companion's puzzled frown, Henry explained that the strange clicking noises was the way they communicated among themselves.

* In Book I The Winds of Destiny

'A native... your friend?' Edward's face registered shocked surprise.

'Yes. Tell you about it later.' To Edward's amazement, Henry dismounted and went towards the young native with his right hand raised in a gesture of greeting. Placing the point of his spear on the ground and with the haft resting against his right shoulder, the dark skinned native returned the greeting.

Edward watched in fascination as by a series of gesticulations and simple sketches in the dust, the two friends communicated. He smiled as he looked down upon the dark fuzzy hair of the young native and that of Henry's straw-coloured shocks as they concentrate over their visual exchanges.

At last they straightened up from their unusual exchanges. Henry then indicated by signs to "Gicky" that all three of them should be friends. Edward's smile and raised arm reassured the young native that he had another friend among the strangers who had invaded his land. After exchanging salutatory gestures, "Gicky" had disappeared as quickly and as silently as he had emerged from the shrubs a few minutes previously.

'My friendship with a native, puzzles you, Edward?' There was a hint of amusement in his voice as he questioned his companion's bewilderment. 'You are probably wondering how it came about?'

'I must confess, Henry, your relationship with one of the natives did cause me some surprise.'

'Then I shall enlighten you, dear friend.' Henry's face became serious as he related his initial encounter with "Gicky" and his family group. He described how they were being attacked by three escaped convicts about four years previously. 'I came upon them as they were being beaten and tied up by the convicts. It was as they began to molest the hapless females that I arrived and interceded on behalf of the victims.'

'What happened about "Gicky"?' Edward had been listening with rapt attention.

'He, like his father and other male members and been ill treated. Beaten almost senseless by the convicts as they tried to protect the female members of their family.'

'What happened about the attackers? Did they escape?' Edward was shocked at his friend's disclosures.

'Not before I had dealt with them.' A chuckle suddenly softened his grim features. 'I used by stock-whip on their backs as I chased after them. Their ragged clothing was no protection against the leather thong. They were still cursing me as they scrambled into a patch of bushes to escape.' The memory induced a wry smile.

'I was angry, Edward. Very angry. By the time I had regained my composure, the marauders were in a bad way. I allowed them to stagger off into the bushes whilst I returned to comfort the natives. Eventually I led them to a secluded area on the farm, indicating to them that they were welcome to stay there. After they were settled I rode off and shot an animal for them.

'Since then, "Gicky" and I have developed a friendly relationship. On occasions we have gone off into the bush together, where he taught me a great deal about hunting and tracking – and about his people.' Henry reflected a moment. 'If it is your wish, I can ask them to move on, Edward.'

'Move them! Why on earth would I want to do that?'

'I was unsure how you would react to finding natives on your land. In a way they earn their keep.' Henry noticed his companion's frown of uncertainty. 'They keep an eye on our sheep when they are in that section of the pastures. Protecting them from other groups of wandering natives who would otherwise kill and steal from our flocks. As a sign of my appreciation I do occasionally kill a sheep for them. A luxury they enjoy.' Henry waited apprehensively for the new owner's reaction.

'I see no reason to change the situation.' A look of relief passed over Henry's face as he heard the words endorsing his act. 'They're welcome to remain, Henry.'

* * * * *

Covered with dust and tired after a day in the saddle, Edward was thankful to see Newacres ahead of him. Home, he thought at that moment was a very welcome sight. Despite his weariness, he was still able to appreciate the beauty of the countryside that surrounded him. The cool evening air was filled with the ubiquitous fragrance of the eucalyptus trees that lined the approach to Newacres. Stretching as far as the eye could see were rolling acres of pastures arable land, now owned by Becky and himself.

Rebecca, who had been watching Edward's approach experienced a moment of longing. A warm excited emotion that his presence seemed to arouse within her healthy young body. In fairness to Edward, she tried to keep these feelings subdued during their time together. Especially of late when she had been aware of his eyes resting on her for longer periods that protocol would normally permit. For them, however, the situation was far from normal. To their friends and neighbours they were man and wife and out of respect for her and the memory of Stephen, she realised that Edward was finding their façade an emotional struggle.

With each passing day her desire for his warm and loving embrace was becoming increasingly stronger. She also sensed that Edward's emotions were as urgent as hers. She felt that the moment was fast approaching when they would have to decide on their future relationship.

Rebecca was now sure that Stephen must have realised that the circumstances he had encouraged between her and Edward before his passing, would eventually lead to a more passionate and lasting relationship between them.* Now, as she watched Edward hand his horse to Jem, their convict groom, she unashamedly hoped that he would decide to stay on. She needed his help – and his love.

'Rebecca!' she waited excitedly for him to climb the veranda steps before reaching out for the light embrace and the perfunctory kiss that they enacted for appearances sake. No suspicion of their true state of affairs must become known to the staff in case their curiosity became aroused. Expecting a quick release from his routine embrace, Rebecca was taken by surprise when Edward's arms tightened around her and his kisses became more fervent.

Her natural reaction was to press closer against the hardness of his body. Straining towards him, Rebecca realised that she

* In Book I The Winds of Destiny

was fast losing control of her emotions. Dusk settled around them as their passionate responses incited a desire to share each others love. Their emotive feelings evaporated quickly as footsteps approached from the shadows.

They eased apart, their emotions still visible to each other as Grace, carrying Marian came to inform them that the evening meal was almost ready. She sensed that her appearance had interrupted a passionate interlude between the mistress and her husband.

'Beggin' y'pardon, mam... sir.' She kept her eyes lowered as she moved demurely towards Rebecca before handing over the baby.

'Thank you, Grace. We shall be along in a few moments.' Edward gave the baby a benign look as he and Rebecca walked slowly towards the house entrance. Their eyes met as they entered the candlelit room, each noticed the flame of desire that still lingered on each other's face. A longing that was becoming increasingly stronger and one that must someday be fulfilled.

It was early morning a few days later that Rebecca looked out of her bedroom window, just as the sun was rising above the distant tree lined hills. It's dazzling brighiness spread over the gentle undulating acres of lush grassland and sparkled on the ruffled surface of the stream that skirted the Westwood Acres. It's brilliance gave a silvery glitter to the narrow strip of water.

Deep in thought and with an inner sadness she watched through tear misted eyes, the birth of a new day. Her twentieth birthday. She was alone as Edward had gone into Sydney for a few days. He must have been unavoidable delayed as he had promised to get the farm business transactions over quickly and be home in time for her birthday.

In silence, Rebecca continued to gaze from her bedroom window, recalling her birthdays that she had spent at home with Josh and her parents. She prayed softly that when her letter carried by the Porters reached them, that they would answer with forgiveness in their hearts. She had told them little of her present circumstances, a secret that she must, for the time being, keep in case it endangered Edward's freedom – his life. Perhaps, an affectionate smile softened her serious features, the news that they were grandparents would overcome her parent's opposition and help them to find forgiveness in their hearts.

Rebecca was hopeful that it would be so. She had pleaded in her letter, begging them to write and tell her that the past was forgotten and that her love for them would be reciprocated. Should they wish the situation of their renunciation to continue, the absence of any correspondence from them would confirm that their opposition remained unchanged. Writing the words had caused her great distress, but she had prayed for their blessing and forgiveness. Both hers and Edward's letter should have been received by now and hopefully a favourable answer would reach them by the years end.

Unknown to the writers and their intended recipients, the letters were lost at sea when the Porter family, along with all others on the Cyebele, went down with the ship in cyclonic winds while sailing for England.

Her mediation's were disturbed by the servants moving around at their early morning chores. Rebecca finished her dressing before going downstairs and then on to the stables. Training the horses was her responsibility and one that gave her great satisfaction. Anticipating an ever increasing demand for horses in the new colony, she and Stephen had selected a pair of stallions and half a dozen fillies for breeding.

*Van Doren had kept his word; the cattle, horses and Merino sheep that he had promised to send, had all been of a high class. Thanks to the two drovers who had taken passage with the livestock, all had arrived in good shape considering the journey.

When the horses first arrived they had been almost unmanageable, but the two stockmen had remained until the stallions had settled down and got used to the lunge reins being attached. Rebecca had been glad of their initial help as the horses, not used to being fenced in, had reacted aggressively when approached. With their ears laid back and their teeth bared, they had at first resisted the attachment of a rope head-collar, used initially to bring them to Newacres.

By gentle persuasion, Rebecca had gradually earned the horses trust. Using a lunge rein in the early stages, she began

* In Book I The Winds of Destiny

their preliminary training. For hours on end she worked with the horses, patiently coaxing her young charges to accept and answer to the bit and bridle. A click of her tongue would set the horse circling around at a gentle trot, her only contact was the lunge-rein fastened to its nose band.

'Whoa!' Rebecca's command brought one of the stallions to a halt. She approached him quietly. 'Well done, Nelson!' Patting the horse affectionately, she whispered words of encouragement. 'Think you can manage the felt saddle and leathers?' Fondling the horses neck, she continued her one way conversation with Nelson, 'I'm training you for the master. Don't let me down.' He whinnied softly, sensing her affectionate mood.

Later in the paddock, she approached Nelson with the intention of putting the felt saddle and leathers on to the young stallion. 'You beautiful creature!' Rebecca's whispered compliment caressed Nelson's ears, bringing reassurance as he became aware that something strange was happening. He arched his graceful neck, but soon relaxed under Rebecca's gentle fondling. 'Good, Nelson! Good!' She looked into his liquid dark eyes as she spoke quietly to him.

Once saddled, Nelson stood quietly waiting for the next move that his intuition warned him was imminent. He trembled slightly as Rebecca, gently and with continuing words of encouragement, eased herself into the saddle. Once settled and with her feet in the stirrups, she gently urged him to move, but for a moment there was no response. She was aware of Nelson's uncertainty at having her on his back.

'Walk on Nelson!' Her quiet word of command settled the horse and with a quiet determination he began to walk round the paddock. 'Trot Nelson!' Urging the horse into a gentle canter they circled a few times before Rebecca pulled him up and dismounted. 'Well done, Nelson!' She gave him an affectionate pat. 'You were wonderful!' Eyes misted with excitement, she reached up to remove the saddle, but a movement behind her made her turn. It was a smiling Edward. Unobserved, he had been watching her for several minutes.

'You're an excellent trainer, Becky.' His admiring eyes were fixed on Nelson. 'He's a magnificent creature... so beautiful.'

'I'm so glad you think so, Edward. He'll be ready for you to ride in a few more days.' Rebecca's smile reflected her affectionate feelings, its warmth sent a tremor of excitement pulsing through his body. Then the meaning of her words penetrated his impassioned senses.

'For me to ride?' Rebecca chuckled as she noticed the look of surprise on his face.

'For your birthday next week! Your twenty first!' She was still smiling as Edward dismounted and walked towards her. Rebecca's face became serious as she noticed the amorous look in his eyes. Next moment they were in each other's arms and exchanging kisses that expressed their silent, pent-up emotions.

For a few moments as their passionate feelings struggled to remain under control, time appeared to stand still. Breathless they at last eased apart, suddenly aware of the love they were trying to conceal from each other. Their eyes sparkled with a fiery excitement, confirming a love that was already becoming obvious.

Edward reached into his coat pocket and withdrew a small parcel. 'Here, Becky...' he passed it to her, '... and happy birthday.'

'What... what is it, Edward?' He smilingly shook his head as he watched her puzzled frown.

'You'll need to open your gift to find the answer.' Edward watched her closely as she carefully unwrapped the small parcel.

'Oh, Edward!' Rebecca looked up excitedly through tear filled eyes. 'My... brooch!' Involuntary she reached out and embraced him. Her affectionate reactions were a spontaneous response at receiving back the brooch she had so fondly cherished. Rebecca had never expected to see it again. Through eyes misted with tears, she looked again at the repaired brooch sparkling as new in the sunlight.

*Rebecca was remembering the occasion in the dinghy when she had offered it to Edward. By using its pin as a fishing hook, he had managed to catch fish for their starving bodies. It had probably saved their lives.

'I promised you it would be repaired, Becky.' His eyes were warm with love.

* In Book I The Winds of Destiny

'Yes!' she nodded, 'it now seems so long ago. I thought...' Edward's nearness and his passionate look was exciting her amorous emotions, her voice was barely audible as she continued, '... it had been lost.'

'May I, Becky?' Edward moved closer to fix the brooch on her dress.

'Thank you... Edward.' Her voice was shaking with enamoured longing as their eyes met. There was no mistaking the urgency of their feelings as they walked hand in hand towards the house. Edward dropped the saddle on the veranda and walked with Becky to their bedroom.

With a shy-like movement, Rebecca drew the curtains to soften the light before unfastening her dress. Edward's desire for her became an overwhelming passion as he watched Becky undressing in the subdued glow. Throbbing with amorous anticipation, he quickly followed her example.

Tenderly, Edward lifted Becky up in his strong arms, where he stood for a moment as she snuggled against him. As his lips felt the sensuous touch of hers, he gently eased her down onto the bed in which she had spent so many lonely and restless nights. Now her loneliness would soon be over. Excitedly she stretched her arms to receive him as his hard, powerful body pressed urgently against hers.

Their inhibitions and frustrations of the past months were swept away in tidal waves of loving emotions. A passion that carried them into realms of ecstasy, climaxing in a whirlpool of pounding ardour before drifting into the peaceful haven of tranquillity. As Rebecca lay with her head resting on Edward's chest, she could feel his heart pounding after what had been an urgent, almost tempestuous act of love making between them.

Rebecca snuggled closer, seeking the protection and reassurance of Edward's strong muscular body. Her affectionate movements against his body aroused his longing once again, but as he smilingly reached out for her, Becky eased away.

'Wait until tonight, Edward dearest. Otherwise the servants will be thinking ...'

'I don't care what thoughts they might harbour...' he drew her tight against his aroused body, '... I can't wait until tonight, Becky love.'

'Neither... can... I,' she giggled as once again they gave way to their sensual longing. An overwhelming desire that could only be calmed by the shared ecstasy of their love-making.

That night, for the first time, they slept together. After their bodies had become satisfied with love, they had eventually drifted off into an exhausted, but satisfying sleep. Becky's deep, emotional sigh before she succumbed to her tiredness, reflected her relief. At last Edward and herself could now act naturally – as 'husband' and wife. No more frustrated longing and restraint in their relationship.

From this wonderful night, Edward would share her bed and her love. It was as if a burden had been eased from her shoulders. His passionate love-making had left her tender, but emotionally satisfied. She smiled in the darkness as she remembered Edward's concern in case she became pregnant.

With his ardour, she had little doubt that his apprehension would soon be a confirmed phenomenon. 'If only you realised...' she whispered to his sleeping body, '... how much I long for your child, Edward.' She smiled reflectively in the darkness. She hoped it would be a boy so that he could be named after Stephen, her late husband.* Rebecca was sure that Edward would agree to her sentimental wish.

* In Book I The Winds of Destiny

Chapter Four

'Happy, my love?' Sebastion leaned closer to Maisie.

'I feel... wonderful, Seb.' Her affectionate smile warmed his heart. 'Just wonderful.' Behind the smile in his young wife's eyes, Seb discerned a fleeting look of sadness. He understood its meaning. Maisie, like his cousin Julie, had been devastated by the news of the Badger's sinking with the loss of all the convicts and crew. Under the impression that Edward had been lost in the catastrophe, Maisie and Julie had comforted each other when the traumatic news first reached them.

As the carriage trundled through the East Anglian countryside, Maisie snuggled closer to Seb. During the three days since their wedding he had been a great comfort to her as she tried to overcome the distress caused by her brother's loss at sea. Edward had promised to be their best man when they married, a pledge that fate had prevented him from fulfilling. Her brother-in-law's perjurious evidence had been not only responsible for his transportation to the penal colony, but also for his death at sea.*

'You look sad, Maisie! Will going back to Foxleigh be too distressing for you?' Seb turned an anxious face towards his wife.

'There will be poignant reminders of Edward, but when I think of dearest Julie and her little son, George, I can see my loss in perspective, Seb. She will never be able to share her happiness with the man she loved, or experience the shared joy of parenthood with Edward.' Maisie heaved a deep sorrowful sigh. 'Whereas...' she gave Sebastion a melancholy smile, '... I have your love to remind me that our future promises so much happiness. Oh, Seb... I love you so very much.'

'And I love you also, my dearest. To such an extent that I feel...' With their lips upon each others, no further explanations of their amorous feeling were necessary. As Seb eased from their passionate embrace, Maisie shyly straightened her bonnet.

'Oh Seb! What will people think if they see us kissing inside the carriage?'

* In Book I The Winds of Destiny

'Their deliberations will be of no consequence, my love.' His affectionate smile was a blithe reflection of his love for his young wife.

'In that case...' Maisie reached out and put her arms around Seb's neck, '... I would love a repeat of your last affectionate act.' Her lips were caressing his as she whispered her invitation. Their carriage's swaying and uneven motion appeared not to disturb their embrace or diminish the ardour of their kisses. They were thrown apart when the carriage lurched into a deeply rutted section of the road. Maisie became concerned as the sudden movement caused Seb to grimace in pain. His hand went involuntary to his shoulder as if to protect it.

'Your injury, Seb!' Her face became serious as she glanced anxiously at his injured shoulder. 'It continues to give you pain?'

'Only on occasions, my dear. It is almost normal again. My protective movement just now...' he paused to kiss her troubled face. '... was but a reflex action to the carriage's sudden lurch. Next month I have to report back to my unit.' Seeing the sadness in her face, Seb did his best to reassure her. 'There is no likelihood of my being involved in any fighting, Maisie. It will be mainly exercises and training in preparation for any future conflict.'

'Is that a... possibility then, Seb?' He was aware of Maisie's troubled look as she waited for an answer. Intuition warned him that a truthful one was expected.

'I honestly don't know, my dearest. It seems unlikely that there will be war, but...' Seb hesitated knowing that he was not being honest with his worried wife.

'But what... Seb?'

'I was going to say that with the French anxious for revenge, war is a possibility. During our last campaign, Wellington concentrated out attacks on Soult's troops to such an extent that they were forced to retreat. We spent a quiet period waiting for the weather to improve as dry conditions favoured our manoeuvres and gave us the advantage when we attacked. Our first objectives was to cross the river lines to permit the concentration of our forces. Having satisfactory completed this strategy and gathered his troops together, the storming of Toulouse began.

Seb paused as if lost in the horrors of battle. Maisie remained silent as if speech had been taken from her. When her thoughts calmed and words seemed to become fluid once more, she realised that Seb was talking again.

'My group…' Maisie noticed that he was staring with unseeing eyes at the passing Norfolk countryside as memories of Wellington's forces storming ever forward echoed in his mind. Cannonade, rifle-fire, sabres flashing, curses and the anguished cries of fallen comrades drifted across his tormented memories. He remained silent as the recollections of that April day filled his thoughts. Eventually, he recommenced his narration.

'My group… were the first of the cavalry to attack. Initially we encountered stiff resistance, but as our forces pressed relentlessly forward, the enemy after a spell of fierce fighting surrendered. The Peninsula War was over.'

'And you… were badly wounded in the action, Seb.' Maisie looked solemnly at her husband as she reached for his hand.

'Nothing too serious, my dear. A shot in my shoulder that incapacitated me for a few days.'

'Oh, Seb. You… you might have been… killed.' Maisie spoke in a shocked whisper. 'Must you return so soon?' Seb noticed the pleading look in his wife's eyes as they gazed emotionally into his.

'Yes. Now that my shoulder is healed, I must return. It is my duty, dearest.' Slowly he leaned towards her and gently kissed her lips. 'There is, however, a promise I solemnly give to you. After my next tour of duty, I shall resign from the cavalry to take over the running of my father's estate.

'That will be wonderful, Seb. Sir Roger er… father,' she smiled shyly at her slight confusion. 'Running Homefield and caring for Lady Anne must be a great burden upon him. I have been helping whenever possible, but your mother… shows so much animosity towards me. Her silent accusing look follows me about the room whenever I am attending her.'

'Accusing look?' Seb turned a shocked face towards her.

'Yes. She still holds me responsible for Andrews departure and she… objected most vociferously to our marriage, Seb. Your father overruled her and he was kind enough to reassure me that our wedding had his full blessing. He also told me that he was looking forward to my living at Homefield during your absence.' Sadness returned to line her troubled features.

'When I return...' Seb gave her an affectionate look, '... we are to live in the East Wing. Father is having it renovated over the next few weeks, to ensure it is ready for us on my return.' Maisie nodded her head silently, without displaying any enthusiasm. 'Are you not in favour with the arrangements, my love?' Seb looked deeply concerned as he waited for her reply.

'Oh yes, Seb. It's just that... if only... Lady Anne would show...'

'Father has spoken of my mother's er... feelings towards you. How it is fast becoming an obsession with her. Needless to say, he is greatly perturbed at her attitude, especially as you have shared in the nursing and care of my mother. According to him,' his smile as he gazed into her eyes reflected benevolent connotations, 'you have cared for her with sympathetic understanding and with great patience.'

'I have done my best, Seb. Since Alison married Josh and moved into Highfield, I have at y... er, father's request taken over the management of the household. A couple of senior staff members were inclined to be obstreperous at first, but when they were made aware that I had full authority to do so, they became more co-operative. Our marriage will make my duties there much easier.'

'I know. Father speaks highly of your capabilities, Maisie. He is very fond of you and appreciates what you are doing at Homefield. Especially when you have acted as hostess to family guests, he told me that on those occasions he now relies on you completely. There is one other item of news that I have been waiting to inform you of, my dearest. Now...' he took her hands in his as he noticed her perplexed expression, '... seems the appropriate moment.' His gentle kiss was meant to reassure her before he elucidated on his announcement. 'Father has arranged for me to inherit his title and Homefield Hall by legal succession in the place of Andrew.'

'That's wonderful news, Seb. I'm so pleased, but... will Andrew not be greatly upset?'

'Despite every effort to locate my brother, there has been no information of him for several months now. He appears to have vanished completely.'

'How did... Lady Anne...' Maisie could not bring herself to call her mother as yet, '... accept the news of your inheritance, Seb?'

'With little grace, I'm afraid, but...' Seb could not bring himself to tell Maisie of his mother's near hysterical ranting when she became aware that her title might one day pass to 'the fisherman's brat', '...father managed eventually to er, pacify her.'

Maisie was not fooled by her husband's diplomatic statement. Lady Anne had spoken to her and made it known that as far as she was concerned, there was to be no daughter-in-law relationship between them – ever. She thought Seb should be made aware of his mother's intent.

'Contrary to my wishes, Seb, your Mother refuses to acknowledge my marriage relationship. I'm afraid it must remain Lady Anne...' a whimsical smile spread over her face, '... she would never consent to my addressing her with such an endearment as mother – despite our marriage, Seb.'

'Perhaps one day she will appreciate all that you have done for her... for all of us. Especially since Alison's departure to Highfield last year.'

'I sincerely hope that someday she will look upon me in a more favourable light, but...' she shrugged her shoulders forlornly.

'Speaking of my sister, reminds me of a conversation I recently shared with her. She informed me that Josh and his parents are deeply upset that they have received no word from Rebecca and Stephen. Having read full details of their survival in the newspapers, they had expected words of assurance from her.'

'It was Sir Rog... father who called me into his study one day while you were away, who gently broke to me the details of the Badger's sinking and of my brother's loss.' She paused as she recalled that heart breaking moment. 'Father... was very kind to me. He sat beside me and held me gently while I submitted to my sorrowful emotions.' In the ensuing silence, they heard the drumming of the horses hoofs on the hard dusty road and the creak of leather as the animals took the strain on an incline. Seb tenderly placed a comforting arm around Maisie.

'I also was deeply shocked when I received the news about Edward from father. He blamed Andrew's irresponsible lying at the trial – his false evidence, for your brother's death. Despite the urgency of sending Edward's pardon on the first available ship to New South Wales, unfortunately its arrival will be of no consequence now.'

'Perhaps we should not blame Andrew entirely, Seb. He was not to know of the Badger's eventual fate. Apparently it was a severe storm and hurricane winds that caused the ship's loss.' Maisie was struggling to maintain her composure as she spoke.

'Your magnanimous attitude does you credit, my love. A salient part of your character that I find so appealing in such a beautiful wife.' As their carriage trundled down the hill into the outskirts of Norwich, they were oblivious to any of the local populace who might by chance be a witness to their emotional kisses.

Inside the carriage their embrace continued until a sudden stop jolted them apart. Their amorous moment was disturbed by the shouted words from their coachman as he had an altercation with a driver who had obstructed his progress. Seb lowered the carriage window to ascertain the trouble. Cattle being driven to the cattle market milled around in front of them.

On seeing Sebastian's face gazing out from the window, the drover's attitude became obsequious as he apologised and touched his bedraggled forelocks. Turning to the nearby citizens he entreated their support to help him clear a passage for the carriage.

The cattle were soon herded to the side, permitting the carriage to make steady progress towards the remains of Ber Street Gate. Having safely negotiated this partly demolished entrance, they were soon in sight of the Norman Castle that dominated the city around it. With a deep sigh of relief Maisie beheld the welcome façade of 'The Maid's Head' where they had arranged to spend the night.

As Seb helped his wife from the carriage, Maisie's eyes beheld the Cathedral's majestic spire reaching ever upwards into the evening sky. A dazzling sun, low down in the western heavens reflected a golden glow on the mellow stonework of the beautiful Norman edifice.

While staff bustled around attending to their luggage, Seb escorted Maisie into the confines of 'The Maid's Head', where he ordered food to be sent to their room. From its window they would be able to watch the hustle in the street outside.

Horses pulling carriages, or carrying their riders, kicked up little spurts of dust as they progressed along Tombland. Groups of local people strolled and chatted as they enjoyed the cool evening breeze after a scorching hot summer's day. Maisie was captivated at so much activity, so different from the tranquil surroundings of Homefield.

By the time they had eaten their meal, shadows were lengthening and deepening in the street outside. Rose coloured hues of the sunset still lingered in the sky above the roof tops. As they sat in the twilight there was a discreet knock on the door. A maid entered and asked permission to clear the table. Before leaving she started to light the lamp in their room.

'You may leave the light for now,' Seb spoke quietly to the girl. 'I shall attend to it later.'

'Very good, sir.' The girl curtsied nervously before leaving with the dirty crockery. Once they were alone again, Seb's eyes rested excitedly on Maisie, as sentimental thoughts filled his mind.

'It's much more romantic sitting together in the twilight. Don't you agree, my love?' Maisie's soft, evocative chuckle came like an invitation from the soft shadows beside him. He reached out to embrace his young wife and found her response was as urgent as his emotional longing.

With haste they undressed and before the last rose-pink hues of the sunset had disappeared from the evening sky, they had found fulfilment in their passionate love-making. As they lay satisfied with love, they experienced a feeling of contentment...

ecstatic happiness. Exhausted, they lay in each others arms as the room darkened to a starlit softness.

Next morning as Seb prepared to enter their carriage, he asked Joe Lambert, now the coachman since Ben Sharp's retirement, to drive to the market place. 'Thought you might like to visit the market, Maisie. Being Saturday, there will be much hustle and bustle around the market stalls.'

'Oh, Seb, how exciting. Shall we be able to make any purchases?' Her eyes sparkled with excited anticipation, especially as they neared the crowded market place.

'If it is your wish,' he smiled at her exuberant spirits.

'The place seems so crowded, Seb!' Maisie gazed eagerly from the carriage window as they came to a stop close to the rows of canvas covered stalls. Throngs of shoppers bustled around them as they waited to alight. Ahead of them, horses, carts and carriages were aligned along the edge of the market. Customers, attracted by the shouting stall owners extolling their wares, gathered momentary to inspect the goods before moving on to a more vociferous trader.

Farmers gathered to discuss topics of mutual interest such as the weather, harvest prospects and livestock prices; housewives searched for bargains among the stall displays; men haggled with the stall holders, endeavouring to get a penny or two off the price of clothes and footwear, while stray dogs scampered around between the legs of the crowd. Occasionally there was a disturbance as the dogs snarled and growled at each other over a morsel of discarded food. Their canine display of aggression ensured a few minutes entertainment for the onlookers.

Serene and majestic, the church tower of St. Peter Mancroft overlooked the busy market place. Sentinel-like, it appeared to be watching the frantic activity around the market stalls below. The cacophony of the market transactions was in marked contrast to the solemnity of the largest of the city's parish churches.

Seb experienced a moment of apprehension as he handed Maisie down from their carriage. People appeared to be milling about everywhere and the passages between the stalls were crowded. The activity was typical for a Saturday market day crowd. Smiling graciously, the crowd gave way to the happy looking young couple who had just walked from their carriage.

Seb and Maisie's presence soon attracted the attention of the stall holders. Wares were almost forced into their hands for closer inspection, but the good-natured refusal of the trader's goods in no way discouraged or offended the loquacious traders. After walking round the whole gamut of stalls, they made their way back to the carriage, relieved at being able to relax in the comfort of its interior. Their sole purchase was a hobbyhorse for George.

'I very much doubt that the little lad will be able to ride it yet awhile, Maisie.' Seb inspected the brightly painted toy that Maisie had purchased as a present for their twenty month old nephew. 'However, we shall soon know the answer to that,' he chuckled expectantly.

'Direct to Foxleigh, Joe!' Seb was now anxious to be on the road again. With mountain excitement at the prospects of seeing Julie again, Maisie tried unsuccessfully to relax as their carriage trundled out of Norwich. From the window she watched the city fall behind them until only the spire of the cathedral was visible above the tree tops. Gradually this towering edifice disappeared and the gentle undulating countryside of fields and woods surrounded them.

It was this environment that induces a gradual change in Maisie. She was remembering a cold winter's day nearly six years previously when Edward had walked beside her as they tramped hungry and almost pennyless towards Foxleigh Green.* Memories of that day came poignantly to mind. She tried to hide her tears, but Seb noticing her sadness, understood the reason for her distress. Gently he embraced her in a gesture of sympathy and understanding. Words, he realised would be of little solace just at the moment, but time he hoped would ease his dearest wife's heartaches.

When Maisie was composed again, he ventured a question about his cousin Julie, who unknown to Edward had borne his child.

'Julie seems to have recovered from the shock news concerning Edward's... drowning on the Badger.' Seb glanced towards his wife for confirmation.

* In Book I The Winds of Destiny

'Yes. It came as great shock to her. Poor Julie. Perhaps…' Seb noticed the sadness in her voice as she continued, '… George will help take her thoughts off her… heartache.'

'My uncle informs me that in addition to nursing her mother and attending to George, she also assist him on the estate.' Maisie could well imagine Julie's urgency to keep herself fully occupied. Anything rather than have to think of the past, the present, or the future without the man she loved. Her silence drew an anxious look from Seb as he hesitated. Eventually he went on to relate how concerned his uncle was at the way Julie was burdening herself unnecessary. 'Yes…' he shook his head despondently, '… despite his remonstrations with her to leave the practical side of the state work in his hands, she still persists in helping my uncle.'

'My brother's death was a devastating experience for her, Seb. Edward was not even aware that she was carrying his child . It was such a tragedy that he was… transported before becoming aware of Julie's condition. Her pregnancy.' Shaking her head sadly, Maisie spoke of their futile journey to visit Edward. 'We had gone to the prison in the hope of telling him the wonderful news, but it was too late.

Edward was already on his way to Portsmouth where the convict transport, Badger awaited him. Now he will… never… know,' her voice faded away as she struggled to control her emotions – her heartache.

* * * * *

'Anything you require, my dear?' Colonel Markham gave his wife an anxious look. He tried to hide his concern by glancing out of the bedroom window as he waited for her answer. He was remembering Doctor Bamford's warning that time was gradually running out for her.

'Nothing Granville, thank you. I'm quite… comfortable.' He was aware, that despite her reassurances, she was as usual trying to hide her distress from him. Her pallor and frailty, the colonel realised, were reflections of the pain she was enduring as her terminal illness entered its final stages. 'I hope that Maisie and Sebastian will soon be with us,' she nodded expectantly towards the door.

'They'll not be long, I expect...' he turned just in time to see her face grimace with pain. 'Oh, my dear! Let me...'

'It's alright...' her weak smile of reassurance did not deceive him, '... the pain will... soon pass.' He nodded apprehensively, feeling so helpless when the spasms of pain overcame his dear wife. As she closed her eyes to rest, he turned to gaze pensively across the park lands, recalling as he did so the many happy years they had shared together. Behind him he heard his wife's deep sigh. When he turned she was lying back on her pillows with closed eyes – and so still.

'Dora!' The colonel's voice was a harsh whisper. 'Dora, my love!' Panic edged his voice as he came towards her. Relief flowed through him as her eyes fluttered open. For a moment he had feared the worst. 'I... feel... little tired... Granville... dear.' Once again her eyes closed as she drifted into a restless sleep.

'I will leave you to rest then, my dear.' Gently he made her comfortable before moving again to the window. A few seconds passed before the significance of the carriage trundling down the drive registered in his thoughts. As it drew near he suddenly recognised it as his brother-in-law's conveyance. It must be Sebastian arriving with his new wife, Maisie.

Quietly he left the room and hurried down to join Julie in preparation for receiving his young guests —the newly weds. He glanced thoughtfully at his daughter, wondering what she must be thinking as she waited beside him to welcome her friend Maisie and Seb. Did their marriage remind her of what might have been, had Edward not been imprisoned?

As if understanding his deliberations, Julie turned towards her father with tear filled eyes. 'I shall... never marry father... in case Edward should one day return.' Julie paused for a moment to compose herself, then taking hold of her father's arm she waited with him to greet their guests. 'Come father, let us go and welcome Maisie and Seb.' A warm smile was already covering her sadness as they walked down the steps.

The carriage had barely stopped when Maisie, abandoning all decorum, climbed down the carriage steps and lifting her skirts clear of the gravel, rushed across to embrace Julie and the colonel. It was like coming home again for the excited young bride.

'It's so wonderful... to see you both... again,' Maisie was breathless from her excitement and happiness. 'Where is your mother, Julie?' she glanced round expectantly. A momentary silence caused Maisie to give her hosts a worried look. The troubled glance that passed between Julie and her father only served to increase her alarm. Maisie's exuberant mood faded as she waited for Seb to greet his uncle and cousin.

'Mother is... resting at the moment, Maisie. She is... very ill.' Julie tried not to show her anxiety. 'I will take you both to see her as soon as she wakes.' Her voice was weak from distress as she continued. 'You... must be prepared to see... changes in her. Mother is... gravely ill.'

'Oh, Julie! I'm so... sorry.' Maisie's face was sad as the impact of her friend's words penetrated the shocked emotions that she was experiencing. 'Your mother was always so kind... and loving. A real mother to me.' She reached out to take hold of Julie's hand as they walked into the hall. Seb and the colonel followed closely behind.

'How did your wedding day turn out, Maisie?' Julie made an attempt to change their sombre mood.

;Oh, Julie... it was wonderful!' Eyes sparkling with excitement, she turned towards her friend, 'Just wonderful!' The radiance of her smile induced a beautiful glow to her face. 'I wish you could have been there, Julie.'

'Believe me, Maisie...' her face was grave as she continued in an emotional voice, '... it was my wish to share in your most precious day... but...' She paused to regain her composure. 'Mother's health has deteriorated so... so rapidly of late.' Julie's sadness gave her voice a warm softness. 'We were all so sorry at missing your wedding, Maisie dearest. It was a decision not taken lightly as we have always looked upon you as one of the family.'

'Speaking of family, Julie, when will I be able...'

'We can go up now.' Maisie's request had been anticipated. 'I believe mother is awake.' As they ascended the stairs, Julie gave her friend a pleading look. 'Please remember, Maisie... you will see changes in mother... great changes.' Her voice choked slightly from her suppressed emotions.

'Maisie! Dearest Maisie!' Julie watched anxiously as her mother reached out weakly to accept Maisie's embrace. 'How lovely to see you again.' Dora Markham eased her protégé from her to gaze into a radiant and smiling face. 'Aha! I see marriage... is already enhancing that very... attractive face of yours.' She laughed quietly as a blush caressed Maisie's cheeks. 'I hope you and Seb will be very happy, my dear.' Catching sight of her nephew, she reached out and drew him down beside his young wife. 'That goes for you also, Sebastian. Take care of your lovely wife... she's a wonderful person.'

In the ensuing silence, the soft ticking of the bedside clock seemed an ominous warning that time was passing for all of them – especially for the dying member among them.

'Julie!' Dora Markham's voice startled the silent visitors. 'My jewel case, dear.' Trance-like, Julie took a key and unlocked her mother's casket before passing it to her.

'Thank you!' Smiling to herself, Dora Markham opened the lid to disclose a magnificent collection of exquisite jewellery. From the case, she removed a necklace, an adornment of flawless workmanship. There were gasps of admiration as the diamonds sparkled brilliantly in the shaft of sunlight that penetrated the partly drawn curtains.

'Here, Maisie!' She invited the startled face in front of her to lean forward. Involuntarily, the head of corn-coloured hair was lowered so that the necklace could be placed over it. Maisie remained speechless as she gazed from the necklace back to the woman who had been her mentor – her mother over the past six years. At last she found her voice.

'They're... so... so beautiful!' Tears filled her eyes as she spoke. Maisie began to unfasten the necklace.

'Keep them on, Maisie,' a frail, but gently hand rested upon hers. 'They are your wedding present... from the family.'

'Yes... and with our blessings, my dear.' The colonel who had joined them, bestowed a benign smile upon the young lady who was continuing to stare at the lovely necklace around her neck. Choking with emotion, Maisie embraced all the family in which she had spent the recent years as an accepted member. Her smile was radiant as she expressed her gratitude.

'Thank you...' she was still breathless with excitement, '... thank you all. It's the most precious gift I've... ever known.'

'This, Seb, is for you... your wedding present.' The colonel handed him a brand new saddle. Seb expressed his thanks as he inspected the new saddle with mounting pleasure. A smile of appreciation spread over his face as he looked in turn at his relations. 'It truly is a magnificent saddle.'

'Don't think it will be suitable for the Cavalry, but when you leave, as I believe that is your intention after your next turn of duty, it will be suitable for riding around the estate – and hunting.'

'Hunting?' Seb gave his uncle a questioning look.

'Yes, I'm hoping you'll start the hunt up again... when you return. Your father says he can spare you for a few weeks in the hunting season. So what d'you say?'

'A wonderful idea,' Seb was excited at the prospect of leading the hunt. 'I'll attend to it as soon as I'm released, uncle.'

'Good!' The colonel slapped Seb on the back as all offered their congratulations. 'Thought you'd be in favour.' A quiet knock on the door interrupted the conversation.

'Come in nanny!' As Julie called the invitation, the door opened to admit a young woman. She was holding the hand of the small boy who was toddling a little unsteadily beside her. Maisie gasped as she watched his scamper towards his mother.

'Mama!' He smiled as Julie reached out to take him in her arms. His shock of dark, slightly curled hair and greenish eyes caused Maisie to catch her breath in surprise. George's looks and colouring were a poignant reminder of Edward, when he was young.

Maisie was endeavouring to control her distressed emotions as Julie carried her small son towards her. Through misted eyes she watched as the little boy was held out for her to hold. It was a special gesture and she found herself involuntarily reaching out to receive him. Maisie held him close as she greeted him with a kiss.

It was as if the boy had known that Maisie was someone special, a person full of affection for him. Chuckling, he reached up to touch the face that was smiling so warmly close to his. She smelt his freshly bathed fragrance as she cuddled and repeated her good-night kiss. Reluctantly she handed little George back to his mother.

As Maisie did so, she was aware of Julie's eyes anxiously seeking hers. A look that was pleading for confirmation that her son had a likeness, some characteristic of his father, Edward. Maisie's benign smile eliminated any need for verbal ratification. She watched compassionately as Julie handed her son over to his nanny, a young woman whose face was familiar.

'It's Ruth' Later, while the two men were discussing farming and the threat of war in Europe, Julie had enlightened Maisie as to the nanny's identity 'She was a maid to my aunt, Lady Amelia. When George was born she became his nurse and with my aunt's blessing, Ruth returned to Foxleigh as his nanny.

'She has become my friend and companion, in addition to being a very efficient nanny. George adores her – thinks there's no one like, 'nana Ruth'.' Julie's elucidation induced an affectionate smile as she remembered how the young maid had befriended her while she was staying at her aunt's until her baby was born.

Warm, early morning sunshine was already dispersing the skeins of mist that lingered over the park as Julie and Maisie finished breakfast. With so much to discuss, the two friends had lingered over their meal long after Seb and the colonel had made their excuses and retired from the table. An inspection of the estate was a prerequisite to any other activity for the two men.

'Seb and your father are concerned at the strenuous duties you have imposed upon yourself, Julie.' Maisie's worried look also reflected her own concern as she waited for her friend's reaction. Julie nodded pensively.

'Yes, it has been demanding at times, but…' leaving the table she walked silently towards the window. '… one day I hope to see… Edward returning down the drive.' There was a catch in her voice as she looked towards the hall's tree-lined approach way.

'Oh, Julie, my dearest!' Maisie rose and hurried to embrace her friend. 'You must try not to... expect such... miracles. Edward was reported lost... drowned.' The two friends remained silent for a few moments, finding consolation in their shared grief.

'She... told me Edward... was alive! That... one day... he would return!' The words came between Julie's quiet sobs.

'She? Alive... Edward alive? Who spoke to you of such things?' Maisie was shocked, bemused at Julie's statement.

'Widow Jenkins. I came... upon her once... when I was out riding.'

'How could she know?' Maisie gave her companion a puzzled look. 'What induced her to predict such an... impossible event?' She shook her head in disbelief as Julie explained their brief encounter.

'She was fond of Edward. I believe he often delivered a rabbit or some other game. On one of his visits she persuaded Edward... to have his palm read.' Julie paused, aware of her friend's sudden pallor. They were both reminded of Seb's visit to the palmist at the village fair a few years previous.* Then, the palmist had reluctantly forecast an early and tragic death for him. A discreet knock at the door broke their silent thoughts. Jameson, the butler, looked enquiringly towards Julie.

'Yes. It's alright, Jameson... we've finished breakfast.'

'Thank you, miss Julie. I'll arrange for the table to be cleared.' The door closed quietly behind his retreating figure.

'What... did Edward's palm... foretell?' Maisie was anxious to hear what had been prognosticated, but dreading that which she might hear.

'That Edward would have... a long life. That he was destined to travel a long distance across the sea.' Julie looked uncertain as she related the elderly widow's predictions. 'I concurred with her... regarding the travel, but remarked that unfortunately his... death had been officially confirmed...' her voice faded to silence as she stifled a sob.

'What was her reaction?' Maisie was aware of the facts but was grasping for some indication of hope.

'He's alive! You'll see... you'll see! She almost screeched at me. After staring at me for a few moments she turned and

* In Book I The Winds of Destiny

hastened away. As she departed her head was nodding vigorously and at the same time she was muttering some incantations.' Julie's face became sad as she recalled the elderly witch-like creature scurrying away towards her tumble down cottage.

'If only... her predictions... were true, Maisie.' Her tear-stained cheeks glistened in the early morning sunshine. 'Ah, well!' She sighed heavily and long. 'Wishful thinking... I'm afraid.' Quickly composing herself, she enquired of Maisie's plans for the day.

'I had hoped to ride over and see my uncle and Nelly at the forge and to see how their little lad, my cousin, John is progressing.'

'When I paid them a call a few weeks back, the two boys appeared to enjoy each others company. George, despite being about six weeks older than John, is the smaller of the two. Nevertheless, both boys are well developed for their ages.'

'John was just a baby when I last visited them. I'm looking forward to seeing them all again, but I shall not be away long, Julie.' Maisie's voice was warm with excitement as she anticipated her call.

It was widow Jenkin's grandson Dick, who took the horses from the colonel and Seb when they returned late that afternoon. 'Well, Seb! What is your honest opinion?' The colonel gave his nephew a shrewd look after handing over his horse.

'The estate looks in excellent shape, uncle. A credit to you.' The colonel corrected Seb as they walked from the stables towards the hall.

'A credit to Julie and myself, Seb. Without her help I would not have been able to manage. Ah! Here comes Julie now.' They waited for Julie to dismount and hand her mount over to Len Baxter, the head groom. As she did so they noticed her animated discourse with him. Julie eventually nodded and turning, walked pensively towards them.

'Is something amiss, my dear?' The colonel was aware of his daughter's worried frown.

'It's... Maisie. She appears to be overdue from her visit to the forge. Before leaving she told Baxter that she expected to be back from visiting her uncle by mid-afternoon.'

‘Perhaps she has prolonged her stay. I’ll ride over after I have freshened up.’ Seb’s reassurance failed to ease Julie’s concern.

‘Baxter informed me just now that Maisie had taken Thor.’ Julie’s voice reflected her anxiety.

‘Thor! Surely Baxter...’

‘He tried to dissuade her, but...’ she shrugged her shoulders resignedly, ‘... you know Maisie. She can be very persuasive.’ Julie had a wistful look as she spoke of her friend’s determined attitude.

‘Is there reason to doubt her safety. You both look deeply troubled.’ Seb had become conscious of their increasing anxiety.

‘Thor is a very temperamental horse, Seb. Baxter has been trying to train him to become more reliable... less nervous.’ The colonel’s apprehension was apparent as he explained the situation.

‘Maisie is an excellent rider, I’m sure she will be able to manage him.’ Seb’s hopeful words did little to dispel the anxious look on his companion’s faces.

‘I hope your faith in Maisie is soon confirmed, Seb, but...’ he shook his head slowly, ‘... I’m worried about her nevertheless.’

‘I’ll ride to the forge immediately. Put our minds at rest.’ Seb was already walking towards the stables.

‘Mind if I ride with you, Seb?’ Julie was hurrying to catch up with him, her face grim with worry. He gave her an anxious look before nodding a silent acquiesce.

I reck’n its nearly two hours since she rode off.’ Nelly’s smile of welcome gave way to a look of alarm as Julie and Seb questioned her about Maisie’s movements. Clutching her little son’s hand, she gave her two visitors and anxious look as they prepared to continue their search.

‘Did Maisie give any indication as to where she was going, Nell?’ There was a moment of silence as Nell tried to recall any information that might indicate Maisie’s movements after her departure.

‘Yes... I remember...’ She nodded her head to emphasise her recollections, ‘... Maisie was goin’ t’ride back by way of the common, Master Seb.’ Just as they were preparing to ride off, Ben walked over from the forge.

'Something wrong?' Their anxious faces alerted him to some misfortune.

'We are worried about Maisie,' Julie was trying to hide her emotions. 'We had expected her home before...'

'She was havin' some difficulty with her horse. Quite a handful he was.' Ben gave the two riders a troubled look. 'Took all her time t'hold 'im in check a'fore they galloped off towards the common.'

'Thanks Ben! Julie and myself will ride over and search the area.' As they turned to go on, Ben had a premonition that all was not well with his niece. Had some calamity befallen her?' With mounting fear he watched her husband and friend ride away to continue their search. Nelly sensing his deep concern came and stood beside him.

'Come, Ben. I'll make us a drink.' She took hold of his muscular arm in a reassuring gesture. 'There's not much we c'n do – but wait.' It was a very worried Ben who walked beside his wife and small son back into the cottage.

'Julie... if you ride round by the bushes, I'll...' Seb's face was by this time pallid with worry as he pointed towards the woods that edged the common, '... I'll search the trail through the trees.' Urging his horse into a gentle canter, he set off to search the eerie surroundings of the wood. He came upon no sign of Maisie or her horse. Seb fought to control his emotions as panic threatened to overwhelm him. His whole body was now trembling with distress as he sensed something had happened to his dearest, Maisie. His horse, aware of its rider's nervous disposition was becoming unsettled. Realising this, Seb leaned forward and patted his mount's neck in an attempt to calm the animal.

From the depths of the wood Seb thought he detected a horse's snicker. He pulled up immediately in case there was a repeat. There was nothing – only a deep silence. A wood pigeon exploded into flight from the branches above him, startling both horse and rider. Seb's horse began to whinny as it pranced nervously about. As his mount calmed down, Seb heard the answering neigh from deep in the wood. Taking a side trail he urged his horse towards the sound.

Suddenly in a clearing ahead stood a rider-less horse, which could only be Thor. There was no sign of Maisie. No answer to his frantic call. Seb secured a restless Thor to a tree stump before remounting to search further along the trail. He was now shaking with fear at what he might find. Overhanging branches were become an increasing hazard as he rode deeper into the wood. On two occasions, low spreading boughs forced him to lean forward in his saddle to avoid being brushed from his horse.

A fork in the trail caused him to hesitate. 'Maisie!' His voice echoed in the silent wood. 'Maisie!' Fear gave his voice a harsh sound. Silently he prayed for an answering call. None came. An ominous silence settled over the woodlands after his echo had faded. He pressed on dreading the worst as he guided his horse round a narrow bend.

'Dear, God! No!' His anguished cry shattered the tranquil wood. 'Maisie!' Fear urged him towards her crumpled body. She lay in the shade of an oak. Seb noticed its low spread branches and surmised what had transpired. As he jumped down from his horse, his shaking legs almost gave way beneath him. Scampering in a trance-like scenario, he eventually reached Maisie's inert body.

Seb forced himself to remain calm as he glanced down upon his wife. Blood had trickled down her cheek from an angry abrasion above her right eye. Her pallid features were in stark contrast to the crimson gore that marked her cheek. Her stillness and paleness alarmed Seb.

'Oh, Maisie... no, my love!' In stunned silence he gazed down at her, his brain momentarily incapable of functioning. Then he remembered Julie. Twice he called to his cousin, hoping that his voice would reach her ears. After his second call, he noticed Maisie's eye lids flicker open. A brief movement, but one that stirred him into immediate action.

Yes, there was a pulse. Relief swept through him. He could just feel it. Very faint, but he could just detect Maisie's weak heartbeat. Anxiously he checked for any indications of broken or dislocated limbs. All seemed well. Her prone position appeared a natural one, but... why was she so still?

Julie appeared just as Seb was raising Maisie's head onto his folded coat. 'I'll not be a moment, Julie.' Removing his neckerchief he hurried to the stream that edged the woods where he emerged the cloth into the water. Seb retraced his steps to where his cousin was anxiously watching Maisie and began to gently bathe his wife's face.

'Perhaps we should summon help, Julie?' His voice was soft with worry as he looked up at her. 'If we can get her to the Forge, the doctor could then attend her.' His cousin was already mounted by the time he had finished speaking.

'Leave everything to me, Seb. You just take care of Maisie.' Soon she was out of sight, speeding on her way for assistance.

Seb gently cleaned Maisie's face of the blood from her injury, but she continued to remain very pale and still. 'Maisie! Maisie dearest!' He spoke her name softly as he watched for any response. Was there the merest flicker of her eyelids? Perhaps it was his imagination. An illusion of his agitated emotions. 'Oh Maisie, my love!' he whispered. 'Can you not hear me?' He prayed silently for a sign that she was not severely injured.

Had there been a slight movement? Seb held is breath as he gazed with suspense into his wife's ashen features. Yes, he was sure that his whispered supplications had encouraged some slight reaction. His heart ached with expectation as he noticed Maisie's eyes slowly flicker open. Blue eyes that he loved were staring bewilderingly up at him. For a few moments they look silently into each other's eyes.

'Seb... dearest Seb.' Her words were barely audible as she falteringly continued. 'Thank you... for... coming.' Tenderly he bent over and lightly kissed her lips.

'Try not... to worry. We shall soon have you in bed at the forge.' Maisie felt reassured by the warmth of his smile. An answering one lingered on her lips, but the effort of orientating herself became too exhausting. Once again her eyes closed and she remained still while Seb held her gently in his arms.

That was how Ben and Julie found them a few minutes later. Ben had driven his pony and trap along the rough woodland track until reaching the fork. The narrow track beyond forced them to stop there and walk the short remaining distance to where Seb waited anxiously beside Maisie.

'How is Maisie, Seb?' Ben's voice was hoarse with worry as he looked down upon his beloved niece.

'She... has opened her eyes... spoken a few words. A good sign... I pray, Ben?'

'Amen t'that, lad!' Between them they carried her carefully to the waiting trap. With Maisie reclining in her husband's arms and Ben driving with extreme care along the woodland track, they made their way back to the forge; the two rider-less horses trotted behind them. Julie urged the horse into a gallop to enable her to help Nelly prepare for Maisie's arrival.

They soon had the spare bedroom ready. It was the same one that Maisie had slept in when she and Edward first came to live at Forge Cottage. Their refuge after fleeing from Yarmouth.* Maisie was still in a semi-conscious state when they arrived, unaware of her surroundings, or able to tell them what had caused her riding accident.

Anxiously, Seb and Julie bathed her face, hope to see some reaction from their administrations. They were deeply worried at her negative responses. Downstairs, Ben and Nelly kept an expectant lookout for the appearance of Doctor Bamford. Their anxiety increasing as the minutes ticked away.

* In Book I The Winds of Destiny

Chapter Five

'Farewell, father.' Sebastian embraced Sir Roger before turning to Maisie standing close beside him. As he did so he noticed the healing scar above his wife's right eye and the tenseness in her face as she waited to kiss him goodbye.

'I'll be home again soon, Maisie,' he whispered. 'Then I shall...'

'Oh, Seb!' She buried her face upon his chest as he embraced her. 'Please hurry back, my dearest.' Maisie forced a smile to her face as she raised her tear-filled eyes to gaze into her husband's troubled features. 'Please don't worry about me, Seb. I feel...' she paused to kiss him. '... fine again.'

Seb was apprehensive about leaving. Despite Maisie having made a remarkable recovering from her riding accident, he was still worried about her. He had waited at Foxleigh until she was well enough to travel, before escorting her back to Homefield. The waiting had delayed his departure for a few days. Now with his wife almost fully recovered it was imperative for him to report back to his unit with all possible haste.

'Goodbye... and God Bless you, my dear.' With a hastened word of farewell, Seb mounted his horse and after a last anxious glance at Maisie, he began to walk his mount towards the drive. As he did so, he called over his shoulder, 'I shall be calling briefly at Highfield. I will convey your sincere regards to Josh and Alison.' He gave a final wave to his two watchers before urging his horse in to a canter down the drive.

'Come Maisie, my dear.' Gently Sir Roger guided his daughter-in-law back towards the hall entrance. 'Seb will soon be back with us. Then if all is as planned.... It will be permanently.'

'I sincerely hope so, father.' He noticed the sadness in her voice as she fought to control her emotions. What pleased him greatly was the natural way she now called him father, an endearment that warmed his heart towards her.

'Why, Seb!' Josh gave his brother-in-law a surprised look as he emerged from the milking shed. 'What brings you over this early?'

'A chance to see you and that charming sister of mine, Josh.' His face became more serious as he continued. 'Unfortunately, it must be but a short visit. Duty calls, I'm afraid.'

'You'd best come in then, Seb. Alison, I know, will be glad to see you and hear news of Maisie.' Josh placed his arm around Seb's shoulders in a friendly gesture as they walked, still in conversation, towards the house.

'What news do you bring of Maisie, Seb?' There was an anxious look on Josh's face as he questioned his brother-in-law immediately they were inside. 'We received the disturbing news about the accident from Sir Roger.'

'Is Maisie alright?' Alison eased from her brother's embrace to enquire of her dearest friend's welfare.

'Good news, I'm happy to report.' He gave his sister a reassuring smile. 'It was a nasty fall.. but fortunately her injuries were not too serious. Abrasions and bruises mostly.'

'Good news indeed, Seb.' There was relief in his sister's voice as she expressed her elation.

'Yes...' Seb nodded confirmation, '... Doctor Bamford has instructed her to rest and take things easy for the next week or so. Recommendations...' a smile spread over his face as he spoke of the doctor's instructions, '... that my wife is finding it difficult to comply with, as you can imagine.'

'How did it happen? Maisie is such a good rider?' Alison shook her head as she gave her brother a puzzled look.

'Apparently, a man who she believed was a gypsy, suddenly emerged with his dog from the bushes, directly in front of her and Thor. His sudden appearance and the dog's aggressive barking upset the temperamental Thor. He reared up unexpectedly, causing Maisie to be thrown. As she fell from the horse she knocked her head against a low branch and lost consciousness.'

'Is Maisie back at Homefield, Seb?' Alison had missed her sister-in-laws company of late.

'Yes. She is hoping to visit you in a day or two.'

'What of yourself, Seb? What plans for your future?' Josh gave his brother-in-law a concerned look.

'I'm on my way to rejoin my unit.' Thee was a gasp of dismay from his sister. 'Hopefully…' he gave Alison a reassuring smile, '… by the end of the year, I shall be home and running Homefield for father.'

'Oh Seb! That's wonderful news!' She smiled her relief. 'I'm sure that Maisie and father will be pleased to have you home… permanently.'

'Yes…' he nodded, '… unless circumstances change drastically, I should be home in about three months.' Unknown to Seb, however, circumstances were changing – the finger of destiny was already pointing towards him.

* * * * *

'I'll not be away long, my love.' Josh, gently eased himself from his wife's tearful embrace. 'A week at the most…' an affectionate look passed between them, '… but sooner if possible.'

'Sooner, I hope, Josh. I shall be lonely while you are away.' She stood on tip toes to give him a quick final kiss.

With one foot in the stirrup he turned towards her. 'Clem has promised to take care of things in my absence. He's an honest man.'

'Yes… but hurry back, Josh. It will be so lonely without you.'

'Then… I shall promise a speedy return.' From the saddle he smiled down and raised his hand in a farewell gesture.

'God Bless you, my dear.' As she whispered the blessing to her departing husband, Alison experienced a strange feeling. An uneasy emotion that continued long after Josh had disappeared from her sight. She found herself shaking as she walked unsteadily back into the house. What was it that troubled her, she wondered.

Josh traversed the first few miles in silent contemplation. There was much to appreciate as he observed the sun drenched fields of stubble, where crops had been good that harvest. Now, in the first week of October, there was already a mellowing look to the countryside as the leaves displayed their first traces of scarlet and golden hues of autumn.

Josh's thoughts, however, became more disturbed the further he progressed from home. He hated leaving Alison on her own at Highfield with so much work to be done on the farm. He was thankful that Clem Gibson, his herdsman, would be there to ensure that the farm ran smoothly in his short absence. With this comforting thought he continued on his way in an easier frame of mind.

His cogitation turned to the business that was taking him to the city. While at the solicitors he hoped it would be possible to arrange for his letter to be dispatched with the documents relating to the farm in New South Wales. There were still one or two details that needed finalising as regards the transfer of his share to Rebecca. Now that the amendments had been legally sanctioned, the solicitors were anxious to terminate the transaction. He refreshed his memory as he rode along towards London.

He frowned as he recalled the reference to some unclaimed money being held for a Matthew Porter. Josh removed the solicitors letter from his pocket to check the details.

'...we received a letter from Mrs. Rebecca Burstow informing us that the Porter family had sailed from New South Wales and were expected to call and collect the money on their arrival in England.

Mrs. Burstow had intended sending the letter by Matthew Porter, but in the bustle of the family's departure, it was overlooked. The letter has now been in our possession since September (1813) last year. As there has been no news of the Porter family since they sailed from Sydney, just over eighteen months ago, we feel the matter requires urgent attention.

We would appreciate a visit from you as soon as it is convenient so that the matter can be discussed and hopefully resolved....'

Josh replaced the letter without reading the concluding paragraphs. His serious meditations induced a deep frown as he tried to assess the situation. The solicitor had mentioned other letters that Matthew Porter was believed to be carrying. What had become of them? Who were they for, he wondered. Perhaps there was one from Becky. She had promised to send him one as soon as they were settled on their farm. Josh was remembering his disappointment when he had received no word from his sister he adored. It was so unlike Becky, but his spirits rose when he realised that there might well be news from her at the solicitors.

Involuntarily he felt inside his coat. Yes, his letter to Becky and Stephen was still there. Thinking about his words as he rode along, he wondered if he had been too severe in his reprimand to his sister. In his letter he had explained how upset they all were at home when no news of their welfare had been received. They were deeply concerned and distressed after reading of their terrifying ordeal in the Badger's lifeboat.

He had written of the tragedy that her and Stephen had been very fortunate to survive and explained the shock it had caused to them all at home. Josh had also expressed a hope that his sister would write to their parents as they were anxious to receive news of her health. They had, he explained in his letter, expressed regrets at their selfish attitude and hoped that she would forgive their wrong and find it in her heart to love them again.

Josh realised the words wee his own interpretation of his parent's unspoken thoughts. He was sending the letter without them being aware of its contents. It was because of their distress and misunderstanding that existed between them and Becky, that he had considered it an acceptable action.

'I'm sure...' he had pleaded in his letter to his sister, '... that their suffering would be greatly eased if you, my dearest Becky, could find it in your heart to offer them your love – and forgiveness.' To ensure that his letter would reach his sister quickly, he was arranging it to be forwarded with the signed documents. Assuming the solicitors would agree

Josh's thoughts about his letter to Becky were interrupted by a coach travelling towards him. It eased up as it passed, so that the driver could shout a warning. 'Beware... young man! Highwaymen about!' He pointed his whip in the direction Josh was travelling. Josh raised his hand to acknowledge the thoughtful warning, at the same time reminding himself to remain ever alert on the road.

He wished now that he had his pistol with him. Its presence would have given him more confidence in the unlikely event of being waylaid. A short ride ahead of Josh lay the village of Brentwood. A settlement he was destined not to reach. His thoughts were of Allison when it happened. A narrow stretch of road lay in deep shadow from overhanging trees and the tall hedge that shaded the road beside it. Suddenly a masked rider emerged from the hedgerow and manoeuvred his horse to obstruct Josh's progress. Gripping his whip, Josh prepared to defend himself against his assailant. For a few seconds the two men confronted each other.

'Orf yer 'orse!' he snarled. 'An' givus y'money!' There was no mistaking the threat in his voice.

'I'm damned if I will. Get out of my…' Unaware of the second man behind him, Josh threatened to lash out at the masked rider. Suddenly an explosive blow on the back of his head sent a shudder through his falling body. A curtain of darkness enveloped him as he rapidly drifted into an unconscious state. Before he crashed to the ground, he vaguely remembered another painful blow to his head. Then an all enveloping darkness.

'Yer's kilt 'im Sam!' The first rider paused in his ransacking of Josh's valuables.

'Don't fink so!' His smile appeared unconcerned. 'Any 'ow it don't mat'er!' he wiped his nose with the dirty sleeve of his shabby coat.

'Best git 'im orf t'road.' Having removed all of Josh's belongings they dragged him into the hedgerow before riding off.

'Wot about 'is 'orse Will?'

'We'll take it wiv us. Git rid of it later.' The two robbers were soon lost to sight among the trees. They rode deeper into the wood and further away from the highway- and Josh.

CHAPTER SIX

Jason Smith, his wife May and teenage daughter, Doreen were returning home from a reunion, shared in meditation and prayers with their Quaker Friends. Wherever they had gathered for worship, the family had been made welcome by Friends they had once shared their lives with in the city. Now, with pleasant memories of their stay in London still fresh on their minds, they were returning home to their small farm.

Their partly covered cart trundled slowly over the rutted road, pulled by an elderly looking horse that found the leisurely pace and the light load much to his satisfaction. Mostly, the man in dark sombre clothing walked beside the cart while his wife and daughter sat meditatively upon the driving seat. A black hat with a broad, half cocked brim was placed slightly high on Jason's brow to permit the cool caress of the light breeze upon his perspiring forehead.

His wife and daughter's clothes though mainly dark, were neat and modest, a reflection of the purity of their souls. A white apron like covering was worn as a protection to their dresses, an adornment that was as pure and carefully ministered to as their minds. Both the women were wearing velvet bonnets as a protection from the sun and out of reverence for their religious faith. Their conversation as they progressed on their journey was spoken in low, courteous tones.

It was with shocked emotions that these three Christian souls came upon a semi-conscious, blood spattered being. Bemused and in great pain, Josh's blood-shot eyes watched the mirage-like approach of the horse drawn cart, led by a person in clerical attire. Alerted by the injured man's appearance, Jason had hurried forward to offer comfort. As he arrived beside the badly injured stranger, Josh felt himself once again slipping into a coma.

Jason raised his hand to bring his entourage to a halt. 'We shall need water and a cloth,' he spoke quietly to his wife, who had climbed down from the cart to inspect Josh's injuries. Shaking her head sadly, she retraced her steps to the cart where Doreen, their sixteen years old daughter handed her a bowl of water and a small piece of cloth.

'Can I be of any help, mother?'

'No. Thee stay where though art, my child.'

While his wife bathed the wound on Josh's head, Jason watched for any signs of movement. After a few moments, the injured man's eye lids fluttered open and a pair of blue-grey eyes stared disconcertedly into his.

'Have no fear, young man... we are friends. We shall care for thee.' Josh turned his eyes towards the voice, bemused by the activity that surrounded him. He found himself gazing into the serene face of a middle aged woman who was kneeling on the grass beside him. She held a saturated cloth in her hand and was about to immerse it into a bowl of discoloured water. 'Your wound is clean now. How does thee feel. . thy colour is rather pale?' May gave Josh an anxious look as she tipped the water from the bowl and wrung out the cloth.

'May we enquire thy destination? Perhaps we may be of some help to thee?' Josh gazed slowly around, unable to comprehend his situation. He buried his head in his hands as he tried to remember, but he could draw no recollection from his mind. Shaking his head despondently, he raised his head to gaze in bewilderment at the kind friends who had stopped to help him.

'I'm... sorry... but... my mind seem... incapable... of remembering.' Josh continued to shake his head as he tried to reach back in his memory. It was useless, no thoughts materialised. It seemed as if they were permanently locked behind a curtain of impenetrable fog. He experienced a moment of panic as he realised that he was unaware of his identity, or what was happening to himself. If only the throbbing in his head would subside, then he might be able to concentrate his thoughts. Josh made an effort to stand, but his legs were weak and had it not been for Jason's strong arms around him, he would have collapsed.

With Jason's support, he managed to reach the waiting cart. 'Best if thee rides in our cart, young man. We have friends at Chelmsford where we can perhaps arrange for a doctor to examine thee.' Josh attempted to express his appreciation for their help, but Jason raised his hand. 'No need for talk... thee must rest.' Sitting in the back of the cart, Josh drifted in and out of coma-like spells as they jostled slowly towards their unscheduled destination.

Each time Josh's vision cleared he became aware of the young woman sitting on the seat of the cart. Once, aware of his scrutiny, she turned and gave him a warm friendly smile. 'Are thee comfortable, sir?' Her voice was a soft comforting sound. He nodded a silent affirmation, still bemused by the peculiarity of his mind. Once again the lovely vision before him faded, darkness once again enveloped him. It was as if a curtain was being drawn across his vision... his thoughts... his past.

Josh watched anxiously as the doctor straightened up from his examination. In the ensuing silence he heard the distant sounds of voices from the street and the terse shout of a driver warning pedestrians that they were impeding his progress. Voices and noises appeared to come through veils of mist. He was endeavouring to comprehend their significance.

'Good-day to you, young man!' The doctor gave him a puzzled look before leaving the room. Josh could hear voices in deep conversation just beyond the closed door. The muffled words were inaudible and these gradually faded as the speakers moved away. After a few minutes, the door opened and a very worried looking Jason entered.

Josh watched his silent approach with trepidation. He eased back as an invitation for his rescuer to sit on the edge of his bed. Jason remained silent for several seconds as he gazed uncertainly into Josh's bewildered countenance. 'It would appear...' he eventually broke the silence, '... that thee has suffered severe head damage. From the doctor's observations it would seem thy memory has been seriously impaired. To what extent he is unable to confirm, but...' he continued to stare intently into Josh's troubled eyes, '... the degree of its severity will probably manifest itself in the next few days... perhaps weeks.'

'How long have I been here?' Josh looked trance-like around the room.

'Near on a week, lad!'

'A week!' Josh was shocked. He had remembered very little of the time in its passing. 'I'm sorry... to have brought... trouble upon you... and your friends, Jason. I shall leave as soon as I am able.'

Jason scratched his head thoughtfully as he considered his companion's words. Eventually he expressed that which was on his mind. 'Hast thou considered where thee might go?' Jason's face was serious as he raised the question. 'Thee has no idea who you are or from whence thee came – your home.' The two men looked at each other in silence as Jason waited for his statement to be comprehended. 'No money was found on your person. We found no means of identification... nothing. All you possessed was taken by the robbers. Even your horse, as we must assume that you were riding at the time of the attack.'

'Oh, Jason!' Josh buried his head in his hands. 'What am I to do? I may have left a family. Perhaps a wife and children.' His face reflected his anguish as he looked up with a tear-stained face. 'Who am I, dear friend?" With tears trickling down his cheeks, Josh lifted his eyes to the cloudless sky beyond the window. 'Dear God,' he whispered in veneration, 'Please help me.'

'He will, young man! He will!' Jason's reassurance induced a feeling of peace in Josh's troubled mind.

'This note...' Jason displayed a crumpled piece of paper. 'We found it in the grass, near to where we found you. Hopefully it may give us a clue as to who you are. Perhaps by reading it carefully... the words may stir some part of your memory.' Filled with expectancy, Josh reached out to take the creased segment of paper.

'Thank you, Jason.' For several seconds Josh continued to stare at the letting, wanting to, yet apprehensive about reading it.

'Best if you read it, friend.' Jason's voice was sympathetic and understanding. Josh shook his head sadly.

'The lettering is... so... so confusing.' A frown of concentration creased his brow. 'Perhaps you will be kind enough to read it for me, Jason. 'Dearest Joshua,' he commenced without any sign of emotion.

'When you write to your sister, please ask her...
obdurate disposition towards her marriage...
reflection, we now realise that our attitude was...
Please reassure her of our love and inform...
We hope that she will find it in her heart to pardon...
Sinfulness.'

Jason lowered the torn piece of correspondence. 'It is signed with words of love from your father and mother.' Josh was struggling for remembrance, but there was nothing in the segment of the letter to stir his memories. The note may not even be his. Raising his face to meet Jason's troubled eyes, he slowly shook his head.

'I'm sorry...' Josh struggled dejectedly, '... the letter conveys nothing.'

'On the assumption that this piece of correspondence belongs to thee... and as we have no other clue to thy identity, we should perhaps accept that Joshua is thy rightful name.'

'Yes. In the absence of no other identification, Josh must be acceptable.' He was not to know that it would be well into the future before unusual circumstances confirmed his true identity.

'What plans would thee be having for thy immediate future, er... Josh?' for a few minutes, Josh was bemused, almost shocked as the implication of Jason's words gradually penetrated his dulled senses. He had forgotten that life despite his uncertain disposition must carry on.

'With no money... no identity and no remembrance of the past. My future, assuming I have one, would appear to be very uncertain.' Josh shook his head despondently as he meditated on his unusual circumstances. 'The truth is, Jason...' he gave his companion a worried look. 'I feel lost. Can you help me?'

A knock on the bedroom door interrupted their conversation. Jason glanced round as his wife opened the door to check on the invalid.

'Ah, my dear. Thy arrival is most opportune. We...' he nodded towards Josh, '... were just discussing this young man's future. Joshua, as we believe his name to be, is uncertain as to what course it should take.' Jason gave his wife a meaningful look. A covert glance that induce the flicker of a smile to her benign face as she gleaned its meaning.

'Perhaps er... Joshua would considering travelling home with us. We are Quakers, dear friend.' She gave the injured Josh a benevolent smile. 'Thee may find our way of life austere, but we shall be glad to welcome thee into our Christian home'

'Thank... thank you both.' Josh's smile was one of relief as he accepted their kind invitation. 'When do we resume our journey home?'

'Tomorrow... if you...'

'I shall be well enough to ride with you... and gladly look forward to sharing your Christian way of life.'

* * * * *

'Oh, Alison, dearest!' Maisie, now fully recovered from her riding accident, dismounted and hurried across to embrace her deeply worried friend. For a few moments they shared an affectionate embrace, both aware of the uncertainty and loneliness that was blighting their lives. After a few moments of comforting each other, they eased apart as their visions became misted by unshed tears. Their smiles of welcome barely altered the tenseness of their features. Each was acutely aware of the others suffering. With arms around each other they entered Highfield, their silent thoughts recalling the last occasion when they had last been together in the house.

Josh had been at home with Alison then. They had been discussing the happy event that was but a few days away. Maisie and Sebastian's wedding. It had been a joyful and exciting occasion. Their spirits and moods a complete contrast to the sadness they were now enduring.

'Have... you heard any news... of... Josh?' Maisie was uncertain about the subject that was dominating their thoughts – their lives.

'No ...' Alison was endeavouring to maintain her composure, '... nothing whatever. We know that Josh... did not keep his appointment with the solicitors. Father contacted Seb at his barracks. On receiving the letter, Seb requested and was granted a few days off duty to enable him to make enquiries.'

'Yes...' Maisie looked across at her friend, '... Seb mentioned his search when he wrote.' She pulled a letter from her pocket. 'I received this three days ago, but it would appear that you have more recent news, Alison.' Maisie nodded towards the envelope in her friend's hand.

'Yes...' she looked disconsolately at her letter, '... this was delivered only yesterday.'

'From Seb?' Alison nodded as she unfolded the letter to refer to the contents.

'He was able to trace Josh's movements as far as a small hostelry a few miles beyond Chelmsford. It was there that the landlord remembers serving a meal to a man answering Josh's description. He also remembers warning the traveller that robbers were operating in the area.'

'Was Seb able to obtain any further information?'

'No... none whatever.' She shook her head sadly. 'After leaving the hostelry, Seb rode along the road a few miles towards Newham. Josh's destination,' she reminded Maisie. 'After about an hours ride...' Alison hesitated, 'Josh was... attacked.' She was unable to continue. Alison buried her face in her hands as sobs shook her body. Maisie moved quickly across to comfort her.

'Thank... you... Maisie.' Alison forced a smile to reassure her friend. 'It's... alright...' her hand reached out for Maisie's, '... I just... needed to tell someone.' After a few moments of silence to regain her composure, Alison related further details of Seb's search.

'Quite by accident as he was riding along a lonely stretch of road, he noticed something shining in the hedgerow. The area was in shadow from overhanging trees, but a shaft of sunlight filtering through the leaves glittered upon a bright object in the grass. Seb dismounted to investigate and came upon Josh's... whip.' Alison made a determined effort to control her troubled emotions. 'It... was the one... I gave him... last Christmas. His name was engraved on the silver band that decorated the stock. Seb believes that the... robbers... cast it aside because of Josh's name on the band. If they were caught with it in their possession, it would be sufficient evidence to incriminate them.'

'Was there any other sign... of Josh's presence?'

Alison shook her head. 'None!' In a voice that was strained with sadness she continued. 'Seb made... a thorough search of the area. There was nothing... nothing... nothing!' Maisie held her sobbing friend close in her arms. Silently she waited for Alison's emotive outburst to subside.

'We must continue to hope... and pray for Josh's safe return.' Alison nodded a silent affirmation, but intuitively both realised that Josh's safe return after nearly two months was becoming increasingly doubtful.

'I have other news for you, Maisie.' Tears glistened on Alison's cheeks as once again she reached out for the reassuring touch of her companion's hand. 'You are the first to know.' Maisie noticed the sadness that lined the face of her dearest friend, yet she also beheld a glimmer of excitement in the eyes that gazed into hers. 'I am expecting a... baby. Our... first!'

Maisie was speechless. For a few moments she just stared unbelieving at Alison, then words tumbled from her lips as she held her friend close in a congratulatory embrace.

'I was intending to ride over and tell my parents when you called. I'll ask Clem to get the trap ready, then we can ride over to Homefield together. On the return journey I shall call and tell Josh's parents. Perhaps the news will ease their distress.'

Sir Roger's embrace was warm and affectionate as he congratulated his daughter on her wonderful news, but Alison was aware that something was troubling her father.

'Is something amiss, father? You look troubled.' She wondered if her condition and being alone at Highfield was worrying him. She was about to reassure him when the reason for his solemn disposition was explained.

'It is your aunt Dora. I have just received news of her... her passing.' There was a moment of silence as the sad news penetrated their thoughts. Maisie, who had heard the news, was the first to speak.

'I'm sorry about the sad loss of Mrs. Markham,' her voice was quiet as she gazed into the blazing fire. 'Julie and the colonel will be greatly distressed.' She gave a deep melancholy sigh.

'She was a kind and... understanding... person. Like a mother to me when I first stayed at Foxleigh.'

'Yes, Maisie, we are all saddened by the news. However...' Sir Roger gave his daughter an affectionate glance, '... we must think of the life just beginning.'

* * * * *

Josh was in deep meditation as he walked across the snow covered field towards the flock of sheep that he tended. They were huddled in the lee of a tall hedge that separated the field from a small wood. Since arriving at Jason's small farm, he had taken on the work of shepherd and herdsman as a way of compensating the Quaker family for his keep.

It was among the animals that he had experienced strange sensations of ambivalent thoughts. Their presence reminded him of an unknown manifestation that he was unable to explicate. Jason, noticing his skill with the sheep and cattle, was sure that the young man he had taken into his household, had before his loss of memory, been associated with farming.

Despite enquiries around the area where they had found him, nothing had been gleaned as to his identity. Where he came from also remained a mystery. The Quaker communities had promised to extend their quest for information, but no definite clues had been found.

Josh paused to check his flock as a flurry of snow sprinkled his clothes. Near the hedge there were a few patches of exposed grass where the sheep, despite the wintry conditions, were finding sustenance. Above the intermittent bleating of the sheep, he heard the staccato-like sounds of a woodpecker rapping away at the bark of a tree. The sound was crystal clear as it drifted on the frosty air. Crows glided like shadowy wraiths against the ice-blue morning sky. Their raucous cries, as they flew over the landscape, disturbed the silent, snow-covered land beneath.

Josh's inner sense appeared captivated by a distant church. Whenever his eyes rested on the flint-stone edifice he experienced a stirring of some inner emotion that he was at a loss to understand. Was it something to do with his forgotten past, he wondered. After attending his flock, some supernatural power seemed to draw him towards the church that was used by the villagers as their place of worship. Before Josh realised the significance of his actions, he was standing at the entrance to the weathered flint-stone building.

An unknown presence seemed to draw him inside. As he stood within the sacred edifice, he was overcome by a strange emotion. It was as if a veil had been lifted briefly, revealing a scene that seemed familiar to him. He glanced silently round at the box-pews, wooden galleries and the font with its ornate features and pulpit. Something strange and imperceptible was troubling his mind, but he could not relate their implications.

Josh continued to stare trance-like at the church's interior, struggling to orientate his feelings in what appeared to him, familiar surroundings. A quiet spoken voice startled him, dissipating his unaccountable sensibilities. He turned to find a man in clerical robes approaching him from the rear of the building.

'May God's Blessing be with you throughout the New Year, young sir!' Josh found himself looking into the smiling face of an elderly man. His attire confirmed his status as that of the village parson. Suddenly, Josh remembered his surroundings and quickly removed his hat.

'Please forgive my laxity. I was...' A hand was raised to indicate that no apologies were necessary.

'You are more than welcome to our place of worship. A stranger... yet your face...' he gave Josh's countenance a searching look, '... does seem familiar. Perhaps if I might know your name... it might refresh my memory.' His close observation continued as he spoke.

'Unfortunately, I am unable to impart that information, reverend.' Seeing the old parson's surprised look, Josh elaborated on his statement. 'It would appear that I was the victim of a brutal robbery in which I sustained head injuries that resulted in the loss of my memory. Since I was found semi-conscious by the roadside, I have been cared for by the family that found me... Jason Smith and...'

'The Quakers!' His voice sounded a little sharp.

'Yes!' Jason nodded. 'Kindly people who have taken me in and cared for me when love and understanding were my urgent needs.'

'Hmm!' His face had a frown of concentration. He was still wondering where he had seen the young man who now stood before him. Still puzzling, he watched pensively as Josh turned to leave.

'Good-day, reverend!' He gave the elderly parson a benign look. 'And may the New Year be a blessed one for you also.' Quietly he walked out into the open. As he replaced his hat, a thought suddenly struck him. Turning to the watching cleric, he requested a favour. 'If by chance you should recall anything that might help in my identity, reverend, perhaps you will be kind enough to relay that information on to me.'

'Oh, that would be old Reverend Woods. A kindly old soul.' Jason nodded across the table to confirm Josh's description of the village parson.

'He thought thy face was familiar, Josh?' May seemed interested in that piece of news.

'Yes, ma'am.' Josh had settled on the more formal mode of address in his relationship with May, the matronly wife of his mentor, Jason. Her dignity and motherly bearing encourage such respect. 'He scrutinised me most comprehensively.' Josh gave a little chuckle as he remembered the elderly parson gazing at him from under his bushy eyebrows.

'Did... he give thee any hope. Any expectation that thy identity might be confirmed?' There was an anxious note to Doreen's voice as she asked the question.

'None whatever. His thoughts seemed somewhat... vague.' Josh shook his head sadly. 'I did however...' he glanced round the table at their expectant faces. '... request that should he remember anything relating to my identity, such information would be greatly appreciated.'

'We shall pray for thee, Josh and hope that the Almighty will in His own good time deem it necessary to restore thy lost memory.' Such silent prayers were deliberated by the Quaker congregation at their place of meditation on the following Sunday.

Josh experienced a feeling of nervousness as with Doreen beside him, they followed her parents into the Friends meeting place. A place of meditation would better describe the building, thought Josh as he remembered Jason's words of explanation. His mentor had been preparing him for this special occasion, Josh's first visit to the Quakers place of assembly.

'We believe in meditation, where...' his serious countenance was indicative of the sincerity with which he imparted his religious beliefs to the young man his family had welcomed into their home, '...our silent prayers descent into our thoughts as we await the inspirations of virtue in our hearts.' Josh was remembering Jason's inspiring words as he was guided to an area where the men sat apart from the women, while they bowed their covered heads in silent meditation.

Before leaving the farm, Josh had been presented with a black hat, similar to the one worn by the male members of the Quaker community. Surreptitiously, he had tried it on in his room. Looking back at him fro the mirror was a clean shaven man with blue-grey eyes that stared dispassionately into his. His fair, sandy coloured hair was in sharp contrast to the hat he was wearing.

As he observed his reflection, he experienced a strange sensation that had troubled him. A transformation of his image was taking place. In an ethereal-like way, another man appeared to be staring back at him from the mirror. Briefly, his Quaker reflection had faded, replaced by a blurred familiar countenance that induced in him a momentary confusion of thoughts. The vision had disappeared before he could ascertain any characteristics regarding its presence.

The image he had glimpsed seemed that of a young clergyman, but it had faded so quickly and been replaced by his Quaker reflection. Josh turned quickly from the mirror, wondering what it could mean. What was the significant of the celestial-like appearance? Had he in his forgotten life been connected with the church? He had considered that possibility, before shrugging it aside as an unlikely vocation.

Now, as Josh sat down beside his mentor on the simple bench that acted as a seat, he tried to concentrate on his meditations.

A principal facet of the gathering. Covertly, he slowly raised his eyes to observe his peaceful surroundings and the Quaker Friends offering up to God their hearts and silent prayers.

There was a dazzling whiteness about the walls that reflected the pureness of the congregations hearts. The bareness of the place was deliberate. There were no places for statues, altars and such normal accessories as found in the churches. Nothing was permitted to distract the thoughts and meditations as the men on one side and the women opposite them offered up their silent thoughts and prayers.

With bonnets, mainly of silk or velvet, the women covered their heads as they lowered them in search of heavenly inspiration. Josh's eyes rested upon the delicate features of Doreen. Her presence induced an emotional response within his young powerful body. Ashamed of his thoughts, he forced himself to concentrate on his prayers of forgiveness.

Josh lowered his eyes humbly towards the floor as he endeavoured to force out any extraneous thoughts that might disturb his meditation. It was at that moment that he realised to what extent his thoughts and actions were becoming Quaker orientated. Josh watched silently as one of the congregation walked quietly towards the slightly raised platform at the end of the hall. From this tribune the man, zealous from heavenly inspiration, began to express his emotive feelings to the assembly. In a loud voice, strained with passion, he inspired those present to offer up to God acts of virtue and to display warm benevolence towards their saviour and earthly brothers.

The meeting ended with a prayer and as Josh walked home beside Doreen, he once again experienced an aching in his body – a longing that troubled him. He tried to force such amorous thoughts from his mind. He must restrain himself as there was no way of knowing if he was free to share a serious relationship with the daughter of his mentors.

Easter found Josh busy with the lambing. Long wearisome hours among his flock kept him from the house for lengthy periods – both by day and night. Occasionally when he paused in his labours, his troubled thoughts would dwell on his unique situation.

He was still no nearer to solving his dilemma – his true identity. Twice he had visited the old parson, but other than confirming that he thought Josh's face was familiar, there had been nothing further to encourage hope.

It was the anxious bleating of an ewe that interrupted his thoughts. Hurrying across to the animal, he noticed that one lamb was already born and experiencing its first tentative contact with the world, while another was reluctant to leave the warmth of its mother's body. 'Twins!' Josh exclaimed apprehensively as he lowered himself down beside the ewe to encourage and assist it in the delivery of the recalcitrant lamb.

After gently stroking and reassuring the mother, Josh with his sleeves rolled up began the delicate task of helping the lamb to enter the cold world outside. 'Come on... you... young scamp!' With a deft final pull, a young lamb emerged. Gently Josh wrapped it in his coat and carried it towards the barn where he had made a bed of straw for such contingencies.

A few ewes and their lambs bleated nervously in the barn, both recovering from births that had been troublesome. Josh took his new arrival to a sheep that had lost her lamb, but the ewe would have nothing to do with the small creature that she realised was not her own. While he was considering alternative means of keeping the lamb alive, the barn door opened behind him. Suddenly Doreen was standing beside him.

'Trouble, Josh?' She looked anxiously at the new born lamb in his arms.

'Twins! I was hoping to introduce it to another ewe, but...' he shook his head solemnly, '... it hasn't worked.'

'Shall I take it, Josh? I can nurse it until it's stronger.' She came close to take the lamb from him. Silently he handed the lamb to her, his heart throbbing at her closeness. As he did so, their eyes, sparkling in the gloom of the barn were fixed on each other. Their faces were almost touching as Doreen received the small creature into her arms.

Josh, his heart racing with excitement lowered his lips onto those of the young woman in front of him. Emotions of ecstasy surged through their young, eager bodies as their kisses became more sensuous.

As the door crashed open, they quickly moved apart. Still standing close to each other they looked around to see who had entered. It was her father. Fortunately the gloom in the barn had prevented Jason from seeing their kiss, but he realised that he had interrupted some sensitive act that had passed between them. Their excited faces reflected the exciting experience they had just shared.

'I wish thee to leave us, Doreen!' Jason's voice was terse as he gave his daughter a searching look.

'But the lamb father! I was only...'

'Do as thee are told, girl!' The guilty flush on her face confirmed his worse fears.

'Yes... I'm sorry, father.' Her words were little more than whisper as she turned to leave with the lamb still in her arms. Slowly with lowered eyes she walked from the barn.

'I assure you that...' Jason raised his hand to stop Josh's explanation.

'In the future, Josh, thee will refrain from any clandestine meetings with Doreen.' Before Josh could explain that his meeting with her had been unpremeditated, Jason continued his reprimand.

'I have noticed they covetous glances in my daughter's direction of late and would ask that thee refrain from such licentious observations. It is my wish that her pureness of mind and body is not tainted by such nefarious thoughts or deed.' There was an angry look to his face as breathing heavy he paused to watch Josh's reaction.

'Jason, you must believe me when I confess that my thoughts of Doreen have always been chaste and sincere. I would not wish to abuse the trust that you and your family have placed in me. My admiration for your charming daughter is heartfelt and I can assure you that my feelings are virtuous ones.'

Well... er... that's as maybe and I thank thee for thy honesty, Josh. Nevertheless, I feel it would be prudent for thee to share thy meetings with Doreen... in the company of others.' Josh nodded his understanding.

'You have my word, Jason. I shall respect your wishes.'

'Perhaps I was hasty in my castigation, Josh, but my daughter's welfare and purity of being are of paramount concern to her mother and myself.'

'And mine also, Jason. I give you my solemn oath that Doreen's virtuousness will be venerated. I would not wish it otherwise.'

'I thank thee for thy veracity, Josh.' His glance was uncertain as he elaborated on his initial outburst. 'My anger was at finding you and my daughter alone in the barn. I would not want...'

'Doreen was collecting a new born lamb... the last born of twins. An ewe that had lost its own, refused to take it. Our only hope for its survival was to hand nurse it. A twin lamb in need of warmth and care was being offered a chance of life.'

'Yes... I er... understand. We appreciate all that thee has done for us on the farm, Josh. Thanks to thee our lambing has been a successful one. Thy long hours of conscientious working has ensured a gratifying outcome.'

'And I owe your family my thanks for the kindness they have shown to a stranger. Someone unknown not only to you and your family, Jason, but also to myself. My identity, despite our enquiries still remains unknown.'

'Until that happy occasion arrives, Josh, thou art welcome to continue as one of our family.'

'Thank you. There is but one favour I would ask of thee, Jason.' Josh found himself gradually settling into the Quaker's way of life – and speech.

'If it is within my jurisdiction, thy request will be considered and granted, if it be at all possible.' There was an expectant look in his face as he waited for Josh to speak.

'If by chance my life is destined to continue in the Quaker community, I...' he hesitated, wondering if his solicitation would be misconstrued. Perhaps he was being too impetuous... but it was too late to retract his request now, '... I would like... one day... to ask thee for thy daughter's hand in marriage.' He watched the conflicting emotions play across Jason's face. There was a long silence before the answer he was waiting for was confirmed.

'Thee is an honest and Christian-like man, Josh and thy intentions regarding my daughter are sincere, but...' he was aware of the young man's concentrated gaze as he waited an answer. Jason hesitated, not wanting to hurt the man whom he and his family, as well as the Quaker community had come to respect. Here was a good man, who in normal circumstances he would have unhesitatingly accepted into his family – as Doreen's husband.

Jason's eyes filled with sorrow as he prepared to explain why he must refuse the marriage request. Why it would be impossible for Josh and his daughter to become husband and wife – in the near future at least. 'Until we know thy identity, Josh, there is nothing we can do regarding such a union. I'm truly sorry, but we must at least know thy name, or wait a few years in the hope that our enquiries will by then have revealed who thee are.' Sadness filled his eyes as he continued to gaze at the young man his family had found severely injured by the roadside.

'Has't thee not considered that somewhere a family, perhaps a wife may be grieving for thy absence. Such possibilities must be given serious consideration.' Josh nodded his understanding before walking thoughtfully from the barn. He paused in the doorway and turned slowly to face Jason who had remained by the sheep.

'I pray that thee are wrong, Jason... about my being a family man. If that should be so, my absence will have been the cause of much distress – even hardship.' Josh looked bemused as he hesitated in the patch of sunlight by the door. 'Dear, God!' he whispered uncertainly, 'Please help me to find... myself.

Chapter Seven

'She's... so... so beautiful, Alison.' Maisie was gazing adoringly at the small baby that nestled in its mother's arms. When news of her friend's imminent confinement had reached her, Maisie had hurried over to Highfield to be on hand when the baby was born.

Both her and Jenny, the housemaid who had come from Homefield, had ensured that all was ready for the doctor's visit. Jenny, now ensconced as the housekeeper at Highfield, had stayed to assist during the birth while Maisie had remained to comfort an anxious Sir Roger, who had come over to be near his daughter. 'I know there's not much I can do Maisie, but with Josh... away...' He shrugged his shoulders forlornly.

Their anxious waiting had ended in the early hours of the morning, when a tired Doctor Wallace had informed Sir Roger that he had a healthy and charming granddaughter. 'Everything is fine, Sir Roger. If only... her... husband...' he shook his head sadly, unable to express his feelings for the tragedy that had befallen the young mother.

'Drink, John?' Sir Roger looked towards the old family physician as he hesitated over the misfortune that had brought sadness to the house.

'Oh... er, yes. Yes, thank you.' He watched pensively as Maisie placed the brandy and glasses close to Sir Roger. Having ascertained that the drinks were at hand, she spoke quietly to the old doctor.

'I would like to see Alison and...'

'Of course, my dear,' he had anticipated her request. 'Your presence may help ease the melancholy feeling that has prevailed since confinement.'

Alison, as she became aware of Maisie's presence, turned her pale face to smile weakly at her friend. 'Oh, Maisie... if only Josh...' her sobbing tore at Maisie's heart. Fighting to keep her emotions under control, Maisie reached out to embrace her friend in an effort to comfort her.

'I'm sorry... Maisie!' Alison wiped the tears from her cheeks before glancing towards the cot beside her bed. 'What do you think of my baby... my daughter?'

'She's so... so beautiful!' Maisie looked down at the little girl sleeping so peacefully. 'Have you... decided...?'

'Jane!' Alison had expected her friend's question. 'I shall call her Jane.' She sighed wearily as her eyelids closed momentarily.

Noticing her tiredness, Maisie suggested that she try and rest... sleep.

'I shall be here should you need me.' Reassured by her friend's presence, Alison with a smile upon her face lay back on her pillow.

'You're so kind...' She gave Maisie a tired look. 'I must confess to feeling a little tired.' Having made her friend comfortable, Maisie went over to the cot.

'You must be so proud of your baby, Alison!' She turned to smile her congratulations, but the new mother was fast asleep.

The greyness of the dawn was filtering through the curtains as Maisie, anxious for the night to be gone, eased them apart. She was thinking of Seb as she watched the sun rise over the flint-stone structure of the village church. East Wensum with its few scattered cottages lay across the meadows. Standing by the bedroom window she watched the sun's crimson orb, climb slowly above the trees that sheltered the church.

As the early morning sunlight spread its golden glow across the landscape, it disclosed signs of natures new life that were synonymous with the month – May. A feeling of expectancy lingered in the air as the dawn shadows disappeared to reveal the season's fresh beauty. Blossoms decorated the trees and hedgerows. Fresh green buds breaking from their protective cases complemented the colourful blooms of the merging spring flowers.

Maisie, sighed deeply, wondering if Seb was also beholding the beauty of the morning. In silent meditation she watched the swallows in acrobatic flight as they searched for insects in the cloudless sky. Twisting and diving they graced the heavens outside her window. With a few rapid wing-beats they gathered momentum before swooping down to skim low over the surface of the stream, sipping from the water during their continuous flights.

Suddenly their excited twittering turned to a series of alarm-like shrieks. As she watched, the swallows began to close into a more compact flight formation. Danger, she realised had caused their agitated actions. It was then she noticed the sparrow-hawk closing in at speed. Its aim was to catch one of the swallows before they reached the shelter of the trees.

Maisie, watched fascinated as, despite their fear, a small group of the swallow turned and flew towards their attacker. Their strategy, although a dangerous one, was successful. Their concerted mobbing eventually forced the hawk to abandon his attack. Maisie smiled with relief as she noticed that the swallows were continuing their mobbing tactics until the predatory hawk had been driven beyond the meadows. Perhaps it's not hungry, she thought, but she was pleased the swallows had survived.

'Good morning, Maisie!' Alison's voice startled her.

'Alison!' She hurried across to embrace her friend. 'Have you rested well?'

'Very much so... and I feel... fine!' Her glance went towards the cot where a movement indicated that the baby was stirring also. Maisie lifted Jane from the cot and placed her into her mother's arms.

'I'll get Jenny to arrange for some breakfast to be sent up. You'll like a warm drink, I expect?' Alison nodded her agreement, still looking down at her baby daughter as she expressed her thanks.

Now that you are awake, I shall have to leave you, Alison. Your parents will need my help at Homefield, but I shall return as soon...'

'Oh, Maisie. What would we do without you?' She looked affectionately into the cornflower-blue eyes that sparkled with joy as they watched mother and daughter cuddling together. But beneath that façade of happiness, Alison realised that Maisie also shared her heartbreaking loneliness.

Josh and Seb had both been gone for several months now, bringing an emotional emptiness to their lives. In her own case, there had been no news of Josh since his departure for London, eight months previously. Edward's loss at sea must have caused Maisie so much heartache and sadness, yet she had remained a cheerful companion to them all.

'I'm afraid that we are the lonely ones, Maisie. We must endeavour to live our normal lives, despite the uncertainty on not knowing when, or if our loved ones will ever return to us.' Maisie paused to give her companion a warm and understanding embrace before moving to the window. She tried to blink back the tears to cover the heartache caused by Alison's melancholy words.

'We must... hope and prey... for their safe return, Alison.'

'Yes!' She looked with dismay towards her friend. 'Yes of course. I'm sorry, Maisie. I didn't mean to sound so... so despondent. It's not knowing... about Josh...' She looked down at her baby, wondering if he would ever share in the happiness of their daughter's childhood or her future.

Maisie was about to turn and offer her commiseration's, when she noticed the horseman riding towards Highfield. She blinked hard to clear her tear filled eyes in an endeavour to ascertain the rider's identity.

'I believe you have company. A gentleman is approaching.'

'A gentleman... do you... think...?' Alison's voice faded. Her hopes had been dashed all too often over the past few months. 'Can you identify... the rider, Maisie?' Once again she had her thoughts and emotions under control as she awaited her friend's confirmation.

'No, he has just passed behind the stables.' Maisie gave Alison an expectant smile before turning back to the window. After a moment of silence, she gave a startled gasp.

'It's... Seb! Oh, Alison...' she turned from the window, her eyes ablaze with excitement. 'It's Seb. Will you mind if...'

'Oh, Maisie, there's no need to ask...' her words changed to joyful laughter as Maisie, picking up her skirts dashed from the room. At the door she almost collided with a startled Jenny who was entering with the breakfast tray.

'Oops, sorry Jenny! Can't stop!' With a happy exclamation she continued her excited progress down the stairs and out into the yard.

'Mistress Maisie... will never change, ma'am?' Jenny smiled benignly as she shook her head after the departing figure.

'I would not wish her to do so, Jenny. She's such a wonderful person.'

'And a caring one, ma'am, as they will tell you at Homefield.' There was a silent agreement in the room as they heard Maisie's distant greeting to her husband.

'Seb! Oh Seb!' before he had time to collect his thoughts, his wife was dashing towards him. Despite her slight limp, she raced across the yard to greet her smiling husband.

'Maisie!' He called, as with sparkling eyes he waited to greet her with open arms. She rushed directly into them. Maisie's face was aglow with happiness as Seb held her in an affectionate embrace. Unconcerned at the smiling faces witnessing their passionate greeting, they continued to exchange amorous kisses.

'Oh, Seb... are you home to stay?' She paused in her kissing. 'It will be wonderful to...' Seb placed his fingers gently over her lips.

'I shall explain shortly, my dearest.' Arms around each others waist, they walked towards the house. 'How is my dearest, sister? I understand that we have a charming little niece.'

'Yes, her name is Jane. She's...' there was a radiant look to her face as she spoke of the baby, '... so beautiful, Seb. Come, we must visit both mother and child.' Laughing excitedly she took hold of her husband's hand. 'Seeing you will cheer Alison considerably.'

'Last night? Oh, Seb why didn't you ride over?' Maisie gave her husband a hurt look as they rode back to Homefield. After seeing his sister and briefly holding his small niece somewhat nervously in his arms, he had suggested to Maisie that they take a ride on the estate.

'Father has already informed me of your involvement with the farm work. Quite proud of your efforts as a matter of fact.' Maisie noticed his apprehensive look as he turned towards her.

'I enjoy helping out on the estate, Seb, but now that you are home…' Seb pulled his horse to a stop, inviting his smiling wife to do the same.

'There's a quiet spot up by the old Abbey ruins, Maisie. Perhaps we can ride up there so that we can be alone when I tell you why I must return to my unit first thing on the morrow.'

'Return… tomorrow?' Maisie's face was pale with shock. 'Oh no, Seb! Please say… you're… not leaving again.' She felt a cold shiver of fear surge through her trembling body.

'We'll ride to the Abbey. I'll try to explain…' He hesitated, how could he explain to his beloved Maisie that he must return – to war? Gently he eased their horses from the road so that they could ride side by side through the Glades and on to the Abbey's crumbling edifice. It was a quiet spot with a lovely view of the countryside he loved. In these idyllic surroundings he had wanted to discuss with Maisie, plans for their future.

After dismounting they walked hand in hand through the grass until they reached the shade of a large oak. Few words were spoken, Seb's thoughts were on the devastating news that he must soon impart to Maisie. She was trying valiantly to suppress fears that intuition warned her to prepare for. His deep sigh of resignation as he sank down on the grass only served to increase her perturbation.

It was as if a shadow of foreboding had settled over them. Seb looked greatly distressed as he reached out to clasp his wife's hand. In the ensuing silence they heard the soughing of the breeze as it stirred the leaves above them. A soothing whisper that did little to alleviate their emotional turmoil.

'You are deeply troubled, Seb?' Maisie had become increasingly aware of his anguished look. Something, she realised, was profoundly tormenting him. She remembered her asperity, when Seb had first informed her of his arrival at Homefield late on the previous evening. She wished he had called at Highfield and seen her, but her pique had soon vanished as she became aware of his sadness. His sombre mood. It was when he explained the reason for his unexpected visit that Maisie understood the reason for his distress.

'It was late when I arrived home yesterday evening, Maisie dearest.'

'Please, Seb, I understand. There was no need to...' her voice trailed away as she realised that her husband has continued his explanation.

'Bates informed me that you and father were at Highfield with Alison as her baby was due. After a short rest, I had intended to ride over, but...' he shook his head sadly, '... the next thing I remember was father gently shaking me with the news that my sister had just given birth to her baby.'

'If only I had known you were home, Seb.' He shared her yearnings as they looked into each other's eyes.

'I understand your feelings, my love.' Releasing her hand, he placed his arm affectionately around her waist. As dawn was already breaking when father woke me and explained why you were remaining with Alison, I changed and rode over as soon as possible.'

'I'm sorry if I seemed so upset, Seb. It's just that...'

'There is no need for apologies, my love. I wanted so much to be with you, but...' he paused to kiss her lips that were so tantalisingly close to his, '... I was near to exhaustion, Maisie. I had been in the saddle best part of three days.'

'Never mind we can share...' She placed her cheek against his, excited at the prospects ahead of them. Then she remembered his words. 'You... you spoke of returning tomorrow.' He noticed the concern on her face. 'I thought you were resigning from the Cavalry?' Troubled eyes watched him from beneath her frown-wrinkled brow. 'Must you return so soon...' Her voice faded as Seb gently nodded his head.

'I shall not be permitted to resign while the situation in Europe remains so tense. As you may have read in the papers, Napoleon escaped from Elba and has been back in France since early March.'

'Yes, father informed me when the news was published. He said it was very disturbing.'

'Disturbing! The Sovereigns of Europe have ordered an immediate mobilisation of the Continent's armies to combat the threat of the forces that Napoleon is assembling. I was with Wellington who commands the advance guard in the low countries. Urgent dispatches wee entrusted to me with instructions to proceed to London with all haste.'

'Have you... to return, Seb?' Maisie's face was white with shock as she asked the question. She was already dreading the answer that she waited for.

'I'm afraid so, my love. I must leave early on the morrow. At dawn.' He held her tight in his arms as he thought of the war that was imminent. Seb mentioned nothing about the large forces of Prussian, Austrian and Russian troops that were being mobilised against the French. He felt disinclined to distress her more than was necessary. 'I have to collect dispatches... government dispatches, for the Duke of Wellington and return immediately with them to Flanders.'

'Seb ...' she smiled affectionately as she cuddled closer against him, '... I'm thankful that you were able to get home.' She kissed him provocatively on his lips. 'Even for such a brief visit.'

'That is also my sentiment, Maisie dearest.' He stood up to remove his coat and place it upon the grass beside his watching wife. 'We must try, however, to forget the threat of war... the present is much more important.' Maisie felt herself being embraced and eased back until she was lying on Seb's coat and smiling invitingly up into his passionate gaze.

'Sir!' She gave her husband a feigned coquettish look. 'Are you suggesting that we should indulge in an... improper act,' she giggled at her advocacy, '... in public?'

'Truth is fair maid...' Seb gave her a seductive look, '... my amorous intentions can not be deferred until tonight.' He was endeavouring to keep his features solemn. 'So... I was wondering if this might not be an opportune moment.' Their frivolous banter induced a feeling of carefree abandonment. In the tranquil surroundings their joyful laughter echoed their happiness and love.

'Is it your wish that I should disrobe, good sir?' Maisie gave her husband a bewitching smile.

'Either that, or...' with a tantalising movement he made as if to life her riding skirt, '... it is my intention to proceed with the act myself.'

'You would not dare?' Her happiness was infectious as she incited her husband with a teasing look.

'Your challenge leaves me no option, but to carry out my preferred act of...' Seb rolled half onto Maisie and began to ease her skirts above her ankles.

'Oh no, Seb! We must not indulge in such an intimate act her in the... open!'

'Why not? No one ever comes here because of the curse.' He was smiling into her face, his lips seeking and finding hers. There was a long silence, broken at last by their passionate sighs as their lips at last separated. Breathing heavy with emotions they lay close in each others arms, aware only of their urgent longing that craved fulfilment.

'Perhaps... just this once... Seb.' He nodded longingly while continuing to ease her skirts higher. Excited at the thought of sharing love with his beloved Maisie, he was trying to ease her clothes aside. His fingers fumbled evocatively with her under garments. Their light hearted frivolity had now given way to an urgent longing. Uncontrollable desire for passionate love was in need of urgent fulfilment.

'Let... me help you... Seb.' Eagerly she began to raise her clothes higher so that her amorous husband would have an easier access to her excited body Suddenly, Maisie hesitated, half raising herself as she strained to listen.

'What... what troubles you, my love?' Seb paused in the act of lowering his wife's underclothes.

'I believe...' she looked anxiously towards the dense vegetation that edged the wooded side of the clearing, '... that someone is watching us.'

'Few, if any people visit this...' They both heard the faint wicker of a horse from the thicket. As if to confirm another presence, their two horses whinnied in answer and looked towards the unknown interloper. As they watched, there was a brief glimpse of a horse and rider disappearing into the woods.

By the time Seb reached the bushes, there was not sign of horse or rider. Checking the position from whence the watching rider had been covertly observing them, he noticed the trampled grass where the horse had been standing in the deep shadows. Seb shrugged his shoulders, dismissing the incident as an obnoxious act by an unscrupulous person. He walked pensively back to where Maisie, her clothes rearranged and tidy, awaited him. His annoyance faded as he helped his wife up onto her horse.

'Any idea who it was spying on us, Seb?' She looked pale and distraught as she questioned her husband. Their happy, carefree mood was abruptly replaced by one of consternation.

'No!' Seb shook his head. He hesitated, his brow creased in concentration as he tried to contemplate who would want to spy on them – and why? 'It is of no consequence, Maisie.' He hid his worry, not wishing to alarm his distressed wife more than was necessary. 'Whoever it was, sneaked off in a cowardly manner. Best that we try and forget about it.' Seb tried to sound unconcerned as he suggested that it was time for them to ride home. The incident however, had cast an ominous shadow over their happiness and, as they rode back to Homefield, they were subdued and pensive.

* * * * *

Seb looked at the clock. Almost ten and he was still unable to retire. Maisie had gone to their room half an hour previously, where he had promised to join her as soon as possible. Now, with precious time passing, he was still no nearer joining her. His father had detained him, anxious to impart information about facts and figures relating to the estate.

Details which would have been appropriate had he been remaining to run the estate. Now, he found them mundane and in direct conflict with his amorous emotions that he was yearning to share with his waiting wife. He forced his concentration back to his father's words.

'... an exceptional harvest, Seb. Best returns per acre we've ever experienced. Your introduction to the Norfolk four course system is certainly paying dividends. A most satisfactory development. Wonderful... prospect... when you...' Seb watched his father straighten up and hold his chest. Colour dashed from Sir Roger's face as he looked anxiously towards his son.

'What... is it, father?' Seb moved quickly across the room, alarmed at the sudden transformation.

'Been... overdoing things. I shall be... alright in a...' He grasped the mantelshelf as sharp pain in his chest made him gasp in agony. Seb reached out to support his father and to help him to a chair.

'I think we should send for Doctor Wallace?' Seb's face was grave as he looked at his father's drawn features.

'Yes... yes...' his voice was weak, barely above a whisper. 'It's... it's frightening, Seb.'

'Is something wrong?' both men looked round to see Maisie standing in the doorway.

'It's father... Maisie. I fear that he is... gravely ill.' She noticed her husband's drawn features as he watched his father. Aware of Sir Roger's distress, she hurried across to comfort him.

'I shall remain with father while you arrange for someone to call the doctor. Then perhaps two of the men servants can help us get him into bed.'

When the doctor put in an appearance at one of the clock, he was directed immediately to Sir Roger's bedroom. 'What in tarnation's been going on Roger?' The old family doctor queried euphemistically as he became aware of the patient's condition.

'Pains... in my chest... John. Feel... wretched.' He tried to sit up, but the physician's restraining arm, gently eased him back on to the bed. 'I can check you... as you are... no need to sit up!'

As the clock chimed two, Maisie, now fully dressed, glanced towards the troubled countenance of her husband. 'Seb, you should rest.' There was a note of concern in her voice. 'Tomorrow you will be in the saddle all day.'

'It's father, Maisie. I must stay...' He began to protest, but was cut short.

'I shall be with him, Seb. If... if there is any need, I promise to awake you.' As Seb moved towards the stairs he met a tired Doctor Wallace coming down.

'How is my father? Will he...'

'Rest and quiet... for a few days should see him strong enough to get up. However...' he gave them a stern warning, '... his future activities must be er, curtailed. No strenuous work must be attempted – whatever.'

'Thank you, doctor. I shall ensure that your advice is heeded.' Maisie was sure her father-in-law would co-operate to make her nursing easier. Looking towards Seb, the doctor wondered why confirmation of his advice had been reaffirmed by his old friends daughter-in-law.

'I have to leave in the morning, doctor. Return to Flanders.'

'Oh!' There was a surprised look on the old physician's face. 'In that case I wish you a safe journey... and a safe return.' He refused Maisie's offer of a drink. 'Thank you... but two late nights... need some sleep. Good night to you both.' He turned at the door to impart further advice. 'It would be prudent to have someone with... Sir Roger... just for a night or two.' This time he was looking at Maisie as he spoke. She nodded her understanding.

'I shall see to it, doctor. My husband must rest before his long journey.'

Don't worry about me, Sebastian.' Sir Roger gave his youngest son an affectionate embrace. 'I shall be in good hands with Maisie to care for me.' There was a moment of silence as father and son looked into each other's eyes. They were alone as Seb had come to bid his father farewell. 'I know your concern, but I hope to be up and about in a day or two. We can't have Maisie burdened with two patients to care for.' He smiled as he noticed the tension ease in his son's worried face. 'I'm also insisting that your mother accepts a full time nurse to ease the load placed on Maisie.' Seb nodded a silent approval.

'Have you seen your mother?'

'Yes!' Seb's voice betrayed his alarm. 'Mother was not very, er... receptive. She has never forgiven me for marrying... a 'fisherman's brat'... as she persists in calling my wife.' Sir Roger noticed his son's distress.

'I understand your frustration... your anger, Sebastian,' he patted his son's arm sympathetically. 'I'm sure that given time, your mother's prejudice will be overcome and Maisie's care and devotion appreciated.'

'I sincerely hope so father. How she tolerates mother's aggressive and abusive attitude towards her, beggars all understanding.' Sir Roger nodded his head solemnly before giving a little chuckle.

'That also concerned me until I inadvertently heard Maisie giving your mother a taste of her own medicine. I remained outside the door unseen as Maisie informed her that she was an ungrateful and selfish woman. That was only the start of the chastisement.' His eyes were sparkling with merriment at the recollection. 'To be honest, Sebastian...' he shook his head as he recalled the unbelievable incident, '... I had to agree with every word that Maisie uttered.'

'What was mother's reaction?' A smile was hovering on Seb's face as he enquired.

'Your mother...' Sir Roger paused as his chuckle developed into a guffaw, '...was for once shocked into silence. Before she could respond, Maisie had turned and left the room. As she passed me outside the door she gave a beatific smile, knowing well that I must have heard her castigation's.' Smiles wreathed his face as he looked towards his son.

'You have no cause to be concerned about Maisie. She is more than capable of taking care of herself... and us also it would appear.' Seb acknowledged his agreement with a nod of his head.

'Thanks for your reassuring words, father...' As he hesitated his face became serious at the thoughts of leaving home with both his parents indisposed. 'God willing, I shall soon be back with you – permanently. Now, it's time for me to leave, father... reluctantly, I hasten to add.'

'Farewell then, Sebastian. We shall be thinking of you and praying for your safe return to us. We need you here at

Homefield.' He reached out to embrace his son, little realising that it was to be their last time together.

Maisie walked beside her husband down the drive. Placing her arm around his waist, she looked sadly up into his face. 'Oh Seb, darling... to think that you have been home and we have been unable to share our... love... our passionate desires.' Disappointment gave her face a sadness that drew an understanding smile from Seb.

'It was our fate, my darling. Destiny decreed that our passions should remain unfulfilled – at least until my next homecoming.' His suggestive smile warned her that on his next leave coming there would be no restraints of their lovemaking.

'I pray that your return will be soon, Seb.' She cuddled against his as they came to a stop. 'I need you so very much, my darling.' Raising herself on tip toe she kissed Seb on the cheek.

'Maisie!' There was a huskiness in his voice and tears glistened in his eyes as he gave Maisie a final embrace and kiss. 'I'm sorry... but... I must leave you now.'

Through tear-filled eyes she watched him ride down the drive until he was lost to view. She heaved a deep sigh of desolation, then blinking back her tears, turned and wandered disconsolately back inside the house to check on her patients.

'Seen the brave warrior off, Maisie?' The sarcastic words startled her as she entered the hall.

'Andrew!' She gasped. 'What are you doing here? You are not supposed...'

'I'm fully aware of my obligations. I certainly don't need a reminder from you.' Maisie experienced an uncomfortable feeling as she became aware of his eyes upon her body. A lascivious stare that made her tremble.

'Your father is very ill. He... he needs rest and quiet.' She was anxious to distract his attention.

'So Howard has just informed me. I shall pay him and my mother a visit after I have changed and taken some er... refreshments.' Maisie for the first time became aware of his appearance. As he moved from the shadows she noticed that his clothes showed signs of wear and lack of attention. Faded and scruffy, his attire verified the type of life he had been experiencing. Andrew noticed her glance and misconstrued her feelings. He thought that she was demeaning his appearance, whereas she was experiencing a modicum of pity for his situation.

'No need to be so condescending. You're the last one to put on airs and graces.'

'I was unaware that I was.' She gave him a challenging look. 'As a matter of fact my feelings were of sorrow for your irresponsible behaviour. You have let your parents down... betrayed their trust. Humiliated yourself.'

'What's that to you?' Maisie noticed the anger in his eyes as he glared across at her.

'If you are unaware of the degradation you are inflicting upon yourself... then there's nothing can be done to help you, Andrew.'

'And who needs your help?' he sneered.

'Your father and mother do at this present moment. So if you will excuse me...' She turned and departed, wondering if she had been too critical of her brother-in-law.

Maisie was almost staggering from exhaustion. Throughout the day sine her encounter with Andrew she had been nursing and caring for Sir Roger and Lady Anne. One redeeming feature of her day's toil, had been her father-in-law's slight improvement and now, as she wished him good-night, she gave him a word of warning.

'Remember, no heated arguments when you see Andrew. You must remain quiet. No excitement or anger.' Maisie gave Sir Roger a cautious look as she made him comfortable for the night.

'I warned Andrew not to return until...' But he was cut short.

'Father!' She came across and gently admonished you. 'You promised!'

'Sorry, m'dear. It's just that Andrew and I... never seem to... agree.' He gave her a sheepish look, not wanting to upset his daughter-in-law. His initial doubts about Maisie had been overcome and he had become very pleased with Sebastian's choice of wife – the woman who might one day become Lady Douglass.

'Well, just see what Andrew wants. He has been waiting all day.'

'Very well... you're the nurse. His benign look followed her to the door, where she hesitated before turning.

'Good-night father... and please, no disagreements.' She tried not to sound too severe.

'Good-night, Maisie and... sleep well.' He was still chuckling long after she had gone.

'Come in!' At the proffered invitation, Andrew entered his father's bedroom. After a change and a wash, he felt some of his old confidence return. This amicable state had been induced by an evening's indulgence of drinking. A fact that was not lost to Sir Roger as he watched his son shuffle across the floor. Even allowing for his limp, he realised immediately that Andrew's gait was unsteady because of his insobriety.

'Evening father... I trust you are feeling... better?' Andrew made every effort to keep his speech low and not slurred, but he was aware of the anger reflected in his father's eyes.

'Yes. Thanks to Bamford's help and Maisie's nursing, I feel quite er... comfortable.' Andrew felt uneasy under his father's piercing look. 'However, I'm sure that your unsolicited visit is for reasons unconnected with my health?'

'As a matter of face... there, er... was...' he paused to give a suppressed belch, '... another sub... subject, father.' Sir Roger's face remained stern as he waited for his son to continue.

'I, er... urgently require... few pounds.' His voice faded as he watched an angry flush colour his father's face.

'How much?' Sir Roger's voice was terse.

'I need... five... five hundred... guineas.' There was a startled gasp from the invalid. Sir Roger was fighting to control his emotions.

'No arguments... you must not become angry.' Maisie's words came to him as he struggled to contain his temper. 'Five hundred guineas?' he stared angrily at his son as he repeated the sum, his temper barely under control.

'Yes, father. I face the possibility... of prison unless...'

'No!' Sir Roger was white with anger. 'You'll get nothing... now leave this house immediately.' He was aware of his quickening heartbeat as he turned away from his eldest son. Andrew, having given his father a savage look, retreated sullenly.

Later, Maisie went to make her final visit to Lady Anne before retiring. She paused outside the partly open door as she became aware of animated voices in the bedroom. Through the chink she noticed a man's back as he bent over to inspect something hidden from view.

'What of these, mother dear?' Jewels sparkled in his outstretched hand.

'I don't think... you should, Andrew.' Lady Anne shook her head uncertainly. 'Your father will be very angry should he find they are missing.'

'That possibility should not arise, mother... unless you inform him.'

'Oh, Andrew! What am I to do? Must you take them?' She nodded towards the beautiful necklace and matching bracelet that Andrew continued to hold in front of him.

'It's either these...' he held the jewels up, '... or prison for me, mother.'

'Prison!' Maisie heard Lady Anne's anguished gasp. 'Oh no, Andrew! Not prison!'

'I have no choice. My debts... unless...' he looked eagerly at the jewels.

'Take them! Say nothing to your father. If ever he finds out...'

'No one will ever know... I promise you mother.' He brushed her cheeks with his lips. 'I shall be gone by morning.'

'So soon?' There was a pleading look in her eyes.

'Afraid so, mother.' He noticed her wince as he belched alcohol fumes towards her. 'Father has tolerated this visit... but he has informed me that my presence here is undesirable. I'm no longer welcome in my own home.' Andrew was aware of the tears in her eyes as he bent over to kiss her cheeks. 'Goodbye, mother... heaven knows when we shall meet again – if ever.' Maisie heard Lady Anne's anguished cry as she hurried away from the door. Andrew must never know that she shared their secret.

* * * * *

It was still very hot as she undressed for bed. Pale moonlight gave the room an ethereal look as she turned back the bed clothes. Maisie felt a cool caress as a gentle breeze whispered against her naked body. It was so refreshing after the heat of the day that she decided to sleep as she was – naked. There was one person who would have approved her decision, had he been at home to share her bed. Thinking of Seb, she drifted into a gently sleep with just a sheet to cover her.

Maisie awoke with a start. For a few moments she lay motionless, waiting for her heart-beats to become normal. Something, she was certain had disturbed her slumber, but she cold hear nothing as she strained to hear in the darkness. Her fear began to fade, there was no sound or movement in her room. Reassured, she was about to turn over when a scuffling sound reached her ears. Once again she became alert, sensing danger as she peered into the dark shadows of her bedroom.

'Is... someone... there?' Her mouth was so dry she could hardly speak. 'Who's there?' Again her words were little more than a muttered croak. She raised herself into a sitting position, holding the sheet tightly around her shaking body. 'Wh... who... are... y... you? Wh... what is it y... you... want?' Her anguished words produced a soft chuckle from the shadows. She watched in fear as the shadowy form of a man edged silently towards her bed. Suddenly her terrified feelings eased as she noticed the man's limp.

'Andrew! What are you doing here? Is father worse?' Maisie was about to pull the sheet aside and reach for her dressing-robe when she suddenly remembered her nakedness.

'There is no need to worry about father... he's sound asleep.' She detected the uncertainty of his speech and realised that he had been drinking. 'As for my presence...' he whispered, '... I've come to sh... say... my farewell.' By this time he was standing over her, a silken robe covered his body.

'You must leave... Andrew. Please go.' She pulled the sheet closer around herself, afraid that he might see part of her body. 'Farewells can be said in the morning.'

'Not the... farewells... that I have in mind, Maisie.'

'I shall call to have you removed... unless...' she turned her face away, hoping that her threat would induce him to leave.

'No one would hear you. You're isolated in this wing.' His sardonic chuckle frightened her. She turned to remonstrate with him, to please with her brother-in-law to leave her and then realised that he had thrown off his robe. He was naked.

'No, Andrew! No! I am your brother's wife. Have you no... no... shame?' Maisie was fighting to control her fear as she watched Andrew lean over her.

'After witnessing... your flir... flirtatious display with my brother, I have a burning desh... desire to I'dulge in some serioush... love play... m'self.'

'So it was you spying... on Seb and myself,' her words were caustic with disgust. 'You... you despicable... creature.' He grabbed her wrists, bringing an anguished gasp as the pain made her grimace.

'Andrew! Please! You're hurting me.' She could smell the brandy fumes as he bent closer to her. There was no chance of easing herself away from Andrew's presence. Suddenly he snatched the sheet from her grasp. She tried to cover her nakedness with the pillow as she felt Andrew's lustful gaze upon her body. His heavy breathing as he began to force himself on top of her sent a chill through her trembling body. Her cry for help was but a frightened croak, but even this was cut off as he placed his hand over her mouth.

'Shut up!' His harsh command stirred Maisie's fighting instinct. She reached up and clawed ferociously at his face. Her sharp nails ripped the skin from his left eye and down over his cheek to his mouth.

'Damnation! You cursed bitch! I'll...' but before he could grasp her hand, he felt the nails tear once again at his cheek. Andrew tasted blood as it trickled into his mouth, but the savagery of Maisie's attack only spurred his desire to have her.

As her efforts weakened, Maisie realised that she would eventually have to accept the inevitable. She tried to force her mind... her being from her body as the man on top of her indulged in his obnoxious act.

Maisie lay motionless long after Andrew had left her room. At first her mind refused to accept what had taken place. When her thoughts eventually became more lucid, she felt sick with revulsion. She was still staring silently at the fading stars as the first glimmer of the dawn softened the night shadows. Her dry, convulsive sobbing gradually subsided. Calming emotions began to replace her shocked state that had prevailed since the repugnant act forced upon her.

'Oh, Seb! Seb!' She cried in a sobbing whisper. 'Please... please... forgive me!' Tears streamed down her face as she watched the first golden streaks of the sunrise brighten the early morning sky. 'Oh, Seb! Where are you my love?' Her disconsolate whisper was a call from a breaking heart. 'I need... you so... my darling.'

Maisie hurriedly dressed into her riding clothes. She was anxious to be out in the open so that the cool, refreshing touch of the morning breeze could cleanse her of the obscenity that had defiled her body. Her long, corn-coloured hair streamed in the wind as she urged Blaze into a full gallop. Gradually the turmoil raging within her eased and once out on the heathland, the tranquil surroundings induced in her a confused and restless peace.

As she paused to enjoy the serenity of the countryside around her, Maisie was suddenly aware of an approaching rider – a man. His coat collar was turned up and is hat pulled down low over his forehead. It was as if he was trying to hide his identity. She experienced a brief moment of alarm as her eyes focused on the rider's horse. There was something familiar about...

'Oh, no! Please... don't let it be...' her whispered invocation died on her lips as she recognised the rider – Andrew. Maisie endured a moment of panic, but her fear soon gave way to anger. She gripped her whip until her knuckles were white with tension. If he came too close to her, she was determined to use her whip on his face.

Her surprised gasp as he removed his hat caused Andrew to smile capriciously. Lacerations down the side of his cheeks had congealed into blood red scars. His left eye was blood-shot and bruised and there was another deep scratch above his inflamed right eye.

Andrew's expression became serious as he noticed her shocked gaze surveying his injuries. 'No more than I deserve, Maisie.' Seeing her distress as he halted his horse a few paces from hers. Andrew assured her that he bore her no malice. 'In the hope that you would be riding this morning, I waited, to observe the hall covertly. Having ascertained your direction, it was easy to take a short route to...'

'I would have thought that after your... degrading action of... last night...' Maisie was struggling to remain articulate, '... you would have... saved me... from this further... humiliation.'

'I meant no disrespect to you, Maisie. My sole intention this morning was to apologise for my contemptible behaviour and ask for your... forgiveness. The face that I had been drinking... was no excuse for my abominable actions.'

'It may be possible to forgive you in time, Andrew, but I can never forget your humiliation of my... being. When I inform Seb of your actions, he may not be prepared to...'

'Tell, Seb? There is no need...' Andrew looked startled.

'Seb is my husband. It would be wrong not to...'

'But you need say nothing, Maisie. It was a most... despicable act that I, er... inflicted upon you and known only to ourselves.' He waited for her confirmation, but received instead a contemptuous look from Maisie. There was a long silence as they stared into each other's eyes.

'Your trouble, Andrew...' her voice was harsh as she informed him of his capricious character, '... is that you think evil is easily forgiven with a few expressions of regret. Your irresponsible behaviour and the way you take advantage of your mother...' Maisie was suddenly aware of Andrew's surprised reaction.

'Has... my... mother...?'

'No. Through her partially open door I accidentally observed your loathsome conniving as you inveigled your mother into handing over the jewellery that was not rightfully hers to give.'

'Not hers? Of course it belongs to my mother. She is free to part with what ever she wishes.' There was an angry flush to his face as anger began to build up inside him.

'They are part of the family heirloom... as you are well aware.' Disapproval of his imprudent action was reflected in her intonations as she continued her condemnations. 'You had no right to force your mother to...'

'Maisie!' He held up his hand. 'It was either the jewellery – or my imprisonment.'

'Then perhaps you should have considered the latter. Its humiliation might have induced a feeling of remorse and encouraged a more responsible attitude... on your eventual release.' There was no sympathy in the accusing look she gave Andrew as he prepared to ride off.

'One final word... if you will permit me another moment of your time,' his anger had faded as the truth behind Maisie's imputations touched his conscience. A hesitant smile lingered around his lips as he solicited her attention. 'I promise that the jewellery will be returned – however long it may take. You have my word on it. When I next return to Homefield... it will be with our family's heirloom.'

Before she could comment on his pledge, he had turned, replaced his hat and was urging his horse into a fast canter across the heath and away from Homefield. She watched him impassionedly as he rode away, wondering when or if his promise would ever be fulfilled.

Eventually his avowal would be honoured, but a few years and much tragedy would touch their lives before that day of reunion. Maisie watched Andrew's departure until he was lost to her view beyond the common's tall gorse bushes.

A lonely, disconsolate emotion overwhelmed her as she turned Blaze towards home. Andrew's distress and remorse had softened her anger, but she felt depressed and humiliated when she remembered the vicious act that he had subjected her to.

'Please... please forgive me, Seb.' She pleaded in a passionate whisper as tears ran down her cheeks. 'I tried not to betray you, my dearest.' Eventually a feeling of calm permeated Maisie's being, the degradation of the night faded as she thought of her husband. His forgiveness was all that concerned her. She was certain that her explanation of the circumstances under which her molestation had been perpetrated would elicit Seb's compassion. What of his reaction to his brother, Andrew who had committed such a heinous act? Only the future would know.

Chapter Eight

Trusted with the responsible duty of carrying the Prime Minister's dispatches from England, it was a relieved young captain who eventually handed them over to the Duke of Wellington in Brussels. He remembered his apprehension on receiving the documents from Lord Liverpool himself. Knowing that Seb had seen action on the continent, the Prime Minister questioned him on the situation regarding the troops preparation for battle.

'Yes, I understand from the Duke of Wellington...' the Prime Minister tapped a couple of documents on his desk, '... that many veteran fighters from the Peninsular campaign are there and have recently been joined by the regiments just returned from America.'

'We shall give a good account of ourselves when the time comes, sir.'

'Of that I have no doubts, Captain Douglass.' He nodded solemnly in acknowledgement of Seb's salute. 'My regards to the Commander-in-Chief's headquarters', he had glanced at the date on the campaign diary. It was June 15th, a Thursday, nearly two weeks since he had bid his dearest wife, farewell. Seb thought of Maisie as he rode to join up with his fellow officers, wondering when he would be with her again. He eased his horse into a trot as they passed through the city of Brussels. All around, he detected a sense of urgency in the air. A feeling of expectancy. Troops were passing through the city in a scene of military pageantry. They were being cheered on by the citizenry, who themselves were revelling in spontaneous gaiety.

Seb, dry and dusty after his ride from the coast, edged his horse through the city throngs. The celebrations perturbed him. A spasm of disappointment infiltrated his exhausted body as he wondered if his frantic dash from the coast had been in vain. 'Hope we haven't missed any of the fighting, old friend,' he whispered to his horse as he gave the weary animal a reassuring pat.

'Charles!' Seb called across the street to one of his fellow officers. 'What's happening?' He swept his arm in a half circle, indicating the revelry and carefree laughter of the populace. 'Have I arrived too late?'

'No, Seb,' his companion shouted above the din. 'Welcome back... you're just in time!' His eyes were sparkling with excitement. 'We expect to engage the French within a day or two.' Eventually Charles managed to edge his horse along side Seb's grey charger.

'What are our plans?' Seb looked anxiously towards his friend.

'We move up on the morrow!' he pointed in a southerly direction. 'Tonight, however, we shall celebrate your return with...' Charles's words faded as he became aware of the tenseness reflected on Seb's countenance. 'Is... everything... all right, Seb?' He gave his friend a worried glance. 'Did you manage any leave... when you were in England?'

'Just a few hours.' As Charles leaned closer to hear his friend's reply, he noticed the tension on Seb's dust-strained face and the sadness in his eyes.

'Why the sadness, old friend?' Charles was deeply perturbed by Seb's melancholy appearance. 'Your wife... she is well?'

'Fine, Charles! Fine!' Seb was glancing around him as he spoke, in an endeavour to orientate his bearings. 'It's my father... he was taken ill on the night before my departure.'

'Is the situation grave... is he in er...?' Charles was searching for words of consolation, but with the gaiety and raucous laughter, he was finding it difficult to concentrate.

'With rest... I feel sure he will... improve. Nevertheless, my presence is most urgently needed at Homefield, Charles. After this campaign, I shall be retiring to run my father's estate.' Seb did not notice his friend's surprised – almost shocked look. Seb was thinking of Maisie and wondering how she was managing to keep Homefield running. A deep sigh escaped his lips as he endeavoured to bring his mind back to the present.

'What's been happening during my absence?' Charles shook his head apprehensively as he gave his companion a searching look.

‘Tell you later, Seb. First I intend to see that you have a chance to rest and freshen up. Then over a meal and a drink you shall have details of our imminent activities – our preparations for the battle ahead.’

* * * * *

‘We shall move up with the Greys, come the morning, Seb. There has been much activity in that direction over the past few days.’ He indicated beyond the southern section of the city. ‘Information gathered suggests that a confrontation with the French forces is imminent.’ Charles lifted his drink. ‘Here’s to our success, Seb!’. He watched his friend push his empty plate aside before reaching for and raising his glass in acknowledgement of Charles’ toast for their victory.

‘To our success!’ He repeated before taking a long draught of wine.

At a more ostentatious party, a ball given by the Duke of Richmond in the more select area of the city, a similar toast had also been drunk by the party-goers. A notable guest at that social evening had been the two friends’ Commander-in-Chief. Throughout the evening dispatches and messages of a perplexing nature had caused the Duke of Wellington to issue a succession of discreet orders to his staff. Officers began leaving as the ball progressed and by the early hours of the morning, it was obvious that something of great importance was pending. By dawn the next morning, Seb and his fellow officers had their horses and equipment ready to depart the town. By then the shadowy streets and squares were echoing to the sound of trumpet and drum beats. Troops were being called to arms. As Seb’s cavalry contingent rode clear of the outskirts they began to overtake the marching troops. He noticed the green-jacketed riflemen, scarlet clad infantry and the tartan dress of the Highlanders. They had also passed the blue-coated Belgian troops, who like their allies, were laughing and joking to cover their apprehension of what awaited them in the coming battle.

Around the capital, the British troops, like their German and Dutch allies, were marching towards predetermined assembly points. As the army moved forward they could already hear the distant action as Napoleon,, with lightning precision drove his forces at the outposts of Blucher's army. His ploy was successful in driving a wedge between the Prussian forces under Blucher and those under Wellington. Napoleon's objectives had been to defeat one or the other force before they had time to concentrate their combined attacks on his troops.

Throughout that Friday, the sound of cannonading drifted through the hot, sultry air to reach the citizens of Brussels. A few miles south of the city, Marshal Ney was trying to sever the communications link between Prussian and Anglo-Dutch armies.

Seb, with a few quiet words of assurance, steadied his horse. With mounting nervousness he waited for orders that would send the cavalry to join in the battle. His group were to reinforce troops who had been subjected to a fierce attack from the French cavalry. Around him the dust drifted in clouds above the battle ground in a choking haze.

'Greys! Prepare to charge!' An icy shiver ran down Seb's spine. He glanced at his grim faced companions, who like him had their eyes fixed on the approaching enemy forces.

'Charge!' Seb's fears evaporated, adrenaline accelerated his heart beats as he galloped at speed towards the French ranks. Next moment he was plunged into the depths of hell. Horses neighed and milled amid clouds of dust as riders manoeuvred them into strategic positions.

Occasionally a horse's scream of terror was heard above the cacophony of battle as a sabre missed its rider and slashed open the creature's body. Shrieks of hate and pain rent the air as combatants slashed with razor sharp sabres at their enemies and in some cases, were themselves cleaved open as a sword sliced through their flesh.

Seb's horse shied onto its hind legs as it found another horse and rider obstructing its progress. Fighting to control his charge, Seb was only just time to parry a sabre blow from a French officer. Before the man could regain his balance, Seb's sword had swished venomously through the air and sliced into the French officer's throat. Blood poured from the open wound as the man reached up in a futile attempt to staunch the flow.

It was a useless actions, the injury was fatal. Slowly the injured officer slid from his prancing horse and was dragged a short distance by his entangled foot before disappearing under a melee of stamping hooves. Death came quickly – and mercifully.

Before Seb had fully recovered from his encounter, he was once again engaged in mortal combat. Only just in time he moved his horse to avoid the flashing blade of a sabre. He felt a sharp pain on his shoulder, but aware that he was again under attack, Seb urged his horse sideways in an endeavour to dodge the sabre thrust at his body.

A warning shout made him turn just as a French cavalry officer was riding in to attack. Swivelling his horse in a half circle, he was just in time to parry the flashing sabre. Recovering with trained speed, he flashed his sword at the attacker's face. It wasn't a deep cut, but the pain and agony of his cheek wound caused the officer to retreat from Seb's concentrated assault.

Having met stiffer resistance than expected, the French as a whole were moving back. Eventually they abandoned the fight and returned to their lines leaving behind several of their dead and injured comrades. There was little chance to help any of the wounded as the area came under fire from the French forces. Seb's group had barely cleared the combat zone before the guns of the enemy were concentrating on the recently evacuated battle area.

Seb reached up to feel his injured shoulder. His sliced shoulder strap was damp and sticky with his blood, but apart from a slight tenderness, there seemed little to trouble him. He would have it dressed after the battle, which as the sun dipped low above the woods appeared to be easing.

If rumours were correct, Napoleon's troops had inflicted a defeat on Blucher's Prussian army, killing several hundreds. Fortunately, a large number of his troops, along with the Field Marshal himself, had withdrawn along the Charloeroi-Brussels highway. An important stratagem that was to bear fruitful results, as by keeping his army in touch with Wellington's troops they would eventually by their combined forces, deliver a decisive blow to the French at Waterloo on the morrow.

* * * * *

Seb's teeth chattered from the damp and cold as he tried to sleep on the night before what was to be a conclusive confrontation. Both armies were experiencing an unpleasant night. Despite his weariness, he could only sleep fitfully under the unpleasant conditions.

Lightning lit up the surrounding countryside in a macabre-like scene. Tomorrow's battlefield took on an eerie glow. Winds swept across the landscape; lashing rain saturated the animals and men who sought to find some comfort against the extreme elements.

Unable to sleep, Seb lay shivering in the darkness. He tried thinking of Maisie, wondering how she was managing to cope with caring for the two invalids in addition to running the hall and estate. If only he could be home again soon to ease the burden that she had so gallantly and willingly accepted in his absence.

He thought of their wedding day. A smile ruefully touched his lips as he recalled how proud he had felt while waiting for Maisie at the altar. Memories of his young bride stirred amorous emotions inside him. Impassionate longing's which, despite his physical discomforts from the stormy elements, filled him with a warm passionate glow.

How he longed for their reunion when, God willing, they would be able to share each others love. A shared love, that because of unforeseen circumstances during his very brief visit home, had been denied them. The thought made him long for their joyful reunion. Thinking of that wonderful moment, when once again he and Maisie would be able to share and enjoy their rapturous affections, Seb drifted into a restless sleep.

Seb tossed and turned continuously on the ground as rain and wind, easing slightly in the early dawn, still tried to enter his crude shelter. Emotions drained from his body as he awoke and realise how near they were to the crucial battle. Indications were that it would be a bloody one. As he stood and stretched himself in the cold and cheerless dawn, he experienced a feeling of disquiet. A strange chill of fear gripped him.

Must be the weather, he thought. Shivering, he watched as his orderly prepared a small fire on which to cook a makeshift breakfast. Uniforms, splashed with mud, showed signs of their previous encounter with the enemy. Although the rain had passed, the storm had left their camp site almost a quagmire. Involuntarily, Seb's thoughts drifted back to Homefield's pleasant park lands in the spring. How he wished that he was there now.

There was a feeling of expectancy in the air as the morning sun broke through the clouds to spread its warm, brilliant glow over the saturated countryside. Seb gazed solemnly across the area that would soon resound to the clamour of battle. How peaceful it all looked in the sunrise. Each blade of grass, every leaf, appeared to hold a shimmering drop of moisture that reflected the sun's brilliance. A myriad sparkling crystals, dazzles the beholder's eyes, tantalising them with reminders of home – and peace.

Time for action was fast approaching. Seb, heaved a deep sigh as he took a last look at the tranquil setting. Soon all would change. The peaceful silence that pervaded the rural scene, was even now exuding an ominous manifestation. Reluctantly, he turned in readiness to make his rounds. Moving attentively among his men, Seb ensured that all was in readiness with the horses and weapons. Other officers were already making their rounds, checking that the troops were drying their ammunition and that their arms were ready for battle.

Seb rode pensively to the top of a ridge, intending to get an image of the area on which their Commander-in-Chief had elected to do battle with the might of Napoleon's army. Thoughts of the conflict ahead filled him with apprehension – and a sense of foreboding. Try as he might he seemed unable to shake off these emotions.

He nodded his approval, the Beau, as Wellington was referred to by his officers, had chosen wisely. With his army halted on a rolling plateau, their leader had selected a favourable area for the defence from the village of Waterloo. The plateau on which Seb found himself that morning was close to the village of Mont St. Jean.

A burst of brilliant sunshine gave added lustre to the colourful and composed group riding towards his party. Startled at their approach, he acted with alacrity on recognising his Commander-in-Chief among the officers. He brought his men to attention just as the Duke of Wellington paused to acknowledge Seb's professionalism.

'Captain Douglass! Your troops appear in fine fettle?' Seb was proud to have been complemented by the Duke.

'Thank you, sir!' There was a note of gratification in his words.

'What of their feelings for the battle ahead?'

'Of great expectations. Of a resounding victory, Sir.' Seb's salute reflected his pride. At the same time he noticed the trace of a smile flicker in the Duke's bluish-grey eyes as he nodded his farewell.

'Good luck to you all!' Turning his horse, the Commander-in-chief, closely followed by his retinue of senior staff officers, continued his rounds of the line.

Seb's brief encounter with his leader had induced a temporary easing of his sombre mood, but as the morning progressed a deep, more ominous feeling prevailed. He was glad when the order came for them to move into battle positions to the right of Wellington's disposition.

Hidden from the enemy lines by a slight ridge that edged the forest at their rear, Seb cantered across the plateau. Away to his right as his men trotted to their lines on the western flank, Seb noticed the fields ripening corn. These waist high crops were to be the invisible hiding place of Wellington's infantry. Just beyond the orchards and woods of the Hougoumont estate, Seb intended to hold his group of light cavalry in readiness for immediate deployment as and when they might be needed.

He had barely reached his position when the first shots of the battle echoed round the area close to Hougoumont. His mouth, dry from the suppressed tension, made it difficult to swallow. He glanced up at the sun's position, estimating that the fighting had commenced around noon. Soon, the area around the wood and buildings was the scene of bitter fighting between four of the French battalions and the British forces comprised mainly of the Guards. Seb found himself and his troops involved in a few skirmishes as the main fighting centred around Hougoumont. Fierce opposition had forced the enemy to abandon his attempt to capture or by-pass it.

Seb's face was bathed in perspiration as he rejoined Charles's group after another aggressive sortie against a French flanking attack. Suddenly, the sound of British guns rolled across the battlefield. Wellington's scheduled bombardment had commenced. Smoke and fumes enveloped the area as Seb tried to estimate the course of battle.

With the forest behind him, Seb took up his new position. He gave his horse a reassuring pat as they took a brief respite among the cavalry. There, as he awaited the order to charge he noticed that the French were concentrating their bombardment on Wellington's centre and right flank. Seb experienced a moment of relief as he and his group had just been recalled from that area centred around the Hougoumont estate.

'Just as well we're not there now, old boy,' he spoke softly to his restless steed. Because of the saturated ground conditions, the round shot from many of the bursting shells was not ricocheting as intended, but was being embedded in the mud. Seb noticed this phenomena and heaved a sigh of relief.

Distant drums and shouting heralded the advance of the French infantry against the British left and centre. Sulphurous smoke drifted across the battlefield as the artillery opened up on the advancing enemy. Seb was alerted by the infantry's musket fire. It was an indication that the enemy troops were in combat with the British infantry. He caught glimpses of the action through a smoke hazed battlefield.

Fiercely and inevitably the battle raged, each side gaining some ground here and losing a position there. Smoke, shouts and the roar of the guns reverberated around the battleground. The incessant throb of battle, a cacophony of martial resonance throbbed against Seb's ear drums. He wiped the sweat from his face, his smoke soiled hands leaving a grimy smear in their wake. All fear had deserted his tiring body. Despite the fatigue his skirmishes had induced, he was however, ready and eager for action.

'Cavalry, at the ready!' The order took him momentarily by surprise.

'Charge!' With alacrity, Seb and his troops followed the Household Brigade's Chief, Lord Uxbridge, into action against the charging French cavalry. Their momentum soon had them among the attacking enemy. Sabres flashed and clashed, steel upon steel as the French, surprised at the ferocity of the attack began to fall back, only to be confronted by the Life Guards coming at them from behind. Trapped between such ferocious forces, the French cavalry joined their infantry in a hasty retreat.

Seb found himself riding after the fleeing French cavalry, unaware until too late that their charge had carried them into the enemy positions. Cut off from any chance of support, they were compelled against overwhelming odds to extricate themselves from the enemies counter-attack by the reinforced French cavalry.

Courageously, the scattered and near exhausted units of Seb's cavalry endeavoured to fight their way out of the enemy positions. Tired horses could not respond quickly enough to their riders' defensive manoeuvres against the superior and fresher reserves of the French. It was a desperate situation as separated and bewildered men who had just helped save Wellington's centre, were now being systematically isolated and hacked down.

Sweat trickled into Seb's eyes, his arms wee aching and weak from continuously wielding his sabre. Eventually, just as help was arriving, Seb found himself surrounded by retreating French cuirassiers and lancers. Sabre flashing in the sunlight, he fought valiantly against overwhelming odds. Two of his attackers became victims of his sword before he felt the searing pain of a lance as it pierced his chest.

Seb struggled in vain to fight his way clear. If only I could reach our reinforcements, he thought as his vision began to fade. With blood flowing copiously from his chest and dribbling from his mouth, he tried to fight a way through the enemy ranks. Weakness overcame him, faintness blurred his surroundings. Swaying in the saddle, Seb could sense darkness descending. Gradually he slipped to the ground amid the stamping and kicking hooves.

Horses and faces drifted before his misted vision as his life ebbed away. 'Maisie... Maisie... my love!' Seb's cry for his beloved was lost in the din of battle. His vision clouded and his utterances went unheard and unheeded as thoughts of Maisie eased his last moments. Death came quickly to the young cavalry officer who had died amidst the retreating enemy forces. A death that had been foretold.*

Mist wreathed the macabre scene where thousands of dead and mutilated bodies lay like grotesque statues upon the battlefield. The wounded, weak and shocked stared silently with pain filled eyes towards the heavens. Daylight, like the life in their bodies, was fading into darkness. Unfortunately, for many of them, there would be no new dawn of hope to follow.

Charles, his head and arm wrapped in crude, blood stained bandages, stared in stunned disbelief at the mutilated body of his friend. Still stupefied from his wounds and the holocaust of battle, he had insisted on searching for Seb's body. At last he had located it.

Gently, he removed Seb's belongings. 'I promise they will be delivered to your family dear friend.' Tears streaked his battle-grimed face as he walked sadly back to the temporary headquarters to await transport to the capital – and eventually home to England. He had promised to inform Seb's family as soon as he reached home.

Waterloo had been a victory, but at what cost? Charles felt shattered as he gazed through melancholy eyes across the body strewn landscape for the last time. Tears distorted the gruesome sight. He shook his head in disbelief and was about to move away when he became aware of someone else viewing the battleground.

He turned to find his Commander-in-Chief standing beside him. Silently, the Duke of Wellington gazed with tear-filled eyes across the scene of his greatest victory. In a halting voice, filled with emotion, he spoke of his sadness for the lives that had been sacrificed in the battle against tyranny. Later, as we wept for the fallen, he spoke a supplication that Charles felt was an embodiment of all their emotions.

'I hope to God I have fought my last battle.' His hope, like Charles' was to be fulfilled.

* In Book I The Winds of Destiny

Chapter Nine

'You look troubled father! Perhaps we should turn back?' Maisie's concern was instigated by Sir Roger's pale and solemn features as they began their journey to Foxleigh.

'No, my dear, but thank you for your anxiety.' He gave his daughter-in-law a compassionate look which broadened into a smile as he met her troubled eyes. 'I'm in excellent health, thanks to your sympathetic nursing, Maisie.'

For several minutes they remained silent as they watched the Suffolk countryside pass their carriage window. They had started early on their journey so as to arrive at Foxleigh by the evening. Maisie noticed the ripening corn, a good sign for the end of June. At Homefield where only the previous day she had made her rounds of the estate, there had been encouraging signs that the harvest would be a good one providing the weather remained fair.

Thoughts of the harvest reminded her of Seb. There had been no news of late, but Maisie was hoping for his return before harvesting started. How wonderful it would be to see him again, but the thought also troubled her greatly.

In recent editions of the 'Morning Post', there had been references to a great battle in Belgium. A place called... Waterloo. Yes, that was the place her father-in-law had mentioned one morning as he looked up from his paper.

'What news of our victory, father?' she nodded towards the paper lying on the seat beside him. Maisie noticed his reluctance to discuss the latest news despite the fact that he had made a few attempts to read it since their departure. In the brief ensuing silence, a sudden fear gripped her body. Had something gone wrong with the fighting. Colour drained from her face as she waited for Sir Roger's reluctant answer.

'We had a magnificent victory, but... the losses on both sides...' he shook his head sadly, '... were er, high.' He refrained from using the editorial description... horrendous. 'However...' seeing her shocked look, he continued. 'We must try not to er, prejudge events, my dear.' Sir Roger was trying to hide his uncertainty – his fears. 'A few days have passed since the battle. Had there been any news, I feel sure it would have reached us by now.' Neither could have been more aware, that an injured Captain Charles Roberts was at that very moment nearing Homefield, bringing with him the tragic news of Sebastian's death in battle.

Sir Roger called to his coachmen to stop in Bungay. 'Give the horses a rest, my dear and us a chance to partake of some refreshments.' Maisie smiled her agreement.

'While they are preparing our meal, I would very much like to take a short walk. Is it possible, father?'

'Of course. Good idea. Perhaps you will permit me to accompany you?' He proffered his arm for Maisie to rest hers on as they strolled along the narrow streets of the small market town.

'That, my dear…' he pointed across the square towards a dome-shaped building, '… is the Butter Cross.' Further down the High Street, he indicated beyond the houses, the crumbling remains of the castle. After a few minutes in the warm sunshine, Sir Roger suggested they should return to the hostelry and enjoy their refreshments.

'You look tired, my dear. Are you feeling unwell?' Maisie was aware of her father-in-law's glance at the barely touched food on her plate.

'No!' She shook her head. 'It is nothing. A little faintness that will pass when we resume our journey.' How could she tell her kind and understanding father-in-law that she believed she was expecting a baby – Andrew's child.

Since she had become aware of her condition, Maisie had experienced many sleepless nights. Hours of anguish had been endured as she considered how best to inform Seb of her traumatic experience when his brother had forced himself upon her. Reflecting on the ordeal induced a shiver of revulsion. The memory continued to cause her great distress and a feeling of degradation.

Sir Roger noticed her tremor and the distressed look that was reflected on her pallid features. 'Come, my dear. We shall leave immediately.' He pushed his plate aside and assisted Maisie outside. Within minutes they were in their carriage and trundling down the street. After a short run down the hill, they crossed the bridge and headed out of town along the Norwich road. Maisie felt better as the breeze from the partly opened window fanned her cheeks.

'I'm feeling much better,' she smiled her thanks in answer to Sir Roger's question.

'Good!' He leaned across and patted her hands. 'I'm relieved to see the colour coming back to your face. Must have you better before Seb's return, m'dear.' Maisie returned his concerned look with a joyful chuckle before kissing his cheek.

'Yes, father!' her longing for Seb's return, however, was now being replaced with emotion uncertainty. Her feelings of anxiety prevailed as she wondered what Seb's reaction would be when she informed him of Andrew's attack upon her. Throughout the remainder of the journey that agonising thought continued to trouble her, bringing with it a feeling of despondency.

Maisie's depressive emotions were swept aside as the carriage came to a halt outside Foxleigh Hall. Awaiting to greet the new arrivals were Colonel Markham and his daughter Julie. During the exchange of warm greetings and the bustle of the servants attending to the luggage, Maisie's spirits began to revive. Especially after refreshments when Julie had taken her to see George, now an active and robust child. Meeting Julie's son had induced a few moments of disquiet for Maisie. She had been reminded that her worst fears had almost certainly been confirmed – Andrew's child was developing in her womb.

'Any news from Seb?' Julie gave Maisie an anxious look as she sat on the bed while her dearest friend changed from her travelling clothes.

'Nothing... Julie.' She shook her head pensively. 'Nothing since he wrote a few lines before he left London. He was about to depart for Brussels.' Her voice faded so that Julie barely heard the last few words. Reaching out she clasped Maisie's hands and pulled her gently down beside her on the bed.

;What troubles you so, Maisie? Can I help... in any way?' Julie had seen the torment and deep sorrow in her friend's eyes as they had gazed steadily into each others. She was anxious to help the friend she cherished above all others. 'After all, you have always willingly shared and helped to lighten our burdens over the years.'

Maisie's deep sigh broke the following silence. 'Thank you, Julie. Should I ever be in need, rest assured that your kind offer of help will be gladly accepted.' That day of commiseration was but one day from her.

Parson Jameson's sonorous voice reverberated in the small village church. His hair, longish and white, straggled over his clerical collar and was in urgent need of some tonsorial refinement. His voice, however, apart from the now more frequent croaking attacks, was just as forceful as ever. Beside him on this first Sunday in July 1815, stood the young man who was about to take Parson Jameson's place. A smile flickered across the clean shaven face of Robin Darvell as he listened to his predecessor haranguing the congregation on this, the old parson's last service before retirement.

Robin's glance wandered to the Markham's pew where two strangers had joined the Colonel and his daughter. His eyes rested a while on the latter, before moving on to the strangers. They looked like father and daughter, but he would enquire from his mentor when they were back at the Rectory.

As he watched, the young woman's eyes held his for a brief moment. A moment of revelation. What he beheld made him lower his eyes. It was as if he had witnessed the inner most secrets of her soul. There was so much pain and suffering in their fathomless blue depths that he could almost feel her sorrow across the chancel.

Robin took his place in the pulpit towards the end of the service, when he thanked Reverend Jameson for his long and faithful services to the community. He stood beside his mentor as the congregation filed from the church. As their new parson he was anxious to introduce himself to his future parishioners.

Daughter-in-law, thought Robin Darvell as he was introduced to Sir Roger and then to the young woman beside him. The woman into who's eyes he had briefly glimpsed so much sorrow. He noticed her slight limp as she walked beside the young mistress from Foxleigh Hall.

Behind the two ladies, Sir Roger and the colonel were in deep discussion abut Wellington's victory at Waterloo. In both minds the high casualty figures were causing concern. Each man was disinclined to mention the lack of news about Seb. Unknown to them, the matter was just about to be taken out of their hands.

'I believe we have a visitor, father!' Julie, who was walking ahead with Maisie, turned and pointed to an unrecognised horse standing outside the stables. For a moment, Maisie's heart raced with excitement as she anticipated running into her loved ones arms. They could see no sign of the horseman, but there was an urgency about her walk as she hurried to see who their visitor was.

There was no sign of anyone in the hall. The butler, hearing their voices, came to inform the colonel that a visitor had called to see Sir Roger and mistress Maisie. 'I've directed him to the library, sir. The young officer appeared somewhat distressed. I offered him a brandy, sir... I hope that was in order?' He gave the colonel a questioning look.

'That's alright, Jameson. You, er, mentioned an officer...'

'Yes, sir. Same uniform as Mr. Sebastian, I believe.' His statement brought a gasp from Maisie. She turned a startled face towards Sir Roger.

'Come, my dear. We shall see what news the young man has for us.' Intuition warned him to be prepared for the worst. His hand tightened involuntarily on Maisie's arm as he escorted her to the library.

As they entered, their visitor rose briskly to attention. 'Sir Roger Douglass?' He saluted with his left hand as his right was heavily bandaged and in a sling. 'Captain Charles Roberts at your service, sir.' He introduced himself in a voice broken with deep emotion. His uncertain glance went to the young woman beside Sir Roger.

‘My daughter-in-law, Sebastian’s wife.’ He had guessed from the young officer’s uniform that it was Sebastian that he had called about. Seeing the distress on the young man’s face, he realised that his worst fears were about to be confirmed.

‘Please!’ Sir Roger indicated that the officer should be seated. Maisie, followed by her father-in-law, had apprehensively taken a chair. They were anxious to take the weight off their trembling legs. The young captain was about to comply with Sir Roger’s invitation, when he suddenly straightened himself upright again.

‘I think I would prefer to stand... if you have no objections, sir?’ Sir Roger nodded, anxious yet dreading the information he was about to hear.

‘I received my wounds at... Waterloo. Many of our brave men were wounded. Some, much more seriously than myself.’ He paused as if gathering strength before continuing. Maisie’s eyes were fixed rigidly upon Captain Roberts’ face. Already a numbness was infiltrating her body as she waited for his next words about her beloved, Seb. ‘Losses on both sides were heavy and... all those that died did so gallantly. None more so than my dearest friend, Seb.’

A low plaintive moan escaped Maisie’s lips. Her pallid face was taut with shock. ‘No... no ... not, Seb!’ She pleaded in a voice choking with despair. ‘Please... tell me there has been... a mistake.’ Maisie’s voice trailed into silence as she looked at Captain Roberts through tear-filled eyes.

‘I’m sorry... deeply sorry, Mrs. Douglass... Sir Roger.’ He walked slowly towards the window to hide his own emotions as he looked out at the park lands. Behind him he heard Maisie’s heartbreaking plea.

‘What are... we to do... father?’ Already she was fighting to regain her composure, but her sadness, her desolation was disclosed as she continued her lamentations. ‘We... we shall never... see him again!’

How do you feel this morning, Maisie?’ Julie gave her friend a compassionate look as she drew the curtains to allow a shaft of sunlight to fall on Maisie’s bed.

'Oh Julie, dearest. I feel as if I have experienced a dreadful nightmare.' Distress overwhelmed her, but tears that had flowed copiously at first, had now dried up as she endeavoured to maintain her composure.

'Captain Roberts is about to leave. Is there...?'

'Leaving!' Maisie had hoped for a few words with him before his departure.

'Yes. He sends his commiseration's and...'

'But I must see him, Julie. I would like to thank... him... for...'

'Are you sure, Maisie?' Julie gave her an uncertain look as she gathered up Maisie's clothes that lay across the chair beside her bed. She gave a few tidying pulls to the bed clothes before handing her friend a brush and hand mirror. 'Place them under the pillow when you've tidied your hair, Maisie,' she whispered conspiratorially before leaving to fetch the young captain.

Julie was soon back with Charles, who seemed uncomfortable as he entered the bedroom. He appeared slightly embarrassed at having to make an appearance in such intimate surroundings. His uneasiness soon passed as Maisie thanked him warmly for conveying the sad news about Seb to them personally.

'My only regret is that I was not the bearer of more comforting news, Mrs. Douglass.' He hesitated as he silently contemplated his next action. 'Your... your husband's possessions.' Gently he placed a small package on the bed beside Maisie. 'I promised that... they would be delivered to you in the case of Seb's...' he was finding it difficult to continue. 'We... we were... sincere... friends.' Distress showed on his face as he saluted and turned to leave the room. At the door he paused and turned towards Maisie. 'I'm... truly sorry, Mrs. Douglass. Truly sorry it had to be this way.' She barely heard his compassionate words as his voice faded to an emotional whisper.

In the silence following his departure, the two friends looked sadly at the package lying on the bed. At last, Maisie reached out and with trembling hands began to unwrap the parcel, wondering what if could contain. Julie, not wishing to observe her friend's anguish, walked towards the door. Maisie's soft, almost pleading words, brought her back.

‘Please, Julie. I would wish you… beside me.’ Maisie’s face was taught with sorrow. Julie, not wanting to leave her friend, yet unable to watch her distress, walked towards the window. There she observed the departure of the young captain as he gave a farewell salute to her father and uncle. Despite his badly injured arm, he had effortlessly eased himself into the saddle and was urging his horse into a gently canter.

An agonising gasp caused Julie to turn anxiously towards her friend. Maisie, with ashen features, was staring in shocked silence at a brooch. ‘The village fair!’ she whispered. ‘It’s the brooch I won at the fair… so long ago…’ With a harsh, sobbing sigh she fainted.

* * * * *

As Doctor Bamford came down the stairs, Julie rose from her chair, anxious to be with Maisie to offer her comfort. The doctor, anticipating her action, detained her with a few quiet words.

‘I would like you to stay a moment, Julie.’ Gently he laid a restraining hand upon her shoulder. ‘the news I have will, I believe, be of interest to you all.’ His gaze moved from her to the colonel and then onto Sir Roger. With his eyes resting on the latter, he spoke of his findings.

‘There is no cause for concern. The young lady has obviously suffered a great shock -- emotional distress. A few days rest and quiet will help her over the shock. Time alone will be the healing factor in her great loss.’ He took the drink that the colonel offered him. ‘thanks Grenville!’ He half raised the glass in acknowledgement before taking a sip. ‘There should be no adverse affects to… your daughter-in-law’s pregnancy, Sir Roger.’

‘Pregnancy!’ Three voices spoke in unison. ‘We… but we had no idea…’ Sir Roger spoke for them all.

‘Well…’ the elderly family doctor chuckled before taking another sip, ‘… after talking with the young lady I can confirm that her condition is as I have already mentioned.’ He replaced his empty glass and made his way towards the door. ‘I shall call again should you need me, but I’m sure that the patient will require no further attendance’s from me.’

He did not mention the melancholy look that had come into Maisie's eyes when he had confirmed her pregnancy. Anticipating a look of joy and excitement, he had been taken aback at her sorrowful look of silence. Thinking about it later, he assumed her reaction was probably from the shock of her husband's death.

Maisie reflected on her condition immediately following the physician's departure. Seb would be spared the shock of knowing about the baby. The hurt of how it had been conceived would never cause him pain. Everyone would think that the baby was his. Only herself would ever know the real father. Another person had however, watched silent and unseen as a drunken Andrew had intruded upon Maisie's privacy. Her cries and struggles had been ignored by the figure watching covertly from the shadowy recess of the landing.

Unaware of the unseen observer, Maisie thought her secret safe. She had considered telling Julie, but having to talk about Andrew's depraved act upon her person, would only reawaken memories that induced feelings of revulsion – and guilt. She received her father's congratulations with a forced smile of happiness, wondering what Julie's reaction would be had she confessed the name of her child's father.

After a few days rest, the morning of their departure arrived. Maisie had visited Ben and Nelly to inform them of the devastating news about Seb. Joyful, but subdued congratulations were exchanged when she told them of her pregnancy. Ben, thinking that Nelly and his niece might prefer a few moments along together had taken his two and a half year old son, John, out into the garden.

'At least you will have a permanent reminder of... of Seb. Having his child will be a... great consolation to you, Maisie.' Nelly had meant to ease the heartache, but as she looked into the blue eyes watching her, she realised her words had brought not comfort, but pain. Maisie, she realised, had turned towards the window in an attempt to hide her distress.

As Maisie spoke, her whispered words were like an emotional soliloquy. 'I wish... that... the baby... had never been... conceived.'

Nelly watched aghast as Maisie, staring solemnly across the surrounding meadows appeared to be communicating with herself. 'I hate the... child... within my body! Seb! Oh, Seb! Please... forgive me...' Nelly had held a distraught Maisie in a comforting embrace, not fully understanding the meaning behind her near hysterical outburst.

'Yew'll feel better... when t'babe is born, Maisie dearest. Then yer'll know the feeling' a love 'as come with...'

'Never, Nell! Never!' With these words, Maisie had broken down completely and been comforted by an understanding and motherly Nelly. In the course of time, a deep sympathetic love was to develop between the young mother and her as yet unborn son. As Nelly had predicted, Maisie's motherly emotions would prevail.

At last the time of departure was at hand. Sir Roger was anxious to return as he still had to break the news of Seb's death to his invalid mother. He was concerned at how she would react to such devastating news. His enigmatic wife's behaviour was already troubling him. Another shock might cause her mind to become... unstable. Alison would also have to be informed of her brother's death. Another trauma was the last thing he wanted to subject her to. She was still deeply distressed at the mystery surrounding her husband's disappearance as he travelled to London. He was aware that the news would come as a shock to her.

Sir Roger's apprehensive silence in the carriage and the tense look of concentration on his face cause Maisie to reflect on his emotions. As if understanding his solemn contemplation, she made a suggestion that startled him. It was as if she had been aware of his thoughts.

'Would you like me to break the news to Alison, father?' His sadness was obvious as he stared silently into her eyes. There was a brief glimmer of relief as her words penetrated his deliberations. A momentary easing of his heartache that was soon over.

'Thank you, Maisie, but... I feel it is my responsibility to...'

Then, may I perhaps accompany you on your mission?'

'Of course you may, my dear,' he continued to watch her intently for a few moments and then as if a decision had stemmed from his contemplation, he signalled Joe Lambert to bring his horses to a stop. As the carriage rolled to a halt, Sir Roger issued fresh instructions to his coachman.

'Highfield, Lambert! Go direct to Highfield!'

'Very good, Sir.' As his master's head disappeared back inside the carriage, Joe flicked his whip and clicked his tongue to set his team of horses into motion again. They were tiring a little, but an inborn instinct encouraged them into a spirited effort over the last few miles. Joe smiled to himself as he became aware of their renewed efforts. 'Yew'll not be the only ones anxious to git home,' he whispered to them as he gave a little flick of his whip to acknowledge their liveliness.

'Oh, father...' Alison sobbed, '... how can fate be so... so cruel?' Tears trickled down her cheeks as pale and in shock she found solace in her father's affectionate embrace. 'First, Edward...' she gave Maisie a sympathetic glance, '...then... Josh... and now... Seb.'

Maisie, her eyes brimming with tears rose and moved across to the window. She was hoping the familiar view from the house would help to calm her emotions. Suddenly she felt Alison's hand clasping hers in a commiserative and understanding gesture. An emotive action that softened the heartache of their loss – and loneliness.

Sir Roger silently shook his head, a wordless affirmation that he had no answer to Alison's original question. He felt grieved that two young wives should have to endure so much anguish and sorrow. In an attempt to reassure his daughter, he spoke of his conversation with Doctor Bamford while at Foxleigh.

There is still a chance, according to Bamford, of us seeing Josh again. From his medical experience, he recalled a person being severely concussed, who on recovery from his coma had no knowledge of his past.; Sir Roger noticed his daughter and Maisie observing him with startled expressions.

'What... what was the outcome of this unfortunate person's experience then, father?' Tension had dried Alison's mouth, making it difficult for her to speak.

'For several months he existed as a... a, er, different person, having no knowledge of his previous life. His condition continued so until he suffered a heavy fall while out riding. Apart from breaking his arm, he was also concussed from a knock on his head as he fell.' Aware that her father was about to impart some crucial information, Alison waited with breathless anticipation. She wanted to ask her father what connection there was between the unknown rider's accident and her beloved, Josh, but she was incapable of speech.

Shock had numbed her reasoning inducing a moment of near panic. Sir Roger seeing her distress, hurriedly explained the circumstances of the unconscious man. 'When he recovered from his comatose state, his memory had return. His name, his original existence, were all vividly remembered as if he had suffered no interruption to his earlier way of life.' Seeing the uncertain look on Maisie's face, he waited for her expected question.

'What of the... the period between his bouts of unconsciousness? Did that not affect his return to... normality?' Sir Roger shook his head reflectively.

'Strange as it may see, he remembered nothing of the months while his memory was impaired. That intermediate part of his life remained a complete blank. Had never existed as far as he was concerned.'

'How can such happenings bring us hope of Josh's return?' Alison's shock was reflected in her bemused look as she gazed solemnly at her father. Sir Roger moved closer, reaching out to hold her hand as he continued.

'Alison, my dear...' his face remained serious as he hesitated to consider his reasoning for hope. 'We know that Josh was beaten and robbed and that there has been no sighting of him...' he refrained at the last moment from using the word body, '... er, person. It is possible therefore, that he may be suffering from loss of memory and is living among strangers who may have befriended him. His old life, his home, his family...' he indicated the three of them in the room together, '... could be erased from his memory.'

'Should that be so, father... that would mean...'

'That he does not remember who he is, or from whence he came. Should these circumstances apply to Josh, we must hope that our continuing enquiries will soon bring results and rehabilitation with his true family.' Alison in the comfort of her father's embrace, sobbed for the uncertainty of the man she loved – her dearest husband.

'I'm glad that you are able to stay for a few days, Maisie. Your companionship with Alison will help ease the loneliness and heartache that you are both experiencing.' Sir Roger paused, one foot already on the carriage step as he gave Maisie a teasing glance. 'You'll be needing a few... er, clothes and such things... no doubt...?' Maisie nodded as she pointed to her trunks strapped to the rear of the carriage.

'If Joe could bring the smallest of the two, it will be sufficient.'

'Lambert!' The young coachman, anticipating Sir Roger's order, was already preparing to unfasten Maisie's trunk.

'Good bye, m'dears.' He gave the two sad and silent women a wave before settling back in his carriage. 'I'll be over to fetch you in a day or two, Maisie.' She waved her understanding and then watched with Alison as the carriage disappeared towards Homefield. After a few contemplative moments they walked arm in arm back into the house.

'I'll get Homes to take your trunk up later, Maisie.' Once in the house, Alison invited her companion into the nursery where her daughter was gurgling with happiness.

'Would you like to hold her?' Alison, seeing the startled look on her friend's face, mistook it for apprehension. 'It's alright, Maisie...' she laughed good naturedly, '...you'll not hurt her...' Alison's voice faded as she noticed the tears in her companion's eyes. 'Oh... Maisie, dearest... please forgive me. I didn't mean... to...' Alison was deeply upset, believing that in her eagerness to show off little Jane, she had triggered thoughts of Seb in her friend's mind.

'There is no need to apologise...' she hesitated a moment before continuing. 'Its... just that... I'm... pregnant.' Her words came in a harsh whisper.

'Maisie! How wonderful! Does Seb...?' In her excitement Alison became slightly confused, '... was Seb aware of...?' She was lost for words as she noticed the distress on Maisie's face.

'No!' Maisie shook her head. 'Seb was unaware of... my condition.' She wanted to confide in Alison, tell her that the child was not her husband's, but something kept her silent. Her secret must remain untold.

'Look at the crops, Maisie.' Alison pointed anxiously towards the ripening corn. 'I don't know how we shall manage the harvest.' She gazed despondently across the fields of maturing crops. The two friends had wandered a short distance down the lane while waiting for Sir Roger to call and take Maisie back to Homefield. They had paused by a gateway to look across the undulating landscape of Highfield's arable acres. Fields of corn formed a chequered mosaic of bronze and golden hues. Each field divided by the dark criss-crossed strips of summer hedgerows. A light, early morning breeze stirred the rustling corn into a harsh whisper. An integral sound of the rural landscape in summer.

Maisie, her heart aching with sadness, was thinking of Seb as she gazed at the cornfields that would soon be ready for the reapers. Her eyes were drawn to where the petals of the poppies splashed the ripening corn with scarlet patches. In contrast the cornflower's petals reflected the colour of the cloudless summer sky – a lovely shade of blue.

'If only Seb... and Josh were here!' Maisie sighed. 'Before Seb departed...' she turned towards a pensive Alison, '... Seb promised me that it would be... his last... campaign. He was going to retire from the Cavalry to concentrate on running Homefield for father.' Fighting to hold back her tears she looked into her friend's grey-green eyes, 'Why has fate... been so... so hurtful to us, Alison? What have we done to deserve such suffering – so much anguish?'

Peace replaced the sadness as they once again observed the tranquil landscape before them. Composed at last, the two friends walked arm in arm back to the farm. Just as they arrived, Sir Roger drove up the lane in his gig. Behind him, to their surprise, came a rider on horse back. As they reached Highfield, there were startled gasps from the two women as the recognised the rider. It was Captain Roberts.

'How is your arm, Captain?' Maisie's, enquiry elicited a benign look from the young man as he dismounted and removed his hat. Out of his cavalry uniform he exemplified the comportment of a country gentleman. A trait that was soon to be confirmed as Sir Roger informed them that Captain Roberts, or Charles as he now wished to be called, was to combine estate stewardship duties at Homefield and also at Highfield, until Josh hopefully returned.

'Almost recovered, Mrs. Douglass, thank you.' Charles flexed his arm rather stiffly as if to demonstrate its limited movement. Charles' presence disturbed Maisie, it reawakened memories of her dead husband. Seb had failed to recover from his injuries, he would not be returning to her. Maisie's meditation was suddenly interrupted by Alison's mild remonstration with her father.

'Jem's done a capable job of running Homefield during my indisposition. I would not wish him to...' Sir Roger, noticing his daughter's piqued look, realised that he had erred in his arrangements. He should have consulted his daughter before employing the retired Captain Roberts to manage both his estate and Highfield. Although his omission had been partly unintentional, it was a miscalculation that would now require some diplomacy in rectifying.

'Of course, my dear.' Sir Roger walked across and gave Alison an apologetic embrace. 'Gibson has managed very well and should continue to serve you in that capacity. Charles...' he turned towards the man standing a few paces from him, '... will I'm sure wish for your man to continue as your... charge-hand. My reason for urging Charles to take over as steward to our estates, was to permit you more time to devote to your parental duties, my dear.'

Charles nodded his agreement. 'It is not my intention to disrupt the efficient running of your estates, I assure you Mrs. Kennard, my desire is for both Homefield and your farm...' He indicated the adjoining fields, '... to remain viable and well organised.' He paused to give Alison and Maisie a friendly smile of assurance before continuing. 'My presence will, I hope, ensure that you both have a well earned break from your... estate duties.'

'Thank you... Captain Roberts. Please forgive my acrimonious words, but Jem has worked very conscientiously to ensure...'

'I fully understand your concern, Mrs. Kennard... and apologies are not required.' Replacing his hat, he then spoke in a less formal mood. 'I would esteem it a great favour if you and... Mrs. Douglass...' his glance went towards Maisie, '... would call me Charles.' He was about to remind that that as a civilian he was no longer entitled to his military nomenclature of captain when he realised that its connotation might be a distressing reminder of Seb to those around him. He remained silent out of respect.

'Good! Glad we are in accord.' Sir Roger heaved a sigh of relief as he cast a furtive glance in his daughter's direction. He was also aware of Maisie's reproachful look, which like Julie's, warned him that he had not heard the last of the matter from them. He smiled inwardly at his subterfuge, but knowing the stubborn nature of the two young women before him, there was no way they would have agreed voluntarily to cease their estate work. With his new steward ensconced, they had little choice but to accede to his wishes.

Sir Roger nodded to Bates, indicating to the butler that they were ready for the meal to be served. With silent gestures, Bates alerted those serving as to their duties. With quiet efficiency the staff executed their evening ritual of serving table. It had been agreed that Charles should join them in the last meal of the day. An estate cottage had been prepared for his accommodation.

Once the meal was served, conversation dropped to a minimum and eventually ceasing altogether as the diners concentrated on their meals. In the silence the only sound to be heard was the tinkling of cutlery on the porcelain plates.

'Will you be going home for Christmas, Charles?' Maisie's voice broke the silent mastication's of those around the table.

'Christmas?' He looked up in surprise. 'I, er... really hadn't given the matter any thought.'

'Well...' Maisie chuckled, '... time you did so. It's barely five weeks away. Your parents will need to be informed if you are going home for the festivities.'

'Yes!' He looked uncertainly towards Sir Roger. 'Yes... I suppose I should. Christmas, to be honest had eluded my thoughts.' He nodded his thanks to Maisie for her timely reminder.

'Go, Lad!' Sir Roger butted in. 'Go and enjoy yourself. It's a quiet period... we'll manage for a few days.'

'Thank you, Sir Roger. I shall inform my parents immediately.'

'Good!' Sir Roger's face became tense as he glanced sadly towards his daughter-in-law. 'I'm afraid that our Christmas will be a rather melancholy one. Our first without Sebastian. However, we must rejoice in the knowledge that come early February, we shall be blessed with the birth of his child.'

Maisie, through tear filled eyes, smiled her acquiescence, but eventually she was overcome emotionally. Blinded by tears she stumbled from the room, sobbing her apologies as she departed. There was a deep embarrassing silence after her departure, broken after a few moments by Sir Roger's sympathetic sigh.

'Poor Maisie!' He shook his head, dismayed that he had been responsible for her distress. 'I had momentarily forgotten her other loss.' Noticing Charles' puzzled features, Sir Roger apprised his listener of her previous sorrow. 'It's about three years since she lost Edward.'

'Edward?' Charles looked from his employer towards Maisie's vacant chair.

'Yes... poor girl's suffered a double tragedy in her young life.' Seeing the uncertain frown on Charles' face, he explained. 'Maisie's brother Edward was drowned at sea while on his way to the penal colony of New South Wales.'

'A long and hazardous journey.' Charles was intrigued by the penal reference.

'Yes. He was on a prison transport...' but before he could explain all the circumstances relating to Edward, Maisie returned to join them at the table.

'Please... forgive my... departure.' Now composed, Maisie had returned to ask their forgiveness.

'It's alright, my dear. I had momentarily forgotten about... Edward. I'm sorry I caused you so much distress.' A warm smile softened his features as he reached across to affectionately pat her hand.

'You must not blame yourself, father...' Maisie gazed solemnly into his eyes, '... it is something that I must learn to accept... it is my fate.' She did not mention to Sir Roger that the cause of her distress was the child developing within her womb.

They were all anticipating the birth of what they all believed was Seb's child. What would be their reaction, she wondered, if I told them the truth? That the baby had not been conceived in love, but as the result of a lascivious attack upon her. She struggled to control her emotions until the meal was finished. Later, alone in her room, she undressed in front of the fire and then thankfully climbed into her bed. Tears instead of prayers calmed her into a gentle sleep.

Next morning, refreshed and composed, Maisie looked across the park lands to the distant woods. Recent frosts and strong autumn wind had caused the fading leaves to release their hold of the trees and fall silently to the ground. Their multi-coloured shades had disappeared, leaving behind a sombre outline of skeletal boughs etched against the grey autumn sky.

A veneer of frost covered the park land grass and silvered the hedgerow twigs and bushes. Early morning sunlight on the frosted landscape was a reminder of winter's approach.

Maisie felt lonely and sad. She was thinking of Seb and how they used to ride across the park together. 'If only the baby had been yours, my darling.' She whispered as she gazed at the frost sprinkled landscape outside her window. Then her thoughts turned to Edward, her lost brother.

He would never know that his beloved Julie had given birth to his son. The happiness of watching his child grow up would never be his. 'He is so much like your Edward.' She raised her eyes upwards to the heavens as she spoke, unaware that her brother was still alive - another world away. 'If only you could have survived to see him... Edward.' Her whispered lamentations were lost in the soft sounds of the dawn.

Chapter Ten

Stephen grows more like you each day, Edward.' Robert Morrison on a break from his surgery in Sydney, nodded towards a dark-haired child. An affectionate smile spread over Edward's face as he turned to watch his son toddling excitedly on the lawn in front of Newacres. Stephen was making the most of the occasion, his second birthday, but Marian, his sister and senior by eighteen months was keeping a wary eye on him. His impulsive actions in the past had often terminated in awkward predicaments.

Robert and Elizabeth with their son Mark, had joined other friends who had accompanied their children to celebrate Stephen's special event. Most were local settlers and their families on a brief visit to share a drink and a chat with the man they had great respect for, while their children enjoyed the occasion of Stephen's birthday.

'Becky says he has my uninhibited nature.' Edward gave a light chuckle as he described Stephen's latest escapade. 'He was dressed ready for his party and while everyone was busy with the last minute preparations, he suddenly went missing.'

'Missing?' Robert sounded surprised.

'Aye!' Edward, still chuckling, shook his head in disbelief at the memory. 'We eventually found him in the pig-pen. He was trying to lift up one of the squealing piglets. His mother as you can imagine was most displeased.'

'Understandably so...' Robert joined in his friend's laughter, '... he must have been in a mess?'

'He needed a bath... and a complete change of clothes. Marian...' he nodded towards his two children, '... is keeping him under close supervision. There's always the chance he might decide on another escapade.'

'Mark's joining them now,' the surgeon indicated his son running over to join his two young friends. 'Mark is always excited when we come to Newacres. I believe it's the freedom... his activities are somewhat restricted in the town. In addition there are the animals... he's captivated by them.' He watched proudly as his son, carrying a present, hurried towards Stephen. 'You've certainly amassed a large number since your arrival, Edward.'

'There are times when I think we have too many,' he heaved an exasperated sigh. 'Especially at sheep sharing time and again when the lambing season is with us. In addition the numbers seem magnified when we herd the cattle ready for their drive to the market.' Edward's mood changed as he watched his son unwrap Mark's present.

It was a small dog's collar and lead. Stephen looked puzzled as he held the gift in his hand. Uncertain as to what he should do with the collar as he had no dog. Edward and Robert, aware of the secret, watched expectantly as Elizabeth released a small puppy from the veranda. Seeing the children, it ran excitedly towards them.

On hearing the commotion behind him, Stephen turned in time to see a small creature scampering towards him. His face registered extreme happiness as the puppy made directly for him. An instant reaction that was to fuse a life-long friendship between them.

'Mine?' He asked Mark as he fondled the animated puppy.

'Yes!' The onlookers chorused. 'Now you have to name him.'

'Name?' Stephen gave his father a bewildered look.

'He'll need a name... for when you have to call him. Try and think...'

'Curly!' He looked up with a radiant smile. 'Yes... 'cause he's got lovely curly... fur.' Edward nodded, appreciating the connotation of the puppy's name and its short curly hair.

'Curly it shall be then, Stephen.' His father looked proudly from his son to the woman who had borne him. Their warm affectionate glance did not go unnoticed by their friends, Robert and Elizabeth.

'Ah! Here's Henry and Linda with Tess.' They waved a greeting to the new arrivals as they approached. An excited Tess, who had celebrated her second birthday a month previously, ran on ahead of her parents. She couldn't wait to give her friend Stephen his birthday gift.

There were joyful exclamations as the parcel was carefully undone by the two year old host. His eyes sparkled when he became aware of the contents. For a few moments he gazed in wonderment at the beautiful wood carving of a horse. Stephen's eyes sparkled with pleasure as he thanked Tess, his favourite playmate. Catching sight of his father, he scampered across to show his latest birthday present. Edward admired the magnificent carving of a trotting horse.

'It's truly a wonderful carving. Life-like in its actions.' Robert spoke with veneration as he watched Edward scrutinising the sculpture closely before handing it back to Stephen.

'Yes... and here's the sculptor now.' He extended a hand of greeting to Henry.

'Congratulations, Henry. A magnificent carving.' Robert also complemented the young farm steward as they exchanged greetings.

Henry appeared embarrassed at the interest his carving had aroused, but pleased that Stephen had appreciated his present. The men watched as the excited two year old, followed by three of his small friends hurried towards their mothers. Elizabeth and Linda, both expecting their second child towards the end of the spring season, were helping Becky set the table for the children's tea-party.

Edward was the first to notice the dust cloud approaching along the lane that connected his two farms. A smile flickered across his face as he realised that it was James and his family racing over the join the celebrations.

'Here comes James and Maggy with young Ralph and the baby.' His information alerted the remainder of the group. All eyes turned towards the West Lane where the manager of their second farm was speeding towards them with his family. Their gig bouncing and swaying over the rutted track, jolting the occupants into a confusion of body shaking convulsions. Maggy, laughing with excitement, was clinging to her baby, Peggy with one had, while the other was steadying a bouncing and jerking, Ralph. Their dust cloud trailed ever longer behind them.

James brought his horse to a sudden halt as they reached the edge of the lawn. Having helped his family down, he handed over his horse and gig to a young convict labourer, Gerry White, who had been on the farm for the past four years. Because he was a conscientious worker and quite an intelligent young man, he had become a reliable and trusted member of Newacres' farming hierarchy.

After a few words with the young convict, James rejoined the group. He was just in time to see his son tottering over to join the other children. Solemnly, Ralph made his presentation to Stephen. Once again all eyes riveted on the young host as he unwrapped his latest present.

It was a coloured ball. The recipient with an excited gesture tossed it in to the air. There followed a hectic scramble as all the children and Curly set off in pursuit of the bouncing sphere. Their charge culminated in a mass of tangled legs and arms and hilarious shouts as they sprawled in a joyous heap of youthful animation.

'Any one hungry!' Becky's call rapidly terminated the excited scramble. Their laughter ceased, faces appeared from out of the tangled bodies and suddenly with gleeful shouts they stampeded for seats at the table. Once the children had settled, they needed little encouragement to help themselves from the assortment of drinks and sweetmeats. Consummation of the delicacies induced a silence that allowed the parents sitting apart to enjoy peaceful conversations.

Shadows lengthened as the fiery red sun dipped towards the tree-line horizon. Unaware of the time passing, the men were in deep discussion about the farming prospects beyond the Blue Mountain range. Edward spoke little, the conversation had reminded him of the struggle two summers ago when a severe drought had almost defeated their efforts to survive the catastrophe.

Since that drought of 1814, when the farming communities had suffered great losses, Edward had been considering the possibility of farming on new pastures in that area. Newacres had survived the drought, but only just. Even so, the harvest had been a near disaster, barely sufficient to cover the cost of the seed. Cattle and sheep on the farms had perished, but thankfully his losses, because of the river's nearness, had been low. The river had been reduced to little more than a slow flowing stream.

Edward was thinking of that hot, dry summer as they discussed the prospects of farming beyond the mountain range a few score miles to the west. He wondered what their reaction would be when he announced his future plans for farming in the area toward Bathurst. No one noticed his furtive glance in James' direction. He was the one man that Edward was hoping to receive a positive response from when he made his statement.

Despite every effort, the farm managed for him by James, had suffered badly because of the drought. He had struggled valiantly, as indeed they all had, to save the crops and animals, but in spite of their exhausting efforts the harvest had failed disastrously and many cattle and sheep had perished. It had been a heartbreaking and despondent period for them all.

Seeing the dead and dying cattle scattered over the dried up grazing acres and the vast acres of stunted and ungerminated crops, had reminded Edward of man's vulnerability against the harsh realities of the elements in their more severe forms. Anger and frustration had been Edward's companions throughout these long burning hot days of drought. He was brought back from his reminiscing by the sound of James's voice.

'... hear say there be fine farmin' land a'yond the mount'ns,' James gave his young boss an encouraging look. 'Loamy soil... should get some excellent crops. Good grazin' an' all.'

'James, I do believe you've got the wanderlust urge.' Edward gave his manager an expectant look, wondering if the time was appropriate to announce his hew transaction. James' reaction was not long in coming.

'Don't rightly know 'bout that,' his grin widened as he pushed his hat to the back of his head and meditatively scratched his forelocks. 'A few years back... I done a scoutin' trip out that way. Hopin' to farm there, but...' Edward curtailed his excitement as James shrugged his shoulders before continuing. '... 'twas the fire... left me penniless.' He shook his head disconsolately at the memory of the fire that had destroyed his farm and taken the life of his first wife.

'Mind you...' he looked into Edward's face as a sparkle flickered in his sorrowful eyes, '... I'll say this in its favour... 'twere a fine bit a'country. Gentle hills with deep gullies and clear, sparkling streams running through them. Aye!...' he nodded his head reflectively, '... a grand part a' the country, Edward.' His weathered features, mostly concealed behind a grey-flecked bushy beard, broke into an embarrassing grin.

Sounds like a wonderful place to farm in, James.' There was a mischievous look on Edward's face.

'Oh!' The dreamy look faded from his face as his thoughts returned to the present. 'Guess I'm a gittin' carried away. Don't take any notice a'my ramblin's.'

'Nevertheless you would like to farm there, James?' Edward received his answer in the form of a smile and a silent nod. He watched with amusement as he notice the wistful expression spread over his manager's face.

'Aye... but don't s'pose that chance'll ever come...' he paused, fascinated as he noticed Edward's conspiratorial smile in Becky's direction. Something was afoot, he realised.

'Your chance has come, James!' Becky indicated a batch of documents in her hand. 'We've said nothing before... in case negotiations were unsuccessful. It is official now. My farm, the one you manage, has been sold to a new arrival in the colony.'

'Will... that mean... you no longer...' James' uncertainty brought a smile to Becky's face.

'Edward and myself would like you and Maggy to manage Greenacres for us. Our new farm is a score, or so miles this side of Bathurst.' Surprised exclamations greeted Becky's unexpected statement. Maggy walked over to her husband as if to reassure him of her full support. James, who was still recovering from the disclosure, was trying to think which question, of the dozen he had in mind, he should ask first. Aware of his Manager's bemused state, Edward elucidated on their sale.

'We shall be herding all our cattle over as the new owner is mainly growing crops. What few cattle and sheep he requires will come from his own stock. He has arranged for them to be shipped in from Cape Town.' He waited for any comments before announcing his plans for the new farm.

'Greenacres, consists of two and a half thousand acres, permitting an increase in our crop acreage. I'll see you tomorrow about labour requirements. You'll be needing additional labourers, James. Perhaps you could give me your answer then. You and Maggy can consider the prospects overnight.

'No need a'that!' Glancing at Maggy as if seeking affirmation, he continued, 'I er... that is Maggy and myself accept your offer – here an' now.'

Excited congratulations were interrupted by Grace Wellings, who since her emancipation had remained at Newacres as housekeeper. Taking her cue from Becky, she arrived with glasses of sparkling wine to toast their new venture's success. Becky had arranged for this exciting moment and it was with a joyful smile that she now proposed the toast. 'To Greenacres and its success!'

'To Greenacres!' Wine sparkled in the evening sunlight as they drank to the new farm's prosperity.

'Henry will bring a few men over and help with the cattle when you are ready, James. Arrange the drive between you. Oh, and should you require the oxen and wagons, they'll be available for your move.' James, his face wreathed in smiles, was the very epitome of happiness. A new challenge awaited him beyond the mountains.

'I'll be riding over to Greenacres in a day or two to make final arrangements.' Edward paused, visualising the place when he had last visited the farm. 'A few of us could have the place ready in about two weeks. Think you could make the drive by then, James... Henry?' He received a smiling nod of confirmation from both.

As if anticipating James departure, the young groom arrived with his horse and gig. Maggy, with the baby in her arms and a sleepy looking Ralph beside her entered the conveyance. James was the last to climb into the gig. Although he was trying to curtail his excitement, his eyes reflected his elated emotions. Smiling benignly, he clicked his tongue to send his horse trotting down the lane. Maggy and Ralph waving farewells until they were lost in the gloom.

'There goes a very happy man, Edward.' Robert's remark produced a few chuckles among those watching the family's departure.

'Aye. I'll have no worry about Greenacres with James in control.' Edward was still thinking about their new farm as he continued looking along the darkened trail that had engulfed his manager's happy family. It was Henry's voice that brought his thoughts back to the present.

'... ride over to the East Pastures in the morning, Edward.' Henry, with Linda and Tess was about to walk back to their house when he stopped to mention his plans for the morrow. 'Fences are being pulled down... Harrison an' his men are causin' trouble again.'

'Want me to ride over with you?' Edward was a little concerned at the prospect of further trouble from his neighbour.

'No... I don't expect any trouble. I'll just see that the fences are repaired and check if any of our sheep have wandered.' Henry and Linda said their farewells before moving away into the twilight. Tess, with her hands in theirs was skipping playfully between them.

With the children in bed, Becky and Edward shared the remainder of the evening with their friends Elizabeth and Robert.

Stars sparkled like diamonds in the night sky. The pale orb of a nearly full moon had just appeared and was spreading a silvery glow over the landscape. An ethereal setting from which nocturnal creatures called and challenged from ghostly shadows.

Edward frowned as the peace was disturbed by the barking of his two dogs. Their agitated baying was suddenly silenced and the farm once again reverted to a nocturnal tranquillity. Edward assumed that Jem Playford, or one of the other labourers had gone to investigate and calmed them down.

'Sorry, Robert! The dogs distracted my attention from what you were saying.' Robert looked across to where Becky and Elizabeth were in serious conversation. He considering interrupting their talk, changed his mind and transferred his attention to Edward.

'Shame to interrupt their tête-à-tête. You'll be able to pass our news on to Becky at your leisure.'

'News?' Edward's eyebrows rose in surprised anticipation.

'Mmm... we're having a new house built. To the south of Sydney. It's on a site overlooking the Parklands. We hope to move in at the beginning of December. About a month after our baby is born.'

'That's wonderful news. Becky and I look forward to visiting you after your have settled in.'

'Elizabeth has a much better arrangement than that. She is planning to have a New Year Ball to celebrate our new home – Acacia House. We shall of course expect Becky and yourself as our special guests.'

'Perhaps we should interrupt...' Edward glanced towards where the two women were still in serious conversation, '... our good ladies and discuss the arrangements with them. I'm sure Becky will...' Shouting from the direction of the stables caused Edward to pause and turn in annoyance at the disturbance. Then he noticed the flames through the trees.

'Fire! In the stackyard!' He pointed to where flames were spreading rapidly, showering sparks into the moonlit sky. 'Alert Henry!' Edward turned to Robert. 'I'll get the labourers organised.'

One of the stacks was well alight. Flames roared and crackled as the tinder-dry straw ignited and sent sparks floating into the air. Thick acrid smoke engulfed the stack yard, making it difficult to fight the fire.

Realising that the blazing stack was beyond control, Edward directed those forming the bucket-chain to concentrate on damping down the adjacent stack.

'We must try and prevent it spreading...' he shouted above the turmoil, '... otherwise the barn and stables will be in danger.' Noticing his horseman near by Edward called him over. 'Jem, you and Gerry go over to the stables. Try and reassure the horses.'

'Yes, Mr. Burstow... shall I.... Release 'em if...'

'Should there be any danger of the fire spreading to the stables... yes... release them.' Jem hurried away to find Gerry so that between them they could try and pacify the restless and frightened horses.

As the fire continued to roar fiercely and threatened to jump the gap between the adjacent stack, Edward called for Henry to bring ladders. 'We shall need to dampen the top.' He pointed to the sparks drifting high above them and threatening to ignite the nearest stack.

Intense heat, forced the men to gasp and turn away from the flames. Edward dipped his cravat into the nearest water-bucket before trying to round the lower half of his face. As soon as the ladder arrived he grabbed a bucket of water and climbed hurriedly to the top of the stack. He was just in time. A small blaze was on the point of spreading. Water doused the flames, but he sparks were floating across in a pyrotechnical-like display.

Through the acrid, black smoke swirling around him, Edward became aware of Henry helping to curtail the flames, close behind him. Buckets of water continued to arrive via the human chain that consisted of everyone who was available. Before leaving the yard he had seen Becky, Linda and Elizabeth helping the female workers to fill the buckets.

Robert was directing operations from the water tanks, ensuring that the buckets were quickly filled and handed along the line of workers to the seat of the fire. Eventually their determined efforts began to show signs of success. Flames began to die down, flickering into life only at intervals. Black, suffocating smoke thinned as the original stack burnt itself out. Other stacks had been saturated sufficiently to prevent sparks from the blaze igniting the straw. All now appeared safe and under control.

'Dampen the fire down! Make sure the fire is out!' Edward called his instructions and then directed the last buckets of water onto the glowing ashes. Gradually they were all able to relax, pleased that their efforts had not been in vain. They had curtailed the fire to just one stack.

'Well done! My thanks to you all!' Edward passed among the tired fire-fighters, praising them for their efforts. Exhausted and smoke-grimed he walked over to his wearied charge hand.

'Expect the workers would like a drink, Ned? They certainly deserve one.' Ned Fuller, an emancipist, nodded his head. 'Don't reck'n as how they'll refuse, Mr. Burstow.' His chuckle started a spasm of coughing that eventually subsided as the smoke drifted away.

Edward grinned as tears ran down Ned's blackened face. When he had become an emancipated man, Ned had requested to stay on at Newacres. 'I got nothin' a'go back for, Guv,' he confided in Edward. 'Like t'stay on if yer've a mind t'employ me.' Edward had willingly agreed as Ned was a good worker and being a senior member of his workers, was highly respected by them. Seeing his potential as a leader, Edward had promoted him to charge hand. His intuition about the one time convict's capabilities had been confirmed as Ned had proved an excellent leader.

'Best come up to the house, Ned. I'll see that a cask of ale is available for your and the workers.'

'Thanks! That be mighty kind o'yer, Mr. Burstow.' He fell in beside Edward as they walked towards the house. 'Drink'll be greatly 'preciated I c'n, assure yer.'

'Strange about the fire, Ned.' Edward frowned meditatively in the moonlight. 'What started it, is what puzzles me. Something suspicious about it to my way of thinking.' His conjecture was about to be confirmed.

* * * * *

'Edward! Edward!' Becky's voice sent a chill running down his spine. She sounded hysterical – frightened, which was so unlike her.

'Edward!' Her call was becoming frantic. Realising that something serious must have happened, he raced towards the house.

'Becky... what is it, my love?' She was almost incoherent as she tried to explain what had taken place. 'Please, Becky... try and keep calm... and tell me what the trouble is.' At that moment, Elizabeth appeared supporting a bruised and battered, Grace. He looked aghast at the semi-conscious girl and then back to Becky.

'What... what's happened?' Edward was shocked at the developing situation.

'They've... taken... Stephen...' Becky was sobbing

convulsively as Edward reached out to take her in a consoling embrace.

'Who has taken, Stephen? Please... Becky.' He was trying to calm her in an effort to find out the cause of her distress.

'I'm... sorry... Edward.' Becky was fighting to control her composure, to overcome the shock. 'While we were... distracted... by the fire... three men forced their way... past Grace. She...' Becky looked anxiously towards their housekeeper, '... tried to prevent their entry. They... they beat her... and tried to make her... take them to the children's room.' Tears were running down Becky's face as she hesitated in an endeavour to steady her distraught emotions.

'They grabbed... Stephen... took him...' She was choked with worry and distress. 'They want ... money... for his... safe return...' Becky eased from Edward's embrace to turn a sympathetic glance towards the still shocked housekeeper. 'Grace has ... Suffered badly... in the struggle.'

'How are your feeling now, Grace?' Edward walked across, noticing as he did so the extensive injuries the intruders had inflicted upon her. 'If... you... are able to give me some details... it would help ..' He was reluctant to cause her further distress, but it was essential he had all the information about the bush-rangers.

There was no doubt in his mind that the men were escaped convicts and that the stackyard blaze had been a ploy to draw their attention from the house. It was obviously a well thought out operation. Edward struggled to contain his anger, but the thought of little Stephen in the hands of those lawless fugitives induced a feeling of rage. He was determined to see that they were captured. Extreme care would be necessary, otherwise his young son's life would be in danger. Grace's voice penetrated his cogitation's.

'... done my... best... Mr. Burstow...' her voice was weak from the shock of her beating. Distress brought tears to the bruised eyes that grazed uncertainly into his.

'You did very well, Grace... a very brave effort. There is no need to reproach yourself in any way. If... If you could tell us...

what happened and… their demands…' Gently, Edward guided her to a chair and eased her down into it. 'Now, in your own time… try and tell us what happened, Grace.' His sympathetic words and actions seemed to reassure the distraught housekeeper. Edward's understanding encouraged her to talk about the ordeal she had experienced.

'Apart from the children… I was alone in the house… when three men rushed in…' she hesitated, remembering their forceful entry and the way she had been mauled by the one who had clamped his dirty hand over her mouth. At the same time he had threatened to kill her if she screamed. '… they tried to get past me… to reach the stairs. I… managed to struggle free… by biting the hand of the man trying to gag me. My screams for help were… cut short. One of the men punched me in the face… another grabbed me from behind. . I could do… nothing…' Grace shook her head sadly, fighting back the tears as she relived those terrifying moments.

Edward squatted down in front of her and took her hands in his. 'It's alright, Grace… if you feel unable to…' Her forced smiled exemplified her determination to continue with her frightening confrontation.

'Stephen must have heard the noise… he came to the top of the stairs. Seein' him, the men became very agitated. One of 'em shouted to grab the kid as they continued to… knock me…' Grace bowed her head as tears threatened to overwhelm her again. Knowing the importance of her words, she took a deep sobbing breath and struggled on. 'While I was trying to prevent them reaching little Stephen, one of the men knocked me out and… that's all I remember… until Mrs. Burstow was bending… over me.'

'Thank you, Grace… you have been very helpful … and brave.' He squeezed her hands in a friendly gesture as he turned towards the others.

'We found this scribbled note beside Grace.' Elizabeth handed Edward the grubby piece of paper. He had difficulty in deciphering the illiterate writing, but the meaning was clear. Three hundred guineas ransom – or else. He was being allowed five days to collect the money and to deliver it to Emu Ford – alone. Failure to meet their demands would mean death to his son.

Henry, having received word that three horses had been taken from the stables, hurried over to investigate. In one of the stables he found the beaten up and unconscious form of the young stableman – Gerry White. He sent one of the labourers to inform Edward of the situation and requesting the doctor's services – urgently. Robert hurried over, but he could do nothing. Gerry White's young life had been brutally terminated.

They found Jem Playford outside, badly shaken and dazed. He also had been brutally beaten, but there seemed every chance that he would survive. Robert confirmed this after examining the horseman.

'Where's Gerry?' He looked around as if expecting to see his young companion. Edward glanced at Robert, his head shaking warned against imparting the truth for the time being.

'It's you we're concerned about, Jem!'

'Oh... I'll be fine ...' but he staggered a little as he tried to walk unaided.

'What happened Jem? Can you remember?'

'Oh, ay! I c'n remember right 'nough...' Jem winced as a spasm of pain shot through his body. 'They ambushed Gerry an' m'self as we went to tend the horses, Mr. Burstow.' Edward nodded his understanding.

'Best you don't talk, Jem. Just concentrate on getting better.' Robert nodded his head in approval.

'Just take it easy for a day or two. After that you should be fine again.' Edward gave Jem a friendly pat on the shoulder before walking with Robert, back to the house.

It was only then that Henry learnt of Stephen's kidnap. 'The... fiends... I'll have them... dead or alive. I care not which.' With anger burning in his eyes he looked from Robert to Edward for confirmation of his reaction.

'We understand your feelings, Henry, but we must do nothing impetuous that might well put Stephen's life in danger. We are dealing with unscrupulous thugs, who, it seems, have no compunction about killing.

Henry's initial anger subsided. 'Yes... yes of course. I'm afraid I let my anger... upset me.' Slowly his emotions became more calm as the three men discussed a planned response to the bush-rangers' kidnap and murder.

CHAPTER ELEVEN

'I'm not sure, Henry.' Edward frowned thoughtfully as he considered his manager's suggestion. 'If those murderers realise they are being followed, Stephen's life could be in danger.' He was deeply disturbed. The thought of his little son in their hands filled him with anger and dismay.

'They'll not be aware of our presence, Edward. Gicky and I can track them to their hide-out. We'll keep them under observation until you arrive. If...' Henry hesitated, uncertain if his scheme would meet with Edward's approval, '... if conditions become favourable and it's possible to rescue Stephen safely. Gicky and I will do so, but only if we are sure...'

'Take no risks, Henry.' Edward shook his head apprehensively. 'Attempt no rescue... unless it is absolutely safe to do so.' Edward shuddered at the though of what might happen to little Stephen, should the kidnappers realise they were cornered. He did not trust the fiends. Their insistence that he hand over the money alone, was an ominous sign, but he had no option.

'They'll be on the look out, alert for any sign of being followed. Take care at all times, Henry.'

'They'll not be aware of our presence... I promise.' Aware of the anguish in Edward's eyes, Henry gave his promise. 'With Gicky's skill, we shall track those murderers to their hide-out.'

'I have to hand the money over at noon, Friday. If all goes well you should see my approach over the last mile or so. Keep a look out at the hand over area. Keep out of sight, unless...' Henry nodded grimly, understanding Edward's consternation.

'We'll give you cover. You'll not see us, but when you hear the repeated call of the crested parrot...' he gave a demonstration. 'Keel-keel... keel-keel.' He lowered his hands from his mouth. 'When you hear that call, you'll know we're at hand.' Despite his concern, Edward smiled at Henry's perfect imitation of the native parrot-like birds, with their upturned crests. 'Good luck... but remember, take no chances, Henry.' It was a deeply worried Edward who wished his friend farewell.

* * * * *

As he rode into Sydney to collect the ransom money from his banker, Edward experienced a feeling of foreboding. His features were grim as he entered the small office.

Joseph Silvester had from a long experience become adept at assessing his customers requirements. By watching their facial expressions, their deportment as they entered his office, he could evaluate their requirements. As he watched Edward's entrance, intuition warned of a distressing problem ahead.

'Good day to you, Mr. Burstow.' He extended his hand in a formal greeting. 'What can I do for you?' Involuntary he massaged his delicate hand after extricating it from Edward's strong but friendly handshake.

'I need money urgently, Jos, er... Mr. Silvester.' Just in time he remembered that the elderly banker was a stickler for protocol. Always ensuring that the correct address was accorded to each of his customers and in return expecting the same propriety.

As he eased himself into the proffered chair, Edward became aware of the banker's grey, hawk-like eyes upon him. Joseph eventually inclined his balding head as an indication that he was ready to hear the reason for his customer's urgent visit.

'I'll come direct to the point. I'm here because my son has been kidnapped by bushrangers.' Joseph's eyes opened wide in astonishment.

'Kidnapped?' He had difficulty in getting the word out.

'Yes... his young life is in danger. The kidnappers are demanding three hundred guineas... by noon on Friday.'

'Three hundred... guineas?' A surprised gasp escaped the lips buried beneath the neatly trimmed whiskers. Edward nodded silent affirmation, aware that the amount would seriously deplete Newacres account. Since their financial disaster because of the 1814 drought, life had been a struggle for survival. Two years of hardship and travail had gradually pulled them round.

Now, a bunch of escaped convicts was about to relieve him of money that had been hard earned after long, wearying days of exertion against a harsh environment. Edward remembered the exhausting days of the harvest, long periods of alertness during the lambing and the back-breaking work of shearing the sheep. Each passing day had been an enervating effort to keep Newacres solvent.

Natural disasters, such as floods and fires were an accepted hazard, but kidnapping. Edward experienced a pulsating fury at the barbarous act instigated by the escaped convicts. Anger overwhelmed him. He had no option but to comply with their demand... Stephen's life must not be placed in jeopardy.

'Were it not for endangering my son's life, I'd have the murderers back behind bars – or hanged.' There was a note of asperity in his voice as he vented his anger.

'You and Mrs. Burstow have my sympathy. We must hope that your er... actions will be concluded satisfactorily and that your son is returned unharmed.' He stood up, walked to the inner office door and called his head clerk. A few quiet words were exchanged before Joseph returned to his chair.

'Abraham will have your money ready in a few moments.' His face was grave with concern as he turned towards Edward. 'Would it not be prudent to inform the er, army of...?'

'No!' There was a sharpness to Edward's voice. 'On no account must details of the kidnapping be made known – to anyone. Only yourself, my family and close friends at Newacres are aware of the situation. That is how is must remain – until Stephen is safe.' In the ensuring silence, the only sound was the clock ticking in the corner. Edward felt he should pacify, Joseph as his intentions had been genuine. 'The army will be notified once the risk to my son has been eliminated.'

'Of course!' Joseph inclined his head in acknowledgement. 'Your wishes will be respected, Mr. Burstow. I sincerely hope that your encounter with your son's kidnappers will be successfully concluded.'

A few minutes later, Edward with the ransom money in his saddle-bags left the bank, anxious to return to a distraught Becky.

'My respects to Mrs. Burstow, Edward.' As an indication of his sympathy, the decorous banker for once relaxed his sombre propriety.

'Thank you, Joseph!' A flicker of a smile softened the sternness of Edward's face as he acknowledged the banker's subtle display of compassion. With a final wave, he urged his horse through the busy throng in the town centre. Now that he had the ransom money, Edward was impatient to be clear of the town and on his way home to Becky.

He was remembering her distress and tears as she urged him to get Stephen safely home. Holding her close, he had promised that their son would soon be back with them.

He had appreciated Robert and Elizabeth's decision to stay on at Newacres until his return. Their presence would bring some comfort to Becky during the traumatic period of waiting. Edward realised there would be continued distress until Stephen was safely back home again. Anything less... such consequences he tried to obliterate from his mind.

He tried thinking about Henry in an attempt to dispel any thought of failure. 'I hope all goes well with you both,' his words were a spontaneous whisper, an extension of his thoughts. Doubts abut Henry and Gicky trailing the kidnappers were beginning to trouble Edward. It had seemed a logical solution at the time, but if their presence became known... The thought filled him with fear. He continued his journey home with his thoughts in a constant turmoil.

* * * * *

Gicky held up his hand to bring their progress to a halt. Henry dismounted and walked over to where his companion was closely studying imprints in a sparsely grassed clearing. As he reached the young aborigine's side, Henry was shown the hoof and foot marks on the ground. It had been difficult to follow their tracks at first, but here was confirmation that they were on the trail of the kidnappers.

Henry watched Gicky's gestures intently as he demonstrated by signs that a woman had been picked up by their quarry and was riding pillion on one of the horses. He indicated the slightly deeper prints among those of the other horses as they continued along the track that took them deeper into the wood.

A woman's presence among the kidnappers aroused Henry's interest. It was unusual for a female to be riding with a gang of bushrangers... unless she was there to care for the victim – little Stephen. If so, was she there voluntarily, or was she like

Stephen an innocent victim. That possibility induced a silent nod of agreement at his speculation. The developing situation meant that extreme care was imperative.

With his native companion loping beside his horse, Henry followed the trail left by the gang. As dusk fell he became concerned that their prey might have stopped for the night. He indicated to Gicky that they should call a halt before they were seen. Henry was under no illusion as to the kidnappers actions should they discover the presence of their trackers. It was best they call a halt and make camp for the night.

With diagrams drawn in the dust and by a series of gesticulations, Henry alerted his companion to the dangers of pressing on. Gicky nodded and indicated that he would go on ahead and check the area was safe before they decided on their camp-site.

It was moonlight when he emerged quietly from the shadows. There had been no whisper of sound, or any sign of the young native's movements as he approached the sheltered area where Henry waited. Nodding his head and smiling, he indicated that it was safe for them to build a fire.

Pointing to the moonlit sky, Gicky made a movement with his hand that Henry interpreted as a segment of an arc travelled by the moon in about two hours. Henry smiled his understanding and gave a nodded affirmation action that was reciprocated with an infectious grin. Close but not too near, the pursuers were pleased with their progress.

Just like old times, thought Henry as, having enjoyed the meal prepared by Gicky, they settled down for the night close to their camp fire. Later, as the flames died down, a silvery moonlit glow accentuated the wild loneliness of the surrounding bush. Nocturnal creatures ignored the human presence and continued their foraging for food.

The sun's crimson tip had barely edged above the distant hills, before Henry and his companion were already proceeding with stealth as they tracked the kidnappers. Throughout the day they remained in the wake of the gang. By the position of the sun, Henry estimated that they had been riding in a north-westerly direction since clearing the river. He guessed they would hide up near Emu Ford until Friday, when the ransom was due to be handed over.

Shadows were lengthening as they neared the edge of the woodlands. Intuition warned Henry that they were nearing the designated area as the day drew to a close. His concentration had wandered as he tried to estimate their position in relation to the ford. He was just about to ride from the shadows of the trees when he felt Gicky's hand tighten on his. An emergency. Quickly he eased his horse deeper into the protective shadows of the wood. He was only just in time. On a slight ridge, barely a quarter of a mile ahead of them, three riders suddenly came into view.

In the last rays of the setting sun, Henry watched their silhouettes moving against the evening sky. One horse had two figures on its back, confirming that the woman was riding behind one of the men. At first there was no sign of Stephen, but as the trailing rider made the summit on the ridge, his outline was clearly defined. In front of the last rider was the small form of Stephen, the small child they had so callously snatched from his parents' home.

Henry's anger precipitated an urgency to attack the kidnappers, but as he watched the procession of riders dip below the ridge, he remember Edward's warning – and his promise The situation called for a calm assessment as they must do nothing to jeopardise Stephen's life.

'We'll close in on them, Gicky!' As if understanding what was required, his dark-skinned companion swept his hand in a half circle, indicating that they should use the woods as cover. Their shadowed cover would make it almost impossible for their movements to be discerned.

By the time they eventually reached the ridge and picked up the gang's trail again, dusk had settled over the bush. They followed the signs with extreme care, aware that the kidnappers were now very close. A sudden movement in the bushes just ahead brought them to a sudden halt. Henry reached for his gun, just as two creatures came bounding towards them on their strong hind legs. He relaxed with a grin as they two animals changed course and disappeared back into the bushes, their progress eventually fading away to silence.

A tranquil feeling prevailed. The bush seemed deeply quiet in the transitional period between daylight and darkness. Diurnal creatures were settling down for the night while lethargy was being replaced by increased activity for those that were nocturnal.

Forcing such distracting thoughts from his mind, Henry dismounted, anxious not to alert their quarry. Progress now necessitate extra caution. With dusk already upon them, it was possible that the gang had already made camp. As he prepared to make his, Henry estimated that they must be in the area of Emu Ford, the location to where Edward had been instructed to deliver the ransom.

As Gicky returned from his reconnoitre, he pointed ahead and then clamped his hand over his mouth indicating silence. Quietly, the two pursuers edged through the starlit bushes until a signal for the young native halted their progress. They were now very close to the bushrangers camp. A horse whickered softly in the shadows, causing them to remain motionless.

In the deepening darkness, they noticed ahead of them, the flickering flames of camp fire. As they edged closer the sound of voices reached Henry's ears. '... c'mon woman... stir yer arse off that log. No need t'nurse the kid... he'll come a'no 'arm – yet.' His meaningful guffaw brought a sharp rebuke from one of the men round the fire.

'Keep yer trap shut, Will!' There was a hint of malice in his words that stung the first man into a retaliatory observation.

'Damnation, Bert... can't yer see as 'ow she's motherin' the boy? I don't trust the bitch.'

'Leave her be. She's doing' the job we got'er for.'

Henry glimpsed the woman as she came into the firelight. Truculently, she picked up a pot and fixed it over the flames as if to disclose her objections to the situation. Henry's heart ached with sorrow as he noticed little Stephen walking close beside her. He had an urge to rush in and rescue the child, but the odds were stacked against him and the apparently two victims. Stephen obviously found the woman's presence comforting as he kept close to her while she prepared the meal for the gang.

Henry indicated that they should retrace their steps and locate a safe camp site for the night. Gicky nodded silently and quietly edged away into the deep shadows. Crouching low, Henry turned to follow, but as he did so his foot caught against an exposed root. Snatching at a branch he managed to keep his balance, but his actions caused a slight disturbance in the undergrowth.

'What the 'ell is that!' A note of alarm was reflected in the voice. Henry crouched motionless in the shadows, not daring to make any movement. From his position he could just discern the silhouette of the nervous lookout as he came towards the bushes and looked anxiously in his direction.

'F'git it Will. Prob'ly an animal, or suffin'' Will, however, was not convinced, he continued to stare into the shadows. Henry never moved, he had the feeling of being fully exposed to the observer as he peered into the shadows from the edge of the firelight. It was the woman's call informing them that the food was ready, that eased the man's alertness.

Slowly, almost reluctantly he turned away and walked towards the campfire. As he did so, Henry inched his way deeper into the shadows and safety. Once clear of the campsite he met up with a worried Gicky. Together they walked silently away from what was obviously the gang's prepared hide-out. They made their own camp a safe distance from the kidnappers.

Throughout the next day, Henry and Gicky took it in turn to keep the kidnappers' hide-out under careful observation. Henry, who was on lookout when one of the gang rode off, considered the possibility of going in to try and rescue Stephen. He remembered his promise to Edward and remained on watch. Desperate as he was to rescue the little lad, he realised the odds were still stacked heavily against him.

Failure would bring not only his own death, but Stephen's also. Perhaps the woman's life would be at risk as well. Henry found her presence an enigma as she did not seem the type that would willingly associate with escaped convicts. He shook his head reflectively, unable to comprehend her presence.

His restraint proved propitious as the other rider soon returned. Henry heaved a gentle sigh of relief, especially when he noticed the musket slung over his shoulder. Its presence induced an ominous feeling as he watched the man dismount and start giving instructions. The man's words were inaudible to Henry as he watched covertly from his cover, but on seeing the leader's arm sweep in a circle, Henry deduced that a search was planned around their campsite. Henry decided it was time to make a stealthy retreat to alert Gicky. Gently he brushed the grass to eliminate any sign of his presence before moving to their camp that was some distance away. He was sure that they were far enough away to be safe from the search, but he wanted to be sure. Carefully he made his way back to Gicky and their concealed shelter. They neither heard nor observed a sign of the kidnappers throughout the day.

It was evening by the time Henry silently returned to the gang's hide-out. The last crimson strands of the sunset were just fading from the sky as he edged himself through the deepening shadows that surrounded the kidnappers campfire. Stars were flickering through the overhanging boughs as he carefully approached his observation post. His caution proved prudent, as the shadowy form of a guard alerted him to the danger of a careless move.

Each step had to be cautiously considered as he edged closer. One false move would bring revengeful retaliation. Intuition warned Henry of some hidden danger. Step by silent step, he eased ever closer towards the camp, pausing to take one further step, he heard the unseen sentry's cough from the shadows just ahead of him. Henry froze, not daring to move.

Footsteps shuffled from the direction of the campfire. Another dark silhouette moved away from the firelight to join the lookout. From his hidden position, Henry could clearly hear their subdued conversation. Their exchange of words sent a chill of fear pulsing through his body. It was their off hand callousness that shocked him rigid. The horror of what they intended to do after receiving the ransom money, filled him with rage as he listened to their plans.

‘Be glad t’git away from ‘ere, Jim…’ he paused to belch loudly before continuing, ‘… gives me the creeps.’

‘Me ‘n all!’ the man on lookout muttered. ‘Bert…’ he nodded in the direction of their shelter, ‘… says as ‘ow we best split up once we got t’money. Hide up a while in the mount’ins. One fing’s f’sure…’ he chuckled satanically, ‘they’ll be searchin’ f’us when they finds the bodies.’

‘… ‘as true, but by then,…’ his companion reflected loudly, ‘… we’ll be well away from ‘ere. They’ll not find any sign o’us in the mount’ins.’

‘What about the woman, Will?’

‘That stuck up bitch! Treats us like we was dirt.’ He paused to clear his throat and spit into the bushes. ‘Just she wait. I intend to ‘ave me fill o’her…’ he disgorged a lecherous laugh, ‘… a fore she’s finished.’

‘How in damnation did yer git her t’join us in the first place? She’s hardly our type, Will.’ There was a cynical note in the questioner’s voice.

‘Bumped in to ‘er… accidental like o’course.’ He gave a suggestive chuckle. ‘Said as how ‘t’were fate that I should a met ‘er. Wiv’ a solemn e’spression an’ tears in me eyes, I said as ‘ow me wife were very ill an’ unable to see to our little lad.’

‘And she fell f’your story?’

‘Aye! Said ‘ow sorry she was an’ could she ‘elp in any way until my wife was better.’ He made a sympathetic grimace as he mimicked the woman’s concern. There was a burst of raucous laughter from both as they gave a contemptuous glance towards the shelter. Inside the victim, now fully aware of the way she had been deceived, was doing her best to protect and care for the child kidnapped by the gang.

‘I’ll say this for ‘er. She’s looked arter the kid an’ kept ‘im quiet. Even promising to take ‘im back ‘ome again.’

‘She’ll be lucky!’ Their sadistic laughter sent a chill down Henry’s spine.

‘They’re going to kill them both!’ His whispered thought filled him with horror. Henry realised that he now had the responsibility of saving them… but how? The men’s voices faded as they walked away towards the shelter.

'... once we 'ave the money... 'is father'll not be able t'report us... tha's f'sure.' Henry was straining in the shadows to catch their conversation as they walked away. '... dead men... as they say... c'n tell no tales...' Their derisive laughter was indicative of their intentions. 'Once we 'ave the money...' but Henry could not hear their plans for murdering Edward.

It was dark, the moon had yet to make its appearance as Henry cautiously made his way back to where Gicky awaited him with a succulent meal. Having experienced his native friend's cooking on their past hunting forays, Henry settled down to the mouth-watering food. Thinking of the gang's murderous intentions took the edge off his appetite. During his meal, he tried to formulate a plan to save Edward as well as Stephen and the innocent woman. They were all in grave danger of being murdered once the ransom was paid.

Henry remembered Edward saying that the money was to be paid over at noon. This meant he only had tomorrow morning to execute any plan that he might conceive. By gestures and signs he indicated to Gicky that he would try and rescue Stephen and the woman in the morning. That was if he could think of a plan – a safe plan.

His best chance, he considered, would be after one or even two of the gang had departed to collect the ransom. Speed would be essential as Edward's life was also in danger. Somehow he must think of a plan to save them all.

By early dawn, Henry was in position close to the kidnapper's shelter. He still had conceived no definite plan. At the moment he was alone, Gicky was due to join him after clearing their campsite. Action of some kind was become imperative if Stephen and the woman were to be saved. Henry was becoming impatient, he had the urge to charge the shelter. To force a show down with the murderers. He quickly discarded the thought, remembering the vulnerability of the two hostages. Time was getting short, he must somehow take the initiative.

His break came suddenly and unexpectedly. Two members of the gang walked towards their horses. Once in the saddle, they turned and headed their horses in the direction of Emu Ford, leaving at a gentle canter. Time for action.

Cautiously he crept nearer the hide-out. As he settled behind the bushes on the edge of the clearing, he heard the woman's voice raised in anger. '... get away from me... you... you loathsome... oaf!' Realising that a struggle was in progress, Henry prepared to charge in. He hesitated as he noticed the man, cursing and threatening to retaliate emerged from the shelter.

'I'll have yer... yer snobbish... bitch!' As he walked away, the woman and Stephen came out into the clearing. Henry smiled, despite the critical situation as he noticed the ball in Stephen's hand – his birthday present. The man watched them sullenly as they played with Stephen's ball. All the time his gun was balanced menacingly in his hand.

Henry remained in the bushes, watching and waiting for a chance to strike. If only he could attract the woman's attention, warn her of his imminent rescue attempt. He continued his observations unobserved, knowing that if Stephen spotted him he would call out in his excitement.

Henry noticed how at ease he seemed with the woman as the two of them played with his ball. Suddenly it rolled under the bushes close to his hiding place. 'Leave it, Stephen! I'll get the ball... for you.' She hurried round the bushes to retrieve it. Her startled gasp faded as she noticed Henry's finger pressed against his lips.

'I'm a friend... here to rescue... you and Stephen,' he whispered.

'Here... take this. Use it if you have to!' Henry quickly and silently handed over his knife which the woman hastily concealed. 'Your lives are both in danger!' She picked up the ball and scrambled back into the clearing.

'Come Stephen, we shall go inside.'

'I wish .. daddy would come.' Henry noticed the bemused look on Stephen's face as he spoke to the woman leading him by his hand.

'He will be with us soon... I promise.' She gave the little lad an affectionate hug as they entered the shelter. Watching them with a sullen look was the man left behind to guard the captives.

'Keep inside... damn you...' he swung his fist as she passed. The blow landed on the woman's cheek. Her gasp of pain as she was sent staggering into the shelter, induced a feeling of rage in the unseen observer.

Henry's attack caught the man momentarily off guard. With difficulty he managed to turn and just avoid the fist aimed at his face. Nevertheless, there was an audible grunt of pain as the blow landed against his shoulder. There was sufficient force to send him staggering backwards. Before Henry could follow up, Stephen came running towards him.

'Henry! Henry!' Stephen's excited shouts as he raced towards him, disturbed Henry's concentration. Taking advantage of the situation, the guard made a grab for his gun.

'Stay with the lady... Stephen.' Henry gently guided him towards the anxious woman, who snatched the lad and shouted a warning at the same time. Henry flung himself sideways as the guard's gun butt powered past his head. Thanks to the woman he had been able to evade the brutal blow. Unfortunately, his evasive action caused him to stumble to his knees. Henry could only watch helplessly as his opponent raised the gun butt to deliver a fatal blow to his unprotected head.

In that moment of helplessness, Henry was suddenly aware of a hurried movement behind his attacker. There was a flash of steel as the woman flung herself at the brute who had taunted and attempted to force himself upon here. Anger erupted within her as she became aware of his intention to kill the man who had come to their rescue. Without hesitation she jumped at his back and plunged the knife deep into his body. As the blade entered his back, he emitted a strange gurgling roar as the gun dropped harmlessly from his hands and his legs collapsed beneath him.

Horrified at what she had done, the woman watched mesmerised as blood spilled from his mouth and his eyes gradually glazed over. She looked from the still figure on the floor to Henry with a shocked silent expression. Henry, grateful for the changed situation, rose to his feet and walked slowly over to the thug. As he bent over to check his condition, he realised it was an unnecessary act – the man was dead.

'Dead!' Henry looked at the woman to nod his confirmation. 'You've killed him... but saved our lives.' She seemed in a state of shock as she murmured uncertainly about protecting him... protecting Stephen.

'Never... realised... what I was... doing...' Her silent sobbing suddenly changed to alarm as Gicky made his appearance.

Stephen, silenced and bemused by the recent actions, suddenly ran towards Henry and the dark skinned new arrival. Two people he was able to identify with. Henry picked the lad up to comfort him and at the same time reassure the woman that Gicky was a friend. 'He's been helping me to rescue Stephen... and yourself from these murderers.' His words had a calming affect and as she became aware of the friendlier atmosphere, a warm smile reflected her relief.

Realising that her presence with the kidnappers must appear suspicious, the woman began to explain her circumstances.

'No need to explain.' Henry assured her. 'We...' he indicated Gicky, '... have been watching this site since you arrived. As regards the killing...' he nodded towards the dead man, '... it was your life, or his. They had planned to kill both you and Stephen once the ransom was paid.'

'Ransom?' She gave Henry a puzzled look.

'Yes. The other two are due to collect the money... at noon.' His mention of the ransom alerted Henry to the passing of time. He glanced at the sun, noticing with a shock that it was nearing its zenith. If he was to save Edward, he must leave immediately.

'Stephen...' he gave the little lad an affectionate look, '... you stay with the lady until...'

'Amy... Amy Carver!' Her voice had an educated ring to it as she introduced herself.

'Thank you... Amy. Henry Coleman... at your service' There was a brief flicker of a smile before he continued with his instructions. 'You stay with Amy and Gicky, Stephen,' he gently handed the little lad over to Amy.

'Daddy... mummy... come...?' Stephen was near to tears – bewildered.

'Soon. Very soon, Stephen. I'm now going to fetch him.' He

tried to sound reassuring, but... Once again he glanced anxiously at the sun's position.

'Gicky!' He turned and made signs to his silent friend. He indicated that he must leave for Emu Ford immediately and that he wanted him to follow with the woman and Stephen. A smile spread over his dark features as he nodded his understanding of what was expected of him.

'Follow Gicky, Amy and he'll take you and Stephen to where I hope his father will be waiting.' Without a backward glance, Henry mounted his horse and rode off towards the ransom hand-over place.

Involuntarily, his glance was once again directed into the heavens. He experienced a tremor of fear as he noticed that the sun was almost at its highest point. He urged his horse into a full gallop, praying silently that he would be in time to save Edward's life –prevent his murder. He barely noticed the stinging lashes of the low, outstretched branches as he sped towards his destination – Emu Ford.

Gradually, the trail narrowed and became very rough. Henry, because of the danger to both him and his horse was compelled to ease his speed. A fork in the trail eventually brought them to a stop. As his horse stamped impatiently, Henry tried to ascertain which track the kidnappers had taken. There were no visible signs to help him. Looking round for some indication of their progress, he felt momentarily lost... defeated.

'Damn them!' he cursed out loud enough to startle the local avifauna. His frustration soon gave way to determination as he remembered how Edward had risked his life to save him from the blazing barn. Intuition directed him along the right hand fork – there were no other signs to guide him.

'Thank God!' he whispered reverently a few moments later as he noticed hoof prints clearly visible on a patch of sandy ground. Further conformation followed a few minutes later. Fresh horse droppings verified that he was close behind the kidnappers. Their destination could not be far ahead. He prepared his gun for immediate action, hoping that his race against time would not have been in vain.

* * * * *

'Have we much further to go, Robert?' Becky's voice was terse with anxiety. She was near to exhaustion after a day and a half in the saddle, but still desperate to reach Edward and their small son, Stephen. She prayed that they were both safe and that Stephen had not suffered in the hand of the kidnappers.

Since he had been abducted, Becky had experienced many long hours of agony as she waited helplessly at home. Stephen had been continuously in her thoughts. Night and day she had suffered untold agonies as she wondered how he was coping in the hands of those uncouth villains. Eventually, she could stand the uncertainty no longer. The waiting had become unbearable after Edward's departure. She yearned for action, anything to prevent her thoughts from dwelling on Stephen's predicament. In a moment of extreme anguish, she had decided to ride after Edward.

'In which direction is Emu Ford?' Becky had enquired casually at the breakfast table on Thursday.

'North-westerly from here. Towards Bathurst.' Robert had answered with an uncertain frown furrowing his brow.

'I intend to ride there after breakfast... I must do something. Waiting is... becoming... unbearable.' Robert and Elizabeth both gave her a sympathetic look. Understanding her impatience – her restlessness.

'If that is your intention, Becky...' there was a note of anxiety in his voice, '... then I must ride with you.' His firm statement precluded any protest that she might have considered. 'Elizabeth can remain with the children until we return... with Stephen and Edward.'

An hour later, Robert and Becky, accompanied by the trusted Jem, who was now fully recovered from his encounter with the kidnappers, set off for Emu Ford. 'If we maintain a steady canter we should be in the area by noon on the morrow, Becky.' Robert's reassuring words calmed her mounting apprehension. He gave one word of warning, however. 'Our presence must not become known to the kidnappers before the ransom money is handed over.'

Robert explained as they continued their journey, 'that a sign of their approach would endanger the lives of both Edward and Stephen. We must proceed with extreme caution, Becky. We are dealing with unscrupulous thugs.' She nodded her agreement, her terse unsmiling features reflected the agonising suspense that she was enduring. Robert gave her a furtive glance as they rode deeper into the bush.

Since the kidnapping, Becky had become very quiet and withdrawn – symptoms that had greatly perturbed him. It was with a feeling of relief that he became aware of her change of emotions. Gradually, as they maintained a steady progress towards Emu Ford, Becky became more like her usual, vivacious self. Her phlegmatic mood was disappearing, replaced by a feeling of hope as they cantered along the dusty road towards Edward and Stephen.

A smile lingered on Robert's face as he realised how much their positive actions were helping to restore her faith and optimism. It augured well for the outcome of their journey. He hoped that nothing untoward would destroy her returning happiness. As Becky's eyes gazed momentary into his, he became aware that beneath her attempt to happiness, she was suffering deep anxiety for her loved ones.

They stayed the night at a small farm, owned by acquaintances who called at Newacres on their rare visits to Sydney. Jenny's motherly figure in her faded bonnet and sombre clothing, was shocked to hear of the kidnapping. 'We've heard as how there'd been trouble from bush ranger in the area…' she nodded towards a gun standing in the corner of the room, '… for some weeks now. There's been raids on a couple of local settlement – but kidnap…' Jenny shook her head in shocked disbelief. She gave Becky a comforting embrace as she guided her into the farmhouse. Frank, her angular husband followed them while listening to details of the ransom arrangements.

'Emu Ford!' he frowned in thought as he absently stroked his bushy beard. 'Be around a dozen miles or so, I reck'n.'

'We need to be in that vicinity around noon tomorrow.' Robert explained the reason for their time of arrival.

‘I’ll ride with yer… if you’ve a mind?’ Robert was about to refuse Frank’s offer when he noticed the trap in the yard. A conveyance that they might be glad of come the morrow. There was a possibility that little Stephen might be exhausted after his ordeal with the kidnappers, or even worse. That frightful thought he kept to himself as he suggested that their host should accompany them in the trap.

‘If it’s convenient, Jenny…’ Robert glanced across to where she was anxiously tending to Becky, ‘… we would like to make an early start.’

‘Breakfast’ll be ready when you are… and there’s no need t’worry about farm.’ She picked up the gun with the skill of an expert and demonstrated how she would use it should the need arise. Jenny’s actions induced a few chuckles as they prepared to settle down with welcoming drinks to await the evening meal

Robert and Becky were in the lead, closely followed by Jem who kept his pace to that of Frank in his trap. They were able to maintain a steady pace over a well used road. Before leaving, Jenny had handed her husband a blanket. His protest had been stifled by his wife’s furtive look, an expression that informed him why he was to take it with him. Robert’s worried features also explained why his presence in the trap was required.

‘Have we much further to go, Robert?’ Glancing anxiously up at the sun’s position Becky repeated her question. Some time had elapsed since she had enquired originally. Looking across she had noticed his deep state of concentration.

‘Oh, er… sorry, Becky. I was lost in my thoughts… dreaming.’ He gave her an apologetic smile. ‘I’ll enquire.’ He dropped back to pull along side Frank.

‘…’bout another half mile… just b’yond that ridge.’ Frank pointed his whip ahead of them in answer to Roberts question.

‘We’ll stop in the shade of those trees. Just before we reach the summit.’ Robert indicated a small thicket. ‘Don’t want to disclose our presence… yet.’ He cast an anxious glance towards the heavens. It was around noon as far as he could estimate.

‘When we get to the trees, I’ll ride on ahead… alone.’ Frank and Jem nodded their agreement. As he urged his horse into a canter to rejoin Becky about fifty yards ahead of them, the sound of two shots fired almost simultaneously shattered the silence. Alarm showed on their faces as they gazed in shocked silence at each other.

'Quick… we must hurry!' Robert reacted quickly. A pistol shot reached their ears as they cleared the ridge. Involuntary, he reached for his pistol as ahead of them they watched as Henry aimed and fired at a retreating rider. Two bodies were lying on the ground close to him.

Edward experienced a strange sensation as he neared Emu Ford. An instinctive feeling warned him that he was being followed. He felt exposed – vulnerable. He had no option but to ride on for Stephen's sake. As he became aware of the figure shadowing him, Edward's concern gave way to anger. There was something ominous about the furtive movements of the man trailing him.

Reaching down, he touched the butt of his gun as if seeking comfort from its presence. If it came to a shoot-out, he was ready and determined, but care was of paramount importance. Any false move on his part would place his son's life in danger.

A lone horseman emerged from the bushes, just a few paces ahead of him. His appearance induced in Edward a feeling of rage. Through eyes misted with anger he surveyed the ruffian who had been responsible for Stephen's abduction. Edward's fists clenched in an involuntary gesture as he struggled to control his urge to punish this savage who had kidnapped an innocent child.

'Calm yourself!' he entreated himself. 'You'll need a cool head to deal with these barbarians.' His whispered commendation induced a feeling of calm as he rode slowly and vigilantly up to the waiting figure. Edward smiled grimly as he noticed how he would be exposed at the moment of handing over the ransom.

Three men had been reported on the night of the kidnap. Where were the other two, he wondered. Concealed in the bushes with their guns trained on my back, Edward conjectured. He felt defeated – helpless. Something warned him that not only was his life in danger, but also Stephen's. What could he do with the odds stacked heavily against him? If only Henry had accompanied him, they might have worked out a plan between them, but there had been no news of his friend and Gicky.

'Keeel... keeel.' Was he imagining things? Tense with anticipation, he waited for a repeat of the crested parrot's call. 'Keeel... keeel.' The sound brought joy to his heart. He was not alone, help was close at hand. A quiet determination pervaded his body as he realised that there was every chance of capturing these murdering scum.

The man's neckerchief covering the lower half of his face was watching him intently. Edward's hand was resting close to his gun as he brought his horse to a stop just a dozen paces from the kidnapper.

'Where is my... son?' Edward glanced quickly round him 'There's no money until...'

'I'll tell yer where t'find 'im after I 'ave the money,' he indicated Edward's saddle bags with a loathsome sneer.

'Then you had best take me to him... for there will be no payment – until I know he is safe.'

'I'll 'ave the money.. NOW!' There was a threatening note to his demand.

'After I have seen my son... and I know he is safe.'

'Unless I'm back at our hide-out within the hour... and with the money, there's little chance of yer seein' 'im... alive that is.' His repulsive laugh sent a spasm of anger pulsing through Edward's body. It took all his control not to rush forward and grab the satanic being in front of him. His fists clenched until the white of his knuckles showed. Edward was just about to attack the obnoxious creature before him, when the kidnapper drew his pistol.

'Giv'us the money... NOW!' He waved his pistol menacingly. As Edward began to slowly remove the saddle bags, his mind was contemplating a way to overcome his predicament. It was Henry's shout that alarmed him and with lightning reflexes Edward reached for his gun, but it was too late. Helpless, he watched as the kidnapper raised his pistol and aimed directly at him. He vaguely remember two reports, as if from behind him. Before he could react, a grey mist of pain dulled his senses and he experienced a feeling of falling... falling... into the unfathomable chasm of darkness that gradually engulfed him.

Crouched in the bushes, Henry paused to take stock of the situation. From his concealed position he could make out the figure of the gang's leader, Bert which he had heard the others call him. Thinking of the other two, reminded him that the body of one was back in their camp, while the other was hiding somewhere around. As he anxiously swept his gaze over the surrounding bushes, Henry noticed Edward riding slowly along the road. With mounting apprehension, he watched as his friend rode assertively towards the kidnappers leader.

There was something sinister about the rogue as he waited for Edward to hand over the ransom. Intuition warned Henry that the hidden kidnapper was planning some murderous action. Somehow he must warn his friend that he was in a dire situation. Then he remembered his promised call of identification.

'Keeel... keeel...' his call drifted across the clearing. Immediately after the call he noticed with relief how the cry had alerted his friend. After a pause he repeated the crested parrot's cry, 'Keeel... keeel...' as they had arranged. There was a subtle movement of Edward's hand, a furtive sign of acknowledgement.

From his concealed observation point, Henry peered closely at the surrounding vegetation. A perfect place for an ambush, he thought as he continued his survey of the shadowy depths of the bushes. Gripping his gun, he watched as Edward brought his horse to a stop a few paces short of the kidnapper's leader. As he heard their initial exchanges, Henry's eyes were alert for any danger. 'Where the hell is that other blackguard?' he silently asked himself. The man's absence worried him... an ominous sign.

'There!; he whispered as his eyes caught a brief movement in the bushes behind Edward. With horror, he watched the man raising his gun at Edward's back. At the same time he noticed that the leader had suddenly produced a pistol and was about to fire it – at Edward.

Henry acted instinctively. His warning shout reached Edward's ears just as the hidden kidnapper fired. Henry's aim although quick, was accurate. The concealed man was dead before the echoes of the shots had died away. Seeing Edward collapse, the leader lowered his still loaded pistol and prepared to make his escape.

Bluffing for time to recharge his gun, Henry called to the leader to surrender. When the man hesitated, he shouted a final warning. With his gun almost ready, Henry noticed the leader's covetous glance at the saddle bags lying beside Edward's still form. Realising his hopeless situation, the kidnapper decided to abandon the ransom and make his escape. Freedom was more important that capture and hanging.

Suddenly aware of riders and a trap approaching along the road, the gang's leader vaulted on to his horse and at the same time fired a deterrent shot in Henry's direction. He ducked involuntarily as the shot narrowly passed him and landed harmlessly in the bushes. He fired randomly at the retreating figure, but how near he came to hitting the escaping kidnapper was a matter of conjecture. Henry could only watch as the rider swerved and disappeared into the thicket, anxious to depart the scene of his abortive kidnap.

Henry's main concern was for Edward who lay recumbent a few paces away. He hurried over only to hesitate with shock as he noticed the blood running down the side of his friend's face. 'Dear God!' His disconcerted exclamation was an involuntary reaction as he gazed down upon the pallid features of Edward.

Robert's sudden appearance seemed to startle Henry out of his shocked state. He watched anxiously as the doctor carefully inspect Edward's injury, before turning a worried face towards Robert as he crouched beside his friend. 'Is... is he...?' Henry could not bring himself to ask the vital question. He eased aside as Becky joined them. Her face was ashen with anxiety as she looked down at the man she loved and then glanced round for any sign of Stephen.

Robert broke the tense silence. 'It's serious. A scalp wound... but...' he looked round anxiously until his glance rested on Frank. 'We must get him to shelter... as soon as possible.'

'Of course...' He acknowledged Robert's meaning. '... my place is at yer service.' He turned towards Becky. 'I'll take Edward t'our place in the trap. He'll be fine...' he tried to reassure her. Becky thanked him reflectively as her frantic gaze searched for signs of her little son. Distraught with grief, she turned her tear filled eyes to enquire of Henry.

'Where... where is Stephen, Henry?' Becky could contain her emotions no longer. Edward was being cared for by Robert, but where was their son? Fear gripped her as she realised that he might be dead. Murdered by the kidnappers.

'He's on his way Becky... safe and in good shape.' He hesitated before reassuring her further. 'For that, we must thank the young woman who has been caring for him.'

'Young woman?' Becky gave him a cynical look, wondering how he could be so gracious towards a woman who had been in league with the kidnappers.

'You have much t'thank her for, Becky. She was an innocent party in the kidnapping. After the care and protection she has bestowed upon Stephen, I think you should hear the circumstances of her involvement with those scum.'

'Stephen! Oh, Stephen!' Becky suddenly noticed her son stepping out of the bushes that edged the track smiling and affectionately holding on to Amy's hand, he watched excitedly as his mother ran towards him. 'Oh... darling... you're safe!' Becky held a bewildered Stephen in a warm and loving embrace.

After a few moments of their joyful reunion, Becky was suddenly aware of the young woman's uncertain presence. Her troubled face reflected the ambivalent emotions she was experiencing as she waited to see what reaction Stephen's family and friends would accord her. Instinctively, she picked up the child's ball that had eluded his grasp during his mother's embrace.

Becky lifted Stephen up in her arms as Amy returned the birthday present to him. His hearty chuckle as he accepted it was a reassuring sound to his mother. His sojourn with the kidnappers appeared to have affected his bravado very little. Someone must have protected him from the gang and also ensured that his welfare had not suffered while he had been away. It could only be one person, the woman standing beside her. Becky's eyes met Amy's troubled gaze.

A warm smile spread over Becky's face, as still hugging Stephen, she assured the young woman of her gratitude. 'Thank you for taking care of Stephen,' she gave her son a gentle caress. 'He looks well considering his ordeal.' Becky turned again to Amy. 'You have been very kind to him.'

'I did my best... to protect him, ma'am.' She gave Stephen a benign smile as she turned to depart. Where she could go to, she had no idea – she was alone again.

'Amy! Amy! Don't go!' It was Stephen's shrill voice pleading with her to stay that caused her to pause and smile sadly at him. She would certainly miss the little lad. 'Mummy... please!' his eyes filled with tears as he turned towards his mother. 'Please... let... Amy... stay.' Becky nodded, aware of his concern for the woman who had protected him.

'You'll be very welcome... Amy.' She gave the forlorn figure a warm smile of encouragement. 'We would love to have you.' Gently she eased Stephen into Amy's eager arms as the need to ascertain the extent of Edward's injury overwhelmed her.

Becky turned a worried face towards Robert and Henry, still crouched over Edward's inert form. 'Please, God!' She pleaded in silent prayer. 'Please... don't let him die.' Her prayers appeared to be answered as she noticed Edward's eyes flicker open and rest upon her.

'Becky... love...' His smile faded as dizziness overcame him once again. With eyes closed he whispered Stephen's name.

'Yes... Stephen is safe, Edward. He's been asking for you.'

'Good!' His eyes flickered open as if searching for signs of his son. Becky fetched Stephen into his vision.

'Daddy!' His face lit up as he looked down at his father.

'Hello... Stephen...' Edward's voice was little more than a whisper.

He reached out weakly to touch his son's face. 'You've... been... a brave... lad... Stephen.' But dizziness caused him to close his eyes as he felt himself falling once again into the darkening depths of a fathomless abyss.

CHAPTER TWELVE

Edward straightened his back gradually. Every sinew, every muscle ached as he walked past the other shearers towards the barrel of ale. Sweat glistened on his dusty face, dampening his beard where it trickled down his hirsute features. For days it seemed, he had endured the back-breaking task of sheep shearing.

Henry and James with a few other experienced staff, had a sheep locked between their legs as they skilfully continued with their shearing. With a dexterity borne of familiarity they manipulated their shears to remove the sheep's fleece. Henry glanced up as Edward took a long swig of ale.

His thoughts reflected on the incident of a few months back when it had been doubtful whether Edward would survive the scalp wound caused by the kidnapper's gunshot. Involuntarily his eyes lingered briefly on the scar at the side of his employer's head An angry cicatrix that was a lingering reminder of that near fatal encounter.

'Nearly finished...' Edward sighed wearily, '... and I for one will not be complaining.' He nodded towards the few remaining sheep as he handed Henry a pot of ale.

'My sentiments exactly.' Henry paused to wipe the sweat from his face. 'Thanks...' after eagerly accepting the refreshments, he imbibed long and deep. 'Ahh... that...' he wiped his mouth with the back of his hand, '... was more than welcome.' Next moment, with an exaggerated gesture he tipped the tankard to his lips and gratefully emptied it of its contents.

James, the more experienced of the shearers, placed his fleece on top of the bale before claiming his drink. 'Good fleeces, Edward...' he indicated the bales of fleece at the end of the shearing shed, '... reck'n as how they'll be nigh on eight pounds each.' Edward nodded confirmation. He passed James a tankard of ale before picking up his shears in preparation for the next sheep.

Working in shift with the experienced shearers, the three friends had toiled strenuously through several days of shearing.

Now, with the end in sight, there was a feeling of relief as they selected their next sheep from the few remaining in the pens.

It was dusk as the last of the skittish sheep left the shearing barn. Shorn of their thick wool covering the sheep, now that the temperatures were climbing, showed their relief by bounding away from the shearers. As the last sheep disappeared, Edward cast a satisfying glance over the bales of fleece. Next thing was to transport them into Sydney for the wool auction.

Edward had already made arrangements for two trading hoys to carry his wool down river from Parramatta to Sydney. To ensure that it was safely transported to the government warehouses, he intended to sail on the leading craft. First, they must cart the fleece into their nearest town, Parramatta.

A few days later, Edward supervised the loading of the wool bales into wagons at Newacres. 'That's the lot Henry!' Edward nodded towards the wagons onto which his wool from both of his farms had been loaded.

'Aye... we're already to move off.' Henry gave a warning shout to the four drivers standing by their wagons, before jumping onto the leading one. He was anxious to be under way now that the loading was completed. Each conveyance carried two men, the driver and a guard. The latter being armed against attacks from roaming bands of bushrangers.

'See you in Parramatta!' Edward called across to Henry before springing into his saddle and urging a frisky Nelson into a gentle canter. Henry acknowledged by waving his whip. Then with a flamboyant gesture he sent the convoy of wagons rolling along the road.

Slowly the hoy drifted away from the wharf. Edward, from its bows watched as his empty wagons trundled away from the jetty, to start their return journey to Newacres. A smile twitched his lips as he noticed Nelson hitched to the rear of Henry's wagon. There was a dispirited look about him at being subjected to such an ignoble role. Henry, as if aware of Edward's glance, turned and raised his arm before the wagons were lost to view.

Edward and his four helpers settled down for their sail down river to Sydney. As they drifted between high banks, thick with trees that straggled down to the river's edge, Edward was alert in case of trouble. Thick vegetation edged the narrow reaches of the water for the first mile or two. Ideal hiding places from which to launch raids on the passing craft. Attacks were rare, but he had warned his men to keep a sharp lookout. It was easy to get lulled into a feeling of false security in such idyllic surroundings.

In the trees and high bushes, Edward noticed crested parrots and parakeets flitting among the branches, their plumage dazzling in vivid displays of colour. As the boat with its single sail neared their habitat, its presence induced discordant cries of alarm from the avifauna.

Occasionally, Edward glimpsed dark-skinned natives fishing from their bark constructed, canoe-like craft. Their flimsy structure caused him to ponder on how the fishermen managed to keep their craft afloat. He watched with consternation as an aborigine manoeuvred his craft with great skill in an endeavour to paddle clear of their hoy. It seemed like a deliberate attempt on the part of their steersman to disrupt the fishermen. An act that annoyed Edward. He shouted a warning to their helmsman, indicating that he should take avoiding action.

Acres of pastureland gradually replaced the thick riverside vegetation. Small herds of goats and domestic pigs grazing close to the river, raised their heads to watch the passing hoys. Wild duck took to flight as they approached, proclaiming their annoyance with a cacophony of harsh rasping calls.

White-washed buildings, gleaming in the later afternoon sunlight, identified the isolated settlements dotted about the flat pastures just a few miles from Sydney. These small farms gradually gave way to tree clad slopes sweeping down to rocky inlets as they neared the town. Sandy beaches, golden in the brilliant sunshine, warned Edward that they were nearing Cockle Creek where produce from the Hawkesbury farms was landed and stored in the nearby warehouses.

* * * * *

Thankful to see the unloading of his wool completed, Edward walked from the wharf into the town. A short distance past Government House, he came upon Robert's cottage, where a welcome always awaited Becky or himself. Edward was surprised to see so much activity in the place. Then he remembered, Robert and Elizabeth were shortly to move into their new home, Acacia House.

'You'll have to forgive the chaotic welcome, Edward.' Robert looked up from his surgery desk where he was packing his medical books and instruments. 'I'm afraid we're rather disorganised at the moment.' In the next room he found Elizabeth, heavy with child and almost wilting under the heat, trying to cope amidst the turmoil of preparing for their pending move.

'Perhaps I can help...' Edward glanced round, wondering how best he could assist Elizabeth, '... just tell me what's required.'

'I wouldn't entertain such an idea...' she demurred good naturedly, '... the servant are conversant with what is required. It was kind of you to offer, Edward, but we've almost finished packing.' Despite her warm smile of appreciation, he noticed the tired look in her eyes.

'Now...' she took hold of Edward's arm and led him towards the main room, where much calmer conditions prevailed, '... tell me how Becky and your family are... all well, I sincerely hope?'

'In excellent health... and spirits... I'm glad to say.'

'What about Stephen... did his ordeal with the kidnappers...?'

'He's in good shape. Fortunately, Amy shielded him from the brunt of their attentions.' Elizabeth's surprised look caused Edward to chuckle. 'Truth is, all he talks about is the food he helped Amy to prepare over the campfire and the games he played with her. So on your next visit...' he jokingly warned Elizabeth, '... expect to partake of a meal prepared over a campfire.'

'I shall look forward to that...' her confirmation was accompanied by an amusing smile, '... but first I have a very agitated child to bring into this world.' She placed her hands over the swollen belly.

'When do you... expect to... to...?'

'Two more weeks,' she sighed. 'The beginning of next month.'

'What of your move? Will it delay...?' Edward began to enquire pensively.

'No. We shall be able to move as arranged. I trust I shall be well again... by then...' Elizabeth paused as a maid appeared with the teas. 'Thank you, Mary. I shall serve.'

'Very good, Ma'am.' She placed the tray beside Elizabeth before leaving.

'Robert has already seen to the furnishing of our new house...' Elizabeth continued her conversation as she poured the tea. 'We hope to be settled in by the end of November. Then, if all goes well...' excitement sparkled in her eyes as she handed the refreshments to Edward, '... we hope to celebrate with a New Year's ball.' She gave her guest a questioning look. 'You and Becky haven't forgotten?'

'No chance of that...' he laughed. 'It's costing me a small fortune. Becky's new gown and... a new outfit for myself.' Edward shook his head in feigned dismay as Elizabeth joined in his laughter.

When her husband joined them later, Elizabeth excused herself when she realised that the two friends were anxious to discuss business. In particular Edward's new enterprise – his forge at Newacres. Aware of the local area's urgency for a blacksmith, Edward had built a forge on his farm. Skilled from his previous experience in his uncle's forge, Edward had already achieved a respected reputation among the settlers and land owners.*

'What about that... er, contraption you were working on ... 'Robert was trying to recall its name, '... is it ready for trials yet?'

'Not under field trials...' he shook his head, '... but test experiments have proved very satisfactory.'

'You'll be the envy of the other farmers, if your... er, machine works.' Robert's hesitant words revealed his doubts about a machine that would sow seeds in drills.

'Jethro Tull proved it could be done. His horse-drawn drills allowed the seeds to be sown more efficiently than the hand

* In Book I The Winds of Destiny

broadcast method. It also ensured that sufficient space remained between the rows to permit the use of a horse-drawn hoe to operate. My drill is based on his machine.'

'You believe... you have faith that your er... drill will work, Edward?'

'I have every confidence that it will. We shall know for sure come sowing-time.' Edward sounded optimistic about his drill machine being a complete success.

* * * * *

There was an air of excitement, of great activity as servants scurried between kitchen and dining room, where tables laid for supper awaited the guests. Acacia House wore a festive look as preparations reached the final stages for Robert and Elizabeth's New Year ball. Not only would the festivities introduce friends to their new home, but also, thought Robert, a chance for them all to welcome in the New Year together.

To the south of Sydney, their new two storied brick house overlooked the Park that now graced that area of the town. Their six bedroom structure, sheltered by the acacia shrubs and eucalyptus trees, was an imposing landmark. It was from the profusion of mimosa shrubs surrounding their new home that first gave Elizabeth the idea for its name – Acacia House.

Edward and Robert were conversing on the veranda. Beyond the newly laid out garden, the feathery foliage of the acacias trembled in the golden glow of the late evening sunlight. As the shadows deepened with the approaching twilight, the cicadas announced their presence with a vibrating rhythm of their calls.

'You have a magnificent house, Robert...' Edward wearing his new dark green brocaded coat, turned towards his friend, '... a just reward for the community work that Elizabeth and yourself had contributed to the town's residents over the years.'

'Thanks... Edward.' Robert appeared a little embarrassed by his friend's laudable commendations. 'I...' there was a hesitancy in his voice, '... that is, Elizabeth and I are very fortunate to be sharing this celebration.' There was a deep silence as the two companions walked thoughtfully down the veranda steps into the garden. Above the wooded hills in the distance, a crimson and golden sunset displayed its fading hues. A piercing reminder of the passing day – the dying year.

'Yes...' Robert's voice was soft with remembrance, '... very fortunate indeed. When our baby, Carol was born, Elizabeth's life was in danger.' He shook his head sadly as he recalled the exhausting time of the birth. Robert's deep emotive sigh reflected the agony he had endured in his struggle to save his wife's life – and his daughter's.

'I wanted Elizabeth to postpone the party,' he nodded back to the activities in the house behind them, 'but she begged me to let it go ahead as planned. Believe me, Edward... I'm more than grateful for Becky's help. I honestly don't know how we would have managed without her.'

'When we received your letter detailing your crisis, Becky was anxious to visit Elizabeth immediately. She very soon issued a series of instructions to ensure the smooth running of the house in her absence. Once satisfied of our welfare,' he chuckled at the memory, '... she gathered a few items of clothing together and requested that I escort her to Sydney without delay.' Smiles lingered on the faces of the two friends as they remembered Becky's fervent reactions to the news of Elizabeth's crisis.

'Our gain has been your loss, dear friend. Now that my wife is better we must, reluctantly I might add, allow Becky to return home with you. We shall most certainly miss her.'

'As I did... I can assure you, Robert.' Their shared laughter drifted across the silent, lantern-lit garden.

I wonder what our husbands find so amusing, Becky?' Elizabeth turned from the open window.

'Whatever it is appears to cause them much hilarity.' Becky walked over to join her friend at the window, from where they could see the shadowy forms of their spouses deep in conversation as they paced the garden.

'How can they remain so calm... when we are sick with worry, should our careful preparations go wrong?'

'I'm sure your party will be a success, Elizabeth. You'll see, every thing will be fine.' She gave her friend a reassuring kiss on the cheek. 'As for our men…' Becky nodded towards the garden, '… I doubt if they have given the party a passing thought.' Her face softened as a tender look came into her eyes. Beneath her was the shadowy form of the man she loved – passionately.

'Farming and medicine, if my guess is correct.' Elizabeth turned, shaking her head gently as she gave her companion an understanding smile.

'Becky… you look beautiful. Radiant. Your appearance…' She gave her friend an evocative look, '… will, I feel sure, disperse any thoughts of farming from Edward's mind.' Elizabeth's gaze was warm with admiration as she noticed how the pale green ball-gown complemented her companion's attractive features. There was the whispered caress of silk as Becky walked across the room to pick up her gloves.

'Thank you… Elizabeth… but you helped by introducing me to your dressmaker. This is my first ball-gown since we came to the colony.' Excitement sparkled in her eyes as she smoothed her long gloves over her arms. 'Do you think… Edward… will approve?' Becky pirouetted before giving Elizabeth a pensive look. A blush touched her cheeks as she anticipated his admiring – sensuous appraisal.

Edward's amorous reactions came later that night as they lay in each other's arms. The consequences came nine months later, when their second son, Roger, was born. Such developments, however, were far from Becky's mind as she finished dressing for the ball.

Picking up her skirts, Becky walked gracefully out into the garden. Edward's conversation with his friend died away as he turned to stare speechless with admiration towards his wife. Lantern light reflected the sheen of her silken gown as she moved towards him.

'Becky… you… look… wonderful. Charming.' Edward was finding it difficult to express his admiration. Excitement stirred within him as he gazed at Becky in her beautiful ball-gown.

Robert, aware of his friend's emotive reaction, excused himself. 'Must see to my guests… soon be time to greet them.'

As he came level with Becky, he paused to whisper, 'My sentiments are the same as Edward's. You look very charming… and I hope you will honour me with a dance later in the evening.' Becky's face was radiant as she lowered her eyes demurely. To hide her shyness, she made a pretence of smoothing her gloves over her arms.

She smiled her thanks and promised that a dance with him would be to her delight. As soon as Robert had departed, her eyes, glowing with love were raised to behold Edward's admiring glance. A surreptitious smile lingered on Robert's face as he glanced back from the veranda. The look on the faces of his friends reflected their emotional excitement – and affection.

'Do you like… my gown, Edward?' She spoke shyly, almost breathlessly as she became aware of his admiring glance lingering upon her. Not that she needed confirmation, his eyes revealed the answer. A warm smile spread over his face as he reached out and took her gloved hands in his.

'You look beautiful… just wonderful, my love.' There was an urgency about his kisses as he held her close in his arms. Their affectionate embrace evoked amorous desires within their yearning bodies.

As they eased apart, Becky gently touched Edward's cheek with her fan. 'Perhaps we should go inside before…' Her emotive thoughts remained unspoken. Smiling his understanding, Edward offered her his arm as they paused to look across the Park now fading into the dusk. With the last trace of the sunset erased from the evening sky, they turned and walked arm in arm to join the guests.

Garlands bedecked the room set aside for dancing. A small orchestra was busy tuning up in anticipation of the evening's dancing. Vases of flowers displayed their exotic colours and filled the air with their fragrance. Supper tables groaned under the weight of food that had been prepared to appease the guest's appetites.

Carriages were arriving in a procession to discharge their immaculately dressed occupants at the steps of Acacia House. Each guest was introduced to the gathering as they arrived.

Ladies in their beautiful silk, brocade or satin dresses flounced in on the arms of their escorts. Candlelight gave a soft sheen to their colourful gowns and sparkled on glittering jewelled adornments displayed, ostentatiously in some instances, by their owners.

Becky remained by Edward's side as she watched the guests circulating to greet friends and acquaintances. Contrasting with the colourful gowns of the ladies were the more subdued shades of the men's clothing. A few scarlet uniforms were conspicuous among the assembly as officers from the local garrison flirted evocatively with a few of the unattached ladies.

There was a slight lull in the conversation as Governor Macquarie and his wife, Elizabeth, were announced. Becky fingered her beautiful necklace pensively as she watched the new arrivals circulating among the guests. Their progress was spasmodic, as they paused to exchange a few words here and a smile there, as they greeted friends from the outlying districts.

Above the murmur of voices came the lively notes of a gavotte, an invitation for the dancers to take the floor. Soon, a few were executing skipping-like steps as the fiddles scraped away above the soft shuffle of the dancers' feet. There was a caressing rustle of the silk and brocaded gowns as the ladies swirled to the lilting music; a gentle whisper following their every movement.

Becky, watching from a window alcove, opened her fan to its full width as she swayed to the lively strains of the music. She felt the soft caress of the gentle breeze through the partly opened window. The fragrant filled evening air drifted in from the garden, bringing a touch of freshness to the warm room.

Edward removed two glasses of champagne from the tray, proffered by a servant. He passed one to an uncertain, Becky. Candlelight sparkled on the effervescent liquid as Edward whispered a toast in her ear.

'To the most beautiful lady present!' Their eyes met as he raised his glass. His look that revealed his longing, his love for her, induced a feeling of excitement to her aroused body. She was constantly reminded of his love for her. Yet, occasionally, in his unguarded moments, Becky was aware of Edward's thought and reflections contemplating on distant episodes. She endeavoured to suppress her jealous emotions as she wondered if he was thinking of England – of Julie, the girl he had loved before his transportation.

'Hello, Becky! Edward!' Her thoughts were interrupted as the Governor's wife came over to them. 'How are you both?' Becky was surprised that Elizabeth Macquarie had remembered her, as they had only met on three occasions. The first meeting had been when Edward and she arrived as survivors. On that eventful occurrence, the whole town, including the Governor and his wife, had been anxious to meet the young couple who had been rescued as they laid at death's door. That was four years ago and they had conversed on only two meetings since.

They were soon joined by the Governor, who had followed their progress with keen interest since their arrival in a weak and emaciated condition. 'How's that young lad of yours, Edward? Frightening experience for him... being kidnapped?' Governor Macquarie's face reflected his genuine concern.

'Strange as is may seem...' Edward gave the Governor a wry smile, '... he appears to be the one least affected. Fortunately, a young woman that the gang had more or less abducted to care for him, protected Stephen from the kidnappers anger and abuse. She was able to shield him from their uncouth actions.'

'A most fortunate coincidence indeed.'

'Yes!' Edward nodded thoughtfully before continuing. 'Stephen in fact, became quite fond of her, insisting that she stayed on with us at Newacres.' He chuckled as he remembered his young son's concern for the young woman who had protected him. 'Now...' he shrugged his shoulders good naturedly, '... we find ourselves with a young nanny.'

'Yes, I er...' the governor frowned in contemplation, '... I remember the young woman's circumstances. Unfortunately, the couple she was travelling with as companion and nanny died. The man died on the voyage out to become a settler, while his wife died in childbirth just after their arrival. Alone and with very little money...' Governor Macquarie shook his head sadly at the recollection, '... she was anxious for employment when accosted by one of the gang. Her refined upbringing made her gullible to the rogue's persuasive patter.'

'It was most fortunate for Stephen – and us, that he inveigled Amy into going with him. She shielded our son from the kidnappers' malevolence. Since being in our employ, she has become both friend and companion to Becky. One of our family in facet, but she still insists on being foremost, the children's nanny.'

'Good! Glad to hear that some good came out of your traumatic situation.' He suddenly noticed the scar on Edward's scalp. 'How's your injury? Heard they nearly shot you?' His eyes were still fixed thoughtfully on the healing wound.

'Thanks to Robert... I'm fine. That's twice he has been on hand to save my life.'

'An excellent surgeon. We're thankful for people like him in our community.' As he paused for his wife to terminate her conversation with Becky, he enquired about the harvest.

'Corn will be coming to the warehouse any day now, Governor. It's been an exceptionally good harvest.' Edward mentioned their crop, but he guessed that the Governor was already conversant with Newacre's yields. Not much escaped his alert mind.

'Edward... I think we owe the ladies a dance... for being so patient.' With a friendly smile he offered Becky his arm, while Edward reciprocated with a similar action to the Governor's wife. As they took the floor, Edward was aware that all eyes were upon them. He felt a little tense to begin with as dancing, because of his farming, had been denied both Becky and himself in recent years. Gradually he became more relaxed and his movements more graceful. He found himself enjoying the occasion as he guided his pleasant partner elegantly through the musical movements. At the end of their dance, Elizabeth, who was a few years younger than her husband, thanked Edward for an enjoyable dance. Still smiling excitedly, she rejoined her husband to circulate among the other guests.

Captivated by the lilt of the music, Edward and Becky were soon dancing together under the flickering candlelight. They became lost to the music and each other as their feet glided lightly over the floor. Unaware that their dancing was attracting the admiration of the onlookers, they continued to skip and twirl to the music of the dance. At times, their closely executed dance movements induced sensuous excitement as their bodies reacted to the exhilarating actions of their impromptu steps.

Still unmindful that their dancing was the focus of the other guests, Edward and Becky continued dancing until the music ceased. Breathless and excited they remained in each others arms, their eyes shining with desire and longing. It was the spattering of applause that brought their thoughts back to reality. Both experienced a moment of embarrassment as they realised that their dancing had been under observation by the other guests.

'Who is that gentleman – the one we have just seen dancing?' The man, an officer from the naval frigate in the harbour, enquired of Robert. They had been in conversation and had paused to watch Becky and Edward's dancing display.

'Edward.... Edward Burstow.' Robert turned towards the officer. 'A friend of mine. He has a large farm...'

'That wasn't the name I had in mind...' the officer shook his head, frowning concentration as he tried to recall where he had seen Edward previously.

'You know Edward?' Robert's interest was aroused.

'Well... I er, that is... I thought his face was... familiar.' The captain's face was furrowed in thought. 'Was he... ever a naval man?'

'First and foremost a farmer... of that I can assure you, captain.' He glanced across the ballroom to where Edward and Becky were resting after their exuberant display of dancing. 'Come captain... let me introduce you to my friends.'

'What is it, Edward?' Becky glanced around as she noticed Edward's look of surprise. 'We must be careful of our words.' He whispered to her. 'That naval officer with Robert... his face reminds me of someone...' he shook his head as he tried to relate its significance. Both Edward and Becky were composed by the time Robert reached their sides. Even as they came to a halt, the captain's eyes focused on Edward as he tried to remember where they had met previously.

After the introductions, it was Robert who mentioned the captain's belief that he had seen Edward on a previous occasion. 'Is that so, captain?' He gave the watching officer a brief scrutiny as if trying to recollect the encounter. With a start, Edward remembered. It was the officer who was in charge of his watch when he served on the Saracen. A tremor of fear pulsed through his body as he became aware of the captain's searching look.*

'You remind me of someone who once sailed with me. The man in question, if my memory serves me correct...' Edward watched the officer's brow crease in deep concentration, '... deserted ship.' As he made the statement, Edward was aware of the captain watching for his reaction. Edward, who had steeled himself for just such a contingency, remained calm —his response was negative.

'Captain Greenwood,' there was a teasing smile on Becky's face as she addressed the naval officer. 'My husband is a farmer, who I doubt could differentiate between the main royal stay-sail and the main-sail of a ship.'

'I take your point, ma'am.' The captain's stern features relaxed to a smile as her turned to acknowledge her statement. 'I must confess however, that he has a remarkable likeness.' Shaking his head as if still in doubt, he directed another piercing look towards Edward. His deportment conveying the impression that he was unmistaken in his assumption. 'Perhaps...' he turned courteously towards Becky, '... you will permit me the honour of sharing a dance with you, ma'am?'

'Certainly, captain!' Becky smiled her accord, anxious to draw his attention away from Edward. There had been a growing assurance about the captain's enquiries that reflected ominous connotations. His questioning during their dance confirmed to Becky that he was still harbouring some doubt as to Edward's true identity. The sooner we get back to Newacres, the better for our piece of mind, she thought. Fate very nearly prevented that return.

On the eve of their departure to Newacres, a positive reaction by the captain, nearly caused Edward's exposure as an impostor. Edward, out of curiosity had walked down to the water front to identify the frigate anchored in the cover. In the evening sunlight,

* In Book I The Winds of Destiny

he had difficulty in observing the naval vessel against the low sun's dazzling brightness.

Edward heaved a sigh of relief as he noticed that the frigate was not his old ship, the one on which he had served as a press-gang victim. As he turned to walk away, he became aware of the captain and another officer approaching Not wishing to attract their attention, he pretended to show an interest in a ship riding at anchor a short distance along the cove. Silently he prayed that his presence would not be noticed.

'Ah... Mr. Burstow... good evening to you!' It was the captain who greeted him, but Edward was aware of the other officer's close scrutiny.

'Oh...' he tried to sound surprised, '... good evening... captain.' Words choked in his throat as he returned the captain's greeting. The captain acknowledged Edward's salutation with an exaggerated salute – a sardonic action that puzzled him. It was when Edward turned to greet the other officer that he realised it was the midshipman who had been in charge of the captain's barge when he had deserted from the Saracen.

Edward experienced an uncomfortable feeling as he recalled their previous encounter in Sydney when intuition had warned him that the officer appeared to have recognised him. A critical situation was developing. He was now confronted by the two officers, who, it appeared, were showing an uncomfortable interest in his true identify. Care was needed, a false move on his part might bring retribution upon him. He felt himself being forced into a worsening situation. One from which he must extricate himself as soon as possible.

Thankfully, there had been no confirmation that he had been positively recognised. Edward's observation of his ship, had however alerted the captain to possibilities. Although he suddenly became quite friendly, the captain's manner did not fool Edward.

'I noticed your interested observation of my ship, Janus... Mr. Burstow. I'm sure you will find a visit most rewarding... and refreshing.'

'That's very kind of you, captain, but I er... leave for my farm come the morning. Otherwise I would gladly...'

'Then why not come aboard now?' Before Edward could refuse, the captain assured him that his barge would return him to the jetty well before dusk. Against his better judgement, Edward found himself sitting beside the officers as they rowed back to their frigate.

'I've just remembered our last meeting.' The young lieutenant suddenly turned towards Edward. 'It was when I came to Sydney about... four years ago.' Edward felt the tension evaporate from his body – an anticlimax. Nevertheless, he had been aware of the captain's sudden interest as the speaker recalled that occasion.

'Yes... even then I had a feeling that you were someone known to me. You reminded me of a seaman who once served under me aboard the Saracen.' Edward was aware of both officers intense gaze as they watched for his reactions. Forcing himself to remain calm, he feigned a casual demeanour as they continued to observe him closely. His acting was superb, but Edward was unsure if he had fooled them. Their countenances gave no indication of their thoughts.

As he set foot on the Janus, he experienced a disquieting sensation. Furtively, Edward swept his gaze around the deck, half expecting to see an armed escort waiting for him. 'Why should I harbour such ideas?' he asked himself. While he surveyed the familiar activities of the crew, he tried to disperse the ominous thoughts that troubled him.

'If you would care to follow me... Mr. Burstow.' The captain stepped out in the direction of his quarters with Edward and the younger officer walking in his wake.

They had almost reached the quarter-deck when the captain paused to confer briefly with the officer of the watch. Momentarily alone, Edward was concentrating on the once familiar surroundings of the frigate, when a voice startled him.

'Payne! What yer bleedin' well doin' on 'ere? Come back t'sea 'ave yer?' Edward had partly reacted to the shouted comment. With dismay, he realised that both the captain and the young lieutenant's eyes had been upon him. Watching for his response – his reactions.

'Boson... Mr. Burstow is my guest. You appear to have mistaken the... gentleman's identity.'

'Begin' yer pard'n sir,... I never f'gits a... face.' Edward was aware of the Boson's intense gaze as he spoke. 'This one 'specially... a bloody... deserter.' Edward glanced round, fighting back the panic that was endeavouring to overwhelm him. Any attempt to escape on his part would only help confirm his guilt. At all costs he must remain calm. Taking a deep breath to control his emotions he decided to bluff his way out of a delicate situation. They have no proof, he reassured himself as he returned the boson's stare with a puzzled look. 'Who is this man, captain? He appears to be mistaking me for some other person.'

'As we all are... Mr. Burstow...' the captain's voice was noncommittal as he turned and inclined his head to include the young officer. 'However... his eyes took on a hard glint, '... you will be given a fair trial to defend yourself when we are at sea' The impact of the captain's words brought a gasp of dismay from Edward.

Anger surged through his body as he furtively ascertained his chances of escape. There were none. He was trapped. A shouted command from the captain would have the crew members upon him before he could reach the ship's side. He must remain calm, any attempt to escape would only confirm his guilt. By feigning innocence, he might cast doubt in their minds and induce a momentary relaxation on their part.

Edward's protestations at being incarcerated and watched over by a sentry, were very vigorous – and unsuccessful. 'Captain Greenwood... I must protest at such... discourteous conduct. Your unwarranted actions will be reported to the Governor in the morning.' Edward noticed the sardonic smirk on the captain's face as he made a show of considering his objections.

'Unfortunately...' he gave Edward a belligerent stare, '... your report will be somewhat delayed, Mr. er... Burstow... or is it Payne? We sail at daybreak for China.'

'What of my family... my farm? I demand that...'

'Demand... Payne.' Edward realised that he was trapped on the frigate. 'Demands...' the captain withered him with a scornful look. '... are not the prerogatives of deserters.' Edward tried to hide his anguish as he realised that he was already guilty in the captain's mind. Guilty of deserting his ship.

As for his punishment, he gave a shudder. Flogging, or… he tried not to think of the alternative, but the gruesome spectre of his body hanging from the yardarm sent a tremor of alarm pulsing through his body. He turned sharply, prepared to make a dash for freedom, but the boson and two crew members were lined up behind him.

There was no mistaking the boson's actions. He was holding a belaying pin in his right hand while gently, but menacingly tapping his left palm with its rounded end. He made not attempt to hid his intentions of dealing with any escape bid.

'Perhaps you would be kind enough to follow boson Macaulay to your er… accommodation.' He noticed the captain's cynical smile that he exchanged with the boson before turning to the young officer who had remained silent throughout. 'A temporary one until…' there was no need for the captain to elaborate on the expected outcome. The young officer's shocked expression warned Edward of the dire consequences ahead.

A whistle sounded as the colours wee lowered for sunset. The once familiar routing was a reminder to Edward that he must consider calmly what means of escape were available His quick glance round induced a feeling of despair – there seemed little, if any, chance of escape.

Before he could protest further, he was forced into a confined structure – a kind of makeshift storage. A coil of cordage acted as a seat while he contemplated what action, if any, he could take. A barred open port-hole permitted a view of the deck outside where an armed sentry had taken up his post.

After a few futile attempts to strike up conversation with the taciturn sentry, he realised that the seaman had been warned against communicating with him. Perhaps the middle watch sentry would be more receptive. Edward hoped it would be so as his plan of escape relied on getting the seaman's confidence. Once out of his lock-up there were two escape options open to him. He could attempt to swim across the cove, a dangerous undertaking, or purloin the frigate's dinghy.

Edward concentrated on the second – and safest option. His keen observation had revealed that the frigate's davits were empty. A sign that the dinghy was still in the water, waiting to be hoisted just before the frigate sailed. Should... the chance of escape arise, getting to the dinghy must be his first objective. A hazardous undertaking but one that must be attempted if he was to escape an uncertain fate. Calming his frustrated thoughts, he tried to formulate a plan of escape, but as darkness enveloped the harbour, he began to lose hope.

Murmured exchanges alerted him to the changing of sentries. Edward hoped that the relieving seaman would be more gregarious. He waited patiently by the open port, hoping to catch the young seaman's attention.

'You... alright, mate?' Edward realised that the sentry was addressing him.

'Not much chance of that under these abominable conditions. An innocent man should not...'

'Innocent? I heard as how yer were...'

'Enticed aboard...' Edward whispered harshly, '... and detained under false charges. Treated worse that a press-gang victim.' He waited for the sentry's reaction. It was immediate and bitter.

'What d'yer know... 'bout press-gang victims?' Edward noticed the seaman hesitate as he came close to the barred port opening. 'Yer lookin' at one and believe me...'

'I know how heartbreaking it can be for the victim's families,' Edward interjected. 'Dying of starvation and privation because of their men being forcibly snatched from them.' Quietly he went on to tell the sympathetic listener about his friend, Geoff Rawlings. 'When he eventually returned home, both his wife and child were dead. Starved because there was no one to care for them.' In the emotional silence that followed, he heard a stifled groan from the young sentry. 'You married?' Edward enquired of the distressed seaman.

'Ye...yes. I have one little girl... two years old.' He paused overcome with grief. 'My... wife... was expecting... our second...' He was speechless with sorrow, his distress obvious. Edward watched as the young sentry buried his head in his hands.

'Help me, Lad! We can escape together!' Edward spoke quietly and sympathetically. 'I promise you a quick passage home, or the money for your family to join you out here. I have two large farms, one just over a hundred miles away. You'll be safe there… should you decided to stay. There's a job waiting, but we must…'

'Don't know about that. They'll come after us and…'

'No! I shall report my ordeal to the Governor, a friend of mine. They'll not dare step foot ashore.' That is, if I can get ashore to report the captain, he thought. Edward remained quiet to give the sentry time to think about his proposition or the alternative.

'What… have you in mind…?' Edward noticed his continued uncertainty.

'If we're caught… they'll…'

'If we escape… get ashore, the captain will be anxious to up anchor and be under sail come dawn. What he has done is illegal. Once the Governor is aware of my ordeal, your captain will be in serious trouble. He'll be anxious to leave for China as soon as possible, once my escape is known.' Edward stressed the destination. 'Unless you escape with me, I doubt you'll see your wife and family again. Who will care for them?'

Silently he waited for the young seaman's reaction. Edward noticed the despairing emotions on the man's face as he did so. Lamplight revealed his sorrow. Edward was becoming increasingly anxious. He decided to strike openly while the sentry was vulnerable.

'Here!' He reached inside his pocket and withdrew two guineas. 'Once we reach shore, I promise you freedom and a free journey home.' He eased the coins through the bars for the sentry. 'There'll be more when we get ashore.' Edward was aware of the man's irresolution. It was imperative that he win his confidence quickly.

'Remember… if you decide to bring your family out here, they'll be a job waiting for you – and a home.' A tense silence followed his offer. 'A free passage out for you all.' Water lapped against the frigate's bow. Further along the deck, the quarter-master leant over the side-rails and gobbed into the sea.

'I'll do it! Damn them!' His voice was harsh with anger. 'I hate them for forcibly separating me from my family – my wife and child.' He came close to open the port. 'What's your plan?' The whispered question was music to Edward's ears.

'But it's so unlike Edward.' Becky's face was tense with worry as she waited for Robert to finish his report.

'I've made enquiries around the town, Becky and the only information gleaned was down on the wharf from an old boatman who remembered some one resembling Edward being rowed out to the frigate. He was in the company of two officers... the frigate's captain and one other officer.'

'Do you think...' Becky was remembering the captain's interest in Edward at last night's ball, '... that he has been enticed...?' The very thought forced an anguished gasp from her lips. Despair was reflected in her eyes.

'Perhaps he went as their guest. In which case they will be rowing him back before darkness.' Robert tried to reassure Becky as he noticed her agitation. Her distress puzzled him, the situation did not appear to warrant such anguish. Edward had probably met the captain and been invited on board ship for a drink. It frequently happened when naval ships were visiting the town. Robert could see no reason for Becky's concern. His absence did not appear to suggest portentous consequences.

Elizabeth's attempts to console Becky only succeeded in worsening her distress. 'If Edward is a guest, my dear, he will soon be back as I believe the Janus sails for China at daybreak.' She glanced for confirmation from her husband, who concurred with a nod.

'Oh, No!' Becky's hand went to her mouth. She stood transfixed as the impact of Elizabeth's words penetrated her disquiet thoughts. 'China!' she gasped. 'But... but...' Becky was now on the point of revealing Edward's identity when Robert, noticing how distraught she was, volunteered to make further enquiries.

'If necessary, Becky... I'll get a boatman to row me out to the Janus.' Edward would probably object to his drinking session with the captain being interrupted, but at least he could warn his friend to the worry he had caused Becky by his clandestine action. This behaviour was completely out of character for Edward.

'I'll not be long! See you at dinner!' Edward's last words as he had strolled off into the evening sunshine, did not infer that he would be visiting a naval ship. Robert himself was now experiencing a feeling of uncertainty. He had now been gone five hours and already the stars were flickering in a darkening sky.

Dinner had been delayed in the hope that Edward would soon be with them. Eventually, over the meal they had discussed the possible justifications for Edward's absence. Becky, silent and tense, had eaten very little. Her distress had induced an uncertain atmosphere around the table. Edward's seemingly irresponsible action had been so unlike him, that Robert was suspecting there was more to the incident than Becky was prepared to admit – but what?

Becky's apprehension gave way to alarm as the hour grew late and there had still been no news of Edward. Robert, as promised, had departed in his carriage to enquire once more in the town. His tentative enquiries at possible venues brought negative replies. Then he remembered the old boatman he had spoken to when he had visited the wharf. From the man's remarks he had assumed that his friend had joined the captain on his ship for a drink. Had that been so he would surely have been back on shore by now. He experienced a moment of guilt as at the time his thoughts had been dulled by annoyance at Edward's apparent discourteous behaviour.

'To the wharf!' There was an urgency in his command that alerted his coachman as he urged the horses into a fast canter. It was dark down by the water's edge. There was no sign of the old boatman, in fact there was no life of any description on the wharf. He directed a startled coachman towards a nearby tavern. Robert sprang from his carriage as it came to a stop, eager and yet doubtful about his next action.

What if it was not Edward whom the old boatman had seen being rowed out to the Janus? He would feel ridiculous boarding the frigate, only to find that the captain had now knowledge of Edward's whereabouts. On the other hand, if his friend was enjoying drink with the officers, his presence would certainly not be appreciated. What was to be done? Faced with a perplexing dilemma, he decided to risk acrimony and visit the frigate.

Robert, a little apprehensively, stepped across to the tavern. As he opened the door, his appearance caused the cacophony of inebriated voices to subside gradually. Through a bluish fog he spotted the boatman. All eyes were upon him as he walked purposely across the room and asked to be rowed out to the Janus.

'Dun'now as I c'n managed in t'dark, sir. Bit risky... that be, y'see.' There was a reluctance on his part to leave the comfortable surrounds of the tavern – and his drink. Robert offered him a sliver coin. It glistened momentarily in the dim candle light before being snatched at by the boatman's scrawny hand.

'I'll do it f'yer!' Robert heaved a sigh of relief as he followed the man out into the darkness. As they made for the jetty, Robert called to his coachman to follow and wait there for his return. The boatman's shuffling suddenly stopped as they reached some wet and slimed steps leading down into the water.

'Git y'self in!' He pointed to the dark shape of his boat. Robert carefully eased his way down the slippery slopes to reach it, closely followed by the unsteady owner. The boatman pushed off and as they drifted away, Robert's apprehension returned.

Ahead of them the frigate was a dark silhouette against the starlit sky. It's dark outline broken only by a few flickering lights that seemed to draw them mesmerise-like towards them. Robert forced his eyes from the shadowy form of the frigate to glance at the ruffled surface of the seemingly dark fathomless waters around them. Their progress was slowed by the breeze and tide being against them.

Robert was still meditating on the wisdom of his impulsive acting. What, he wondered, would be the captain's reaction to his late and uninvited visit to his ship. Not a welcoming one, especially as the hour was well past midnight and all appeared calm and quiet on board the anchored frigate.

Robert was still experiencing uncertain thoughts as the Janus drew closer. Perhaps he should turn back. A tranquil atmosphere hung over the frigate. He was reluctant to disturb the peaceful ambience. Suddenly the situation changed rapidly.

It altered just as Robert was about to order the boatman to row him back to where muffled shouts from the ship's upper deck drifted across the silent waters. Frowning with concentration, Robert half rose from his seat. He remained silent as he endeavoured to pierce the darkness with his eyes on the Janus.

Edward stepped out of his cramped prison on to the upper deck, relief flowing through his body. 'Thanks er…' he kept his voice low because of the quarter-master.

'Andy! Andy Gregson!' The young seaman whispered his introductions.

'Thanks again, Andy. Now, we must try and get to the dinghy.'

'First we got t'get past him.' Andy pointed to the shadowy figure of the quarter-master.

'Try and divert his attention…' Edward spoke low, '… give me a chance to make for the dinghy. Once in the boat, I'll cut it adrift then…'

'Quick!' With a push, the young sentry sent Edward staggering into the shadows. He was only just in time.

'Everything under control, Gregson?' The question came in a harsh articulation.

'Yes… yes, boson. All's well.' Andy's voice reflected his nervousness. Its shaky inflection went unnoticed by the senior member of the crew.

'Good!' The boson gave a sinister chuckle. 'It'll be a pleasure ter d'liver the first lashin's on the prisoner's bloody back, or…' he gloated with anticipation, '… be the one as pulls t'rope to stretch 'is damned neck.'

'You… speak… as if the man is… already found guilty. He hasn't appeared before the captain yet…'

'Oh, I'll see as 'ow he's guilty alright… just yer mark me words.' His guttural laugh held satanic threats. Andy experienced a moment of fear as he watched the boson move towards the door.

'What the 'ell is this doin'… open?' He pointed to the partly open door through which Edward had just escaped. 'I'll 'ave yer flogged if you've...' he turned to look into the lock up. As he did so Edward stepped from the shadows just in time to see Andy swing the butt of his musket down onto the boson's skull. He grimaced in anticipation as he heard the dull thud.

'Well done, Andy!' Edward whispered his satisfaction. 'I'll drag him inside and lock the door.' He turned the key on the locked up boson, then tossed it into the water.

'Watch out!' Andy's warning came as the quarter-master walked across to investigate the commotion. As his shadowy form neared them, Andy tossed his rifle over the ship's side. There was a loud splash as it hit the water.

'Quick, mate...' Andy turned to the approaching seaman, '... man overboard!' The quarter-master hesitated as if uncertain of the situation. Andy took advantage of his confusion. 'We'll...' he pointed to Edward's shadowy frame, '... get the boat away and make a search.' There was a bewildering silence as the bemused quarter-master tried to assess the position.

'Quick man... raise the alarm!' Andy pointed to where his musket had entered the water. He was anxious to drawn the man's attention from Edward who was edging towards the stern of the ship and the tied up dinghy.

'Man overboard!' The cry sounded as Andy reached the after part of the ship. Edward was leading when his progress was abruptly halted. Barring his way was the officer of the watch on his way to investigate the disturbance.

'What's going on up here?' Edward could see the officer straining to identify himself and Andy as they stood before him.

'M... man... overboard... sir!' Andy indicated the forward part of the ship, just as the bellowing roar of the recovered boson penetrated the darkness.

'Prisoner's escaped!' There was no mistaking the shouted warning.

'We're... manning... the dinghy...' Andy tried to bluff his way past the officer, who had now got his eyes used to the darkness. The officer of the watch eased aside to let Andy past. Edward followed close behind, but even in the starlight his clothes were conspicuous and attracted the officer's attention.

'Stop!' He peered closely into Edward's face. 'You're... the prisoner.' He stopped in front of Edward, intending to prevent his escape. By this time crew members were beginning to stagger onto the deck, slightly confused at the mounting activity in the darkness. They had been called in answer to an emergency, but were momentarily confused at the disturbance around them.

As the officer made a move to detain him, Edward sent his fist crashing into the man's solar plexus. There was an audible groan as the victim's legs buckled under his winded body. With a lightning reflex action, Edward followed his first punch with a powerful blow to the dazed officer's jaw. As it connected, Edward noticed how the officer sank slowly and silently to the deck.

'Quick, Edward! Down the rope!' They slid down the rope and into the dinghy. Once in the boat, Andy released the securing line and gave the dinghy a push off from beneath the frigate's stern. As the space between their drifting boat and the frigate widened, faces began to appear, gazing down into the darkness where the two escapees were now pulling on their oars.

As Edward and Andy began to disappear into the darkness, a stab of flame flashed in the night. Shot splattered on the water and against their dinghy. By now the escapees were straining on the oars in an effort to get well clear of the frigate. There was another stab of flame in the darkness, but this time no shot splashed around them. By then they must have been but a shadowy target for the marksmen on the Janus.

Concentrating on their escape, they had failed to see the other boat in the darkness until they almost collided. The boatman cursed them, while his passenger advised them to be more careful.

'I'm sorry... if we...' Edward stopped as he recognised his friend's voice.

'Robert... is that you?'

'Edward! What in damnation is going on?' He pointed in the direction of the frigate's dark shape behind them.

'Quick, Robert! We'll join you.' Edward reached over and grasped the other boat. 'I'll explain later...' he paused to concentrate on keeping their two boats together, '... when we get ashore.' There was a precarious manoeuvre as Edward and his companion abandoned their dinghy and clambered into the other boat beside Robert. In the darkness they watched the frigate's boat drifting away on the tide.

'What if they come searching for you this morning, Edward?' Becky had her arm around him as they sat close together on the couch. She had been listening anxiously to his ordeal on the frigate and despite his assurances, was still greatly troubled at the possibility of Edward being charged as a deserter and taken back to the Janus.

'After their infamous behaviour, they'll be anxious to escape the Governor's wrath and be away by daybreak. Thanks to Andy...' he nodded towards the young seaman, who, overawed by his surroundings, was nervously ensconced in a corner chair, '... we managed to foil their dastardly plot.'

'Arresting an innocent citizen and accusing him of false misdemeanours, will not go down well with the Governor.' Edward hoped that his voice sounded acrimonious as he had not related the whole truth to a perplexed Robert. He had managed to give the impression that his arrest was because of his likeness to a seaman who had served under the captain a few years back.

Edward glanced out of the window as he paused to reflect on his good fortune. His escape. He could so easily have been taken from Becky and their family – forever. Silently, he watched as the greyness of the dawn gave way to the gold and crimson hues of the sunrise. Night clouds vanished as the early morning sun replaced them in the cerulean blue of the sky. Sleep was far from Edward's thought as he watched the crimson orb of the sun edge itself above the wooded hills.

'Come, Andy! We shall watch to see if our adversaries sail off into the morning mist.' As they reached the wharf, the frigate with her sails spread was weathering the two rocky headlands standing sentinel-like at the cove's entrance. A sight that induced a feeling of great relief to both observers.

'They'll not trouble us again, of that I feel assured,' he gave Andy a confident smile before turning his gaze for the last time at the departing frigate. 'I shall explain your situation to the Governor and your wish for a quick voyage home.'

'My sincere thanks to you all...' Andy turned and nodded towards the house, '... especially Mrs. Burstow.'

'Our hope and prayers, Andy...' he placed his arm around his companion's shoulders, '... is that you'll find your family well... and your small farm prospering.'

'Should that be so... then my prayers also will have been answered.' Tears glistened in his eyes as he turned to shake Edward's hand in a firm grip of friendship.

'Don't forget...' Edward's sincerity was obvious as he continued, '... you and your family will always be welcome. Also, my offer of employment will also be valid.' As he spoke, Edward took from his pocket a letter addressed to Becky's solicitors in London. 'This letter...' he handed it to Andy, '... authorises the solicitors to pay you and your family's passage out to New South Wales, should you change your mind – in the future.'

With comforting emotions they watched the Janus disappear round the headland before returning to Acacia House. As they walked along the wharf, Edward pointed to a ship anchored further along the cove. 'That's the Hercules, bound for England in two days time.' He noticed Andy's wishful look as he gazed across the water towards the ship. A deep emotional sigh escaped his lips as he paused to watch the Basque being prepared for her voyage home – to England.

Governor Macquirie exploded in anger when he heard of Edward's treatment on board the Janus. He assured him that an official reprimand would reach the naval authorities regarding the captain's disgraceful conduct in apprehending a respected member of the local society.

Gradually the Governor's anger against the naval officers eased, especially when Edward confirmed that he had suffered little from the ordeal. 'In fact...' Edward tried to conceal his delight, '... one officer is probably suffering from the after effects of a blow to the jaw and the boson a throbbing headache.' Edward was aware of the sanguine smile that flickered across the

Governor's features as he lowered his eyes to straighten some documents lying on his desk.

'Now, concerning yourself, Mr. Gregson. He gave Andy an understanding look. 'I understand you are anxious to return to your family at the first opportunity?'

'As soon as it can possibly be arranged, Governor.' Andy sounded a little nervous in the official's presence.

'Providing you have no objections to working your passage Captain Boswell on the Hercules, will be glad to accommodate you.'

'I'd be prepared to row, if it meant getting back to my family, sir.'

'The need for such a drastic action will not arise, of that I feel sure.' The Governor's sombre features softened as he continued. 'The Hercules has a fine spread of sail and is a fast ship under the command of an experienced captain.' He began to gather his documents together as an indication that the interview was coming to a close.

'Call here in an hour's time,' he glanced up into Andy's apprehensive eyes. 'By then all will be in order for you to join Captain Boswell. Your experienced seamanship will ensure you a quick passage home.' He walked with them to the door of his office where he reiterated his intention of reporting the episode of Edward's incarceration on the Janus.

'Good luck, Andy... and once again, my sincere thanks.' Edward watched the dinghy from the Hercules pull alongside the wharf.

'It was a pleasure... helping in your escape, Edward. For some reason that sadistic boson was drooling over the thought of flogging your, or... even er...'

'Hanging! I know, Andy... I heard him.' Silently the two men exchanged firm handshakes. 'Hope you find your family well.'

'Thanks. Don't suppose we shall ever meet again, Edward. Then again...' he shrugged his shoulders, '... who knows?' In fact, it was to be nearly two years before Edward heard from Andy again. The letter reached him in late spring of 1818.

* * * * *

Edward cast a perfunctory glance around the office. It had changed very little since his last visit to Sydney. A musty-like atmosphere still prevailed. Even Joseph, his friendly old banker seemed to blend in with the banal surroundings. The correlation induced the flicker of a smile, necessitating an effort to force his concentration back to their conversation.

They had been discussing the fleece Edward had just delivered to the warehouses. It had fetched a good price and most of the money had just been deposited in the bank. As they conversed in general terms about the prospects of the coming harvest and the good price obtained for the last consignment of fleece, Joseph suddenly paused and opened his desk drawer. From it he withdrew a sealed paper. This arrived only yesterday...' he handed the letter over to Edward, '... from your solicitors in England.'

'Thank you, Joseph,' Edward put the letter in his pocket, with the intention of opening it in Becky's presence. 'What other news have you for me?'

'Reports...' Joseph's countenance was serious as he continued, '... have been received of bushrangers raiding a few of the outlying farms. Some settlers have been killed – murdered. These marauding gangs are a threat to decent folk.' The old banker shook his head sadly as he spoke of the mayhem caused by these roaming gangs of escaped convicts.

'Ay!' Edward nodded his agreement. 'You're right about that, Joseph. I'll alert our neighbours to the danger. At the least they'll be prepared.'

'Good!' He appeared relieved as he gave Edward a look of approval. 'These... murderers recently raided a farm in the area and killed the family and a couple of convict labourers who worked there.'

'Thanks again for the warning.' Edward, his face grim at the news he had just received, had paused to reiterate his appreciation of Joseph's warning.

Reflecting on the reports of the gangs that were rampaging the area, Edward walked back to their small town house. Becky and himself had decided that a dwelling would be convenient to stay in when they visited Sydney. It was an unpretentious house, but with three bedrooms and a small garden, it gave them some privacy during their social or business visits to town.

Becky, he guessed, would be discussing the latest social gossip among the friends she had made since arriving in Australia, nearly six years ago. His thoughts drifted back across the years as he strolled down the main thoroughfare towards Jasmine Cottage, their town house. Becky had suggested the name, Edward smiled at the romantic connotation, but then she was a sentimentalist at heart... and I love her for being one, he thought. As he strolled in the warm sunshine a kind of reverie settled upon him. Edward found himself thinking of his sister Maisie and wondered if her friendship with Seb had developed into a more serious attachment. What of his beloved, Julie? He experienced a feeling of guilt as he reminisced about their relationship – their love. Perhaps she was married by now. There had never been any reply to his letter. At first he had hoped, but...

'Edward...? Edward Payne?' There was an uncertain pause. 'How are you...?' Geoff Rawlings voice faded as he received a startled look from the person he had almost bumped into. He had been so sure, yet the man's startled reaction had put doubt in Geoff's mind. No... it just had to be... his old friend.

Edward, confused at the unexpected encounter, turned away quickly to hide his face. He was too late; he realised his mistake. Lost in his meditations, he had reacted positively to the man's greetings. He hastened his steps to evade the man. Regretting his incautious actions his lapse of alertness. 'Damnation!' He cursed silently to himself, as the man followed him down a side street.

'Edward?' There was still some uncertainty in the voice that hailed him. 'Edward... it's your old mate... Geoff. Geoff Rawlings!' Edward's footsteps faltered. He hesitated for a few moments before turning. Still unsure and with his emotions in a turmoil, he gazed into the bewildered eyes of his one time ship-mate.

'Geoff!' Recognition dawned. 'Forgive my unmannerly reactions, but...'

'I was unsure myself... in the first instance, Edward. You being so far from England.' A friendly embrace prevented further conversation. Eventually words began to tumble from both, but Edward paused furtively raised his hand in silent gesture of warning as they retraced their steps to the main thoroughfare.

'There's much to explain, Geoff, but not here in public.' Edward directed their footsteps towards Jasmine House, with a silent and puzzled friend beside him. 'You'll understand the necessity for my reticence later, old friend.' They conversed but briefly as they continued their walk to the cottage.

'...that Geoff... is... the situation in which you find Becky and myself. Landowners and highly respected members of the local society.' There was a long, emotional silence after Edward had concluded his explanation. Geoff had listened with increasing amazement as Edward had related his circumstances from the moment of his wrongful arrest and incarceration in Norwich Castle,* until their unexpected encounter earlier that day. 'You're the only person aware of my true identity. Our...' he smiled across at Becky, '... true relationship.'

'Needless to say, that is how I intend it to remain.' Geoff's reassuring look left Becky and Edward in no doubt as to his trustworthiness and integrity.

'Thank you, Geoff.' Becky rose from her chair. 'Now, if you will excuse me, I shall arrange for an extra place to be laid for dinner. You will stay, I hope?' She gave Geoff a questioning look.

'Delighted... Becky... and...' he rose and walked across to open the door for her, '... my sincere thanks. It will be a pleasure to share your hospitality. Shipboard food, as Edward will confirm, becomes very monotonous after a few weeks of repetitive diet.' Becky smiled her understanding as she departed.

'When do you sail, Geoff?' Edward broke the reflective silence following Becky's exit.

'Next week... for Calcutta!'

'A great pity. I was about to invite you to visit our farm, Newacres.' Disappointment was reflected in his voice when he realised that his one contact with the past would soon be leaving him again.

* In Book I The Winds of Destiny

'A boson on the Conquest, I shall be in a position to obtain silks, satins and other exotic goods, should it be your wish Edward.'

'Does that mean that you will be returning to Sydney?'

'Yes!' Geoff nodded his head. 'Our commission is to transport goods between the colony and India. China also, should trade warrant it.'

'Then we shall probably see you between voyages?' Edward seemed cheered by the prospect.

'Indeed you will... and I shall be holding you to your promise. A visit to Newacres.' He hesitated as a smile wrinkled his eyes. 'Perhaps, one day, I'll buy myself a farm... settle in the colony. I have no ties with the old country... since...' his voice faded as painful memories returned.

'You have friends here, Geoff. There'll always be a welcome for you in our home.'

'Yes...' he whispered sadly, '... I'm more than grateful for the kindness that you and Becky have extended...'

'As it shall ever remain so... whenever you call.' Edward refilled their glasses before relaxing back in his chair. 'Now, tell me what you have been doing since our last meeting... in Portsmouth, I believe it was?' Edward frowned as he tried to recall their last encounter.

'Yes...' Geoff raised his glass to Edward before taking a sip. '... that would be about... seven years ago. I was on the Georgina at the time.' Reminiscing continued through dinner – and beyond. Time passed quickly, soon bringing the time for Geoff's departure. As they exchanged farewells, Becky reiterated their invitation for him to visit Newacres. 'You'll see me at the farm... early in the New Year... I promise.'

It was only after Geoff's departure that Edward remembered the letter that Joseph had given him earlier in the day. Becky's interest was aroused when she realised that it was from England. 'Who is writing to us, Edward?' Excitement sparkled in her eyes. Perhaps it was from her parents... Josh... Maisie. Her heart raced with elation at the expectation of a few words from England.

'It's... from... Andy.' Edward glanced up from the letter. Becky tried to hid her disappointment... but tears dimmed her eyes as she waited to hear what news it contained. 'He and his family have received confirmation from the Colonial Office to farm in the Bathurst area. Andy has reserved grants from 2,500 acres and a passage has been reserved for them on the Penelope.'

'Did they give any expected date of their arrival?' Despite her disappointment, Becky was thrilled at the prospect of meeting Andy and his family.

'They were due to sail...' he glanced down at the letter, '... in early June. That means...' he hesitated as he mentally worked out the voyage time, '... under favourable conditions they could reach here in 160 days, or so.'

'Which means...' Becky's voice became quite excited, '... Andy and his family can be expected almost any day now.' They both smiled with pleasure at the thought of the family's arrival in Sydney.

'I'll check daily what ships are expected and from whence they sailed. We can arranged for them to stay in the cottage until they get themselves organised.' Becky quickly nodded her agreement, aware that Jasmine House was always kept ready for such contingencies.

'Grace must be kept informed of the developing situation, in the event of our absence when Andy arrives.'

'Ay...' Edward looked thoughtfully towards her, '... you made a wise move getting Grace to come as housekeeper at the cottage. She certainly keeps the two maids and handyman busy... the place is always spotless when we come into town.'

'It was more a move of convenience...' Becky confessed, '... Grace and Amy worked together under an uneasy truce. A strained tolerance realy.' Becky chuckled as she recalled their silent innuendoes about their status in the household hierarchy at Newacres. 'Grace was very enthusiastic when I mooted the idea of her being our housekeeper in Jasmine Cottage.'

'What about Amy?' Edward's features remained passive as he waited for Becky's answer.

'With Roger now over a year old...' she reminded Edward, '... and with Marian and Stephen now able to care for themselves, I thought Amy would be more helpful to us as a housekeeper at Newacres. 'Unless…' she gave Edward a teasing look, '… you are contemplating a further increase in our family.'

Grace, who was just passing the partly open door, smiled as she heard their shared laughter. A gaiety that was soon to fade. Their joy was to turn to sorrow and heartache before the arrival of Andy and his family.

Chapter Thirteen

Edward paused in his dressing to look out of his bedroom window at Newacres. As far as his eyes could see, acres of ripening corn waved in the early morning breeze. Beyond the corn, he visualised the distant sheep grazing on the arid pastures and his cattle searching diligently for succulent areas of grass. It had been a very dry spring and much of the pastures had wilted under the dry spell.

Now, as harvest approached, Edward experienced a moment of anxiety as he gazed out over his arable land. The corn was tinder dry. A careless spark could cause an uncontrollable conflagration – crops and even the buildings could be at risk from the flames. All staff had been warned against smoking and lighting fires, other than in their quarters.

As a precaution against fires, Edward had large tanks of water placed strategically around the buildings and a central storage of buckets for use in case of emergencies. All his labourers were aware of their duties should such a conflagration occur. A long metal tube, suspended from a frame was to be banged repeatedly by an attached hammer for raising a fire alarm.

A troubled sigh escaped Edward's lips as he looked out over the golden acres of corn. Despite all his precautions, he realised how hopeless their fire-fighting efforts would be against a fire that raged across the dried fields of ripening corn.

He was about to turn from the window when he noticed a horseman riding at full gallop from the direction of the east pastures. As the rider turned by the paddock, Edward recognised him as one of Paul Harrison's men. There had been a quiet truce of late between the two farms. Since the dismissal of Grant Medler because of fraudulent activities, there had been no further confrontations concerning the ownership of east pastures. In fact, over the past year, the owner of White Gables had become much more friendlier and tolerant towards them. A mood that had pleased Edward and Becky.

Becky's visits to his wife, a nervous reclusive-like person, may have had some bearing on Harrison's less antagonistic behaviour. These thoughts flashed through Edward's mind as he hurried down to meet the rider. There had been an urgency about the man that had troubled him. As he stepped from his veranda, the rider came to a stop in a cloud of dust.

'Bush rangers ... Mr. Burstow!' He shouted breathlessly to Edward. 'They've shot ... Mr. Harrison ... and... now... they're ransacking... White Gables.'

'How is Harrison? Is he... badly...?' Edward was cut short in his enquiry.

'He's dead... I believe.' The rider shook his head forlornly. 'I managed... to evade... the gang... and come for... help.' Edward had been hurrying towards the stables as they exchanged words.

'What of Mrs. Harrison?' Edward gave the man an anxious look.

'Don't rightly know.' He still seemed in a state of shock. His distraught expression indicated his troubled thoughts.

'Jem...' Edward called his stableman, '... my horse as quick as you can manage.' There was concern in his voice. 'I'll get my gun!' The man from White Gables nodded approvingly.

Becky came down the stairs as he was leaving. Quickly Edward explained the situation. Henry, also disturbed by the commotion, hurried out in time to hear the disturbing news. His reactions were immediate. 'Be with you as soon as possible.' Without hesitation, Henry picked up his gun and was soon running towards the stables.'

As the three riders approached White Gables, a dark column of smoke drifted lazily into the sky above the trees. 'Looks as if they've fired the place.' Edward pointed towards the smoke as he urged his horse into full gallop. They soon reached the east pastures where they crossed the gully and then up the incline that rose gradually from the river. Once they had crested the ridge, White Gables came into view. Flames were leaping from the barn as they raced towards the Harrison's farm. Briefly, beyond the smoke they glimpsed four horsemen riding at speed from the conflagration.

Their furtive actions, as they urged their hoses across the pastures, identified them as the culprits. Henry, sensing their direction, shouted that he would try and intercept them at the river crossing.

'Take care, Henry! They're armed... and will not hesitate to kill.'

Edward and the labourer from White Gables pressed on towards the farm, dreading what mayhem awaited them. As they entered the yard, small flames flickered against the door to the house.

'Quick' Edward commanded his companion. 'Round up what men you can and concentrate on saving the house,' he pointed towards the smoke drifting out through the half-open door. When he dashed inside, he found more smoke than flames, but the fire was on the point of flaring up. Edward snatched down a heavy curtain and began beating out the smouldering flames. Excited voices sounded outside. Suddenly the labourers, who had been hiding from the raiders, began appearing with buckets of water. Edward directed their efforts on to the source of the fire. Buckets brimming with water began arriving in an organised manner and very soon they had the flames contained and eventually out.

'Can't do nothing' about t'barn, sir!' One of the men pointed in its direction. It was engulfed in flames and thick black smoke billowed from it as the flames continued to roar ever higher. Edward could feel the heat as he watched anxiously at the sparks showering into the air around. He noticed some fall on to a small building, but they were soon dealt with by the labourers.

One factor in our favour, thought Edward, is the isolated position of the barn. He felt confident that any sparks drifting across from the blazing pyre could be dealt with by the men fighting the fire. Nevertheless, he issued a warning to them.

'Take your buckets...' he cautioned, '... and watch out for sparks drifting across and igniting other buildings.' The worst of the fire appeared to be over but he wanted to keep them alert.

He returned to the house, calling Harrison's name as he went from room to room. Edward was shocked to see how the place had been ransacked. Broken furniture, smashed pictures and shattered ornaments lay strewn across every room. He pushed wide the partially open door to the veranda. As he stepped through it he almost tripped over a body lying there. He involuntarily stopped and checked Paul Harrison's pulse, but the pool of blood spreading from his shattered head warned him is was a futile action.

There was no sign of his wife. Edward began to dread the worst as he called her name and received no response. He rechecked each room in the house. Each one he entered with a feeling of trepidation, expecting at any time to come across the poor, inoffensive woman's body. His search was fruitless, there was no sign of her anywhere in the house.

Outside again he organised the removal of Paul Harrison's body. Edward was reminded of their past differences which of late had become forgotten contrarieties by them both. The ex-colonel had certainly not deserved to be murdered so callously. Thinking of the murder caused Edward's frustration to give way to distress – then anger.

A movement across the paddock caught his eyes. He glimpsed a piece of coloured material as it appeared briefly in the small entrance to the hen house. As he watched, a young woman scrambled hesitantly out of the small wooden structure. Edward's wave and friendly call reassured her that she had nothing to fear. Her confidence grew as she realised that friends and labourers were now back in charge.

She turned after waving and spoke to another person who had been hiding inside the shelter with her. Soon, another head appeared and, on hands and knees, Emma Harrison emerged.

'Thank, God... Emma is safe!' Edward was startled to hear Becky's voice close beside him.

'How did you...' He gave her a surprised, almost shocked look.

'I came in the curricle. Thought I might be of some help.' Before Edward could reproach her for the risk she had taken while the bushrangers were on the rampage, she had walked over to comfort and console Emma Harrison.

Edward called Becky aside to enlighten her as to the situation. 'Best take Emma over to our place,' he spoke softly. 'Her husband is dead in the house...' Edward's despairing gesture towards White Gables said it all. 'I'll arrange to have the place tidied up and his body seen to...' He pointed towards the remote corner where trees surrounded a small burial plot.

'I'll break the news to Emma...' Becky's sympathetic gaze never moved from the frail figure being led towards her. The girl who had shared her refuge in the chicken shelter was supporting her employer's unsteady progress. Edward watched from the veranda as Becky helped a weeping Emma into the curricle beside her. Just a they were leaving, Henry returned with the news that the gang had made good their escape across the river.

'I believe I hit one of them... there was blood on their tracks near the river. One of the gang was...'

'Grant Medler!' Henry gave Edward a surprised look. 'One of the labourers recognised him. Revenge for his dismissal it would seem. We must be on our guard, Henry.' Edward's expression was thoughtful as he considered the possibility of a retaliatory raid on Newacres. 'Medler owes me no favours... that's for certain.' Henry nodded his agreement.

'They ransacked the house... it will need cleaning up.' Henry glanced at the smoke-blackened doorway as Edward described the chaos inside. 'Emma Harrison is staying with us, until the situation becomes more settled. Paul Harrison and two of his labourers were... murdered.'

'Witnesses say he deliberately attracted their fire while one of the maids slipped out to warn his wife. Fortunately, she was on her morning ritual of collecting the eggs...' Edward paused reflectively. 'It probably saved her life on this occasion.' Noticing Henry's perplexed look, he elucidated. 'The girl and Emma Harrison both hid in the chicken's house throughout the attack.'

Becky clicked her tongue to send her restless horses away. The pair had been especially trained to pull the curricle, a present from Edward on her 25th birthday a few weeks previous. Noticing Edward's apprehension, Henry turned his horse and escorted the two women back to Newacres.

'I'll get the harvest underway. Everything is ready for the reapers to begin.' Edward raised his hand in acknowledgement. Henry's expertise in running Newacres was greatly appreciated.

Edward had been thankful of his help, when in his earlier days on the farm he had struggled to come to terms with farming. Henry still took on much of the organising at Newacres. As Edward watched his manager escorting Becky and Emma back to the farm, he wondered how he would have managed without him. 'Thankfully...' he sighed before turning to organise the cleaning up at White Gables, '... that is one problem which will never cause me worry.'

* * * * *

'You are sure that is what you want, Emma?' Edward looked from the solicitor back to Emma Harrison. A month had passed since the gang's attack on White Gables. In the hectic weeks since her husband's murder, Emma had come to terms with her widowhood and, after consultations with her solicitor, had decided to sell White Gables. With two of her maids she planned to retire and live in Sydney.

Emma's decision had surprised Edward, but his astonishment had increased more so when she offered him the farm on very favourable terms. Elation showed in his face as the final signatures were being appended to the sale documents in the solicitor's office.

'Yes, that is my wish, Edward. Becky and yourself have been very kind to me. I'm aware that you and Paul had altercations over the boundary dispute...' Emma paused to give him a mischievous smile, '... but that in no way distracted from the friendship I shared with Becky and yourself.'

'A friendship that I hope will continued for a few more years, Emma.' His benign look, as he gazed into her strained and tired features, reflected his sincerity.

'That is also my... wish,' her look softened as she nodded her head approvingly. Their hopes for continued friendship were interrupted by the solicitor's discreet cough. He was anxious for the business to be concluded. They were reminded that further signatures were required on the legal document to finalise the sale. Silently the signatories watched as the solicitor dried the ink on the papers. White Gables was now the property of Becky and Edward.

As Emma heaved a deep nostalgic sigh, Becky sitting beside her, reached across and took hold of her hands in a comforting gesture. She understood the heartache and the distress that these transactions must be causing her elderly companion.

Edward glanced at the copy of the official document that he had just received from the solicitor. He noticed that nearly three and a half thousand acres of prime arable and grazing land had just been added to Newacres. Becky and himself are now among the largest landowners in the colony. Their hopes had been fulfilled beyond their wildest dreams.

* * * * *

'Why are we waiting, Andy?' Nancy Gregson looked anxiously at her husband as she spoke. There had been times on the voyage when she regretted acceding to her husband's wish to settle as farmers in Australia. She had experienced so much anguish when the ship's motions made her wonder if death might not have been a happy relief from the nauseous suffering.

Now at last her affliction was over. They had at last reached their destination –Sydney. 'Why are we anchored out here?' There was a hint of asperity in her voice which was not lost on her husband.

'Firstly my dear…' Andy gave his wife a sympathetic look, '… we have to await the arrival of the Harbour Master.' He pointed towards a pilot cutter heading towards them 'Once he is on board and conditions are favourable, then we shall sail for our anchorage position in the cove.'

'Will it mean a long wait… before we can go ashore?' Seeing the anguish on his wife's face, Andy tried to reassure her.

'It will not be long, Nancy… the wind appears to…' His voice hesitated as he watched the approaching cutter.

'What… is it… Andy?' She had noticed his frown of concentration as he watched the Harbour Master's boat. Just before it reached the ship's side, Andy raised his arm and gave a shout of recognition. 'Hey Edward!' On hearing his name called, Edward glanced up at the faces lining the Penelope's side.

'Andy!' Edward waved and smiled his acknowledgement when he noticed the young seaman who had helped him escape from the frigate, Hercules. Beside his rescuer he noticed a fair-haired young woman clasping the hand of a small boy. Andy was pointing his presence out to a little girl who stood beside him. Edward returned her elfin wave with a solemn raising of his hat. Her innocent smile captivated his happy heart.

'How did you know that we...' Andy looked round at his family, '... would be on the Penelope?' Introductions had been completed as they stood on the ship's deck.

'I didn't, Andy.' He shook his head, chuckling at his friend's surprised look. 'We anticipated the time of your arrival and when I heard the Penelope was due, I had a word with the Harbour Master and... well... here I am.'

'We shall soon be underway!' Andy's experienced seamanship had alerted him to the change in wind direction. Crew members were already scrambling aloft, while on the deck the seamen began to haul in the anchor. Soon the ship was easing gracefully into Sydney Cove.

As they conversed, the Penelope sailed past white-painted timber constructed houses and the occasional larger dwelling of brick and stone built along the wooded slopes. Silhouetted against the clear azure sky were a few windmills used for pumping up the water. Government House, because of its height, was a conspicuous building overlooking Government Wharf and the cove itself. All were visible from the ship as she finally dropped anchor after her voyage from England.

Later that day, Jasmine Cottage resounded to the joyful laughter of Andy's two children. Relieved to be free of the restricted confines of the ship, they were enjoying themselves in the garden. Standing beside their parents, Edward watched their boisterous antic as they charged about in happy abandonment. Molly, the eldest at four years, was always the instigator of their games, whereas Danny, her junior by two years, was ever eager to follow into whatever escapade his sister might lead them.

Nancy's long drawn out sigh, drew a surreptitious glance from Edward. Her quiet reactions had troubled him at first. Because of her formal disposition, he wondered if she regretted the upheaval of bringing her family all the way to the new colony. As if she had understood his uncertainty, her next words contradicted his reflections.

'Thank goodness that awful experience is over.' Her face, still pallid and drawn from her suffering, broke into a warm smile as she turned to Edward. 'I have yet to thank you for your kindness, Edward. A kindness that I'm afraid we shall never be able to repay.' As she looked into his eyes, he noticed the sparkle of determination that her long, distressing sea voyage had not succeeded in quenching.

Nancy's next words confirmed that her courage would ensure the family's success. 'Thanks for making it possible for us to start a new life out here. Andy and myself intend to make it a successful one... we are determined to succeed.'

'Then... you have no regrets... in coming out here?' Edward was anxious to have his intuition confirmed.

'None whatever. Already I can feel my strength returning. I hope soon to accompany Andy to see the acres held in reserve for us.'

'Conditions, according to information gleaned, suggests that life will be exceptionally rough to start with.' Andy gave his friend a worried look. 'Perhaps it would be prudent to leave Nancy and the children behind until... conditions have improved and a more permanent accommodation awaits them?' Edward nodded agreement, but seeing Nancy was about to protest, spoke first.

'There is a possibility that such a separation can be avoided.' Aware that he now had their full attention, Edward spoke of his alternative for them. 'It's a proposition actually. Your answer can wait until the morning, before we leave for Newacres.'

'We hope that you will stay with us until you have decided on your future plans. A future I sincerely hope will be associated with Becky and myself.' Noticing Andy's puzzled look, Edward proceeded to explain. 'So that you and Nancy can discuss my proposition later, this is what I have in mind.'

By the time Edward had explained his plans in detail, the evening sky was a blaze of crimson and gold. In the irresolute silence that followed, he watched the sun descend behind the wooded slopes on which the town was established. Edward had been aware of the interested glances that had transpired between his listeners as he concluded his conceptions. Nancy's eyes sparkled as her unshed tears reflected the brilliance of the sunset.

Edward turned from the window and raised his hand as he noticed Andy was about to speak. 'First... we'll have dinner. Afterwards, Becky and I will leave you alone to talk over and consider what I have spoken of. Sleep on it, if necessary, and give me your answer in the morning.' He helped Nancy to her feet and escorted her to the table.

'There you are... White Gables.' Edward gave his two companions an expectant look. 'Your home... I sincerely hope?' His doubts vanished when he heard their appreciative gasps. Intuitively, he had made the proposal to Andy and Nancy to take over as manager on his newly acquired farm. Edward realised that his instinctive feelings had been justified when the couple's answer had been on enthusiastic affirmation., Now, a few days later, as he showed them over the farm that he hoped would be their home, he experienced a feeling of gratification at his companions' acceptance of his offer.

'You've not changed your mind after seeing the place?' Edward was aware of the answer; Andy and Nancy's faces reflected their admiration as they excitedly observe the farm that would be their new home. During the journey from Sydney, Edward had explained the unfortunate circumstances surrounding its purchase. They had not vacillated their decision and now as Andy and his wife walked into White Gables, their joyful expressions were indicative of their acceptance.

All signs of the fire and wilful damage resulting from the raid had been eradicated. Edward was pleased that he had arranged for the house to be decorated and cleaned up after the raiders had vandalised much of the interior. The joyful look on the faces of his companions, vindicated his decision to purchase and renovate White Gables.

'It's ... wonderful, Edward!' Nancy's relief showed as smiling happily she walked over and endowed him with a kiss. 'Just like a... a dream,' she enthused as, taking hold of her husband's hand, they continued their tour of the house.

'Don't know how I'll ever repay yer, Edward.' Andy continued to shake his head, still trying to take in the good fortune that had befallen him and his family. There was little to indicate, as they concluded their inspection, that his chance to return Edward's benevolence would come sooner than he expected – under circumstances that were to result in tragedy.

Crimson and apricot hues streaked the evening sky as the sun edged below the horizon. Another hot, stifling day was fading, but with the twilight came a gentle breeze. A soft wind that would be greatly appreciated by the reapers on the morrow, when their scythes would slice through the last brittle stems of the standing corn. Harvest was almost over, only the corn down by the river and then finally the aptly named Home Acres remained for the reaper's scythe.

Later that evening, a sigh as gentle as that of the passing breeze, escaped the lips of Becky as she stood beside Edward in the silvery moon-glow. Hearing her sigh, Edward turned towards the woman who shared his life, the woman who had borne his two sons and shared in his early struggles. Together they had overcome adversity and heartache in their endeavours to tame a rugged environment and bring success to Newacres. After nearly six years of struggle they were at last beginning to see signs of prosperity. Success.

After an exhausting day in the harvest, Edward appreciated these quiet, reflective moments when twilight deepened the shadows to a deep purple and a cool breeze caressed his tired frame. Henry, as usual, had been there among the reapers, encouraging them during the long hours of tiring work. An excellent manager and friend, one who was respected for his honesty and fairness. Edward nodded his head in silent approval.

It continued to nod as he thought of Andy. With White Gables' crops ready for harvesting, Edward recalled the problems he had anticipated. There had been none. To his astonishment, Andy had gathered his labourers together and, leading by example, had proceeded to harvest the crops. It had been a well organised operation that had greatly impressed Edward when he had visited the farm. His presence, the thought brought a smile to his lips in the darkness, had been superfluous.

Yes, he reflected contentedly, it had been a very good year. High yields per acre. There was no doubt in Edward's mind, that the recent good harvests were due to his method of machine drilling. He chuckled softly as he recalled his first attempts a couple of years previously. His first primitive efforts had been accompanied by good natured banter, as, marching behind his oxen drawn drilling machine, he had disappeared in a cloud of dust.

He had stopped often to make adjustments. Each time these mechanical alterations were made, onlookers had proffered suggestions of a humorous nature. The laughter had gradually faded as the operation continued. After a few tentative starts, Edward had got his adjustments correct and had drilled a successful strip across a section of land to the amazement of the spectators.

It had been the three hundred adjoining the paddock that had been used for the experimental section. When the corn had speared through the soil, it was noticeable for its uniform spacing and reasonably straight drills. Realising that Edward was inclined to wander off course, one old ploughman had told him his trick of placing a marker at the opposite end of the acres to be ploughed. 'Aim for't, master... an yer'll be 'orlright.'

The sound advice had been followed and proved successful. From the reapers' favourable remarks, he had realised that the corn growing in straight lines had lightened their arduous labours. Something they gratefully appreciated.

Starlight and a segment of moon gave the landscape a soft eerie glow, that, if anything appeared to complement the tranquillity of the scene. A moment in time when the world gave the illusion of standing still. A moment that was to leave an indelible impression on Edward's mind. He would always remember this treasured instance, when Becky, sitting beside him beneath the flittering stars, had reached across to take hold of his hand. Everything had seemed so peaceful and reassuring – just perfect. A time when their hearts were united in love – no words were necessary.

In the shadows Edward turned towards his silent companion. Becky was looking across the moonlit landscape of her home. Lost in an act of deep meditation. Involuntarily she smoothed the skirt of her voluminous silk dress, unaware that its close fit complemented her still youthful figure.

Edward's observations were more enlightening. Her attractiveness induced a stirring; a longing within his strong healthy body. In the fading light her lilac dress with its white collar and matching cuffs, reflected the silvery glow of the waning moon. Oblivious of Edward's thoughtful eyes upon her, Becky continued to gaze out across the land, opaque in the fading moonlight.

'Troubled thoughts, Becky?' He squeezed her hand that still rested in his. For a few moments she remained silent as if Edward's words had not penetrated her reverie. He was about to repeat the question, when another emotional sigh escaped her lips as she turned towards him.

'Not troubled ones, Edward.' A wistful smile displaced her thoughtful features. 'I was thinking of my first harvest with Stephen. How happy we all were at Highfield as the reapers and their helpers arrived at the barn for a well deserved harvest supper. The last stack had been gathered safely in and a feeling of great satisfaction prevailed. We were joyous at such a bounteous harvest.' She looked sadly into Edward's eyes. 'So long ago. Sometimes I wonder if it was just a dream.' The two shadows joined as Edward embraced a pensive Becky. Gently he kissed the tears that trickled down her cheeks. Tears that glistened in the reflective starlight. 'Oh, Edward!' Her voice seemed choked with sadness as she looked up into his face. 'What would I have done without your help – your love?' Easing back from their close embrace, he gazed lovingly into her eyes.

'It is I who should be grateful, my love. Without your help and Stephen's, my fate would have been a very uncertain one. In all probability I would have gone down with the Badger.' Their reminiscing evoked emotions of passion and longing to share each other's love. Hand in hand they moved from the veranda, back into the house. They were eager to be alone where their passionate longings would bring ecstatic fulfilment – a loving union.

'Edward! Edward!' He awoke with a start. Someone was calling his name. Startled he sat up in bed, unsure if he had been dreaming. Then the urgent call was repeated. 'Edward! Fire!' Naked, he hurried to the window. Down in the yard he could see a distressed Henry on horse back, gazing up at the window.

'Fire... down on the river acres, Edward.' As he shouted the news, he pointed in a northerly direction where a glow was already lightening the horizon. 'I'll take a couple of men and ride over... assess the situation.' Turning his horse he galloped away into the night

'What... what... is it, Edward?' A sleepy Becky looked up as Edward scrambled into his clothes.

'Fire! River acres!' Still fastening his breeches, he dashed from the bedroom. 'See... you... later... Becky...' his voice faded as he dashed down the stairs to where the groom waited with his horse. Labourers, who had arrived for the harvest, were dashing across the Home Acres towards the fire. Already the acrid smoke was filling the night air.

'Damnation!' Edward cursed silently. 'Wind's blowing this way.' He realised that with the fire heading towards Newacres, the situation could become dangerous. He dismounted, aware that he needed to organise their defences against the raging fire. A line of flames was already flickering across the darkened skyline. Sparks drifted and swirled upwards in the thermal disturbances. Fire snatched at the stems of the tinder-dry corn, devouring them in flames that leapt towards the starlit heavens.

When the flames reached the dusty track that divided the river and Home Acres, Edward was hoping that the fire might be curtailed. If they could keep it in check, they might be able to prevent the fire jumping the track. Wielding besoms, kept around the farm for just such contingencies, he was hoping that the men would be able to hold the fire along the edge of the track.

Smoke billowed above the roaring flames, blotting out the stars as the ominous black clouds drifted and swirled low over the burning crops. Flames leapt ever nearer towards them, devouring the brittle dry corn and filling the air with the pungent smell of smoke. Aided by the light breeze, the flames soon reached the dusty track that Edward was praying would act as a fire-break.

Urging and cajoling, Edward was everywhere as he directed the fight to curtail the conflagration. It was imperative that the fire be prevented from jumping the track, failure would place the farm buildings and stack yard in serious danger. A few gum trees on the eastern boundary of the river acres had been engulfed by the roaring flames. With an explosive roar the fire had swept up the trees, showering sparks and flaming debris into the smoke filled air.

Horrified, Edward watched as the eucalyptus tree exploded into a fireball and sent flaming timber across the dusty track. He realised that the inevitable was imminent. Heat from the fire was forcing his men back behind the dusty track. Retreating from the fierce heat, Edward tried to organise his fire-fighters, but suddenly it was too late. Home Acres had ignited as the flaming debris exploded across the break and settled among the dry stems of the mature wheat.

'Hurry! Everyone back to the farm!' Edward's shouted warning was almost lost in the cacophony of roaring and crackling flames. He acknowledged Andy's arrival with a thankful wave of his hand. 'We're... falling back... to the lane. Take your men...' he was shouting to make himself heard, '... to the east section. I'll try and hold the fire at the paddock end.'

Andy was already directing his labourers as they retreated towards the lane. Their last line of defence before the farm complex – and the living quarters. If they failed... the thought stirred Edward into frantic action as he organised his men to combat the approaching wall of fire. 'Dear God... Help us!' he prayed fervently for divine assistance as the enormity of their task was revealed. As they raced back towards the farm, Edward directed men to fetch the two mobile tanks that were used to transporting water in emergencies. Another group he detailed to try and damp down the barn. He shouted across to Andy and at the same time pointed towards the sky-line behind them. It was a chilling spectacle. A roaring wall of flames appeared to be advancing upon them, like some threatening holocaust. He rushed across to Andy with a warning.

'We must try and burn a wide strip beyond the lane, Andy. If we are successful we should contain the fire.' Both men were grim faced as they set about arranging the operation. Their worried glances towards the farm buildings reflected their fears. Failure to control the raging fire this time would mean complete devastation to Newacres.

Smoke, thick and acrid rolled towards them, reducing their vision as they spread controlled fires alongside the lane. Its intensity caused choking as they battled courageously at their tasks. Edward had directed his men with their flaming torches to ignite the corn about twenty, or so paces from the dusty track. There was soon a line of flames creeping beneath a smoke filled sky towards the strip of track. Sparks rose and drifted towards the barn and stack yard. Andy directed operations a short distance away, urging his men with their water filled buckets and besoms to any spot where danger threatened.

Just as the fires over the pre-scorched strip were dying, the fierce heat from the main fire hit them with scorching ferocity. Flames stirred up by thermals of the advancing wall of flames, flared at intervals across the scorched fire-break. Smoke became so thick that Edward had difficulty in seeing his men.

'Fall back to the stack yard and barn!' Edward shouted above the roar of the flames as they advanced menacingly towards the scorched and smouldering strip by the lane. Anxious faces watched in stunned horror as the main flames reached their scorched fire-break.

'Please God... let it work!' Edward prayed softly as the flames that had crackled and exploded in their race towards the farm, appeared to ease and gradually lose their intensity. Sparks that drifted across the lane were soon smothered to eliminate any chance of the flames taking hold again. Choking, gagging and near to exhaustion, the men battled on in the swirling smoke, attacking with alacrity every potential fire threat. Their discomfort and anger were disregarded as they fought the final threats of the fire.

Imperceptible at first, but more discernible as the smoke cleared, Edward realised that the flames were gradually dying down. As the thick swirling smoke lifted, he was surprised to see that it was early dawn. The sky was already reflecting the first rose-pink blushes of the sunrise. As the sky gradually brightened, the men saturated with sweat and blackened from the smoke, eased their backs for the first time since the emergency began. Success had been an agonising effort, but they had managed to save the farm and nearly all the harvest.

'Well done... everyone! You were truly magnificent!' Edward looked back over the blackened acres. 'We've lost a few hundred acres of corn, but more importantly, we saved the buildings and the harvested crops... and thankfully no one was hurt.' Looking up, he noticed Becky and her helpers coming towards them with flagons of ale and a hamper of food.

'Help yourselves to refreshments... and I don't expect any refusals.' Edward's statement produced a good natured burst of laughter. A sudden release from the tension they had all been under. Fate, however, was just about to deliver them a fatal blow.

'What is it that troubles you, Edward?' Becky had noticed his anxious glance back across the scorched acres. Smoke still spiralled lazily into the morning sky, glowing as the embers were stirred by the dawn's breeze. Occasionally a dying flame would flare up momentarily before it finally became extinguished.

'Henry! There are no signs...' he looked around, his features tense with worry, '... of Henry or his companions.' Once more, as a premonition of doom filled his emotions, he looked agitatedly back across the blackened cornfields. 'They should have been back with us by now. Best if I ride over and see what...'

'Please... Edward! Drink this first!' Becky poured him another mug of ale. 'You look exhausted, dear!' He gave her a reassuring smile as he took the tankard and quaffed the contents. Edward's dispassionate demeanour hid his real feelings. Inside, his emotions were in a turmoil at Henry's continued absence. Ominous thoughts were troubling him.

'I'll not be long, my dear.' Edward gave Becky a reassuring kiss as he handed her his empty tankard.

'Be careful, my love!' Her apprehensive look as he mounted his horse confirmed to Edward that his feigned casual actions had not deceived Becky.

'I promise…' he nodded grimly as he looked down from the saddle, '… no heroics.' His involuntary action of touching his gun, did not go unnoticed by Becky. 'Come Nelson!' He spun his horse round in a cloud of dust and blackened ashes and soon had his horse at full stretch towards the distant river acres. Hopefully, he kept a look out for Henry and his companions, but there were no traces of them.

His anxiety increased the further he progressed. Surely he should have encountered Henry or his companions by now. He had almost reached the river when he noticed a native hurrying towards him. He recognised Gicky as he neared the agitated figure. He looked strange in a pair of Henry's old faded breeches and a shirt given him by his long time friend. Edward's smile of welcome faded as he became aware of the look on Gicky's face. He pulled his horse to a stop beside the young native.

Gicky's usual polite greeting, his ritualistic protocol was missing. His face was solemn. Silently he pointed towards a cluster of trees. Dumb with anguish, he indicated that Edward should follow him. Running ahead he guided an apprehensive Edward to the distant trees.

Beneath them on the grass lay the bodies of three men. As he watched, there was a feeble movement as one of them endeavoured to attract Edward's attention. He urged his horse across and then leapt from the saddle and bent down beside the dying man. He first paused by his friend, but Henry was dead. Murdered.

'What happened?' Edward's voice croaked with anguish as he knelt beside the fatally injured man.

'Bush rangers… started fires. Tried… to… prevent… ambushed.' He had to stop as a spasm of coughing racked his body. 'They… shot… us. No chance…' Blood trickled from his mouth as the labourer slowly shook his head. Edward removed his neckerchief and indicated to the distraught Gicky that he should soak it in the river.

'Try and hold on.' He encouraged the injured man, but by the time the young native had returned with the saturated cloth, the man was dead.

Tears of anguish trickled down the dusty and smoke-blackened cheeks of a grim faced Edward, as he silently gazed down at his dead friend. 'Why, Henry! Why?' For a few moments he stared solemnly down at his friend. 'This I promise... dear friend... I shall seek revenge... for your... murder.' Edward's voice was cold with anger as he removed his coat and laid it gently over his dead friend.

Numb with shock he rode back to the farm. Before him was the heartbreaking task of breaking the news to Linda and the three children. That thought filled him with consternation as he pondered on the trauma and distress he was about to bring to a mother and children. Close friends of his own family.

'Please take care, Edward.' Becky's tear stained face looked anxiously into his.

'I will, my love... I promise.' Edward could feel Becky trembling as he held her gently in his arms for their farewell kiss. Since his return with the news of Henry's murder, there had been hasty preparations for his dangerous task of tracking down and bringing to justice the three murderers. Now it was time to leave, while their trail was still fresh.

'I'll bring those scum back dead or alive. I care not which. I shall return with them, I promise... if they live.' Becky had never seen Edward so grim, so emotionally disturbed. 'Andy is riding into Parramatta to inform the authorities. They'll probably catch up with me in a few days.' His words were meant to bring some comfort to Becky, but he could tell from her strained features that she was deeply troubled for his safety.

'How is Linda... taking... the news?' With one foot in the stirrup, he paused to enquire in quiet words.

'Very shocked ... I'm on my way to see her now.' Becky shook her head sadly as she gave Edward an incredulous look.

'Why? Why did they have to resort to... murder? Wasn't firing our crops... sufficient revenge for those... murderers?'

Edward could give her no answers, their barbaric behaviour had stunned him completely. He reached down from his horse and gave Becky a reassuring pat on the shoulders. 'Who knows how the brains of such scum work? They're beyond... normal comprehension.'

'Oh Edward... you will be careful?' He noticed the fear in her eyes as she reached up and clasped his hand. 'I love you, my dearest!'

'And I you, sweetheart.' Gently he eased away to set off in pursuit of the murdering bush rangers His first step was the native camp down by the river where he had arranged to meet Gicky.

When Edward indicated that he should ride Henry's horse, the young native declined with a sad smile and a shake of his head. There was no necessity to explain their mission to him. Intuition had alerted Gicky that his skill would be appreciated in tracking down the men who had killed his friend, Henry. He was determined to find and kill them, as far as he was concerned.

Nodding his head gravely, the young native pointed to the ground under the trees where Henry and his two companions had been ambushed and murdered. He pointed in a north westerly direction beyond the river as if expecting a positive reaction from Edward. Edward realised that while he had returned with news of the murders to Newacres, Gicky had utilised the time to locate and follow the gang's trail as far as the distant woods.

As they moved swiftly across the territory beyond the river, Edward maintained his horse's speed at a gently trot, compatible with Gicky's jogging run. He would have to rely on the young native's expert tracking to follow the murderers trail. When they caught up with the killers, what then, he wondered. He touched his gun with a feeling of reassurance, he would have no qualms about using it, should the necessity arise. He would not hesitate to shoot them, if they resisted his attempt to take them back to the authorities.

Chapter Fourteen

The sun beat down remorselessly upon the two figures clambering over the mountainous terrain; reflecting back at them with scorching intensity. Edward was gasping the rarefied air. Sweat ran down his dusty face and into his eyes. He was uncomfortably aware of his saturated clothing clinging to the contours of his near exhausted body.

For ten days now, he and his native companion had been on the trail of the murdering bush rangers. Gicky had in the first few days found their trail easy to follow, especially as one of the gang appeared to be injured. Probably shot by Henry as he defended himself against their ambush.

Edward had noticed that Henry's gun had been fired when he had recovered it from beside his dead friend. Before he died, the fatally injured labourer had told him that the fire had been started deliberately. It had been ignited by the gang to lure either Henry, or himself, or both into an ambush. Unaware of the danger, it had been Henry and two of his labourers who had ridden into their trap. There had been no warning, they had been shot down in cold blood. Murdered.

Gicky had indicated at the start that there were four riders and the occasional trace of blood confirmed that one at least was badly injured. The gang had several hours' start, but their progress had been hampered by the injured rider.

A makeshift grave on the lower slopes of the Blue Mountains was an unmistakable manifestation of his fate. Three killers still remained, however, a reminder that they must remain alert at all times. One of the riders was a heavy man according to Gicky. Evidence seemed to indicate that they were tracking the same gang that had been terrorising the region of late. Possibly the group that had attacked White Gables and murdered Paul Harrison.

If that were so, thought Edward, the heavily built man riding with the gang was almost certainly Grant Medler, the uncouth brute who owed him no favours. Demonstrating to his dark-skinned companion that they must proceed with extreme care, Edward remained alert for any sign of an ambush.

Despite their cautious pursuit, they had made favourable progress. They were within a few hours of their quarry when the trail led them into the mountains. Edward realised that the terrain of rocks and scree would make tracking very difficult, even for Gicky. In addition there was now more chance of an ambush, especially if the gang were alerted to their presence. Each rock, or overhang could be concealing the murderers.

Edward marvelled at his companion's skill in following the gang's trail among the rocks. Eventually the tracks came to a boulder strewn watercourse where the hoof prints in the damp soil were clearly defined. They searched for almost an hour along the opposite bank before coming across signs of where the gang had emerged from the water.

Once again, because of the rocky terrain, it was becoming increasingly difficult for Gicky to track them. By their continuous evasive actions, Edward was beginning to think that they were aware of being followed. Either that, or they were making it almost impossible for any one to track them later. Whatever their intentions it was imperative to remain alert for any unexpected attack.

With several days of tracking behind him, Edward felt his energy enervating under the burning sun. Even the rocks were hot to his touch. He became aware of this phenomenon when he dismounted to scramble over the boulders to discuss with Gicky any potential ambush situation ahead of them. These possible dangerous situations had to be carefully reconnoitred before moving on. They dare not take any chances.

Despite the rugged conditions and the difficulty of tracking the gang through the mountainous landscape, Edward was determined to press on. During the journey, he had become aware that Gicky was as resolved as he was, in seeing that the men who had murdered Henry and his two companions should pay for their maleficence. As to how that objective would be achieved, Edward was uncertain. That matter could be determined after their capture.

Nelson's whicker startled Edward. Adrenaline sent his heart pounding as he involuntarily flung himself from his saddle. He dived for cover, expecting to hear the sound of gun shots as he did so. There were none, all remained quiet.

Gicky, from the shelter of a boulder, eased his head above the rocks for a cursory inspection of the area. Indicating to Edward that he would reconnoitre the surrounding boulders, he disappeared as silently as his following shadow. There were a few anxious moments for Edward as he awaited his companion's return.

Carefully he moved from his cover to view the situation himself. Scrambling from cover to cover he eventually reached a high position beneath an overhang. There was no sign of an ambush, Nelson's whicker must have been a natural reaction to his own nervousness. As he waited for Gicky's return in the shade of the boulder, he tried to envisage the possible route of the bush rangers, who were obviously familiar with the mountain territory.

Gicky's sudden appearance disturbed his cogitation's. Shaking his head, the native confirmed that his search had revealed no signs of their quarry. Once again they resumed their pursuit of the gang. Before emerging from the shade into the sun that would beat remorselessly upon them, they refreshed themselves with a few sips of water.

Edward experienced a moment of concern as he realised how low their water had become. Involuntarily he glanced at the dried up creek and wondered where their next water would come from. Edward realised just how much he was relying on the young native beside him. Not only for his tracking expertise, but also for his ability to keep them supplied with food and water.

Gicky seemed capable of producing a meal from the most unlikely surroundings. Just a few minutes disappearance was usually sufficient time for him to find their next meal – animal or vegetable. There were occasions when Edward felt it prudent not to enquire too closely about the constituents of the meal handed him. If tastes were the criteria, he had little to be concerned about.

Edward was near to exhaustion as he gasped for air in the rarefied atmosphere. Their apparent lack of progress was also causing him moments of uncertainty. His despondency induced a feeling of hopelessness and frustration. He was aware of a silent Gicky observing him closely. As his companion stood there in faded shirt and tatty breeches, he looked a comical figure, but his serious features contrasted with his factitious appearance.

Materialistically, his appearance had connotations of the settlers civilised society, but spiritually he was of a world that had arrived in that country with his dark skinned ancestors some thirty thousand years previously. Edward realised that the settlers were the interlopers in a land that had since antiquity been the home of Gicky's people. Their way of life, their ritual hunting grounds and even the sacred land of their ancestors were now in danger of being despoiled.

Edward's thoughts returned to their critical situation. At the same time courage flowed back to disperse his pessimistic emotions as he realised that Gicky was expecting some form of reprisal for Henry's murder. He pointed ahead, indicating that they should continue their mission. Gicky's face reflected his desire to find the man who had killed his friend. Revenge, thought Edward, would come swift and final if his companion succeeded in reaching them first.

The knife, partly concealed under the young native's faded shirt, brought a nod of approval from Edward. He felt sure Henry would have sanctioned his hunting knife being passed to his native friend. That thought reassured Edward as he confirmed to Gicky his intention of pressing on. The murderers must be caught – dead or alive.

Gold and crimson hues fading above the shadowy peaks reminded Edward that another day's pursuit of the gang was almost over. He stretch out by the camp fire to enjoy the succulent meat of a small creature caught by his companion. It had taken only a few minutes for Edward to prepare camp, but by then a smiling Gicky was already back with their meal.

As they relaxed near the fire's warmth to enjoy their meal, Edward noticed how reverently Gicky handled Henry's hunting knife. He realised that its touch must feel strange to a native whose only means of defence against adversaries, were normally clubs, spears and blowpipes. The same weapons that were sometimes used for killing wild creatures for food.

Next morning before riding off, Edward demonstrated to Gicky his prowess with a knife. From just over twenty paces he threw his knife at a small exposed area of bark on a stunted tree. An impromptu act, but one that displayed to his watching companion, how the weapon could be used to kill game at a distance.

As the point of the blade buried itself in the exposed trunk, Edward smiled as he heard the watcher's excited gasp. One he had retrieved his knife, Edward encouraged his companion to try a throw himself. After a few futile attempts, Gicky was becoming dispirited. Frustrated at his lack of success.

Edward then explained the signs and in slow movements how he should hold the knife; how to aim and throw the weapon. Under close supervision the young native aimed and threw the knife once more at the target. It was a good throw, but the knife just missed its mark. The thrower's gasp of surprise brought a smile to Edward's lips as he prepared to set forth on their more solemn task of bringing the murderers to justice.

By continued practice and determination, Gicky soon became an adept knife thrower. Henry's knife had now become, not only a revered keepsake to the young native, but a potentially lethal weapon in his skilled hands. Edward quickly realised that his companion had a natural aptitude for throwing. Once shown the correct technique, he quickly mastered the art of hurling his knife at targets.

Suddenly, Edward's senses were alerted as Gicky, who was a few paces ahead, swiftly raised his hand. They had just climbed out of the rift close to where a stream splashed over scattered boulders. He pointed silently to a scar on the bank, indicating with mime that someone had slipped and dislodged a small piece of rock.

After studying the marks closely, he directed his arm towards the sun before moving it back along it imagined trajectory a few degrees. Four or five hours. Edward acknowledged his companion's sign. They were closing in on their quarry.

He waited anxiously while Gicky searched for other marks. There were none. It looked as if the gang had walked their horses along the rocky course of the stream. A perplexing situation that caused Edward a moment of uncertainty. Were the murderers aware of being trailed? The present terrain would make an ideal place to lay an ambush. Alertness must remain a paramount factor as they continued their chase.

Shadows began to creep across the mountains. Edward glanced up at the sun just before it disappeared behind a formation of dusky indigo clouds that were accumulating above the rocky peaks. There was not a movement of air. In the oppressive heat, Edward was perspiring profusely. He felt exhausted, enervated in conditions that were sapping his strength.

Nelson's ears pricked as distant thunder rumbled angrily over the mountains. Chain-lightning cavorted along the rugged contours of an escarpment ahead of them. Edward glanced anxiously round for shelter as rain began to splatter and hiss on the burning rocks.

Just ahead of him, Gicky suddenly disappeared between the cleft of a large boulder. Almost immediately he reappeared and indicated that there was some kind of shelter beyond the fissure. Edward urged a nervous Nelson over the slippery rocks and through the cleft as the rain intensified. Beyond the opening he was thankful to see his companion beckoning him to an overhang. With great relief, Edward guided his horse into a cave-like shelter beneath a projection of rocks.

Thunder rolled and reverberated in a deafening cacophony above the mountains. Rain swept down from the darkening rain clouds, completely blotting out the landscape. Edward glanced reassuringly around the cave, thankful for its shelter.

Noticing the ashes of a partly covered fire, he glanced enquiringly at Gicky, who nodded as if understanding his unspoken question. Here was confirmation that the gang had spent the previous night in the shelter. Both experienced a moment of elation and excitement as they realised just how close they were to their prey.

It was dark by the time the storm had passed. As Edward emerged from the shelter, stars were already flickering brilliantly in a clearing sky, bringing a soft velvety glow to the mountainous surroundings. There was no point in proceeding with their quest in the darkness. With the gang so near, they would be exposing themselves to unnecessary risks. An early start would be more prudent.

Next morning, as Edward paused by the edge of the stream, the first rays of the morning sun sparkled in rainbow hues above the spray of the splashing water. As they resumed their mission along the edge of the stream, Edward noticed that the sunlight occasionally reflected on a glittering object just beneath the surface of the cascading water. He was intrigued, but time and circumstances did not allow for an investigation. They must now keep contact with their quarry. Just as the sun neared its zenith, Edward signalled that they should pause, an inner instinct had warned him that they were very close to the gang. In the scorching heat of the noon-day sun, he indicated his intuitive feelings to Gicky, who nodded concurrence. Realising that hoofs clattering over the rocky terrain would warn their approach, Edward decided to leave his horse in the shade of an outcrop and continue with his companion on foot.

He had just dismounted when Gicky touched his arm and pointed ahead. Before he fully realised his companion's intentions, he had turned and disappeared like a dark shadow among the rocks. Once he had secured Nelson, Edward followed the path of the young native.

Gicky, as if by a pre-arranged plan, had left a series of signs to ensure that Edward would have no difficulty in following him. Gasping and sweating profusely he trailed his friend in the rarefied air. Scrambling over the rocks, he eventually came to a wide gully that led sharply up an escarpment. At the summit he collapsed, near to exhaustion. While squatting on a boulder to regain his breath, his gaze wondered beyond the rock edge to a sight that brought a surprised gasp from his lips.

Far below him on the edge of some rough pasture land was a timber shack. It stood in the shade of a cluster of eucalyptus trees and close to a small stream. Four horses stood grazing behind the building. A blue-hazed column of smoke spiralled lazily into the still air from a chimney-like structure. Edward's heart raced with excited anticipation. They had discovered their quarry's hideout.

He heard movement behind him, but thinking it was Gicky returning, he continued to survey the area below. Involuntarily, Edward drew back from the ledge he was standing on. The sheer drop of two hundred or so feet to the boulder strewn plateau below, induced a moment of fear. Perhaps Gicky had found the track that would lead them to the lower level.

He turned to enquire what his companion had located, but fund himself looking into the evil eyes of the man who had demanded Stephen's kidnap money. Recognition increased the hatred in the man's eyes. The leader and only survivor of the abortive kidnap gang now had Edward at his mercy. Shock numbed his senses as the killer raised his gun and walked menacingly towards him.

Perspiration trickled down Edward's back as he waited for each deliberate step towards him by his adversary. Their eyes were locked on each other's as the man came to a stop just two paces away. Edward was aware of the gun still pointing directly at him. Anticipating a sudden move from his prisoner, the bush ranger paused just beyond Edward's reach. A tantalising action, the outcome was just about to be revealed.

'Yer 'as y'choice, mister! Shootin'... or...' he gave a heinous laugh as he indicated the sheer drop behind Edward, '... a nasty fall.' Still grinning odiously, he edged forward at the same time, giving the gun a sudden jerk. Instinctively, Edward retreated a half step. For a moment he almost lost his balance as his heel caught against a projecting boulder. After a brief, heart stopping moment tottering on the ledge, he managed to regain his balance. His situation was desperate. The possibility of attacking his tormentor crossed his mind, but the odds were stacked heavily against him. Then again... what have I to lose, he thought.

'Don't try it... or I'll blast yer over t'edge.' It was as if he had anticipated his captive's intention. His finger caressed the trigger as he deliberately prolonged the final moment of execution.

A guttural shout momentarily diverted the gunman's concentration. Gicky's sudden appearance and strange call had attracted the killer's attention. It was a brief lapse, but one that Edward took full advantage of.

Jumping forward, he careered into the gunman and sent him staggering backwards off balance. He tried to steady himself and raise his gun, but before he could recover his equilibrium, Edward sent a crunching blow into his midriff. There was a clatter as his gun slipped from his grasp and bounced over the rocks.

He raised his arm in an endeavour to protect himself, but before he could do so, Edward smashed another punch against his jaw. Groaning and dazed the man staggered backwards from the impact of another punch. He stumbled almost to his knees, caught his foot against a boulder and disappeared over the edge of the ridge. His screams came to a sudden stop as he smashed on the rocks far beneath.

'Thanks... Gicky!' Edward smiled his gratitude. There was a moment silence as the dark skinned native drew his knife and indicated his uncertainty about using it on the murderer – a white man.

'If you need to protect yourself...' Edward mimed as he pointed to the two men who had emerged from the shack to investigate their companion's screams, '... use it Gicky.' He accompanied his explanations with gestures and silent demonstrations that left his native companion in no doubt about using the knife if they were threatened by the murderers running for cover in the rocks below. Edward was unaware just how vital his instructions were to prove in the crucial time ahead.

Forewarned, the two gang members were soon lost to sight among the rocks that edged the rear of their shack. Momentarily, the sun glinted ominously on their guns as they ran for cover afforded by the terrain. We have now become the hunted, thought Edward as he looked around for cover from which to meet the imminent attack.

Edward moved behind some rocks that edged the steep track leading down to the plateau and indicated to Gicky that he should hide behind the same boulders on the opposite side. From their concealed positions they watched and waited for the gang's next move. Had they kept the shack under observation for a few seconds longer, they would have noticed the stealthy exit of a third member as he scampered for the rocks.

Shadows began to lengthen and deepen among the boulders. There was a refreshing coolness in the air as the sun descended behind the distant mountain range. Darkness would introduce a difficult period for both hunter and hunted, but with the gang's obvious knowledge of their hideout area, night would be to their advantage.

When the two men had scurried for the shelter of the rocks, Edward had recognised the large bulky form of Grant Medlor leading them. He was sure that the man was responsible for Henry's murder and, if his supposition was correct, that of Paul Harrison also. Medler was a man with no principles – a murderer who would not hesitate to kill again.

Edward eased himself from boulder to boulder, taking advantage of the deepening shadows to conceal his movements. Gicky followed few paces behind, ensuring no surprise attack came from their rear. As Edward crouched and moved silently across a small clearing near the bottom of the track, one of the gang emerged from the shadows. He raised his gun to fire, but before he could discharge the weapon, a knife flashed in the fading light and thudded deep into the bush ranger's back.

A strangled groan rasped from the man's bloody lips. As his legs began to collapse, he tried once again to raise his gun. Before he could do so, Edward leapt forward and delivered a shattering kick to the dying man's jaw. He watched as the killer sprawled face down on the rocks. After a few spasmodic jerks the body remained still. Edward was under the impression that only one of the gang were unaccounted for – Medler.

Bending down, he withdrew the knife from the dead man's back. As he handed it back to Gicky, he acknowledged his thanks with an approving smile. Close by they heard a stone clatter over rocky ground. Edward, noticing his companion merging into the shadows, was about to follow his example when he stumbled over a small boulder in the gloom. He was still partially off balance when Medler suddenly leapt out of the shadows.

On recognising Edward, his anger turned to burning hatred. Instinctively he went to raise his gun, but it was too late.

Helplessly, Medler looked from the gun levelled at him into the eyes of his one time adversary. Greenish-grey eyes returned his gaze with a steely determination.

'I'm taking you back to face murder charges, Medler.' Edward's laconic words were greeted with an impudent sneer. Some intuition warned Edward that he was in a dangerous situation. A metallic click behind him, made him spin round quickly. His worse fears were confirmed. With a shock, he realised that another member of the gang had emerged from the shadows of the rocks. Even in the near darkness he noticed a pistol being aimed directly at him. Edward realised too late that he had miscalculated their number.

'Not s'sure now are yer, Burstow?' There was a sardonic note to Medler's voice as he waited for Edward's reaction to the stalemate situation. Nerves were stretched to breaking point as the three antagonists waited for the first signs of irresolution. A shadowy movement broke the tension. Gicky, brandishing this knife leapt at the man with the pistol.

Medler took his chance while Edward's concentration was momentarily broken as he glanced to check on his companion's action. Too late, he realised his mistake. Powerful arms wrested the gun from his grasp, just as he heard the pistol shot behind his back. There was no pain. Perhaps Gicky had diverted the bush ranger's aim, causing him to miss. He was unable to turn and ascertain the situation, but the gurgling gasp behind him sounded ominous.

Edward concentrated his attention on Medler as he manoeuvred into a position to use the gun now in his possession. While scrambling to reach the shadowy recess behind some rocks, Edward tripped and fell just as Medler fired. The explosion stunned his senses, but miraculously the shot missed him as he sprawled among the rocks. Still dazed he crawled silently for the shelter of a large boulder. From the shadows he had a glimpse of Gicky and the fourth member of the gang. Both were lying completely still on the ground. He called softly to the young native. There was no response.

Shadows deepened as clouds raced across the starlit heavens. Edward and Medler stalked each other with the stealth of skilled huntsmen. Medler carried the gun to use as a club, while Edward held his knife at the ready. Both were waiting for the other to present himself as a target. His expertise as a knife thrower could now mean life or death. There would be no room for error. No second chance.

Drifting cloud formations occasionally obliterated the stars and deepened the shadows among the rocks. In the darkness a stone clattered over the rocks, drawing his attention to the left of his position. He was about to move in that direction, when intuition warned him to remain silent and motionless. It was an old trick, throwing a stone to attract attention away from a concealed position. He had nearly fallen for it.

Medler was a big man, but Edward was realising just how stealthy his stalking had been, silent and menacing. Slowly, Edward eased along a narrow ledge, anxious to reach the lower plateau. Once there he could hide close to the shack and keep it under observation. He had a feeling that Medler would try and reach his horse.

Edward froze in the shadows. A soft shuffling sound, the scuff of a boot against a rocky surface alerted him. He could hear his heart beating in the intense silence. For long moments he remained completely still in the deep shadows. Above him, he heard the soft whisper of sound. He glanced upwards and there silhouetted against the stars was the bulky form of Medler. With his gun raised high, he was about to deliver a shattering blow to his head.

Edward's reflexes, born of his days as a prize fighter, saved his life. Springing sideways, he managed to evade the full force of the blow, but as the rifle butt smashed against his shoulders, he could not contain his agonising gasp.

'Dam yer… Burstow. I'll hev yer… this time!' Despite the numbness in his arm, Edward had reached out and grabbed the gun as Medler was about to raise it in another attempt to batter him. It was a surprise tactic that cause his opponent unawares. Medler's curses as he struggled to recover the gun, reflected his anger.

A titanic struggle for possession of the gun developed in the darkness. An unexpected wild kick from Medler landed against Edward's injured shoulder, numbing it temporarily. Realising that his chances of survival were fading rapidly, he gave a strong, final pull on the gun, but his inured arm could not maintain the grip. As the gun slipped from his grasp, Edward staggered backwards and eventually collapsed on to his knees.

From a half crouched position, Edward watched the shadowy figure of Medler holding the gun by its barrel in preparation for delivering the fatal blow. Edward realised that he was trapped and made a final attempt to get clear. As he did so, his hand knocked against his knife.

Snatching it from his belt, he flicked it over instinctively so that the blade tip rested between his thumb and finger. Just as the butt reached its spex, Edward threw his knife directly at Medler's heart. There was a brief glint of steel in the fading starlight as it flashed towards its target The blade sliced deep into the body of the murderer.

Medler's hoarse cry of pain rasped the silence of the night. Edward remained crouched as he watched the shadowy silhouette stagger on the ledge above him, before pitching forward to land on the rocks at his feet. There were no further movements. As Edward recovered his knife he experienced a feeling of satisfaction knowing that Henry's murderers had suffered their deserts. All now were dead.

'Gicky!' Edward stood silently by the young native's grave as he whispered the name he had carved on a rough wooden cross. 'Thank you for saving my life... dear friend.' Sadly he turned from the small heap of rocks that covered the shallow grave and silently mounted his horse.

'It's alright.... Nelson!' Edward calmed his nervous horse. He gave his steed a reassuring pat before urging him into a steady canter away from the blazing shack. Because of the energy-sapping work in excavating even a shallow grave, Edward had taken the bodies of the gang into the timbered building before setting it ablaze.

* * * * *

It was three days later that Edward came down from the mountains into an area that was unfamiliar to him. It had the appearance of being remote with no sign of human presence. He tried to get his bearing from the sun that was just about to sink behind a tree lined ridge.

It was almost dark when Edward reached a dried up gully. A good place to camp, he thought, as he started a fire to prepare for the approaching darkness. Placing a piece of wood onto the fire, he watched thoughtfully as the flames suddenly flared up to send sparks rising up into the starlit night.

Darkness, with its accompanying nocturnal sounds, settled over the bush as Edward pondered on his circumstances. He estimated that Greenacres, his farm near Bathurst, was about two day's ride away. 'Think I'll call there while I'm in the area.' He nodded silent agreement as he spoke his thoughts aloud. Having reached his decision, he placed some wood on the fire and settled down beside it. A smile flickered across his face as he thought of the welcome that always awaited him when he called on James and Maggy – and their children. Three at the last count.

Edward was awake early, anxious to be on the move as his family must be wondering about his long spell away from home. The sun was a blood-red orb as it cleared the haze of the tree-lined ridge. As he attempted to scramble up the steep side of the gully, he slipped and dislodged some lose rocks and scree. The debris cascaded around him as he fell to his knees. His silent cursing suddenly stopped as a glittering object caught his eye.

Slowly he reached out and picked it up. 'Gold!' The word escaped his lips as he stared in shocked disbelief at the piece of shining ore in his hand. 'Gold!' he repeated in a croaking voice as he continued to inspect the material closely. A shaft of sunlight gave it a dazzling radiance as he turned it in his hand.

He searched among the fallen debris in an unsuccessful search for more. Then he concentrated on the exposed stratum where signs appeared more hopeful. He took his knife and prized away a sections of lose rocks that tumbled down into the gully. As he looked amongst the fallen rocks, he noticed some smaller pieces of the shining metal. Further probes sent pieces of scree cascading into the dried up water bed. He picked up a medium sized segment of the sparkling mineral. Before continuing his journey, Edward placed his find in a makeshift pouch beneath his coat.

First thing, he must get the gold assayed, assuming it was gold. He was confident that the mineral was gold, but doubtful thoughts kept troubling him as he rode towards Greenacres. If gold was confirmed, as he was sure it would be, its presence could start a mad scramble over a lovely fertile valley. The thought worried him greatly. Edward decided to keep the gold's presence a secret, until he had spoken with the authorities in Sydney. He must first find someone he could trust, but who?

The Governor. He would speak in confidence with Governor Macquarie. Yes, he nodded his head pensively, that would be the safest procedure. Nevertheless, even as he rode across the remote bushlands, he was trying to estimate the value of the gold in his pouch. If it was confirmed as gold, it would certainly make him a rich man.

As he considered the consequences of his find, he remembered the shining object in the stream, as Gicky and himself had climbed the rocks in pursuit of the killers. Was that glittering object in the water gold, he wondered? Any indication that gold had been found in the mountains would start a stampede that could only bring chaos. Mayhem. It was essential to remain silent, if the area was to remain a peaceful one.

'You er, say that no one else is aware of your... find, Edward?' Governor Macquarie looked up from the gold he had just tipped from Edward's pouch on to his desk.

'No one, I can assure you, Governor.'

'Good! With your co-operation, I should like it to remain so.' He frowned as he gave his reason. 'The last thing I want is a gold stampede across our farm lands.' He waited for Edward's reaction. His concurrence.

'My sentiments exactly, Governor. However, I wondered if...

how to... get my gold assayed.' He nodded towards the glittering pieces of ore lying on the desk. 'I'd like to know if it really is....'

'Oh, it's gold alright. We've had previous sightings reported. Small quantities in all cases, but it had been the policy of myself and also that of my predecessor to keep the findings secret. Fearing the catastrophic effects such discoveries would have on the population, we suppressed such reports and discouraged further searches.'

'Then I have no hesitation in abiding fully with your recommendations, Governor. You have my word on it.'

'Thank you. As regards your, er... find...' Governor Macquarie indicated the pieces of gold on his desk, '... I'll arrange for it to be assayed and disposed of through official channels.' Edward nodded silent agreement on seeing the Governor's questioning look. 'Its worth, I feel sure...' his stern features were softened briefly by the flicker of a smile before he continued, '... will make you a very wealthy man, Edward. Congratulations!' The Governor rose and extended his hand. Edward felt the firm grip of it and, as he stared into the Governor's eyes, he was aware of the silent plea in their depths.

With suppressed excitement, Edward stepped into his phaeton, anxious to be on his way back to Newacres. As he settled back in his carriage, a wistful expression settled upon his face. He was recalling his return home after his confrontation with the murderous bush rangers.

A momentary sadness touched his eyes as he remembered his first call on Gicky's family group. He had explained to them by gestures and diagrams drawn by a stick in the dust, how their family member had died bravely. Edward had indicated that they were free to remain, but by their gesticulations the natives had intimated their intentions to move to their warrior's resting place.

Seeking the young native's father, Edward had solemnly handed over Gicky's knife. Proudly the old man received the weapon, holding it high so that all cold see. He then commenced a strange chant-like intonation that was soon taken up by the group. When Edward had looked back, the knife, flashing in the sunlight, was still being held aloft as if in some ritualistic manifestation.

Edward had then continued on towards Newacres, leaving the natives to their lamentations. Foremost in his thoughts as he rode away was the undying gratitude he would always have for one of their family – Gicky. Had it not been for his bravery, Edward realised that he would never have returned to Becky and the children. That thought had induced an ache in his heart. So tired and so near to exhaustion, Edward recalled how he had crossed the westwood acres towards home and his family. Gradually, he became aware that the burnt out acres, although still showing signs of the fire, were in the process of being ploughed.

When distant voices attracted his attention, he had paused in the shade of some trees. It had been a moment of nostalgia, bringing a lump to his throat as he had surreptitiously watched his children from the shadows. Marian was leading an unsteady Roger as they inspected the horses and fed them tit-bits. Stephen, with his faithful companion, Curly, scampering beside him, was chasing after a couple of piglets that had managed to escape from their pen.

Edward remembered how his smile had turned to silent laughter as his eldest son dived on to one of the escapees and, after carrying the squealing and wriggling piglet back to its pen, then unceremoniously dumped the complaining animal inside. As the second one, having received identical treatment, was safely returned to its pen, Edward eased Nelson out into the open.

For a few moments as he approached the farm, no one had noticed him. Stephen was the first to pause in his activities and gaze in his direction. With recognition came an excited shout as he bounded towards his father.

'Pa! It's Pa! He's back!' His call alerted family and staff alike Edward dismounted in time to catch Stephen in his arms as he flung himself against his tired body. Marian, struggling to make progress with a tottering Roger, eventually reached his side.

'Oh pa! We missed you lots. Ma has been worried... upset.' Edward embraced her affectionately and assured her that he was home to stay. He lifted Roger up in his arms, but his youngest son just gazed solemnly at him while he continued to suck irresolutely on his thumb. Suddenly the wet digit was removed and a damp hand was wrapped lovingly around Edward's neck. That was how Becky found her family when the children's excited shouting had drawn her to the veranda.

Through misted eyes she watched the children's reunion with their father. 'Oh, Edward!' she whispered. 'Thank God you're safe.' Her softly spoken gratification was a reflection of the relief she was experiencing. An easing of the tension and worry she had endured since his departure. Gathering her skirts, she hurried to welcome home the man who she thought had been killed in his quest to bring the murderers to justice.

As Edward continued his ride back to Newacres, he smiled as he recalled that wonderful reception that had greeted his return from the mountains. Later, after he had bathed and changed, he had shared a seat with Becky on the veranda while relating his adventures.

'The gang... they are all dead?' She looked uncertainly towards Edward as he had nodded affirmation. 'What about Gicky? His companionship must have... been...' Her voice had faded as she noticed the sorrow in Edward's eyes.

'Gicky...' sadness made it difficult to speak, '... was killed in saving my life.'

'Oh, Edward! I... I had a feeling that you were in danger... that you were...' She could not bring herself to say the word. Instead, with tears in her eyes, she had reached out silently to embrace the man who shared her life – her love.

A man's voice sounded in the distance. As the voice intruded on their intimate moment, Edward strained to listen. He frowned as he tried to remember the voice, one that somehow seemed familiar. Becky smiled up into his puzzled face. 'A surprise for you, my dear!'

'Surprise?' he gave her a nonplussed look. Taking his hand she led him to the end of the veranda, where a wider view of the farm complex could be seen.

He could still hear the man's voice as he emerged from the barn to come into Edward's sight. 'Geoff! Geoff Rawlings... what...?' Becky laughed at his statement.

'Geoff arrived on the day after your departure. Andy came over to assist while Geoff established himself, but since then he's been running the farm in your absence.'

'And very efficiently... if my supposition is correct...' he pointed towards the freshly ploughed acres just as a smiling Geoff walked over to join them.

'I was sorry to hear about...' Geoff's face became solemn as he continued, '...your friend. His murder must have been very distressing for you.' Geoff had hesitate a few moments before offering a proposition. 'My qualifications are not of Henry's standard, but if you are in need of help, Edward...?'

'If...' Edward smiled as he remembered how he had given his friend a serious look, '... you are applying for the job as manager at Newacres ... don't, Geoff.' His chuckle, as he recalled the shocked looks on the faces of Becky and Geoff, caused Nelson to prick his ears up. Still continuing to gaze at Geoff with a pensive countenance, he had given his reason. 'Any application is unnecessary... the present administrator is requested to continue ad infinitum.'

Geoff's apprehension gave way to a burst of laughter as he stepped across and embraced his old shipmate.

'Thanks, Edward. You'll not regret it... I promise.' A promise that was to be fulfilled a thousand fold in the ensuing years at Newacres.

Edward's thoughts returned to the present as he negotiated Parramatta's crowded streets to reach the road leading out to his farm. He still suffered the effects of his adventure into the Blue Mountains and was anxious to be back at Newacres – and Becky. He had stayed only briefly at the farm before departing to Sydney, wanting to report as soon as possible the details of his encounter with the bush rangers to the government authorities. Also, he was eager to report his gold find to the Governor. Thankfully, that was now all behind him and soon he would be in sight of Newacres.

Still drowsy from an exhausted sleep, Edward reached out to embrace the woman who had shared his love, only a few hours before. His hand encountered an empty space. There was no sign of Becky. Drowsiness gave way to confused emotions as he became fully aware of her absence.

'Becky?' There was an anxious note to his voice as he called her name. Edward sat up in bed wondering where she was. Against the early dawn sky, he noticed her silhouette by the window. 'Becky?' he called her name softly once again. 'Is something wrong?' Anxiety gave way to concern when she turned towards him with tears glistening on her cheeks. 'What troubles you so, my love?' He spoke tenderly as he scrambled from their bed. Aware of his nakedness, he snatched his robe and slipped it on as he walked towards a disconsolate, Becky.

Gently, he placed comforting arms around her. 'What is it that distresses you so?' As he pressed his cheeks against hers, Edward noticed the sadness in her eyes. While waiting for her to speak, he noticed how the tears that trickled down her cheeks, sparkled in the first blushes of the dawn.

'Oh, Edward... what is to become of us... our future? Shall we ever be able to marry... lead a normal life... together...?' He shared her melancholy emotions as they held each other in a warm embrace. While contemplating Becky's questions, he buried his face in her hair, caressing her crown with his lips.

'Becky, love... please forgive me.' He held her close, feeling the warmth and excitement of her body through her thin night-dress. 'I had no idea our... our way of life... was causing you so much distress...'

'Oh no, Edward. You must never think that.' She leaned slightly away from him to look lovingly into his face. 'Our years together have been so wonderful... full of happiness and love.' As if to stress her sincerity, Becky affectionately placed her lips upon his.

'Why so pensive then, my love?' He eased away from their kiss to ask the question.

'It's... a... kind of... homesickness... I suppose...' She buried her head against Edward's naked chest as she slid her arms lovingly around his waist beneath his open robe.

'Homesickness?' Surprise sounded in his voice. 'Would you... like to... return to England, Becky?'

'Oh, no! I did not... mean...' she was uncertain of her emotions. 'I have no... yearning... to return.' Becky snuggled closer, pressing affectionately against his body. Her nearness aroused a physical longing that Edward had great difficulty in containing. He forced himself to listen dispassionately to Becky's nostalgic words. 'Its just that we have been out here for six years or so and not one word has reached us from home.'

Edward noticed the sadness clouding her eyes as she looked up into his face, awaiting his reply. He remained silent, his emotions sympathetic to Becky's dilemma. He nodded his understanding and indicated with a wistful look that she should continue to unburden her troubled thoughts. Share them with him. After a few reflective moments Becky spoke once again of her disappointments.

'I had hoped for words from Josh... we were always so close and tolerant towards each other. News of home... of my family... would have been so welcome, but it would appear that our letters did not... warrant... an answer...' Becky heaved a deep, emotional sigh as her voice faded to silence. A deep silence prevailed as close in each other's arms they watched the first rays of the morning sun edge their way across their land.

Edward spoke in a pensive voice about his disappointed expectations. 'I also had hoped for some response from Maisie or Julie.' The mention of his betrothed's name induced a moment of nostalgia as he recalled the young woman he had loved.*

'Did you... love... Julie, Edward?' Becky had noticed the changing emotions reflected in his eyes. A brief surge of jealousy made her press closer to him.

'We were to have been married in the summer of my departure, but...' he gave a deep sigh, '... the rest you know. I do not suppose I shall ever see her again.' Quietly and tenderly they remained in the close embrace as their thoughts returned to their homeland and loved ones so far away.

'I also doubt if I shall ever see my brother or my parents again.' A sob of despondency escaped her lips. After a few

* In Book I The Winds of Destiny

moments of silence, Becky gave Edward an affectionate smile. 'I'm glad we still have each other.' She whispered seductively as she pressed eagerly and provocatively against Edward's excited body.

'I concur whole heartedly with your sentiments, Becky.' His embrace was passionate and his kisses aflame with desire as the dawn heralded the new day. Gently he eased from their closeness. 'Perhaps we should share our love...' he looked expectantly towards their bed with an impassioned longing. Becky, glancing down beneath his open robe, experienced a passionate urgency to comply with his emotive suggestion.

Josh... Julie... and their homeland were soon obliterated from their thoughts as they shared each other's love. The nostalgic thoughts faded as they shared an act that reflected their love and passion for each other. As the early morning sunlight slanted in through their bedroom window, it glowed softly on two exhausted bodies that continued to share a close embrace, even in exhausted sleep.

Far away across the boundless waters of the raging ocean, Josh was covertly longing for the moment of love-making that he would soon be sharing with his bride – Doreen. They were soon to be wed. Julie's thoughts were less emotive. She was considering how best to discourage the advances of the young curate, Robin Darvill.

PART TWO (1820-1828)
THE COLONISTS

Chapter Fifteen

Josh walked from the cottage a happy man, yet deep within something troubled him. He paused on his way to the barn to consider once again his disquiet, but he could think of no reason for his uncertain emotions. Shrugging aside his vacillation, he resumed his walk towards the timbered structure.

Inside an anxious Doreen awaited his arrival. Her parents' blessing for their wedding was the reason for Josh's visit to the cottage. Now, as he came into the barn, her heart raced with excitement as she looked into his eyes for some sign that her parents' permission had been granted. She deeply loved Josh, the stranger who had spent the last few years in their Quaker community.

It was a pensive Josh who came silently toward the woman he loved. The woman he was soon to marry. Doreen's parents had given their blessings for them to marry. An acquiescence that had pleased Josh and yet induced a feeling of torment.

'What... were my parents... reactions, Josh?' Despite his smile of welcome, she had noticed the sadness in his eyes. 'Have they given their blessings... for our... wedding?' Puzzled by his reticence, she waited for his answer.

'Yes... yes, Doreen. All is... well.' He reached out to take her hands. 'Your parents have agreed... to our marriage.'

'Yet... thou hast... doubts?' Her questioning look was not lost on Josh. He hurried to elucidate his disquiet thoughts.

'Not doubts, Doreen. It's... just that...' Irresolutely he paused to shake his head. 'If only I could remember... my past. My true identity.'

'I understand thy troubled emotions, Josh...' she moved closer so that she could kiss his cheek, '... but after five years and despite all our efforts, my love, we still have no idea as to thy identity.' For a few silent moments she gazed lovingly into his eyes. 'Oh, Josh... I love thee truly.'

'And I thee, my dearest.' Their lips were joined in an affectionate kiss. 'When I return from Norwich, we shall make final arrangements for our wedding.' Their yearning for each other gave way to amorous emotions as they held each other closer and their kisses became more passionate.

'Now...' reluctantly, Josh eased from their close embrace, '... I must prepare myself for the journey. Your father has the horses ready and is anxious for us to be on the road.' At the door he paused to give Doreen an affectionate smile. A look that urged her to hurry forward to share a parting embrace – and kiss.

'May our wedding day be soon, my love.' There was an urgency in his voice. 'Waiting has become an unbearable... burden.' His enamoured excitement induced a blush to her waxen cheeks.

'Tomorrow... were it possible, dearest Josh.' Her teasing smile and flushed cheeks stimulated an emotional longing in the departing beau.

'I shall keep you in my thoughts until I return... and then our desires... our love will know fulfilment.' Excitement, actuated by the meaning of his words, stirred within her young body.

A short time later, Doreen and her mother waved farewell to the two riders from the cottage doorway. As Josh and Jason trotted their horses down the lane, they responded with a final wave before settling down for their ride to Norwich. Jason smiled covertly as he became aware of Josh's one last lingering look back at his betrothed.

Neither of the riders were to know that Josh's backward glance was to be his final view of Doreen. They were destined never to see each other again.

'How many sheep are thee thinking of buying, Jason?' Josh turned to question his companion as they progressed along the dusty ribbon of road. They had moved into the cool, dappled shade of some overhanging elms before Jason enlightened him as to their expected purchase at the city's cattle market.

'How many will mainly depend on the price asked, Josh.' There was a confident ring to his voice as he mentioned his expectations. 'I have in mind a figure of three score.' He gave a gleeful chuckle as he noticed the surprised, almost shocked look on Josh's face.

'Having thee as family...' he continued to smile benignly at his companion, '... was sufficient encouragement to speculate on an increase in our flock.' Noticing his future son-in-law's interest, he continued his explanation. 'They will be thy responsibility, Josh, so I shall be relying on thy judgement when we buy.' As their journey progressed, they continued to discuss future prospects for the farm and their Quaker community.

Behind them, the gold and crimson hues of the sunset streaked the evening sky. The elongated shadows of the two riders preceded them on the ochered stretch of highway. Spurts of dust kicked up by their horses hooves drifted in the still evening air before settling on the roadside grass.

'Massingham Heath!' Jason pointed ahead as twilight engulfed the rural landscape around them. 'We have relations in the village. Shelter and food awaits us there.'

Skeins of mist drifted low over the fields, fusing ethereal-like with the deepening shadows, as the riders approached a small cottage on the outskirts of the small village. A lamp flickered at its uncurtained window, a tiny beacon that proffered a welcome to the weary travellers. Dogs began to bark as they dismounted outside the thatched white-washed building.

A door opened and a soberly dressed man emerged from the cottage. His grey hair, almost silvery in the flickering lamp light behind him, accentuated his dignified appearance. He stepped across the yard to view the two arrivals while his wife, a small nervous creature peered anxiously from behind the window curtains.

'How are thee friend, Jonathan?' Jason moved in to the light as he spoke.

'Bless me! 'tis Jason... welcome old friend.' Jonathan hurried forward to embrace the recognised visitor. 'Hannah!' he called over his shoulder towards the cottage. The worried face disappeared from the window and emerged smiling from the rose-surrounded doorway. Hannah, on seeing her cousin Jason, shuffled forward to receive his warm embrace.

'Greetings Hannah... how fare thee, my dear?' Jason stood back to smile enquiringly into her joyful features.

After Josh had been introduced, a small lad appeared in the doorway of a barn-like structure. Jonathan beckoned the lad over. 'Billy will see t'yer horses.' He indicated to Billy that he should feed and water their guests horses and then bed them down in the stable.

As the silent boy took his horse, Josh noticed the straw adhering to his back and mop of unruly hair. 'I thank thee, Billy.' Josh gave the boy an appreciative smile. Without a word or change of expression, he nodded before leading the two mounts away.

'Billy's a mute! A deaf one!' There was a sympathetic note in Hannah's voice as she explained the lad's silent behaviour. 'We found him bruised and battered in Norwich, nearly two years since. He was alone and unwanted.' As Hannah watched Billy remove the saddles and reins from the two horses, Josh noted the tender look in her eyes.

'We feed him and he has a cosy corner in the barn for sleeping. In return he does odd jobs around the place.' Josh's eyes remained on Hannah's face as she informed them of Billy's disabilities. He noticed the care, almost motherly look she cast in the lad's direction.

'Well...' their host indicated the open door, '... come thee inside.'

'I thank thee friend, Jonathan.' Jason, after acknowledging his friend's invitation, followed his cousin Hannah into the small, cosy cottage.

News of family and friends were exchanged during and after the meal. Josh became the centre of attention when it was known that he was to marry Doreen. Congratulations were still ringing in his ears as he and Jason rode off early next morning.

A few hours later, Jason left the highway to traverse a narrow lane that lead to an isolated farm. Their arrival was greeted by the usual barking of dogs in this instance, by the hissing of geese. A cacophony of farmyard sounds warned the owner that strangers were present. Eventually the farmer emerged from the cattle sheds. Jason noticed his frown of annoyance. An almost belligerent look crossed his countenance as he studied the two interlopers.

'Good day to thee, friend.' Jason's friendly greeting was met with a silent stare. Reluctantly, it seemed, the farmer eventually returned their greeting. Condescendingly, he appeared to acknowledge their presence.

'We seek a favour of thee.' Jason's amicable attitude appeared to reassure the taciturn farmer. When he spoke for the first time, his speech was terse and gruff.

'Speak yer favour!' He gave them an uncertain scrutiny as Jason explained his need for a night's pasture for his sheep, when the drovers passed this way en route for his farm.

'Sheep! Don't reck'n t'have 'em on my farm.' He was about to turn away, the matter closed as far as he was concerned.

'There would of course, be recompenses for thee!' Jason's words brought him to a stop. 'You have...' Jason pointed back down the lane, '.. an ideal meadow by the roadside and your farm is a good day's drive from Norwich.' Seeing the man's avaricious look, he continued. 'Your farm would make a suitable overnight stop for the drovers.' Jason waited for the farmer's reaction.

'What be yer... comp'sation?' There was an eager, almost covetous expression when he realised that money was on offer.

'Payment for services. A meal for the drovers and a night's grazing for three score sheep.' Jason explained his requirements.

'How much... yer offerin'?' His greedy look was obvious as he waited Jason's offer.

'Er... two shillings.' Jason noticed the farmer's sly expression as he shook his head.

'Two'n a half... I reck'n on.' Quickly he countermanded Jason's offer. As he waited confirmation, he extracted a blackened piece of tobacco from his pocket and proceeded to cut a sliver of the dark textured material. He popped the slice into his mouth and, after pushing it towards his cheek with his tongue, began to chew with his stained molars. His straggled beard, discoloured with tobacco blemishes, testified to his obnoxious habit of squirting nicotine-tainted saliva at frequent intervals.

Jason frowned, as if giving the farmer's offer serious thought. He deliberately prolonged his cogitation's. Originally, he had intended offering the farmer his asking price, but seeing the avaricious gleam in the man's eyes, went back to his first offer.

'Two shillings, or...' Jason turned his horse as if to ride away. An act of bluff that the cantankerous farmer fell for.

'Two shillin's... agreed!' He gave Jason a contentious look as he continued to chew his wad of tobacco.

'Agreed! Jason turned his horse towards the lane. 'I shall pay thee on my return from market and confirm the details,' he called over his shoulder.

'As y'wish!' The farmer watched the departing riders for a few moments. Then squirting a globule of tobacco-stained spittle in their direction, turned and shuffled away to disappear inside the dilapidated barn.

'A mean fellow, Jason?' Josh looked back just as the surly farmer entered his ramshackle structure.

'Aye... but we need overnight stops for the drovers and the sheep.'

'This will be their first stop after leaving Norwich market?' Jason nodded confirmation as they rode out onto the main thoroughfare.

'Yes... and thankfully our two previous requests for overnight stops were received in a much friendlier manner. Mostly, the farmers respond favourably.'

'And offer refreshments...' Josh chuckled.

'A hospitality that was sadly lacking by...' Jason jerked his head in the direction of the farm behind them, '... our last, somewhat belligerent agrarian.' His companion's ironic remark caused a wry smile to flicker across Josh's face as they headed their horses towards the city, now but a few miles away.

* * * * *

Andrew sank wearily down on his knees. Another exhausting and humiliating day was drawing to a close. His fingers were raw and tender from picking heaps of oakum. His last session of labour before his cell was locked for the night.

Absently he picked away, recalling the monotonous daily routine as he did so. Not very different, he thought, from the last two hundred days he had endured since his incarceration in

Norwich Castle. His spirits plummeted at the thought of his term still to be served.

Tomorrow it would begin as usual with his awakening at six of the clock. A hurried dress and then a scrub round his cell before breakfast. Prior to commencing his work at nine, he would join the other prisoners in the chapel for half an hour's service. The only time they would be allowed to relax throughout the long wearisome day.

Andrew was not a religious person, but the time spent in the tranquil surroundings of the chapel was beginning to induce a spiritual peace to his troubled mind. Meditating on the circumstances of his imprisonment, he wondered about his uncertain future. He was an outcast and deservedly so, he now acceded.

His past sins returned to haunt him as he instinctively continued with his oakum picking. Gambling, drinking and… he shuddered with remorse as he thought of the wrong he had done Maisie. The woman who was his own brother's wife. Then the debts had begun to pile up as he gambled heavily to try and force the memory of his incestuous misdemeanour from his mind.

As his debts mounted, he had moved around to avoid a confrontation with his debtors. Eventually he was tracked down and apprehended. Now, with just over six months of his prison term behind him, he dare not dwell too much on the immediate future, if he had one.

A sceptical chuckle escaped Andrew's lips as he recalled how his creditors had demanded he cleared his debts or face the consequences. He had no option but to face the outcome - incarceration in Norwich Castle. When informed of his son's imprisonment, Sir Roger had promised to pay each creditor half of their debt, but insisted that his eldest son must stand trial for the remainder.

Andrew shook his head to disperse his tormented thoughts. Gathering up another handful of oakum, he looked at the passing jailer, tempted to throw it into the man's sardonic looking face. Involuntarily, he gripped the fibrous material in preparation for throwing it. Premonition caused him to stay his hand.

An inner voice warned him to refrain. Any aggressive action on his part would only bring some sadistic retribution. He had suffered acutely over the past few months. If he were to affront the jailer now it would only aggravate the situation. Further punishment would only bring him additional humiliation. Unseen by the warder, the oakum spilled from Andrew's relaxed hand.

'How much longer?' Andrew whispered. He was weary and irritable, anxious to cast the damned oakum aside and finish for the day. 'Does it matter?' His sigh reflected his despondency. Tomorrow he would be subjected to the repetitive routine once again – and for every following day until... He groaned inwardly as he thought of the months of imprisonment ahead of him.

Frustration and anger overwhelmed Andrew as he meditated on the weeks ahead. On the morrow with the cleaning of his cell, his humiliation would start all over again. Rage pulsed through his tired body as he thought of the monotonous routine. Scrubbing the cell floor on his hands and knees with filthy cold water mortified his senses. After chapel, it would then be the wheel room.

How he loathed the morning and afternoon spells on the human tread-wheel. Andrew likened it to walking up a never-ending flight of steps. Hatred, resignation and chagrin; he experienced all these feelings as he endured his fifteen minutes spell on the wheel. The five minutes rest between sessions never seemed long enough for his weary body.

Andrew's frustration had been building up over the past six months or so and was now nearing a climax. He was afraid that his anger might erupt and result in his incarceration being prolonged. It was a struggle to remain calm, but whatever happened he must not be provoked into a hasty act of retaliation. Antagonising the jailers would soon bring a swift and agonising retribution. He was remaining submissive, but it was taking immense will power.

Andrew was under no illusion that he was reaching the limit of his endurance. With his senses dulled by anger and fatigue, he realised that he would not be able to endure much more of this degrading existence. Each day was now becoming a challenge to his frustrated emotions, a raging battle against his despondency. A fight to control his anger. Intuition warned him that it could not last much longer.

'Yes... wanted!' The jailer gave Andrew a sardonic look. 'this way!' He followed the surly warder along narrow corridors and finally up two flights of steps. The jailer made no attempt at conversation, appearing to resent this departure from routine for his prisoner.

'Wait in there!' He jabbed his finger towards a small ante-room. The bare, white-washed brick walls gave the place a Spartan look.

'Do you... er, know why...?' Andrew was perplexed at the sudden change of his routine and was anxious to ascertain the reason.

'Shut yer gob!' The jailer's words angered Andrew. He bunched his fists and moved forward to strike the sullen brute just as the door opened. A sombre, quiet-spoken man emerged and invited Andrew inside the large, well-furnished room behind the door. Andrew experience a guilty feeling as he entered, the official must have realised his intention of striking one of his jailers.

'Carry on Fenton.' Quickly the senior official dismissed the man and closed the door. Andrew was surprised when he was invited to sit in the chair facing a desk-like table.

'You're probably wondering why you've been sent for?' There was a hint of friendliness in the official's voice... and manner. It had certainly not been so when he had first arrived at the prison. Andrew remembered how the senior jailer had quietly threatened him with further punishment if he so much as showed rancour towards any of his staff. 'Do as you're bid – and you'll not suffer.' An exhortation he had managed to comply with, despite provocation by a few of the jailers.

Andrew recalled that initial meeting as he now sat before the senior official, wondering what discipline he had broken. He could recall no deed or words spoken that could warrant disciplinary action, but... He silently nodded his head, still trying to think what rule he had broken. It had to be something serious for him to be in front of... Andrew's thoughts were interrupted by the official's voice.

'This...' the head jailer picked up a document from his desk, '... is authorisation for your release. As of now you are a free man. Free to leave this prison.'

'A... free... man?' Andrew's surprise left him almost speechless.

'As you say... a free man, Mr. Douglass.'

After the door shut with a clang behind him, Andrew paused to breath in the air of freedom and to look across the roof tops towards the setting sun. Its brilliance reflected on the windows, dazzling his eyes that had been used to the gloom of the castle's interior.

'Where now?' he whispered uncertainly as he tried to orientate to his freedom. Andrew glanced down as his scruffy clothes. His breeches and stocking, once white and fresh, were soiled and rumpled from long continuous wear. His bottle-green coat, once fit for a gentleman, was faded and worn and because of the weight he had lost while in prison, hung loosely on his person. At least I'm fit... an ironic smile touched his lips as he thought of the treadmill.

It was twilight, the first evening stars flickered uncertainly in a darkening sky. Andrew found himself walking intuitively towards the heath. He had no money and since his dinner of prison 'stirabout', a kind of porridge made from oatmeal and maze, he had eaten nothing. Hungry and in need of companionship, he remembered a friend who lived nearby in the city.

His visit had been ignored, an insulting rebuff on the doorstep had caused him a moment of consternation. He had even been refused an audience with his friend. The servant had conveyed contemptuous replies from his one-time companion to the effect that his presence was both inopportune and undesirable.

'Damn them! Damn them all!' Andrew's anger erupted as he looked for a sheltered place to sleep on Mousehold Heath. Even his so-called friends were ignoring him now. Refusing to acknowledge his existence. So be it, he thought, I can well manage without their support. Nevertheless, as he settled down to spend the night sleeping in the heather, a melancholy feeling engulfed him. He felt unwanted and alone. There was no one he could turn to. He slept fitfully under a star spangled sky.

Andrew stretched his cramped and aching limbs. The first rays of the sunrise glided silently over the heath, bathing the weathered stonework of the distant castle in a mallow glow. He shuddered as his gaze rested on the edifice in which he had been incarcerated for the past six months or so. Andrew experienced a loathing for the Norman Castle that stood predominantly on a high mound overlooking the city.

His gaze moved on to the cathedral's majestic spire as he made his way down from the heath. It was an inspiring sight in the early morning sunlight as it stretched up into the cloudless azure heavens. There was something ethereal about its presence that attracted Andrew towards it.

Brushing the grass and heather from his clothes, he crossed the river and made his way towards the upper close and Tombland. Hunger and thirst were troubling him as he arrived in the vicinity of the close. With no money, he had little chance of satisfying either, but he was optimistic that something would turn up.

It was late afternoon when fortune took pity on his despairing soul. As his wonderings brought him to the crowded market place, he noticed a penny lying on the ground. His prayers were answered. Perhaps it would buy a stale loaf. Eagerly he reached down to pick-up the coin, but as he did so a large boot stamped down hard on his hand.

'Tha's mine! Leave it be!' Andrew gasped with pain as the man's weight squashed his hand against the ground.

'Damn you!' Andrew snatched his hand clear, straightened up and in one continuous movement delivered a powerful blow to the man's leering face. The swiftness of the attack caught the man completely off guard Before he could recover, Andrew landed another punch with his injured hand. Andrew winced from the pain, but seeing his antagonist sinking down to his knees was compensation for his suffering. He enjoyed a moment of gratifying satisfaction. With the penny safely in his hand, he hurried off into the crowd.

'Stop, thief! Stop!' As the man called after Andrew, one or two made as if to pursue him. There was a moment of confusion... of uncertainty. Taking advantage of the commotion, Andrew dodged deeper into the crowd and was soon lost to any would-be pursuers. Gradually his pace eased as he realised that his agitated progress was attracting attention. Curious glances were being cast in his direction, the last thing he wanted was to draw attention to himself. A furtive look behind assured him it was safe to walk.

Casually strolling, he turned into a narrow cobbled road. It was the smell of fresh-baked bread that attracted him in that direction. The pleasant aroma accentuated Andrew's hunger pangs. Eagerly he clasped the penny in his sweaty hands and hurried towards the bakery.

From the doorway of his shop, the baker, a short rotund man, watched Andrew's approach with an inquisitive look. Aware of the man's interest, he experienced a moment of uncertainty, but hunger drove him on. To draw back now would only arouse suspicion.

He paused outside the shop to look longingly at the display in the window. With a shaking hand he withdrew the penny from his coat pocket. Andrew's salivary glands secreted a tasteless moisture into his mouth as the appetising smell of the fresh baked bread wafted from the bakery.

'Good day t'yer, young man. Yer... face...' Andrew was aware of the baker's close scrutiny, '... seems familiar...' He frowned in deep concentration as he tried to recall his previous meeting with his potential customer.

'I'm... a... stranger to er... these parts.' Andrew's half truth was an attempt to cast doubts in the baker's mind. He was hoping the man would not recall their last meeting. A confrontation would perhaps be a better way of describing their previous encounter. Its sudden remembrance filled Andrew with remorse and shame.

'An... in that case...' he continued to look closely into Andrew's face as they stood just outside the doorway of the shop, '… 'tis a remarkable likeness.' Shaking his head slowly, he enquired if he could be of service. A customer was always welcome.

'Have you… a, er… small loaf?' Andrew watched the baker's frown deepen as he was offered the penny.

'Well… can't say as how…'

'Perhaps a slightly… stale one.' As Andrew made his plea, the baker became aware of how pallid and gaunt his customer looked. A hungry and woeful appearance that touched the baker's sympathetic nature.

'Here!; Reaching inside his shop he took a small pie from a shelf. 'Baked Wednesday… only a couple of days old.' Andrew's hand stretched eagerly towards it. As he did so the baker suddenly withdrew his ware as enlightenment came into his eyes.

'Now… I remember. 'as just come t'me.' Andrew was aware of the baker gazing knowingly into his face. 'It were you as took food from my shop…' his heart sank, Andrew was hoping that the incident had been forgotten. Now, of all times, he was being reminded of his indiscretion. 'Two of yer… rather drunk…' the baker continued without waiting for Andrew's confirmation, '… helped y'selves an'… refused to pay.' He gave Andrew an accusing look while he waited a response.

'Yes…' Andrew nodded ruefully, '… a most unfortunate incident. An irresponsible action that I sincerely regret.' He realised that his chance of food was rapidly fading. 'You have an excellent memory.' A wry smile crossed the corner of his mouth as he waited for the baker's next move.

'An a long'un, young sir.' Andrew nodded silently.

'A small recompense…' he offered the baker the penny, '… and I promise that one day you shall be repaid in full.'

'Aye… I reck'n yer will… but keep yer penny. It would appear that yer need is greater'n mine.' With a benign look, he gently eased Andrew's hand away. 'An' yer can have this here pie with my blessings.'

Andrew accepted the pie with a feeling of deep humility. Such kindness and understanding from a person he had once wronged, deeply moved him. With sincere humbleness he thanked the baker for his benevolence. 'I shall not forget my promise. One day when...' sadness was reflected in the baker's eyes as he watched Andrew's disconsolate figure shuffle away to the city centre.

For the remainder of the day, a weary and near exhausted Andrew wandered the streets hoping for a glimpse of a past friend or companion. Only once was his perambulations rewarded. Catching sight of a friend at last, he hurried across to exchange greetings. A warm smile brightened his pallid features as he neared his friend. It was Captain Ralph Fitzgerald. Now an ex-army captain and a prosperous one, if appearances were any criterion.

The irony of their meeting was not lost on Andrew. Their last time together, nearly three years since, had been the occasion when drunk and aggressive they had entered the baker's shop and taken goods to satisfy their besotted whim. A strange coincidence that he should be meeting Ralph on the very day that the victim of their mindless behaviour had been truly magnanimous in forgiving them their transgression.

'Ralph!' Calling his friend's name he hurried across the street to greet him. 'Ralph!' On his second call, his friend turned with a scowl on hearing his name spoken. As recognition dawned, he gave Andrew a silent contemptuous look. 'It's... Andrew... remember?' His voice faded to silence and disbelief as he noticed a look of sheer disgust cross Ralph's scowling features. With a repulsive sneer he gazed silently at Andrew for a few moments, then, turning abruptly away, he stepping into his carriage. Not a word was exchanged, but the silent look of contempt from his one time friend hurt and humiliated him deeply.

It was not only the evening chill that made Andrew shiver. His spirits had plummeted to the depths of despondency. He felt alone and forsaken as he wondered aimlessly around the city. Once he stumbled and almost fell as hunger caused him a spell of dizziness. Apart from the pie and a basin of broth that had cost him his last penny, he had partaken of no other sustenance since leaving prison. Now, hungry and dispirited, he shuffled down Bishop Gate towards the heath. Pausing to regain his breath, he glanced up at the towering edifice of the cathedral where the last rays of the setting sun reflected a celestial-like glow upon its tall spire.

Gradually the shadows deepened as the first flickering stars spangled the darkening sky. Another night sleeping out on the heath, thought Andrew. The prospect of that unpleasant ordeal made his footsteps falter. A sense of desolation overwhelmed him... was there no one he could turn to for comfort and hope?

Andrew's footsteps dragged as he approached the bridge. It appeared that he was doomed to spend another night shivering in the bracken out on the exposed heath. Just thinking of the wretched conditions filled him with despair, but he had no option – or had he?

He stopped to rest his weary body against the brickwork of the bridge. From above the centre archway of Bishop's Bridge, he gazed down into the dark depths of the river as it swirled beneath him. Was the River Wensum the answer to his utter despondency? Andrew continued to stare silently into the murky waters as if seeking an answer.

Its rippling surface held his gaze in a mesmerising grip. So easy, he thought. A peaceful end... no more worries. Distorted visions of his parents appeared to be gazing back at him from the water's depths. His father's angry features as he bade him leave and never return until he had safely returned the family jewellery.

As the vision of his father faded, it was gradually replaced by that of his mother's tearful and conniving countenance. Her hands were outstretched as if she were handing him a casket – the family jewels. The vision faded. In an attempt to disperse the hallucinatory apparitions, he shook his head vigorously.

What was he thinking of? Taking his own life was inconceivable. With an effort, Andrew controlled his trembling, but the river seemed to whisper his name as it splashed under the arch beneath his feet. A magnetic force seemed to draw his eyes back to the swirling waters.

As he looked down upon them, a vision of Maisie's pale and frightened face evolved in their gloomy depths. It was as if she was accusing him of the obscene act he had perpetrated. Forcing his body upon his own brother's wife had been the most despicable deed of his iniquitous life. He covered his eyes with shaking hands as if trying to erase the picture of that unforgivable moment, when his depravity had plummeted to its lowest depths. An act that he sincerely regretted... one that continued to torment him.

From the water's shadowy depths a voice seemed to berate him. Imagination, he tried to convince himself as he lowered his hands and peered again into the swirling river. The curses continued as he gazed into the distorted features of Maisie's brother. From the waters, he was accusing him with an expression of deep suffering.

The vision of Edward shocked Andrew. Because of his false evidence –perjury – he had been responsible for Maisie's brother being taken from the ones he loved and in doing so, had been indirectly the cause of his drowning on the prison transport.*

Involuntarily, he flung his hat to the ground and with an agonising groan began to clamber on to the brick parapet. Beneath him the water whispered harshly in the shadows. Their depths offering a tranquil haven from the troubles and strife of a world that held no future for him.

'Don't look back! Jump!' Andrew forced the words from between his gritted teeth. Moaning at his many tribulations, he forced his shaking body up onto the bridge.

'It's getting dark, Josh. Perhaps it would be prudent for us to return to our lodgings?' Jason cast a wary eye at the shadows that edged the river path. 'We must be early at the market. It is then that bargains may be...'

'Look, Jason! On the bridge!' Josh interrupted his companion's conversation to point to the shadowy outline of a bridge that spanned the river beside them. They had strolled, deep in confabulation, along the riverside path and had almost reached the structure, when Josh noticed the silhouette of a man acting strangely above the centre archway.

As the two walkers paused to listen, the man's tormented murmuring reached their ears. 'I do believe... he is about to

* In Book I The Winds of Destiny

cast himself into the...' Josh's words were lost as he raced towards the man. Just as the shadowy figure was preparing to cast himself into the river, Josh reached out and drew the man back.

'No friend! No! I beg you...' Josh pulled the man from the parapet. 'We can offer you help... salvation. Please share your troubles with us.' Josh was taken completely unawares by the man's reaction.

After closely peering at him in the gloom, he suddenly became very violent. Josh felt strong hands grab the lapels of his coat and almost jerk him off his feet. Even in the darkness, Josh could detest the hatred on his antagonist's face.

'I... mean... but... to help... you... friend.' Josh felt himself being forced back against the bridge. He offered no defence, hoping that his appeasing action would calm the stranger before him.

Jason, realising that something was amiss, hurried to intervene. He was almost upon them, when to his horror the man landed a punch on Josh's jaw. The force of the blow sent him staggering backwards, causing him to trip and fall. Jason intervened to prevent another blow being delivered to the hapless Josh. As the man struggled in his arms, Jason was aware that the stranger was berating a fallen Josh.

'You detestable cur! Deserting... Alison... and the ... baby.' He raised his fist as if to strike again, but Jason managed to restrain him. Andrew, anger straining his features, was being held in a bear-like hug that left him gasping.

'Enough! My Friend... meant but to... help thee.' Andrew was trying in vain to escape the strong arms circling him from behind.

'I want... no help... from a... despicable bounder.' Andrew was continuing to break free from the arms holding him as he spoke. 'A cursed... creature... who deserts... his wife... and child.' Realising there was no escape from the Quaker's grip, Andrew began to calm down.

'Does thee... know my companion?' Jason released Andrew as he raised the question.

'Yes! My brother-in-law...' Andrew snarled. 'And...' Jason raised his hand to stop further accusations.

'Then thee had best let me explain... our situation...' he looked round for Josh, only to see him stretched out on the ground with blood trickling down his chin.

'Dear Lord!' Jason gazed down at Josh's still form. 'Thee... has killed... him.; He turned angrily towards Andrew as he made the accusation. Dreading the worst, he hurried to where Josh had fallen after staggering backwards and striking his head against the bridge.

'I hope... so.' Andrew's vehement statement occasioned a strong rebuke. He was shocked into silence as Jason turned to glare at him.

'Hold thy tongue... thee... wicked infidel. You are mistaken about this good man's nature.' He nodded down at Josh, 'Thankfully...' Jason glanced up from his inspection of his injured companion, '... there is a pulse. He is alive... but unconscious.'

'He is... a rogue. A sinful...'

'Quiet!' Jason's voice left no room for argument. 'There is much thou needs to know concerning... this good man. To our community he is known only as Josh... but neither himself nor any of our Quaker community are aware of his true identity.' A worried frown wrinkled his brow as he noticed Josh's pallid features. 'If thou would kindly help me carry... then I shall enlighten thee as to his unfortunate circumstances.

'... thus, for about five years, Josh has farmed for me and become integrated into our Quaker Friendship near the Lincolnshire border. Every effort to ascertain Josh's true identity has failed...' Jason paused in his narrative, looking across the hearth as if expecting some reaction from Andrew. There was no response. Andrew could only shake his head in silent amazement as Josh's predicament infiltrated his stunned senses.

'In fact...' Jason continued, '..., Josh was to have married my daughter on our return... now an impossible situation.' With a melancholy look he watched the flames in the fire as if seeking an answer to his dilemma. 'Doreen... my daughter... will be heartbroken.' Jason's heavy sigh stirred the flames of the fire.

'I am deeply sorry, Jason. I did him a great injustice.' Andrew spoke the words sympathetically.

'Thou were not to know, my friend... he...'

'Saved my life.' Andrew interrupted. 'I was about to cast myself into the river...' He paused to reflect on what might have been his untimely fate. 'Now, 'tis Josh's life that is in danger.' Andrew buried his tear-stained face in his hands as his heart ached with remorse. He was suddenly aware of a comforting hand being placed on his shoulder.

'Perhaps thou would like to join me in prayers for Josh's recovery.' For the first time in his life, Andrew sank to his knees and shared in Jason's litany. Muffled footsteps eventually disturbed their meditations. Curtains at the foot of the stairs parted to reveal the puzzled face of the doctor.

'Your prayers...' he waited for them to rise, '... appear to have been heard, the injury is not as severe as I had expected but...' his frown deepened, '... he is very confused. Completely disorientated.' The doctor continued shaking his head reflectively. 'Seems to think he is on the road to ... London. To his solicitors in Newham. Strange... very strange.' The bewildered physician paused in front of the fire to give his recommendation. 'A few days rest should restore him to er... normality. There is little else I can do.'

Andrew and Jason exchanged shocked glances. In the ensuing silence, the doctor coughed discreetly. 'Oh, sorry, doctor. Thy fee of course.' Jason reached into his purse to pay the physician.

'Thank you... and good night, gentlemen.' He hesitated at the door. 'It would be prudent for someone to stay with your friend until he is fully recovered... his confusion troubles me. Otherwise all appears fine.' With these words of indefinite comfort, he turned and departed.

'What does thou make of it, Andrew?' Jason was deeply disturbed by the doctor's diagnosis. 'Josh's confused state is most puzzling.' Andrew could only nod a silent agreement. He was at a loss as to what their actions should be in dealing with Josh's confused mind.

'Perhaps we should confer with Josh?' Jason waited for the confirmation from his companion. 'If he is well enough, we will try and ascertain that which is confusing him.' Taking Andrew's silence as agreement, he continued.

'According to the doctor, he appears somewhat bewildered as regards time and surroundings.' Andrew agreed, still trying to get the situation into perspective. Events had moved so quickly, that he also seemed somewhat confused.

'A delicate situation for us all, dear friend.' Jason's voice reflected his concern. 'Come, let us speak with Josh.' Together they climbed the narrow stairs, apprehensive as to how they would find the patient.

'Why, Andrew... what brings you here?' As he spoke, Josh noticed the startled look that was exchanged between his brother-in-law and the soberly dressed stranger. 'Is... something... amiss? That is, apart from my aching head.' Gently he touched the side of his bandaged skull.

There was an uncertain silence as each of them waited for the others to speak. It was Josh who eventually broke the quietness in the room. 'Your friend...' he indicated Jason, '... will you not introduce us?' Josh had been aware of the man's close scrutiny since he had entered with Andrew. He smiled an acknowledgement in the stranger's direction. There was a moment of disconsolation following his words. Josh was suddenly aware that their distress was the consequence of something more serious than his injury. What then could it be? He remained silent – uncertain.

'Josh...' it was the stranger who came forward to address him, '... can thou not remember me... Jason?' A bewildered Josh stared uncertainly at the man pleading recognition. Slowly he shook his head as he tried to recall any remembrance of the man calling himself Jason.

For a few moments, Josh had continued his long, silent scrutiny of the man who had just claimed his friendship. Sadly he shook his bandaged head. 'I... must beg your forgiveness, but...' his voice was an uncertain whisper as he turned towards Andrew as if for support, '... I have no recollection of your... name.' As Josh's gaze returned to the stranger, he noticed the sadness that lined his face. 'I mean you no discourtesy, sir... but I cannot recall our acqaintanceship. Perhaps the attack... by the robbers...' Frowning, he paused to consider their attack upon his person. 'Concussion from the blow... may have dulled my senses...' Andrew noticed his brother-in-law's voice fade as his eyes closed. A deep silence settled over the room as the two visitors watched the still, pale face relax in an exhausted sleep.

Jason was the first to react. He indicated with a silent movement of his head that they should retire downstairs. 'We must discuss matters relating to... dear Josh,' he whispered to Andrew as they quietly descended the stairs.

'I agree with thee Andrew. The situation is very serious. Most confusing.' While meditating, he combed callused fingers through his shock of greying hair. Jason was finding the situation a very distressing one. 'Thou will need a horse to reach your uncle's place?' Andrew nodded. 'Best take Josh's mount then.'

'Foxleigh is but a few miles outside the city. I shall wait and ride back with my relations.'

'Good. A carriage will make Josh's journey... less fatiguing. Once at your relation's place, his recuperation will be less... distressing.'

'If, as seems confirmed by his confused state...' Andrew looked in the direction of Josh's room, '... my brother-in-law is suffering uncertainty in his memory, you could perhaps enlighten him as to his missing years, while I ride to Foxleigh. He has no recollection whatever of my fracas with him on the bridge.'

'None whatever.' Jason's unsteady voice reflected his shocked senses. 'He believes that his concussion was caused by the robbers who attacked him nearly five years ago. That was when we first found him. It would seem...' Andrew was aware of the tears in his companion's eyes as he reflected on the situation. 'That Josh has recovered his full faculties... but that his past five years with us...' Jason's voice was now little more than an emotional whisper, '... are now but a blank in his memory.'

Andrew nodded agreement as he prepared for his departure. It had been his idea to ride to Foxleigh and return with the carriage so that Josh could be taken there until he was well enough to make the journey to Highfield and his family. Jason's voice broke in on his meditation.

'... and while thou art away, Andrew... I shall enlighten Josh as to his missing years – his life in our Quaker community. His time spent praying and farming with us...' his distress was obvious as he hesitated before continuing his commendations of Josh, '... he was sincerely respected by all who met him.'

Jason shook his head forlornly as he thought of the young man he had taken into his home... his family. 'He will be greatly missed, especially by my daughter.' Sorrow filled his eyes as he spoke. It was a silent, reflective Jason that Andrew left behind as he set off for Foxleigh on his mission of mercy. A mission that was to culminate in his salvation.

Chapter Sixteen

'Comfortable, Josh?' Julie bestowed a friendly smile upon her companion as she fused over the travelling blanket covering his legs. There was a sparkle of excitement in her eyes as she anticipated the wonderful surprise awaiting his family. His unexpected return would be a wonderful surprise to Alison and his parents who had been distraught by his disappearance nearly five years ago.

Julie was confident that Josh's return was a good omen; a sign that one day, Edward would return to her. She had never given up hope of seeing again the man she loved. Julie's faith was to remain with her over the years.

'Yes, thank you, Julie.' Josh returned her smile rather apprehensively. 'I'm fine.' He had been in deep contemplation, still finding it difficult to comprehend all that the friendly Quaker had told him abut the past five years of his life. A period of which he had no recollection. Years, that as far as Josh was aware, had never existed.

'Coming to terms with my present situation has been something of a shock. It has caused me much distress, to think of the anguish and uncertainty that my family must have suffered during my absence.' His face was strained with concern as he looked into Julie's sympathetic eyes. 'Alison, especially must have been deeply upset at my sudden disappearance... not knowing what had befallen me.'

'You also have a charming little daughter, Jane. She was four last May.' Julie reached out gently and clasped his hand. 'We have sent word on ahead to prepare Alison for your arrival home. She always had faith that one day you would return.'

'According to Bamford...' the colonel spoke across the carriage, ' ... it was the blow to your head when you struck it against the bridge, that erased your period of amnesia.' He gave Josh an anxious scrutiny before continuing. 'Bamford, our physician, is of the opinion, that what you now remember is your life prior to the attack upon you by the robbers and all that has transpired since the... er, incident on the bridge.' He refrained from informing Josh that it had been an aggressive punch from Andrew that had caused him to fall and hit his head against the stonework of the bridge.

There was a pause as the colonel waited for a still weakened Josh to absorb his statement. As he waited for Josh's full attention, he placed his arm gently around his grandson's shoulders. George, who had been sitting beside his grandfather, had lost his initial excitement of visiting Homefield and was dozing fitfully as their carriage trundled through the East Suffolk countryside.

Julie's benign smile brought a radiance to her face as she glanced across the carriage towards her son. Snuggling close against his grandfather, he was trying unsuccessfully to keep awake. Satisfied that his grandson was comfortable, the colonel gave Josh a serious look before imparting information that he had hoped would elucidate any uncertainties regarding his missing years.

'For nigh on five years, Josh, you suffered what Bamford described as amnesia... loss of memory. Although it now appears your memory has thankfully been restored, those five years are... will remain a blank in your mind – possibly forever.'

'That would appear to have been my fate, Colonel Markham. The Quaker who found me unconscious by the roadside and took me into his family, enlightened me as to those lost years. I thanked him most sincerely for his kindness and asked for his name and the location of his community. That information was not forthcoming. I was informed that it would perhaps be best if those details remained untold... for the present at least.' For a few moments, Josh's face reflected his emotive thoughts as he tried to remember what had transpired during those missing years.

'I know the Quaker's name was Jason, but so little else about him and his friendly community.' Josh heaved a deep sigh of regret. 'It would appear that a personal friendship concerning myself and his daughter was causing him some distress. However, despite my questioning, he gave no indication as to that which troubled him.'

'When we arrived with the carriage,' the colonel leaned closer to impart his information, 'Andrew and the Quaker were exchanging confidences before departing together.'

'Andrew... accompanied the Quaker?' Josh seemed surprised.

'Yes. Andrew accepted the man's... er, Jason's invitation to travel with him. An invitation that my nephew seemed very glad to comply with.'

'Oh... look, Josh!' Does that not remind you of home?' Julie's excited voice interrupted the men's discourse. She was pointing towards the magnificent knapped-flint church that rose majestically from the marshlands of the river Blyth.

'Blythburgh church!' Excitement overwhelmed Josh as he recognised the church that he had attended on many occasions in his capacity as a rector. As they crossed the river, he realised that his journey was nearly over. Home was but a few miles away.

An emotional longing stimulated his elation as he thought of his beloved Alison waiting to welcome him home... to Highfield. Had she changed much, he wondered. How had she managed during his absence? It must have been a struggled for her to keep the farm solvent in addition to attending their home – and little girl. A daughter he had never seen. He felt Julie's hand rested gently upon his, as if she was aware of his irresolution.

'You... will notice changes, Josh.' He realised that Julie was trying to prepare him for the meetings ahead. 'Since Seb's... death, Maisie has been running Homefield. My uncle relies upon her expertise in the day to day running of the hall.

The news of Seb's death at Waterloo had come as a shock to Josh. When Julie had broken the news of his friend's death in action, Josh's sympathetic thoughts went out to Maisie, who he realised must have suffered much heartache at having the husband she dearly loved taken from her in such a cruel manner. Perhaps the birth of their son had helped ease the anguish, he had suggested to Julie, on being informed of the young Jonathan's birth. As the thoughts returned, he shook his head sadly, remembering the happiness of Maisie and his friend in the immediate years before Seb's departure into the cavalry.

Julie had also brought him up to date with the news of his parents. They had suffered poor health, but he had been assured that despite their infirmity, there were signs of gradual improvement. 'Your father...' she had compassionately informed him, '... has found it necessary to curtail his ecclesiastical duties to give more care to your mother.' Her words had distressed Josh as he thought of the anguish his parents must have endured because of his absence.

'Why did my father not retire, Julie?' He remembered how distressed he was when making the enquiry, but Julie's reply had eased his troubled mind.

'It was your father's wish...' she had turned a smiling face towards him before answering, '... to remain rector of Homefield until your return. He was confident that at some future date you would return and take over his duties.'

Now as they neared Homefield, he spoke of that which had been causing him much distress. 'What... news have they received from Becky?' Josh had noticed the colonel and Julie's reluctance to discuss news of his sister. It was as if they were trying to hold back news that might delay his recovery. It was Julie who had replied after his enquiry if any correspondence had been received during his absence.

'None... to my knowledge, Josh. Their distress at receiving no news was aggravated by your... disappearance. Alison informed me that the two misfortunes devastated their lives.' Josh grieved in silence for his aged parents. How they must have suffered during the uncertainty of the past few years.

He shook his head as if trying to shake off his despondency as he gazed out of the carriage window. His spirits rose and a feeling of elation overcame him as he noticed the familiar countryside. Soon he would be able to visit his parents and reassure them that all was well. First, he must hurry to Highfield where his dearest Alison and Jane, the daughter he had never seen, awaited his return.

With mounting excitement, Josh watched Homefield Hall come into view. He experienced a strange sensation as he glimpsed the Jacobean edifice through the trees. Its reflection on the unruffled surface of the lake, mirrored its grandeur. Thankfully, he was almost home.

Would Alison, he wondered, see in him a reflection of the man she had lost for five years. Although he had come to terms with his period of lost memory, he was apprehensive as to how his wife would react. Anxiously his gaze kept returning to the carriage window where he expected at any moment to see his lands – his home, Highfield.

Deep in meditation, Josh rode down the lane towards his old farmhouse. After the hectic arrival at Homefield, where he had been warmly made welcome, he was now nervously anticipating his homecoming. Holding a tearful Maisie in an affectionate embrace, he could not fail to see the deep sorrow in her lovely blue eyes. His homecoming must have been a reminder to her that the man she loved would never return.

War, with all its horrors had claimed the only men she had ever loved. Then Josh remembered her brother, Edward, who had been wrongly accused and transported to the penal colony of New South Wales. He had been reported as drowned, when the ship taking him and other convicts to the colony, had gone down in mountainous seas. Her sadness was understandable.*

'I'm sorry, Maisie… truly sorry.' He had gently whispered his commiscration's.

'Thank you… Josh. Your homecoming… has reawakened… such poignant memories. A reminder of…' She could not continue. Choked with emotion, Maisie eased from his embrace and hurried to greet Julie and the colonel.

Now as he rode down the lane toward his home, he shook his head sadly. He was remembering Maisie's distress at their reunion back at Homefield. He sighed emotionally as he watched Highfield draw ever closer. He would soon be with Alison. What would be her reaction after their long enforced separation? He would soon have the answer, as he had reached the outer yard of his farm. Beneath the shade of the old walnut tree, he pulled his horse to a stop. Slowly, his misted eyes moved round the farm and the outer buildings. All seemed in a well maintained condition. Beyond the barn he could see the surrounding fields, now mostly stubble after the harvest.

* In Book I The Winds of Destiny

He brushed the tear from his cheek with the palm of his hand as he beheld the idyllic scene before him. His home... his farm. Eventually his eyes came to rest on the woman emerging from the dairy. It was Alison, his beloved wife. Josh wanted to rush over and embrace her. To kiss her dear face. Hold her close in his arms again.

'Alison!' Softly he called her name. She paused, uncertain at first from whence the call had come. Josh moved out into the sunlight and quickly dismounted. For a brief moment they surveyed each other in silence. A precious moment that would forever remain a treasured memory. An instant of bliss, a greeting that would stay a perceptible image in their minds through the remainder of their lives.

'Josh! Oh, Josh!' Alison hurried across the yard to welcome her husband. Tears of happiness glistened on her cheeks as they shared an affectionate embrace. 'Oh, Josh...' she sobbed, '... it's so wonderful... to have... you back. Just... wonderful.' Alison was endeavouring to express her feelings between kisses. Her prayers had been answered, she was reunited with the man she loved. They eased apart to gaze silently at each other. No words were necessary to describe their emotional empathy. Love was reflected in their smiling eyes.

'Mummy!' It was Jane's small voice that interrupted their affectionate embrace. Alison, overwhelmed by the occasion, had momentarily forgotten their daughter. She reluctantly moved from Josh's arms and walked over to the little girl. Holding her by the hand, Alison walked proudly back to Josh, a loving smile hovering on her face.

'Jane... this is your daddy. The one we said our prayers for each night, remember?' Jane nodded uncertainly, events had left her slightly bewildered. 'Perhaps you should say hello... and tell him your name?' For a moment his daughter silently surveyed him with her bright grey-green eyes. Her chestnut brown hair, ruffled by the wind, had a sheen of burnished gold in the dazzling sunlight. After a few moments her solemn voice broke the silence.

'Hello, daddy... I'm... Jane!' Her face gradually relaxed into a cherub-like smile as she stood shyly before him.

'Hello, Jane.' Josh squatted down beside her and held out his arms. Without a trace of hesitation she rushed into her father's fond embrace. As he held her close, he glanced over her head towards Alison. As he did so, tears of happiness trickled down his face and onto Jane's chestnut hair that was so like her mother's.

Josh experienced a feeling of contentment. An emotion of complete happiness as he held his daughter close in his arms. Peace overwhelmed him, satiating him with loving thoughts. He stood up and, holding Jane's tiny hand in his callused one, walked over to join an emotional Alison. They were together again, a family united in joy – and love.

As Josh looked into Alison's eyes, he became aware of those emotions. His warm smile creased the corners of his eyes as he gave her an enamoured look. For the first time he became aware of the flecks of grey in her hair and how the lightly furrowed brow reflected the strain of running the farm in his absence.

With a tender look, she waited for his reactions. Alison wondered if the intervening years sine his departure had diminished his love for her. Relief induced a radiant smile and a blush to her cheeks as she became aware of her husband's sensuous gaze upon her. His look held a promise of love being gratified at the first opportunity. Their enforced abstinence would soon be forgotten as they shared their amorous longings in a new awakening.

* * * * *

How's your lad making out, Jem?' Josh had been walking down the lane with his herdsman when he put the question. Alison had praised Jem's support when she had struggled to keep the farm operational on her own.

'He be doin' fine, Mr. Josh.'

'That also confirms my observations, since my return last September, Jem. He's a good lad... a good worker.' Josh nodded as if confirming his own assessment. They paused by the new cottage that had been the cause of much speculation among the labourers and villagers alike. Josh and Alison's silence on the eventual resident had only served to increase the mystery.

'Think Tommy is capable of taking over your Job, Jem?' Josh watched the emotions flicker across his herdsman's face. Shock, disbelief and uncertainty. He smiled inwardly as he awaited an answer.

'Well... er, yes... but...' Jem was bemused, a little upset to think his job was in danger, even if it was to his own son.

'Good!' Josh nodded emphatically. 'I'd like him to take over as herdsman... from today.' There was a deathly silence as the two men looked across the hay field to where the grass was just coming into flower. Almost ready for cutting, Josh speculated as the silence intensified.

'I... er, don't... rightly follow... yer, Mr. Josh. Does... yer mean... that my services... be no longer... required...?' Jem's voice faded to silence as sadness filled his eyes. He had been at Highfield for well over thirty years. His first and only employment. Now it seemed as if...

'Goodness me! Nothing like that, Jem. I need you as my new manager.'

'Manager?' There was a gasp of surprise.

'Yes. I'm taking over my father's church duties in the parishes of Homefield and East Wensum and I'm hoping that you will run the farm for me during my absence.' He waited for Jem's response, but the long serving herdsman was temporary lost for words. 'As you are aware, Jem, your mistress is for the moment indisposed.'

'When... is the baby... expected, Mr. Josh?' His voice was still shaking from the surprise of the offer of manager.

'Any day now, but... she has been unwell of late.' Jem noticed his employer's worried look. A sign that all was not well. He remained silent, waiting for Josh to speak first.

'Think you can do the job for me, Jem?'

'I'll hev a good try. One thing yer c'n be cert'n of... I'll not be lettin' yer down, Mr. Josh. That be a promise.'

'I'm sure of that, Jem. That was my reason for wanting you as my manager.' Josh watched his companion's face as he continued. 'This...' he pointed to the newly built cottage, '... goes with the job, Jem. You can move in when you like.' Josh smiled inwardly as his newly appointed manager tried to thank him. An emotional Jem could barely nod his acceptance, but the excited look in his eyes was a reflection of his appreciation.

Josh stood quietly by the window, the warmth of the early June sunshine upon his face as he watched the distance reapers in the hay field. 'Josh!' Alison's voice was weak with fatigue as she called his name. He turned and hurried anxiously to her bedside, a warm smile softening his solemn countenance as he did so.

'Alison, my dearest. I thought you were sleeping.' He eased himself into the chair beside her bed. Then taking her hand in his, he leaned over and kissed her pale cheeks.

'I... I feel... that I have... let you down. . dearest, Josh.' Her voice was soft with distress as she looked forlornly into his eyes.

'No! No, my love!' He sounded perturbed as he noticed how distraught Alison had become. 'You must on no account harbour such thoughts. It... it was God's will that our baby girl should be taken from us at birth.' Tenderly and with loves shining in his eyes, he tried to console his tormented wife. 'She will be at peace in God's loving care. Please Alison, my dearest...' he paused to gently kiss her lips, '... there is no reason to reproach yourself.' His sincerity and sympathetic words induced a feeling of peace to a weak and exhausted Alison.

'I shall pray for your continued recovery, my love.' His embrace so gentle and affectionate eased away her heartache in her fatigued body. For her husband's and little Jane's sake, Alison was determined to share in their activities again as soon as possible. It was this determination that accelerated her recuperation from her unfortunate ordeal of having her baby stillborn.

On her first outing, Alison accompanied Josh to the village church. There in a quiet and sheltered corner of the grounds stood a small wooden cross by a fresh mound of earth. Beneath the canopy of elms that shaded the area, Alison stood beside her husband and read the words through misted eyes. Carved on the cross were the words that were the cause of their emotional reflections – Emily Kennard. Died at birth. 31st May 1820.

* * * * *

'Happy birthday, George!' Julie greeted her son with a proud smile. Colonel Markham, sitting opposite at the breakfast table, had however, noticed the sadness in his daughter's eyes. For just over ten years she lived in the hope that her son's father, Edward, would one day return. The colonel shook his head imperceptibly at his daughter's obduracy in refusing to accept that the man she loved was dead. Refusing, despite his name being listed among those who had perished on the transport Badger when she was lost in a tropical storm. Julie intuitively continued to believe that Edward was still alive. That one day he would return to England and share her love.

'My blessings and good wishes on your birthday, George.' The colonel gave his grandson a benign look. 'Ten years old... double figures at last, eh?'

'Thank you mother... thank you grandfather.' His smile was expectant as he cast a covert glance around the room. He could discern no sign of a present. This negative observations cause a disappointed frown to flicker across his face as he took his place at the table. He failed to notice the conspiratorial wink that his grandfather gave his mother.

'I've arranged with your tutor for you to have a free day, George. No lessons on your birthday and...' his mother glanced insouciantly out of the window, '... and it's such a glorious day.'

'Thank you, mother.' A disappointed George was wondering during his breakfast how best to fill his free day. After the meal, he thoughtfully followed his mother and grandfather down the steps and on to the lawn. They paused for a moment to admire the sweep of the park lands. A magnificent view with the deciduous trees displaying their autumnal hues. George's observation of the scenery was distracted by a movement in the stable yard. Captivated, he watched as Jim, the young undergroom, walked towards them leading a large pony.

Its chestnut coat had a lovely sheen, while a white flash down its forehead gave the animal a distinctive appearance. George had never seen the pony before. Must be a new one, he thought... a recent addition to the stables. He was about to enquire, when his grandfather's voice interrupted his contemplation.

'What do you think of the new pony, George?' By this time, Jim was standing directly in front of them with the pony. A wide grin spread over the young stable lad's features as he handed the reins to a bewildered ten year old boy.

'A beautiful pony, grandfather... but...' he turned a puzzled look towards the colonel and then to his mother. Enlightenment gradually dawned as he became aware of their happy, smiling faces.

'He's yours, George. A birthday present from your mother and myself...'

'It's a... wonderful present.' Breathless with excitement, he turned and thanked them both. With gentle hands he patted and rubbed the quiet pony as he spoke. 'May I... ride him today?; He enquired over his shoulder as he continued to stroke his precious birthday surprise.

'That, George...' the colonel chuckled, '... was the reason your mother and I bought him.' George shared in their laughter. 'If you can contain yourself for a few moments,' the colonel nodded towards Jim, '... you can ride with me on my rounds of the estate.' The stable lad was already hurrying towards the stables to prepare the colonel's horse.

'I'd love that, grandfather.' He led his pony across to his mother. Tears filled her eyes as she received his embrace. 'Thank you mother, it's... it's a wonderful present.' Still in an ecstatic mood, he turned and smiled at his other benefactor. 'Thank you also, grandfather.' He walked over and warmly embraced the colonel, who swallowed hard at his grandson's act of affection.

A few blooms still lingered in the garden, attracting Julie's attention. She experienced a melancholy feeling as her father and son departed on their ride. A wistful expression crossed her face as she watched George proudly leading the way on his new pony... Flash. She wiped the tears from her cheeks with her lace handkerchief before turning to walk into the garden. Her original intention had been to gather a bouquet for the house, but realising that they would be among the last of the season, decided to take them to the churchyard.

Silent with remembrance, Julie stepped back to gaze at the flowers she had just arranged on her mother's grave. She was thinking of the treasured moments they had shared as she looked pensively at the lovely bloom. She turned to go but paused as she became aware of the young rector, Robin Darvell, walking slowly towards her.

Since the death of the old parson Jameson, he had been living at the rectory with the ageing Agnes as his housekeeper. Taking pity on the charming sister of his predecessor, he had invited her to continue in the duties that had always been hers. 'Just until I'm settled, Miss Agnes.' Julie for some reasons that she could not explain, had reservations about him.

'Good morning, Miss Markham... a very beautiful one, is it not?' He stopped close beside her as she smiled a greeting and confirmed his assessment of the weather. Julie was apprehensively aware that his encounters with her were occurring more frequently and if she was not mistaken – predetermined. Realising that his intentions towards her were becoming serious, she had continually tried to ensure that their meetings were never shared alone.

On this occasion she had been unsuccessful and now found herself greeting the handsome young rector with uneasiness. 'I'm glad I find you alone... Julie.' She noticed his hesitation before he used her name. Familiarity that only increased her nervousness in his company.

'I am at your service, Mr. Darvell,' she was trying to get the conversation on a more formal footing. 'Unfortunately, I am... expected back...'

'Oh, please, Julie...' His manner induced an invidious feeling, a disturbing emotion. 'We are friends and it would bring me pleasure to hear you call me Robin.' His eyes held hers as he invited her friendliness. As the colour came to Julie's cheeks, he looked around as if to ascertain that they were not under observation.

'Thank... you ... Mr. er,... Robin.' She endeavoured to hide her irritation as she realised that he had deliberately conspired to meet her in the churchyard alone, where there was little chance of their privacy being interrupted.

'Christian names make it sound much friendlier, don't you agree, Julie?' His intimate smile as he awaited her answer, only increased Julie's nervousness. She nodded silently, trying to think of an excuse to leave as she did so. 'It is my dearest wish...' the look in his eyes filled her with anxiety, '... that we should become friends and confidants.'

With his insincere smile lingering on his face, he reached out to take her hands in his. Julie fought to remain calm as she realised that he was about to kiss her. She was aware of the impassioned gleam in his eyes as he gradually lowered his face to place his lips upon hers.

'I think...' Julie eased away from him, '... that we should refrain from such indiscreet behaviour, especially in public, Mr. Darvell... er, Robin.' She noticed the frustrated frown as she disengaged her hands from his. 'Such conduct, were our meetings to become public knowledge, would be an embarrassment to us both.'

'Please forgive my... actions, Julie. I was momentarily carried away by your nearness. Your attractive person. I am deeply sorry.' She noticed the strange look in his eyes. One that troubled her as she recalled it later. 'My only excuse...' he continued, '... is my love for you.' In the deep silence that followed his words, George's anxious call reached her ears.

'Mother! Mother!' Julie caught her breath as she noticed her son riding his pony at great speed towards them. 'Oh... mother... it's grandfather!' He pulled his pony to a stop. 'He... he collapsed... at the forge.' He was breathing heavily as he turned towards the rector. 'Please forgive... my interruption, sir... I...'

'That's alright, George. Your mother and I will be over immediately.' Walking beside Julie they hurried together down Forge Lane.

'George...' Julie called to her son, '... ride over and inform Doctor Bamford of your grandfather's... illness.' She watched anxiously as her son urged his pony into a gallop to comply with her instructions. He was soon lost to their vision as he turned by the green.

'A prudent... precaution... Julie.' He was having difficulty in keeping up with her as they crossed the field towards the forge.

* * * * *

'What day is it, my dear?' The colonel eased his head off the pillows to glance across towards his anxious daughter.

'Friday... but you are not to...'

'Friday?' There was a moment of silence. Julie watched the frown deepen on her father's face. 'That... that means...' he gave her a shocked look, '... I've been lying her... two... no, three days?'

'Yes, father... and Doctor Bamford's orders are that you are to remain for a few more. At least until he calls on the morrow.'

He tried to ease himself up in the bed. After a few unsuccessful attempts, he gave up. 'Don't seem to have... much strength in me, my dear.' Julie noticed the distress in his face. There was an uncertain almost pleading look in his eyes as they met hers. To hide her tears, Julie walked across to rearrange the pillows and to assist him into a raised position against them.

'Your weakness, father...' sitting on the bed beside him, she reached out to hold his hand before continuing, '... is the result of your... heart.'

'What did Bamford have to say?' He gave her a quizzical look.

'That you had suffered a mild stroke. Rest is important...' Julie gave her father a meaningful stare, '... and that your weakness would trouble you for some time.'

'Nonsense, my dear. I'll show you... how...' She watched in distress as her father slipped helplessly across the bed when he tried to raise himself.

'Oh, father!' Julie helped him into a comfortable position. 'You must not... over exert yourself... please. Doctor Bamford is arranging for an attendant to help me care for you until you are... well again.'

'I'm sorry, Julie, my love. I shall endeavour to be a good patient...' he gave her a loving look, '... and to do as I am advised.'

'Thank you father. Between us we shall soon have you well again.' She did her best to hide the deep concern in her voice.

'I hope so, my dear! I sincerely hope so!' Closing his eyes, he sank back on to the pillows and remained quite still. After a few minutes silence, Julie, thinking her father was sleeping, walked quietly from his bedroom.

With sadness in his eyes, the colonel watched her departure. 'If only you would marry.' His whispered words did not reach her troubled mind. 'Without a husband the burden of running the estate will fall heavily upon you, Julie, my love.' He recalled the two potential suitors who had tried to court her without any success. Now, the third and latest, unless he was mistaken in his observations, was the young rector, Robin Darvell. A possible choice, but one again it would appear that Julie was avoiding any affectionate involvement with a serious suitor.

'It's no good, Julie dearest...' he spoke his thoughts aloud once the door had closed behind her, '... Edward unfortunately is dead. You cannot live with a memory, my dear.' Gradually the colonel's eyes closed and sleep obliterated his melancholy cogitation's.

* * * * *

Beside the grave, the man dressed in sombre clothes that identified him with the Quaker community, stood with his head lowered in silent prayer. Motionless, he remained staring down at the freshly made mound as tears trickled down his cheeks to moisten a grey-flecked beard. His dark curly hair, streaked with grey was ruffled by the early autumn breeze. Through tear misted eyes he read the words on the newly erected headstone.

Doreen Douglass.
Wife of Andrew.
Died 24 September 1823. Aged 25 Years.
'Your love was my Salvation.'

Andrew did not look up when he heard footsteps behind him. Since his wife's death just over a month ago, grief seemed to have numbed his senses. He continued to stand in prayer, his black hat with its broad half-cocked brim was clasped low down in front of his body.

He was suddenly aware of an arm gently encircling his shoulders. A sympathetic voice came to him as if in a dream. 'We all share thy grief, Andrew... Doreen was loved by us all.'

I know, Jason,' Andrew's eyes never moved from his wife's grave as he spoke of their past, 'my only regret is that Doreen and I shared so little time together. Barely a year of marriage... eleven months of joy and happiness, then...' Andrew's shoulders drooped in a disconsolate gesture as his gaze continued to rest on the grave of the woman who had given him love, peace and honour. The baby they had waited for with love and excitement, the cause of his wife's death, had also been taken from him at birth.

'Come, Andrew. Come and share in our prayers...'

'Prayers, Jason! I sometimes wonder if they may not be in vain?'

'Nay... Andrew. Prayers can bring comfort from the Almighty... but thou must have faith and understanding.' Gently he led Andrew away from the burial ground. 'Hast thou given any thought... to thy future?' Andrew gave his companion a bewildered and silent look. 'I realise that it is early days yet and thy sorrow is great, Andrew... but life... must continue...'

'My future?' There was a note of uncertainty in Andrew's voice. 'Why my future is with the community... if it is thy wish?'

'We shall be pleased to have thee, Andrew. Thy help on the farm will be greatly appreciated, but we would like thee to stay, mainly because thou has accepted our religion in a true and sincere manner.'

'While sharing our lives... our prayers, thou has earned the respect of the whole community. Unfortunately, it was God's will that thou were not to find a lasting happiness among us. The Friends have offered their prayers as a comfort against thy great loss. Should it be thy desire to remain with us, thou can be certain of their lasting support.'

Andrew nodded a silent acknowledgement to Jason's words of comfort. Realising that his father-in-law had additional words to impart, he refrained from any comment. Words seemed irrelevant somehow in his shocked and heartbroken situation.

'After Josh, thy brother-in-law had departed, thou not only replaced him in our fields, but also in our hearts. With kindness and true humility, thou showed our heartbroken daughter that moments of deep sorrow can eventually give way to a reborn happiness.' It was the reference to his dead wife that once again filled Andrew with sadness.

'When...' Jason cast a sympathetic glance in Andrew's direction, '... after three years n our community, thou asked for Doreen's hand in marriage, we realised that our prayers for her happiness had been answered. Your acceptance by our community made our decision an easy one. Our blessings for you both were but an echo of the feelings of every member.'

'If only our happiness could have continued... our years of joyfulness together been a more lasting experience. If only...' sadness choked off Andrew's words, curtailing his soulful speculation.

'It was the Almighty's will, my son. Perhaps we shall find the answer within.' He stood aside for Andrew to enter their place of assembly. Inside, friends and relations awaited the appearance of Jason and Andrew so that prayers of remembrance for the kind and gently woman they had lost could be offered to the Almighty. Doreen's presence among them would never be forgotten.

As Andrew lowered his head in prayer, he meditated about his old ways. Drink, gambling and carousing among the sinful, such thoughts filled him with remorse. His prayers asking forgiveness became more fervent. As if animated by heavenly inspiration, he moved to the tribune at the furthest end of the meeting place where he exhorted the assembly into prayers for his forgiveness.

A strange phenomenon occurred during Andrew's emotional beseechment. As he continued his passionate speech, pleading forgiveness for his past sinful ways, a brilliant shaft of Autumn sunlight pierced the gloom inside the hall. The slanting brilliance of light was centred upon the man leading prayers from the tribune.

There were those present who believed that the vision they observed was caused by dust motes dancing in the ray of brilliant sunlight. Others were of the opinion that the vision was the result of the dazzling sunlight reflecting a sheen from Andrew's greying, sweat-moistened hair. All those in attendance were in accord that they had momentarily glimpsed a halo-like apparition above the man seeking salvation. As the aureole gradually faded and the sunlight paled, Andrew sank down onto his knees in a final act of supplication.

'Thee hast shown true humility, Andrew.' Jason reverently laid his hand upon the shoulders of the still kneeling man. 'I feel sure that thy remorse for past transgressions will find favour in the Almighty's eyes.'

'Jason...' slowly Andrew rose to stand before his mentor, '... one day soon I shall depart on a mission that will take me to a distant land across the seas.' Jason nodded his head understandingly as he became aware of the light burning in his companion's eyes. 'It is my desire...' Andrew continued with a kind of inspirational look, '... to sail for the new colony of Australia. There, I hope to spread the words of our faith and at the same time search for evidence that the man I falsely accused and caused to be transported as a convict is alive or as is more probably – dead.'

'Thee must do as thy conscience says, Andrew...' Jason's whispered concurrence encouraged his son-in-law to speak further of his distant mission.

'Before my departure, I intend to visit my parents and...' Jason noticed the sadness and sorrow that lined his protégé's face, '... to beg their forgiveness for the anguish I have caused them.'

'I feel sure that thy parents will respond favourably to such a sincere offer of repentance, Andrew. Your leaving will sadden us all, dear friend, but in thy absence, we shall all pray for thy mission to be concluded successfully. In return, the favour we request is that thou remember us who love thee, in thy prayers.' Andrew lowered his head in silent assent.

The hands of destiny, however, had already set in motion, circumstances that were to prevent Andrew's reunion with his family and their absolution. Fate was slowly and inexorably directing the participants towards a tragic conclusion.

Chapter Seventeen

With their coat collars turned up against the cold, late February wind, the two riders guided their mounts along the grey ribbon of road in the direction of East Wensum. A chill wind swept the sulphur-yellow pollen from the hanging 'lambs tails' that dangled from the roadside hazel bushes. As they passed over the bridge, the woman pointed out the lesser celandines that spangled the banks of the meandering beck.

'Spring messengers!' Maisie smiled as she indicated the celandines golden blooms to Jonathan. Her son nodded his understanding at her information as he rode proudly on his black pony beside her. The pony had been a given to him by his grandparents, Sir Roger and Lady Anne Douglass. Since that celebration at the start of the month, Jonathan had been out riding every day.

'There is still traces of ice in the shallows, mother...' he gave her a cheeky smile. 'I hope you're right about the spring messengers.' Maisie laughed her agreement as they continued their ride between banks lined with gorse. A brief spell of late winter sunshine had already prompted the sprinkling of golden-yellow flowers on the spiky stems of the bushes.

A male yellowhammer was proclaiming his territory with a series of quick, harsh notes from a vantage position on one of the thorny bushes. In front of them, a blackbird swept low over the road, its harsh alarm-notes 'tchinking' a protest at their appearance. The bird's activities were a reminder to Maisie, that the labourers would soon be busy sowing the fields.

Thinking about the estate made her glance in Jonathan's direction. Eventually, he would become heir to Homefield Hall. Maisie experienced a moment of trepidation as she wondered if he would ever know the truth of his conceivement. Sadness overwhelmed her as she recalled the heinous act perpetrated by Andrew, her brother-in-law, on the night when he had furtively entered her bedroom and forced himself upon her.

Recollections of her ordeal on that night after Seb's departure to Belgium still tormented her. Andrew's distress and his sincere expressions of remorse on the following morning had barely eased the trauma she was experiencing at the time. The shock of Seb's death in action at Waterloo had removed much of her apprehension about the child she was carrying. Everyone had assumed that Jonathan was her husband's child. Only she was aware of the truth, that Andrew was the father.

'There's Jane!' Jonathan's voice broke in on her uneasy meditations, he was pointing ahead to where his cousin was waving a greeting as they approached Highfield. Alison, alerted by her daughter's excitement, joined her with the latest addition to her family cradled in her arms. An affectionate smile spread over Maisie's face as her friend with seven week old baby William in her arms waited to greet their arrival. Over the years, the shared misfortunes and heartaches of the two mothers had cemented a lasting friendship of trust and empathy.

'Josh is visiting his parents...' Alison paused as they walked towards the house, her face reflecting her deep concern, '... his mother's health has greatly deteriorated. She now spends most of her time in bed.' Alison shook her head sadly as she invited Maisie to sit in one of the chairs. 'I believe the distress at receiving no news from Rebecca has aggravated her condition.' She stood at the window, looking back towards the unseen rectory as she spoke of her mother-in-law's infirmity.

'It's nearly twelve years since Becky and Stephen departed.' Alison turned towards Maisie as she continued her disclosures regarding her in-law's distress. 'Since then they have suffered much anguish for their obdurate action in refusing to bless Becky's marriage to Stephen. An action they now most sincerely regret.' A deep sigh escaped her lips as she thought of her husband's enfeebled parents. 'If only Rebecca would write and reassure them... accept their forgiveness.'

'Father-in-law suggested several months back that Josh should write a letter to his sister and explain their regrets and how sorry they were for what had transpired between them. There has been no reply, it's as if Rebecca has been.... Taken from us.' That possibility induced a few moments of sad contemplation's, as all three had been friends before Rebecca's departure.

A commotion out in the yard drew them both to the window. Josh had returned and was patiently listening as Jonathan proudly explained all about his pony. After listening attentively for a few moments, Josh thanked him for his information and then encouraged the children to continue their play. He was anxious to join his wife and Maisie, as inside the letter he carried was some wonderful news.

Seeing their thoughtful faces at the window, he raised the letter that had caused his joyful elation. A feeling of expectancy filled the room as they awaited Josh's entrance. 'The letter must be important, Maisie. I wonder who it is from?' They were soon to be enlightened.

'It's from, Becky!' Josh waved his sister's letter as he entered the room. 'Dispatched last October... just over four months ago.' Excited exclamations escaped the lips of the two women.

'Please, Josh... read it.' Alison was anxious to hear news of her long departed friend. 'Don't keep us in suspense.'

'Perhaps you would rather I....' Maisie was preparing to leave.

'You will do no such thing.' Alison placed her arms around Maisie and guided her back to the couch. 'You are one of the family. We want you to share in our news from dearest Rebecca.'

'Indeed you must, Maisie. Some of the news concerns you directly.' Side by side the two friends sat and listened while Josh read from the letter. Silently and with tear-filled eyes they heard of Becky's traumatic experience when the ship taking her and Stephen to the new colony had gone down in heavy seas. Anguish showed on their faces as Josh related how his sister, when close to death, had eventually been rescued. They listened in shocked silence as he read on.

'... tell Maisie and Julie not to despair about Edward. I am still unable to inform you of the unusual circumstances surrounding his fate. Suffice is for me to say that there is hope for their eventual reunion one day. His safety is...'

Maisie's quiet sobbing caused Josh to pause in his reading. With tears running down her cheeks she looked up into his face.' Oh, Josh... do you really think... that Edward is... is...?' Overcome with hopeful emotions, she was rendered temporarily speechless. Alison's comforting embrace gradually induced a feeling of calm that pacified Maisie's overwrought state. 'Sorry, Josh. It's just... that...' She sighed in bewilderment, unable to explain her emotions.

'We understand, Maisie.' Josh tried to comfort her. 'Alison and I also share your optimistic expectations.' It was a compassionate look that he bestowed upon her before raising the letter to continue reading some other news items in its neatly written pages.

'...now have three farms, two adjoining and the third is about a hundred miles away. A total of nine thousand acres in all...'

There were gasps of amazement as they tried to imagine the size of all the farms. 'That's an area...' Josh frowned in concentration, '... nearly twice as large as our two villages, Homefield and East Wensum, combined.' They could only shake their heads in amazement. Alison, anxious to hear more, encouraged her husband to continue his reading of his sister's letter.

'... I have three children. Marian who is eleven, Stephen was nine last June and Roger celebrated his sixth birthday last month (September).

Tell dearest Alison that Elizabeth, the girl we had an altercation with at Newlands, is out here. The incident regarding the necklace has been pardoned and we have become dearest friends.

Elizabeth is married to Robert (Morrison), an experienced surgeon who came out to practice in Sydney...'

Josh continued to read about the fire that had nearly destroyed their farm... their home. Her details of Stephen's kidnap brought gasps of horror from the two mothers. Becky in her letter had stressed the part played by Henry in her son's rescue. Edward's part, indeed his existence, was tactfully avoided. His safety was still of paramount importance to her life. His true identity, even to friends and relations, must still remain a secret.

There was a long silence after Josh had finished reading Becky's letter. Maisie was first to break their quiet deliberations. 'Do you not find it strange, that Becky never once mentioned her husband, Stephen?'

'Extraordinary indeed, Maisie. That fact had not escaped my notice.' Josh reflected for a moment before folding the letter. 'We must assume that he is well and prospering.'

He waited until the excitement of the letter had eased before mentioning its final words. 'The most exciting part of the letter is in the post script.' He smiled as their faces were turned expectantly towards him.

'Oh, Josh! You are deliberately keeping us in suspense.' Alison gave her husband a playful rebuke. 'Now you must tell us immediately what Rebecca's good news is.'

'Gladly, my dear. Becky informs us that at the first opportunity, she is hoping to return to England to spend a few months with us.' Josh chuckled as his wife and Maisie squealed their joyful response. After the initial excitement had passed, Maisie's smile faded and was replaced by a puzzled form. 'Rebecca's letter raises my hopes regarding Edward, but her information is so... so ambiguous. Almost mysterious as to his... circumstances. His fate remains as uncertain as before.'

'I must agree with your conjectures, Maisie. My sister's statement that she is still unable to convey any definite news of your brother appears to indicate that Becky has previously communicated with us regarding his situation.' Josh shook his head as he again opened the letter and perused once again the few lines relating to Edward, but he could find no clues as to the whereabouts of Maisie's brother – or if he was even alive. Josh found his sister's news regarding Edward so very imprecise.

'What am I to tell dearest Julie when I next write her?' Maisie looked anxiously from Alison back to Josh, seeking their suggestion... their help.

'We must try not to raise her hopes without...' Josh indicated the letter as he folded it, '... any corroborated evidence to confirm his existence.' He frowned as he replaced the letter in his pocket. 'You can but mention that my letter from Becky appears to infer that...' Josh tried not to sound too pessimistic as he made his suggestion to Maisie, '... Edward may have survived the Badger's sinking. Perhaps...' noticing Maisie's sadness, he tried to sound more positive... more helpful for her sake, '... Becky is intending to enlighten us on her visit.'

'Oh, Edward...' Maisie sighed, '... if you are safe, please... please let us know.' Sorrow lined her face as she reflected on the uncertainty surrounding her brother's fate.

* * * * *

In the evening sky, the fading colours of the sunset imparted a crimson glow to the heavens. Behind the distant trees, the sun, a blood-red orb was sinking from view after another warm day. In the meadows, conical haycocks basked in the sun's fading light. On the still evening air lingered the fragrance of freshly mown hay.

Maisie sat by the lake, her evening refuge after the hectic routine of running Homefield and nursing the acrimonious Lady Anne. Each day Maisie found herself the target of the invalid's increasing animosity. Her every effort to placate her bedridden mother-in-law was repulsed. Now, with her patience waning, Maisie was finding the strain of nursing her almost unbearable.

A despondent sigh escaped Maisie's lips as she tossed a pebble into the lake. A moment of tranquillity pervaded her thoughts as she watched the ripples radiate over the mirror-like surface of the water. A moorhen, disturbed by the splash, flapped frantically over the lake in an endeavour to reach the safety of the reed-lined shallows opposite.

'May I join you?' Maisie's smile faded, the moorhen's amusing actions were forgotten as she turned towards the person who had intruded upon her seclusion. Her peaceful interlude... her solitude was being disturbed.

'If it is your... wish.' Her reply held a hint of asperity. She appreciated the organisation and effort with which Charles managed the estate, but of late their relationship had been a strained one. Despite her attempts to avoid being alone in his company, he still persisted in paying court to her whenever the chance arose.

'Thank you for the warm invitation.' Maisie was aware of the sarcasm behind his words. Not that his attitude troubled her greatly. There had been an uneasy peace between them since the incident near the old Abbey ruins a year or so back. Thinking of it even now induced a chill of fear as she recalled their encounter. While Charles settled on the seat beside her, visions of that skirmish flashed through Maisie's memory.

Its occurrence was on the eighth anniversary of Seb's death at Waterloo. Maisie's emotions as she remembered Seb's passing had reached a restless state. At the time she had just wanted to be alone... at peace with her melancholy thoughts. Memories of that last afternoon they had shared together near the old Abbey's ruins. By noon, under an azure sky with just a whisper of cloud to stain its vastness, she had ridden off towards their last trysting place.

Once there, she had stretched out upon the grass in the secluded and peaceful surroundings of the crumbling Abbey. There, her sadness had faded. Peace and a warm, satisfying serenity had overwhelmed her. 'Oh, Seb!' She had sighed. 'I still miss you so, my darling.'

Slowly her melancholy emotions had faded. Lying on her back in the warm sunshine, she had experienced a strange feeling... as if Seb was stretched out on the grass beside her. She had smiled as his happy laughter seemed to drift across the years. Her eyes had remained closed as she tried to hold the vision of Seb in her thoughts.

It was then that a dark shadow had crossed her face, interrupting her meditations. A puzzled frown had replaced her smile as she opened her eyes to see the silhouette of a man against the sun. Anger drove out any feelings of fear as she began to rise.

'Charles!' She suddenly recognised the intruder. 'What... are you doing up here?' Anger gave her voice a sharp edge.

'Such a quiet and lonely place...' Maisie experienced a moment of shock as she realised his intentions. 'I thought that we might share...' he lowered himself down beside her and pressed her back on to the grass, '... a few moments of... pleasure.' She recalled how her efforts to release herself from his hands had been thwarted. His grip had been far too strong for her.

'Please! Please Charles! You're hurting me.' Maisie had struggled inwardly to remain calm, hoping that her impassive plan would deter further action on his part. It was only when he released her hand and was trying to lift her dress, that her composure erupted.

Anger, hate and revulsion gave her a maniacal strength to fight off Charles' improper advances. He was not to know that Maisie's violent aggression was a reaction to the humiliation that she had once suffered.

Once again the vision of Andrew's lecherous look as he had forced himself upon her became a vivid imagination. Her response was a reflex action that caught Charles completely by surprise. Before he could protect himself, Maisie's finger-nails scratched deeply into his cheeks and across his eyes.

With a cry of anguish he straightened up and was preparing to kick her half recumbent form. Anticipating the move, she had jabbed the heel of her riding boots hard against his shin. As he staggered back in pain, Maisie had scrambled to her feet ready to defend herself.

'You... you, whore!' Rage burned in his eyes as blood trickled down his pallid features.

'How dare you use such a... a term. Your vile... insinuation demeans yourself, an...'

'If... if you're not a whore... how is it that you have a child... that is not Seb's?' Maisie fought to control her emotions as the impact of his accusation struck her senses.

'What... obscene thoughts your... anger has induced.' Maisie had tried to remain calm, but had found it difficult to hide her shock... her guilty emotions. 'You have no justification for making such... indecent imputations against me. Against the wife of your one-time companion and friend.' Her quiet dignified charm appeared to calm his temper.

'It would appear... that I er... must have misunderstood, Seb.' Charles had paused as if trying to recall his friend's confidence as they had prepared themselves for their attack on the French cavalry at Waterloo. It was as if Seb had a premonition that he was not to survive the battle.

'If... I should be killed... my one regret is that I shall leave no heir... to Homefield.' Aware of his friend's melancholy thoughts, Charles had good naturedly suggested that his two nights at Homefield might well have fulfilled his wish.

'No such good fortune, dear friend. Maisie and I, because of our family commitments, were unable to share each other's arms. No chance of an heir this time,' he had shaken his head at his disappointment. 'fortune may perhaps bless us next time... if there should be a next time.' As the vision of Seb faded, Charles was suddenly aware that Maisie was watching him closely, expecting a formal apology for his salacious innuendo.

'Yes... I must have misunderstood, Seb.' Charles, calmed by his remembrance, turned towards Maisie to beg her forgiveness. His act of remorse turned to deep concern as he noticed the pallor of Maisie's face and the shocked look in her eyes.

'Please allow me to escort you back to Homefield, Maisie. I, er... completely lost my senses. I'm deeply sorry... for the distress my... accusations have caused you.' He extracted his kerchief and used it in an endeavour to clean the blood from his cheeks.

'I very much regret any torment that my injudicious remarks may have caused you.' Gently, he helped a shocked and silent Maisie to mount with but a minimum exchange of words they rode back to Homefield.

Since that day, a feeling of enmity had existed. Outwardly they had displayed a shared friendliness, but their original trust and understanding towards each other had been irrevocably broken. Visions of their past confrontation vanished as Charles settled on the seat beside her.

Silently, Maisie watched the fading hues of the sunset shimmering upon the ruffled waters of the lake. A breathtaking kaleidoscope of rippling patterns influenced by the gentle caress of the evening breeze upon the surface of the lake.

'I am leaving Homefield, Maisie.' Charles was the first to break their uneasy silent. Turning towards her in the twilight, he informed her that Sir Roger had been made aware of his decision. 'No doubt, he will discuss it with you later.'

'Yes... yes, I expect so.' Maisie was not surprised at his statement, but she nevertheless experienced a moment of regret.

'We... shall miss you Charles.' All traces of asperity vanished from her voice as she turned towards him. 'Thank you for your help and... comfort in the early days of my... my loss.' Her smile was a little strained, but sincere as she thanked him. 'When will you be leaving us?'

'I promised Sir Roger that I would stay until most of the harvest is gathered in.'

'That was most considerate of you. Thank you again.' She hesitated a moment before reaching out to take hold of his hand. 'I'm sorry... truly sorry, if the... situation turned out contrary to your expectations. Perhaps it was for the best.' Her last words were little more than a sigh.

'Sounds rather like a well-used cliché, Maisie... but I understand and appreciate your sincerity. Thank you.' He raised her hand to his lips before rising. 'Now I shall leave you to your peaceful meditations.'

* * * * *

Andrew, after a brief stop at Scole, continued on the last stage of his journey to Homefield. If his progress continued on schedule, he should reach home by the evening. Apprehension induced a feeling of strange emotions as he meditated on the reception he would receive. Should I have contacted my parents first? Warned them of my visit in advance? He was hoping to share a few days with them before he continued his journey on to Portsmouth, where he planned to take a ship to his ultimate destination – Australia.

It was his third day on the road. A life time it seemed since he had bid farewell to Jason and Mary, his dead wife's parents. On the morning of his departure they had shared a tearful parting, unsure if they would every meet again.

Andrew sighed with remembrance as he recalled how tired they had been after a night spent in discussion and prayers. Their worship had been for his safe passage into a harsh, uncertain country. His last view of them was of distant figures waving after his retreating figure. Their kindness and love, together with that of their now dead daughter, had been his salvation. Andrew felt a new person... a better man for knowing them and in sharing their lives.

His first day, riding through the fens and the flat arable lands of West Norfolk, had taxed his weary body to the full. On two occasions his lethargic state had caused him to sway in the saddle. In an attempt to overcome his lassitude, Andrew had decided to dismount and walk beside his horse for a mile or two.

Vaguely, he recalled passing landmarks from the journey he had first made with Jason, nearly five years previously. Five years that had changed the course of his life, thanks to the friendly and caring Quaker community. Despite his feeling of inertia, he spent long periods of his journey remembering the happy and contented years he had shared with Jason's family and friends. The Quakers had made him, a stranger, welcome in their homes – and in their hearts.

In his hour of need they had helped him find salvation and an inner peace. Andrew recalled with humility how they had invited him to join in their activities, their prayers – their lives. Gradually he had become captivated by their sincere and devout approach to life and soon found himself sharing in their meditations.

For several months he had helped his mentor's daughter, Doreen, overcome the heartbreak of Josh's departure. Carefully and sympathetically he had explained to her the illness that had caused her betrothed's vagueness about his early life and its sudden re-emergence. How his involuntary disappearance from his family and friends had caused heartache and tears for his wife and little daughter. Gently and with a kindness that previous to his Quaker correlation would have been incongruous to her character, he had persuaded Doreen that it was God's will that Josh should be reunited with his family.

Eventually she had come to understand the reason for Josh's actions and his wish not to return to a place and people he no longer remembered. Five years of his life that would probably forever remain a blank in his memory.

Andrew had shared Jason and May's concern as they helped their daughter to overcome gradually her traumatic experience. A heartbreaking process that Doreen found it difficult to transcend before she once again settled back into her family routine.

Realising that his friendliness with their daughter was troubling her parents, Andrew assured them that their concern was unnecessary. Once he had promised that his intentions towards Doreen were honourable and that his respect towards her was most sincere, their apprehension had eased.

As Andrew rode along the dusty road, his thoughts lingered on those days he had shared with Jason and his family. Inevitably, his friendship with Doreen had blossomed into love, a precious affection that had been fulfilled in their marriage.

Sadness creased Andrew's eyes as he remembered his wife's death. He continued to miss her greatly, despite the eleven months since her passing. Involuntary he wiped the tears from his dusty cheeks with the back of his hand. Overcome emotionally, he heaved a deep sign and brought his horse to a stop.

In the shade of a roadside oak, he dismounted to rest his horse and to stretch his legs. While he rested he watched the reapers and their gatherers at work in a field of wheat. The harvesters reminded him of home. Perhaps it would be possible to help in the last of the harvest at Homefield, but that would depend on how his father reacted to his offer of regrets for the disgrace he had brought upon the family.

'Perhaps not!' He sighed as he shook his head thoughtfully. 'My destiny...' his whispered words carried softly on the gentle breeze, '... has been ordained.' In a moment of deep meditation, he had seen a vision of himself sailing to fulfil his mission of mercy in a distant land. A self-imposed retribution for his perjurious statement that had sent an innocent and honest man to transportation and possibly to his death.

Andrew had been overcome with remorse for his past iniquitous life. An existence that had been changed by a spell in prison and a period of reformation among the friendly and forgiving Quakers. Silently he prayed that his father and Maisie would be as understanding. His behaviour to both had been abominable.

'Dear, Lord!' his voice was little more than a whisper, 'Help them to find forgiveness in their hearts for the iniquities I once inflicted upon them.' Andrew's head remained lowered in prayer

– and shame. He was remembering the hurt and distress that his wicked actions had caused the two people he greatly admired. Slowly he raised his head, then, after replacing his hat, he mounted his horse and continued upon his homeward journey.

As he approached Homefield, Andrew experienced an unusual sensation of expectation, but his elation was tempered with a deep uncertainty. His elongated shadow moved ahead of him as he rode down Hall Road between the woods. Home at last, but it would only be for a day or two. Hopefully the reunion with his parents would be a welcome and forgiving one. Andrew prayed that he would be able to continue his mission with their blessings.

He was expecting no encouragement to stay at Homefield. Andrew fully concurred with his father's actions regarding the estate's future. Receiving their pardon for his past misdemeanours would bring peace to his troubled mind. By his nefarious deeds he had forfeited the heirship to the lovely old hall and estate that would rightfully have been his after his father's death.

'You were right to disown me, father,' he whispered as he turned nervously into the West Drive past the now empty lodge. Andrew pulled his horse to a sudden stop as he became aware of two distant figures. One, a woman, was sitting alone by the lake, while a man was walking down from the hall towards her.

He recognised both Maisie and his father. As he watched, Maisie shaded her eyes with her right hand to look directly at him. Andrew experienced a moment of indecision. His thoughts were in a turmoil as he turned his horse back on the road again.

Realising the distress that his sudden appearance might cause her, he decided against meeting his sister-in-law that evening. Highfield would be his destination He would stay overnight at his sister's farm. Spending the night with Josh and Alison would prepare him for the meeting with his parents and Maisie on the morrow.

His decision was to prove a fateful one. An action that was to have repercussions to haunt him for the remainder of his life.

As Andrew guided his horse slowly down the road towards the village, he paused occasionally, still undecided whether to return to Homefield. He experienced a restless feeling, an instinctive emotion that seemed to be urging him to return to the hall.

'In the morning...' Andrew voiced his thoughts as if trying to dispel his uncertainty. He continued on his way to East Wensum away from the pending tragedy.

Andrew did not see his father join Maisie down by the lakeside, where all appeared so tranquil after a day that had started so disconcerting for both of them. Sir Roger's early morning confrontation with his wife had troubled him greatly throughout the day. It was still on his mind as he walked pensively down towards his daughter-in-law.

He had gone as was usual each morning on arising to greet his invalid wife. That morning as he had entered her bedroom, Lady Anne had screamed demonic abuse against Maisie, that had momentarily shocked him. Her vitriolic outburst had caused Sir Roger to remonstrate angrily.

'You're... being very... irrational, Anne.' Struggling to control his temper, he had interrupted her unwarranted tirade against Maisie. 'You would do well to show your appreciation for the care and nursing she has ministered to you over the years, instead of vilifying her'.

'Trust you to... defend her. I hate her... hate her.' His wife's demented look as she spat out the words shocked Sir Roger. 'She is nothing but a... pretentious strumpet.' Lady Anne glared defiantly at her husband as saliva drooled from her lips.

'Quiet, Anne!' Anger made him shout to stop her vituperation. 'You're an irascible woman, constantly venting your enmity on a daughter-in-law who should be the recipient of your grateful thanks. I wonder at times how she can be so caring towards you. Especially after the malice that you have subjected her to.' Sir Roger paused to ensure that his meaning was clear to his disturbed wife. 'As for your injudicious remark...' his eyes as his gaze met hers glinted with anger, '... I consider it a most hateful and imprudent assertion. It is nothing but malicious fabrication in your... tormented mind.'

'Mad! So that's what you think I am... Mad!' Sir Roger had watched in anguish as his wife's reasoning became once again poisoned with vindictiveness. 'Malicious fabrication is it?' She snarled. 'Well, ask her who... fathered her child!' A shocked silence settled over the room.

Lady Ann realised that her anger had stimulated her into an injudicious remark. As the words penetrated Sir Roger's anguished mind, she had recoiled from his shocked and outraged look. It was the innate feeling of respect for his wife that prevented him from striking her. As his anger was replaced with a sensation of disgust, he had turned sharply and hurried from the room.

Fighting to control his emotions of anger, Sir Roger had paused in the open doorway. 'You're... disturbed, Ann. Your mind is filled with hatred.' As he turned and walked away, her voice taunted him.

'Ask her then. Ask her when you're sitting beside the lake talking with the fisherman's brat this evening. You've spent the last few evenings talking with her and...' He walked rapidly away from the spiteful, hate-filled voice.

Maisie eased herself onto the grass, close to the rustling reeds that edged the lake. She felt tired and confused after a hectic day in the house and later in the harvest field. For a break from the household complexities she had gone to check on the progress of the reapers and to organise refreshments for the harvesters. She sighed as she settled down on the grass, wishing that Charles could have stayed for just a few more days. His departure had meant a frail Sir Roger and herself overseeing the final stages of the harvest.

Now, as she relaxed by the lake side, she was remembering the days worrying problems.

It had started with Liz Fuller's temperamental outburst before breakfast. An unusual outburst from the matronly, grey-haired cook, when she realised that her carving knife was missing. Her staff had all pleaded innocence, suggesting that she may have temporary mislaid it. An idea that she had vehemently denied.

When Maisie had made her routine visit to the kitchen, Liz had emphasised that mislaying the knife had not been possible.

'I remembers sharp'n an' cleanin' it yisterd'y evenin'. When I finished, it was replaced in the drawer.' She pointed defiantly towards the cutlery cupboard.

'Never mind, Liz... I'll see that you have a replacement.'

'Carn't un'nerstand it,' she shook her head while a puzzled expression clouded her face. 'Why should anyone want 'a take me knife. Don't like it, mistress...' she continued to shake her head in a forlorn manner, '... 'tis like losin' one a' me family...'

Maisie had smiled inwardly at the simile and at the same time given an agitated Liz a comforting assurance that the knife would probably turn up before the day was out. Her optimism, however, was not to be confirmed.

Soon Maisie was to find out that her frustrations had only just started. As she made her way cheerfully towards Anne's bedroom, she was closely followed by Lucy carrying the breakfast tray. As they progressed on their morning ritual, Maisie spoke to the young maid about her friendship with Denis, the Head Groom.

'Oh, Mistress Maisie...' Lucy's blush gave her surprised features an attractive look, '... didn't realise that yer knew 'bout it.' Her nervous giggle was a reflection of her shyness.

'We're all...' Maisie paused to whisper in feigned confidence, '... waiting an invite to the wedding.' Lucy nearly dropped the breakfast tray at her mistress's words.

'Oh... but... we have no place t'live... as yet.' She stammered.

'Haven't you noticed what has been going on at the two Lodges since they became vacant?' There were confidential connotations to Maisie's question.

'Why yes, Mistress Maisie... builders seem t'be workin' on 'em.'

'That is correct, Lucy. They are in the process of being renovated.' Maisie smiled at the maid's puzzled look. 'The West Lodge is almost ready for occupation. Now... if you and Denis...' Lucy received a suggestive look as they stood together on the landing, '... were to become married, there is every possibility that the lodge would be available for you and your husband to move into.'

'Oooh... Mistress Maisie...' Noticing that the breakfast tray was in danger of slipping from Lucy's excited grasp, Maisie relieved her of Lady Anne's breakfast.

'I'll see to the tray, Lucy. You just slip over and have a word with your young man.' An extremely happy Lucy hurried away, smiling and crying with a joyful heart. Maisie also experienced a brief moment of happiness as she watched the young maid disappear in search of her betrothed. It was but a momentary peace. A serenity that was soon to be shattered.

'Good morning, mother-in-law.' Maisie realised that her warm greeting would be ignored, but her feeling of joy was something she wanted to share.

'Don't call me, mother-in-law, you... you... wanton strumpet.' Her venomous words induced a shocked numbness to Maisie. She was used to and came to expect abuse from Lady Anne, but this vitriolic attack momentarily stunned her. Her hands were shaking as she placed the tray down on the bedside table. She pretended not to have heard the slur on her character.

'I don't want that offal.' Lady Anne looked with burning hatred from the food tray into Maisie's bewildered eyes. 'You can take it back...' she leaned over, grabbed the tray and then tipped the contents onto Maisie. As the food and drink spilled over Maisie's dress and down onto the floor, a fiendish laugh escaped the perpetrator's lips.

'You're an... evil woman...' Clenching her fists, Maisie struggled to control her temper. To give herself time to regain her composure, she started to gather the mess from the floor.

'That's all you're fit for...' Lady Anne's demented ranting continued, '... gathering dirt from the floor... you... you... slut.' Maisie straightened up, her face white with anger as she walked towards the invalid. Anger blazed in her eyes. Now, aware of the acrimony that her tirade of abuse had aroused in a normally placid Maisie, Lady Anne tried to ease away from her daughter-in-law's ominous approach.

'Don't ever... use that degrading word to me again. Ever. You... you ungrateful creature.' Maisie spoke quietly, but the steel in her voice held a threat that quietened the cowering invalid.

There was a strained silence as they gazed into each other's eyes. Maisie eventually broke the inert ambience.

'Now you can eat it!' Maisie place the tray of gatherer up food on the bed and stood back with a determined look. Her features stern and unforgiving. Lady Anne whined her protests. 'Eat it... now!' Maisie ignored the look of hatred bestowed upon her and the gagging attempts of her mother-in-law to swallow the mixed up food. Her pleading looks were ignored by an obdurate Maisie.

'Only if you apologise for your obnoxious remarks.' Lady Anne's look of malice directed at Maisie was a mask of her determination not to make any gesture of remorse. Time and again she gagged with food in her mouth, unable to swallow the contents.

'I'm... sorry...' There was a vibration of enmity behind her words, despite her spoken regrets.

'Thank you, Lady Anne.' Maisie turned and walked slowly and with dignity from the room. The harsh, angry whisper of her mother-in-law's words, as she left the room, caused a frown of consternation.

'I know! You... you... fisherman's... bitch!' What, or how much of the truth did her mother-in-law know, Maisie pondered. Was she aware of what took place on the night of Andrew's attack upon her? Impossible. Unless... no... She shook her head at such an impracticable idea. Nevertheless her words troubled Maisie, who was meditating on the accusations as she made her way to Jonathan's room.

Despite the early hour, she found the room empty. Her eight year old son had already departed for the harvest field. Maisie shook her head as a benign look softened her worried features. At least she would receive no querulous words from her son. Their relationship was trusting and – loving. If only he had been Seb's son. Maisie's sigh of regret was a whispered lamentation.

Her son's absence to be with the harvesters reminded Maisie of Charles' recent departure. It troubled her to think that she was possibly responsible for his leaving. Her earlier refusal to accept his proposal of marriage had placed a strain on their unsettled relationship. She thought of that afternoon up by the Abbey ruins when he had tried to... Maisie endeavoured to shut the incident from her mind. Her angry rejection... refusal, had been the cause of his eventual departure. Of that she was certain.

'We shall manage!' Her determined whisper was a reflection of her mood as she relaxed in the evening sunshine.

Even after the remembered visions had faded, Maisie had continued to gaze thoughtfully into the ruffled waters of the lake. Their crimson hues of the reflected sunset held no portentous significance to her tormented mind.

Maisie's troubled thoughts returned once again to that morning's confrontation with her mother-in-law. Lady Anne's acrimonious words had induced a feeling of guilt. Emotional distress. The insinuating words were still ringing in her ears.

'I know! I know! I know!' the words kept repeating themselves in her agitated thoughts. How could she possibly know... Andrew would certainly not have confided such... Maisie's thoughts were interrupted as she shaded her eyes to watch a rider hesitate at the West Lodge entrance. She felt disappointed when the soberly dressed man turned his horse and continued on towards the village. Her emotions would have become more troubled had she recognised the rider as the man she had just been thinking of -- Andrew. The rider's appearance had however, transferred her thoughts to the present.

Maisie had decided to inform her father-in-law when he came down to talk with her that evening. Throughout the day she had been meditating about telling him the truth concerning Jonathan. Her confession regarding Andrew's behaviour would cause him much distress, but it was right that he be informed of the truth. Over the years she had often considered confessing to Sir Roger, but her courage had failed whenever the moment had seemed appropriate.

As there had been no news of Andrew since Josh's return, nearly five years previous, Maisie had decided to keep her secret. Lady Anne's outburst that morning had caused her to reconsider the situation regarding her son. Whatever the consequences, Sir Roger must be informed – that evening.

Three evenings ago, while sharing confidences on the seat beside her, Sir Roger had informed her that Jonathan would inherit Homefield after his death. He was heir apparent. Maisie had been startled by the revelation. It was then she had reconsidered her decision and to confess the truth to her father-in-law that Jonathan was the outcome of Andrew's violation of her body. That moment had now arrived. She felt tense and nervous as she pondered on how best to broach such a sensitive incident.

'May I join you, Maisie?' Despite being aware of his approach, his words startled her.

'Yes... yes of course father.' Her worried smile touched the old man's troubled mind. He was greatly concerned about the strain and burden being placed upon her.

'I'm glad of your presence, father... there is something... serious I must discuss with you.' Maisie realised that now was the time to make her confession.

'As I gathered from your troubled expression, my dear. First I have an urgent message from Jonathan...' As he paused, Maisie turned to look back towards the hall. A frown creased her forehead as she wondered what the urgency of her son's message was. Just then, as her gaze was resting on the house, she was just in time to catch a glimpse of Lady Anne observing them from her bedroom window. Aware that she had been seen, she stepped back behind the curtains. On past evenings, Maisie had been conscious of movement at her mother-in-law's window whenever Sir Roger had joined her by the lake.

There were occasions when she experienced feelings that her innocent meetings with her father-in-law were under close observation. Now she had proof. Personal verification that Lady Anne was not completely bedridden as she would have them believe.

'... he wishes to discuss some urgent observation with you.' Sir Roger's words interrupted her speculations. Noticing Maisie's hesitation, he expressed a further reflection. 'Jonathan did appear rather agitated.'

'What can be so... so urgent?' Her evening confession seemed to be in jeopardy. As Maisie hesitated further, Sir Roger's next words confirmed that Jonathan was anxious to see her as soon as possible.

'That is what your son informed me, my dear. He did seem rather distressed and was eager to confide in you. My assurance that you would be with him immediately seemed to ease his... agitation.'

'Than, if you will excuse me, father, I shall leave you to...'

'Of course. My impression...' his face was clouded with concern, '... was that he was rather upset about something.' The last statement encouraged Maisie's hurried departure.

'I shall not be long.' She spoke over her shoulder as she walked quickly away. 'I have serious thoughts... a confession to discuss.'

'Then I shall wait for your return, Maisie.' His benign look gave way to a chuckle. 'Your promise of a... serious talk intrigues me. As a matter of fact...' Sir Roger's face became stern with uncertainty, '... I also have a rather sensitive matter... that I must discuss.... Er clarify with you, Maisie.' His hesitant words caused Maisie to pause briefly. Intuition warned her that their discussions would be on a related subject – Jonathan's birth.

'In that case I shall return as soon as possible, father. I feel our concerns are mutual.' It was a very apprehensive Sir Roger who watched his daughter-in-law walk back to the hall with her characteristic limp.

Compassion replaced his concern as he reflected on her courage. He was full of admiration for her tenacious spirit in coping with his wife's enmity and aggressive behaviour. Maisie's management of Homefield and her help in running the estate had also occasioned a feeling of veneration for her competence.

Glancing away from his daughter-in-law's retreating figure, he was unaware that her departure was related to the tragedy that was about to affect them all at Homefield. Sir Roger experienced a feeling of guilt that his wife" derogatory words about Maisie and her son, should have raised any doubts about her probity.

As Maisie entered the hall, a figure moved furtively from a side door. Gliding ethereal-like from bush to bush, Lady Anne in her night gown made her way unseen down to the lake. She crouched briefly behind some lake side bushes, waiting an opportunity to confront her husband and the fisherman's bitch. From her window she had observed them talking by the lake and was hoping to attack them both unexpectedly.

'Damn the bitch!' She cursed under her breath. 'Where is she?' Lady Anne, her eyes glazed with insanity, searched the area with her eyes in the hope of seeing Maisie. She held her responsible for the disinheritance of her favourite son, Andrew. Hate blazed from her eyes as she looked around for a sign of Maisie. Shivering from the chill of the dusk air, she settled down among the shrubs to wait. When she found the girl... her hands gripped the handle of the carving knife until her lust to kill became an overpowering obsession.

'Jonathan, what troubles you... what is so urgent? Grandfather thought that you were... a little distressed.' Maisie, a little breathless from hurrying from the lake side, gazed down at her son as she walked over to his bed. 'Could your information... not have waited?' She gave her son a puzzled look.

'It's about Grandma!' He hesitated. Uncertain about what he was about to relate. 'She had... a... knife.'

'A knife?' Shock waves pulsed through Maisie's trembling body. She tried to control her moment of fear.

'Yes... when I visited grandma to say Good-night, I glimpsed it sticking out from under her pillow. She tried to cover it with the sheet when she realised I was looking at it.'

'Was... it... a kitchen knife, Jonathan?' Her voice was little more than an anxious whisper.

'Yes...' He nodded his head, '... one like Liz uses in her kitchen.'

'Dear God!' Maisie looked around frantically as panic threatened to engulf her. What was happening? What did it all mean? Forcing herself to remain calm, she turned to Jonathan. 'Stay here... until I return.' She tried not to show her concern as she paused and turned to face her bewildered son. 'Remember, Jonathan... please remain in your bedroom.'

Having imparted that advice, Maisie hurried along the landing towards Lady Anne's room. Trembling with misgivings, she knocked sharply on the door before entering. She steeled herself for an attack of some description, but all was quiet. The room was empty.

Maisie rushed to the pillows and lifted them. In her haste she cast them aside, but there was nothing under them. The knife and Lady Anne were missing. Where was her mother-in-law and what was going on in her mind? Involuntarily, she swept a searching glance round the room before walking across to the window.

She had a panoramic view of the parklands fading into the dusk. The drive was a pale ribbon in the shadows and as her gaze centred on the opaqueness of the lake, she noticed Lady Anne.

The sight she beheld shocked her. A scream rose in her throat, but the horror of what she was witnessing constricted her throat muscles so that only a choking sound emerged from her lips.

Maisie watched, momentarily paralysed with fear as the knife flashed in the fading light before it sliced into the neck of Sir Roger. As his wife prepared to strike again, he turned to defend himself against her frenzied attack. Blood from his fatal wound, splashed his face and clothing.

As they struggled, Sir Roger and Lady Anne became a blurred image to a shock and vertiginous, Maisie. Forcing off her faintness, she dashed unsteadily from the bedroom and down the stairs, alerting the staff as she went.

Her startled calls forewarned the staff. Pausing briefly in the hallway, Maisie directed a bewildered Bates to send one of the staff for Doctor Wallace and to bring him down to the lakeside on arrival. Then, gathering her skirts, she scampered off in the direction of the confrontation. Breathless and trembling with shock, Maisie raced to intercede in the struggle she had seen from the window.

Panting from her exertions, she pulled up in horror by the edge of the lake. She was too late. Sir Roger, still gripping his wife's hand that had held the knife, was floating in the lake.

Lady Anne, her white night-dress wrapped around her like a shroud, drifted face down in the water beside him. Both were dead.

It appeared to Maisie, that as blood had pulsed from his severed jugular vein, the dying Sir Roger had staggered into the lake dragging his wife with him. There, unable to release herself from his hold, she had drowned beside her dying husband.

Maisie could only stare in disbelief as the water around her dead in-laws became stained with blood from Sir Roger's fatal stab wound. Had she remained with him by the lake, she also might have been a victim of Lady Anne's frenzied attack.

Maisie's head began to spin as dizziness overcame her. The parkland faded and swirled as she staggered in anguish from the shock she had just experienced. A grey mist came to her eyes. Slowly her legs gave way as she collapsed on the grass in a faint.

Chapter Eighteen

Maisie, weakly raised her head from the grass. Bemused and dizzy, she gazed around through misted eyes. Shock had caused a momentary blackout. As she tried to orientate her situation, she notice the water lapping the reeds close to where she was lying. It was the sight of the lake that shocked her into immediate awareness. Her gaze shifted to the reed-lined shallows. Sir Roger and Lady Anne floated lifeless in the water. They were gradually drifting away from the lake's edge.

Taking some deep breaths to restore her numbed senses, Maisie staggered out onto the short landing stage. She attempted to grasp the bodies, but they were just beyond her reach. Fighting back her fear, she held onto one of the upright iron stakes that secured the landing boards. By hanging on with one hand, she was able to reach out over the water with the other and take a grip on her dead mother-in-law's ankle.

Lady Anne, she realised, must have drowned when her husband staggered back into the lake still firmly grasping her wrist. A defensive act on his part as he endeavoured to prevent his wife using the knife again. Weakened by the loss of blood and knowing his life was ebbing fast, he had maintained his hold on his wife's arm.

Their violent struggles must have sent the knife into the lake, for there was no sign of the murder weapon. A distressed Maisie realised that her dying father-in-law must have decided to drag his wife into the lake, determined that she should suffer for her evil deed.

Weak and exhausted from her struggles, Lady Anne would soon have succumbed to the tranquil-like embrace of the water. Knowing that there was no escape, she must have given up the struggle and just let the cool water engulf her.

Maisie was concentrating on her struggle to pull the two bodies to the bank when she became aware of staff approaching. As she shifted her hand position on the stake, a stabbing pain in her hand caused her to gasp and almost release her hold. Despite the discomfort she managed to maintain her grip and drag her in-laws' bodies closer to the staging.

'Here, mistress. Let me.' She turned to find the head groom already crouching down beside her.

'Thank you... Wilson.' Maisie was greatly relieved to hand over the gruesome task of recovering the two bodies.

'Your... hand, Mistress. Best hev' it seen ter.' Wilson had noticed the gory state of Maisie's hand as they exchanged places.

'I er... must have cut it on the... stake.' She pointed towards the rusty iron support. Even as she poke an idea was formulating in Maisie's mind. She directed covert glances around the area while walking towards the shocked group waiting anxiously by the lake side. There was no sign of the knife. She was relieved to have her previous observation confirmed. The murder weapon was definitely at the bottom of the lake.

Another groom went out on the staging to assist a shaken Wilson. As Maisie staggered towards the staff, Millicent Cranford, who had joined as housekeeper only a few months previously, rushed forward to help her.

'Let me help you, Mistress Maisie.' She placed a reassuring arm around Maisie's trembling shoulders and supported her as she gradually regained her composure.

'Thank you... Milly...' She hesitated as she looked at the shocked staff gathered on the bank. 'Such an... unfortunate... accident.' Maisie was hoping that her words would create the impression that an unpremeditated mishap had befallen Sir Roger and Lady Anne.

'Ah, Bates...' she had noticed the butler standing in front of the watching group, '... did you manage to...'

'Doctor Wallace has been informed, Ma'am... and news of the tragedy has been conveyed to Highfield. Because of the urgency, I er... took the liberty of ordering the use of horses for the messenger.'

Good. Very thoughtful of you, Bates.' Her voice was still weak from shock. 'Now...' she directed her observations to the silent group, '... I think we should retire to the house. There is nothing further we can do until...' Maisie glanced back at the two men positioning the two bodies side by side on the grass, '... the doctor has been.

A stable boy arrived with a roll of canvas. As they moved away, Maisie noticed Wilson take the material from the frightened youngster and place it over the bodies. As she led the solemn procession back to the house, Maisie became increasingly aware of the pain in her hand. She half raised it to inspect her injury and was surprised to see a nasty gash under the partially congealed blood.

Milly, who had noticed the observation, frowned her concern as she commented on the injury. 'You will need the doctor t'treat your hand, Mistress. It looks a very bad gash.' Maisie nodded silently, she was too weary and distressed for words. The shock of what she had just witnessed had induced a trembling to her limbs that she felt helpless to control.

Doctor Wallace, a quizzical look on his face, drew his pony and trap to a halt outside Homefield and hurried inside.

'Ah...' Maisie heaved a deep sigh of relief as she met him in the hall. 'I have grave news doctor. Such... a... ghastly... tragedy.' As she walked beside him down to the lakeside, Maisie spoke of the incident that she had witnessed from Lady Anne's bedroom window. She never mentioned the knife.

Doctor Wallace spoke very little, nodding occasionally as Maisie related her observations concerning the deaths of Sir Roger and Lady Anne. When they reached the victims, she remained silent. As the doctor bent down to examine the bodies of his friends, Maisie averted her gaze away from the scene. Involuntary her gaze went to the darkened water. Under the first evening stars the lake reflected their silvery brightness in rippling configurations. The tranquil surroundings seemed an improbable setting for such a horrendous murder... accident.

As Doctor Wallace looked up to confirm their deaths, Maisie moved nearer to him. Even in the starlight, she noticed the sadness that lined his face. He placed the canvas back over the bodies and, after expelling a deep emotional sigh, began to walk slowly back to the house beside the new mistress of Homefield.

'What's wrong with your hand, Maisie?' He paused while she raised it for his examination. 'It needs cleaning and dressing, my dear.'

'You... watched... from the house as Lady Anne staggered towards the lake?' Maisie nodded silently, her eyes fixed on her injured hand as the doctor applied a dressing. 'You... also witnessed Sir Roger's unsuccessful attempt to save Lady Anne from falling into the water?'

'Yes, doctor. I had gone to my mother-in-law's bedroom expecting to find her in bed. Her absence shocked me momentarily. I looked out of her bedroom window just as the incident by the landing stage was taking place.' The old family doctor nodded silently, watching her anxiously as he did so. Maisie's distress and shock troubled him. To prevent her suffering further torment, he made a few of his own observations.

'It would appear that the effort of reaching her husband down by the lake, completely exhausted Lady Anne...' the family physician observed Maisie closely as he continued, '... and that she arrived at the lake side in a... distressed condition.' Maisie nodded and in a strained, faltering voice reiterated what she had purportedly witnessed from the window.

'Weak and near to fainting from her exertions, Lady Anne appeared... to stagger against... Sir Roger. Her... unsteady action caused them both to stumble... out into the staging...' Words at last failed the distraught Maisie. Doctor Wallace spoke quietly and reassuringly to her, before repeating her observations.

'It was then that Sir Roger... collapsed onto the iron support that secured the staging.' As he confirmed her statement, the doctor's eyes rested momentarily on Maisie's injured hand. Sighing heavily, the old family doctor rested his hand on her shoulder in a sympathetic and understanding gesture.

Gently he took hold of Maisie's bandaged hand and placed it in her lap. 'You... have no idea... how this came about?' He indicated her injury. Maisie shook her head, aware as she looked into his eyes, that he was conscious of her withholding important information. That she was endeavouring to protect her in-laws.

After a few silent moments of contemplation, he indirectly confirmed Maisie's belief.

'You were correct... in sending for me, Maisie.' As he gathered his surgical instruments together and placed them in his bag, he continued to nod his head in approval. 'A wise move, my dear. I shall confirm your observations to the authorities. Needless to say, I fully concur with your, er... sentiments.' His look as he bade her good-night told her all.

As Maisie waited with the doctor while his pony and trap was brought from the stables, he gave a final reference to the tragedy, confirming her evidence with his own observations relating to the fatal accident. He was anxious that no stigma should be associated with his departed friends.

'Everything appears to confirm with your observations, Maisie.' The doctor nodded pensively before elucidating further. 'Sir Roger's fatal neck injury was caused by...' he stared towards the distant starlit landing stage, '... a sharp angled spike.' The doctor recalled the traces of blood he had noticed on one of the supports. 'It would seem, that in his struggle to support his wife, Sir Roger must have stumbled and fallen onto the spike, causing the main vein in his neck to be punctured.' Maisie nodded silently in the shadow of the doorway.

'His grip on Lady Anne's wrist...' doctor Wallace continued as if aware of his companion's silent assent, '... must have been maintained as he collapsed onto the spike and thence into the lake. Lady Anne being weak would have been unable to break free and had consequently drowned. Her death would have been quick.' Maisie nodded in silent agreement. Quick and deserving, she thought.

Just as the doctor was settling in his trap, prior to leaving, two horsemen emerged from the darkness of the driveway. Twilight made identification difficult, but Maisie was sure that one of the riders was Josh. His presence was confirmed as they brought their horses to a stop close to the entrance. The other horseman seemed familiar, yet... Then Maisie remembered the horseman she had seen earlier in the evening. It was the rider who had hesitated at the entrance to the drive earlier, but so much had happened since then.

She tried to put the tragedy that had shattered Homefield's tranquillity to the back of her mind as she prepared to greet Josh and his companion. Despite her efforts to suppress the memory, it kept returning to torment her. Maisie was beginning to have reservations about her statement. Had she done the correct thing in suggesting that Sir Roger's death was accidental? Maisie's self-reproachment continued as the men exchanged information.

The more she contemplated her statements, the more sure she became that her half truths were best for the family. Her family. The truth, if known, would be so distressing and cast a cloud over Homefield. A stigma of murder would always be associated with the family. Maisie was determined to protect their respected name.

It was then that she suddenly recognised the soberly dressed man by Josh's side. It was Andrew. Her shocked gasp caused the doctor to turn a worried look in her direction. Maisie's startled reaction had him wondering if the events of the evening had become too much for her. The appearance of Josh and Andrew eased his troubled mind, but the latter's appearance surprised him. Nevertheless, he was reassured and felt confident that he could now leave the new arrivals to deal with the grievous situation.

Although his countenance revealed little of his emotions, Andrew's homecoming perplexed the old family doctor. He had offered his commiseration's to Andrew and informed him briefly of the circumstances that had claimed his parents' lives. A still shaken Maisie noticed Andrew's face turn ashen in the lamp light as his family doctor related the details. She became aware that her observations of the tragedy were being spoke of as Andrew's bewildered glance met hers.

Moving slowly and fighting to control her agitated emotions, she walked over to Josh and her broth-in-law as the doctor made ready to leave. 'Thank you for coming over, Josh and...' she turned towards his companion '... you also, Andrew. I had no idea... of your presence... at Highfield. Such a dreadful... homecoming... for you...' Maisie realised that she was trembling. A socked reaction to the trauma of the evening's events. 'Is dearest Alison… aware of…?' her voice trailed away as dizziness made her stagger.

'Allow me… to assist you… Maisie…' She was suddenly aware of Andrew's arm around her as he aided her to a chair inside the hall. Josh poured and offered her a small drink. Unsure whether to accept because of her abstemiousness, Maisie held the glass uncertainly in her shaking hands.

'It's mostly water, Maisie… just take a few sips.' Josh reassured her in an encouraging voice. She was aware of their anxious eyes upon her as she swallowed a drop of the liquid. The unusual taste of the brandy caused her to choke slightly. After two further sips she placed the glass down. Maisie took deep breaths to still her trembling and after a few moments she was able to assure them that her faintness had passed.

A tearful Alison arrived at that moment. Josh hurried to console his distressed wife, who had learnt from the departing doctor of her parents' tragedy. He had imparted the barest details, informing her that her husband would explain the circumstances. Shaking his head forlornly, their old family doctor had offered his sympathy before riding away into the night.

During the next few days, there was hectic activity at the hall as Homefield prepared for the final departure of its much loved squire and his wife. Throughout this traumatic period, Maisie was more than grateful for Andrew's help and support. At first she had been reluctant to accept his offer, but as she became aware of his changed demeanour and sincere feelings, she acceded to his offer of help without reservations.

'I'll not… trouble, or cause you further… distress, Maisie.' Andrew's words of assurance came when they were alone together in the study at Homefield, discussing the funeral arrangements. 'I'm fully aware of how my past… misdemeanours have brought you much heartache… and suffering. Unfortunately my irresponsible actions of the past cannot be erased – nor forgotten. I do, however, pray…' Maisie was aware of his distress and the hopeful look he accorded her, '… for your forgiveness and understanding.'

'Thank you… Andrew.' She was endeavouring to come to terms with his enigmatic behaviour. Since his return he had been so quiet, his manner so... unpretentious. A characteristic so different from the imprudent person she remembered. Despite these observations, Maisie continued a cautious relationship with her brother-in-law.

'If you are in agreement... and should it be your wish, Maisie... we could discuss Homefield's future. Next week, perhaps... after the funeral.'

'Yes.' Maisie nodded her agreement. 'I think we... Alison, yourself and I should meet to consider what is to become of the estate.' A matter that had been causing her much concern, especially now that Andrew had returned. It was obvious to her that Andrew's presence would have an important bearing on the future of Homefield and its estate. First, there was the ordeal of the funeral on the morrow.

'Regarding... tomorrow, Andrew...' Maisie gave him a sympathetic look, '... your presence beside Jonathan and myself... will be greatly appreciated... and understood.'

'Thank you, Maisie, but I'm not sure if my father would have agreed had he...'

'I'm sure he would have approved... as we all do.'

'Then I shall be honoured to join you tomorrow. Until then, good-night, Maisie... and thank you.' She noticed the moisture in his eyes as he turned to leave for Highfield.

* * * * *

Late summer sunshine spread a warm golden glow over the maturing countryside. Acres of stubble gave the fields a barren, almost forsaken look. A few wisps of cloud feathered across the vast expanse of an otherwise clear blue sky. Even nature seemed to be paying its silent respect to the man who had spent so many years in harmony with the ever changing seasons. A gentle sighing of the breeze in the foliage of the trees was nature's whispered lamentations to the passing cortege.

Black cloth and ribbons draped the haywain that carried Sir Roger and Lady Anne to their final resting places. Two majestic black horses from the estate pulled the wagon silently along the lane towards the church. In their sombre harness and with dark plumes fastened to their headbands, the two horses stomped their muffled hooves towards their dead master's burial place. It was as if they also were aware of the honour accorded them in carrying him on his last journey. Their quiet behaviour seemed to reflect the sadness of the occasion.

Maisie and Jonathan, with a melancholy and silent Andrew beside them, immediately followed the wagon. She noticed her brother-in-law's sadness and understood his feelings. Last night he had explained to her that his continued abstinence while living with his Quaker friends had encouraged him to call and seek forgiveness from his father, before he departed for New South Wales.

Now, such understanding would not be possible – he had arrived too late. Maisie's covert glance rested briefly on his bowed head. 'Oh, Andrew… if only you had called at Homefield first.' Her whispered thoughts were reflected in the sadness of her eyes.

Close behind her, Maisie heard Josh's quiet words of comfort to a distressful Alison. Immediately in their wake a sombre looking Colonel Markham walked beside his daughter, Julie and grandson, George.

Local dignitaries, friends and villagers fell in respectfully after the cortege had passed. There was a very large following by the time the funeral procession had reached the church. At the gate an elderly Reverend William Kennard waited to receive them and to officiate… his last ecclesiastical duty. Josh had asked his father to officiate at the burial of his long-standing friends. It was a silent and sorrowful person who watched the approaching cortege.

Maisie realised that Jonathan's hand was reaching out for the comforting touch of her own. Because of the affectionate friendship that had developed between him and his grandfather, she understood the emotional stress that he must be enduring. Gently she squeezed his hand in a sympathetic act of reassurance.

In a celestial-like ambience, the service and burial were conducted by the saintly figure of the Reverend Kennard, a long time friend of the deceased. Josh watched anxiously as his father in a hesitant voice rendered the last honours of friends who had shared his confidences over many years. It was with Josh and

Alison, his daughter-in-law, that the aged parson rode to Homefield after the funeral.

* * * * *

There was an autumnal chill in the air as Maisie enjoyed her early morning ride over the estate. Sheep stopped their grazing to watch her passing. A sight that these ruminant mammals were familiar with, as on most mornings Maisie enjoyed a ride after breakfast. Often she was accompanied by Jonathan, but on this occasion she was alone, as her son was already out riding with Andrew.

Maisie was glad to be alone on this particular morning, she was hoping that her ride would help to stabilise her confused thoughts and apprehensive mood. Later, she was meeting Andrew and the family's solicitor to discuss the future of Homefield. It was a very pensive Maisie who turned her horse to ride back to keep the appointment.

She had become increasingly aware, that Andrew's unexpected presence would in all probability affect her stay at the hall. Leaving Homefield after residing there for so many years, induced a feeling of sadness and heartache. An enforced move would also upset Jonathan. Under his grandfather's guidance, he had become conversant with all farming activities on the estate, now all might have to be forfeited.

Could she appeal to Andrew? He seemed so changed... more compassionate and understanding. When she recalled his truculent nature of the past, it was if she was seeing a different man. A much more gracious and... attractive person. Nevertheless, Maisie still had misgivings about requesting any favours from him. If her son's welfare was in jeopardy, then she would not hesitate to ask with true humility.

Should the situation demand it, she was even prepared to inform Andrew that Jonathan was his own son. These ultimate circumstances never arose because of Andrew's magnanimous gesture.

'If that is your wish, Mr. Andrew,' the old family solicitor gazed over his spectacles towards the man who by law should now be squire of Homefield... Sir Andrew Douglass.

‘That most certainly is my wish, Mr. Stevens and if I am not mistaken, it was also my father’s.’ The solicitor nodded a silent agreement. After a few moments, his quiet voice broke the reflective silence.

‘Your, er... changed... demeanour, if you will forgive the expression, Mr. Andrew, would I’m sure have elicited an... alteration in Sir Roger’s directions.’

‘Yes, Andrew, I am of the same opinion as Mr. Stevens. Your father I feel sure would have reconsidered and... authorised your reinstatement as heir to Homefield.’ Maisie had hesitated before expressing her thoughts, but a more compassionate Andrew to deal with, she had experience no compunction about agreeing with the old solicitor’s sentiments.

‘Thank you, Maisie... but I have a mission that I must fulfil in the new colony of New South Wales. An undertaking that reflect upon yourself and my cousin, Julie. A recent communication of which you are aware, indicated that there is some uncertainty regarding your brother’s fate. Indeed, it seems he may have survived when the transport on which he was taking passage went down in mountainous seas. Becky’s letter was rather ambiguous when referring to his survival... his existence.’

‘Edward’s survival, is something Julie and myself have always prayed for, but...’ sadness moistened Maisie’s eyes as she shrugged her shoulders disconsolately, ‘... twelve years is a... long time...’

All the more reason for my mission then, Maisie. If Edward is alive, especially if he is a convict, I shall seek his pardon and present it to the governor of the colony. Until there is proof to the contrary, I shall assume that your brother is alive.’

‘Thank you for your kindness, Andrew.’ These were words she thought never to use in relation to her brother-in-law, but she was sincere in her continued praise. ‘I shall be most grateful for any news that you might send regarding my brother, as will Julie, I’m sure.’

‘Ahemm...’ In their talk of Edward, they both had forgotten about the family solicitor. His discreet cough, a gentle reminder of his presence, generated their profound apologies. ‘Thank you...’ his features remained solemn, ‘... perhaps we should consider what immediate actions are necessary to ensure the progression of the estate over the next few months?' He looked at them both in turn as he considered his next words. 'Your wish, Mr. Andrew, was that your nephew, Jonathan Douglass, became heir apparent in your protracted absence... and that his mother, Mrs. Maisie Douglass...' he turned an uncertain look in her direction, '... becomes, er... a kind of consort. A guardian of the estate.'

'That is my wish... my requirements, Mr. Stevens. If I have not returned by his eighteenth birthday, Jonathan, my late brother's son is to inherit the title and the estate of Homefield.'

'Very good, Mr. Andrew.' The old solicitor bowed his head respectfully. 'I will ensure that the documents are drawn up immediately. Perhaps you will be available to sign the legal forms in my office next... Tuesday?' His glance included Maisie in the invitation as they both nodded confirmation of their agreement.

Silently, Maisie stood beside Andrew as they watched the family solicitor drive off in his pony and trap. She was experiencing a strange feeling, an uneasy emotion. Andrew's nearness was having the opposite affect to what she had anticipated. Revulsion and anger that she had once suffered in his presence had gradually been tempered with emotions of forgiveness. During the three weeks since his return, Maisie had become aware of Andrew's sincere and impeccable behaviour towards her.

His conduct had been above reproach. Whether working on the estate or sharing meals with them in the house, he was always thoughtful and courteous. Maisie's surreptitious glance lingered on the man beside her. Streaks of grey in his dark curly hair gave him a mature look, while his sombre clothing attributed to his quiet and pleasant appearance.

Aware of Maisie's eyes upon him, he turned and met her glance with a warm and friendly smile. Before she realised the implication of her reactions, Maisie had reciprocated with one that revealed her affectionate emotions. Noticing her confusion, her blush, Andrew remarked on the maturing landscape and the stubble covered fields.

‘Which reminds me of your helpful proposition, Andrew.’ Maisie had soon recovered her neutral composure.

‘One that meets with your approval, I trust, Maisie.’ He turned once again towards her.

‘Indeed it does. A very generous offer on your part, Andrew. One that would be churlish of me to refuse. Thank you.’ He experienced a moment of gratification as he noticed the happiness in his sister-in-law’s eyes.

‘I’m glad you approve. To ensure that you suffer no embarrassment, I shall take up residence in the Lodge during my stay at Homefield.’

‘A most understanding and considerate act, Andrew, but...’ he received an inviting look, ‘... Jonathan and myself, hope that you will join us for meals in the house.’ In the ensuing silence following his acceptance of her offer, she watched the sheep and cattle grazing peacefully on the park meadows. An idyllic scene that reminded Maisie how her life at Homefield had been tottering precariously in the balance. Now, thanks to Andrew’s unselfish action, her existence at Homefield, a place that she loved, was guaranteed... for the immediate future at least.

‘You have no cause for uncertainty, Maisie. You deserve the security... the guardianship of Homefield...’ She realised that Andrew must have been aware of her concern for the future as she listened to his reassuring words. ‘In your hands...’ his statement filled her with hope and gladness, ‘... its keeping will be assured and prosperous. Homefield needs you, Maisie.’

‘Thank you.’ Her voice was but an emotional whisper. She was finding it difficult to speak... to express her feelings. ‘I... have for many years... looked upon Homefield as my... home. Your very generous and understanding act will now ensure that it will continue to remain so.’

* * * * *

Maisie’s smile softened the serious lines of her face as she pulled her horse to a stop. She watched the season’s new lambs as they gambolled, half grown over the lush meadow grass. High above in the cloudless sky, a skylark hovered on fluttering wings as its sweet melody of joyful trills cascaded down to her receptive ears. An exuberant song that to Maisie epitomised Spring.

In these tranquil surroundings, the somnolent droning of the bumble bees induced a relaxed feeling to Maisie's uncertain emotions. Deep in thought, she gazed at the bees as they settled on the field-side flowers in search of the early nectar-bearing blooms. A passing breeze ruffled her corn-coloured hair. She brushed the strands from her face with an involuntary movement of her gloved hand.

A distant shout broke her contemplation's. Cornflower blue eyes wrinkled into a smile as she became aware of its source. Jonathan was racing his pony across the meadow towards her. Closely following him was the man who was the result of Maisie's restless and uncertain feelings.

Sensations of conflicting emotions had been troubling her of late. She was experiencing stressful feelings of uncertainty. Time and again she had tried to subdue her natural sentiments, but always there was that deep desire to share her affectionate feelings... with Andrew.

It was nearly eight months since the tragedy by the lake and throughout those lonely, uncertain months, he had always been available to help in the running of the estate. Life, Maisie realised, had been less arduous because of his willing support in organising the daily routine at Homefield. Not once had he taken advantage of his position. Always courteous and complaisant towards their guests and displaying a great empathy towards the labourers who toiled willingly in response to his caring manner.

Over the past few months since Andrew's return, Maisie had noticed the change in his demeanour. A complete change of character. His pleasing disposition was reminiscent of his father's caring and tolerant nature. When she had spoken to him of this, he had smiled and attributed the change to his new found religion.

Often, he would talk to her of the happiness he had found during his stay among his Quaker friends. It was then that Maisie noticed the deep sorrow in his eyes as he remembered the woman he had loved. It was the one thing they especially shared, heartache for a love one lost forever.

As Maisie watched her son Jonathan and Andrew galloping their horses towards her, a benign smile lingered on her thoughtful face. The two had been constant companions since Andrew's arrival at Homefield. A father and son-like relationship that Maisie had not failed to notice. Often of late she had wondered if their friendship was inspired by any suspicious thoughts that Andrew harboured regarding Jonathan. Just as often she dismissed the idea. She was the only person aware of the circumstances relating to his conception.

'Mother!' Jon, as her son now preferred to be called, brought his pony to a stop close to the field gate. 'I race... Andrew... from the... wood.' His breathless and excited chatter drew a warm smile from the two adults. As their eyes met above the young rider's head, Maisie found herself holding Andrew's gaze longer than propriety permitted. That was when she had glimpsed the look of humility and sadness mirrored there.

She was reminded of the time when she had first contemplated the reason for his absence on the Sabbath. When she had casually mentioned the matter, he had willingly informed her that he visited the Quakers assembly house near Aldeburgh. 'As a follower of the Friendship...' he had confided to her, '... I enjoy attending their gatherings for prayers and meditation.' In a quiet and emotional voice he had then spoken of his life among the friendly Quakers.

'They were kind and understanding in my hour of need, Maisie. Had Doreen survived, I would gladly have stayed and shared the remainder of my life with them, but...' Sorrow precluded his continuation of words.

Maisie had been deeply touched on that evening when Andrew had spoken of his five years in the Quaker community and of his marriage to a member of the sect. It had been Doreen's love and kindness that had greatly influenced his conversion to the Quaker Religion.

Andrew's confession on that occasion had somehow clarified the enigmatic emotions that had been troubling her. The reason for his reticent manner had been lifted by his fortuitous revelation of his life of abstinence among the Quakers. As he had spoken of his wife's tragic death, Maisie had been aware of the deep sorrow he still suffered from her passing. He had walked across to the window in an attempt to hide his emotions, but she had noticed the tears before he turned away.

She was reminded of that sorrow as her eyes now gazed deeply into his. Maisie's smile faded as she turned her gaze towards her son. Like Andrew, she was aware that their eyes had revealed the sincere, silent longing that lingered within them. They both realised the emotive issue that was preventing an affectionate relationship from developing. An act that they were both reluctant to mention. It was an unspoken barrier.

'You have done extremely well to win the race, Jonath.... Er, Jon.' She had almost forgotten that since Andrew had commenced using the shortened version of her son's name, Jonathan himself had preferred the abbreviated one.

'Jon it shall be then...' She had laughingly ruffled his hair as he had seriously asked her permission. Now he was known to all as Master Jon.

'Now...' she gave him an affectionate look, '... having won the race, I believe a prize would be in order. Do you not agree, Andrew?' A conspiratorial smile passed between them.

'A reward is certainly called for, but... er... what?' he glanced towards Maisie, who shook her head in mock uncertainty.

'Ah! Here comes Wilson!' The groom had arrived as if on cue. He walked towards them leading a colt fully saddled. Excitedly and with a knowing smile he led the horse towards Jon. He had been part of the covert operations in preparing the mount for this auspicious occasion.

All eyes were on Jon as he silently observed the head groom's approach. At first, he had been perplexed by the adults secret-like behaviour, but the reason for their reticent actions gradually dawned on him. A radiant smile brightened his face as he looked from the horse towards his mother and then on to Andrew. Momentarily speechless, he could only stare at the lovely creature that pranced gently before him.

'Mine?' Jon's voice was hoarse with emotion as he looked expectantly in his mother's direction.

'Yes...' she nodded, '... Andrew and I agreed that a horse would be more in keeping with your new status. When Andrew leaves…' Maisie, aware that her brother-in-law's departure was near, gave him a solemn glance, '… you will be mainly responsible for the estate work. A serious obligation, Jon.'

Maisie felt proud of her son, who since the association with Andrew had become more mature in his ways. Just a few weeks past his ninth birthday and already he was developing into a sturdy and intelligent lad. Jon, she realised was familiar with all aspects of the estate work, thanks to his grandfather's tuition and now in recent months under Andrew's guidance, he had become a confident and skilled manager.

Very soon now he would be called upon to organise the running of the estate with only her support. Maisie was sure that the estate would be in safe and capable hands, as, since an early age, Jon had shown a keen interest in Homefield's welfare. He was young, but determined and sufficiently skilled to take on the responsibilities of an estate manager – especially his own.

Maisie was thinking of these coming changes as she watched her son mount his horse for the first time. Before jumping into the saddle, he first spoke to and then gently patted the placid creature.

'His name's Swift, Master Jon… b'cause a' his speed.' Wilson gave the horse a parting caress as he handed the animal over to the proud, 'young squire', as some were already addressing him.

Maisie had at first been concerned at this form of address, but when she realised that it was a sincere mode of speech and that Jon acknowledged it in true humility, she refrained from discouraging it. After all, she thought, on day Jon could possibly be their squire and if his initial reactions were any criterion, then Homefield's future was ensured.

She acknowledged his wave as proudly she watched him ride away beside Andrew. A born horseman, confirmed by the way he seemed to become as one with his horse.

'What of Andrew?' Maisie questioned herself quietly as she returned to the house. 'How much longer before he departed?' She realised how much she would miss his helpful presence on the estate. Since his return, when both were initially apprehensive about the situation, there had been a gradual easing of her enmity towards him.

At first, Maisie had wanted to refuse his offer of help in the wake of his parents' tragic end. Realising that she had little option, she had reservedly accepted his assistance. It was not long before she became aware that she was dealing with a different personality... a changed Andrew.

His pleasing demeanour had gradually dispelled Maisie's antipathy towards him. A guarded friendship had developed and now when that relationship was being threatened by his departure, Maisie was beginning to realise how deep and sincere their feelings were.

She brushed aside the thoughts of love. Impossible, she told herself. Nevertheless, she was becoming increasingly aware of the affectionate emotions stirring within her, when they were together. A physical reaction that she had not experienced for many years. 'It will pass!' she tried to console herself, but the thought of Andrew's departure caused her a moment of heartache.

Maisie did not want him to leave, but sadly that day was drawing ever closer. Once he had sailed for that distant land, she doubted if they would ever meet again. His leaving was inevitable, she had known that it must be so, but despite this, his announcement when it eventually came, caused her a heart-stopping moment of sadness. It came at the time of the harvest supper.

Chapter Nineteen

Autumn sunshine warmed the maturing landscape into a resplendent panorama of russet and golden hues. Fields of stubble were already disappearing under the plough as the soil was turned in preparation for the sowing. Leaves of bracken along the hedgerows, glowed in shades of yellow and ochre as the early morning sunshine caressed their dew-saturated forms. Gossamer webs sparkled among the fretwork of twigs in the overgrown hedges.

Maisie was deep in meditation as she rode her horse through the October landscape. Her thoughts were not on the pleasant surroundings or the chill in the air as she cantered between hedgerows still glistening from the early morning mist. Her silent contemplation's were not only of the time when just Jon and herself would have the responsibility of running Homefield, but also of an emotional nature. Andrew's imminent departure was causing her heart-searching deliberations of an impassioned kind. She was trying not to think of them as romantic sentiments.

As Maisie pulled up at the barn door, the murmur of voices reached her ears. Dismounting, she entered the building and stood for a few silent moments watching the labourers at work with their flails. Threshing was both laborious and dusty, requiring skill and dexterity on the part of the workers.

Fascinated by the work, Maisie continued her observation as the men in their smocks wielded flails to separate the grain from the chaff and straw. Their flails she noticed consisted of two pieces of wood, a handstaff about seven feet long and the beater, a short piece joined to the main staff by thongs.

As the red-faced workers paused to acknowledge her presence, Maisie reminded them of that evening's harvest supper. Later than normal, but after the previous year's supper had been cancelled because of Sir Roger and Lady Anne's deaths, there had been doubt in her mind about it restoration.

'Why not, Maisie? I'm sure my father would have approved.' Andrew had encourage its reinstatement when Maisie had questioned him on the matter.

'I'm glad you agree, Andrew. I shall arrange for it to be held on the first Saturday in October. That will give Liz and her staff time to prepare the food.' Maisie had hesitated before turning towards him. 'You... will attend... Andrew?'

'Yes... that is... I hope to be there.' Maisie had noticed the hesitation, the uncertainty in his voice. Then she remembered that his Quaker philosophy might debar such entertainment.

'Perhaps... for the supper only.' She tried not to show her disappointment. 'You have contributed so much towards our successful harvest.' When he failed to answer immediately, she sympathetically reminded him that his presence would be greatly appreciated by the workers and their families. Maisie was remembering that conversation with Andrew, when she realised that the threshers were acknowledging her question.

'We'll be there, don't yer worry, Mistress Maisie.' Benign smiles reflected their happy expectations and also expressed their respects that they nurtured for the new 'Lady' at Homefield. At a call from their leader, the men resumed their threshing of the wheat.

Maisie stayed a few minutes longer watching the eight men who formed the group. She estimated that they would on average thresh about sixty bushels in a day. With barley, the amount would be almost doubled, while the threshing of oats would produce around seven score bushels by the group.

'I'll send some ale over shortly.' She called. Cheerful nods and smiles confirmed the workers' appreciation... and anticipation.

Maisie, still smiling at their response, departed to continue her rounds of the estate.

It was a beautiful autumn morning. Warm sunshine had spread over the fields and woodlands. A myriad pearls of dew sparkled in the brilliance of the early morning sun. Wild fruit and berries glistened in the hedgerows as she rode across the meadows to where Danny, the head shepherd, was tending his large flock. 'Morning, Danny! Sheep look in good condition.' She pulled to a stop by the elderly shepherd.

'Aye. Reck'n all be well, Mistress.' He glanced in the direction of his flock with a caring and expert eye. If appearances are any criterion, thought Maisie, the sheep are in excellent shape.

'See you tonight, I hope Danny... and Mrs. Carver.'

'We'll be there, Mistress... thank yer.' Maisie turned her horse for home, anxious to see how the preparations for the harvest supper were proceeding.

On her way back to the hall, she called at the West Barn where the supper was to take place. There, Maisie found a group of villagers already busy, clearing space for the large table and forms. They were also ensuring that there would be space for the dancing and games that would follow the supper. All appeared to be going well, with the excitement among those present increasing by the hour.

'Oh, Mistress Maisie... we're s'glad that harvest supper be a start'n agen.' Hearing their happy voices expressing the pleasure at its resumption, Maisie realised that her decision to hold it had been vindicated. It was as she circulated among the happy women that she experienced a moment of uncertainty. A sense of foreboding.

Despite the happiness emanating from the helpers around her, she was overcome with a feeling of sadness. Her emotions troubled her, including an irresolute sensation. Maisie could think of no reason for her disquiet. Past harvest suppers had always been cheerful occasions. There was no reason why tonight's celebrations should be different... but her pessimism lingered and worried her.

Once she was back at the house, her apprehensive mood faded. Maisie found herself caught up in the euphoric state that prevailed among the staff as they good naturedly prepared food and drink for the supper. Liz in the kitchen, her face red and damp from exertion, dashed around directing operations with the expertise of one who has experienced it all before.

'Everything alright, Liz?' Maisie enquired above the hubbub. Smiling to herself as she noticed how cook's white bonnet was set slightly askew on her greying head of hair.

'Fine, Mistress Maisie. Only wish I had 'nother pair a'hands.' Her whimsical notion was momentarily forgotten as she paused to remove bread from the oven. 'We'll manage. Hev no worry,

Mistress,' she called over her shoulder, before turning to issue instructions to one of her helpers. Shaking her head at Liz's ability to remain so calm and good humoured under such pressing demands, Maisie retreated to the much quieter surrounds of the library.

For the past few years, Maisie had tended to the financial side of the estate's working. Sir Roger had been reluctant initially in allowing her to look after the accounts, but her adroitness with figures and records had so amazed him that he had willingly relinquished that side of the estate business to her. Now deep in concentration she perused the current year's entries.

It had been a very good year. Wool had fetched top prices and the sheep taken to market had rewarded their efforts with a satisfactory price. Their harvest had been a bounteous one. Good crops that had fetched excellent prices on the market. Maisie felt very pleased as she checked through the figures. Their grain had been early on the market, thanks to Andrew's incentive in getting the corn threshed early.

As Andrew entered her thought, she paused to reflect on his presence. Maisie continued to be amazed and greatly appreciative of his changed character. His attitudes were so different from the irresponsible and obstreperous person of old. She wondered if she would ever be able to forgive him completely for the hurt and humiliation he had subjected her to. Her one consoling deed resulting from that awful act was the birth of Jon, a son who shared her affections.

Maisie admitted to herself that Andrew's changed personality had attracted her and that there were times in his company when she experienced sympathetic emotions towards him. So concentrated were her thoughts of Andrew, that she failed to hear him enter the library behind her.

From the shadows he watched in silence as Maisie, deep in meditation, gazed unseeingly at the autumn landscape beyond the window. How beautiful she is, thought Andrew as his eyes took in her still attractive figure. Her shoulder length, corn-coloured hair had a halo-like sheen as a shaft of brilliant sunlight caressed its fairness. She was sitting so that her skirts were raised sufficiently to reveal her ankles. A stirring of excitement was aroused within his being as he gazed upon them, but sadness lined his face as he noticed the one that was deformed.

Andrew was reminded of his stupid action many years previous that had resulted in Maisie's injury. Had it not been for a branch falling into the men-trap as it snapped shut on her ankle, she could have lost her leg – perhaps her life.* Remembering the incident, now caused him much distress. It seemed on reflection, that it had invariably been Maisie who had suffered most from his past misdemeanours – yet he had always been attracted to her. Even loved her.

His dreams had been shattered when his brother Seb had captivated her heart and then married the girl that he had secretly admired. It was their marriage that had induced a feeling of frustration and enmity in himself. It had come to a head on the night after his brother's departure to Waterloo He had envied his brother's marriage to Maisie, the woman he had covertly wanted for himself. Realising that he had lost her and upset by the frosted reception from his ailing father, Andrew remembered how he had found solace in drink. Eventually the brandy had only exaggerated his jealousy and desires.

Drunk, miserable and driven to despair, Andrew realised on that fateful night just how much his habitual drinking and incessant gambling was ruining his life. He had become a useless member of society – a parasite. In his inebriated state he had gone to Maisie's room, hoping to find understanding and forgiveness. Someone to talk with. To hear a few reassuring words from someone he cared for.

Once in her room, the situation had somehow all gone wrong. He shuddered as he recalled his sensual reaction to Maisie's nakedness in the moonlight. Suppressed impassioned emotions had overwhelmed him, inducing a sensuous desire to make love to the woman he admired. Losing control of himself, he had forced his violent love upon her. Initially his attack had been gentle, but Maisie's struggles had increased his longing, both emotionally and physically. Before he was fully aware of his actions, he was holding her down while he continued his evil act.

* In Book I The Winds of Destiny

Later, he remembered how in his own room he had been filled with shame and remorse for the sinful deed he had perpetrated. Gathering his few possessions together, he had departed from Homefield in the early dawn. Facing Maisie's silent accusing looks, would be a shameful reminder of the odious act he had forced her to endure. He had felt the need to apologise to her first.

In the morning, anticipating Maisie's ride, he had waited for her on the heath. There he had hoped to meet her and offer his sincere regrets for his abominable behaviour. Her shocked appearance and the hurt look in her eyes as she stared disbelievingly at him in the moon-glow continued to haunt him. Andrew realised that he would forever see that distressed look in her tear-filled eyes.

Sadly he shook his head, endeavouring to dispel his distasteful memories. As he continued to watch Maisie in her deep reverie, he wondered if his sinful action would ever be forgiven. If only he could hold her close in his arms and tell her how much he loved her – had always loved her. Andrew realised however, that such a passionate embrace would have to remain an impossible dream. His past indiscretion precluded any hope of such emotional actions.

'Maisie!' His words were revered with connotations of love. 'May I join you?' Startled from her meditation, she turned a surprised look in his direction.

'Oh... Andrew! I'm sorry... I had no idea... of your presence.' She displayed a momentary loss of composure as her thoughts returned to the present.

'Please forgive my interruption...' he was surprised at her startled, almost guilty-like reaction, '... but I was er... just wondering if...'

'It's nothing... just reminiscing,' her smile was welcoming, but uncertain. 'Please... join me.' Maisie indicated the chair by the window.

'Thank you.' Andrew experienced an uncomfortable moment as he lowered himself into his father's favourite seat. He was wondering what reaction Maisie would have to his news.

Maisie had a premonition that her brother-in-law was about to disclose a momentous decision that would affect her directly. She waited with deep apprehension, knowing that she was about to be informed of his departure to the distant colony. Jon will miss him, she thought and if I speak truthfully… I shall also.

A widow for ten years, Maisie had not shared any amorous thoughts or experiences since she had lost Seb. She had of late, however, found herself physically aroused whenever she was along in Andrew's company. At first she had tried to suppress any impassioned thoughts, but the sensations had been so pleasurable that she had accepted them as the stirrings of reawakened… love. Aware of her emotional feelings, Maisie tried to hide them from the person concerned.

As she silently waited for Andrew to explain the reason for his visit, she experienced once again an affectionate longing for the man who had gradually won her admiration for his impeccable behaviour since his return to Homefield. His changed mannerisms had helped her overcome the fear and revulsion she once experienced in his presence. From the unscrupulous person she had once know, he had become a temperate, kind-hearted and a more understanding person. She nurtured affectionate feelings towards Andrew, but their circumstances forbade her acknowledging such a possibility.

'I wanted you to know… that I shall be… leaving on the morrow.'

'Oh… Andrew… no.' Her anguished gasp was an involuntary response that surprised him momentarily. As they silently gazed into each other's eyes, their true emotions were revealed. They were in love. There was a deep serenity in the room as the depth of their affections became apparent. An emotional love that both were afraid to disclose.

'I shall miss you, Maisie… and Jon. To ease my conscience and to try and make amends for my past deeds, I promise to seek news of your brother. I hope it will be possible to send you some news of… Edward.'

'Thank you, Andrew… but his… departure, was so very long ago…' Gently he raised his hand as he prepared to offer her words of regret.

'I owe you... and Edward an enquiry at least, Maisie. It was a great and evil wrong that I did to him.' She lowered her head in sorrowful remembrance as tears misted her eyes. Her sadness eased and, after a few moments, she regained her composure. It was then that she recalled the evening's celebrations –the harvest supper.

'What of the harvest supper... to night, Andrew? Will you... circumstances permit...?'

'The very first...' Maisie could feel the blush of excitement burning her face as she made her promise, '... and the last dance shall be yours, I promise.' His heart raced as he noticed the warmth in her eyes, but Maisie's emotional tears went unnoticed, as fighting to control her excited feelings, she rose and walked across the room. As she retraced her steps towards the desk, she enquired if goods, or money was needed for his journey. He assured her that he was in need of nothing but her blessings on his departure.

'Then you shall have them, Andrew... without reservations.' In her thought, Maisie also offered her love. 'What plans have you for New South Wales?' Now composed, she turned to enquire of Andrew.

'I shall most certainly seek news of your brother and also seek his pardon; if the documents are still in existence after all these years. My other aim is to encourage a Quaker community in the colony. A meeting place where Friends can meet and share in our meditations and prayers.'

'I wish you every success in your venture, Andrew. My thanks are also extended to you for the kindness and help that you have given us these past seasons.' She noticed the sadness reflected in his eyes before he rose and prepared to leave.

'I shall look forward to our dances this evening.' Andrew paused in the doorway to accept her promise.

Maisie confirmed her agreement with a smile and continued to stare at the closed door for several moments after Andrew's departure. 'Oh, Andrew... why do you have to leave me now?' Her whispered words were a manifestation of the heartache she was experiencing.

* * * * *

That evening as Maisie and Jon walked together across the park, she noticed the glorious sunset above the West Wood. Crimson and golden hues spread across the sky, silhouetting the tress against the sun. Already there was a refreshing coolness in the air as the slanting rays of the sinking sun sparkled on the rippled surface of the lake.

From the barn came the sound of excited voices. A hubbub of cheerful conversations and the occasional outbreak of laughter as the happy villagers waited for the harvest supper to commence.

A call from behind made both Maisie and Jon turn. The distant figure gave them a wave and hurried to reach them. 'It's Andrew, mother!' Maisie noticed the happiness on her son's face as he spoke. She had yet to tell him of Andrew's departure in the morning. Let him enjoy the evening, news of his companion's leaving can wait until later... after the supper.

'Glad I reached you before you entered the barn. I'd like you to have this... gift, Jon.' Andrew handed the astonished lad his decorated riding crop. As he did so he gave Maisie and enquiring glance. She shook her head surreptitiously. An indication that her son had yet to be informed of his departure.

'A... present...' Jon was holding the crop uncertainly, '... but... it's not my birthday.' His eyes reflected his excitement as he admired Andrew's gift.

'I know, but you've er... worked hard and... helped me on the estate. It's a kind of er...' Andrew was searching for an explanation.

'Harvest supper present!' Maisie had interrupted with a reasonable elucidation.

'Yes... of course...' Andrew smiled his thanks to her above Jon's head, '... a harvest supper... souvenir.' Together they continued their walk towards the barn.

From the partly open door came the cacophony of excited laughter and joyful talk. It appeared to Maisie as she entered the gaily decorated barn that the whole village was in attendance. The trestle tables strained under the weight of the food and drink.

Maisie's glance took in the appetising menu. Cold chicken, cold roast beef, pigeon pie, cold veal, tongue, cheesecakes, trifles, creams, jellies, sweetbreads and biscuits, all waiting for the eager appetites of her guests. A mouth watering display that all were eager and anxious to sample.

'Thank you, Liz. You and your staff have prepared a wonderful spread.' Maisie on her way to the reserved space at the top of the table, paused to express her gratitude to all concerned in the presentation. She took the empty space between Jon and Andrew.

Conversations died to whispers and eventually faded completely as the villagers noticed Mistress Maisie standing at the head of the table. She experienced a moment of sadness as she remembered past harvest suppers when Sir Roger had presided over the celebrations.

'Welcome... and thank you all for coming.' Maisie glanced round with a benign smile at the happy faces gathered around the tables. 'We...' she indicated Andrew and Jon standing each side of her, '... welcome you to the harvest supper and sincerely hope that you enjoy the evening.' At the conclusion of her introduction, Maisie had a sudden idea that would involve Andrew.

'Before we commence Mister Andrew and Master Jon wish to join me in offering our sincere thanks for the hard work you have put in towards making our harvest a very bounteous one. Perhaps Mister Andrew...' she turned towards her brother-in-law, '... will say grace before we partake of this lovely food?'

It had been a spontaneous gesture on Maisie's part and for a moment she wondered if Andrew would respond to her invitation. It was not reluctance that made him slow to respond, just his emotional feelings – of love. Saying grace and prayers were now a natural undertaking for him.

While Maisie had been speaking, Andrew's eyes had rested lovingly upon her. Her natural beauty as she stood beside him to address their guests, had drawn a warm, admiring glance from him. He was aware of how the pale-lemon silk dress complemented the fairness of her shoulder length hair and accentuated the attractiveness of her mature figure. From close beside her, Andrew noticed how her sparkling blue eyes appeared to be smiling at him as she awaited his response.

A fragrance of spring flowers pervaded the air around her. Maisie's perfume was encouraging forbidden thoughts that Andrew was trying to suppress. It was during this battle with his emotions, that he became aware of Maisie's request for him to lead grace.

Slowly, to cleanse his mind of all extraneous thoughts, Andrew rose and stood for a few moments with his head bowed in meditation. A deep silence gradually settled over those present as they waited for his words. All eyes were upon the man they had come to respect and trust since his return to Homefield.

'Lord, we thank thee for the bounty of the harvest we have safely gathered in and for the food we are about to receive. We ask that thee may make us truly grateful.'

'Amen!' Voices echoed ratification's.

'Enjoy your harvest supper!' Andrew bestowed a radiant smile upon his guests as they settled at the tables.

Eagerly the villagers reached for the food, anxious to enjoy the appetising treats prepared for them. Wine and ale had been provided to compliment the meal and to ensure a supply of sustenance for the exuberant, if unskilled dancers. The hubbub of conversation continued interrupted by an occasional peal of joyful laughter.

'Our guests appear to be enjoying themselves, Maisie?' Andrew glanced happily at the masticating diners and at the rapidly emptying dishes.

'Yes...' she chuckled her agreement as she paused to look around the tables, '... a compliment to Liz and her hard working helpers.' As Maisie took a sip of rhubarb wine she noticed that Andrew's glass contained water. How he has changed, she thought as her glance momentarily rested upon his benign features. A pain of sadness stabbed her as she remembered his words about departing in the morning. There was little chance of her becoming too melancholy as no sooner was the meal over than the floor was being cleared for games and dancing.

A fiddler scraped a few introductory notes with his bow before settling into a lively rhythm that encouraged a few dancers to skip and twirl about the floor. The music was infectious, causing Maisie to glance at her companion with an inviting smile.

'May I have the pleasure, Maisie?' Andrew, his face serious, but his eyes smiling, feigned the strict protocol associated with gentlemen as he bowed exaggeratedly before her.

'Oh, Andrew!' Maisie giggled excitedly. Then reciprocating his mood, she rose sedately and extended her hand for him to hold and guide her onto the floor.

Once there, their acting stopped and very soon they were joining in the happy, carefree dancing of the villagers. Maisie found herself swept gaily over the floor by the enthusiastic actions of the dancers. Occasionally Maisie and Andrew would come together, then clasping each other's hands they would skip and twirl to the lively music.

As Andrew sent Maisie skipping away from him, he noticed as he awaited her return, how agile she was. Despite her deformed ankle, her actions were as light and delicate as any of the dancers around them. He wondered if his own actions, the result of his slightly twisted leg, were as conspicuous as his partner's.

Of late he had come to believe that his own deformity, the result of an indiscreet action concerning Rebecca, was a form of retribution by the Almighty.* He forced a smile to his face as Maisie came dancing back towards him. A prolonged chord brought the dance to its close, allowing the breathless dancers a few moments respite.

It was nearly midnight as the last of the villagers departed. A small group who had delayed their departure to ensure that all was safe and secure in the barn. Andrew thanked them before closing the barn door. As he turned he was surprised to see Maisie beside him. Only a few minutes ago he had seen her and Jon walking with a few of the household staff towards the hall.

'Maisie!' She experienced a momentary thrill at the excitement in his voice. 'I thought... you had returned to the house with Jon.' Seeing her alone reminded Andrew of their last dance they had shared so happily together. Joyfully they had clasped hands as they swirled and skipped through the final steps.

* In Book I The Winds of Destiny

Andrew was remembering the thrill of gazing into Maisie's sparkling eyes as the music faded. Her vivacious, fun-loving demeanour had captivated him throughout the evening and as the final chords of the music had died away, he had smiled into her cornflower-blue eyes and seen her forgiveness. Her nearness as they now stood together beneath a starlit sky, reminded him of their last few hours together and his imminent departure from Homefield – and Maisie.

Maisie's presence reminded Andrew of the affectionate emotions he had experienced during their last dance. An excited reawakening of the love he had always felt for her, but one that had never been reciprocated – until that evening. Maisie's blush had reminded him that they were alone on the dance floor and continuing to hold each other's hands. Protocol had been forgotten as they enjoyed their shared emotions. Gently he had lowered her hands before escorting her to the side where the guests were already preparing to depart.

Now it was finished and, as Andrew turned to walk home to his lodge, he found the woman who had been dominating his thoughts all evening, close beside him. Tomorrow he must leave and there was every possibility that their paths might never cross again. Andrew realised that his future was filled with uncertainty.

'I came... to say goodbye... and to wish you success... on your journey... your mission, Andrew.' As she hesitated because of her nervousness, he reached out and took her hand in his. An encouragement for her to continue. 'As... you are leaving early... to visit Highfield, I wanted to say my... farewell now while we are alone.' She paused a moment, uncertain of her emotions. 'Jon, I believe has already wished you... a safe voyage?'

'Yes...' he nodded in the darkness, '... I spoke to Jon of my departure. I reminded him that as Homefield's new master, he had a great responsibility to shoulder. My reminder eased his distress somewhat.

'He will miss you greatly, Andrew. You have been good for Jon... an excellent mentor. I would also like to thank you for being so understanding.'

'What of yourself, Maisie?' he was looking into her eyes as he spoke. 'Shall you... also... miss me?' In the deep emotional silence, the prolonged and quavering call of a tawny owl drifted ethereal-like across the starlit park lands.

'Yes, Andrew...' her voice was a sentimental whisper, '... I shall miss you – very much.'

'Whatever befalls me, Maisie... I shall never forget... you.' His affectionate words aroused her amorous feelings.

'Oh... Andrew!' Maisie was trembling with excited anticipation as she felt him close against her. She thrilled as his arms gently encircled her and as their bodies pressed closer, his lips eagerly sought hers. For a brief moment, past memories returned, inducing a moment of near panic.

Andrew felt Maisie stiffen momentarily in his arms. Aware of the reason for her distress, he eased away from their passionate embrace.

'I'm sorry Maisie. It was... unforgivable... of me.' She noticed his distress and the anguish in his voice. 'It was an... impulsive reaction to my... feelings.'

'There is no cause for apologies, Andrew. It was... just a fleeting... memory of an incident best... forgotten. Something that should never come between us again – ever.'

'Thank you for being so... compassionate, Maisie. May God bless you for your magnanimity and should... when I return from my mission... I would like to...'

'Oh... there you are, mother!' A breathless Jon appeared from out of the shadows as Andrew was about to express his desires. Maisie was filled with disappointment. She felt sure that Andrew had been about to express something important regarding their relationship. Now the magical moment had passed. Their close embrace already a fading memory of what might have been.

'I was saying my farewell to Andrew...' she reached out to clasp her son's hand, '... tomorrow he starts off on a long and dangerous journey.' They exchanged emotional farewells in the starlight before finally parting. Maisie, paused and walked back to Andrew on impulse to give him a last endearing smile. 'Come back to us some day, Andrew... you will always be... welcome.' Starlight glistened on her tears as she turned to walk away.

Andrew stood silently watching Maisie and Jon disappear into the shadows. 'I shall… my love. That I promise, thee.' With these whispered words he walked away to prepare for the hazardous journey ahead of him. A journey that was to tax his courage to its limit – and beyond.

Chapter Twenty

'Men that is born of woman ... hath but a short time to live... and is full of misery. He cometh up… and is cut down, like a flower…' Andrew, uncertain of the service for those buries at sea, was struggling to remember extracts of the burial service from memory.

He experienced a moment of sadness as he glanced at the canvas shrouded body about to be cast to the waters of the deep. It was only a few weeks since his first meeting with the old surgeon, but during their short time together, they had become firm friends.

Andrew's offer of help had been accepted gratefully. While assisting the elderly physician during the course of his official duties, Andrew had come to respect his skill as a medical officer and also as the government representative on the prison transport, the Leonore.

'… he fleeth as it were a shadow… never continueth in one stay. In the midst of life we are in death…' Andrew was endeavouring to recall words said at his parents' funeral, nearly twenty months previous. He was aware that on that occasion, the service had been in a church, here at sea the words and routine were probably different, but…

Shrugging his shoulders uncertainly, he looked over the mourners gathered at the ship's side. An officer, a few crew members and a small group of convicts. Andrew doubted if they were familiar with the burial service – or even cared. Continuing with words, vaguely remembered from the past, he closed his eyes to concentrate on the service.

'… O holy and merciful Saviour thou… most worthy judge eternal, suffer us not… last hour…' he stumbled over the words, unable to remember their sequence. '… pains of death, to fall from thee…'

There was a pause as he nodded towards the men standing ready to slip the deceased overboard. In the ensuing silence he heard the waves slapping against the ship's side and the straining of the ropes as the breeze filled the sails and forced the Leonore's bows through the sparkling water. Andrew forced his thoughts back to the present, aware of the air of expectancy from the onlookers.

'For as much... as it has pleased Almighty God... of his great mercy to take unto himself... the soul of our dear brother here departed.' Andrew nodded a silent warning to the burial party. 'We there commit his body to the deep...' Andrew hesitated as the body slipped over the side with a splash and began to sink slowly beneath the waves. David Jennings was a man he had come to know well since their first meeting at the start of the voyage.

Andrew experienced a pang of sadness as his late friend gradually disappeared beneath the ocean astern of the transport. An uncertain shuffling from those around him reminded Andrew of his responsibility. To finish the service, he led the mourners hesitantly through the Lord's Prayer, before walking back to the quarters he had shared with his now departed friend.

A deep sigh escaped his lips. Andrew experienced a feeling of relief at having struggled through the burial service. There had been so little time to prepare for the ritual that he had never expected to officiate. It had all started with a summons for a meeting with the ship's captain.

A meeting that never materialised. 'Cap'ns ill! Says as 'ow yer c'n see t'the burial.' It had been the boson's visit to his cabin that had alerted Andrew.

'Ill?' He had queried the captain's indisposition. 'Ill... or drunk...?' Andrew had noticed the boson's knowing look as he departed without saying another word.

It had been an emotional ordeal, thankfully it was now over.

What he intended to do now, was to relax and give serious thought to his new and unforeseen status. As he stood on the after deck and gazed sadly astern, his thoughts reflected on the brief few weeks he had shared with the man now sinking into the fathomless depths of the water in the ship's wake. Andrew smiled wryly as he remembered their first meeting.

'You'll be sharin' a cabin with the ship's surgeon... David

Jennin's.' The words had been directed at him as he reported aboard the Leonore.

'Thank you, captain.' Andrew, aware of the captain's petulant attitude towards him during their exchanges, forced himself to remain courteous. As he walked away to collect his few possessions, he overheard the officer's remark, scorning his presence on board.

'Och, man... Quakers. 'tis all I'm needin'.' It was said in a sotto voice, but loud enough, as was intended, to reach Andrew's ears as he walked towards his cabin.

Gently, he eased himself into the smallish cabin. Twin bunks, a couple of stools and a crude locker for storing clothes.

'Perhaps you'll be good enough to take the top bunk, young man?' Andrew looked round to find an elderly gentleman standing at the cabin's entrance. 'My age,' he shook his head solemnly, '... precludes any climbing activity'. He indicated the top bunk with a wistful smile.

'My pleasure, sir!' Andrew liked his companion from the start. 'Allow me to introduce myself. My name is... '

'Douglass! Andrew Douglass!' The man chuckled as he noticed Andrew's surprised look. 'I've just seen the captain. Your... er... vocation is causing... some uncertainty.'

'Guilt... if I'm not mistaken.' Andrew's statement produced another chuckle and a knowing look from his companion. 'And... yourself...?

'Forgive me!' His face became serious as he concluded the introductions. 'David Jennings... at your service...' an infectious smile spread over his bearded features, '... I also have an official title.' He paused to affect a conspiratorial demeanour. 'Medical Officer and Government Agent. The prisoners...' as he had pointed to the convicts being checked into the forward hold, Andrew noticed his compassionate look, '... are my responsibility. Their welfare throughout the voyage will be my main concern.

'An awesome obligation, Mr. Jennings.' Andrew had been watching the human cargo being herded below.

'Yes...' he closed the door and began to remove his coat, '... but I shall do all that is possible to ensure their voyage is a...

tolerable one. However…' A warm smile reached his eyes as he laid his coat on the bottom bunk. 'If we are to be companions, David will be a more appropriate form of address.' He paused to give Andrew a thoughtful look. 'Truth is, I may be glad of your help… support during the long voyage ahead of us.'

'Then it shall be yours for the asking… David.'

'Thank you, Andrew!' His words sounded sincere as he placed a friendly arm around his companion's shoulders. 'Now, I'll let you settle into what little space is available.' Another chuckled escaped his bewhiskered lips as he retreated to check on the condition of the incoming prisoners.

* * * * *

'Cap'n wants t'see yer, sir!' A voice startled Andrew out of his reverie. 'He's in 'is cab'n!' Andrew gave the seaman a perfunctory nod to acknowledge the message. Since he had joined the ship in his Quaker-like dress, Andrew had been aware of the captain's acrimonious attitude towards him. While his late companion had been alive encounters with the senior official had been few. Mostly it had been David who made his daily report to Captain Freestone, but now it would be his responsibility.

With a trace of trepidation, Andrew made his way towards the official's quarters. 'You wanted to see me, captain?' he enquired through the partly open door.

'Aye, I do. Get yourself inside, Quaker.' It was a surly command that engendered a momentary flash of anger in Andrew.

'Captain Freestone, whatever your feelings regarding my beliefs, I would appreciate a more civilised and unbiased disposition in our working relationship. Here is my authorisation…' Andrew produced his late friend's signed letter, '… the transfer of Mr. Jennings duties to myself. Handed to me when David realised that his death was imminent.

'I know little of medicine. Only that which was taught me by my departed friend as I helped him on the course of his duties. Nevertheless, the prisoners' welfare will be my concern from now on and I intend to execute my responsibilities as expeditiously as possible.' There was a charged silence in the room as Andrew waited for the captain's reaction.

There was none. Andrew's impulsive statement appeared to have stunned the inebriated captain. Bleary eyes, he gazed at Andrew with his mouth open as if wanting to reply, but only incoherent muttering's escaped his lips.

When Andrew realised that a statement was not forthcoming, he excused himself and made to leave. At the door he paused before turning to give the bemused captain a friendly smile. 'I'm sure we can rely on each other's co-operation... full support, captain. Good day to you.' He never waited for any response – if there was any.

Andrew was recalling the early weeks of the voyage as he walked pensively back to his quarters. How when David's health began to deteriorate, he had suggested that perhaps Andrew would like to visit the convicts and check if all was well. Any ailments arising were to be reported to the medical officer on Andrew's return. They would then diagnose the symptoms together and under the surgeon's guidance, Andrew would administer any treatment found necessary.

Now, with the ship's health his sole responsibility, Andrew found himself appreciating those medical duties he had shared under the auspices of the elderly, but skilled surgeon. David's death had placed a great burden upon his inexperienced shoulders. Thinking of the uncertain prospects awaiting him, induced a momentary tremor of alarm. His obligation on the prisoners and crew over the last leg of the voyage to New South Wales was an enormous responsibility.

In the quiet of his cabin, he knelt in silent prayer and meditation. Later and easier in mind, he made his rounds of the convict holds. There, the conditions although Spartan and cramped, were at least tolerable. There was a smell of lime and tar despite the holds adequate ventilation. David had expressed the importance of keeping the convict quarters disinfected and the convicts clean and in good health.

Andrew smiled to himself as he remembered his late friend's solemn advice. 'Keep them well, lad. Prevention is better than cure.' Heaving a sigh of relief, Andrew turned to climb the hold with an easy mind.

'Sir! Could you please look at my boil?' Andrew paused to see who had spoken. A young woman stepped forward, pointing to her neck as she did so. Andrew noticed her shyness as she waited his response. He moved closer to inspect the angry swelling, trying as he did so not to display his nervousness.

'What is your name?' Andrew was hoping to gain a little time while he assessed the situation.

'Hester, sir. Hester Collins.' He noticed the distress in her dark eyes as they stared hopefully into his. She was placing her trust in him. Andrew hoped he would not fail her.

'How long have you had the swelling, Hester?' An idea was already stirring in Andrew's thought as to what form of treatment he was going to administer.

'Three... maybe four days... sir.' She flinched as he gently touched the inflamed area around the boil.

'Painful?' There was a sympathetic concern in his enquiry.

'Throbs quite a bit.' He was aware of her distress, but his close inspection of the girl, also revealed how pallid and listless she appeared. Undernourished would be a better description, but why should that be so? The situation caused him some anxiety. Andrew decided to pursue the matter later. The present situation presented a more immediate problem as the boil needed urgent treatment.

'Bread poultice, Hester. You'll need to come with me for the medication.' Andrew noticed her uncertainty... a reluctance on her part to leave the convict quarters.

'It's alright... you have my promise that no harm will befall you.' Briefly their eyes met. Seeing his concern and genuine sympathetic look, convinced Hester that she was in safe hands. As he escorted her back to his quarters, Andrew explained his intended treatment.

'Every four hours I shall crumble a slice of bread into boiling water before wrapping it in a porous material. Once the water has drained, I shall then apply the poultice to your boil. You may find the treatment a little... uncomfortable, Hester.' He tried to reassure her with a commiserate smile.

Andrew was less assured next morning, his treatment had proved unsuccessful. The carbuncle, as he now considered the inflamed swelling, had not diminished and was causing his patient considerable discomfort. He realised that he would have to lance the swelling so that the pus could be drained away. The thought of the minor surgery filled him with apprehension.

'Hester...' Andrew looked closely at her drawn and wan features, '... the treatment has not been a success?' She shook her head carefully as her eyes reflected the agony she was in. 'It will be necessary to make a small cut to relieve the pus.' He was trying to sound confident although he was deeply worried at the prospect of having to lance the festered swelling.

During the voyage, Andrew had become friendly with the Gordons. They were a family immigrating to take up residence on a small farm in the new colony. Their destination was a settlement close to Bathurst, an unknown place to them, but one where they were hoping to find security... and a settled future.

James Gordon and his wife, Mary, had been turned off their farm in the Highlands and with their four year old son, Billy, were sailing out to farm in Australia. Their passage and a deposit on the distant farm had been paid for by the laird; an act of compunction to ease his guilty conscience.

Andrew had shared many happy hours of the voyage with them, listening to their plans – and hopes for the future. If strength and determination were a criterion for success, then their future seemed assured. Now, as he approached them, he wondered what their reaction would be to his unusual request.

His uncertainty stemmed from his observation of the frail, pallid looking young mother. Andrew was aware that Mary had been indisposed for long periods at the start of the voyage. Due, he had assumed, to the adverse weather conditions. He was now beginning to wonder if that was the real cause.

Recently, he had noticed her spells of affliction occurring more frequently, even when conditions were fair and the sea calm. On those occasions, James became very reticent, his thoughts troubled because of his wife's illness. At times she looked tired, listless and haggard from pain. With a feeling of apprehensiveness, Andrew now approached Mary and explained his predicament regarding the young female convict.

‘Of course I’ll help, Andrew.’ There had been no hesitation on Mary’s part. ‘I know little of nursing, but perhaps you can instruct me as to what is required, then…’ her kind and gentle nature was revealed in her smile, ‘… I shall do my best.’

‘Thanks, Mary.’ He turned and gave her an appreciative smile as they walked towards the patient. Hester appeared more relaxed with Mary beside her. Within a few minutes, her comforting words and gently manner had the patient at ease and ready for the treatment.

Forcing himself to remain calm, Andrew opened his late mentor’s medical case. Deeply perplexed he ran his eyes over the array of instruments. Silently, Andrew prayed that he would never have any reason to use them, especially the saws. Fighting back his moment of panic, he selected a small knife-like instrument and dipped it briefly into the bowl of hot water delivered from the galley.

Mary had encouraged her charge to take a small amount of laudanum while Andrew was preparing to make a small incision. His troubled eyes encountered Mary’s above the patient’s head to concentrate on Hester’s inflamed swelling. His deep breath was more of a sigh as with a positive movement he made the small cut necessary to release the pus.

A sharp gasp escaped Hester’s lips as the knife did its work and the pus spewed out of the wound. Mary bathed the place gently with warm water before clearing the soiled clothes away. Andrew heaved a sigh of relief as he wiped the sweat from his brow. After cleaning the knife he replaced it in the case, praying silently as he did so, that he would never have to use the surgical instruments again.

;Excuse me, Mary…’ he was feeling a little unsteady, ‘ … think I’ll get some… fresh air.’ She nodded without looking up from drying the clean area where the swelling had been.

‘A neat job, Andrew. All the pus appears to have drained off.’ Mary gave a final look before wrapping a piece of cloth over it. Hester remained passive on the bottom bunk as she recovered from her ordeal.

* * * * *

'Our patient appears to be making a good recover?' It was a pensive Andrew who acknowledged confirmation of Mary's prognosis. He had been thinking about the conversation he had shared with the elderly ship's surgeon during the early weeks of the voyage. When he realised that David had sailed as Medical Officer on previous convict transports, he had enquired of conditions in the earlier years.

'At their best, barely tolerable... at their worst...' he shook his head sadly as his eyes reflected revulsion, '... terrible. Shocking. A living hell.' His voice had broken with emotion as he recalled the wretched conditions of the past. 'Thank God, the prisoners' environments have improved.'

'Were circumstances that odious, David? Was there no one responsible for their... welfare?' Andrew recalled his companion's cynical look, his silent anguish confirming his worst fears. With a deep feeling of remorse he remembered Edward's sentence of transportation. Because of his perjurious evidence, Maisie's brother had been subjected to such barbarous conditions.

'... brutal floggings...' David's words had penetrated his disturbed thoughts. '... starvation diets. If a fellow prisoner died, and quite a few did in the early days, his companions kept his death a secret as long as possible so that the deceased's meagre rations continued to be issued.' He hesitated as memories became distressful, but noticing Andrew's shocked interest he had continued his grim narrative.

'Over-crowding... and the stench from the convict's quarters was absolutely vile. Many died in the early years of transportation. It seemed the poor souls had just given up, unable to endure the harsh and filthy conditions any longer. Death was their saviour – their peace.' Andrew's reverie had been so deep – so intense that he had forgotten Mary's presence. Her discreet cough shattered his cogitation.

'Oh, Mary! Please forgive my inattention. I was lost in... meditation.'

'You seemed very distressed, Andrew.' There was a look of concern in her eyes as she smiled at his embarrassment.

'Please forgive my lapse of manners, Mary. It was... most discourteous of me.' As he made his apology, distress continued to line his features. 'My sincere thanks for your invaluable help... support. Now I must enquire about your health.' For a moment they looked steadfastly into each other's eyes. He detected her reticence to discuss her ailment, a reluctance to accept its existence. 'I'm not a physician, but I have noticed how pain causes you so much distress at times. Is there anything I can do?'

'It's... nothing, but thank you for your concern, Andrew. I'm sure I shall feel much better when we reach our destination.' Andrew nodded thoughtfully, aware of the uncertainty behind her words.

'Promise you will let me know if...'

'You have my word, but I'm sure there is nothing to be... concerned about.' For a few silent moments they both looked reflectively across the rolling waters towards the crimson orb that was fast dipping below the horizon. Andrew's words eventually broke their brief reverie.

'I think it's time I checked Hester's condition. See about her return to...'

'She is deeply distressed at the thought of returning to the convict quarters.' Mary gave Andrew a speculative glance before continuing. 'In confidence, Hester mentioned something about starving, rather than submit to the guards' evil demands.'

'Did she say what those... demands were, Mary?'

'No. I tried to get more... information, but...' Mary shook her head, but her concern for the girl was obvious.

'Was she not able to give you... any information?'

'None. She was still drowsy from the laudanum when she mentioned... the situation relating to the guards. When I questioned her later she appeared frightened... afraid to mention the matter.'

'I'm glad you mentioned it, Mary. I'll have a quiet talk with Hester later. Because of her circumstances, it might be prudent for her to spend the night in my cabin.' He chuckled as he became aware of her astute look. 'As for myself...' Andrew gave her a teasing look, '... I shall spend the night under the stars.' A smile spread over Mary's face as she realised his honourable intention.

'You're a very compassionate man, Andrew. A true reflection of your... faith.' She failed to notice the pain and sorrow in his eyes as he turned towards the fading hues of the sunset.

'If only you knew, Mary...' he sighed silently into the dusk.

Andrew nodded approvingly as he eased off the bandage. All seemed satisfactory. He was modestly pleased with his minor surgery. 'It's healing fine, Hester... you can stay another night in the cabin. On the morrow, I shall make arrangements for your return to your quarters.' He was watching for her reactions as he spoke. She was unable to hide the shocked look that flashed briefly in her eyes. Mary is right, there is something that greatly troubles her.

'Hester!' As she turned her dark, troubled eyes towards him, he noticed the lamp light reflected in their depths. 'I want to help you.' Under his steady gaze, she lowered her agonising gaze.

'Th... thank you, sir.' Her voice was an uncertain whisper.

'First...' Andrew emphasised the word, '... first you must tell me of that which is distressing you.' He waited for her response, but she remained silent, her head lowered as if in prayer. 'What is it that troubles you so, Hester?' Gently he covered her hand with his. His touch appeared to stimulate her desire to talk.

'If... if I tell you... they will... hurt me when they deliver the rations.' Her eyes were pleading for his understanding.

'No one will hurt you... that I promise. Who are these people that threaten you?' Andrew spoke firmly as he sought the information about the culprits.

'The guards... the ones who deliver our food. They ask for... expect... favours... from the female prisoners.' Andrew managed to keep his anger in check as he waited for Hester to continue. There was a long silence, she was reluctant to continue.

'Favours?' He guessed the nature of the benefaction demanded, but he wanted to be certain.

'Yes. Unless we... are free with our... responses, our rations are reduced to a minimum... if we are lucky.' Andrew remembered David's words imparted a couple of days before his fatal stroke.

'I'm deeply troubled, Andrew.' He had paused to shake his head slowly. There was a note of uncertainty in his voice as he had continued his contemplative observations. 'Most of the women prisoners appear under nourished. Their rations seem adequate but except for about half a dozen, they look ill... listless. Symptoms of malnutrition it would seem, but...' he had remained silent, stroking his beard as he contemplated the situation.

Now, all was clear. Hester had confirmed the cause; he would rectify it immediately. 'From today, Hester, I shall make certain that I am in attendance when the rations are issued. Everyone will have their fair share. If any guard makes an er... improper suggestion or withhold any ration, he will be severely disciplined.' A knock on the cabin door caused him to pause.

'I've managed to get some food for Hester. She looks in need of some sustenance.' Mary wondered at the whimsical smile that passed between Andrew and his patient. After thanking her benefactor profusely, Hester consumer her food with relish.

'James... would you and Mary agree to Hester becoming nanny for young Billy?' Andrew put the question as the two of them conversed by the ship's side. As the matter was considered in silence, they watched the seamen prepare to meet an approaching squall. Above them, the rigging stirred itself as the inert canvas snapped slowly into life.

'Is there a... personal reason for your request?' James spoke above the creaking braces and flapping sails. Andrew returned his searching look, wondering how best to explain his concern for Mary. He did not want to alarm her husband more than was necessary.

'More of a compassionate reason, James. I was thinking of companionship for Mary... during the remainder of the voyage.' Just then the squall struck the ship, forcing Andrew and James to seek shelter. Out on the swaying yards, the crew continued their struggle to shorten sail.

'I know why you are troubled, Andrew.' James turned towards his friend. 'I'll be honest...' the young farmer's voice cracked with emotion, '... I also am greatly troubled as regards Mary's health.' Seeing Andrew's surprised look, James informed him that he had consulted the old Medical Officer just before he died.

'What was his reaction... his opinion?' Andrew watched the wind swept waves as he waited for his companion's answer.

'Not very encouraging, I'm sorry t'say. He pointed out that the hard and exhausting life on a remote farm would jeopardise Mary's health. The kindly thought as how her weakening constitution would not be able t'stand the strain.'

'I'm sorry, James.' Andrew commiserated with his friend. 'I did not realise the seriousness of Mary's, er... situation. If... if I can help in any way...'

'Thanks for your offer, Andrew...' James nodded his appreciation, '... but if all goes well, Mary's health will hopefully improve.' His companion's false optimism did not deceive Andrew. He had glimpsed James' despairing look before he turned away. They were both aware that Mary's health would never improve... that it was gradually deteriorating.

A sympathetic silence fell between them as they walked out onto the silvery wet deck. Brilliant sunshine had immediately followed the passing squall. As the crew unfurled the saturated sails, its radiance sparkled on the water droplets that cascaded from the yardarm.

'Returning to your original question, Andrew. Yes, having Hester as a nanny, or companion, call if what y'will, would greatly ease the situation for Mary.' James gave his friend a thoughtful look as he realised that the latter had been Andrew's original intention. Hester's presence would greatly ease the burden on his wife, especially when they reached their destination.

'I'll arrange for her to be accommodated with you today. She need not return to the convict quarters.' Andrew hurried away to inform the captain of the new arrangements for Hester.

Andrew made certain that his visits to the convict quarters always coincided with the delivery of the prisoners' rations. His present ensured that all the women had their fair share of the food. When the guards became aware of Andrew's intentions, they became sullen and unco-operative. It took a threat of disciplinary action before they became more helpful. None of them fancied the excruciating pain of the cat-o-nine-tails across their naked back. After Andrew's warning that any interference with the prisoners, especially the females, would be dealt with severely, the guards reluctantly stopped intimidating their charges.

For a week or two, Mary's health stabilised, bringing a smile of relief to her husband's face. Hester's arrival had cheered his wife and induced in James a feeling of optimism. He was now anticipating his arrival in Sydney in a more hopeful mood.

They now had permission for Hester to remain with them. An authorisation that pleased all concerned, especially Andrew, who as government representative had arranged and made it official. James' aspirations and his future plans were however to suffer a traumatic set back before he surveyed the farm that was to be his home in the new colony.

Chapter Twenty One

Andrew, recognising the shadowy silhouette of his friend as he stood by the ship's side, paused to converse with him. 'How is Mary? Any improvement, James?' He experienced a moment of despair as his companion shook his head forlornly.

'None!' There was a huskiness about his voice. 'She is very poorly. Don't know what t'do for the best.' His eyes went to the starlit heavens as if seeking succour for his beloved wife. 'It's the pain, Andrew. She doesn't complain, but I can see the anguish in her eyes.'

'I'll give you some laudanum…' Andrew hesitated, uncertain about his prescription, '… perhaps you could give her a small dose whenever her pain becomes… unbearable.' James turned his troubled face toward the man who had befriended his family on the voyage. 'It will make her… drowsy.' Andrew explained. 'A drugged sleep… but the pain will be less distressing for her.'

'Then I have no other choice,' his voice was an emotional whisper. Reaching out, he clasped his companion's arm. 'Her condition troubles me greatly.' For a few moments, as the stars sprinkled the shadowy ocean with pin-pricks of light and the calm waters slapped against the Leonore's prows, the two men remained silent. Each reluctant to voice his unspoken thoughts. They both realised that the chances of Mary seeing the shoreline of their new homeland – were very remote.

'I'll have the laudanum ready for when you call later, James. You will need instructions as to the required dose.' He began to walk away, then hesitated to add a warning. 'You will make sure that the medicine is kept… secure.' James nodded a silent assurance. 'An overdoes could prove, er… fatal.' Troubled and wondering if he was being prudent in prescribing the opiate for Mary, an introspective Andrew walked back to his quarters. He was fully aware that his knowledge of medicine was very basic. 'I can only do what I believe is best for Mary!' he whispered to the flickering stars.

* * * * *

"James! 'tis best we face fact.' Mary's pain-filled eyes held her husband's gaze for a moment. Silent and worried he sat beside her bunk. Reaching out she took hold of her husband's strong, callused hands. 'My dearest, it is very… doubtful… if I shall live to see… land again…' She grimaced as a spasm of pain racked her frail and weakened body. 'You must have… no regrets, James. No remorse… I have none. Our time together… has been…' she caught her breath as pain once more racked her body, '… has been a happy one.' His wife's warm smile seemed to tear at James' heart.

'Please, Mary…' she noticed his sadness, his anguish, '… I'm sure that there is a chance of your… recovery. When we reach…'

'No, James!' Her eyes filled with tears. 'We both know the truth!'

'Oh, Mary… my love… why?' She held his shaking body close against hers as tears ran down her cheeks. Gradually his sobbing subsided and he eased away to look into her ashen features.

'I'm… sorry… my love. It's just that… I love you so…'

'I know, James.' She kissed him tenderly. 'Life… however… will have to continue… even after…' but words choked in her throat. Both made feeble attempts to smile in an endeavour to cover their emotive silence.

'Billy seems to enjoy Hester's company.' Mary gave her silent husband a speculative look. 'She has been a great comfort to me, James.' He nodded pensively. 'Look after her when…' she hesitated on seeing his distraught look but forced herself to continue, '… should I… succumb to this… illness.' Noticing the sadness in her husband's eyes made her hesitate. 'Perhaps… Hester will be waiting… to… take…' Mary's voice faded to silence. Overwhelmed with despair, she could not continue. Silently they embraced, each distressed because of the other's suffering and torment. Mary's pain induced a feeling of faintness; involuntarily she reached out for her husband's hand.

James waited as her distress eased and a reassuring smile returned to her face. Then he promised that both Billy and Hester would be cared for. Her smile lingered as she whispered her relief, but her eyes reflected the pain she was suffering.

'Now... your medicine, my dear.' James walked over to the locker in which the laudanum was securely stored. High enough to be out of Billy's reach and safe from Mary's temptation. Eagerly she took the small dose from her husband and swallowed the medicine. Gradually Mary became relaxed as the opiate induced a painless drowsiness.

When she was asleep, James made her comfortable and, after gently kissing her cheeks, he departed. Thinking her asleep, he moved quietly from the cabin, he was unaware of the sorrowful eyes that drowsily observed his tormented leaving.

Andrew, after a restless night, made his way thoughtfully along the top deck. It was early, the sun, a crimson disc, edged in awe-inspiring splendour above the grey, indistinguishable horizon. A silvery-grey morning sky was waiting to accept the dazzling sun into its firmament.

Above him, Andrew heard the lazy flap of unfilled sails. For several days their progress had been hindered by lack of winds. Doldrums, he had heard the captain call this natural phenomenon that becalmed the ships and belayed their movement. Their lack of progress and direction was determined by the currents.

On questioning the captain's concern, Andrew was informed that windless days prolonged the ship's time at sea and could mean rations and water becoming dangerously low. Andrew voiced his concern about Mary's health. For once the captain listened sympathetically and promised a quick voyage when the winds were again favourable. He confirmed to Andrew that he intended to shorten the voyage by sailing through the straits that divided Van Dieman's land from that of the southern coast of Australia, the new continent.

The name was new to Andrew, but he understood it was the country that was to be his destination. As he listened to the captain's pensive voice speculating on their passage through the narrow straits, he detected a note of concern.

'Need decent weather. Rocks 'nd reefs await the unwary,' he shook his head as he gazed out across the ocean ahead of them. 'Not a route I would normally consider, but…' he indicated the limp canvas above them, '… my choice is limited.'

Becalmed, the Leonore rolled sluggishly on the swell. It was stifling between decks where the convicts, overcome with lethargy were gasping for air. Andrew noticing their distress, insisted as Medical Officer, that they be permitted on the upper deck. Even there, with the sun burning relentlessly down, the air was sultry and energy-sapping.

The days seemed endless as anxious eyes searched the clear azure sky for signs of clouds that might herald a change in the elements. Another becalmed day gave way to the cool but humid evening. All that remained of the sunset was a faint flush of crimson in the darkening sky.

Andrew sighed apprehensively as he silently reflected on his dilemma. His supply of laudanum was almost gone. Barely sufficient to last Mary until they reached Sydney. Once there, she would be nursed more proficiently in hospital. Their lack of progress over the last few days had forced the captain to reduce their food rations and water for the remainder of their passage.

Mary's health had deteriorated considerably and was causing her acute distress. As Andrew gazed in anguish up at the starlit sky, he was wondering about his patient and friend's medication. Should he decrease Mary's dosage? If he did so, he estimated that his supply of opiate would last until they reached Sydney.

He realised that a reduction would only ease his patient's suffering. On the other hand, continuing with the current dosage would subdue Mary's pains, but leave her without any laudanum for the last part of the voyage. He found it very agonising trying to decide the best course of treatment for Mary. Andrew was still undecided when the answer to his dilemma came unexpectedly.

'Can you come, sir? Mrs. Gordon is… very poorly.' Hester's voice startled him from his meditation. He turned to find her close beside him, her face strained with worry. He noticed how attractive she now looked in the clothes given to her by her mistress.

Even in the deepening gloom, he was aware of her pleasing appearance. Her hair that had become matted and straggly during her sojourn in the convict quarters, was now washed and neatly coiffured. He decided to caution Hester about the dangers of moving around the ship, during the hours of darkness.

'I shall return with you immediately, Hester.' Taking her arm, he guided her back towards the Gordons' quarters. Andrew paused outside the cabin and turned to face his companion. 'It would be prudent for you to remain off the deck during darkness, Hester.' Seeing her uncertain look, he gave a whispered warning. 'An attractive young lady could encourage unwelcome attention, alone in the shadows.'

'Yes... sir.' Hester's blush was visible in the lantern light. 'I shall be with Billy... should you need me.' As Andrew turned to enter Mary's cabin, a cool breeze caressed his face and ruffled his hair.

'A breeze, Hester! I do believe we are...'

'Deck there!' Andrew leaned back to gaze up at the rigging as the lookout's voice warned of a change. 'Squall a comin' from the Nor' West!' With the light almost gone, the man on watch in the crow's nest had suddenly discerned the darker formation of heavy clouds and turbulent waters. Scrambling down from the lookout position, he soon joined the alerted crew members out on the swaying yards. Already the rigging was creaking under the strain as the inert sails filled and snapped into life.

Andrew's spirits rose as the sails billowed out in the sudden wind. Braces squeaked in their blocks as they took the strain and water gurgled and swirled around the rudder as the ship gathered speed. Eagerly, it seemed, the ship swung to embrace the welcome wind. Rain swept across the deck as Andrew entered the cabin in answer to the urgent summons.

James, his face tense with anguish, gave Andrew a pleading look as he entered. Quickly he crossed to the bunk where James knelt to cradle the frail body of his wife. Mary made a wan attempt to smile a greeting as Andrew crouched down beside a distressed James.

'As last we're moving... a favourable... wind...' Andrew realised how hollow his words must sound. Nevertheless, he wanted to try and encourage flicker of optimism for the sake of his friends. 'In a few days we shall be entering the straits. Captain Freestone assures me that our journey… we shall… almost be…' Andrew's voice trailed off into silent.

'Thank you… Andrew.' Mary, aware of his embarrassing attempt to reassure them, whispered her appreciation.

Above the patient's bowed head, his gaze was held by James' agonising glance. They were all aware of the situation… Mary would never survive the voyage. Silently, Andrew prayed that the laudanum would last out.

For a few days the Leonore made good progress. With a favouring wind filling her sails, the transport sliced her way through the waves as if rejoicing in her new lease of life. Mary, with Hester beside her, was able to sit in a sheltered area and feel the warm caress of the sun and breath in the fresh sea air. Unfortunately, like the Leonore, her active life would soon be over. Vanished forever beneath the surging waters.

None had any premonition of the catastrophe that awaited them in the narrow straits. As they entered the treacherous stretch of water, a sense of false security permeated both crew and passengers. They were unaware that the perilous sea awaited them with perfidious expectation. Experienced seamen who should have been alert to the ocean's capricious nature relaxed too soon, lulled into a sense of apathy by the tranquil elements.

Mary, once again in pain, grimaced in agony. Clasping Hester's hand, she waited in anguish for the tortuous spasm to recede. Distress showed in the eyes of her young attendant as they pleaded silently for Andrew to ease the suffering of her mistress. Taking the last bottle of laudanum from the battered bag that had belonged to his mentor, Andrew measured out a dosage. He tried not to think of the consequences after the bottle was emptied. There would then be no relief to ease Mary's agonising pains.

A distressed Andrew waited beside Hester until the opiate had induced a pain-easing drowsiness in Mary. Once he was assured of her relative peacefulness, he rested his hand gently upon Hester's shoulder.

'Watch over her, Hester. I fear the pain will be with her constantly as she nears…' Hester's shocked gasps silenced his dreaded expectation. 'I'll be close at hand... should you need me.'

'Thank you, sir.'

'Hester... in view of our shared concern and close liaison, could you not call me Andrew? I would much prefer it so.' His smile was a warm invitation for her to accept him as a friend.

'Yes, sir... I mean...' she blushed as she whispered his name, '... Andrew.' Yet, even as she returned his smile, he noticed the sadness, the uncertainty lingering there.

'Don't like the look o' it!' Boson Fenton eased along-side Andrew, who was fascinated by the crimson sunrise, an angry-looking phenomenon. 'Them there clouds...' he continued as he nodded towards a dark, turbulent formation gathering ahead of them, '... looks like trouble t'me, Mr. Douglass.'

'Trouble, Dan?' Andrew gave the old boson a puzzled look.

'Aye... we be in fer a blow a'fore long.' Even as his warning shout brought all hands racing to their stations, the first gusts of wind were straining the canvas and stays.

'Shorten sail! Hurry y'selves... an' don't let me see any slackers!' Boson Fenton's commands sent the men scrambling aloft and out onto the swaying yards.

Spume-crested waves lashed by the increasing wind made conditions uncomfortable for the men endeavouring to take in the sails. Their plight was worsening by the minute as storm-force winds and tumultuous seas battered the pitching Leonore.

Andrew's worried features followed the men struggling aloft in their attempts to gather the rebellious canvas. Their work, a precarious operation in normal conditions, was now becoming an almost impossible task. They fought tenaciously to take in the straining canvas. He shook his head in disbelief as, hanging onto a stanchion, he gazed up at the cursing men who were battling to secure the treacherous sails.

With just her tops'ls and jibs set, the Leonore's motion, although easier, was still uncomfortable. Andrew, drenched with spray, was about to go below, when an extra strong gust of wind buffeted him hard against a deck structure. Partially winded, he paused to regain his breath just as a seaman plummeted down from one of the yardarm's high above him. A sudden gust had snatched the unwary seaman from the yard and hurled him into the raging seas. His final resting place.

'Oh... James!' Mary's hand stretched out for him. The ship's motion was causing her great pain as she struggled to remain in her bunk. Conditions were worsening, the pitching and rolling was becoming more severe as the Leonore battled against the storm. 'I don't think... I can stand... much more.' Her pain-filled eyes seemed to be pleading with her husband.

James moved closer to hold her in a tender embrace. He felt so helpless. 'I know, my dear. If only I could do something... to ease your agony.' He paused, frowning as the ship gave a sudden lurch. Above the roar of the storm, he heard a terrific crash as a shattered spar smashed down upon the deck. His troubled eyes rested momentarily on his wife's pain etched face. 'I'll not be long, Mary my love.' He kissed her gently before clambering outside to investigate the cause of the explosion of sound.

Waves pounded the ship as she wallowed sluggishly in the mountainous waters. With her tops'ls gone, the winds were driving her remorselessly towards a jagged reef. The helmsman's cry for assistance was lost in the howling wind. Help in any case would be futile – the ship was at the mercy of the raging sea and gale-force winds.

'We're drifting towards the reef!' Andrew pointed towards the foam-crested waves as they pounded the impregnable rocks.

'Dear God!' James voiced his horror in a shocked outburst. 'I must get back to Mary.' It was not to be, as before he could move an agitated Hester arrived.

'Can you come, Mr Gordon? Billy is unconscious... hit his head...' already Hester was scrambling back to her charge, '... knocked over... when the ship lurched...' she called over her shoulder.

'You go James. I'll see to Mary.' Andrew's voice was barely audible in the roaring wind. Rain, lashed by the wind, stung their faces as with eyes almost shut against the stormy elements, they separated. Both men were aware of the waves smashing against the stricken ship's side, driving her ever closer to the reef.

Andrew, after racing towards the Gordons' quarters, paused momentarily outside the cabin door to regain his breath. A brief interlude amidst the pandemonium of the storm to permit a quick assessment of the situation that was deteriorating by the minute. Already he could hear the seas breaking over the treacherous reef towards which the incapacitated Leonore was slowly and inexorably driven. How much longer had he to rescue Mary? The thought spurred him into action just as an explosion of shattering timber drew his eyes aloft.

With horror, he watched as another spar disintegrated under the strain of the roaring wind. Andrew was unable to get closer as the torn rigging and splintered spar crashed down onto the deck around him. He found himself entangled in the trailing ropes and flapping canvas.

With the fragmented wreckage trailing half over the ship's side, the Leonore was now forced broadside on towards the jagged rocks. Mountainous seas exploded against her sides and sent turbulent water sweeping across the listing deck. Andrew watched helplessly as a crew member was knocked off his feet and swept overboard.

Fear began to penetrate Andrew's stunned senses. The chances of survival were rapidly fading. How could any person live through this maelstrom? 'Mary!' He called her name above the wind. Andrew suddenly remembered his promise to help her. He had been inadvertently diverted from his mission by the mayhem around him.

'Abandon ship!' The frantic cry reached his ears above the noise of the storm. The ship was almost onto the jagged reef. Suddenly the Leonore lurched violently as the hazardous reef smashed a hole in her side. Water poured into the ship while men, who had been endeavouring to clear the deck of the fallen spars and tangled ropes, were now trying to cut the tangled ropes that had fouled the remaining longboat.

Andrew, realising that time was running out for those still aboard the disintegrating ship, dashed to reach Mary's cabin. He felt sick with worry as he thought of her alone in her room. With all the commotion of the storm and the shuddering lurches, she must be feeling trapped. Abandoned... doomed to die alone in her cabin.

Each terrifying movement of the sinking ship must be causing her spasms of excruciating pain. He would have great difficulty in carrying Mary to the longboat because of the ship's acute list. I must hurry, he thought, as he pushed against the cabin door. There was no movement, the door was jammed. He shouted an obscenity to the storm in abject frustration.

Mary, despite her pain, had realised that the ship was doomed. She had seen the anxious, almost frantic look on her husband's face when he had gently kissed her before going out to assess the situation on deck. The violent actions of the ship since his departure had been ominous, a warning that they were in dire trouble.

After her husband had gone, Mary had eased herself gradually into a sitting position. The effort had exhausted her and while recovering she had become aware o the turbulent waves smashing against the ship's side. Every motion... every shudder had sent tortuous pain throbbing through her frail body. They were becoming unbearable.

Mary screamed in agony as another heavy lurch caused the ship to list sharply. The shuddering movement sent her sliding helplessly from her bunk. Entangled among the bed clothes, she found herself stranded on the cabin deck.

Spasms of pain throbbing inside her weakened body, caused her to cry out in pain as she tried to free herself from the bed clothes. Tears of agony dimmed her eyes as she thought of the burden her infirmity was causing James. She looked up with startled eyes as something heavy crashed down onto the deck above her. Next moment, the Leonore, groaning and creaking, eased over a little further.

It was then that Mary realised that the ship was doomed. If James and Andrew returned to rescue her, they would be placing themselves in danger as they struggled to get her to the longboat. This thought gave her the strength and determination to crawl to the locker and reach the laudanum. 'Don't hesitate!' She encouraged herself with a harsh whisper. 'Take it all... there'll be no more pain... just eternal peace.'

Something was obstructing the door. Frantically, Andrew hurled his weight against it, slipping on the wet and listing deck as he did so. Eventually he forced open a small gap in the doorway.

'Mary!' He called her name above the cacophony of howling wind and roaring seas. Silence. He peered through the partially open door. 'Mary! Are you there?' Once again there was no response to his call. Perhaps she had been taken by crew members to the longboat. Squinting against the driving rain, he looked towards the two small boats bobbing perilously on the storm tossed waves. Was she safely in one of them? Andrew noticed one longboat still fouled in the tangled rigging. She was certainly not in that one.

Andrew concentrated on one last despairing effort to open the cabin door. He put all his frustrated and pent-up emotions into one final effort. Time was fast running out for the doomed ship – and himself. Gradually, he managed to get the door sufficiently open to squeeze inside. He looked around the gloomy interior to ensure that Mary was safe.

There was no sign of her. His sigh of relief froze on his lips. 'Mary!' A shocked Andrew slid across the steeply angled deck towards the woman he had come to rescue. His eyes were fixed on the still, lifeless body wedged against the bunks.

Involuntary he felt for her pulse. Nothing. But he hesitated, unsure of his findings. As he bent closer to Mary, he noticed the empty laudanum bottle. He grimaced in anguish as he realised that in an act of desperation, she had taken nearly a full bottle of opiate.

Frantically, he once again checked for her pulse, but he was still in doubt. He could feel no heartbeat, but as the ship gave another shudder, Andrew realised that he was faced with an emotional dilemma, an urgent one. Already he was in danger of going down with the ship as it continued to disintegrate on the reef. A quick decision was imperative if he was to survive.

Whatever course he decided on he was sure that Mary, even if she was alive, would never awake from her drugged sleep. She had decided on a peaceful and painless way out of her agony. Andrew decided to respect her wishes, her unselfish bravery. 'God be with you, Mary!' His blessings were a gentle whisper as he covered her still body. 'Your suffering's... your pains, are over... for ever!'

As he scrambled out onto the listing deck, now being pounded continuously by heavy seas, he wondered if he had left his chance of escape too late. Peering through the spray of pounding waves, he noticed that all the boats were now in the water, with their occupants struggling to manoeuvre them clear of the sinking ship. If he was to survive, he must reach the longboat without delay. There would be little chance of survival in such tempestuous waters.

During a momentary lull in the storm, he heard muffled shouts and screams. As he strained to listen against the cacophonous background of the elements, he heard the cries once again. With a feeling of horror, he realised the shouts for help were coming from the convict hold they had been abandoned to their fate... locked in the darkened quarters.

'Dear God!' Andrew's cry of anguish was lost in the howling wind as he scrambled across the slippery and debris-strewn deck to reach the convicts' hold. Turbulent waters swept knee deep across the deck, at times almost dislodging him from his precarious position on the doomed ship.

Something in the swirling water stuck his leg. Wincing in agony from the blow, he glanced down to see what had been swept against him. With a quick reflex action he grasped the axe before it was washed over the ship's side. It had probably been discarded by a member of the crew, who had been more concerned on abandoning the ship than trying to chop free the tangled ropes and spars.

By the decrease in the volume of sound., Andrew subconsciously registered that the storm was abating slightly. It was too late for the Leonore, wedged on the reef and shuddering under the continuous pounding of the waves. Seas breaking over the stricken ship lifted and tossed the tangle of broken spars and masts across the deck. These splintered timbers and trailing topes were a danger to any unfortunate trapped on the ship.

Andrew, disregarding the danger to himself, slid and tumbled across the treacherously listing ship to reach the padlocked hold. Wielding his axe, he smashed determinedly at the lock. After the third blow, the padlock shattered and fell away. It took an enormous effort to open the hatch and allow the terror stricken and bewildered convicts to scramble out onto the deck.

'Abandon ship!' There was no need for his warning shout, the released prisoners did not hear him. They were already fighting to keep their balance as they endeavoured to seek some means of escape. Unfortunately for them, there were none. 'Poor devils!' Andrew sighed at their misfortune, then remembered that he was in the same situation himself.

Making his way to the side, Andrew was struggling to remain calm as he considered what action he should take in what now appeared to be a hopeless situation. Beneath him the foaming waves crashed against the disintegrating ship's hull. Too dangerous to abandon the ship on that side. He began to scramble back across the listing deck just as an enormous wave exploded against the deck structures. In the resulting maelstrom of surging water, Andrew felt himself being swept helplessly past the chaos of tangled rigging and shattered spars.

Carried by the wave across the deck, Andrew shouted in agony as he felt a stab of pain in his shoulder. He had been swept against a submerged object. Disorientated and stunned, Andrew resigned himself to the inevitable as he was carried away by the roaring surge of water. Helpless, he found himself being washed overboard and forced under the raging seas.

His lungs were on the point of bursting as he was swirled around beneath the waves. He was in a raging darkness, his senses numbed. Was this the end? Just as all seemed lost, his head broke free of the water. He gulped in a lung full of precious air and fought to remain calm. Still gasping, he managed to glance around, but his vision was filled with foam-lashed waves.

Andrew managed to tread water despite the buffeting he was receiving. It was but a moment's respite as almost immediately he was knocked under the water as he again received a painful blow. With water cascading from his emerging head, he glimpsed a section of the shattered mast drifting past. Two powerful strokes towards it, exhausted him, but they allowed him to reach out and grasp hold of the floating timber. Using a piece of trailing rope he managed to lash himself loosely to his makeshift raft.

Although he was weak and bewildered, he was determined to hang on until the end. He was under no illusion about the chances of being seen and rescued in these waters, but... ever the optimist, Andrew prayed silently for the impossible. Around him, the wind and waves were moderating as the storm abated, but he realised that he could not survive much longer in these conditions – time was fast running out for him.

A numbness was already penetrating his body. His mind became confused and he began to hallucinate. Where was Mary? He looked around for her in the surging swells, wanting to help her. Remembrance returned momentarily. Mary was dead, drowned when the Leonore broke up on the reef.

He had forgotten something, he fought against his drifting thoughts to try and concentrate. Becky's letter. He recalled the letter that his sister Alison had entrusted him to deliver to her friend. It was still in his cabin, now submerged beneath the turbulent waters.

He thought he heard voices. Once again his imagination was playing tricks with him. Exhausted and shaking from cold. Andrew was preparing to give up the seemingly hopeless struggle and sink peacefully down into the ocean's depths. Something snatched at his shoulder and in a trance-like condition he heard the voices again.

'... 'ere's another'un! Poor sod's nearly 'ad it... I reck'n!' Andrew was vaguely aware of being hauled unceremoniously from the water and dumped beside two rescued convicts in the tossing whaleboat. In a semi-conscious state he was rowed in rough seas to a large ship where eager hands reached out to haul him on board. Andrew gasped and choked as he swallowed a drink of burning liquid offered him and the other two survivors. Whatever the concoction, the burning sensation eased the shaking and faintness that he had been experiencing.

When he came fully to his senses, he found himself wrapped in a coarse blanket. At least it gave him warmth and his trembling had ceased.

'... 'ere 'ave a sip a'this!' Andrew thinking it was the burning liquid again, was about to refuse when he noticed it was a bowl of steaming hot broth.

'Thank you.' Eagerly he reached out for the hot nourishment and began to sip from the bowl. 'Where am I?' Andrew gave the young crewman a puzzled look.

'Yer on Trojan... a whaler 'eading' for 'bart.'

Andrew nodded his thanks. 'Were... there... other survivors?' He was thinking of his friends, the Gordons and Hester. They would be frantic with worry, wondering if he had managed to reach safety with Mary.

'Only a couple a'convicts... an' yourself.' Andrew tried to encourage the slovenly dressed seaman to talk abut their rescue operation.

'Did you not see any boats from the... sunken ship?' Andrew gave the lad a hopeful glance as he hesitated. 'Two appeared to have got clear of the wreckage...'

'Nah! 'spect they went ont'a the rocks.' He appeared casual and unconcerned. The possible loss of many crew and passengers on the Leonore was accepted with indifference. A philosophical attitude of all seaman, thought Andrew. After all, they must be familiar with the loss of ships – and shipmates.

'I'll bring yer clothes when they gits dried... skipper'll see yer then.' Pausing in the doorway, he hesitated as if meditating on some perplexing problem. 'Sorry 'bout yer mates... but they wouldn't a stood a chance in them seas.' Andrew nodded a silent acknowledgement before weariness and exhaustion overcame him.

He dreamt he was back on the Leonore. Mary was pleading for him to stay, while across tempestuous waters, James, Hester and Billy were calling for his assistance – his help. He felt helpless as the waves washed over him and carried him away. He had failed them all. Restless and tormented, he continued to toss and turn in his restless sleep.

Chapter Twenty Two

A the barque, Hercules eased into Sydney Cover, James heaved a sigh of relief. Since being rescued from the longboat, he had needed all his guile and strength to protect the young woman by his side. He had been aware of the covetous glances bestowed upon Hester by the trading barque's crew and had warned her to keep within the confines of their quarters. Now, at last, James felt able to relax. Their voyage was over.

As he watched the crew preparing to anchor, he wondered what had befallen Andrew and Mary. Had they against all the odds managed to survive the Leonore's sinking? He recalled those hectic moments as the longboats were tossed about in the raging seas. Helpless to manoeuvre the small craft, the survivors had been carried away at the mercy of the turbulent waters. It was then that he realised that his wife and Andrew were trapped on board the stricken ship.

Frustrated and helpless, he had watched as the surging waves had carried the longboats further aware from the doomed Leonore and beyond the reef. He had briefly glimpsed Andrew on the deck, but there had been no sign of his beloved Mary. There seemed little chance that anyone still on board could survive. Waves were continuously pounding the disintegrating wreck and surging with exploding force over the deck.

After a few terrifying hours in the longboat, where conditions had been appalling, they had been rescued by the trading barque Hercules and taken to Launceston. There, all except James, Hester and Billy, had embarked at the small settlement.

A smile flickered across James' saddened features as he recalled the captain's surprise when he had offered to pay his passage to Sydney. When he had learnt that was the barque's destination, he had bargained for three of them to be taken there as passengers.

'Yer fam'ly can hev my cabin, but…' he had given James a meaningful look, '… I strongly suggest that your wife remains close to the quarters, unless accompanied by yourself.' The captain had mistaken Hester for his wife. James decided for her safety, that he would encourage that belief among the crew. He had decided to inform Hester as soon as possible as to his subterfuge – and its reason.

'Yes... yes, I understand, but...' He remembered her deep blush when he had explained why it would be prudent for them to appear as a family.

'You need have no fear, Hester. You and Billy can share the bunk, as for myself, I shall sleep... by the door.' He stopped her words of protest by explaining that his presence would act as a deterrent should any of the crew become... over zealous.

Thankfully all that was behind them, they had arrived at Sydney, their original destination. Soon they would be setting foot in the country that was to become their homeland. Sadly, he wondered if Mary, against all odds, had survived the Leonore's sinking. He glanced silently at Hester and Billy standing at the baroque's rail as they waited for the boat to take them ashore. Their meagre belongings were contained in the small bundle that rested on the deck close to their feet. James had ensure that it was never far from his reach.

James experienced a moment of apprehension as, accompanied by Hester and Billy, he made his way towards the Governor's office. They were surprised and a little nervous at the number of people bustling about the town. Occasionally, a curricle or a carriage would pass them at a slow pace, hindered by the many pedestrians. Hester observed that many of the garments worn by the populace were made from a type of woollen cloth. Later, she was to learn that it was the locally produced cloth spun and woven by female convicts at a factory in a place called Parramatta.

Billy, who kept enquiring about his mother, remained in a small reception room with Hester while his father was interviewed by Governor Darling. To console the distressed child by her side, Hester informed him that his mother would join them as soon as she was well enough to travel. She realised that such a possibility was without hope, but it was necessary to prevent Billy enquiring about his mother in the presence of others.

'Welcome to Sydney... Mr. Gordon.' The Governor had glanced down at the report on his desk to ascertain the new settler's name. 'I understand you were taking passage on the Leonore...' he paused to shake his head sympathetically, '... a traumatic experience for you and your family.'

'Yes, sir. We count ourselves fortunate to have survived.' There was a brief silence as Governor Ralph Darling studied details of the farm that James had purchased. While he waited, James was debating to himself about revealing Hester's status. Wondering if to confess that she was a convict, or should he ignore her criminal status. With the Governor's next words, the dilemma was solved for him.

'You have your wife and young son with you?' He was aware of the Governor's eyes upon him as he made the enquiry.

'My... family took er, passage with me, sir.' James endeavoured not to tell a direct lie.

'Good! Expect you'll be anxious to get settled on your farm?'

'Yes. Unfortunately we, er... lost nearly all our belongings when the Leonore was wrecked. We also lost some of our savings. I was hoping that a small loan... might be available.' He gave the Governor an expectant look, hoping for a sympathetic response. When he noticed the official's frown, he thought that he might have transgressed. He was about to apologise for his indiscretion, when the Governor scribed a few words and signed them.

'Because of your unfortunate circumstances, I'm prepared to make an exception. Take this...' he handed James a note authorising a loan of ten guineas, '... to my outer office and your request will be dealt with.'

'I'm much obliged t'yer Governor. Its taken a load of worry off me mind.' James rose, thinking that the interview was over, but Ralph Darling raised his hand, indicating that the meeting had not been terminated.

'For official purpose, I require from you information relating to the Leonore's loss.' James experienced a momentary shock. What details would he be expected to give? He waited tensely for the questioning to begin.

'Apart from your family and the crew members in the longboat with you, did you know if others survived?' As the Governor waited a reply he noticed the distress his enquiry appeared to have engendered. 'It is necessary for me to make an official report, Mr. Gordon.' There was a sympathetic note to his voice as he explained his need for questioning. James, aware of the empathy behind the Governor's words, nodded his appreciation as he contemplated his reply.

'To my knowledge, there were no other... survivors.' By the official's continued silence, he realised that further information was expected.

'I believe... most of the crew escaped in two boats. One of these was smashed against the reef and the occupants, including the captain, were drowned.'

'What of the convicts? My records show that three score were being transported... twenty of them females.'

'They had no chance. No one thought to release them...'

'Poor devils!' Governor Darling shook his head philosophically.

'That was, until...' James resumed his account of the Leonore's final moments, '... Andrew, er... Mr. Douglass, struggled across the deck to break the lock on the prisoners hatch. By then it was too late for him... and the released convicts.'

The Governor, aware of the emotional distress that his visitor was experiencing, rose and walked over to the window. He was not to know that James was thinking of Mary and Andrew and the uncertainty surrounding their eventual fate. Clearing his throat as an indication that he was ready to continue, James resumed his narration as Governor Darling once again settle behind his desk.

'From the rescue boat we watched as the stormy seas smashed the Leonore to pieces. Waves exploded over the sinking ship, sweeping those who were on the deck into the sea. They would have had little chance of survival... in those... treacherous... waters.' James was unable to carry on. He leant forward, his elbows on his knees as he buried his face in his hands. Reliving those final moments of the Leonore had drained him emotionally.

'Thank you... Mr. Gordon. I'm sorry it was necessary to...'

'It was a most... courageous act, sir.' James words momentarily puzzled the Governor. Then he realised that his visitor was referring to the release of the convicts. To the bravery of the man who had forfeited his life in an attempt to release the trapped convicts. He must remember the name... Douglass. He glanced down at his list until his eyes rested on the name... Andrew Douglass, a Quaker.

'You... believe the man was... drowned?'

'From the longboat we glimpsed his struggles on the sinking transport. There was one enormous wave that seemed to cover the Leonore in her final moments. When the seas had swept past, only floating wreckage remained. I doubt.... He shook his head forlornly, '... if anyone could have survived in such turbulent waters.'

'We must assume that the man...' the Governor once again glanced down at his papers, ... er. Andrew Douglass is dead... drowned?'

'That is my opinion, sir.' James was thinking of his lost wife, Mary, as he nodded confirmation.

* * * * *

Andrew had survived. The whaling ship Trojan was easing herself through the Derwent waters towards the port of Hobart. On board her were Andrew and two convicts, rescued from the stormy seas by the whaler's crew.

Silently, Andrew watched as the whaler approached the anchorage position. In the harbour, a number of whaling and sealing boats were in the process of discharging their cargoes. A trader was unloading manufactured goods from England as well as European wines. On its return to its home port, it would be carrying wool, sealskins, hides and whale oil. Hobart in a few years since its establishment had become a busy port.

Concentrating on the activities around him, Andrew was unaware of the captain's stealthy approach. 'Yer'll be expected to call at Government House.' Turning sharply, Andrew gave the speaker an intense stare before nodding his acknowledgement. He remained silent, intuition warned him that the statement was but a preliminary utterance. 'Best if y'say nowt... 'bout yon fellas,' he nodded in the direction of the two convicts rescued with him. Since their rescue he had noticed the two men labouring with the crew. Their share was always the dirty and hardest work... tasks that would be their lot... until they dropped from exhaustion, then... Mistaking Andrew's silence for dissent, he suggested that they be reported as rescued crew members.

'If that is the situation...' Andrew gave the captain a hard look, '... the men had best come ashore with me.'

'But...' the captain had been on the point of protesting at such an arrangement, when Andrew silenced him. He suggested that once the men were ashore, they could decide for themselves whether they wished to return to the whaling ship, or remain with him in Hobart. He had little doubt as to what their choice would be. The captain's enraged look confirmed Andrew's supposition that the men would have been little more than shanghaied victims once at sea.

'I'll have words with them. Explain the situation.' Andrew turned from the thwarted captain and walked across to converse with the two convicts. As expected, they opted to accompany him ashore, especially when he promised to speak up for them.

Now, as the Trojan rode at anchor, Andrew waited impatiently with the two convicts for the small boat that was to take them ashore. He was anxious to make his report to Government House abut the details of his and the two convicts survival. After conferring with the two men he had recommended that they tell the truth about their convict status. He had promised to speak with the Lieutenant Governor on their behalf and request that they remain under his jurisdiction. Because of their terrifying ordeal on the sinking transport, he had promised the men that he would plead with the authorities for their freedom.

A harbour representative met them as they stepped onto the jetty. In conversation with this loquacious functionary, he learnt that the Lieutenant Governor, Sir George Arthur, had managed to establish good trading relationships with countries such as China, India and the Cape. Trade, which had gradually built up and been instrumental in creating Hobart as the busy port and a relatively prosperous town.

The official continued to enthuse over the Lieutenant Governor's ramifications that had brought prosperity to the developing town. 'Only a few years back, there were only ram-shackled dwellings scattered around the town. Now...' he swept his arm in an arc, '...they have been replaced by these well constructed brick and timber houses.' Andrew's eyes rested on one of the more imposing structures which he assumed was the Customs House.

Following the man's instructions, Andrew passed by this edifice on his way to Government House. His sombre dressed figure attracted a few glances, but the officials noticing that he carried no possessions, ignored his presence. Eventually he found himself in the presence of Sir George Arthur, the Lieutenant Governor.

'You say that the Leonore foundered on the reefs in the straits... driven onto them by heavy seas.' The Governor, who had been listening in silence to Andrew's account of the transport's voyage, suddenly interrupted his narrative. 'Were there other survivors?'

'Two boats managed to get away, but the seas were very rough and appeared to be carrying them ever nearer the reef. At that moment I was swept overboard and found myself struggling to survive in raging seas.'

'You... and two convicts were eventually picked up by the Trojan, a whaler that had been blown off course by the storm. You are indeed a very fortunate man... Mr. Douglass.'

'Yes, sir. It would appear that The Almighty intended me to reach this country and that I, as a Quaker, might encourage its populace to seek the Christian faith.'

'In that case...' Sir George gave his visitor a rueful stare, '... I suggest you build your church... your meeting place–here.' The Lieutenant Governor turned and pointed to an area on the map displayed on the wall behind his desk. 'It's a small settlement, about thirty miles or so north-west of the town.'

Andrew eased forward to glance more closely at the roughly drawn map. He was considering whether to make an offer to buy a piece of land. Fortunately, his money belt, worn under his clothes, had not been confiscated by his rescuers. What money he had was for expenses on his arrival in Sydney – if he ever reached there.

For the time being, it was obvious that the official in front of him was expecting other ideas. Andrew realised that Sir George was expecting him to build a place of worship in the area allotted him, where local settlers and their families would have somewhere to pray. Perhaps it will be possible to purchase some additional land adjacent to the church site. The problem is, how much can I afford? Andrew's contemplation of this difficulty was suddenly broken by the Lieutenant Governor's next words.

'There's a hundred acres available for your… religious meeting place… and grounds.' The official's finger moved across the map to what looked like a wooded area. 'Yours for ten guineas… payment due in seven years.' It was as if his uncertain thoughts had been revealed.

'I'm obliged to you, sir. I hope to leave once I have obtained sufficient stores – and transport.'

'Excellent and er… good luck.' As the official rose to indicate that their meeting was over, his muttered comments that luck would certainly be required, were lost to Andrew. Sir George was remembering how he had encouraged the worst of the settlers and emancipists to farm in that area. Inland and well away from the town.

As Andrew turned to leave, he remembered the two men waiting outside. 'The two men with me, Governor… the convict survivors. Your permission for them to travel with me would be greatly appreciated.' There was a brief pause before the Lieutenant Governor acceded to Andrew's request.

'I have no objection. Leave their details with my official,' he nodded in the direction of the adjoining room.

* * * * *

James flicked his whip above the oxen's head as the wagon moved slowly though the busy streets of Sydney and out into the countryside. As they reached the end of George Street, they found themselves rumbling out on to the Parramatta road where conditions were much quieter.

After six weeks in Sydney, Hester and Billy were elated to be leaving the town behind. My sentiments also, thought James as he glanced with a feeling of relief at his son and the young woman beside him. While in town, he had been dreading the prospect of having her convict status discovered. If Mary had survived, a very embarrassing situation would have developed – and a dangerous one. James was aware of the penalty for harbouring convicts and for knowingly making a false report about Hester's survival.

It was with a feeling of freedom that James, sitting up front with his 'family', guided his oxen-drawn wagon towards the farm that was to be their home. Out of sight... out of mind. James hoped that the old cliché would apply to them all as Sydney disappeared from sight behind them.

Billy's excited chatter gradually subsided as he became aware of his pa's and Hester's preoccupation. Their silent thoughts seemed to weigh heavy upon their minds. Not wishing to disturb them, he remained quiet. Thought of his ma returned and induced a moment of sadness. Each night when he said his prayers, he asked that she might soon be better and able to join them. Billy wished they could have waited a while longer for her, but pa had said that she was not suffering in her new home. He screwed his face up in concentration as he tried to think where heaven was. Not too far away, he hoped... else ma would be lonely.

James gave Hester a surreptitious glance as he wondered if she was having second thoughts about committing herself to what would be, initially, an austere existence. There was also the delicate problem that would have to be determined in the near future. When he had tried to explain what the situation would be like out on the farm, she had appeared unperturbed. Resigned to accepting the inevitable, whatever that might involve.

To ensure that Hester would be under no illusions, James decided to clarify the consequences and expectations of their life together on an isolated farm. So far, he had managed to avoid any emotional intimacies with Hester, but that situation could so easily change. Already he was beginning to experience passionate arousal's at her nearness.

'It'll be a... spart'n life for yer, Hester. Don't rightly know myself what awaits us. Bein' s'close together might cause, er...

certain problems... to arise...' James was searching words to explain intimate personal situations that might arise, without embarrassing her.

'Needn't be a problem, James.' She tried to sound confidently aware of his expectations. 'If you want me as a... a woman, then it must be so.' She spoke softly, a blush burning her face as she continued to stare directly ahead of them. 'When I needed help, Mary and yourself offered me a hand of friendship and comfort. I only wished that she had survived to share this moment with us.' She noticed the sadness in his eyes as their glances met above Billy's head.

'Alas, fate had decided otherwise,' his words were spoken quietly and with deep emotion. 'Billy... and myself are now in need of help... your help, Hester.'

'You have my promise that I shall be as a mother to Billy... and a... comfort to yourself... as a... wife.' Hester's voice faded to silence as she gave Billy an affectionate cuddle.

'A man couldn't ask f'more, Hester. We can but see how things... progress. No one is aware that you are a...' James was determined not to use the word that described his companion's convict status. 'All believe that we are man and wife.'

'Then it is best we... encourage such beliefs, James... if it is your wish?' She could tell by the look in his eyes, that what she dreaded most would be expected of her before many days had passed. Hester wanted to delay that frightening moment as long as possible, at least until after their call at Newacres.

James recalled Andrew speaking of the Burstows, the owners of Newacres on their voyage out from England. As the farm lay on their route, he had decided to call and acquaint them of their friend's misfortune. Andrew had indicated that he knew them well, before they sailed to farm in Australia several years ago.

As James neared the farm, he had expressed his hope to Hester that the owners, experience and help would be of some guidance to them. 'Of course...' he had exclaimed, '... much will depend upon the character of the people concerned.' He also wondered how the owners of Newacres would react to the sad news he was brining, as Andrew's tragic loss would be as yet unknown to them.

Realising that they could not reach the farm before dark, James decided to halt for the night. The sun, a flaming red orb, was already disappearing behind a stretch of wooded hills. 'There'll be shelter by the trees,' he assured Hester as he guided his oxen towards them. 'I'll get a fire started...' James was already jumping down from the wagon, '... while yer seein' t'food.' Hester nodded, aware that her duties would from now on be as mother –and 'wife'. She felt apprehensive about carrying out the obligations of a spouse.

After their meal, they sat round the fire enjoying its comforting warmth against the cool night air. Hester and James sat close together, silently gazing into the flickering flames. Billy was dozing, cuddled close to his surrogate mother. Gently, Hester rose and helped him into the wagon where later she would join him. James had prepared his blanket under the wagon in readiness for his night's sleep. Both adults seemed withdrawn and worried as their contemplative gaze centred on the flames that flared and sent a shower of sparks drifting up into the darkness.

'Somethin' is troublin' yer, Hester?' He reached across and gently took hold of her hand. 'Not regrettin' our er... arrangements?' Her face looked tense and troubled in the firelight. James experienced a caring, protective feeling towards her. He had been aware of her shy, almost innocent demeanour whenever their future together was mentioned. Although she had offered to share his home... his bed, he had glimpsed a look of trepidation in her eyes.

'It's... it's alright, James...' she continued to gaze pensively into the fire, '... I shall carry out... my duties... as I promised you.' Tears glistened in her eyes as she turned towards him.

'I have no doubts regardin' y'promise, my dear, but of your inner emotions.' He watched her face closely in the flickering light before making a quiet plea. 'Can y'not tell me what it is that troubles yer?' Holding both her hands, he gently eased her round so that he could see her features more clearly.

'They... may seem trivial to you... James.' His sympathetic gentleness was easing her distress. She experienced an urge to unburden her fears, to relate the frightening ordeal that had initiated her imprisonment.

'Unless yer tell me, I'll have no way of judging, Hester.' With a benign movement he leaned across and lightly kissed her cheek. His first act of affection towards her. Hester struggled to calm her emotions as feelings of fear... uncertainty cause her to withdraw her hands from his gentle grasp. 'I'm sorry... Hester. It was wrong of me to...'

'No, James! No! It was not... your fault...' She turned her head away sharply to look once again into the fire. 'It's ... just... that...'

Quietly and unemotionally she told him how her step-father had forced his way into her bed one night and committed a painful deed to her virginal body. She had been too frightened to report it, but as the threat of her confession might cause trouble, her step-father had arranged for her to be sent away into service.

While at the large isolated house, she had been beaten and treated like a slave. One night, in an act of desperation, she had snatched a half-sovereign from a table and run away with her meagre possession in a small bundle. The money she felt was owing her as she had never received any payment for her services.

Hester, her voice little more than a whisper, went on to relate how she was stopped as she tramped wearily towards the nearest town, Aylesbury. The half-sovereign that she had retained to help her reach an aunt in London had been used as evidence of her crime – theft.

'I was being transported on the Leonore to... well you know the rest, James.' She buried her head in her hands and sobbed until her heartache and distress began to ease. Suddenly she was aware of a strong protective arm around her shoulders. Through her tears she looked up into the loving eyes of the man with whom she had promised to share her life. Hester realised at that moment, that somehow everything would turn out kindly for her.

'This I promise you, Hester.' His face was serious with understanding as he made his pledge. 'I'll not harm you, or cause thee further distress. Only if... and when you have the er... longing to share my love and it is hoped beyond all doubt that Mary is dead, shall I ask you to become my wife.

'Thank you for your… patience, James.' She stretched across and returned his kiss. 'When and if that day arrives, I shall surrender completely and willingly to your… wishes.' Hester turned, her face the colour of the flames, to look into the starlit night. James had however, glimpsed the silent promised reflected in her eyes.

'Then may it be soon,' he whispered to himself as he watched her climb into the wagon for the night.

Chapter Twenty Three

Edward stirred into wakefulness, aware of the subdued sobbing that had aroused his senses. A sound that reflected the heartache of a troubled soul. For a few moments as the quiet lamentations continued, he endeavoured to orientate his drowsy thoughts.

Realisation permeated his sleepy senses as he reached out for Becky. She was not there. Frantically he scrambled into a sitting position. It was then he noticed Becky's shadowy form silhouetted against the grey light of early dawn.

Barely visible, she stood by the window, silently sobbing as she gazed through tear-filled eyes at the first subtle shades of the sunrise. Edward experienced a moment of anguish as he became aware of her sadness – her heartache.

'Becky, my love... what troubles you so?' Concern was manifest by the sympathetic intonations in his voice. Scrambling from their bed, he hurried across to embrace and comfort her.

'It's... nothing... Edward.' Her sobbing subsided as she tried to hide her distress. 'I... just feel... so...' but her voice faded as Edward held her close in his arms. Outside, he noticed the first rose-pink blushes of the sunrise spreading across the heavens.

'Becky, dearest.' Gently he eased away from her, then, placing his finger beneath her chin, tenderly raised her tear-stained face. Her dark brown eyes, glistening with tears, mirrored the sorrow in her heart. 'Why the sadness... the tears, my love? It's so unlike you.'

'I... feel so... distressed abut us, Edward. I'm worried about... our future.' She was struggling to regain her composure as she looked into his tormented features. 'Of late I have experienced strange... emotional feelings. A premonition that fate is... is about to... violate our lives... to separate us.' Becky choked back the sobs as a vision of the future without Edward clouded her mind.

'Nothing can, or will separate us, my love. Only...' Edward could not bring himself to utter the final word. 'Try not to distress yourself my dear.' Holding her close in his arms, he tenderly kissed her. First her tear-filled eyes, then her damp cheeks, the tip of her nose and finally a lingering kiss upon her eager lips.

'Our future here...' he indicated their land outside, now ethereal-like in the grey, misty light of the dawn, ' ... is assured. We have wealth and have become an integral part of the community in this new country. Most important, we have each other and a wonderful family.' Gradually Edward's embrace eased away her uncertainty. His love induced a tranquil feeling to her being.

'I'm sorry... Edward.' She smiled affectionately up into his worried eyes. 'I think it's the strain of maintaining our secret. I have recently wondered if we should declare our... circumstances.' He was aware of the whispered uncertainty in her voice as she waited for his reaction.

'The matter has also occupied my thoughts a great deal in recent months, Becky. Perhaps, by confessing my particulars to Governor Darling, he may deem it a matter to be viewed in a favourable light. We can but hope so.'

'No matter, Edward. I shall carry on whatever the outcome, but I have a feeling that if we visited the Governor together... our unusual circumstances would be viewed sympathetically.'

'At the moment, Becky...' she could feel the strength of his body pressed against hers, '... I have a more emotional confession to make. I'm in love... and...'

'I'm fully aware of your... urgency.' She chuckled on seeing the yearning look in his eyes. With such a love to cherish, she wondered how she could have felt to unsure ... so insecure. Edward's amorousness seemed to fill her with an urgent requirement as he lifted her in his arms and carried her back to their bed.

Placing her arms around his neck, Becky kissed his lips warmly and tantalisingly as he lowered her gently down. She pulled Edward down onto the bed beside her as passion overwhelmed their naked bodies. The dark thoughts of the early dawn were washed away as impassioned waves of love flowed through their fervent loving.

* * * * *

'We shall see the Governor on my return from Greenacres, Becky. I have decided to declare our full situation to him.' They were enjoying a late breakfast. 'Due...' as Becky had explained on stretching her satiated body in the bed beside Edward, ' ... to natural desires beyond our control.' Laughing happily together, they had dressed between ardent embraces, ready to face the new day. A day that was to bring unexpected visitors – and news of home.

'What is it, Edward?' Becky followed his puzzled look as he gazed out of the window.

'We have... visitors. A wagon is approaching from the Parramatta road.' They rose from the breakfast table to stand by the window and watch as a dilapidated wagon entered the gates to the East Drive.

James, with Hester and Billy sitting nervously beside him, brought the wagon to a halt just as Edward and Becky emerged to greet them. 'Mr. and Mrs. Burstow?' Edward and Becky hesitated a moment before nodding confirmation. 'Names... Gordon. James Gordon... an' this be my... family. Hester 'n Billy,' he nodded towards his two companions.

'Good day t'you, James... Hester... Billy.' Edward noticed the anxiety in their eyes. 'Welcome to Newacres.' His smile of welcome eased their apprehension. As Edward introduced Becky, he was wondering at the nature of their call.

'Can I be of any help...?' Edward was trying to place the family, but he could recall no Gordons. They were complete strangers.

'We're headin' out towards Bathurst. We came out t'settle on a farm just outside the town.' James hesitated, wondering how much information he should pass on.

'Would that by any chance be the Jepson's place?'

'Why, yes.' James seemed taken aback. 'You know the farm?' Edward nodded a smiling confirmation.

'I own Greenacres... the adjoining farm.' He gave his visitor a close scrutiny, wondering if he should warn him of the farm's run down condition. Despite giving Jim Masters, his farm manager at Greenacres, permission to help the elderly and ailing Jepson's with their livestock, the farm had deteriorated considerably over the past few months. Especially as the aged owners had spent longer periods away from their farm while they waited the arrival of the new owners from England.

'You must take some refreshments first.' Becky's invitation caused a moment of uncertainty. Guessing at their embarrassment, she stepped up to the wagon and, holding out her hands, offered Hester support in descending from the wagon. As she did so, Becky noticed the faded and rough-textured material of her dress.

'Thank you, ma'am.' Hester offered a light curtsy.

'Oh, Hester my dear... there is no need for such protocol here. Just call me, Becky.' She turned back to the wagon where a wide-eyed Billy was watching proceedings with a stoical detachment. 'Come... Billy.' Becky held out her arms and helped him down.

'Roger!' His mother's shout brought the youngest member of the family scurrying from the house. He was given instructions to look after Billy while his parents were inside.

That's settled then! James will ride with me to Greenacres. We can inspect your farm en route and I'll arrange for any help you might need.' Edward looked for and received, confirmation from all present.

'While you men are away...' Becky gave Hester a conspiratorial look, '... we shall have much to talk of. I need to know all about the latest news and fashions from England.'

'Which reminds me...' Edward gave James a nonplussed glance, '... how did you know our names... our farm?'

'Well...' James hesitated, knowing that his host was anxious for them to be leaving, '... it's rather a long story.'

'In that case you can impart the details during out journey... and...' Edward glanced at the two women, '... Hester can acquaint Becky in our absence.'

'Yes!' Becky turned excitedly towards Hester, '... I'm longing to hear your news. It's been so long since we conversed with any new arrivals from England.'

'By the way, Hester...' Edward turned towards the young woman, just as her eyes were seeking James. He noticed the flash of fear – uncertainty in her look. He paused a moment on glimpsing the worried frown creasing her brows. Probably she is nervous at being separated from her husband, he thought.

Edward ceased his contemplation as he suddenly recalled the enquiry he had started to ask of Hester. 'I was going to enquire if you can use a gun or pistol.' When the young woman shook her head in bewilderment, he glanced directly at Becky.

'It's alright…' she smiled understandingly at Edward, '… by the time your return, Hester will be a competent gun handler.'

'Good!' He gave Becky a grateful look before gathering his supplies and bidding her and the children farewell.

The two women stood side by side on the veranda silently watching their men until they were out of sight. 'Come, Hester…' Becky placed her arm through that of her companion's in a friendly gesture, '… I'm sure you have much to tell me.' Her smile was beguiling.

'My reason for accompanying you, James, is because bush-rangers have been sighted in the Bathurst area. Quite close to our farms… and I'm rather concerned about the situation.'

'Bush-rangers? What… who might they be?' James frowned as he listened to Edward's warning words about the unscrupulous raiders.

'Escaped convicts on the run. Occasionally they attack the settlers. Burning their farms, pillaging and sometimes – murdering them.' Edward noticed the shocked look on his companion's face. 'You'll need to be alert at all times. Be ready to defend your property – and your life.'

'Now…' James nodded thoughtfully, '… I understand the urgency in training Hester to handle a gun.' He gave Edward an approving glance.

For most of the day they rode side by side, exchanging farming information and experiences. James listened for most of the time, anxious to absorb his companion's valuable knowledge. An exemplary farmer who had learnt the hard way.

'Your farmin' skill has been gained over many years, Edward?'

'Almost fourteen… since we landed as survivors at the end of 1812.

'By a strange coincidence...' James turned towards the man beside him, '... we also were survivors. Hester, Billy and m'self were on the Leonore when she was swept on to a reef. A severe storm hit us when we were in the straits between Van Dieman's land and the southern coast of this country.' Edward was surprised at the news.

Just as the gold and crimson hues of the sunset were fading from the sky, Edward rode towards a familiar landmark. He had taken the shorter, but much rougher route through mountainous terrain. On the occasions he used this trail to reach Greenacres, Edward usually made camp in the shelter of the prominent outcrop or rocks they were now approaching.

A deep purple dusk settled quickly over the mountains. Beneath the outcrop, the two riders soon had a fire started. Few words were spoken as they concentrated on preparing and consuming their food. Once their appetite was appeased, the two travellers prepared to settle down for the night.

'I'll check that the horses are settled, James.' Edward disappeared into the shadows carrying his gun. James had noticed that he never moved far without it. A prudent action that he intended to follow in future. He touched the gun beside him reassuringly. Edward, returning to the firelight, noticed his companion's action and responded with an approving smile. 'Aye keep it handy, James. You'll never know when you might be needing it.' That time was not far off.

After stretching out by the fire, there were a few moments of contemplative silence. Eventually Edward asked the question that had been puzzling him since meeting the man sharing his campfire. 'I'd be pleased to hear who it was that claimed the friendship of Becky and myself.'

'Reck'n as how yer would.' James gave an understanding nod as the flames cast flickering shadows around them. 'He was a Quaker... name of Andrew. Took passage on the Leonore with... us. When the Medical Officer died, he was designated t'take over the surgeon's duties and also that of Government Representative on the ship.'

'A Quaker, you say?' Edward frowned. 'I know... no one of that... sect.' For a few moments Edward lay staring up at the stars as he tried to recall anyone he was acquainted with of that faith. He shook his head at his negative response. 'What... kind of person was the er... Quaker you befriended?'

'A very courageous... and compassionate man.'

'Did he ever speak much of his family... inform you of his family name, or...'

'Perhaps...' James eased himself up into a sitting position, '... it would be best if I spoke fully of the voyage 'as ended in disaster.' He picked up a piece of wood and threw it into the fire as he considered the best place to begin his story.

'Mary and myself had visions of settling in ...'

'Mary?'

'My wife... she was believed...'

'I... thought... that Hester...' Edward kept his thoughts to himself as he realised that James as anxious to narrate his experiences without interruptions. Intuition warned him that his companion's story was going to reveal surprising episodes that would directly... or indirectly touch the lives of his family.

As James continued with his story, Edward became aware of the similar circumstances to that of Becky and himself on their voyage out. He realised that his companion's story was a confession. – a confidence entrusted to him.

One thing that intrigued Edward as he continued to listen, was the references to the Quaker who had professed friendship with Becky and Stephen. Poignant memories returned as he listened to James' account of the shipwreck.

'Andrew braved the dangers and returned to help my dying wife, Mary. He urged me to look after Billy, who had been knocked semi-conscious when the Leonore was struck by the storm. Carrying my son in my arms, I struggled with Hester's help across the tilting deck to the longboat. There was no sign of Mary or Andrew. Before I could return to the ship to assist Andrew, a wave swept us some distance away.

'As we tossed helplessly on the storm-lashed waves, Hester pointed to Andrew who was struggling across the tangled wreckage of fallen masts and stays. As we watched we could see him endeavouring to smash the locks to release the trapped convicts. A brave action… but a futile one. The situation by then had become a hopeless one for the poor unfortunate souls… and for Andrew.'

James was silent as he reflected upon the horror they had witnessed from the longboat. Edward was about to speak, when James, in a voice breaking with emotion, continued his story.

'It was Andrew's last act. We watched with shock and dismay as the towering wave exploded against the ship's side and swept everything before it. Our last glimpse of Andrew…' he hesitated to regain his composure, '… was of the wave sweeping him into the stormy waters. There was no sign… of Mary. Neither of them had a chance…'

'Your Quaker friend… was a man of great courage, James.' Edward noticed his companion's eyes sparkling in the flickering firelight.

'Brave and gentle… a credit to his faith.' There was a note of unmistakable reverence in James' voice as he spoke of his gallant Quaker friend. A man who, it seemed, had sacrificed his life so bravely – but in vain. Edward frowned reflectively at the thoughts that had been worrying him. He was certain that his wild speculations were ludicrous ones… but…

Andrew, who had been responsible for his transportation, and the person described by James could not conceivable be one and the same. Edward never pressed for further details about the Quaker who was unfortunately drowned, so his speculations would be of no consequence.

In the ensuing silence that followed his companion's revelations, he heard the whispered rustling of the trees and the strident call of the nocturnal creatures in the surrounding bush. The fire flared as flames engulfed a fresh piece of wood. Sparks drifted up into the darkness before fading as the stars in the dawn sky.

If was the softly spoken words of James that disturbed the enveloping quietude. 'I'd like t'ask a favour of yer, Edward.'

'Of course. How can I help you?' Edward looked across the flames, expecting to hear James' solicitation, but noticed his companion staring trance-like into the flames. Just when he thought James had forgotten his request, he looked up as if just arriving at an important decision.

'When visiting Sydney, would yer enquire if there is news... of other survivors from the Leonore? Until I receive confirmation of... my wife's death...' he was finding it difficult to continue. 'My... er, relationship with Hester... must remain... unconventional. A kind 'a companionship. I must respect the trust... the faith she has placed in me.' Edward, while appreciating James' concern, was thinking of his own first months alone with Becky.

'Her convict status...' James paused to give an imploring look in the direction of the silent man lying across from him, '... will, I trust, remain a confidence a'tween us?'

'You have my promise of that.' Edward was thinking of his own secret – undisclosed for nearly fourteen years.

'When... if I have news of my wife's death, then I shall be able to ask Hester to act as my wife. Unfortunately, we shall never be able to marry, without disclosing her identity. That she is a convict.' Edward nodded silent agreement; he was all too aware of the problems awaiting James and Hester. Similar circumstances to those experienced by Becky and himself during their shared life together.

'By your description of conditions prevailing at the time of the Leonore's sinking, it seems most unlikely that anyone could have survived in those stormy waters. Nevertheless, I promise to make discreet enquiries when I visit Sydney.' There was no more talking as the fire gradually burnt low and the two men succumbed to the tiredness that had permeated their weary bodies.

It was an unpremeditated remark by Billy that confirmed Becky's intuition, that all was not as it seemed between Hester and James. Aware of Hester's nervousness, she was attempting to put her companion at ease by describing the life to expect in isolation out on their farm. 'You'll find the situation lonely at first, Hester, but Jim, Maggy and their children, who live on our adjacent farm, will...' Becky paused as a tearful Billy entered the room. Sobbing silently, he approached an apprehensive Hester.

'When... is... mummy... comin' back?' he enquired between sobs. Reaching out, she gently pulled him into her arms. A protective and loving gesture that was not lost on Becky, who was momentarily taken aback. She noticed how Hester's sympathetic understanding, gradually eased the little lad's distress.

'We cannot be sure, Billy.' Her words were gentle and reassuring. 'Until we hear from your... mother...' she cast an uncertain glance in Becky's direction, '... you must try and be very brave.'

James had delayed informing his son about his mother, until confirmation about her ultimate fate had been received. Hester's warm embrace helped to reassure Billy, who gave her a tearful smile as he succumbed to her affectionate cuddle. Roger appeared, and at a sign from his mother was encouraged to persuade Billy to join him outside.

After their departure, Hester sat quietly with her head lowered, ashamed that her secret had been disclosed. She was suddenly aware of a comforting arm being placed around her shoulders. With tear-filled eyes she looked up into the friendly and compassionate features of her understanding host.

'Try not to feel too distressed,' Becky was endeavouring to console her distraught guest. 'There is no need to feel guilty, Hester. As for your situation... I'm sure that you have your reasons.' She gave her troubled companion an affectionate hug, assuring her that her secret would be safe.

'Would it help if... we talked about... your circumstances?' Becky realised that something was troubling Hester. She seemed deeply perturbed. Wanting to help her young guest, she had proffered the suggestion of a talk, in the hope of helping Hester come to terms with the problem causing her so much distress.

'I'm... not... sure.' Hester appeared confused... uncertain. She was wondering if a confession would upset the plans for her future... her security with James and Billy. Encouraged by Becky's kindness, she started to tell her story. Words came hesitantly at first, but as Hester's confidence strengthened, words tumbled from her lips.

She described her step-father's attack on the purity of her body. Why she took the money from the people who had abused her. Then with a sob in her voice, she described her arrest and incarceration in prison and the ill-fated voyage on the Leonore.

Becky noticed the changing emotions reflected on her companion's face as she relived her terrifying experiences. Occasionally, she paused, sobs choking her speech as she described Mary's illness and Andrew's courageous sacrifice. Sadness caused her to stop and bury her tear-stained face in her hands.

Hester's description of the shipwrecked survivors and her relationship with James were painful reminders to Becky of her affiliation with Edward. Her heart ached for the attractive young woman sitting close beside her. She wondered how best to help ease her anguish.

'Hester!' Her voice broke the deep emotional silence. 'It would appear that your friend... the Quaker, had little hope of saving Mary?'

'In the circumstances, very little, but...' Hester shrugged her shoulders disconsolately.

'Doubts remain... as regards her survival?'

'We cannot be certain... of Mary's... fate.' Hester's sorrow induced a look of bewilderment. 'Andrew would have known... but he was... drowned.' She dried her eyes on the handkerchief proffered by Becky. 'He risked his life to... to...' she fought back her emotions of sadness to continue, '... release the trapped convicts.'

'There was little hope for those remaining on the ship...' she paused fighting to overcome the shock of her remembered visions of Andrew's last moments. 'Had it not been for Andrew's kindness... that fate... could so easily have been mine. Sadly...' her voice was now choking with emotion, '... his efforts were too late for those poor souls – and himself.' Hester's feelings were obvious as she shook her head forlornly.

'You speak as if you were... fond of Andrew?' Becky noticed the blush that coloured the girl's cheeks before she lowered her head to hide her shyness.

'Yes... he was so kind and friendly. Although he never spoke of her, I could tell that his heart belonged to another. A more fortunate person that I.' Hester's eyes reflected the sorrow, as she recalled her liaison... her friendship with Andrew. 'He was always so understanding... and helpful.' She concluded her reminiscing with a deep sigh.

'It would appear, from your account of his actions, that he was also very brave, Hester?' She gave her distressed companion an affectionate hug. 'Perhaps he survived and is trying to find you?'

'I think not...' Hester shook her head sadly, '... we could only watch helplessly... as the ship broke up beneath him.' Weeping silently, she looked out of the window as if praying for his appearance.

'His family will grieve when the news reaches them of his... death.' 'Sadly both his parents died in a tragic accident. They were... drowned together. in the lake on their Suffolk estate.' She paused as she became aware of Becky's startled look.

'Hester...' Becky was sure that her intuition on this occasion was deceiving her, but, '... did... Andrew have a... limp?'

'Why, yes.' A note of surprise crept into Hester's voice. 'You... know him?'

'It's probably a coincidence, but I once knew an Andrew who was similarly deformed. He however was a waster. A drunkard and a... gambler, nothing like the gentle Quaker you described.'

'Andrew...' she looked uncertainly into Becky's face, '... once confessed to me that he was previously of that nature. Imprisonment and his chance meeting with a friendly Quaker just after his release was the start of his ... reformed life. Since that meeting a few yeas back, Andrew has lived a... rehabilitated life.'

Becky listened in shocked silence. There had to be some mistake. Yet the Quaker had spoken to Hester about his friendship with Stephen, her late husband and – herself. 'Did he ever mention his... home. The estate on which his parents lived when they were alive?' Hester wrinkled her brows in meditation.

'I believe he did... but as it reminded him of his dead parents, he spoke of it very rarely.'

'Was the estate... called...' Becky had to force herself to finish the question, '... called Homefield? Homefield Hall?' She held her breath.

'Yes... yes!' A surprised smile softened the sorrowful features of Hester's face. 'I remember the name... now that...' Her cheerfulness vanished as she noticed the colour drain from her host's face. Realisation dawned. 'Your... Andrew... is it the same person as...?' Her voice faded as she watched Becky silently nodding her head.

'Did... Andrew...' Becky's voice reflected her troubled mind, '... mention the reason for visiting the colony?' If Andrew had survived, then Edward and herself could be in serious trouble. Were these the portentous emotions that had been causing her distressing hallucinations of late? Tense with anticipation, she awaited Hester's reply.

'Only vaguely... something about a mission to fulfil. A past wrong that...' Becky's head sank in despair. The remainder of her companion's words were lost as she reflected on Andrew's possible survival and the threat to her and Edward and their – family. Was their joyous world about to fall apart? Becky struggled to remain clam as the significance of Hester's words stunned her senses.

* * * * *

Edward pulled his horse up sharply. A frown creased his brow as his keen eyesight focused on a distant smudge of smoke. Intuition warned him that danger threatened. As he watched, the smoke appeared to thicken and spiral higher... an ominous sign.

'James!' There was an anxious sound to Edward's voice. 'Your farm lies in that direction.' Edward was already urging his horse into a gallop as he spoke. 'That smoke troubles me... looks like a large... fire,' he shouted his warning to James, who was by then easing up beside him. By the time they crested the hill, his worst fears were confirmed. About a mile or so ahead of them, the farmhouse and outbuildings were blazing furiously.

'We must hurry, James. The Jepsons will need help.' Already Edward was crouched low in his addle and racing his horse toward the conflagration. James, his face a mask of shock, followed close behind.

Before his horse had come to a stop, Edward leapt from the saddle and ran towards the blazing farmhouse. He came to a sudden stop as the intense heat drove him back. Flames roared through the dried timber structure, causing smoke to drift across his vision. He had hoped to find some access to the building, but the smoke and flames prevented any chance of rescuing the elderly Jepsons. A small group of men suddenly emerged from the wooded area at the rear of the farm. Edward called a warning to James as the figures began running towards them. As they approached, he recognised the man leading them. Fran Johnson, a middle aged convict, who had laboured for the Jepson's over the past four years, waved a recognition on seeing Edward.

Breathlessly, he hurried across to the two riders, his face pale from shock at the events that he had just witnessed. 'What's been happening, Johnson?' Edward questioned the man as he came to a stop before him.

'Thank God... Y've come... Mr. Burstow...' Frightened and breathless he looked nervously around. 'They were bush-rangers... as did it... they tried ter... '

'What of the Jepson's... are they inside?' Edward was concerned about the couple's safety, but glancing at the raging fire, realised that there was little hope for them.

'They're safe!' Johnson's voice was hoarse with shock. 'Had... an appointment... Bathurst.' He took a few deep breaths before continuing. 'They left... this morning. 'Twas a blessin'.' His breathing was back to normal.

'A blessing, indeed.' Edward's relief was obvious when he realised that the couple were safe. 'Did you notice how many were in the raiding party, Johnson?'

'Five. When they attacked we...' he indicated three other labourers standing a few paces away, '... ran for the woods.' Edward's glance went to the trees about a quarter of a mile beyond the burning farmhouse.

'When they rode off... did you notice in which direction they went?'

'Rck'n as how they were headin' f'your place, Mr. Burstow.' One of the labourers pointed in the direction of Greenacres.

'Do what you can... we'll be back later.' Edward was in his saddle and riding towards his farm before he had finished speaking.

'I'm ridin' with yer!' James was already in the saddle. 'There's not much I can do here for the time bein'...' Urging his horse into a full gallop he rode with Edward towards Greenacres.

They noticed the spiral of smoke, just before they heard the distant gunfire. As they emerged from the trees, Edward's anger erupted.

'Damn them... the murdering scum.' Gritting his teeth in anger, he took in the sight before him. Flames were licking the outside wall of a storage barn as the bush-rangers attacked the farmhouse. They were being held off by Jim, Maggy and a couple of workers.

'Keep to the right!' Edward gestured their line of approach to James. 'With the wood behind us, we might be able to surprise those damned marauders.' He was already reaching for his gun, when a shot rang out. He grunted in satisfaction as the raider, running from the blazing barn, dropped in his tracks and lay still.

'Well done...' he nodded approvingly towards the farm from whence the shot had come. 'That's one less to worry about.' A grim chuckle escaped his lips as he and James urged their horses towards the confrontation. A series of shots reverberated through the hollow as they did so.

Glass shattered in one of the ground floor windows. James looked anxiously around, a little nervous at the reception awaiting their arrival. He had expected nothing of this description. Edward pointed to the rear of the house where a man was endeavouring to force an entry. 'Take care of him, James. I'll see to those at the front.;

Before he could warn those inside of their presence, Edward spotted one of the attackers creeping under cover towards the house. Held his fire, thinking the man was acting as a decoy to draw his attention from the two men concealed behind the bushes. Glancing towards the thicket, he tried to anticipate the attackers next move. He was soon to find out. In horror he watched as one of the men, carrying a flaming torch raced towards the house.

Edward's reflex action was instantaneous. From his saddle, he aimed and fired just as the man looked like reaching the farmhouse. Just as he fired, the man stumbled and nearly fell. 'Damnation! Missed!' Edward cursed in frustration as he prepared for another shot.

The arsonist, intent on his gruesome task, had almost reached the house, when a gun cracked from one of the windows. It was a relieved Edward who watched the torch bearer sprawl face down in the dirt. Looking towards the window, he was just in time to see Maggy withdrawing her gun as she withdrew from sight.

'Well done, Maggy.' Edward called softly. Turning to check that the arsonist was dead, he found himself watching in disbelief as the flames from the attacker's torch, suddenly engulfed his body. He watched helplessly as the bush-ranger burnt to a blackened corpse.

Glancing anxiously around, Edward was looking for some sighting of Jim, his manager. Perhaps he was inside helping to defend the house against the marauding bush-rangers. If he could safely reach the veranda, there was a chance he could contact his friends inside the house. Leaving his horse, he made a crouching run for the steps onto the veranda. He reached them in safety and began to ease round the side of the building. As he assessed the situation, something beyond the water tank caught his eye.

'Dear God!' Edward gasped with shock. 'Please… not, Jim.' He could see his manager stretched out with his gun lying on the ground beside him. Cautiously, he began to edge across in an attempt to reach his friend, but as shot splattered around him, he realised he was in a dangerously exposed position. There was a low wall about twenty paces ahead of him, Jim was stretched out in its shelter. Edward was determined to reach it and check on his manager's condition – if he was still alive.

Just as he was about to make a dash across the open space, he heard a gun crack. It came from the rear of the house. Next moment he heard James' startled shout, proclaiming his success on the raider at the back. It was an ashen-faced companion who breathlessly joined Edward on the veranda.

'Dead!' He whispered grimly as he pronounced the demise of the bush-ranger. Turning away, he began to retch badly as the consequences of his actions penetrated his shocked senses. He had just shot a man... his first killing.

Edward, aware of his companion's distress, encouraged him into immediate action. 'Cover me, James. I must try and reach Jim.' He gestured towards the still form behind the low wall. Shaking nervously, James reloaded his gun. After a couple of deep breaths to steady himself, he indicated to Edward that he was ready.

Edward dashed from cover, crouching low as he raced across the open ground to reach his manager. Would his efforts be in vain, he wondered... that was something he intended to find out.

He heart the shot just as he reached the shelter of the wall. A sharp pain made him call out, but his momentum carried him to the side of his old friend. With trepidation, he reached across to check Jim's pulse, anxiously watching his ashen face as he did so.

Edward's movements induced a sharp stabbing pain in his shoulder. He grimaced as he clasped the affected area in an effort to ease the pain. As he glance down at his wound, he noticed his hands and his coat were both stained with blood. Shaking his head in an attempt to overcome his dizziness, he remained crouched beside his badly injured manager.

Footsteps were racing towards him. Maggy, unable to contain her emotions, took advantage of the lull to try and reach her husband... and Edward. A warning shout intended for Maggy died on Edward's lips as faintness forced him into silence. He heard the gun blast just as Maggy collapsed beside him.

'I believe... I hit 'im.' James was lowering his smoking gun as he walked across to join them. In silence they watched as the two remaining attackers rode off towards the woods. One of the riders was doubled over in the saddle and looking in bad shape.

'Leave them... Edward whispered weakly, '... they'll not get far… in their condition.' His anxious glance centred on Maggy who was bending over her husband. Worry lined her face as she concentrated on inspecting the bloody wound on the side of his head. 'How… is he… Maggy?' Edward was fighting to remain conscious as a haze began to blur his vision.

'He's… alive. Pulse is… a bit weak. A nasty wound… needs bathing.'

'We'll get… him… inside, Maggy.' Edward looked weakly towards James. 'Can you… see to… it?' James was already walking over to the labourers, who, now that the conflict was over, emerged from hiding. He soon organised a group to carry the unconscious manager into the house.

'How about yourself, Edward?' Giving his companion an anxious look, he indicated to a watching labourer that he should help him take a weakening and shaky Edward inside. Shouting to the remaining workers, he ordered them to collect buckets and to try and contain the fire.

Gently, Maggy bathed and tended her husband's wound. His eyes flickered open, silently he stared around at the anxious looking faces. Then a weak grin spread over his pallid features as he noticed Edward. 'Good on yer, Edward. Thanks fer… droppin' in.' He closed his eyes briefly as an attack of dizziness overcame him. Maggy heaved a sigh of relief, thankful that he was gradually regaining full possession of his faculties.

'It's a clean wound.' James spoke reassuringly after inspecting and cleaning Edward's shoulder injury. 'You've lost a fair amount o'blood, but it appears to have almost stopped now.' He began to apply a dressing.

'I'll see t'it, sir.' Maggy eased James aside to complete the bandaging. As she continued with the dressing, Edward introduced James and explained abut his burn-out farm. 'Best if y'both rest…' Maggy gave both her patients a stern look, '… then we c'n discuss future plans.' Edward was perplexed at the glance exchanged between Maggy and her injured husband.

'You're sure that your decision is the correct one, Jim… Maggy?' A sadness lingered on Edward's face as his glance moved between his friends of many years.

'Yes. We've given the matter a great deal of thought.' Jim, turning to Maggy for confirmation, noticed her nervousness. 'For the children's sake, we have decided to return to England.' There was a deep silence following Jim's statement. 'This latest upset...' he cast an apologetic look in Edward's direction, '... finally decides... our future.' Edward nodded sympathetically.

'I shall miss you both. We've shared so much together.' Gazing up from the couch, Jim confirmed those sentiments. Maggy, her arm resting protectively on her husband's shoulder, called their children over to have them beside her. Ralph, Peggy and Ben hurried forward to see their injured father. Smiles of relief brightened their faces when he reached out to embrace them.

Edward experienced a moment of sorrow as he watched them. He had known the children from birth, been an 'uncle' to them from their childhood. Only forty months separated the oldest, Ralph, now twelve years old and Ben, the youngest. A nine year old whose mischievous ways reminded him of his oldest son, Stephen, in his younger days.

'Don't like leavin' yer in the lurch, Edward, but...'

'Please Jim...' Edward held up his hand. 'No need to distress yourself. While we've been talking...' he looked round at his companions as they fell silent in expectation, '... I've been turning an idea over in my mind.' Now that he had their full attention, it was to James he gave a perspicacious glance before continuing. 'If my plan comes to a satisfactory conclusion, it would solve both my problems... and also that of James'.'

'Me!' James frowned his surprise as he returned Edward's speculative look.

'Why not?' Your farm has been burn down by those rogues,' he indicated the dead bush-rangers being dragged away from the house. 'Jim and his family want to return to England. I shall be needing a new manager.'

A big, understanding grin spread over James' face as he realised the implications behind Edward's words. 'You want me... to take over the management of Greenacres?' The prospect cheered James immensely. Despondency had been infusing his being as he thought of his burnt-out farm; now but a smouldering pyre.

'I'm giving you first offer, James. You'll be most welcome, I can assure you.'

'I'd like to, but...' an uncertain look came to James' face, '... my loan... the farm...' He was thinking of the loan and his small savings that he had invested in the farm. He faced ruin... before he even started.

'The loan is no problem, James. I can repay it in exchange for the Jepson's place. It will mean a much larger farm to manage... should you agree to stay.'

Without further hesitation, James stepped over and clasped Edward's hand. 'Yer just got y'self a new manager for Greenacres. I just hope...' he nodded towards the burn out building, '... that we don't get too many visits from those damned skulking bush-rangers.'

'I think the reception they received today will act as a deterrent, especially the couple who escaped.' Edward's words were greeted with warm approval.

'Aye, let's hope so, but just in case...' James patted the gun beside him, '... I'll be ready for 'em.'

* * * * *

'Well, that's the position, Hester.' Edward noticed the uncertain emotions on the young woman's face as he told her of James' decision to manage Greenacres for him and Becky.

'How soon... before... I join... James?' She hesitated over referring to him as her husband. Then she realised that there was no need for her pretence... her relationship with James was known.

'In about three weeks time. By then James will have established himself and be ready for you to join him.' Hester's apprehension was obvious as she thanked Edward for his kindness.

'There now remains Jim's passage home.' He turned to Becky. 'I've promised to arrange for the family's voyage home. There is a ship, the Veronica, leaving in twelve days time. That should give Jim and Maggy ample time to pack and be ready to sail on her.'

'Were you able to make the financial arrangements for them, Edward?'

'Yes, my dear... all has been taken care of. I have also arranged for a small gratuity to help them start in the old country.'

'We shall miss them...' Becky's sigh reflected her poignant thoughts... her sadness. 'They have been friends since our arrival.'

Becky turned as Hester made a sincere supplication. 'I hope... that we also... might become friends... Becky?' Her voice was shy with uncertainty.

'I'm sure we shall, Hester.' Becky's affectionate smile was both reassuring and sincere as the two women embraced warmly. 'It will be wonderful to share your friendship... and also that of your family.' She smile inwardly as her implied meaning induced a blush to Hester's cheeks. Fate, however, was to tragically rob them of that promised friendship.

Chapter Twenty Four

'What do you think of it, Harry?' Andrew removed his hat to wipe his perspiring brow. Pausing in their labours, the two men had stopped back to view the just completed place of assembly.

'Reck'n as how you've got yerself a splendid church, Mr. Douglass.' Harry Carver, one of the rescued convicts, stood beside Andrew as they appraised the results of their hard labours.

'Much of the credit is yours...' Andrew turned and gave his companion a grateful look, '... without your building skill, I doubt it would have been so... permanent.' There was a proud look on the faces of both men as with feelings of elation, they silently observed the newly constructed place of worship.

There was nothing elaborate about the structure, just a plain timber and stone building with lancet windows and pitched roof. An annex on the west side was to be Andrew's somewhat Spartan living quarters.

'Now, we must concentrate on the completion of your dwelling.' Andrew indicated the partially constructed building that the two men were already using as shelter. They shared meals in Andrew's home, where out of necessity, the food was mostly prepared by him. There was a unanimous opinion, that the food, considering Andrew's untrained culinary skills, was of an enjoyable nature. 'Plain'n wholesome,' was the generous verdict. Andrew smiled stoically, aware that any food is acceptable when you're ravenous.

Paul Jackson, the second convict, brought his horse to a stop beside them. He dismounted from the only mount they possessed and cast an approving glance over the completed church. 'Splendid... building.' Paul nodded his satisfaction; he was economical with words. Andrew's eyes wrinkled at the corners as a smile softened his tired features.

'How're the sheep, Paul?' Andrew waited while their herdsman slapped the dust from his clothes with his battered hat. Looking after their livestock kept him in the saddle for most of the burning hot days.

'They're fine, Mr. Douglass.'

'How about our cattle?' Andrew was proud of his small herd.

'Aye... they be fine.' Paul nodded. 'Could do wi' a bit more space.'

'Yes. Now that the church is completed, we must concentrate on clearing a few more acres.' Andrew noticed their nods of agreement. They were two good helpers; he was grateful for their support. He had never regretted his decision to bring the two men along.

Andrew remembered the evening a few months back, when he and his two companions had arrived at these allotted acres to find them mostly a tangle of bush and trees. Turning to the two convicts he had apologised for what he had let them in for.

'Better'n a lying at bottom o' ocean, Mr. Douglass. Where we should've been had you not released us.' Andrew remembered how he had been a little embarrassed by the men's exaltations.

'Yes. Yer saved our lives...' the second convict nodded solemnly, '... 'twas a brave deed.' He turned to his mate and received a silent confirmation. 'It'll be a priv'ledge to work f'thee.'

Now, after nearly six months of hard and exhausting labour, the assembly room was built and ready for the first congregation of friends. Andrew was also pleased that his small flock of sheep and herd of cattle were become a viable proposition, ensuring his solvency. His money saved for his mission in Sydney had, however, been reduced by half. Andrew shrugged philosophically at the thought. After all, it was the present that matters... tomorrow, who knows?

'I think this joyful event...' Andrew gave his companions a cheerful look, ' ... calls for a celebration.' From the annex he fetched a bottle of wine. 'A special occasion...' he held the bottle up so that its contents sparkled in the evening sunshine, '... calls for a pleasant treat. We shall drink to our success after we have eaten.'

'Here's to our church!' The three men raised their glasses in concurrence. As they imbibed the wine, the two helpers noticed that Andrew barely sipped his. He placed the remainder aside, his face solemn as if enacting a distasteful deed. Seeing their uncertain looks, Andrew assured them it was no reflection on their joyful celebrations, but a reminder of an unpleasant past. 'Even if I don't join you…' he passed the bottle to his companions, '… my heart rejoices with you.'

Andrew eased his horse to a walk. He was suddenly aware of being followed. Unseen eyes were watching his progress along the woodland track. He had set out to speak with Paul, who was shepherding out on the north pastures. Anxious to reach his helper, he had decided to take the short cut through the wooded area. The protection of his sheep as they grazed on the isolated pastures was uppermost in his thoughts as he rode out to discuss the problem with Paul. There was talk of a gang raiding the outlying settlements to plunder and in some cases – to kill.

Pulling his horse to a stop, he listened for any extraneous noises in the surrounding bushes and trees. He could hear nothing, but the normal sounds of wildlife and the whispered rustling of the leaves. Yet, intuition warned him that he was under observation. Perhaps it was the natives, there had been some confrontations with them in the region.

Andrew rode on, trying not to think of a native spear or a bush-ranger's knife being thrown at his back. As he eased his horse into a canter, a strange prickling sensation emanated from his back. Fighting back his fears, he continued to guide his horse along the narrow woodland track, expecting a confrontation at any moment.

Through the trees ahead of him, large patches of sky were coming into his vision. A sigh escaped Andrew's lips. Soon he would be out of the trees and clear of the unseen menace. His relief was of a brief duration as the danger he had been expecting, revealed itself.

Suddenly, he found his way barred by a small gang of natives, carrying long spears. They held their weapons in front of their near naked bodies, with the points resting on the ground. Strangely, Andrew experienced no fear. The natives who watched his approach in silence, exuded no threatening manifestation.

In the clearing behind the natives, Andrew noticed all the paraphernalia of their camp. He slowly raised his hands in front of himself, hoping it would be accepted as a sign of his friendship. While they communicated with strange vocal noises among themselves he remained in the saddle gazing down upon their dark frizzy hair. Gently, so as not to alarm the natives, he dismounted. As he moved to meet the group, his attention was attracted towards a strange moaning sound.

He became aware of a woman crouched over the still form of a child lying on a hide beside here. As he watched, the child made a feeble movement with his hands. Andrew moved towards the woman and her child, but spears were suddenly pointing towards him. Shaking his head and raising his hands, palms uppermost, he endeavoured to reassure them that he meant them no harm. Slowly they retreated with lowered weapons, watching him dispassionately as he walked cautiously forward.

At his approach, the woman backed away in terror, trying to take the sick child with her. Gently he rested his hand on her naked shoulder, indicated with silent gestures that she should replace the child upon the hide. She looked towards the group as if seeking guidance. One, who appeared to be the leader, gave a sign that she do as bid.

Reluctantly, she placed her small son upon the dried skin. There a pleading look in her eyes as they momentarily met Andrew's solemn gaze. As he placed his hands on the child's fevered brow, he heard strange sounds emanating from the onlookers.

Anger overcame him as he realised that the cowardly act must have been carried out by one of his own race. Someone had shot at an innocent child. Why should a bush-ranger or settler perpetrate such heinous attack on a child? He looked down at the injured boy, guessing he was about four or five years old.

Taking the chief aside, he tried to demonstrate with the aid of sketches in the dust that he was leaving to fetch something for the boy. Before leaving, he sketched the outline of a child in the earth. By pointing to the child's wound and then to the same spot on the drawing, he hoped the native chief would understand his intentions. To remove the ball from the boy's shoulder.

Selecting a roundish stone, Andrew then made a hole in the drawing and completely buried it in the wound position. There were startled looks and exclamations as he took his knife and made an imaginary cut above the buried stone. As he did so, he uncovered the small piece of rock and gently removed it from the hole. Andrew hoped that his actions had reassured the chief of the procedure that he intended to carry out.

Gathering a few pieces of wood, he prepared a fire in readiness for his return. As he struck one of his sulphured matches to produce a flame, there were startled cries from the natives as they hurriedly retreated to the bushes. As the wood took hold and flames leapt into the air, he indicated that they should return and keep the fire going while he was away.

Before leave Hobart, Andrew had visited the local surgeon and explained his interest in medicine and abut his mentor, David Jennings. The name brought an instant reaction from the physician, albeit a sorrowful one when he learnt of his old friend's death.

'I shared a voyage with David, when I first came out to the colony. We became great friends.' The surgeon stood silently gazing out of the window as he remembered the man who had helped him in his early days. 'Poor, David!' He sighed deeply as his thoughts returned to the present. 'He was a compassionate man.' Andrew nodded silent agreement. After a few more moments of meditative silence, the surgeon looked round as if suddenly remembering Andrew's presence. 'How can I help you, sir?'

'Before David died he handed me his medical bag and confirmed my authorisation to take over his role of surgeon and Government Representative on the transport, Leonore.' He was aware of the physician's scrutinising look as he continued. 'Unfortunately, the ship went down and...'

'You are in need of a few basic medical supplies to take inland with you?'

'Yes. Being so far from town, I considered it would be prudent to have a few basic items and er... instruments. For minor surgery, of course.'

'You have some knowledge of medicine, I presume?' Andrew thought it judicious not to mention that the only basics had been imparted by his mentor during their short time together. His reply was evasive, he realised... ambiguous in fact, but...

'H'mm... I'll see what can be done. Give me a look before you leave.'

Andrew was recalling that meeting as he placed the shabby medical bag down beside the delirious child. The native boy's shouting and thrashing of limbs troubled him. Harry, who had returned with him, would have to ensure that the patient remained still while he removed the ball. His companion's presence eased his anxieties as he prepared to operate on the young lad.

Andrew looked sympathetically across at the silent, impassive mother. By actions he tried to reassure her that the worst would soon be over. That her son would survive. His smile of confidence faded as a terrible thought suddenly struck him. What if he failed and things perchance did go wrong? If anything happened to the child, would they hold him responsible for his – death? He glanced briefly round at the solemn faces observing his every moment... features that were devoid of any emotion. Perhaps prayers would help. He lowered his head in silent supplication.

Sweat trickled down his beard as he concentrated on feeling for an then easing the ball from the incision with a small tong-like instrument. He had made but a small cut in the inflamed area, hoping his drastic effort would be sufficient to allow access. Slowly he manoeuvred the shot clear of the flesh, must to his relief – and satisfaction.

Quickly, he bathed and closed the wound and with Harry's assistance bandaged the area tightly. Light was fading as he made the sleeping invalid comfortable.

'Best if I spend the night here, Harry.' He noticed his companion's surprised look. 'Just in case complications arise.'

As he was speaking he had been feeling the boy's pulse. He was pleased to find it normal. Harry, who had been observing him closely, was aware of the relief in his eyes as he looked up to nod his satisfaction.

'Why... did yer do it, Mr. Douglass?' Harry whispered his puzzlement in the dusk. 'They're only... natives.'

'Yes!' He answered sharply. 'But human beings, nevertheless. They have the right to wander across the country... their country without being shot at.' Andrew's face was tense with anger as he looked towards the injured boy. 'What kind of person is it that can shoot at an innocent child?'

He moved across to the makeshift bed as the boy stirred restlessly. Slowly, the eyelids of his patient flickered open and a pair of dark eyes gazed solemnly into his. Andrew experienced a moment of elation. A release from the anxiety that had been with him since making the first incision to extract the ball. The boy had survived... all would be well.

As the months passed and he continued to harbour the natives on his land, antagonism arose between Andrew and the neighbouring settlers. When they tried to dissuade him from encouraging their presence, he explained that they were doing no harm. 'I have no reason to move them on.' In fact, Andrew felt a strange understanding had developed between him and the small group, after he had saved the boy's life.

'They're nothin' but thievin'... animals. Sneakin' in an taking our sheep.' The settler's spokesman had protested in vain to Andrew. 'Get rid o' them!'

'The natives are primitive people, Amos.' Pausing to ensure his words were being listened to by the belligerent settler, Andrew continued. 'When we invaded their country and robbed them of their hunting grounds, the land they had owned over hundreds, maybe thousands of years, we made conditions extremely hard for them. Once driven from their food source, they took what they thought was a natural replacement... our stock.'

'Well, they'll not be hevin' more o' mine... and if yer take my advice...' there was a sinister meaning behind Amos Grant's words as he hesitated to give Andrew a meaningful look, '... you'll throw those damned natives off yer land.'

'Thank you, Amos, but I don't recollect asking you for advice.'

'Alright, native lover! If that be yer attitude... I'll... I'll...'

'Good day t'you, Amos.' Andrew realised that his uncooperative attitude had made an enemy, but he was determined to encourage a more friendly relationship with the natives. Quakers precluded any other feeling.

Andrew was soon made aware of his neighbours' changing attitudes as the seasons passed. Subtle changes at first, but as the months slipped by, their behaviour became quite unfriendly. At first, his place of worship although orientated towards the Quaker philosophy, had drawn large congregations. Eventually as word circulated about his friendliness towards the natives, their manner began to change.

Confrontation came to a head after one assembly. Andrew, as was the ritual in the Quaker's place of meditation and worship, mounted the raised platform at one end of the meeting place. After deep contemplation thought were voiced quietly, almost unemotional, but gradually, as if inspired by some heavenly presence, his speech became more agitated.

'Help us Lord to cleanse the hatred from our hearts so that we may offer onto you ones that are pure and filled with beneficence. We ask thee for strength to overcome our blind prejudices against those that are not of our faith – or race.' There was a pause in Andrew's solicitations as he became aware of the congregation's unease. Undaunted by their reactions, he continued to extol the philanthropy of the Friends' doctrine.

'Help us Almighty to look beyond our selfish ways and try to understand the traits and ritualistic acts of others less conversant with the Christian teachings. Give us faith to regard all people as friends, with whom we should share the land, the creatures and the tribulations along life's road that will hopefully lead us to heaven and the Almighty Himself. Amen!' Few joined in the ratification. It was a subdued and morose gathering who shared the final prayer.

* * * * *

'Quaker!' Andrew recognised the surly voice of Amos Grant. The loquacious settler who always appeared to be complaining... an agitator and trouble maker. He now confronted Andrew from the head of a shamefaced group outside the Meeting Place.

'Are we to assume...' he was speaking in a stentorian voice, '... that heaven awaits your native rabble when they are eradicated from this life?'

Aware of the insinuation and animosity behind the question, Andrew paused as if reflecting on the assumption.

'A good question, friend Amos.' Andrew bestowed an uncertain smile upon his disputant. 'However... I think you should communicate your dubiety to the Almighty, Himself. Only He can enlighten us on the matter. One thing is certain, Amos...' he gave the belligerent settler an appraising stare, '... if He is selective... a few of us will be missing from His throne on judgement day.'

Almost spluttered with rage, his face red from humiliation. Before he could speak, Andrew angered him further. 'What have you against the natives? Have they ever harmed you?'

'For good reason...' Amos patted the pistol carried beneath his coat, '... they'll not return to my land in a hurry.'

It was then that Andrew realised who had been responsible for shooting the native child some months previous. Trying not to display his anger, he asked Amos what made him so sure that his land would not be trespassed upon by the natives.

'Because I fired this at 'em, a few months back.' With a flamboyant gesture, he drew his pistol and aimed at an imaginary target.

'Then this is probably the shot you fired in your despicable act.' Andrew withdrew from his pocket, the ball he had retrieved from the native boy. He had no idea why he had retained it; now Andrew intended to use it to his full advantage.

'That's...' Amos started to reach out instinctively, before he realised his action had betrayed him, '... that's... not mine. How c'n yer... tell?' No one answered; his egotism had revealed his guilt.

'Because I removed it from the shoulder of the native child

you hit.' There was a sharpness about Andrew's voice that caused the acrimonious settler to bluster.

'I... didn't... mean to shoot... at the... child.' Shocked faces stared silently at him as he tried to excuse his dastardly action. 'It was... an... accident,' he pleaded.

'No, Amos. Not an accident... it was an act of cowardice.' Before another word could be spoken, Andrew turned with contempt and entered his dwelling.

Thinking that Amos grant had been exposed for what he was, a blustering bully, Andrew's calming thoughts were rudely shattered a few nights later. He awoke with a start. Something had disturbed him. Some extraneous sound had penetrated his sleep. He listened for a few moments, straining to hear in the darkness. All seemed quiet. Perhaps he had been dreaming. Relaxing, he turned over in his bed, preparing once more for sleep. A sleep that never came.

Suddenly, with a deafening crash, his outer door was smashed down, dispelling any supposition that the noises he had heard were fantasy related. Andrew experienced a moment of fear as he forced the drowsiness from his mind. Hurriedly he rose up in his bed, but before he could leave it, two shadowy figures appeared in his bedroom doorway.

In the light of the lantern that one of the men carried, he noticed their dark clothing and the kerchiefs covering the lower half of their faces. Beneath their pulled down hats, two pairs of eyes stared at him from the shadows.

'Hold it... Quaker! Stay jut where y'are!' A muffled voice warned him. The raiders nodded to each other, then one of them turned back into the outer room. Andrew fought down his anger as heard the man smashing up his few possessions. Indignation forced him to rise as if to leave his bed.

'I wouldn't... unless...' There was a flash of steel as the intruder guarding him threatened to use a knife.

'That'll do f'now!' From the shadows the voice of the other man confirmed that his vandalising was finished. 'This be a warnin' t'yer, Quaker.' His voice reflected the malevolence of his nature. 'Just git yer native friends... to hell of y'land...'

Andrew tried to recognise the voice, but realised that it was disguised, muffled behind the kerchief.

'And if I refuse?'

'Then it'll be yer church... next. Should make a good blaze?' he looked towards his companion who nodded a silent agreement. 'Best tie 'im up a'fore we leave.' He stepped forward to assist the man standing near to the bed. Andrew was roughly pushed face down upon his bed before his hands and feet were tied. For a moment the lantern light cast a dull glow on the floor as it followed the departing raiders. Andrew could only see their legs with his restricted vision as he turned his face to watch them leave.

After struggling for several minutes, Andrew succeeding in getting his hands free. Quickly he untied the rope round his legs and stumbled across to light his candle. Holding the flickering light before him, he entered the outer room. Tears of anger filled his eyes as he surveyed the chaos. Furniture had been smashed, his personal belongings destroyed and scattered over the floor.

He looked up as a face peered in through the battered door. 'What... what happened?' Harry's face registered shock and disbelief as he gazed wide eyes around at the shambles in the candle lit room. Furniture that he had so caringly made lay smashed and splintered on the floor. 'When... did it happen, Mr. Douglass?' Harry's face was grim as he asked the question.

'Within the past half hour, or so.' Andrew shook his head reflectively as he tried to identify the men who had caused so much wanton destruction. 'There were two of them, Harry, but I could not...'

'Must 'ave been the two as rode off. 'bout half hour back.'

'You... noticed them... leaving?' Harry nodded in the flickering candle light.

'I 'ad a call o'nature so t'speak. As I went outside I heard a horse whinny. Thinking something was disturbing ours, I walked over to check. It was then I noticed the two riders coming from your direction. Bein' in the shadows, Amos didn't rec ...'

'Amos Grant? You recognised him and his companion?'

'Oh, aye. 'twere Amos and his neighbour, Joe Weston.'

'You are sure... of their identity, Harry?'

'Positive!' He growled his confirmation. 'No mistakin' 'em. I heard Amos tell Joe to keep 'is mouth shut as he passed me.'

'Good. I'll challenge him in the morning.' Andrew was determined to get some compensation from his adversaries.

'Yer have no proof, Quaker!' Behind Amos' bluster, Andrew had detected a note of uncertainty. Because of his guilt, his protestations lacked conviction.

'As it happens, Amos... I do have a witness. A reliable one.'

'Huh, that trick'll not work.' Amos sneered as he walked towards his horse. As far as he was concerned the confrontation was over. Amos paused with one foot already in the stirrup as if expecting further words from his accuser.

Andrew, his eyes fixed on the garrulous settler, felt that his opportunity was slipping away. If it came to Harry's word against that of the settler's, there would only be one outcome, as no one would believe a convict's evidence. For a few seconds the two men glared at each other. Andrew's eyes suddenly focused on the disputant's foot resting in the stirrup. It was a long scuff mark on the boot that held his attention; something about it stirred his memory. Then he remembered the incident as the raiders had walked out of his bedroom, leaving him tied up on the bed.

While he had watched helplessly as the intruders walked away, he had only been able to see their boots in the lantern light. Amos' boot, the left one, had an identical scuff mark as the one he had seen last night. A smile of confidence spread slowly over Andrew's face.

'I not only have a witness, Amos. I also noticed your boots when you left me tied up on my bed.' Andrew noticed the perplexed look on his face. 'You should have changed your footwear,' he nodded in the direction of the frowning settler's left foot resting in the stirrup in preparation for mounting his horse. 'That scuff mark confirms that you were one of the intruders who broke into my place last night. The other was Joe Weston.'

Amos, realising that his identity as one of the raiders had been revealed, mounted his horse and sat there scowling in silent contemplation for a few moments. 'Well... what is it yer want?' He conceded his guilt to Andrew.

'Recompense... for my damaged property... and possessions. Either you pay, or this report will be dispatched to the Lieutenant Governor in Hobart... without delay.'

'What if I am unable to pay?'

'In that case I shall get you to sign this document.' Andrew withdrew a folded parchment from his pocket. An agreement that he had intuitionally drawn up before leaving his quarters to confront Amos and his accomplice.

'What... what's that?' Amos nodded warily towards the document.

'It's to confirm that you have transferred two score sheep and half a dozen cattle to me.'

'The devil it does! I'll sign no such thing!' Amos erupted with anger as he removed his foot from the stirrup and moved menacingly towards an unperturbed Andrew.

'It's your choice,' Andrew stood his ground unflinchingly. 'One way or the other... I intend to have my compensation.' He stood defiantly in the path of the irate settler.

Amos, snatched the document from Andrew's hand, stamped inside his house, where he picked up a quill and scrawled his blotched signature.

'Here!' He thrust the authorisation towards a serene Andrew. 'Yer'll hev 'em tomorrer.'

'Why thank you, Amos... that's most co-operative of you.' There was no reply, only a venomous stare from the inwardly raging settler.

'One day... Quaker... yer'll... suffer for this.' A threat that was never to materialise as a request to visit the Lieutenant Governor was about to be delivered to Andrew. There he would receive news of other survivors, friends that he had thought drowned.

* * * * *

'It was by a chance reference to your situation that the news came about, Mr. Douglass.' Sir George looked across the table, trying to assess the character of the Quaker sitting before him.

He had received a petition from a few settlers complaining of his friendliness towards the natives who had settled on his land. The Quaker was also accused of blasphemous preaching as he had asked The Almighty to look upon all people as equal... natives included.

A smile flickered across the official's face as he watched the sombre dressed man sitting opposite him. My guess is he's a good man, he thought... and a genuine one. A great pity he's required in Sydney. Suddenly aware that he was also under close observation, Sir George brought his mind back to the present.

'In an official report to Governor Darling in Sydney, I mentioned that you and two convicts were the only known survivors from the Leonore. His return communication...' he glanced down at his desk, '... reached me recently. In it he informs me that a family and a few crew members did manage to survive the ordeal.' Andrew experienced a moment of elation, but then he remembered Mary.

'A family, sir?'

'Yes...' once again he referred to the letter lying on his desk, '... the Gordons. James Gordon, his wife and small son.' Andrew felt shaken... guilty. He was sure that Mary was dead when he left her. He was positive that the young mother was dead; he had found no pulse. His head dropped in shame as a feeling of guilt overwhelmed him.

How had Mary managed to get off the ship? She could not have survived. He remembered checking for her pulse and finding none. Suddenly he was aware of the Lieutenant Governor watching him closely.

'Friends of yours... I believe?'

'Yes... yes the news has come as a shock. A pleasant one, sir.'

'Well you'll have a chance to see them again soon. The Governor wants you to sail for Sydney as soon as possible.'

'Sydney? What of my... church... my congregation... farm...' Andrew's voice faded into shocked silence.

'A Quaker from the Parramatta area is being send down to release you. His ship is due in any day now. As soon as the ship has transferred its cargoes, it will be sailing directly back to Sydney – with you on board.

'Th… thank you, sir. I'll er… make sure of my passage.' The news had taken Andrew completely by surprise Why was his passage so urgently needed in Sydney… at Government House? Then Mary returned to his thoughts. He shook his head sadly, surely there must be some mistake.

'Thy speech does not reflect our Quaker's articulation, friend Andrew?'

'Perhaps not…' Andrew hesitated, uncertain about revealing his lack of eminence within the Quaker movement. His companion, who had but recently arrived, was observing him closely as if expecting some explanation. 'Truth is, I'm not a fully converted Friend of the faith.' Seeing the uncertain look in the new arrival's eyes, he decided to elucidate on his situation.

'I became interested in the Friends when I was befriended by a Quaker family, Jason Smith and his kinfolk. They resided in Lincolnshire and it was in that county that I shared their home for a few years.' Darkness fell as Andrew spoke of his marriage to their daughter and of her unfortunate death. He also mentioned his return to his family, only to find that they had just died in a tragic accident. 'I stayed for several months and when the estate was running smoothly, I left for the colony.'

'Why Australia, friend Andrew?'

'To spread our faith and to try and redeem a sinful act that I perpetrated many years ago. On my arrival in Sydney, I had hoped to take the first step towards fulfilling my mission.'

There was a long period of silent as the two men gazed pensively up into the starlit heavens, as the moon spreading an ethereal-like glow over the shadowy wilderness. It was Andrew who eventually broke the quiet interlude.

'On the morrow, friend Anthony, I shall introduce you to your future congregation. What few remain, that is.' He noticed the frown as Anthony gave him a puzzled look.

'I thank thee, Andrew. Your unexpected departure will no doubt come as a disappointment to them?'

'I think not...' Andrew chuckled, '... I also doubt if you will thank me when you realise how strained the relationship is between ourselves and the settlers.' He went on to explain the controversy over the natives using Quaker land when they were in the area and how he had extended to them the hand of friendship.

Andrew had been watching for the newcomer's reaction as he spoke, wondering how he would cope with the complex situation. Pressure would undoubtedly be placed upon him at the start in an encouragement to force him to rid the natives from their refuge on the Quaker land. With Harry and Paul as his allies, he hoped that Anthony would abide by the Quaker's philosophy and see them as friends. Intuition told him that his hopes would be confirmed. His companion's next words validated his instinctive emotions.

'Then I see no need to change the existing situation.'

Andrew nodded his head in approval. 'You'll find your two helpers... I prefer not to use the word convicts, reliable and zealous in their duties. They are good men, friend Anthony.'

'Then these may rest assured that their welfare will be give suitable priority. That I presume is thy... concern.' A smile flickered across Anthony's grave features as he awaited his companion's response.

'Thank you for considering their... well-being. I'm sure your kindness will be repaid in full.' Andrew experienced a moment of sorrow as he though of having to leave his two compatriots behind, but knowing that their welfare was assured helped to ease his sadness. 'It will greatly ease my concern, knowing that they will be cared for after my departure.'

'When do you intend to leave, friend Andrew?'

'On Monday...' he glanced at the calendar for confirmation, '... two days time.'

Chapter Twenty Five

Andrew watched pensively from the upper deck as the Rowena, a small trading ship neared the New South Wales coastline. His eyes were focused on the panorama of towering cliffs, lined with trees spreading their canopy of leaves almost to the summit. Occasionally he glimpsed sandy covers with iridescent surf breaking onto their burning beaches.

His mind as he watched the passing scenery was, however, reflecting on other matters. A momentary look of sadness reached his eyes as he recalled his departure from Hobart. His words of assurance to Paul and Harry, his two helpers, had been received in a sombre mood. Andrew had noticed the uncertainty in their faces when he had confirmed that their new employer would ensure the continuation of their welfare.

Andrew's sadness faded, replaced by a puzzled frown as he remembered his interview with the Lieutenant Governor just before his departure from Hobart. There appeared to be an aura of mystery relating to his summons to Sydney. It had been at Governor Darling's urgent request. He shook his head, perplexed at the circumstances surrounding his appointment with that distinguished official.

Soon now, he would be enlightened as Andrew noticed that the Rowena was already weathering the entrance to Port Jackson harbour. He was aware of the ship sailing past two sentinel-like, rock headlands that guarded the entrance. Once inside the harbour, the Rowena's captain waited for the port's official to board, before proceeding to an anchorage in Sydney Cove.

'Please be seated, Mr. Douglass.' Andrew was aware of being subjected to a close scrutiny by the Governor. An anxious frown creased his brow as he waited expectantly for the official to explain the reason for his appointment. Was his past about to be interrogated, Andrew wondered; but he could think of no reason why that should be so. His past misdemeanours had been paid for… in full.

'From information received...' Andrew became alert as the Governor's voice penetrated his contemplation's, '... it would appear that you are related to Sir Roger Douglass?' The question caught Andrew while he was trying to orientate his thoughts to the present situation. Mistaking the hesitancy as a need for further clarification, the Governor mentioned the estate of Homefield Hall.

'Sir Roger was my father.' Andrew noticed the Governor's surprised look gradually give way to a melancholy one.

'I was a friend of your father's. We met often when he came to the city on business.' There was a poignancy about his words that reflected deep respect for their relationship. 'My commiseration's on your great loss...' he glanced down at his desk, '... Andrew.' In a voice strained with emotion, he continued. 'Such a tragedy... your parents... drowned together...' he shook his head in shocked disbelief.

'Thank you, sir.' Andrew was reliving again those horrendous moments when he had come upon his parents bodies lying blood-stained and saturated beside the lake. His voice broke as he recalled that fateful evening. 'Yes... a terrible accident... indeed.' The ensuring silence was eventually broken by the Governor's deep sigh. A sign that he was ready to continue with the justification for their meeting.

'Let me refresh my memory...' he glanced once more at the papers on his desk, '... you originally came out to er... spread the Quaker faith and to fulfil... a mission.' Andrew nodded his acquiescence. He was quite amazed at the information that had been assimilated regarding his aspirations.

'May I enquire as to your er... mission?' He felt the Governor's intense, almost quizzical gaze upon him as the question was mooted.

'Indeed you may, sir.' After a few moments silence to assemble his thoughts, Andrew enlightened the enquiring official. He explained his part in Edward's wrongful imprisonment and how he had drowned when the ship transporting him and other prisoners had been lost in a storm. 'A pardon was dispatched to Governor Macquarie, authorising the young convict's freedom, but alas he was drowned when the ship went down. It is believed that the document may be filed here in Sydney as there is no trace of it ever being returned to London.' He paused, but a silent nod from the Governor he continued his elucidation.

'My intention was to collect the pardon and deliver it to his sister... my widowed sister-in-law.' Andrew was hoping for a favourable reaction from the Government's representative as his co-operation would be needed in the search for the lost documents.

After a brief moment of thought, the Governor made his decision. 'Have a word with my senior clerk, he may well remember the incident. Rather an unusual request, but...' he spoke with an air of expectancy, '... we shall see.'

'It was because of my perjurious testimony that Edward Payne suffered such a tragic end. Returning the pardon to his sister was to have been my act of atonement for the wrong I perpetrated.'

'H'mm...' the Governor continued his close observation as he meditated on Andrew's statement, '... a commendable action, Mr. Douglass.'

Thinking the interview was over, Andrew rose to make his departure. Raising his hand, the Governor indicated that he should remain seated. An act that filled Andrew with deep apprehension. What other discourses were to be introduced, he wondered, as he settled back somewhat nervously in his chair.

'You were, according to my information, taking passage on the Leonore when it ran onto the reefs and sank?'

'Yes... that is correct.' Andrew frowned expectantly, wondering what information he was about to hear.

'It has been reported, that at great risk to yourself, you remained on board to free the convicts who were still locked in their hold.' There was a moment of embarrassed silence as Andrew waited for the Governor to continue his approbation. 'Witnesses have commended your bravery when you struggled to rescue the trapped prisoners with a complete disregard for your own life.'

'A er... spontaneous act. Anyone in my position would have done the same.'

'You do yourself and injustice, Andrew. What you did took courage... great courage.' Rising from his chair, the Governor walked over to the window. For a few moments he stood silently staring across the ruffled waters of the cover and at the ships anchored there.

Andrew coughed discreetly, wondering if the interview was over. Slowly the Governor turned as if having just made an important decision. His words when they came surprised – shocked, Andrew.

'I would like you to become my representative in the Bathurst area... a temporary post until the new official takes over.' Noticing Andrew's startled look, he enlightened him as regards the duties that would become routine when he accepted the post.

'You will be called upon to visit the settlements in the area and to deal with any disputes. Ensuring that law and order is maintained as well as dealing with any law breakers will also be your responsibility. Working under your jurisdiction will be constables and field police to make certain that the law is respected at all times.

'Major Walters, my present representative is retiring because of ill health and is anxious to leave the post immediately. I would like you to take over until the new official arrives from England. It will only be for a few months at the most.' Andrew was taken aback, yet felt he had no choice but to agree.

'You do me a great honour, Governor. I have no experience of administrative workings.'

'One of the main requirements is courage. Integrity goes without saying.' His steady gaze never wavered as he watched for Andrew's reactions. 'You've proved you have valour, also...' he hesitated as his prospective representative gently demurred his fortitude, '... you carried out the duties of Government Representative on the Leonore expeditiously... after poor old Jennings' death.'

Andrew was unable to hide his involuntary look of surprise 'Yes...' Governor Darling gave a chuckle, '... your prowess as a relief surgeon and Government Representative have been reported upon most favourably.' It must have been James, thought

Andrew, as he considered the Governor's request, or should it be... order, to take on the duties at Bathurst. 'There is no reason why you cannot carry on with your er... Quaker activities. I'm sure the two duties are compatible.'

'Thank you for having faith in my capabilities, sir. I shall be pleased to... accept and promise to execute the duties required to the best of my ability.'

'Good... splendid. I'll keep in touch. Expect you to take up duties at the beginning of next year... 1828. Just over two weeks time.' Andrew was surprised at the short notice, but with luck he would have completed his mission in Sydney by then

'Incidentally, the Gordons are farming in the area. It was Mrs. Gordon who spoke so emotionally about your bravery.' Andrew was stunned... shocked. He had believed Mary dead. Andrew once again experienced shame... a sense of guilt. He had abandoned Mary when she had most need of his help. Nothing would ever erase the shame from his conscience. He had left her for dead and yet it appeared that somehow she had managed to save herself. He shook his head in stupefaction.

'The three survivors...' Andrew realised that the Governor was still talking of the Gordons, '... were expecting to farm near Bathurst. Unfortunately, the buildings were burnt to the ground by a marauding band of bush-rangers – escaped convicts. They were offered and accepted the chance to manage Greenacres, a farm owned by...' he was interrupted by a perplexed Andrew.

'You mentioned the Gordons... was there a young woman with them, Mrs. Gordon's companion? Did she not survive with them?' Andrew expressed his dismay at the lack of information regarding Hester. Surely they had not handed her over to the authorities?

'Apart from the crew members, there were no other survivors.' Andrew experienced a feeling of sadness... shock. Hester must have drowned. It was heartbreaking to come to terms with such a tragic possibility. Especially as he remembered seeing her with James and Billy in the boat as they were swept away from the wreck. Andrew gradually perceived what had possibly transpired. Unknowingly, it was the Governor who confirmed his supposition.

'... surprised at Gordon's highland dialect, while his wife spoke an education form of English. Apart from her shyness, there was one striking feature I noticed about Mrs. Gordon... her dark brown eyes. So full of sadness... even when she smiled.'

'Hester!' Andrew whispered to himself as the Governor walked with him to the door.

'I'll be in touch, Andrew. Leave details of your er... mission with Burton,' he indicated the elderly clerk coming towards them.

* * * * *

Rebecca glanced anxiously towards the hills. Dark, angry looking clouds were accumulating menacingly above them. Occasionally, a vivid flash of lightning seared its path earthwards, followed immediately by rolls of thunder reverberating across the hills and surrounding bush. The storm's nearness and intensity troubled Becky.

With Edward not back from his visit to Greenacres, she was becoming increasingly anxious about East Pastures, the land on their distant boundary. Storms invariably caused the river along this section of land to fill rapidly and in severe storms flood over into the distant pastures. At the fist signs of the storm, Stephen had rode down to drive the sheep away from the threatened acres, a triangular shaped area with the river and gully forming two of its sides.

As Becky looked with deep anxiety up at the darkening sky, the first rain drops splashed refreshingly upon her perspiring face. From experience, she realised that the hot, humid weather of the past two days was about to change – dramatically. Her worried feelings intensified as she hurried towards the house.

Marian watched her mother's approach from the doorway, aware of her troubled look as she scrambled onto the veranda against the increasing rain. There was a deep emotional feeling between them, an understanding that gave their relationship strong impassioned feelings. Emotions that seemed to tie them with some unknown destiny – an unidentified love.

Marian, according to her 'father', was the image of her mother at the age that she would be celebrating in a few days time – fifteen. A slight frown puckered her brow, as, seeing her mother's worried features, she was reminded of the occasion when she had enquired as to what traits she had inherited from him. Marian recalled the sadness in his eyes as he reached out to embrace her and to whisper that his character was such, that it would be to her advantage to inherit none of his traits.

At the time she had shared in his jovial laughter. The covert glance that her parents had exchanged at the time had alerted Marian to the possibility of some inner secret between them. Occasionally she recalled the incident, but nothing had developed to cause her to pursue the matter. It was obvious that her parents were still in love and that their sincere affections reached out and embraced them all.

Marian loved her parents. While she had been away attending school in Sydney, homesickness had been a recurring ailment with her. Staying with the Morrison's at Acacia House had eased her loneliness, especially with their two children as companions, but each night her thoughts and prayers had been in harmony with her family at Newacres.

It had been an upsetting period for them all, following Mrs. Morrison's death after a prolonged illness last autumn. A death, which although not unexpected because of her indisposition during the last few weeks of her life, had nevertheless been a distressing interlude.

With her schooling behind her, Marian now found her duties more demanding as she helped in the running of the house. Gradually, a full burden had been placed upon her as Becky concentrated on her horse training – an enterprise that she fully enjoyed. Her thoughts were shattered as her mother, after a breathless rush, stopped beside her.

'Ask... Amy to fetch... my cloak... Marian dear.'

'Cloak, mother? Surely you are not venturing out in... the storm?' She looked anxiously out at the storm swept landscape.

'I must. I'm worried about Stephen. He rode over to the East Pastures with the intention of driving the sheep onto the higher ground. In these conditions it is possible we could get a flash flood.'

'What about Geoff? Shall I go over and...'

'He's collecting stores from Parramatta... I doubt if he'll be back before... evening. Especially in this weather.' Marian noticed the concern lining her face; she was obviously very worried.

Her brother Stephen, although eighteen months her junior, was an integral part of the daily routine at Newacres. He was never happier than when sharing in the day to day routines of the farm. Tough, active and fearless. If he had a weakness it was his concern for Curly, his ever present companion for the past eleven and a half years. A lively present on his second birthday.

'I had expected Stephen back by now...' Marian was aware of her mother's apprehension as she helped her on with the cloak. Becky pulled her hat down securely and clasped her cloak tightly around her body. 'I'll not be long, dear.' It was a troubled Marian that watched her mother step out into the storm, to be lashed remorselessly by the driving rain as she scampered to the stables.

Becky found the track from the farm in a treacherous condition. By keeping to the edge where the going was slightly better, she was able to make slow progress. As she entered the track that led to the distant pastures, a vivid flash of lightning revealed the gloomy landscape in a dazzling bluish light. Although anticipating the thunder, its deafening explosion of sound caused her to gasp and involuntary cringe in her saddle. She screwed her eyes almost closed against the torrential rain that continued to sweep across the land.

With her eyes screwed tight, Becky had difficulty in seeing the track ahead of her. Cautiously she rode clear of the trees so as to reach the higher ground overlooking East Pastures.

Lightning zig-zagged between the turbulent clouds and the rain soaked earth. Becky jumped as a tree not far from her shattered with an explosion of sound. Lightning had struck it with infinite power; leaving but a charred heap of smouldering debris. The smell of scorched timber pervaded her nostrils as she struggled to calm her frightened horse – and her nerves.

By gently encouragement, Becky eventually calmed her horse so that she could continued on her ride. As the thunder rumbled away in the distance, a ray of sunlight broke through a gap in the clouds. It revealed in dramatic detail the holocaust resulting from the storm.

The murky, mud stained river surged foam flecked along its turbulent coarse. Shattered branches, uprooted shrubs and the occasional body of the drowned animal were swept along in the swirling water. Already the flash-floods had cause the river banks to overflow and flood the East Pastures, a low lying area where the sheep usually grazed. Becky's cry of alarm pierced the abating wind. Momentarily paralysed, she could only stare in horror at the alarming sight before her.

Stephen and Curly were cut off, marooned on a section of high ground. A hillock surrounded by the ever rising and tempestuous flood water. Becky fought against her mounting fear. Already her son's horse was standing knee deep in the water. Unless something was done soon, all three would be in a perilous situation. There was a possibility of them being carried away by the flood water. This thought galvanised Becky into action.

She remembered there was a ridge, running along the submerged terrain towards the high ground where Stephen was stranded. Becky called a warning for Stephen to remain where he was, then forcing the first feelings of panic aside she edged her horse along the edge of the flood water. Frantically she tried to locate the submerged ridge that stretched out towards an anxiously watching Stephen.

'Calm yourself, Becky! You must remain calm.' She reminded herself while assessing the rapidly deteriorating situation. She waved and gesticulated to Stephen, trying to indicate that he should be ready to ride towards her when she called. Perhaps swim would be a better description, she though grimly... but there was no other option. If her son was to survive they would both have to battle against the turbulent water.

Head low against the wind and rain, Becky rode on, sick with worry. She was frantic to find the ridge, her only hope of saving Stephen. Conditions were worsening. Her situation becoming more critical, but despite the risk she was determined to save her son.

Becky was on the verge of despair, when she noticed the partially submerged ridge.

'Thank God!' she gasped. Her eyes followed the ridge down to the water's edge. Pausing for a moment, she tried to visualise its submerged course out towards the hillock that was now well covered by the floods.

Urging her nervous horse out into the swirling water, Becky indicated to Stephen the direction along which he should ride towards her. By gently persuasion they guided their frightened horses out into the flood water. Circumstances were frightening as they eased their horses through the surging, muddy water in the hope of eventually reaching firmer ground.

Slowly, and with a calmness that amazed his mother, Stephen urged his mount into deeper water. Because of the noise he found it difficult to hear his mother's shouted instructions. With mounting alarm, Becky realised that the water was splashing around his horses' flanks. They were both in danger of being swept away in the rushing water.

Stephen slipped from his saddle as his horse began to struggle against the undertow. Clutching precariously to the reins, he edged with grim determination, deeper into the swirling water. Shouting encouragement, Becky coaxed her horse tentatively through the rushing water towards him.

Only a short distance separated them, but the gap still looked formidable as the flood water splashed and eddied across the pastures. Conditions were treacherous as mother and son battled for survival in the turbulent water.

Stephen and his horse were struggling to remain on the ridge, but the surging water was threatening to sweep them from their precarious position. As Becky concentrated on reducing the gap between them, she was aware of a drowned sheep being swept past them. A victim of the sudden flooding.

'No Stephen! No!' Her call was in vain. Stephen's horse, perhaps noticing the safety of the pastures so near, suddenly slipped into the water and began to swim towards the shallows. The unexpected movement snatched the reins from Stephen's hands and left him floundering.

Becky could feel the surge of the water tugging at her legs as she watched her son struggling in the water. Stephen was a strong swimmer, but in these treacherous waters he would be swept away. With a feeling of horror, she realised that he was attempting to swim in her direction. Urging her frightened horse forward, she suddenly found herself hanging on to the saddle and swimming beside the paddling animal.

'Stephen! This way... over here!' Fear gripped her heart as she realised that he was gradually being carried away from her. Curly was swimming beside him as they were swept away. Occasionally, boy and dog came together. Each contact gave Stephen a break as he paddled with his arm around Curly's neck.

Becky's prayers looked as if they were to be answered. She realised that Stephen and Curly might perhaps be swept into the shallows. With difficulty in the swirling water, she managed to turn her horse and scramble back into the saddle. Urgently, she now guided her mount back along the ridge to their entrance point. Scrambling and sliding out of the water, her horse eventually reached firmer ground. Water cascaded from them as they emerged from the flood water.

Saturated clothing hampered her progress as she hurried to reach the area that Stephen was endeavouring to make for. His horse splashed from the water, frightened and nervous after its struggles, but Stephen and Curly were still battling to reach the shallows and safety.

Once again Becky urged her horse into the swirling water that was carrying Stephen closer to the shallows, but also nearer to the river. She could hears its roar as it swirled in turbulent flight between over-brimming banks.

'Please, God! Don't let Stephen drown!' Becky's whispered plea was lost in the distant rumble of thunder. Holding her horse reins in one outstretched hand, she slid from the saddle into the raging flood waters. Snatching her whip, she flicked it out towards an exhausted Stephen.

Tiredness deserted him as he reached out and grasped the leather thong, but as he struggled, it began to slip through his wet fingers. Encouraged by his mother's shout, he made one last despairing effort and managed to retain his grip. Kicking against the surging water he managed with the help of his mother and her horse to eventually reach the shallows.

Becky urged her horse clear of the water. While retaining her hold of the reins with one hand with her whip with the other, she succeeded in gradually pulling him to safety. Once in the shallows, she felt safe enough to release her horse and drag an exhausted Stephen clear of the floods.

'Thanks... ma. I knew... you'd save me...' he gasped as Becky held him close in her arms. Tears of relief were washed from her cheeks by the rain that now fell gently from the clearing sky.

'Oh, Stephen! Thank God you're safe!' Grateful emotions overwhelmed her. Words seemed superfluous as she held her son reassuringly in her arms.

Becky felt Stephen suddenly pull away from her embrace. Shock and anguish were registered on his face as he looked back over the treacherous flood water. 'Curly! Curly!' but his heartbreaking cry went unheard, his faithful old friend was beyond recall. Exhausted and unable to struggle any longer, he had submitted to the strange, stabbing pain within his chest.

His last and most courageous act had been successfully completed. Offering support, when the young master he loved, had needed it most. Curly had closed his eyes as fatigue and pain overwhelmed him. A peaceful darkness ended his faithfulness.

A myriad raindrops sparkled in the early morning sunshine. Each blade of grass and shimmering leaf retained a crystal clear pearl of moisture after the storm. Rain-freshened vegetation and aromatic blossoms filled their air with their fragrance.

From the depths of the protective foliage, the avifauna heralded the new day with their territorial song threats. A smile lingered on the passing rider's lips as the cacophony from the alerted wild life followed his progress along the road. Andrew continued to be amazed at the shape, size and characteristics of the local animals and birds in their natural surroundings.

Gradually, the landscape became moor open. Pastures and arable land that warned him of his nearness to Newacres. His nervousness increased as he noticed the farm in the distance. It was almost sixteen years since his last meeting with Rebecca and Stephen. Even then it had been a brief and wretched encounter. He cringed with guilt as the memory returned.

They had been preparing to leave Highfield, their farm in East Wensum. Under the influence of drink he had gone, not to wish them well, but to taunt them. Rebecca had been his main target, as at the time he still blamed her for his leg injury that was to cause him a permanent limp.

When Stephen had politely asked him to leave, he had threatened the young farmer in front of Rebecca. A confrontation that had deeply humiliated Andrew. Completely ignoring his punches, Stephen had grabbed him by the collar and, after twisting him round, had force-marched him to his horse. Eventually he had managed to get in his saddle and, after muttering incoherent threats, had ridden off flushed with mortification.

Thoughts of the incident induced a flush of embarrassment as he was sure that Rebecca and her husband would be reminded of the unpleasant meeting. A thousand times since, he had regretted his drunken behaviour. If only he could have apologised, but before he was composed sufficiently to consider the implications of his belligerence, it was too late. Rebecca and Stephen had departed, they had sailed for New South Wales.

Was this all Newacres land? He gazed around in amazement at the pastures and fallow land that stretched away to the distant horizon. Vast acres of stubble that had produced a bumper harvest were in the process of being ploughed in readiness for the next crops. In the arable acres, he notice the labourers busy at their work. After yesterday's sever storm, the weather had become much cooler and greatly appreciated by the toiling workers.

Pools of water remained along the road, but these were rapidly evaporating in the warming sun. Andrew had been surprised at the storm's intensity as he was riding towards Parramatta. He had reached the town just before the cloud bust. A fortunate arrival as the storm had caused extensive flooding in the area.

After a night spent with the Governor's Representative, he had departed early, anxious to reach Bathurst. Realising that he would be passing Newacres, he had decided to call, but now, as he neared the farm, he experienced a feeling of considerable trepidation.

Newacres. The name was displayed above a gated entrance that opened onto a long driveway. At the far end of the drive he noticed the large imposing farmhouse and outbuildings. 'Pheew...' Andrew's surprised whistle was involuntarily expelled from his puckered lips. He displayed a look of astonishment as he guided his horse towards the front entrance. Stephen and Rebecca had certainly made good in the colony, but how would they react to his unexpected appearance on their property.

As he pulled his horse to a stop, the young woman on the veranda turned towards him. 'Rebecca!' His shocked exclamation escaped spontaneously from his lips. Andrew found himself staring in disbelief at the woman he had last seen so many years before.

Marian was finding the stranger's close scrutiny an unnerving experience. She was not used to such forthright behaviour and found the situation quite embarrassing. 'It is my mother you wish to see?' Marian's voice was sharp with vexation.

'Your mother? Er, yes... yes of course.' Andrew was suddenly aware that in his confused state, he had acted in a very ungracious manner. 'Please, forgive my discourteous conduct. It was not my intention to be impolite. Seeing you was a confusing reminder of your mother when we last met... about sixteen years ago. Your remarkable likeness to her caused me a momentary lapse of er... composure. You have her... natural beauty.' He wondered if he had been too presumptuous. Marian's warm smile softened her face and assured him that his words were accepted in the sincere spirit they were spoken.

'Thank you...' Before she shyly lowered her head, Andrew noticed the delicate blush that suffused her cheeks. 'Mother is training her horses in the paddock...' she glanced up with a demure look, '... shall I send for her?' With a warm gesture, she first introduced herself.

'I'm Marian... sorry about the cool welcome.' Her attractive smile was a reflection of the one that had haunted him over the years – her mother's. Andrew was about to introduce himself when he noticed an older woman walking towards them. Her arms was placed consolingly around the shoulders of a young lad. Their conversation appeared emotional, if the sadness on their faces was any criterion.

As the woman looked down to murmur commiseration's to the lad's sorrowful upturned face, Andrew noticed the silver threads among her fair tresses. By this time they were close enough for him to hear their intimate conversation.

'Curly's at rest now, Stephen.' His mother nodded in the direction of the family burial plot where a small fresh mound marked the dog's final resting place. 'Life has to go on... that was why Curly helped in your rescue.'

'It's alright, ma.' Stephen blinked back his tears. 'Nothing's for ever... I understand.' Becky's gaze lingered on her son's face as a brief smile softened its sadness. She gave him a reassuring hug before continuing towards the house.

'Here's ma, now.' Marian's voice caused her mother to look in her daughter's direction. For the first time she noticed the visitor standing beside her. There was something familiar about the man's features. Becky's brow creased into a thoughtful frown as she endeavoured to recall their visitor's name. Where had she seen him previously? As she walked towards him her mind was racing in speculation – then recognition dawned. A tremor of dismay caused her to hesitate, but she forced herself to remain calm as she addressed him for the first time in years.

'Welcome... to Newacres... Andrew. We... heard that you had... survived... but...' the colour drained from her shocked face. Andrew was dismayed that his presence should generate such traumatic reactions. Clearly his appearance had upset her as he had noticed the momentary shocked look that she had been unable to conceal. He pretended not to have glimpsed her consternation.

'A pleasure to see you again, Rebecca.' Andrew wondered if his greeting was too effusive considering the circumstances, but he continued his conversation. 'Yes, as you can see I'm in excellent health despite my ordeal of survival. Indeed, I consider myself very fortunate in being able to call upon you and Stephen today.' His smile was hesitant as he watched the conflicting emotions reflected in Becky's dark brown eyes. Was it fear he glimpsed in their depths? Why should his arrival cause her distress? Perhaps she was remembering his debauched past. A period of his life that he was striving to make amends for, but one that seemed destined to haunt him forever.

'I promised Alison that I would... visit you and...' Andrew paused, taken aback by Becky's distraught look. 'Is something wrong, Rebecca... it was not my intention to cause you... distress? Please forgive me if I have...' his attempted apology appeared to pacify her anxiety. Rebecca was however, struggling to contain herself. She was determined not to betray further emotions.

'Surprise... rather than distress, Andrew. You are nevertheless most welcome.' A smile of welcome accompanied her outstretched hand. Andrew held it gently before raising it to his lips in a courteous response. An unpremeditated action that induced a moment of relaxation on Becky's pent-up emotions.

'Your charming daughter...' he smiled towards the slightly bewildered Marian, who had been observing them with more than a little curiosity, '... reminds me of yourself when you were abut her age, Rebecca. She has your charms... your charisma.'

'Thank you for such sincere compliments, Andrew.' Becky was feeling more relaxed. There was something difference about this – changed Andrew.

Despite this observation, it was a perturbed Becky who invited him into her home. 'You must tell me all the news from home. Before that, I would like to introduce you to my children. Marian, you have already met.' Andrew acknowledged this with a warm smile in the young woman's direction. 'This young man...' she turned to the young lad beside her, '... is Stephen and the approaching figure carrying a basket of eggs, is the youngest member of the family, Roger.'

'That leaves just your husband. Is Stephen around?' Seeing the startled look on Becky's face, Andrew apologised. 'Forgive me. I understand that since arriving in Australia, he has used the name of Edward.' Becky found herself speechless. She just managed to confirm this with a slight lowering of her head.

'What ever name he uses...' Andrew chuckled reassuringly, '... he appears to be the same conscientious farmer... if results are any criterion.' Andrew swept his hand in a wide arc, indicating the undulating acres of pasture and arable land that stretched as far as the heat-hazed horizon.

'Edward is visiting Greenacres, our farm near Bathurst. I'm not expecting him back until tomorrow...'

'Greenacres? Isn't that where the Gordons... James, Billy...?'

'Hester is also with them.' Becky was anxious to confirm the young woman's presence. 'They are managing the farm for us, with most satisfying efforts, but... considering...' Becky hesitated as one of the grooms came to take Andrew's horse to the stables. 'Thank you, Jenner.' The young convict touched his hat in acknowledgement as he led the horse away.

'You... have some reservations about their... capabilities?' Andrew fell in beside his host as they walked onto the veranda.

'Not their competence... more their spiritual emotions, which appear er... unstable.' Becky paused uncertainly as they stepped into the reception hall. 'I believe you could help overcome their... emotional problems.'

'Who, me?' Andrew sounded surprised. 'Naturally, if there is anything I can do, but...'

'Hester is very unsettled. Unhappy. The thought of having to remain at Greenacres under the present circumstances is causing her much distress.' Becky noticed the puzzled look on Andrew's face as she invited him into the main living room.

'To what circumstances do you refer, Rebecca?'

'Until confirmation of Mary... James' wife is received, Hester has agreed to live at the farm as housekeeper only. She has promised, reluctantly I believe, to become as a wife to James when news of Mary's death is beyond all doubt. They can never marry without disclosing her true identity.'

'Hester's er, convict status, is known only to you and Stephen... and James of course?' Becky nodded agreement.

'Then I can settle their problem...' Andrew gave an emotional sigh before continuing. 'When I confirm to them that I found Mary dead in her cabin, they will at least feel free to er... cohabit.' Andrew was pleased that his news would help his friends.

'Yes... but...' He was aware of Rebecca's troubled look.

'There are complications?'

'Yes. Yourself, Andrew.' Noticing his amazement, Becky hurried into her explanation. 'Since the news of your survival reached them, Hester's dilemma has become increasingly complicated. She feels that her promise to James must be honoured, but her heart... her love, belongs to another.' Becky was observing Andrew closely as she spoke.

'Another? I don't understand, Rebecca.' He shook his head in innocent surprise. 'Who is it that has captivated her heart?'

'Surely you must know that it is yourself, Andrew?' She could tell by his shocked reaction that he was unaware of Hester's emotional feelings. He had never intentionally given her reason to believe, or hope, that he favoured a more sincere relationship with her.

'Perhaps I should call on James and Hester during my stay in Bathurst?'

'Bathurst!' It was Becky's turn to be surprised.

'Yes. I'm taking up the post of Governor's Representative in the area. A temporary position until the nominated official arrives from England.'

'Speaking of England...' Becky indicated that Andrew should be seated, '... I hope you bring good news... from home?'

'Unfortunately the letter I was bringing from your brother Josh, was lost when my possessions went down with the Leonore.' Seeing her disappointed look, he promised to convey any news of family and friends that she might wish for.

'My parents... and Josh, are they well?'

Andrew's brief hesitation in answering warned her to expect adverse tidings.

'At the time of my departure, your parents were in poor health. Sad, at the forgiveness they had asked from you... but never received. Josh is well and...'

'There must be some mistake, Andrew. My letter of forgiveness was conveyed by the family who returned to England just after our arrival. They promised faithfully that the letters would be delivered.' Andrew shook his head solemnly.

'They receive no such letter....' Becky was about to speak when she noticed Andrew frowning in meditation. 'Was the bearer of your letter...' his face still showed puzzled expression, '... a certain Matthew Porter?'

'Yes...' Becky nodded apprehensively, '... they were caretakers on our farm until our arrival. Mrs. Porter's health was deteriorating fast... it was imperative that they returned to England as soon...'

'They never reached England, Rebecca. Their ship was lost...'

'Then my letter of forgiveness and...' she shook her head sadly, remembering that Edward's letter to Julie had also been carried by the Porters. His letter would also have failed to reach and reassure Julie that he had survived. His words explaining why, for fear of capture, he could not reveal his whereabouts... had never arrived to pacify Julie and Maisie.

'How did you receive news about the Porters?'

Andrew was aware of her sudden anguish as she spoke of the Porters.

'Your brother, Josh. Apparently some money held for the returning family by your solicitors back in England had never been collected. Extensive enquiries eventually confirmed that the family were lost at sea. There were no known survivors from the ship.'

'Then my parents never received my letter, telling them of my love... and forgiveness? For all these years I have waited, thinking they were unable to forgive my obduracy in marrying....' Sadly, Becky lowered her face into her hands as emotional thoughts of her parents' anguish brought tears to her eyes.

'Your marriage to Steph... er, Edward, was forgiven long ago, Rebecca.' Andrew was distressed to see the sadness in her tear-filled eyes as she raised them to his.

'Thank you for your... consoling news, Andrew.' Aware that her distress was causing Andrew concern, she struggled to regain her composure as she mentioned the accident that had killed his parents. 'We were shocked to hear of your parents' tragic drowning, Andrew. What actually happened?'

'As you have received so little news of your family and friends, it would perhaps be helpful if I commenced with news of your family.' Becky nodded her agreement, anxious to hear what Andrew was about to convey.

'Your brother, Josh, is now the Reverend Joshua Kennard,' a sombre note came to his voice as he continued. 'He has taken over the duties of your father. Your parents were in poor health at the time of my departure, just over two years ago. Josh continues to farm at Highfield, but he and his family are frequent visitors to the rectory where your mother and father still live. Combining his clerical duties with that of farming was taxing your brother's ingenuity, but with my sister's help, was succeeding in both vocations.'

Andrew spoke of Josh's missing years, Seb's death in action at Waterloo and of Maisie's determination to continue running Homefield with the help of Jon, her twelve year old son.

'And how is Maisie coping, Andrew?'

'Quite well, I believe. Josh promised me that he would offer help should the situation demand it. I spent the last year before leaving England helping Maisie on the estate. Once the conditions were stable, it became possible for me to leave on my quest – my Australian mission.'

'Your... mission? You are here on a mission?' Becky dreaded to enquire as to what Andrew's quest might be. Intuition warned her that it was in connection with Edward, but what?

'Yes. However, my news of home must be of greater importance. He hesitated before continuing, aware of her nervousness when he had mentioned his assignment.

In trying to anticipate how Andrew's mission would affect her life with Edward, Becky lost the sequence of his continued narrative. It was the mention of Julie's name that induced an immediate response. Was her life, her future with her family, under threat? Fear began to permeate her disturbed emotions. Becky realised that Julie had been Edward's only love until his transportation. A love that had haunted her over the years.

Occasionally, she had noticed Edward's dreamy, far away look as he reclined on the veranda after a day's hard toil. Was he thinking of Julie during those pensive moments? She had often wondered during the precious years they had shared at Newacres. Was that tranquillity about to be shattered? Their family life destroyed. Edward was her man... her life. The thought of losing him now filled her with despair. Becky struggled to pick up the threads of Andrew's news of home.

'... Julie running Foxleigh. Relying more than ever on George, who now practically runs the estate. A remarkable young man.' Andrew paused as he became conscious of Becky's intense interest. 'Takes after his father in many ways, the lad is...'

'Father? I never realised that Julie was married.' Becky tried to hide the relief in her voice. Perhaps it was guilt at her inwardly rejoicing reactions to Julie's marriage. Her joy was short-lived.

'Julie never married, Rebecca. Like Maisie, she has this irrational expectation that Edward survived and that one day he will return to them. It has become an obsession with Julie, who awaits Edward's return with an undying love. A hopeless presumption, I'm afraid, but...' sadly Andrew shook his head.

'You... you mentioned, Julie's... son?' Becky gave Andrew a puzzled look.

'Yes... Edward's son. He was born a few months after his transportation.' Becky felt the foundations of her love ... her happiness... her world starting to crumble. Instinct warned her that her contented existence and days of unbounding happiness with the man she loved were in danger of ending.

'Was Edward... aware of the situation... about his... son?' Becky was struggling to control her emotions. Speech and thoughts were difficult to co-ordinate.

'No. Unfortunately, when Julie and Maisie arrived at the prison on a visit to inform him, they were too late. Edward had already been taken to Portsmouth. Andrew gave Becky an anxious glance as he noticed the shocked look on her pallid face.

'You... feeling alright, Rebecca? Shall I call your housekeeper?'

'No... I shall be fine, thank you, Andrew. A little tired... after yesterday's activities.' Becky realised that it was not her rescue of Stephen that was causing her distress. It was the thought of Edward's reaction when he became aware that Julie had given birth to his son – and was waiting for his return.

'Perhaps I have tired you with all my talk. Now you must tell me about your rise to such eminence in Sydney's society and in the farming community.' Andrew paused, allowing Becky time to gather her thoughts. He was troubled by her obvious distress. It seemed in some way related to his news of Julie. Information that certainly did not warrant the shocked look in her eyes.

'First, Andrew... you must tell me of your... mission.' Her voice was weak as she requested further information.

'Oh, that! Jut a whim, really.' He shrugged his shoulders. 'I wanted to find Edward's pardon... for Maisie. It's possession would, I had hoped, be a small compensation for the wrong I have done him.'

'Pardon?' Alarm caused Becky to gasp out the word.

'Yes. Edward's pardon was sent out immediately following his sailing. Regretfully, it was too late to save his life. Since then the documents had been filed away... and forgotten. Forgotten, that is, until I located the pardon in the Governor's office and...' Andrew leapt from his chair, just in time to catch Becky before she fainted on the floor.

Part Three(1828-1829)
The Tragedies

CHAPTER TWENTY SIX

Robert Morrison was deep in meditation as he drove his phaeton along the road towards Bathurst. Often, as now, his thoughts were filled with memories of Elizabeth, his wife, who had eventually succumbed to a long and wasting illness. It was now ten months since her death and although time had eased the heartache of her loss, he still missed her greatly.

Newacres. The sign jolted him our of his reverie. On impulse, he left the road and drove through the gates towards the home of his special friends. As he came to a stop outside the house, the door was flung open and the housekeeper came scampering across to him.

'Oh, thank goodness... you've arrived...' she gasped agitatedly, '... 'tis Mistress Becky. She's just fainted.' Robert leaped down from his phaeton and hurried inside with a worried Amy explaining as they walked side by side, how her mistress had fainted. 'One min'it she were talkin' to the strange gentlm'n... next thing, she just collapsed inter his arms.'

As they entered the main living room, a pale faced Becky was sitting uncertainly on a chair, while the stranger stood watching her anxiously. Noticing the surprised look at his sudden entrance, Robert explained that he was a doctor and also a friend of the family. A very relieved Andrew was pleased that help had arrived at an opportune moment.

It was an hour or so later, that the two visitors, reassured by Becky that she had overcome her faintness, prepared to depart. 'I'm fine! Truly!' She smiled her thanks to them both as they said their farewells.

'I hope...' Robert gave Becky a meaningful look, '... that you will heed my advice and take things easy for the next couple of days.' Andrew was aware of the doctor's concern when warning Becky about overdoing things.

'You have my promise, Robert.' Her enforced cheerfulness was but a façade to hide her troubled heart. It was a deeply disturbed Becky who watched her visitors ride away together.

On learning that Andrew's destination was also Bathurst, Robert had graciously invited the stranger to share his phaeton. Having secured his horse to the rear, Andrew climbed in beside Robert. 'Wonderful couple... great friends.' Robert looked over his shoulder towards the house as he gave Becky a final wave. 'Pity Edward was away.'

'I expect we shall meet soon...' Andrew sounded apprehensive as he thought of their last meeting. 'I doubt if I shall recognise him now. From information received, Stephen seems a changed man from the person I remember.' Aware of Robert's strange look, he elucidated. 'Back in Homefield we knew him as Stephen. He was a much...' Andrew frowned as he considered how best to describe the young farmer he remembered, '... quieter... more reserved person in those days.' Robert nodded reflectively as he flicked the reins to encourage a little more speed from the horses.

'When do you expect your children to join you?' Andrew noticed his companion's sadness as he turned to reply.

'Very soon, I hope. My information is that the house will be ready in about two weeks. Unfortunately, the hospital will take a few weeks longer.'

'Why leave Sydney? I understand that you have a lovely house and that you are held in great respect by the community.'

There was a long silence before Robert replied.

'Too many... memories, Andrew. Since Elizabeth's death, my heart hasn't been in my work. I have become... very restless. Returning to England was one option I considered.'

'What prevented that option being acted upon?'

'Mainly my children. Mark and Carol. They did not want to leave their home – their country.' Andrew gave an understanding nod. 'When I mentioned my predicament to the Governor, he was most sympathetic. Without a moment's hesitation, he invited me to consider running the hospital being built in Bathurst. It was just the challenge I needed.' Robert paused to concentrate on easing his horses through a fairly deep pool of water before continuing with the conversation. 'How about yourself, Andrew? What brings you to Bathurst?' His questions were accompanied by an enquiring look.

'Governor's Representative for the area. Only a temporary post...' glimpsing the doctor's surprised look, Andrew elucidated, '... until the appointed official arrives from England.'

Dusky shadows were gradually softening the fading brightness of the sunset as they approached a small isolated farmhouse. 'The Baxter's place.' Robert pointed towards the building. 'Usually stay the night here with Meg and Tom. There's always a warm welcome,' he smiled as he looked towards the flickering lantern in one of the windows.

'Settlers I presume?' Andrew looked towards the timber and brick farmhouse as their phaeton trundled down the track towards it.

'No! Pardoned convicts! Governor granted them a hundred acres when they became married... after becoming emancipated...' Robert chuckled as Andrew looked round the vast area of gently undulating pastures surrounding them in the deepening shadows. 'That was ten years or so since. Now...' Robert swept his arm in a wide arc, '... Temmog covers nearly two and a half thousand acres.'

'Quite a success for...' Andrew hesitated, 'er... emancipated folk.'

'I think Tom and Meg, like most of the emancipated farmers around here, would be the first to admit that they owe Edward and Becky a great deal.' Catching Andrew's puzzled look, he clarified his statement.

'It's as if Becky and Edward... have a natural affinity towards the emancipated people. Help in the form of small loans or livestock is available in genuine cases and no repayment expected until the new farmers are settled financially. Needless to say...' he turned towards Andrew as they pulled up outside the house where a middle aged couple were awaiting their arrival, '... you'll not here a bad word spoken against our friends at Newacres. Certainly not in this area.'

Andrew pointed to the farm's name on a signboard. 'Why Temmog? An unusual name?'

'Anagram of their names,' Robert whispered as their hosts stepped forward to greet them.

Stiff and slightly cramped in his legs, Andrew stumbled as he jumped down from the carriage. 'Oh, sir! You've hurt your ankle?' There was concern on the woman's face as she stepped forward to help him.

'No, ma'am. Just an old injury from the past.' Andrew realised that she was referring to his limp. Reassured, she turned to greet Robert before inviting the travellers inside.

'That was wonderful, Meg.' Robert patted his satiated abdomen at the same time as he displayed a satisfied smile over his face. 'I can understand your healthy look, Tom. Don't suppose...' he paused to give Tom a conspiratorial wink, '... you want to get rid of her?' Andrew joined their joyful laughter, aware of the convivial ambience in the room.

They were on the road early the following morning, anxious to reach their destination. Robert spoke of his wife's sincere friendship with Becky as they travelled and of how their children had grown up together to continue the families' friendliness.

Andrew spoke of his mission and survival from the Leonore. Their conversation helped the journey pass quickly. It was almost with surprise that Robert suddenly realised that Bathurst had just come into view.

'There it is, Andrew! Bathurst!' They had just crested a hill and below them lay the expanding settlement, named after the Third Earl Bathurst, secretary for war and the colonies. A few imposing structures dominated the mainly white-washed buildings of brick and timber.

As they entered Bathurst, Robert eased his horses to a walking pace. Beneath the shade of some eucalyptus tress ahead of them, a small crowd had gathered. Frowning at the obstruction to his progress, Robert pulled his horses to a strop and stepped down. With Andrew beside him they walked towards the agitated crowd.

'What is it, Robert?' Andrew cast an anxious glance as the smart carriage standing stationary by the side of the road. Through an inquisitive onlooker they learnt that a young woman had been knocked down. The victim was lying in the road, while a child in obvious distress sat sobbing beside her.

'The child fell in front of the carriage...' the onlooker having witnessed the accident was keen to explain what had happened, '... young woman pulled him free, but was knocked over herself.'

Robert, aware that his services were urgently needed, pushed through the bystanders. 'Make way, please... .I'm a doctor.' His authoritative voice soon cause the people to part and Robert, closely followed by Andrew, were soon standing beside the injured woman.

'Billy!' The tearful lad turned as Andrew called his name. For a few moments he stared bemused-like, then recognising Andrew he hurried to his side where he was reassured and comforted.

'It's Hester,' he sobbed. 'She's... hurt...,' tears flowed down his shocked face. Andrew embraced the little lad to comfort him, at the same time observing the doctor's inspection of Hester through worried eyes. There was no sign of movement and a trickle of blood had traced a scarlet course down her pallid cheek. With Billy grasping his hand, he walked across for a closer observation of the unconscious Hester.

'You know these people, Andrew?' Robert, feeling the young woman's pulse, looked up as his companion reached his side.

'Yes They sailed on the Leonore with me. Survivors, like myself.'

'Pulse is... weak. No bones appear to be broken. Slight concussion... don't think...' he paused as Hester's eyes flickered open.

'Hester!' Andrew softly called her name. Once again there was a fluttering of her eyelids, but no further reaction. 'Hester... it's Andrew!' Her eyes slowly opened and a frown of uncertainty creased her brow. Recognition gradually filtered through her confused senses.

'Andrew...' Hester's dark brown eyes were smiling as she whispered his name, '... didn't expect... to see you... here?'

'You're in good hands, Hester. Robert...' he nodded reassuringly towards his watchful companion, '... is a doctor.'

'Thank you... Robert.' A warm and grateful smile was bestowed upon the man bending over her. Andrew, watching Hester closely, was aware of the sudden sparkle in her eyes as they met those of the captivated doctor. It was an instantaneous response. For a brief revealing moment, each had disclosed their innermost emotions. Their loneliness. Their impassioned urgency for each other's love.

'We must get you to my house... Hester.' There was an emotive huskiness about Robert's voice as he made the statement. 'Just a short ride from here.' Assisted by Andrew, he managed to help his still shaky patient into his phaeton. Hester found herself, weak and longing... his love for her. His nearness excited her as the settled down together in preparation for the journey to Robert's new residence.

Hester glanced down at her faded and crumpled dress. If only I had something pretty to wear, she thought. Tears moistened her eyes as she felt the pain in her head... and in her heart. She gave her companion a reassuring smile to cover her emotions.

Robert paused to give Andrew directions on how to reach his house. Then clicking his tongue, he urged his two horses away from the fragmenting crowd. Billy, pleased to be walking beside Andrew, was now much more composed. As he glanced down to reply to one of Billy's numerous questions, he noticed the sadness still lingering in the lad's eyes. Understandably, thought Andrew. First, his mother's death, then the shipwreck and now the shock of almost being run down by a carriage and horses.

Just as they were preparing to move off, the shocked owner of the carriage emerged to offer her apologies. 'My coachman never had a chance of avoiding the young lady. I pray that she is not badly injured.' She looked very shaken as she glanced anxiously after the departing phaeton. 'Please convey my sincere regrets to the young lady. She was very brave... and if I can be of any help...'

'Thank you. I shall see that your concern is made known to the lady er...' Andrew hesitated, wondering who the lady was.

'Mrs. Walters... wife of Major Walters, the retiring Governor's Representative.'

* * * * *

It was dusk as Andrew pulled up outside Greenacres. Anxious eyes had watched his approach, but before James could ask any questions, Billy had scrambled down from the carriage before it had barely stopped. James' surprise at seeing Andrew again was lost in the welter of words from his son.

'Hester saved me… she got knocked over… doctor has taken her home… until she is well again.' A confused James turned a puzzled face towards Andrew for clarification of the situation.

'It's alright, James…' chuckling, he walked over to greet his friend, '… I'll explain all later.'

'Hester will not be returning for a few days, James.' Andrew was explaining her absence after their exchange of greetings. His words produced an acknowledging nod from his companion. James, aware that perhaps there was more to Hester's episode than Andrew had explained, refrained from questioning him further.

Later that evening when they were alone, James raised the question about Hester's accident and the extent of her injuries. 'Is she badly hurt, Andrew?'

'No, James. She is recovering well. It was, however, considered a prudent precaution to keep her until careful observation for a few more… days.' Andrew was conscious of his friend's searching look as he continued. 'It was a most courageous act on her part. She snatched Billy from the path of the horses and carriage, but was herself knocked over as she pulled him clear.'

'Aye… she's a brave lass a'right – and a good'n. I have me doubts about her returning to Greenacres.' Noticing Andrew's puzzled look, he hesitated before explaining his observations. In the ensuring silence, James selected a paper spill from the mantle and placed it in the fire. When it burst into flames, he applied the light to his pipe. Bluish smoke rose into the air as the tobacco burnt fiercely, while James puffed heavily on the pipe stem.

Satisfied that his pipe was burning to his satisfaction, he knocked the spill against the hob to extinguish the flame. That done, he leaned back in his chair to confess that he had known for some months of Hester's emotional conflict.

'I could tell that Hester was pining f'comp'ny. The farm was too remote… on some occasions it'd be days on end a'fore she would see a soul. Apart from the workers... that is. No Andrew...' he gazed knowingly through the smoke haze, '... farmin' out here in t'wilds... be not for Hester.'

'It will be a few days before she is fully recovered. Then if all goes well I'm sure that...'

'Tell her...' James interrupted, ' ... that I hope that she will soon be feeling better and...' his tanned, bearded face held a look of sadness, '... that I'll not be a holdin' her to her promise. She is free to seek opportunities wherever she wishes... with my blessing. I shall miss her.' He puffed reflectively on his pipe as he considered her companionship.

'She were good t'Billy. Hard wordin' girl... never complained, but...' he sighed heavily, '... her heart and thoughts were always elsewhere. Especially...' he was observing Andrew closely as he continued, '... since we received news of your survival.' Andrew nodded, recalling Hester's look when she regained consciousness and found him beside her. He also remembered the look that had passed between her and Robert. A look that needed no expert to interpret.

'A great pity you were not here a little earlier, Andrew.' Both men seemed anxious to change the subject of Hester's future. 'Edward was here until nearly noon. He said as how he would probably meet up with you sometime.' James removed his pipe, aware that it had long since been without tobacco. 'Your temp'rary post is bound t'bring y'in contact with him, I should reck'n.'

'Business commitments, certainly seem to keep him on the move. He's very elusive... like a phantom.' Andrew chuckled unaware of Edward's true identity.

'Aye. He be that a'right.' James nodded a smiling agreement.

'I shall bring Hester out to see you, when she is better. If she is not returning, she'll probably have a few things to collect and want to share a few words of farewell with you and Billy... before she finally leaves.'

'Tell her, I understand... that I hold no malice. I shall always be in her debt for the way she cared for Billy and m'self when t'goin' were tough.' Andrew was aware of the close scrutiny he was being subjected to as James continued. 'If... if she should change her mind... there'll always be a welcome... here.' Andrew nodded, understanding the meaning behind his companion's words. He, however, had a premonition that Hester's heart had been captivated this time by a man who she was anxious to share her love with.

'It is possible that you may find yourself in need of a housekeeper, James? If it is you wish, I can select a suitable candidate when I receive the next group of... of prisoners?'

'Thanks for the offer, Andrew. I may well be in need o'one later, but then...' His covert glance lingered on Irene, the housekeeper and nanny who had remained behind after the Masters had departed. Since Hester's reluctance to discuss marriage with him, James had been casting enamoured glances in her direction.

He was aware that Irene was a few years older than himself, but she was still an attractive woman with a pleasant disposition. Now, as she stooped to place another log on the fire, he noticed the sheen in her fair hair. The element of capriciousness retained in her character was evident, as, aware of James' gaze, she turned and gave him a saucy smile.

* * * * *

'Well... what do you think of the hospital, Andrew?' Robert's voice reflected his excited emotions. After four months of hard work, the building was ready to receive its first patient. 'I have suggested an official opening. It being a commemorative occasion, I contacted the Governor in Sydney regarding a guest of honour.' Robert found it difficult to contain his exciting news as he smiled at the sombre clad man he had come to respect and trust.

'Did he accede to your request?'

'He was in complete agreement. My choice as to who should officiate at the opening met with his full approval.'

'And... his choice?' Andrew was trying to think who might have that honour. He was taken aback by his companion's response.

'Yourself, Andrew. As the Governor's Representative, you are invited to open the new hospital.' Robert's face was wreathed in smiles as he confirmed the decision.

'Me? But... I've done... so...' The shock disrupted Andrew's line of thought. He eventually gave up... lost for words.

'In the four months since your arrival...' Robert's face became serious as he spoke of the populace's appreciation of Andrew's work since he came to Bathurst. 'You have instilled a sense of responsibility in the community. There is now a friendliness, a feeling of shared interest among all sections of the populace. Your place of assembly is well attended and through your help and interest, the hospital has become a focal point for the area's inhabitants.' Robert suppressed his chuckle, fully aware of Andrew's embarrassment, but he continued his approbation.

'Now, the building stands ready to accommodate those that are sick and in need of care. All that is required is your opening speech, which I sincerely hope will be made in two days time.' A bemused Andrew could only nod a silent confirmation.

'I... er... feel greatly honoured... Robert. Are you sure that the honour of opening the hospital should be mine... after all, it is your project?'

'Our choice was unanimous, Andrew.' Still smiling at his companion's bewilderment, Robert placed an arm around his friend's shoulder and suggested they walk back to the house. The new residence that the doctor had moved into on his arrival in the town.

'We've named it, The Shrubbery... because of the shrubs we had to clear in preparation for the garden layout.'

'We?' Andrew cast an enquiring glance in his friend's direction.

'Hester and myself. Come and see for yourself... it's time you gave us a call.'

'I must admit that I've seen very little of Hester... since her accident. Don't seem to get much time for... social visits.'

'Well, it's time you paid Hester a visit. You'll be pleased with the recovery she has made.

'Andrew!' Hester hurried forward to greet him as they entered the house. 'It's so wonderful to see you again.'

'You also, Hester.' His admiring glance induced a blushing caress to the young woman's cheeks. A pleasurable smile hovered on Hester's lips as she watched Andrew's approving gaze linger upon her. 'You... look absolutely radiant, my dear.' Andrew experienced some difficulty withdrawing his eyes from the happy person he had just affectionately embraced.

Noticing the warm smiles exchanged between Robert and Hester, intuition prepared Andrew for another surprise. Taking Hester's hand, Robert turned towards Andrew and with excitement sparkling in his eyes, conveyed the couple's happy news. 'We wanted you to be the first to congratulate us...' he gave Hester an amorous smile, '... on our forthcoming marriage.'

'That's wonderful news. Congratulations... but...' Andrew's smile faded as he gave Hester a perplexing look, '... what of Hester's er... position, her... social er, status?' He was reluctant to use the word convict when referring to Hester.

'That presents no problem, dear friend.' Robert paused to bestow a benign look upon his future wife. 'I have spoken to the Governor about Hester's situation. In view of the excellent reports of her courage and behaviour on the Leonore and more recently her bravery in risking her life to save Billy, he has granted her emancipation... Hester is a free woman.'

'A freedom greatly deserved. You both have my blessings.' Holding Hester in a gentle embrace, Andrew kissed her cheek. 'God bless you, my dear... you deserve your happiness.'

* * * * *

Andrew paused to glance back at the official residence for the last time. With the arrival of the new Representative, his temporary duty was over. Colonel Farringdon-Hurst had arrived unexpectedly two days previously. He had travelled on from Sydney alone, anxious to be taking up his official duties.

As Andrew exchanged farewells with the staff, there was sadness on their faces as they expressed their regrets at his leaving. Already the friendly relationship Andrew had encouraged between himself and the staff was being subjected to change. The relaxed, charismatic style that had been his way of running the official residence, was already being superseded by a more regimented routine.

The colonel's military-like procedures were not proving popular. Already there were murmurs of discontent among the staff. Andrew, aware of their opposition to such strict practices, had suggested to the new representative that he would perhaps get better co-operation from his staff by a more relaxed routine.

'Nonsense, man!' he had snorted. 'Have t'be strict with 'em!' He gave Andrew a fierce look. 'Let 'em know who's in charge!' Andrew nodded non-committally. You'll find out the hard way. A silent Andrew reflected on his thoughts.

'Carriage is ready, sir!' Engrossed in his cogitation's, he had not heard the coachman's approach.

'Oh... er... thanks, Wellings. I'm ready. We can leave immediately.' Andrew followed Ralph Wellings to the carriage. As they pulled away, he gave a friendly wave to the staff watching from windows and doorways.

As Bathurst fell away behind him, Andrew's face became serious in contemplation. He was thinking of the letter that had instigated his urgent departure. It had been entrusted to the colonel and had come with his official mail. Involuntary, he reached into his coat pocket and withdrew the letter. Its contents were familiar to him by now as over the past two days he had perused the letter a dozen or more times. Josh's writing was firm and neat and made it easy for him to find the paragraphs relating to dearest Maisie.

' ... Sorry to inform you Andrew, but Maisie's health is suffering because of the strain in running Homefield and the estate. Jonathan is a great help, but he is only a lad (nearly twelve) and although I help when possible, I think the burden is becoming too great for them. I think you should return as soon as possible to discuss the future stewardship of Homefield.

In my opinion the matter is urgent and requires your presence. We hope to receive confirmation...'

Andrew looked up as he became aware of the carriage bouncing along the rutted drive that led to Greenacres. He was hoping to see James and Billy before returning to England.

James knocked the dust from his clothes as he walked towards the house. He was deeply troubled about scab, the highly infectious disease that had been reported in the area. For the past two days he had been out checking on Greenacres sheep. James was only too aware of the effect that scab had on sheep. It ruined the wood and had a detrimental affect on the breeding. More worrying was the disease being practically incurable.

It was a relieved James who arrived back at Greenacres itself. With his shepherds he had inspected the flocks and found them in excellent health. He had left them with a warning to be ever vigilant.

James was in a affable mood as he approached Greenacres and noticed Irene gazing with unseeing eyes from one of the windows. Since Hester's departure she had taken on the duties of housekeeper. He had missed Hester, but it had come as no surprise when news was received of her friendship with Doctor Morrison. James realised then, that her destiny would be as the Doctor's wife in Bathurst.

His thoughtful features softened as he glanced at the woman who had been his housekeeper for the last six months. Unaware of his gaze, Irene was thinking about her uncertain future in the new colony. She felt insecure, despite the warm friendship that had developed with her employer and his son, Billy.

'If only I could stay here,' she sighed

'Day dreaming, Rene?' Her blue-grey eyes looked round in startled movement, preceding the smile that accompanied her guilty nod. She realised that gazing in a dream-like trance out of the window, she had not been aware of James' approach. She shook her head to disperse her dreamy thoughts.

'You're a real dreamer, Rene.' He chided her good naturedly abut her silent meditations.

'Aye ... an' a fat lot a good it's done me.' Her wistful laughter brought a smile to his lips. 'Look at me...' Irene raised her eyes in mock alarm, '... well in t'me thirties... an' still on t'shelf.' Their carefree laughter engendered an instant, somewhat impetuous response from James.

'That c'n soon be remedied.' He took hold of her hands and, smiling into her face, asked her to marry him. Irene's joyful laughter gradually faded as she noticed his serious look.

'You ... you... really mean 'at, James?' He nodded, his eyes watching for her reactions. Irene continued to stare at him in amazement, unable to believe that James was offering her marriage.

'Well? Don't keep me in suspense, woman. Be it yes, or nay?' Irene threw her arms around James' neck and kissed him full upon his lips.

'Yes! Yes, o'course!' James found himself responding to her excited emotions. He held her tight against him so that she must be aware of his needs. Their embraces became more urgent, their longing more fervent as lips, moist and sensuous aroused passionate desires through their caress. They were pleased it was possible to share their amorous feelings on their own. Billy's absence with the workers was opportune for the two lovers as their emotions began to cry out for fulfilment.

A loud knocking gradually permeated their emotional feelings. Slowly they separated and Irene after coyly returning James' smile, hurried to see who their visitor was. Andrew was just on the point of leaving when Irene opened the door. 'Why, Andrew... er... Mr. Andrew. Please come in.' Due to her emotional state, she had been guilty of a breach of protocol. Her flustered apologies were gently accepted by Andrew.

'Andrew will suit me fine, Rene. Now tell me what it is that causes your eyes to sparkle and your cheeks to glow as the crimson in an evening sunset?'

'Oh, Mr... er, Andrew.' She giggled. 'Y'are a one.'

'Well... I'm intrigued as to what causes you so much...'

'Should y'care t'step this way...' Andrew looked round to find James inviting him into the large living room, '... I'll be glad t'put yer mind at rest.' Andrew noticed the affectionate look exchanged between his friend and Irene.

'Truth is, Andrew...' he feigned a serious frown, '... I've just asked this lady here t' be m'wife.'

'May I enquire as to what her answer was, dear friend?'

'I 'gree to have'm, Andrew.' Irene's excited voice supplied the answer before James could utter a word.

'Then...' Andrew gave them both a congratulatory handshake, '... you have my best wishes for your future happiness. However, as I shall not be here for your wedding…' sadness lined his face momentarily, '… I would like to claim my prerogative as a friend and kiss the bride now.' As he made to kiss Irene's cheek, she turned her cheek at the last moment and he found his lips pressed to those that were still moist and sensuous from an emotional embrace.

Andrew was aware of the undercurrent of passion as his lips separated from hers. For a moment as their eyes met he noticed the smouldering flames of desire waiting to be unleashed. Realising that his presence had interrupted an amorous interlude, he made ready to leave. Before he could do so, James suddenly realised the significance of his friend's words.

'Not be here for our wedding? Why should that be so, Andrew? As our friend, we…' His voice faded as he noticed Andrew shaking his head.

'By then, my dear friends, I shall be sailing home… to England, where I am most urgently needed. When I arrive…' he informed them with a smile, '… I hope to marry the woman I love.'

As Andrew pulled up outside Newacres, he was surprised to see Amy, the housekeeper, coming towards him down the steps of the veranda. It seemed his wish of finding Becky and Stephen… Becky and Edward, he corrected his thoughts, at home, was not to be fulfilled. It seemed he was destined never to meet the man who had been so successful in his farming enterprises.

'Master 'n Mistress be in Sydney, sir.' She gave Andrew a slight curtsy. 'I be expectin' them back later. Perhaps yer would like t'wait?'

'No thanks, Amy. I'm sure t meet them on the road.'

'Very good, sir.' Seeing Andrew's glance directed towards the paddock and outbuildings where a great deal of activity was in progress, she anticipated his question. 'Children are not around. Marian is with her parents an' the two boys be out riding.'

'In that case, I'll be on my way. Good bye to you, Amy.' He nodded in her direction before clicking his tongue to urge his horse away towards Sydney. He kept a sharp look out for his friends, hoping to meet them on the road, or at least visit them at their town house. Fate, however, was to decree otherwise.

While Andrew rode directly through Parramatta, Becky and Edward had stopped in the town to call on friends as they drove back to Newacres. Because of this, Andrew was to return to England with Edward's pardon for Maisie, still under the impression that her brother was dead.

Chapter Twenty Seven

Frost glistened on the filigree of hedgerow twigs and roadside vegetation as Maisie in her horse and trap, with Jon beside her, drove into the village. A dazzling sun sparkled on the wintry landscape as they made their annual festive visit to the local hamlet. Their mission was to distribute gifts among the elderly and infirm residents of Homefield. Other members of the community would be calling at the hall for refreshments after the Christmas morning service.

Maisie gave a friendly wave to Ben Holland, the son of old Joe, the man who had been blacksmith in her early days at Homefield. Ben smiled and exchanged the season's greetings with mother and son as they passed the forge. Their mission completed, they were on the road to East Wensum and Highfield to issue invitations for Josh, Alison and their family to visit the Hall on the morrow – Christmas Eve.

As usual their arrival generated great excitement among the children. Jane and William came scampering and shouting to greet their favourite aunt, anxious to be the first to enjoy her warm and gentle embrace. Maisie cuddled them both in turn, sharing in their happy laughter as she did so. Jon's greeting was more formal, but given with great affection nevertheless.

After taking refreshments and receiving confirmation that Josh and his family would be visiting them on the eve of the festivities, they all made their way outside for Maisie and Jon's departure. At his mother's invitation, Jon took the reins. Proudly, he guided the horse and trap out onto the drive as farewells were exchanged.

'See you all tomorrow!' Maisie turned with an expectant smile to remind her sister-in-law and Josh. They waved their acknowledgements, but deep concern lined their faces as they watched their dearest friend and her son driving away.

'If only Andrew would hurry home.' Josh heaved a sigh and shook his head sadly. 'Maisie is in need of help on the estate.'

* * * * *

Maisie stretched her tired arms above her head before easing herself wearily into her favourite fireside chair. It was Christmas Eve and she had just completed her morning rounds of the estate. Household staff had been encouraged in their preparations for the family's visitors. They were due in about an hour, in the meantime, Maisie decided to have a few minutes respite away from the hustle of the household activities.

She felt the comforting warmth of the blazing fire as she settled down beside the large open fireplace. Gradually, Maisie experienced a feeling of calmness and tension passed from her body. Completely relaxed, she was aware of her deep tiredness. The comfortable and tranquil surroundings induced a feeling of sleepiness that she gratefully succumbed to.

Voices penetrated her deep slumberous state. Slowly she eased her way back to wakefulness. As she endeavoured to orientate her drowsy thoughts, she became aware of a man standing by the fire watching her. As she recognised the visitor, her eyes opened in joyful surprise. 'Andrew! Oh, Andrew... I'm sorry you find me... sleeping on your return.' Her excited apology was received with an affectionate smile.

'There is no need for apologies, Maisie... and please don't get up.' Andrew placed a restraining hand upon her shoulder. After a brief pause he bent over and kissed her cheek. 'I'll join you, if I may?'

Maisie nodded, her smile reflecting the happiness she felt. Before he moved away, she gently pulled him down beside her. 'Thank you for coming... home, Andrew.'

With a joyful response he leaned over and eased his lips upon hers. His kisses were gently at first as uncertainty about his previous behaviour, restrained his emotions. Feeling Maisie's lips, so responsive and eager against his, made him realise that his past misdemeanours were forgiven, if not completely forgotten.

'I intend to remain at Homefield for as long as you need me, my dear.' He guessed from her benign look that a prolonged stay was inevitable.

'That... could very well be...' she eased away from him slightly to gaze fondly into his grey-blue eyes, '... for a very long period.' Maisie sighed as she relaxed back into her chair. 'I'm afraid the estate work is becoming... too much for me, Andrew.'

'In that case, you must permit me to run the estate, while you concentrate on organising the household.' Before Maisie could reply, Jon walked into the room. A smile of welcome spread over his face as he hurried across the room to great Andrew. It appeared to watching Maisie that their friendship was about to start from where it had left off, before Andrew's departure for Australia.

'You must bring me up to date on the estate work, Jon.' There was a look of pride on the young lad's face when he realised the responsible duty being asked of him. Behind her son, Maisie's covert smile was warm and appreciative as her eyes rested on the gentle and understanding man who had just re-entered her life. Andrew was soon aware that Jon's knowledge of the estate's working was much deeper than the peripheral information that he had been expecting.

Jon informed him of the number of lambs raised in the last lambing as well as the average fleece weight per shearing. After a brief pause to mentally recall the figures, he then gave the number of cattle, sheep, pigs and horses that were currently held by the estate. Andrew was very impressed by the lad's knowledge, but more was to follow.

He received details of what crops had been grown, where they had matured and the bushels harvested per acre. All details given with the solemnity of an experienced farmer. 'What of the crops for the coming season, Jon?' In truth, Andrew had expected a negative response to his question, but to his utter amazement he was informed, not only what crops had already been sown, he was also informed of those scheduled for early spring sowing. Andrew noticed that the Norfolk four course rotation system, where more emphasis was placed on the fodder crops for the cattle, was still being adhered to.

'If you wish, sir... I'll be glad to show you over the estate.'

Andrew, noticing the lad's excited look of anticipation, agreed that after the festive season, nothing would give him greater pleasure.

There was a long silence after Jon's departure. Andrew, standing by the window, watched the lad walk confidently towards the stables. Shortly he emerged leading a well groomed horse and with the ease of an expert was soon mounted and riding off across the park.

'That's Swift... his pride and joy.' Maisie nodded proudly towards the departing horse and rider. 'He grooms and cares for the horse himself. They are almost inseparable companions.'

Shaking his head in amazement, Andrew explained that he was still trying to digest the information he had just received about the estate. 'Your son is a very intelligent lad, Maisie. He has a sense of responsibility that would be a credit to a much older and mature person.' Aware of the proud look in her eyes, Andrew was reminded how pleased his brother would have been at Jon's sense of reliability.

'Sebastian...' he was apprehensive about using his brother's name, but realising that Maisie's memories of her dead husband, although still cherished, had been placed in perspective by the strife and worries of the passing years, decided to continue. 'Sebastian would have been proud of his son, Maisie.'

In the deep emotional silence that followed Andrew's words, the first flakes of snow drifted down past the window. A log dropped in the fire, sending a shower of sparks in a pyrotechnic-like display up into the chimney.

'I'm sorry, Maisie. I did not intend to remind you of Seb. Please forgive me.'

'There is nothing to forgive.' She shook her head thoughtfully. 'It's just that I am uncertain... if I should enlighten you... about Jon.' Maisie's voice faded to a whisper.

'Enlighten... me?' Andrew hesitated, aware of the troubled frown that furrowed her brow.

'Yes...' Maisie rose agitatedly from her chair, paused uncertainly for a few moments, then, as if reaching a decision, walked across the room to stand beside Andrew. Side by side they gazed silently out at the falling snow. Maisie was meditating on what she was about to disclose, aware that it could have adverse repercussions in their future relationship.

‘Yes…’ she whispered as she continued to look out of the window, ‘… Jon was… conceived on the night of Seb’s departure… for Waterloo.’ A deathly quiet followed her words, then she heard Andrew’s shocked gasp as realisation penetrated his thoughts.

‘You… you mean… that… that Jon…?’ He was unable to continue. The thought of what he had done to Maisie on that night filled him with anguish. Remorse overwhelmed him.

‘Jonathan is our son, Andrew.’ The pallor on her face reflected the effort it had taken her to confirm her son’s parentage.

‘That shameful and unforgivable act…’ sorrow lined his face and his eyes filled with tears as he struggled to continue, ‘… that moment of drunken depravity… was the darkest hour of my obnoxious life.’ Maisie noticed his deep distress before he lowered his head in shame. He sank to his knees in despair. Clasping Maisie’s hand, he looked up into her face, begging forgiveness for the hurt and humiliation he had caused her.

‘Your life in recent years, Andrew…’ Maisie helped him rise so that he was standing close beside her, ‘… your help and understanding for those in need, has been a comforting revelation to us all. Endeavouring to make amends for your past… behaviour, has been an admirable and as far as I am concerned, an inspiring quest.’

With true humility, Andrew thanked her for such commendations – and forgiveness. As he did so he noticed the sparkle of admiration and love in her eyes. ‘Here, my dearest, is the culmination of my quest.’ His smile was warm as he handed Maisie the pardon that would have acquitted her brother so many years ago. ‘Proof of your brother’s innocence – and my depravity. However…’ sorrow and disappointment line his face as he turned to leave, ‘… in view of your confession, Maisie, the motive for my return must remain a dream.’

‘May I enquire what the… motivation was, Andrew?’ Her heart ached to see his sadness. Maisie wanted to help the man that she had come to admire for his integrity and kindness of latter years.

‘Perhaps…’ he hesitated thoughtfully, then shook his head sadly, ‘… it is best forgotten.’

'Then...' she gave him a rueful smile, '... at least tell me that which motivated you during your quest.' Andrew stood in silent meditation for a few moments, before focusing his solemn gaze upon the woman he loved. 'I had hoped to ask you to... marry me, but...' he shrugged his shoulders disconsolately.

'But... what...?' Maisie was aware of her heart beating excitedly as she encouraged his reply.

'Don't you see, Maisie... after what happened... that night... Jon...' he stumbled for words as he searched for an explanation.

'Then perhaps, you should let me decide... give you my answer.'

'Will you... then... think... consider... the possibility...?' Andrew realised that his jumbled words were making very little sense. 'Oh, Maisie...' he sighed. 'Will you marry me?' He could hear the pounding of his heartbeats as he waited her answer.

'Yes, Andrew... and welcome... home.' Their embrace was prolonged, but laughter and approaching voices eventually forced a reluctant separation. 'That will be your uncle and cousin Julie.' Maisie's voice was still breathless from their exciting exchange of endearments.

'I didn't realise that they were coming for the Christmas festivities.' Andrew glanced anxiously towards the door. He had not seen his relations since the evening when he had attacked Josh on the bridge in Norwich and knocked him unconscious. On that occasion, after ensuring that his injured brother-in-law was safely in their care, he had departed with the Quaker. Jason had invited him to return and join his family and the Friends' community.

A tall, muscular young man entered the room first. 'My dearest aunt Maisie... how are you?' His greeting was warm as he gently embraced his aunt. 'George...' Maisie gave the young man a benign look, '... you grow taller and more handsome, each time we meet.' Andrew noticed the lad's slight blush of embarrassment. 'Now let me introduce you to another relation who has just returned from Australia.' Maisie turned and introduced them to each other.

'Hello, George. You were but a small lad when last we met. Don't suppose you remember me?'

'Afraid not, sir.' George was uncertain about the man he had just been introduced to. He recalled the many uncomplimentary reports he had heard about his uncle Andrew. Surely this was not the same man?

After a few moments, Andrew greeted his uncle and cousin as they entered the room. Their greetings were warm as they expressed pleasure at seeing him back in England again. As he embraced his cousin Julie, Andrew noticed the melancholy look in the hazel eyes that gazed uncertainly into his. Strands of grey in her dark hair complemented her maturity. He realised, as he observed her closely, that his cousin was as attractive in appearance as she had been in her younger days.

Andrew was aware that she had refused the hand of many suitors over the years in her almost fanatical-like belief that Edward would one day return. She continued to believe this, despite his name being on the official list of those missing, presumed drowned, when the Badger went down on her voyage to New South Wales. Andrew had found no evidence in Australia of Edward having survived. A detailed search of the official records had confirmed his drowning.

Realising that Becky and Stephen had taken passage on the same ship, he had asked her if she could confirm Edward's possible fate. Andrew vividly remembered her strange reaction. An agitated response that had momentarily stunned him. At the time he had found it difficult to assess her emotions. Guilt... fear... or perhaps the memory of that traumatic experience still haunted her. Believing the latter, Andrew had never referred to that episode again.

'Andrew... you seem deeply troubled?' Julie had noticed his reflective expression.

'No... er, not troubled, Julie. Just thinking... dreaming, really.' Seeing her doubtful reaction, he considered whether to disclose confirmation of Edward's drowning. The chance passed. Before he had reached a decision, his contemplation was interrupted.

'Andrew! What a wonderful surprise.' Alison hurried across to welcome her brother. Breathless and excited, she eased from his embrace. 'What news do you bring of dearest Becky and Stephen and...' looking towards Julie, she lowered her voice,

'... Edward?' Alison had almost forgotten her cousin's presence. In the hubbub of excited chatter, her quiet enquire was heard only by her brother.

'No definite news of Edward; as for Becky and Stephen, what information I have regarding them you shall hear later. I shall be relating my experiences in Australia to you all then.' Andrew whispered his intentions before turning to greet Josh.

It was later that evening with the adults, sitting relaxed and comfortable around the blazing log fire, that Andrew spoke of his mission. Flickering candlelight played upon the intent features of the listeners. All eyes were on Andrew as he related his journeys and experiences since his departure from Homefield three years previously. As he neared the end of his narrative, Andrew paused expectantly as he noticed Josh's eagerness to speak.

'You have spoken in detail of Rebecca and her children, but little of Stephen. Did you find him in good health, Andrew?' His brother-in-law's question, he realised, also reflected the uncertainty of the others. All appeared anxious to hear of Rebecca's husband. His success in the new colony had aroused their interest.

'Truth is, Josh... I never met Stephen, or Edward as he is known to everyone out there. Apart from running three farms, he has numerous other commitments that keep him fully occupied. Sometimes his assignments keep him away for several days...' he hesitated on seeing the surprised looks on the faces of his listeners.

'Edward?' Alison enquiry of her brother. 'Why has Stephen changed his name?'

'His second forename apparently; a name that he has used since arriving in New South Wales, or Australia, as the colony is now named.'

'What of my Edward?' Julie spoke for the first time. 'What news do you have of my... betrothed?'

'None... there is nothing... definite... but...' Andrew shook his head, uncertain about revealing Rebecca's reaction... her fainting when he mentioned Edward's pardon to her.

'You... have some... information, Andrew?' Julie had noticed his hesitancy... his reluctance to continue. 'Is he... alive? A prisoner. Incarcerated... somewhere?'

'No. I think not, Julie.' There was a deep, expectant silence as they awaited his further explanation. 'There was, however, a strange occurrence.' Remembrance induced a momentary frown to his brow. 'When I mentioned that Edward's free pardon had reached the colony almost as soon as their arrival as survivors, Rebecca fainted.'

'Unusual for Rebecca to show such emotions.' Alison spoke confidently of her sister-in-law.

'Their friend...' Andrew waited for his listeners' full concentration before continuing, '... a doctor, called just after her fainting. He encouraged Rebecca to rest... insisted in fact. Apparently, the day previous she had ridden out into surging floodwater to rescue her eldest son, Stephen.' Flames from the roaring fire, flickered on the serious faces of his listeners as he spoke of the rescue.

'Young Stephen was marooned on a hillock with the flood water surging around him and still rising. To save him, Rebecca had to ride her horse out into the swirling waters. A dangerous action... .and a very brave one. When she had nearly reached him, the lad and his horse were swept into the flood water. It was his dog that gave his young master support until Rebecca could take her horse near enough to snatch her son from the water. When their doctor friend was told of her rescue attempt by some labourers hurrying to the scene, he had encouraged Rebecca to rest quietly for two or three days.'

'A very courageous act on Rebecca's part.' It was Maisie who spoke for the others. 'Were there any casualties, Andrew?'

'Thankfully there were none. The lad's faithful old dog was the only victim. He apparently died from exhaustion and old age.' Andrew paused as an elderly butler entered the room with a tray of drinks for the guests. 'Why, Bates... I thought you had retired?' Andrew gave the old butler a warm greeting.

'He pleaded to remain on...' Maisie bestowed an affectionate smile upon the old servant, '... so we compromised. Bates does two days a week and helps out on special occasions.'

'Thank you, Bates... but not for me.' Andrew was aware of the surprised glances as he confirmed his abstinence. 'I've not indulged since er... incarceration in the castle. About...' he frowned in concentration, '... ten years ago.'

'A commendable act on your part, Andrew. Well done.' Embarrassed by such praises, he could only smile self-consciously. Anxious to deflect their approbation's, he spoke of Rebecca's plans for visiting them in the near future.

His information generated great excitement and there was general speculation as to how soon her homecoming would be and how long she would be with them. Arrangements for Rebecca's visit were excitedly discussed. Andrew, thankful to have diverted thoughts from himself, heaved a sigh of relief. It proved but a premature one as suddenly he was aware of Julie beside him.

'Andrew... your information regarding Edward seemed rather... evasive. What news did Rebecca have of my betrothed? I would prefer to know the real facts... the truth.' There was no way of him evading her determined stare.

'My dearest Julie, I can only confirm that which Rebecca spoke of when I met her at Newacres. Letters were sent just after their arrival in Australia. Thinking that you, Maisie and Josh had received them, she awaited your replies. When none came she thought that she had been ostracised by us all at home. Unknown to us all, the family bringing the letters to England were drowned when the ship bringing them home was lost in a storm. A hurricane it was believed.' He paused on seeing his cousin's distressed look.

'Did... Rebecca mention the contents of her letters?' Julie was anxious for information on the man she loved.

'Only that...' watching him closely, she noticed the puzzled frown that creased his brow, '... you were not to give up hope – ever. She would say no more despite my pressing for more lucid details. The chance to question her again arose later, but when I gave her news of Edward's pardon... she fainted.'

'Th... thank you... Andrew.' A perplexed and saddened Julie rejoined the other members of the family as they once again settled down in front of the blazing fire.

'Now, Josh... a favour is requested of you.' Conversation around the fire fell away to silence at Andrew's words. He glanced towards Maisie for confirmation to announce their betrothal. Her benign smile was an acquiescence for him to impart their joyful news.

'I have asked Maisie...' Andrew walked slowly to her chair and with outstretched arms assisted her to rise and stand beside him, '... to become my wife, and as soon as permission has been authorised, we shall be wed.' He was looking towards Josh at the conclusion of the statement.

For several moments happy congratulations prevented Andrew from speaking his request. Eventually Josh, who had anticipated its nature, promised that he would expedite the necessary permission from the ecclesiastical body. 'I do not expect any problems and...' he turned to smile graciously at the happy couple, '... I shall expect an invitation to officiate at your wedding.'

'You shall have our promise for that, dear Josh.' Maisie's happy voice induced a feeling of sadness to a despondent Julie. Her joyful news only served to deepen Julie's heartache – and loneliness.

In her mid-thirties, Julie realised that time was passing her by. How much longer could she wait for Edward's return? Aware of her father's affectionate gaze upon her, she forced a smile to her face. He had, however, seen the sadness in her eyes. Julie had not deceived her father.

He was reminded of the conversation shared with her a few weeks back. On her thirty-fifth birthday. He had gently reminded her of the long years of waiting she had endured. Years of waiting and hoping for what must surely be a lost cause.

'You must accept... that Edward is dead, my dear. Your waiting can only be in vain. Why not marry Robin? He seems eager to court your affections... to seek your hand in marriage?' Julie, aware of the parson's complaisant feelings towards her, had remained silent. 'He has been very patient, my dear.'

Her father's words had only incited a sad shaking of his daughter's head and a confession that she did not like him. That she found him very devious in his manners. Secretly, the colonel agreed, but... He sighed deeply as he remembered that emotional conversation.

Noticing her distraught look, he decided that he would make a final attempt to encourage Julie to at least give serious thought to marriage. The Foxleigh parson could very well be her last chance, especially as she was an unmarried mother. It was the colonel's fervent wish to see his daughter wedded before he died and at seventy, he was under no illusions, that time was not on his side.

In the excitement following Andrew's announcement, all eyes had been on the happy couple. Only the colonel had glimpsed the sorrow and heartache reflected in his daughter's eyes. Wanting to comfort her, he rose and crossed to her side. When her tear-filled eyes looked into his, he could only reach out and hold her hand in silence.

Josh, standing beside the pulpit, smiled inwardly as he recalled Andrew's surprised look on being asked to read the lesson. 'Squire's prerogative,' he had whispered to his broth-in-law. 'As that will soon be your position at Homefield, I thought that you might like to re-introduce that ritual.' A speechless Andrew had only managed to nod a silent agreement.

Word of the old squire's son had spread rapidly among the villagers and as news about his coming marriage to the loveable mistress gathered momentum there was increasing excitement. It appeared as if the whole of the local populace had come to church in order to gaze at the happy couple.

Andrew continued his reading, seemingly unaware of the interest his home-coming had aroused. Josh, from his vantage point, noticed the curious glances directed at the man who had, in his younger days, been an enigma to them. Most, however, remembered the changed Andrew. The one who had shared their labours for a year or so before he sailed to Australia.

A smile flickered across Josh's serious countenance as he recalled an overheard comment from the congregation. 'Looks as how prodigal son be returned then, Dan?'

‘Aye ‘n not a’fore time.’ Dan had given his companion a knowing look as they entered the church. ‘Young mistress’ll keep ‘im busy, tha’s f’sure.’ Their chuckles had faded as they disappeared inside.

News of Andrew’s return had generated an air of expectancy and, when news reached the villagers that he was to marry his brother’s widow, there was much head nodding. The populace recognised that such a union would be beneficial to the Hall – and them. Homefield needed a squire and the new Andrew was a favoured and respected candidate. It was proper, they said among themselves, that the old squire’s eldest son should take over those duties. With mistress Maisie as his wife, it was a good omen for the future of the community. Josh smiled inwardly amused at the villagers openly curious stares. His gaze moved over to the family pews.

Maisie, the strain of running Homefield already eased from her face, stood beside her son, Jon. A good strong young man in the making, if I’m not mistaken, thought Josh. Just two months short of his thirteenth birthday, Jon, as everyone now called him, was already taller than his mother. In the next pew, his beloved Alison was ensconced with their two children. An emotional feeling of love and adoration overcame him as he gazed benignly upon his family.

Alison, as if aware of her husband’s eyes upon her, looked up and exchanged an endearing smile. Beside his wife, he noticed Jane, his eldest child, holding the hand of William, his somewhat precocious four year old son. A serious Jane, who was a few years her brother’s senior, was endeavouring to keep him silent during the sermon.

Josh’s eyes returned to the Hall’s pew, where he noticed the septuagenarian Colonel Markham looking very frail and troubled. Julie’s presence seemed to reassure an anxious Josh that the colonel’s welfare was in good hands. As he observed them, he became aware of the loving look that passed between father and daughter. On Julie’s other side, her tall muscular son stood in deep concentration; his thoughts seemingly remote from his immediate surroundings. Josh liked the quiet-spoken George, a likeable young man who, because of his grandfather's weakening disposition, was now managing the Foxleigh estate on his own.

It was Julie, however, that Josh's involuntary glance settled upon. Aware of his attention, she raised her eyes to look directly into his. As she did so, he was aware of the sorrow that lay behind those lovely hazel eyes. One could not but admire her faithfulness and veneration for Edward, the man she refused to accept as dead, despite the evidence that seemed to confirm this fact beyond dispute.

Andrew gently closed his bible, having completed what his father had done for many years – reading the Christmas Day lesson. Josh thanked Andrew as he stepped from the pulpit. With all eyes upon him, the prospective squire joined Maisie and Jon in the Homefield pew.

Josh stood for a few silent moments in deep meditation before addressing his congregation. His thoughts were of his elderly parents and his sister Rebecca, the other member of his family who had been absent for many years now. Andrew's message of love from her would bring comfort to his infirm parents and the news that she was planning to visit them in the coming year would, he hoped, give them the strength and encouragement to struggle against their enfeebled bodies.

From the pulpit Josh gave an erudite sermon on the rituals and ceremonies associated with Christmas and the custom of celebrating it, not merely as a day of thanksgiving, but also one of rejoicing. At the conclusion he wished his congregation a joyful and peaceful Christmas before they silently filed from the church.

Outside, he wished them all well as they departed. As the last of his members walked away, he turned to find Alison and the children waiting. Together, they walked in joyful mood towards the rectory where they intended spending a short period with Josh's parents. After the visit, they would be walking over to the Hall for the Christmas feast.

'Mother…' Josh cast an anxious glance in her direction as he drew his chair closer to her bed, '… Andrew returned recently from Australia and he brings a message of love from Rebecca to you both. He assures me that she is well and loves both of you very much.' He glanced across the bed at the frail and elderly man opposite. 'Also...' he gave them both an understanding smile, '...she hopes to visit in the near future.'

'We shall... look forward... to that joyful reunion... Joshua.' Gently she reached across and clasped her son's hands as if seeking strength to continue her survival until dearest Rebecca was with them again. 'Thank you... for such wonderful news, dear.' Josh felt the slight pressure of his mother's hand. 'A most joyful Christmas gift.'

After a few moments, sleep overcame her and her hand gradually eased from his. Josh rose and gently tucked the bed clothes around his mother before retiring from the bedroom, helping his father as he did so. 'She's determined to survive until Rebecca's return.' Josh noticed the tears in his father's eyes as he spoke.

'Then we must pray for that reunion to be soon, father.'

'Amen to that, m'boy. Amen indeed,' he repeated.

'I shall call again this evening, father, to see that you are both comfortable.' Josh was deeply concerned about his father's health. He appeared so frail and listless these days. As he walked back across the frosted parklands with his family, he decided to send Rebecca a letter urging her to visit them as soon as possible. Intuition warned him that time was not on their side if his sister was to see them -- alive.

* * * * *

'You certainly look very pleased with yourself, Robin. Has the Markham woman finally agreed to marry you?' Dennis Coleman gave his friend a suggestive wink. The two friends were relaxing in chairs that had been carefully positioned each side of the roaring fire. To a background of March winds, the Foxleigh parson and his friend were reminiscing about the years they had shared together at the ecclesiastical college. At the time they had both been studying for entrance into the church.

'A shame you were unable to complete your studies, Dennis.' There was a note of sarcasm in the Foxleigh parson's words. A reminder that he had not forgotten the scandal that had resulted in his companion's dismissal.

'How was I to know that the girl was the Principal's daughter? In any case…' he stared defiantly towards his friend, '… nothing happened to her.'

'Only because her screams alerted the whole damned college.' Robin Darvell chuckled at the recollection. 'You should have used more finesse – been more suave.' He had been on the point of adding 'like me', but noticing the anger on his friend's face, desisted. A tense silence followed, broken eventually by his companion.

'Like you… with the Markham woman? What's her name… er, Julie. Yes, I remember!' He nodded his head agitatedly, still angry at his friend's derogatory insinuations. 'You've made little… if any progress with her.' A note of cynicism edged his words as he turned towards his host.

'All in good time, Dennis. An improper move now could jeopardise all the preparatory approaches I've made since coming to the rectory.'

'I would have thought the woman too refined for your taste, Robin.' His facetious remark stung the Foxleigh parson into an irritable reply.

'That, my dear Dennis… is for me to decide. However…' he gave his friend an angry smirk, '… I intend to have her, ere many weeks have passed. Then Foxleigh Hall will be mine.' His smug countenance reflected his sinister motives. 'Squire of Foxleigh Hall… how does that sound to you, my friend?'

'You might get the woman and her possessions, but squire…' he shook his head emphatically. 'I rather think that her son will be the one to take over after the old man has gone.'

'If he is around…' there was a threatening innuendo behind his words.

'Good Lord…!' his face was pale with shock, '… You surely don't mean to … to kill the boy?'

'Of course not. Nothing so messy.' The parson's voice reflected his irritation as he hinted at the possibility of getting the future owner of Foxleigh out of the way.

'Transportation is much easier!'

'Yes… but the lad's not a criminal…'

'Not yet...'

Dennis shuddered as he noticed the malice in his friend's eyes. He realised that his companion would stop at nothing to fulfil his burning desire to become squire of Foxleigh.

'They trust you as a friend, Robin, yet you are planning to cause them distress and heartache. Isn't that being hypocritical?'

'All's fair as far as money and ambition are concerned. If it's necessary to get rid of the boy to achieve my ambition of owning the estate... so be it.'

'You have no affection – no love for the boy's mother. Marrying her is just a means of fulfilling your ... your avaricious desires.'

'Oh, I shall continue to masquerade as the reserved and gently village parson – respected by all.'

Dennis shook his head sadly, experiencing sympathetic feelings towards the woman and her son.

'If you would heed my words of advice, Robin, I would suggest you take care in your devious manipulations.'

'Thank you, Dennis, but your advice is neither requested or required.'

'How's the contraband situation?' Dennis was anxious to change the delicate subject.

'Shh... not so loud!' Robin warned him harshly as he glanced involuntarily towards the door. 'Take extreme care when you mention smuggling activities. You can never be sure who might be listening these days. Rewards can be an incentive to the most reluctant of witnesses.'

'Well, how goes it for you?' Dennis pursued his enquiry in a low voice.

'Quiet... but good.' The Foxleigh parson nodded his head as he thought of his lucrative enterprise.

'Is the church still used for storing the goods... as in your predecessor's day? I believe the old parson Jameson, used to encourage such activities?'

'Only on a small scale.' There was a smirk on his face as he continued. 'They use the outbuildings these days. More space and... more money for me.' There was an acquisitive look in his eyes as he referred to his prohibited dealings. 'When I explained that I wanted a percentage of the goods sold, in lieu of contraband, there were some protests. A compromised figure was eventually agreed and a satisfactory income is now mine. A welcome addition to my stipend.' His avaricious look gave his features a sinister set. 'Next...' he gave an evil chuckle, '... I must concentrate my amorous intentions on the charming, Miss Markham – and her bastard...'

'Prudence will be required, Robin. I understand the colonel is in very poor health and...'

'He'll not last much longer, I doubt.' The parson's voice was cold and merciless. 'If I press my intentions, display sympathetic emotions, I might catch the woman off balance... entice her to marry me and forget the peasant she keeps yearning for.'

'The one that was lost at sea... a convict?'

'Yes... an uncouth blacksmith that begot her bastard son.'

'Perhaps she may prefer to remain unmarried. The lad looks capable of running the estate. He's strong, intelligent and...'

'In that case, Dennis, I shall have to consider removing him sooner than later. I have the makings of a plan to get him out of the way, but first I must encourage his trust.' There was a cynical edge to his voice as he mentioned the boy.

'Easier said than done He's far from stupid, Robin. Not a gullible lad by any means.' The warning from Dennis was brushed aside.

'My plan requires a little more thought, but...' he gave his companion a sardonic smile, '... it could be the answer. Yes...' he gloated, '... my plan should result in his removal from Foxleigh... England even. Then I shall play upon the distraught mother's sympathy... she'll be glad to marry me then.' He rubbed his hands together in anticipated expectations.

* * * * *

Maisie, wrapped against the early morning chill, gazed across the parkland from her bedroom window. It was mid-April... her wedding day. As she looked across the sunlit fields and meadows, she experienced a strange emotional feeling. A restless uncertainty. Was it excitement or apprehension that made her so agitated?

Unable to sleep, she had risen early and taken her horse for a fast gallop before breakfast. Now, an hour before her noon-time wedding, she sought peace of mind in silent prayers while observing the tranquil surroundings of the park. Moving closer to the window, she felt the warm caress of the sun as its golden glow embraced her thinly covered body.

Overhead, fleecy clouds sailed across a vast expanse of cerulean sky. Maisie watched in thoughtful mood as their shadows chased silently over the landscape beneath. A gentle breeze stirred the lakeside reeds and ruffled the mirrored surface of the water. She averted her eyes as a vision of Andrew's dead parents floating in the blood-stained water induced a momentary tremor to her body.

Her gaze was involuntarily drawn towards the wood where the first penetrating call of a cuckoo heralded the bird's arrival, and also that of spring. Like a flickering dot in the heavens, a skylark warbled its seemingly endless serenade. Liquid-like notes that flowed to earth in a cascade of song. Maisie's eyes searched the firmament for the illusive songster. A smile touched her lips when she spied the fluttering, almost imperceptible shape high above the hay field.

As she continued to gaze from her window, a feeling of peace overwhelmed her. Observing the idyllic surroundings had helped to calm her uncertain emotions.

Swallows, the harbingers of spring, were already active above the lake. Their excited twittering as they twisted and turned in pursuit of insects, complemented the rural peace surrounding the lake. Most of their activity was centred around the overhanging eaves of the Hall, where a few nests had survived from the previous summer.

A deep, emotional sigh escaped Maisie's lips as she moved from the window and began to dress for her wedding. As she removed her dressing coat, there was a tap on her bedroom door. As it eased open a smiling face peeped from behind it. 'May I join you, Maisie?'

'Nell! Oh, Nell!' She embraced the woman who had married her widower uncle some sixteen years previous. 'It's so wonderful to see you!'

'Let me help you dress... and see to your hair, Maisie.'

'Thanks, Nell.' Relief and happiness were reflected in the warm smile she bestowed upon her companion. 'Oh, I'm so pleased to have you and uncle Ben as family.' An expression of joy softened her features. 'I was unsure about asking him to give me away.'

'He would a'been disappointed not to 'ave been asked, I c'n tell yer.'

'I was concerned about the long journey... I know he is not so strong these days.'

'Strong enough... for some things, Maisie.' Nell gave a happy burst of laughter as she helped a smiling bride into her wedding dress.

'Oh, Maisie...' she stepped back to admire the woman close beside her, '... it's so lovely. Yer'll make a gorgeous bride.' Nell gave a nervous Maisie an appreciative look before embracing her warmly.

'How can that be so, Nell? Look...' she combed her fingers through her shoulder length hair, '... strands of grey already.'

'They be honourable ones, Maisie, an' don't yer f'git it. You've worked hard for Homefield since... since... yer been... alone.' Nell realised that she had nearly mentioned Seb's name. To cover her near slip of tongue, she began to dress her companion's hair. The corn-colour tresses, threaded with a few silvery strands, that reached down to Maisie's shoulders.

'I'm surprised that you were able to entice John to the wedding, Nell.'

'It were his own decision an'...' Nell paused in her brushing to admire the lustre in Maisie's hair, '...we've all been anxious t'see yer again.'

'And it's glad I am so see you all again. It's wonderful to have you at my wedding... my only relatives. I only... wish...'

'Now, Maisie... no tears... on such a happy occasion.' Nell laid the brush aside to hold the saddened bride in a warm and consoling embrace.

'Thank you, Nell. I'm sorry... it's just that...'

'I know... and I'm sure Edward would have wanted you to be happy on your wedding day.' The words brought a lump to

Nell's throat. She found herself blinking back the tears as she mentioned the name of the man she had once been passionately in love with.

'Look at 'em, Maisie!' To distract their sombre thoughts, Nell drew the curtains aside so that they could glance out of the window. 'Our two off-springs have serious matters to discuss, it would seem.' Maisie nodded thoughtful as she looked down upon the two lads.

Her Jonathan, or Jon as he liked to be called, although three years younger than Nell's sixteen years old son, was almost as tall as his companion. There was, however, something about the stocky older boy's appearance that reminded Maisie of her brother, Edward.

* * * * *

Andrew smiled nervously at his bride, as, accompanied by her uncle, Maisie came to a stop beside him. Despite her radiance, the sparkle in her eyes could not completely hide the touch of sadness lingering there. She was reminded of her last wedding... and Seb.

'Dearly beloved, we are gathered together...' Josh's voice suddenly reminded Andrew that the solemnisation of his marriage to Maisie had commenced. He hoped the ceremony would not awaken memories for his bride of the occasion when she had stood beside her brother in this very church. Good, honest and trustworthy Seb, the younger brother whose impeccable character had always overshadowed – and dominated – his own irresponsible actions.

Now, as he tried to compensate for his wasted early years, he hoped that his Quaker-like beliefs would have been appreciated by his dead father and brother. In his heart he was confident of their approval. He was determined not to abuse their trust.

'... First. It was ordained for the procreation of children...' as Josh continued with the ceremony, Andrew's eyes went involuntary towards Jon, his son. A relationship known only to Maisie and himself. Would there be other children from his marriage to Maisie, he wondered.

'... why ye may not be lawfully joined together in Matrimony, ye do now confess it. For ye will...' Andrew tried to concentrate on the proceedings as Josh gave him a warning glance. '... Wilt though have this Woman to thy wedded wife...' Andrew followed the words seriously knowing that he would soon be called upon to make his pledge. '... as long as ye both shall live?'

'I will.' Andrew's voice sounded clearly in the silence.

'... Wilt though have this Man...' Josh was already speaking to Maisie. Andrew glanced briefly at his future wife noticing how very attractive and serene she looked as she waited to make her pledge.

Andrew's thoughts once again began to wander. He was recalling his recent visit to the family solicitors. The stipulation laid down by his father, Sir Roger, for his return to full heirship of Homefield had been met and authorised. Written confirmation only was awaited to proclaim him the new baronet of Homefield, Sir Andrew Douglass. His thoughts were drawn back to the ceremony as he heard Maisie's pledge – to love and obey him.

As he placed the ring on Maisie's finger, Andrew experienced a feeling of humility. He realised just how much Homefield owed this remarkable woman. Over the past few years she had been running the estate practically on her own. Without her strength of character and determination, Homefield might well have been lost to him and his family.

Thanks to a courageous woman who had been proud and honoured to carry the name of Douglass, their estate would survive. God willing, it would continue to be the focal point in the community for future generations of the family to come. Yes, Maisie was worthy of her new title... Lady Maisie.

As he smiled inwardly at the thought, he felt his right hand being placed upon his bride's cool, small one. An emotional surge of happiness overwhelmed him as Josh spoke clearly of their union.

'Those whom God hath joined together let no man put asunder...' Josh then turned to the people present to continue with the solemnisation of Andrew and Maisie's wedding.

On leaving the church, the joyful newly-weds were showered with congratulations. Waving and smiling they acknowledged the best wishes of those waiting outside. Eventually they were able to drive back to the Hall, where family and friends waited to toast their happiness.

It was an hour or so later before Andrew and Maisie, now changed for their journey to London, said their farewells. 'Goodbye, Jon.' Maisie embraced her son. 'You'll call uncle Josh if you should require any help?' Jon smiled at his mother, aware that part of her thoughts were still associated with the estate and its working.

'Andrew... er, father...' he hesitated over the dilemma of how he should now address the man who had just married his mother.

'I think... father would be very appropriate, Jon.' His mother's suggestions seemed a sincere compromise.

'Yes. Well... father has given me full instruction, so have no worry and enjoy your stay at Wynham Lodge.' He exuded youthful confidence as he turned to wish Andrew a pleasant journey.

'Farewell, father,' and then in a quiet voice he reassured Andrew. 'Don't worry... everything will be fine.' Chuckling inwardly, Andrew patted his son's back before climbing in to the carriage that was taking them to their honeymoon destination.

'I think we should just put in an appearance at the barn, Maisie?'

'Yes...' she nodded joyfully, '... I think we are expected.' As they came to a stop outside the barn, word soon spread among the celebrating villagers. 'How happy they seem, Andrew...' Maisie had barely spoken the word than they were surrounded by excited and laughing populace. Both acknowledged the kind wishes bestowed upon them during their brief pause.

'We have a long journey ahead of us...' Andrew's voice gradually commanded a silent respect, '... so we shall leave you to continue with your feasting, dancing and...' he pointed to the pots of ale still clasped in the men's hands, '... drinking.' His speech produced a roar of approval. The ensuing cheers followed the newly-weds down the lane and out onto the Hall Road.

Once they were on the main road, Joe Lambert settled his horses into a steady trot, preserving their energy for the long haul ahead of them. He was anxious to reach Colchester before dusk, to ensure that his horses had a good night's rest before continuing their journey on the morrow.

Inside the swaying coach, Maisie rested her head on Andrew's shoulder as she felt his arm encircling her waist. 'It was kind of Uncle Granville to let us stay at Wynham Lodge for our… honeymoon.' Maisie blushed as the implication of her words brought a warm smile to her husband's face.

'My sentiments exactly, Maisie. Although I shall miss the happy eccentricities of dear Aunt Amelia. God rest her soul.'

'Yes. I remember how wonderful she was when Seb and…' Maisie glanced sharply towards Andrew. 'I'm… sorry, Andrew. I did not mean to remind…'

He squeezed his wife's shoulders gently to reassure her. 'There is no call for apologies, my dear.' He leaned across and lightly kissed her lips. 'It's natural that those we once loved should be remembered occasionally. We both have experienced the trauma… the heartache of losing a loved one. Our thoughts from this day forth must be for the present… and future.'

'I agree, Andrew.' She turned her benign features towards him. 'I promise my love shall be yours forever, my dearest… Until the day… I die.' A sad but loving look came into her eyes as she uttered her emotional words.

'Then, I pray that day may be many years from now, Maisie, my love.'

Twilight was falling as Beechwood came into view. As his carriage came to a stop outside his friend's house, Andrew was aware that something was amiss. Lights flickered from every window as excited servants appeared to be hurrying from room to room. As Andrew opened his carriage door, a breathless and rather agitated friend rushed over.

'What's going on, Jeremy? Have we arrived at an inopportune moment?' Andrew hesitated half way out of the carriage, unsure if they would be welcomed.

'Oh, no, Andrew. It's just that I was expecting the doctor.'

'Doctor? Why… is something wrong?'

'It's Ruth… she's expecting our baby… anytime… and there's no one to help her.' He looked shocked and agitated as he grasped Andrew's hand. 'Our first... not expected for two weeks... but... I'm worried. Deeply concerned for her.' Andrew stepped down and took his friend by the shoulders.

'You must try to remain calm, Jeremy. I'm sure there is no need... for panic...'

'Please arrange to have plenty of hot water and clean linen ready.' Maisie's words broke in on Andrew's mild reprimand. Both men looked round, startled by the authority in Maisie's voice. 'If...' she gave the distraught husband a stern look, '... you would be so kind as to take me to your wife immediately. I'm sure that I shall be able to comfort and help her.' She was already walking towards the house as she spoke.

'Oh, Jeremy...' Andrew was trying not to smile as he watched the bemused look on his friend's face, '... may I introduce my wife... Maisie. You had best do as commanded.' Seeing Jeremy's uncertain look, he tried to calm the worried husband. 'Maisie is a mother and has helped in the delivery of my sister's children. Ruth, I can assure you, is in capable hands.'

'Thank heavens... and...' he turned thankfully towards the woman who was entering the house beside him, '... and you also, of course... Maisie.' He was wiping the sweat from his face with a large kerchief as he directed Maisie inside. As they climbed the stairs to reach his wife's bedroom, relief forced a smile to his anxious face.

'You've taken a load off my mind, that's for certain, Maisie.' He paused outside the bedroom door. 'Sorry abut the introduction... afraid I panicked a little. Welcome to Beechwood and believe me, it's a pleasure to have you here.'

'No need for apologies, Jeremy. I understand.' Maisie gave her host a pleasant smile. 'And... thank you for a warm welcome. Now... your wife needs my company... so, if you will excuse me...'

By the time the doctor arrived in the early hours of the morning, Maisie had delivered Ruth of her baby, a lovely daughter. Both were doing fine... there had been no complications. The doctor appeared disappointed that his presence was not needed, as, on checking mother and baby, he had to admit that both were exceptionally well.

'Well, my dear...' he gave Maisie an approving look, '... you've done a splendid job. An excellent one.' The doctor was still nodding his approved as he wished them good night.

'I shall name our daughter after you, Maisie, and hope that you and Andrew will do her the favour of being her god-parents.' Ruth's voice was weak from fatigue and her face pale after her ordeal. Despite her tiredness, there was a sparkle of happiness in her eyes.

Maisie finished fussing over the baby before answering Ruth's request. 'Nothing... and I'm sure that I speak for Andrew, will give us greater pleasure, Ruth.' As Maisie glanced towards the window, the first skeins of sunlight were already glowing in the dawn sky. It would soon be morning, time to resume their journey.

'Oh, Maisie!' The new mother had also noticed the dawn's early light. 'It's nearly daybreak and you've been with me all night. Your wedding night.' Ruth gave Maisie a sympathetic look as she reached out to take hold of her hands. 'You've been caring for me... when Andrew must have... wanted...' She looked distressed as she begged Maisie's forgiveness.

'There is nothing to forgive, Ruth dearest. Andrew, I'm sure, will be most understanding and will be anxious to see his new-born godchild before we make out departure.

Maisie gave Ruth a warm embrace as she prepared for leaving. She paused at the door to smile back at the new mother. 'Mind you keep well... and... we shall call as Andrew and I return from our honeymoon.' Ruth chuckled as she noticed a blush caress her friend's cheeks.

'I hope all goes well for you Maisie. You and Andrew will always find a warm welcome at Beechwood.'

'Thank you, Ruth. Now...' she gave the proud mother a serious look, '... you must rest. Regain your energy.'

Maisie's apprehension returned as she and Andrew sat close together in the carriage as they continued their journey to Wynham Lodge.

Her anxiety was increasing with each passing mile. What troubled her greatly was how she would react to Andrew's love-making. As the time neared for sharing their first night together, she was troubled by the remembrance of the time he had forced himself upon her. Why should those thoughts return now, she wondered apprehensively, as a tremor of uncertainty shook her body. Involuntarily, she clasped her hands tightly in an endeavour to calm her emotions.

That violent act was long ago. Now was the time to prepare herself for the consummation of her marriage to Andrew. Be resolved for his affectionate act of love. She felt a little guilty at the way she had prolonged her attentions and caring for Ruth and the baby. A mindful servant could have taken over after the birth, but Maisie, to delay her retirement and its worrying consequences, had continued her nursing until the dawn.

Andrew's smile when she had appeared at the breakfast table had been warm and understanding. It was as if he had also suffered her unease over what would have been their first act of love. Throughout the remainder of their journey he had been kind and attentive, as if trying to reassure her that she need have no qualms about their shared moments of passion.

Dusk had settled over the city by the time their horses hooves clattered over the cobbled courtyard of Wynham Lodge. Since Amelia's death some seven years previous, the lodge had become Colonel Markham's property. Passed on to him by his sister. Servants, who had been retained, were soon scurrying around the two weary travellers to unload their luggage.

Andrew and Maisie, having exchanged greetings with the older members of the staff, were soon welcomed into the comfortable confines of the Lodge. A blazing fire emanated comfort and warmth as they entered the main room. Candle light cast a soft glow, a beguiling invitation for them to settle in the comfortable chairs standing close to the log fire. A comfortable sight to the weary honeymooners.

They enjoyed a sumptuous meal brought to them by the fireside. A lingering affair as both meditated on their retirement with suppressed nervousness. Andrew moved across to sit on the floor and rest his hands upon Maisie's lap. Gently she squeezed his hand as the firelight reflected the excited sparkle in their eyes. Their intimate contact cause Andrew to raise his wife's hand and press it against his lips. An act that induced an emotional stirring within their impassioned bodies. Both were suddenly aware of each other's amorous desires.

Hand in hand they climbed the stairs to their room. Flames from the fire reflected their brightness on the polished furniture. There was a warm, cosy feeling about the room that was conducive to the romantic excitement of the newly-weds. As they undressed in the flickering firelight, Andrew's desire became more urgent as he noticed his wife's attractive body. On an urgent impulse, he moved across to hold Maisie in a passionate embrace.

'You're so beautiful, my love,' he whispered amorously. Softly at first his lips caressed hers, but as their longing's increased, so their kisses became more passionate.

'Perhaps... Andrew...' she eased back gently from his embrace, '...we should finish... disrobing and...' An unnecessary suggestion as she was aware of him carefully removing her remaining garments. Quickly removing his clothes he came urgently into bed with her. Before she had barely settled, Maisie felt Andrew's arms about her and his lips passionately seeking hers.

Restraining, that had been held at bay for so long, was quickly abandoned as their love, their amorous longing and their bodies became united in the ultimate act of ecstatic loving. A natural response that had overcome their fears, their uncertainties and left them with a feeling of fulfilment – and peace.

Exhausted, they lay in each other's arms, silently wondering why they had experienced such uncertain feelings about their love. For a week they enjoyed the ecstatic fulfilment of their emotional feelings. Each giving freely of the love that so enamoured them towards each other.

What was intended as their last and most joyous act of love on their honeymoon, climaxed as the first light of the dawn filtered through the curtains to disclose their entwined bodies. As the sun edged higher into the early morning sky, Andrew stirred languidly from their warm embrace. Gently he kissed the lips of his sleeping wife. Maisie sighed deeply at the caress of his lips, her slumbers disturbed as she became aware of his embrace.

'Time to rise, Maisie.' His whispered words disturbed her drowsiness. Slowly, Maisie's eyes focused on the man who had for the past few days reawakened her longing for the impassioned ecstasy of sharing in such ardent acts of love.

'Do we have to leave, Andrew?' She sighed slumberously, preparing to turn over and continue her sleep... her dreams of contentment. A laughing Andrew teasingly removed the bed clothes to expose her naked loveliness to the chill of the early morning air.

'Oh... Andrew...' she shivered, '... how unkind.' The reprimand was however, gentle and her smile inviting as she felt the hardness of his urgency against her body.

'Temptress!; He murmured passionately against her breasts as their rising was delayed to satisfy once again their amorous desires. Maisie gave herself completely and passionately in this their final act of love before dressing and returning to Homefield – and normality.

As the carriage cleared the outskirts of London, Maisie and Andrew heaved sighs of regret at the thoughts of leaving behind such treasured moments. They had spoken very little, content in the remembrance of the precious love they had shared in the past week.

'Happy, Maisie?' She nodded silently, her sparkling eyes and radiant smile made words unnecessary. 'Perhaps we can one day return and renew our... troth?'

'I shall look forward to that day with great... anticipation, my dearest husband.' She leaned across to light-heartedly press her lips to his. Andrew's arm encircled her as he drew her close against him in a warm embrace. With eyes closed, she gave herself up to the tiredness that threatened to overwhelm her. A smile crossed her face as she recalled their departure from Wynham Lodge – two hours later than planned.

She remembered how she had blushed as she recognised the smiles of understanding among the staff, who had made their stay a very pleasant and unforgettable one.

'We hope you enjoyed your stay, Lady Douglass?' It was the butler who had unexpectedly reminded Maisie of her new position in society. She could still hear Andrew's hearty chuckle as he noticed her startled reaction to the mode of address that was now rightfully hers.

'Something you will have to get used to, Maisie love, now that my father's baronetcy has been officially handed down to me.' She had nodded acceptance, still a little bewildered by it all. As Andrew thanked the staff for their kindness, she detected a feeling of piety in his gratitude. Baxter, the butler responded on the staff's behalf.

'It has been a pleasure, sir Andrew... Lady Douglass. May we be permitted to wish you both a pleasant journey back to Homefield and a long and happy future there together.'

'Thank you, Baxter,' their response had been in unison. The visions of their departure gradually faded as Maisie slipped into a peaceful sleep.

Chapter Twenty Eight

'England?' Edward gave Becky a questioning look. A log fire blazed against the late evening chill, its flickering flames exuding a cosy glow to the room where he and Becky were relaxing after dinner.

'Yes, Edward.' Becky leaned forward eagerly in her chair. 'It would be wonderful to see our families... and friends again. I am...' her face saddened as she spoke, '... especially anxious to see my parents as they are in very poor health.' Thoughts of home also reminded her of Julie. Recollections of Edward's old love induced a spasm of guilt as she had never informed him of Julie's circumstances. Becky's guilty emotions were eased by her decision not to marry Edward until they had visited England and seen Julie.

It was a resolution Becky had reached after much heart-searching. She had eventually decided to inform Edward during their passage to England of Julie's faithful vigil and of her son... his son. A child that his betrothed had insisted on keeping, despite the stigma attached to her unmarried status.

It was Becky's wish for Edward to be free of matrimony when they arrived in England. After meeting Julia again it would be for him to decide which woman he wanted to marry. His old love, Julie, or herself who had shared so many years of love with him... and given birth to his children. She was fully aware of the heartbreaking choice awaiting Edward, but out of loyalty and love of almost seventeen years, she must offer him the freedom to choose – his future wife.

What if he should decide to marry Julie? Becky's heart ached at the very thought. Yet, it was a possibility that she must face. Perhaps Julie, realising the hopelessness of her waiting, might by this time have decided on marriage. That thought eased Becky's gloom, but she realised that such a hope was a doubtful one.

Edward gave Becky a troubled look. He had become aware of her silent meditation in the ensuing silence. Her thoughtful and serious rumination was so unusual, so out of character for her. Troubled observations seemed to confirm his intuition that something Andrew had spoken of during his visit was the cause of her distress. Josh's recent letter, detailing the gravity of her parents' health, had also caused her much anguish. Becky's torment induced a positive reaction from Edward.

'We shall sail for England as soon as possible, my love.' He smiled at the startled effect his words had on her deep meditation. 'I shall make arrangements so that we can be away by the month's end or early July.' Seeing Becky's hesitant smile, he walked over and knelt down beside her.

'What is it that troubles you so, Becky dearest?' She noticed the concern in his eyes and the softness in his voice. 'Recently I have become aware of your sadness. The news of your parents' illness must be causing you much distress.' Edward reached out in a sympathetic gesture to take her hands in his. Tears dimmed her eyes as she realised his deep concern... his sincere love for her. 'Please let me help you, my love.' The tender touch of his lips upon hers was but a brief release for her troubled mind.

'Thank you... Edward.' Her voice was a soft emotional whisper as she gave him a warm affectionate look. 'I love you... for your understanding sentiments.' Gently she freed her hands from his to reach out and run her fingers through his dark, grey-flecked hair. 'It's... just... that...' she was reflecting on their love as she spoke, '... that I want you for always, my darling.' Lovingly she returned his kiss.

'Then why will you not marry me, Becky? My freedom... my innocence has been proclaimed.' He waited for her reaction, aware of the distress that his question had caused. 'I'm sorry, my love... I did not mean to...' Her question stopped his apology.

'Would marriage...' her smile was enchanting as she continued, '... increase your love... your yearning for me, Edward?'

'You already have my... complete love, Becky, but...'

'We shall have no buts...' With a teasing gesture she placed her finger tips against his lips. 'You gave me hope and inspiration after I lost Stephen and later as our affections developed, you caused love to bloom again in my heart. A love that has become so precious – and special.'

Edward nodded solemnly as he gazed thoughtfully in to the flames. Firelight glinted in his moist eyes and on the strands of silver that threaded his dark, curly hair. Becky reached out affectionately to embrace the man she loved so passionately – and completely. 'What ever happens, my darling... I shall love you... eternally.'

When Edward looked up into her eyes, he became aware of that precious love, despite the tears trickling down her cheeks. 'Yet... you are troubled...' He kissed the tears that stained her face, tasting their saline moisture upon his lips, '... greatly distressed?'

Edward's concern for her only added to her burden of guilt. As they relaxed close together, silently gazing into the fire, Becky experienced an emotional need to confess: to inform the man she loved dearly that Julie had given birth to his son and was waiting faithfully for his return. A hopeful reunion with the only man she had ever loved.

Becky hesitated, uncertain whether to disclose the secret she was holding, that Julie, throughout the long lonely years of his absence, had never lost faith. That she was waiting devotedly for his return. Destiny allowed her moment of confession to pass – never more to return.

Her thoughts were diverted to the day when Edward had first learnt of his pardon. They had been shocked to hear that Edward's certificate of freedom had been filed in the Governor's office for many years. There it had remained throughout the early period of their struggles for survival at Newacres. Edward's pardon now eliminated their need for secrecy, but now would their unmarried status be accepted in the local society? Pillars of respectability in the area's community, they had wondered if their years of cohabitation, if known, might perhaps destroy such an honourable standing.

Edward had suggested a secret wedding to overcome the problem. 'We can carry on as normal after the ceremony without anyone being the wiser.' She remembered his words and how his excited smile had given way to an uncertain look when she had advocated a delay to any wedding arrangements.

'Let's just get used to the... freedom first, Edward.' Her words had puzzled him, inducing a moment of irresolution. In an effort to pacify, she had gone across to embrace and kiss the man she loved. 'After all these years together...' Becky's affectionate look, as she had gazed into his eyes, had eased his disappointment, '... I would prefer things to remain as they are... at least for the present.' Bursting with happiness and love, he had promised to substantiate those emotions that very night.

Becky heaved a sigh of remembrance as she recalled their passionate love-making on that joyful occasion. Glancing down, she became aware that Edward had been observing her very intently. He was still sitting on the floor beside her, his head resting on his arms that lay across her lap.

'An emotional sigh, Becky love.' She smiled affectionately as she lowered her face to kiss him tenderly.

'I was thinking about us, my darling... and our precious love.'

'That emotion has also been in my thoughts,' Edward's voice was warm with passion as he experienced an overwhelming desire to make love with the woman smiling down at him. Gently he eased her face down towards his. As their lips met, Becky became aware of his urgent longing. Their kisses increased their passionate longing. Their bodies became more responsive, pulsing with desire for the consummation of their imprisoned love.

Edward was at first surprised, then thrilled at the urgency of Becky's loving. Her ardent desires had induced in him a passionate response. Their abandoned love-making had left them with an inner glow of happiness... complete fulfilment. Blissful emotions that had been missing in their recent acts of loving. Satiated with love, they slept in each other's arms until the crowing of the cocks disturbed their exhausted slumber.

Reluctantly, they drew apart in preparation for the new day. Edward raised himself to kiss the tempting lips so close to his. As he did so, he felt Becky's arms reach out and pull him back down upon her. 'Love me again, darling... one more time.' Her face was radiant with expectation as he tenderly embraced her. As he became aware of her inflamed passions, he responded with equal urgency to satisfy fully their amorous desires. After their impassioned love-making, they remained in an ardent embrace until their feelings had calmed. Neither was aware that the act of love they had just shared was to be their last. The fingers of destiny was pointing in their direction.

* * * * *

A few days later as Edward was about to leave Greenacres, he spoke to the Gordon's about his intention of selling the farm. 'It's a long journey out here, James… one I don't particular want these days. With Newacres and White Gables taking an increasing amount of my time, I can well do without so much travelling.' Seeing the questioning look on the Gordon's faces, Edward was about to explain his plans for their future, when James surprised him with his request.

'If its possible to delay the sale, Edward… just for a month, or so, there's a possibility I could make yer an offer.' Something about James' eagerness puzzled Edward.

'You… buy Greenacres, James? If you're thinking of a loan ... it would put you into a sizeable debt, old friend.'

'Maybe… maybe not!' James invited Edward into the small room he used as an office. Once in there he shifted the table and lifted a mat that it had stood on. Fascinated by his manager's actions, Edward watched with increasing puzzlement.

Having lifted the mat, James then prized a couple of floor boards up to disclose a recess containing a small bag. From the bag he tipped some shining nuggets. There was an exciting gleam in his eyes as he waited for Edward's reaction.

'Gold?' Edward gave James a surprised look as he spoke the word.

'I… believe so.' He was trying hard to contain his excitement as he handed one of the pieces to Edward. A quick scrutiny soon confirmed that which he feared… it was gold.

'Where? How did you come by…?'

'Natives…' James could hardly remove his glance from the nuggets, '… rememerin' yer wishes, I let 'em stay on the rough land beyond the woods whenever they returned to this area. On one occasion when I took 'em over a dead sheep, I noticed the children playing with some shiny pieces of mineral.' He paused, wondering if he should continue. Edward's nod confirmed that he was interested in his explanation.

'Well... I offered t'exchange some goods for the pieces...' Aware of Edward's worried look, his voice faded as he became uncertain about his disclosure.

'Comes from the mountains.' Edward nodded in the direction of the Blue mountain range. 'I found some there myself a few years back.'

Suddenly, James' eyes blazed with excitement. 'Could we...?'

'No, James. It would start a gold stampede. Bring chaos to the area.' He went on to explain why the Governor had ordered that his find must remain a secret. 'In the interest of the community, James, details of how you came by the gold must not be made known.' Edward noticed his friend's disappointment when he realised that his chances of purchasing Greenacres was in jeopardy. 'I suggest you let me take your gold to the Governor and explain the circumstances of your receiving it. I'm sure that he will arrange to purchase it on the Government's behalf – providing its presence remains a secret.'

'A wonderful suggestion, Edward...' James nodded his concurrence, '... 'tis best if y'take it an do what yer thinks is best.'

'I'll have my banker put the money into an account for you. Whenever you want you can draw on it towards the purchase of Greenacres. Should I be absent, my solicitor will deal with the sale.' They shook hands on the deal.

'Now its time for me to bid you farewell... for the time being, that is. Our departure for England is but a few days away.'

'How long do yer s'pect t'be away, Edward?'

'Twelve months, or so. Any problems... just get in touch with Geoff.' James nodded, smiling proudly as he watched Edward kiss Irene goodbye. 'And mind it's a boy, Rene!' Edward teased her as she wished him a pleasant voyage.

'If it is... we're namin' him... Edward.' With a cheeky smile she placed her hands upon her swollen belly.

* * * * *

Edward heaved a sigh of relief as Newacres came into view. Although there had been isolated reports of bush-rangers plundering and shooting in the area, there had been no pattern to their raids. Their actions seemed that of desperate men – dangerous thugs. Food and money appeared to be their target, attacking where they anticipated that their raids would be successful. Usually on the isolated settlements.

Carrying the gold had troubled him, but with his farm in sight his mission was safely complete. The escaped prisoners seldom attacked the large farms or settlements close to the towns. In a couple of days, Edward planned to take the gold into Sydney and while there make final arrangements for the family's trip to England. As he rode into the yard, he noticed Ned Fuller waiting with the open coach.

'Good day to you, Ned! Special trip?'

' 'tis Mistress Becky. Wants t'go t'Parramatta.'

'Pa!' Roger rushed excitedly out to greet his father. 'We're going to buy some things for when we go on board the ship.' His young voice was quivering with excitement.

'Good... and mind you take care of Ma.'

'I promise, Pa.' Edward would never forget the seriousness of his youngest son's face as he made that promise. A promise that he was destined to keep with courageous fortitude – and his life.

'I know you will, son.' He ruffled Roger's hair as he gave him some spending money.

Edward almost knocked into Becky as he walked inside the house. Making as if to steady her, he placed his arm tight around her waist. 'Just in case you should fall, my love.' Becky's happy laughter stirred him emotionally. He held her close against him as they kissed each other. After sharing a few affectionate moments, they reluctantly drew apart.

'I must go, Edward... so that we can be back by early evening.'

'I'll come with you. Just give me a few minutes to freshen up and change.'

'No, Edward... but thanks.' She had noticed his tiredness. 'I'll not be long. Your company will, however, be greatly appreciated...' she gave him a promising look before climbing into the coach, '... tonight.'

'Becky!' Edward hurried out just as they were pulling away. 'You forgot these,' he passed two pistols to her. 'Keep them ready…' he had always insisted that they carry arms with them in the coach… for protection.

'How about you, Ned?'

'Close 'n 'andy, Mr. Edward,' he pointed to the pistol beneath his seat.

'Good…' Edward nodded his approval, '… but let's hope you never have to use them, Ned.' He turned to give Becky a farewell smile, thinking how attractive she looked in her green dress with matching bonnet.

'See you this evening, my love… you also Roger.' Edward gave them a wave as the coach trundled down the lane.

Becky cast a worried look at the sky as she walked away from her solicitors. It had been her last appointment, but the meeting had been prolonged by her unusual behest.

'Edward Payne?' The elderly solicitor had looked over his spectacles as he questioned the name. 'I… thought that your… husband's name…'

'My husband died many years ago, Mr. Lerkins. The man you know as my husband is Edward Payne…'

'Oh… I er, see Mrs. Burstow. It's just er, that… I… thought…' The unexpected news bemused him.

'Perhaps you should hear the circumstances of our… our relationship.' He nodded in silent bewilderment. He had known Becky and Edward for many years and the information that she had just imparted had induced a momentary shock to the old family solicitor. Her story, although increasing the elderly solicitor's bewilderment, had nevertheless elicited a sympathetic understanding.

Telling the story had taken up much time. Consequently, when she left the solicitor's office, it was late in the day. Despite her concern, she smiled as she remembered her solicitor's face registering first shock, then disbelief and eventually a compassionate response. That the Governor had authorised Edward's freedom… his innocence, was sufficient confirmation of his identity.

Once he had all the facts, Becky's solicitor had soon made the codicil, confirming Edward as the sole beneficiary. In the event of his surviving Becky, all would belong to the man who had sailed from England as a convict and stood resolutely by her over the years.

'Mrs. Burstow...' she recalled the elderly solicitor's serious features as he had spoken, '... under the circumstances, I would urgently recommend that your husb ... er... companion, amend his will as soon as possible.'

'I'll remind him, Mr. Larkins.' She had made the promise as she was leaving his office. 'Goodbye... and thank you.' Her farewell had been hurried as she had been anxious to be leaving for home.

Ned cast a worried glance at the gathering clouds. It was getting late and the threat of a storm did not augur well for their return journey. His deep sigh of relief as Becky approached caused Roger to glance up at the elderly coachman.

'An unavoidable delay, Ned...' she gave her driver an apologetic smile, '... but hopefully we shall be home by dusk. Although, I fear...' Becky gave the darkening storm clouds an anxious look, '... we shall have a wet and gloomy journey before we get there.'

'Aye, Mistress Becky... it don't look too good.' He gave the horses a flick with his whip to start them off on their return to Newacres.

'Trouble, Ned?' About five miles out of town the coach began to lose speed. She noticed that Ned was leaning forward checking his horses.

'One o'the horses has gone lame, Mistress.' He pulled the coach to a stop, before clambering down to inspect the animal's hooves. 'Stone...' he called up to Becky. Then, picking up the horse's hoof he began to free the lodged stone. Becky glanced anxiously up at the sky as the sun disappeared behind the gathering clouds.

'That should do it!' Ned's voice sounded relieved as it had been a stubborn stone to remove. He tried to make up for their lost twenty minutes by urging the horses into a steady canter.

They were making good progress as they approached a length of road edged by bushes and trees, with uneven verges sloping down to a drainage ditch. The road ahead of them looked lonely, dark and – forbidding. Despite a tremor of fear, Becky tried to focus her thoughts on Newacres – just five miles ahead of them.

Intuitively, Becky reached for the two pistols that Edward had remembered to bring her. She experienced a feeling of confidence with the loaded weapons in her hands. Initially, when Edward had insisted on her taking firing practice with them, she had been very sceptical. Gradually, she had been won over to his precautionary methods and soon became a very proficient marksman.

Now, her prowess as a skilled shot with the pistols was acclaimed by all who knew her. Becky always realised, however, that hitting an inane target was one thing, firing at live attackers would be a more nerve-racking ordeal. She was in no doubts about that, but hopefully there would be no cause to fire her pistols in anger.

Becky leaned forward anxiously as she strained in the gloom to see the road ahead of them. Deep shadows lay under the trees, reducing visibility to about forty paces. Ned urged the horses faster, eager to get beyond the wooded section and onto the open section to Newacres. Trees arched above, reducing what little light remained. Every shadow appeared to constitute a threat. At any moment, Becky expected a shadowy figure to emerge from the gloom. Her heart was thumping loudly as she became aware of an overwhelming premonition of danger.

Roger, as if aware of his mother's anxiety moved closer to her. His mother's attempted smile of reassurance did not deceive her eleven year old son. 'Don't worry, ma… we'll soon be home.' His smile was a little uncertain as he looked into his mother's troubled eyes. That smile soon faded as he pointed to where five men on horseback slinked from the shadows.

* * * * *

'We'll call at Newacres and give Becky and Edward a look.' Robert leaned across the carriage to inform Hester of his intentions. It had become very gloomy and to continue in such conditions was a hazard that he was not prepared to take. He was always assured of a warm welcome whenever he called upon his long-standing friends.

Hester smiled her appreciation at her husband's suggestion. Sitting beside her step-daughter, Carol, she had been busy sharing confidences with the young lady whose friendliness had been a blessing during her settling-in period as the new Mistress of the Shrubbery. They often shared many hours together while Robert was away on medical calls and services. This enforced loneliness had drawn them together in an intimate companionship.

Aware of Robert's concern about making the long journey to Sydney, she had assured him that all would be well. He had been reluctant to make the journey, but the Governor's summons had intimated at some emergency. Travelling at a gentle pace, Hester found the journey fairly comfortable, but a little tiring.

Robert's reassuring smile did not completely hide his concern. With his wife nearing the end of her pregnancy, he felt that Becky's friendly advice would be of comfort to Hester. As they approached Newacres, Robert was remembering the early days of his marriage to the young woman sitting across from him.

Hester's timorous, almost fearful reactions to their early acts of love-making had at first disturbed him. Her distress had eventually been overcome by his gentle and understanding acts of love. Robert recalled her inexperienced responses to his urgent needs and the gentleness required to overcome them. Hester's affectionate look as he smiled across at her, reflected the mature love they now shared.

Robert's gentleness had soon dispelled her inhibitions and overcome her naivety. Once her fears had been overcome, their passionate love-making had been both rewarding and stimulating. Glancing down at his wife's enlarged belly, was a loving reminder of just how exciting her passionate responses had been.

Robert, aware of Hester's close observation, gave her a smile that reflected his happiness and longing for her. A blush spread to her cheeks, complementing the adoration that sparkled in her eyes. She experienced a feeling of exaltation at carrying Robert's child; the first of a large family, she hoped.

It was early evening on that fateful day as Robert approached Newacres. Thankfully, a cloud layer had reduced the sunshine and kept the temperature at a pleasant level for most of the day. During the past hour or so, the atmosphere had become very humid. As they came to a stop outside the farm, distant thunder warned of the threatening storm. It was a very apprehensive Edward who greeted them.

Robert noticed the anxious glance that his friend cast at the gathering storm clouds. Having welcomed his guests, Edward explained the cause of his concern. 'Becky and Roger...' he glanced nervously at the darkening sky, '... should have been home by now. It's unlike Becky to be late...' He was pacing the veranda as he spoke. He came to a sudden halt as if reaching an important decision. 'If you will excuse me...' he gave Robert and Hester a troubled glance, 'I think I'll ride to meet them.'

'Mind if I come with you, Edward? We can take my carriage... in case the storm breaks.'

Edward nodded his appreciation as he made arrangements for their departure. 'Make yourself comfortable, Hester... don't expect we shall be away long.'

As she watched their carriage trundling down the lane, Hester experienced a moment of trepidation. A strange emotion that cause her to gasp with shock. She involuntarily cringed as lightning seared its forked path between the darkened sky and the gloomy landscape.

Closing the door against the reverberating thunder, she rejoined Carol, who was sharing reminiscences with her friends, Marian and Stephen. Hester tried to join in their happy conversation, but her feeling of alarm became an overwhelming presence.

* * * * *

Ned was the first to react as the men emerged from the shadows. He whipped his horses into a fast gallop and drove directly at the shadowy figures on horse back. The carriage's momentum carried it through their attempted obstruction. There were shouts and curses as both horses and riders took urgent evasive action. Becky noticed the assailants sinister looks as they realised that they only had to deal with an elderly driver escorting a woman and boy.

The attackers quickly reformed and came in fast pursuit of the speeding carriage. Becky made ready her pistols when the riders neared them once more. Three trailed at the rear, while the other two drew alongside the galloping horses and made efforts to reach over and grab the harness. Another detached himself from the rear group and rode up alongside Ned. He drew a gun and was about to aim it at the coachmen, but Ned was ready for him. Controlling his horses with one hand, he used the other to fire his pistol at his attacker.

He was thankful that his weapon was always kept handy and ready for use. Edward had stressed this to his staff when he had instructed them how to use their weapons in self-defence. That training now proved worthwhile as Ned's aim was deadly despite the carriage's uneven movement.

The elderly coachman nodded with grim satisfaction as the bush-ranger clutched momentarily at his heart. Gradually, with his life ebbing away, the man slipped from his horse and fell under the wheels of the speeding carriage.

He was replaced by another member of the gang, just as Ned lashed out with his whip at the thugs trying to snatch the harness an so bring the horses to a stop. Ned's protection action left him vulnerable to the assailant closing up alongside him.

Becky was finding it difficult to steady herself against the bumping and lurching carriage. As she raised her pistol to aim at the rider along side, he fired his gun at Ned. Their shots were almost simultaneous. Becky experienced a moment of nausea as she noticed her shot slam into the eye of the murderous assailant. She fought to remain calm as the shot Ned half rose in his seat and then began to slip sideways from his driving position.

'Take the reins, Roger.' Her voice was steady despite their critical situation. While her son struggled into the coachman's seat, Becky reached out to help the fatally injured Ned. She was too late. The shot had entered his chest and, as the elderly coachman's life drained away, he slipped from his mistress's grasp. 'Oh, Ned... Ned...' There was nothing Becky could do as the faithful old coachman was dead before he fell from the swaying carriage.

Becky glanced round, thankful for the respite as the three remaining attackers re-grouped behind her. She realised that it would only be a short reprieve as they were already riding in for another attack. 'Can you... manage... Robert?' Concern lined Becky's face as she questioned her young son, who had taken the dead coachman's place as the horses galloped on at full stretch. Roger nodded and gave his mother a grim smile as he endeavoured to keep the nervous horses under control. 'Think so... Ma.' His face showed fierce determination as he glanced anxiously to his side where the bush-rangers were preparing once again to attack them.

'Make for... the.... Gladstones' place.' Becky shouted above the confusion of sound as she held her pistol at the ready. Although Wideacres was only just over a mile ahead, she was beginning to have doubts if they would make it. At the pace the horses were galloping, they must soon tire. Even as she shouted encouragement to Roger, she was aware of the attackers closing in.

As they pulled alongside the speeding carriage, one of the men leaned out of his saddle in an effort to grab the harness of the lead horse. Becky raised her pistol and shouted a warning. His only reply was a lecherous grin as he moved in closer to try and bring their flight to a stop.

It was a reflex action on Becky's part. Aware of what awaited Roger and herself if they were captured, she had no hesitancy in firing the pistol. As she pulled the trigger she noticed the hatred that masked his face. Gradually, the look faded as his eyes glazed over and he slid sideways from his saddle.

Before he fell, she noticed the red stain spreading on his dirty sweat-soaked shirt. His shattered heart had pumped the last of its blood even as he slipped from the saddle. One of his legs remained entangled in his stirrup and his body continued to be dragged along by his horse. It was a macabre sight as his lifeless body bounced and twisted beside the frightened animal.

Becky found herself grimly hanging on as the carriage by this time was swaying and rocking precariously. The startled horses were barely under control as they raced nervous and frightened at full gallop. Robert struggling valiantly to control the animals as Becky scrambled up beside him to help. Even their combined efforts brought little response as the horses raced on without any response to the reins.

As she felt the large raindrops splash onto her face, Becky looked up at the darkened sky. In the murky light, her two remaining assailants were closing in once again in a final attempt to stop the carriage and take the occupants as their hostages. Shouting with rage and cursing Becky, they once again drew level with the horses. They were becoming desperate as they realised that an open road to a farm lay just ahead.

As the horses bolted out of control, Becky indicated that Roger should keep low in the carriage. Thunder reverberated above the din of the chase; an explosion of sound caused Becky to crouch against the noise. Rain cascaded down, stinging her face as she fought to gain control of the horses as they bolted along the lonely road.

As the two remaining attackers drew level with the horses, one reached over and snatched at their harness. His drastic action reflected their urgency to stop the coach before it left the cover of the trees

Becky, anticipating the man's action, lashed out with her whip and drew blood across his cheek. His snarled threats were barely heard above the cacophony of the storm. His face reflected his intentions, leaving Becky in no doubt as to their fate should Roger and herself be captured.

Involuntarily, she flicked her whip above the horses. A meaningless act, she realised as they were already galloping out of control. It was an act born of desperation on Becky's part, she was determined not to fall into the bush-rangers' hands. She shuddered at the thought of what life would be for her and Roger, should they be captured by the bush-rangers. They would use her for their evil and sadistic pleasures before killing them both.

Another flash of lightning gave the darkened countryside a bluish glow as it zig-zagged across the sky. Thunder crashed almost above them, frightening the already terrified horses. Becky pulled back on the reins in a futile attempt to slow their progress.

She gave up eventually and let the horses gallop on, hoping that their speed would carry them safely to the Gladstones' farm.

Both the attackers were now abreast the horses, on the roadside of the carriage. They were frantic in their final efforts to bring the carriage to a stop. Becky was deeply troubled as the horses, frightened by the storm and disturbances around them were reacting in terror. She maintained her grip on the reins and hoped that they would be delivered safely from their perilous situation.

As the horses continued their terrified flight, Becky was fighting valiantly to control them. Ahead of her lay a partially flooded road, bordered by a rough grass verge. A drainage ditch, running parallel with the road, was already filling with flood water. Becky experienced a moment of optimism as she glimpsed the open road ahead. There was every chance now that they might reach the Gladstones' farm and – help.

Anxiously, Becky turned to see how Roger was coping. His attempted smile was an endeavour to cover his inner feelings of alarm. Despite their predicament, he was determined to be brave – for his mother's sake. To be calm and fearless, like her.

Becky screamed at the bush-rangers as she realised their evil intentions. They were gradually forcing the horses onto the saturated verge where they hoped the adverse conditions would slow the coach down. Once this was achieved, they could then clamber onto the carriage and bring the horses to a stop.

'Never! You'll not take us!' Becky's shouted exclamations were lost in the cacophony of the rocking carriage and racing horses. As they emerged into the open, the full force of the driving rain lashed her face, but increased her determination to reach safety. Once again she lashed out at the attackers with her whip, but her aggressiveness was wasted. Their situation was worsening by the minute.

Suddenly, as the horses were forced onto the verge, the carriage began to bounce and sway precariously. The carriage's momentum, combined with the rough terrain, caused it to rock and lurch. Becky was nearly thrown from her seat.

She wedged herself against the seat and the bodywork, struggling to get the horses back on the road. It was then that disaster struck them. There was a sharp crack as one of the wheels hit a piece of rock and shattered.

As the carriage collapsed and rolled over into the ditch, Becky was hurled through the air. Her head struck the ground first as she landed upon the edge of the ditch. She screamed as a pain stabbed her body, but mercifully its duration was short. As the carriage rolled over onto her, she was momentarily aware of a deep shadow engulfing her. A strange, painless darkness. She cried Robert's name as she felt herself falling... falling... into a silent darkness. There was no more pain... just an everlasting peace.

'I'm worried, Robert!' Edward's anxious voice was raised against the storm. 'We should have met them by now.' A feeling of impending disaster sent a tremor of fear pulsing through his body. With mounting trepidation, Edward continuously searched the road ahead of them. As lightning forked across the turbulent clouds, momentary blinding the travellers with its brilliance, Edward's fears increased. He tried to shake off his foreboding, his premonition of disaster as they approached Jem Gladstone's farm. Edward endeavoured to control his shaking as he jumped from the carriage and hurried to his neighbour's door.

'No...' Jem cast an anxious glance towards the Parramatta road as he became aware of Edward's concern, '... we've not seen sign of 'em.' Edward's spirit's plummeted as Jem confirmed his worst fears.

'Pray to God that she decided to stay overnight in town.' He spoke his thoughts aloud as he hurried back to the carriage. Knowing Becky's determination and her need to be back at Newacres with her family, he very much doubted if she would have even considered that arrangement.

'We should meet them soon, Robert. They were possibly delayed...' Edward turned anxiously towards his friend as he spoke. Deep lines of concern lined his weather-beaten face as he gazed solemnly ahead. There was an easing in the storm as they left the Gladstones' farm behind them. Thunder rumbled away in the distance. A shaft of evening sunlight slanted through the clouds. A ray of hope, but Edward's heart refused to accept any such omen.

Edward gasped in horror as he became aware of the horse trotting towards them. The bewildered animal was dragging a splintered section of shaft in its tangled harness. Part of Becky's carriage.

'Dear, God!' Edward's face was ashen as he turned to Robert. 'There's been an... accident!' He scrambled down to stop the nervous horse and free it from the tangled harness. No sooner was Edward back in the carriage than Robert was already urging his horses into a fast gallop.

They were almost upon the coach before they spotted it lying with its broken wheels in the air. It was resting on the edge of the drainage ditch that ran parallel with the road.

'Oh... my God! No!' Edward's anguished cry was a heartbreaking sob as he became aware of the mayhem. Becky's wrecked coach lay shattered, its broken and splintered under-parts exposed to their shocked eyes.

There was no sign of life. The rain, glistening in the setting sun, fell gently upon the macabre scene. The two friends stared in deathly silence for a few sense numbing moments, barely able to comprehend the catastrophe before them. A dying horse, still trapped in the tangled harness and splintered shafts, tried to move. Its action made it cry in agony because of the broken shaft that had pierced its body.

'You see the horse, Edward.' Robert's training alerted him to the situation and he wanted to spare his shocked friend further distress. He had already noticed the small arm sticking out from under the smashed carriage. By focusing Edward's attention on the injured animal, he had hoped to divert his eyes away from the pathetic sight.

With automotive movements and reacting by intuition, Edward drew his pistol and after a comforting word, put the suffering animal out of its agony. The sharp crack of his pistol shot appeared to shake Edward out of his numbed trauma.

Robert by this time had managed to extricate Roger's small body from the wreckage. He looked into Edward's shocked eyes as his friend squatted down beside him. 'I'm... sorry, Edward...' he shook his head sadly, '... truly sorry.' Lifting the lifeless body of his friend's son, he laid it gently on the grass before covering it with his coat.

'Becky! Becky, my love!' Robert turned as his friend's plaintive cry broke the grim silence. With an urgency born of desperation, Edward was noticing Becky trapped beneath.

Robert hurried across to help, but intuition warned him to expect the worse. Beside him, almost sobbing with frustration, Edward struggled to lift the broken sections of the carriage. Feverishly, they tried to reach the saturated and blood-stained dress, that was visible beneath the debris.

As Edward struggled to reach Becky, he had visions of her looking so attractive in that very dress when he had seen her and Roger off earlier that day. He tried not to think of the dress being her shroud. 'Not both of them,' he prayed as he hurled pieces of coach-work aside. Eventually, with Robert's help, the last piece of wreckage was lifted clear.

'Oh, God... Why?... Why?... Why?' Edward clenched his fists as he expostulated heavenwards. Just then, as he was trying to force a calmness into his emotionally distressed body, he became aware of a comforting arm around his shoulder.

'If you would turn my carriage round, Edward... I'll see to... Becky.' Robert's distressing inspection had revealed that there was nothing he could do for a friend who had died in such tragic circumstances. Died as she was excitedly preparing to visit family and friends in England.

'Rest in peace, Becky dear.' Robert whispered the words softly as he laid her beside her youngest son. 'A double tragedy for you to overcome, Edward... old friend.' He spoke sympathetically as he glanced anxiously at his companion's grief-stricken face.

Chapter Twenty Nine

Julie experienced a momentary pang of sadness as she watched her son walking towards her. George is all I have now, she thought, but there was much about him that reminded her of his rather... Edward. As she waited to see him off on his journey, Julie was aware of just how much his determined character reflected that of the man she loved and continued to wait for.

'Farewell for now, Mother...' George kissed his mother's cheek, '... see you this evening.' After mounting his horse, he turned in the saddle. 'Sure there's nothing you want from Norwich?' Julie shook her head, smiling benignly as she wished him a pleasant journey. Memories flooded back as she watched her son riding away down the tree-lined drive.

She had a vision of Edward holding her in his arms on the winter's morning so long ago... nearly seventeen and a half years.* Outside the cottage, the snow had fallen silently as they had succumbed to their amorous emotions. After, as they had lain in each other's arms in front of the blazing fire, they had promised to love each other faithfully – forever. It had been their only act of indiscretion, but one that had been sufficient to conceive the son who now meant so much to her.

Julie had been faithful in her wait for Edward's return. Believing, despite information to the contrary, that her beloved had survived the transport's sinking. After many heartbreaking years of waiting she was now resigned to the fact that her expectations had perhaps been in vain. Edward, she felt sure, would have somehow contacted her by now, had he survived.

Returning George's distant wave, she continued to gaze down the drive with unseeing eyes, even after he had disappeared behind the hedge that edged the lane. She was remembering old widow Jenkins' words; a kind of prophecy uttered by her after news had been received of the Badger's sinking – with all convicts lost.

'Don't y'give up hope... young missy...' the old widow had commiserated, '... y'lad's safe. Y'll see... y'll see...' Before

* In Book I The Winds of Destiny

Julie could answer, the old lady dressed in dark shabby clothes had disappeared among the shrubs and trees.

'I only wish I could believe your prediction, Widow Jenkins...' she had whispered after the departing shadow-like figure. As if aware of Julie's uncertainty, the old lady had paused to peer at her from the bushes. While Julie had gazed in silent amazement at her wrinkled face, fringed with wisps of grey hair straggling to escape her black bonnet, she had experienced a strange phenomenon. A hazy vision of a smiling Edward had appeared before her. The hallucination had faded as the old lady's words had broken the silence.

'I know... read his palm... long life. He'll be back... one day. Y'll see... y'll see.' Once again the shadowy figure had vanished among the bushes, just as Julie was trying to relate her vision to the old widow's prophecy.

At first the strange encounter had revived her faith, but as the years had slipped away, so her hopes had faded. Yet, the old widow, dead these many years, had implanted a strange belief. A supposition that had sustained her faith over the years... since Edward's departure.

Julie sighed deeply as she orientated her thoughts to the present. She had been unaware of Robin Darvell's close observation of her.

'Perhaps I intrude upon your thoughts, Julie?'

'Oh!' She jumped back a pace, startled by his unexpected presence. His nearness induces an uneasy feeling. A vexatious one. Before she could reply he apologised in an obsequious-like manner.

'I beg your forgiveness. It's... just that... I was... thinking of...' She realised that her voice sounded agitated... angry, but his furtive action had annoyed her.

'Now, I have made you angry. I'm sorry to have upset you so, Julie dearest.' He reached out and took hold of her hand as he spoke. Julie wanted to snatch her hand away, but realised it would be a churlish act.

'You wished to see me, Robin?' She tried to sound friendly. 'I was just seeing George off on his weekly trip to Norwich.'

'Ah, yes... the cattle market.' A much longer trip awaits him if my plans come to fruition, he thought. His odious contemplation's were not reflected in his smile as he acted an affected display of sentiment on the woman he was hoping to beguile into marriage. His smarmy words did not deceive Julie. 'A fine lad, my dear... a very intelligent one for his... age. You must be proud of his prowess?' Julie nodded thoughtfully. Somehow his voice lacked sincerity.

'Since my father's death... George has become very efficient at managing the estate. He became very competent under the tutelage of his grandfather and is now running Foxleigh with maturing proficiency. I can now rest assured in the knowledge that the estate is in capable hands.' This statement was contrary to what the parson had hoped to hear.

'Yes, but a more experienced... mature person would ensure complete elimination of your future concerns for the estate, my dear. That is why I am asking you to marry me, Julie. You need someone to shoulder the responsibilities, give guidance and encouragement to, er... George.' His eyes were fixed on her face as he made his proposition. He noticed the vexation reflected in her eyes... a resentful look that disturbed him. Undaunted, he continued with his insincere confessions.

'You must be aware of my love for you, Julie? I feel confident that I could take on the mantle of squire... after our marriage.' He waited for her response. Her reaction.

'A marriage without love... one of convenience, is worse than no marriage at all, Robin. I could not give you the love expected of a wife.'

'That love, intuition tells me, will come eventually. I shall wait with patience and understanding for it to develop... mature.' He made as if to kiss her hand, but Julie expecting the move, eased quickly away from him as they entered the hall. 'You will consider...' her action had taken him by surprise, '... my offer of marriage, Julie?' She had been about to refuse, but realised that she should at least respect his proposal and give serious thought to the offer.

'You have my promise, Robin. I shall inform you of my decision when...'

'Please make it soon, my love. Perhaps I may call within the week for your... acceptance?' He turned and retraced his steps across the park towards the rectory without betraying his sinister thoughts.

Once they were married, he would soon assert his authority. As for her bastard son... it was time to put his plan into operation. His eyes as he walked home, reflected the malice in his heart and the evil-mindedness for permanently removing George from Foxleigh.

'How goes it with you, George?' In the hurly-burly of the market place, the young Foxleigh heir had not been aware of Captain Julian Grant's approach.

'Why, Julian...' a smile spread over his face as he greeted his friend, '... this is an unexpected pleasure. I was unaware that you were back in Norwich.' He shook his army friend's hand warmly as they exchanged confidences.

'I was hoping to find you at the market, old friend.' Julian's smile was conspiratorial as he continued. 'Truth is, I'm heading your way, George.'

'Duty or socially?'

'Both... I hope.' He gave a chuckle as he waited for his friend's reaction.

'In that case, why not ride back with me and stay at Foxleigh until your duties are completed... whatever they may be.'

'Oh, nothing of importance. Just a routine check on smuggling in the Foxleigh area. An anonymous letter purporting inside information has recently been received.'

'In that case you must stay with us. Mother will be most upset if you refuse.'

'How is your mother... and the colonel?'

'Alas, grandfather is dead... he died but a few weeks back.' There was a note of sadness in his voice as he gave the information. 'As for my mother, she is well and gradually coming to terms with our loss. At first, our parson's calls were to offer sympathy and comfort, but of late his visits have become more frequent then I or mother would wish.' Noticing his friend's puzzled glance, George was quick to admit that the parson's early visits had been appreciated, but of late they appear to have become... impudent. Menacing, somewhat.'

'Menacing?' Julian gave his friend a sharp look.

'In a subtle sort of way. At least that is the feeling I experience, Julian. Of late he has become very er... gushing in his attitude. Suggesting that mother should think seriously about marrying him to ensure that a person of authority be in charge of Foxleigh.'

'The devil, he did! The impertinent prig!'

'My sentiments exactly... and mother's. He even suggested that it would be prudent if the marriage was soon.' George's face was flushed with anger. 'Said he would expect an affirmative answer soon.'

'The obnoxious... swine. Bothering your mother when she was still distressed at your grandfather's death.'

'To pacify him, mother consented to consider his proposal, before the week was out.'

'Do you... think... she will...?' Julian left his question open on noticing his friend's troubled look.

'I sincerely hope not. Mother and I can well manage the estate. We certainly don't need some pompous coxcomb acting the squire on our heritage.' George heaved a deep sigh as he turned to his friend. 'Enough of my troubles, Julian... but thanks for listening.' He clapped his friend on the shoulder and suggested that they made arrangements for his visit to Foxleigh.

'An anonymous note, I believe you mentioned?' Julian nodded as they edged their way through the crowded market place.

'Apparently a load of contraband is being transferred by wagon... a week today. Don't suppose you're involved in any smuggling activities in your village, George?' They shared the laughter at such a possibility. 'It looks to me...' the young captain shook his head uncertainly, '... like a betrayal, by a very malicious person.'

'My horse is stabled over there, I'll not be a minute.' Soon the two friends were clear of the city and its busy streets. As they rode towards Foxleigh, their conversation returned to the subject of smuggling. That which was perpetrated in the Foxleigh area.

'I was unaware that smuggling continued to flourish locally...' George gave his companion a questioning look. 'How did you come by such information, or should I have said betrayal?'

'By this...' Julian pulled a torn sheet of paper from his pocket and glanced at it thoughtfully. He hesitated about showing the note to George... no need to involve his friend. Before replacing the anonymous note in his pocket, he glanced once again at the script.

'.... Saturday next... early dawn. Contraband being transferred... Driver is leader of local group. Suggest ambush... near East Copse in Forge Lane... Foxleigh Green...'

It would appear that the writer was well informed, encouraging an official visit. Checking on the suggested interception area had been an excuse for Julian to visit his friend at Foxleigh. George and his family had always made him welcome, often extending an invitation for him to ride with the Foxleigh Hunt. The note was forgotten as they reminisced about the hunts they had shared.

'When is your next meeting?' George smiled as he noticed the excited look on his friend's face as he made the enquiry.

'If your stay in Norwich is an extended one, I'll try and arrange one early in the season. After you've dealt with the smugglers next Saturday morning, come round for breakfast and then we can discuss the most convenient date for the first hunt.'

'I'll take you up on both those generous offers, George.' He raised his hand in a gesture of appreciation as they continued their ride through the Norfolk countryside.

George forgot all about his friend's coming confrontation with the local smugglers. Over the next few days he was busy with the last of the harvest operations and other estate duties. He was not very pleased when the Reverend Darvell delayed his busy schedule on one occasion.

It was mid-week when the local parson approached him with an urgent request. 'I wondered if you might do me a favour er... George.' With a subtle feeling of enmity that existed between them, George experienced some consternation of such a request.

He nodded his willingness to help, a little apprehensive as to what would be required. He was soon to find out.

'On your visit to the market next Saturday, could I trouble you to drop off four crates at the cathedral?' George was surprised at such a unusual request, but agreed nevertheless. 'Good. Didn't think you would mind, George.'

'I'll get one of my men to load the goods, Reverend.' He was always formal with the parson, according him his official title.

'Ah! I'd rather you and I did it as it will mean a very early start.' Noticing George's puzzled look, the parson explained. 'They are valuable church artefacts... requiring delivery to Norwich Cathedral. I need someone reliable in case we are attacked.'

'I don't think you need worry about that, Reverend, but as a favour I'll deliver the goods on my way to market. Just let me have the details so that...'

'They're here. As regards the time and place...' he paused to give George a thoughtful glance, '... it would be prudent if we kept that information to ourselves.'

'As you wish, but...' George glanced down at the note he had just been given.

'Is... is anything amiss?' Robin Darvell had noticed George's frown.

'Well er... no. It's just that it seems rather an early hour to start. We shall barely have sufficient light to see by... for loading.'

'That way, we shall ensure secrecy for our mission.' George nodded a silent agreement, but as he departed he was wondering why all the secrecy was necessary. He could not imagine anyone being interested in their cargo, even if they were aware of the contents. He put it down to a quirk of the parson.

'Well, Robin... how goes the plan? Did the young bastard fall for your ruse?' Denis Coleman looked up from the dinner table as he raised the questions. His companion hesitated, a fork full of roast beef half way to his mouth.

'Like a child.' There was a sinister edge to his voice. 'Perhaps I should have said, like an innocent... bastard.' A cynical chuckle escaped his pursed lips.

'Once you have loaded, will he not expect you to ride with him to the city?' Denis questioned across the table. 'What if the army disregard your anonymous letter?'

'Oh, they'll be there...' an evil smirk creased his face, '... I sent confirmation to the Excise Authorities that the driver would be none other than the ringleader.'

'Surely the lad will deny any knowledge of the contraband when stopped. He'll just refer them to you and plead his innocence.'

'If that be the case, I shall of course disclaim any knowledge of the goods and suggest that the bastard is lying. When the crates are opened by the army and found to contain contraband instead of church artefacts, I'm afraid young George will be in a very awkward situation.' He grinned maliciously as he waited for his companion's comments.

'A very sound plan, Robin. You will of course feign deep anger at the suggestion that the illegal goods were despatched from your church?'

'Obviously, Denis. The onus will be on the boy to prove his guiltlessness.' He burped coarsely as he pushed his empty plate aside.

'After his arrest, what then?'

'I shall act the pacifying parson and offer to marry his heartbroken mother.' His avaricious look, reflected the insincerity of his intentions. 'She will be in need of consolation and sympathy. In her distress she will be susceptible to my, er... charms.' His gloating countenance cause his companion to cringe with revulsion.

It was barely dawn as George flicked the reins to start his horses moving away from Foxleigh Church. He concentrated on manoeuvring his cart out of the church grounds and on to the narrow lane known as the glades.

'I'll see you along the road, George.' The parson's statement was confirmed by a wave of George's whip.

'As you wish, Reverend.' He answered apprehensively. Something was troubling George as he eased his cart into Forge Lane. He was experiencing a strange, uncertain feeling that all was not as it should be. Everything seemed in order, but... he shrugged his shoulders as if to dispel such dubious thoughts. His frowning glance alighted on the crates that he was carrying to the cathedral. They seemed in order.

George's uncertainty continued, intuition warned him that something was wrong. He withdrew the note that contained instructions, but there was insufficient light to read the parson's words. Thrusting the note back into his pocket, he concentrated on negotiating a narrow part of the lane.

Above the trees, skeins of crimson widened as the first reflections of the sunrise began to fuse with the greyness of the dawn sky. George heaved a sigh of relief as the light began to improve. Ahead of him, East Copse cast deep shadows across the road, but around him the landscape was gradually emerging from the early morning gloom as the sky brightened in the crimson glow of the sunrise. His thoughts returned to the near darkness that prevailed as he had made his way to the designated rendezvous.

George had met the Foxleigh parson at the outer buildings in the churchyard, as promised. Assisted by the obsequious Reverend Darvell, he had stowed the four crates onto his cart. His enquiries about the contents had been subtly brushed aside with bland comments. 'Oh, just a few ecclesiastical adornments, George. Artefacts that I feel should be in the care of the Bishop.'

Now as he approached East Copse, George tried to shrug off his qualms. Perhaps he was being over sensitive in his assessment of the situation. Suddenly, the early dawn's light revealed three shadowy figures barring his progress down the lane.

'Halt!' One of the men called a warning. As he stepped forward, George noticed that the man was carrying a gun. Tension eased from his body as he realised that it was an army corporal who was stopping him. It was then as the soldier raised his rifle, that George found he had relaxed too soon.

'Step down!' The brusque command momentary surprised George. 'We intend t'search yer cart f'contraband!'

'Contraband? I carry no contraband... but if you insist on making an inspection, I need to...'

'We do insist. Now, if you'll step down we c'n make a start.' His attitude angered George. He was about to remonstrate, when he became aware of the rifle being pointed in his direction. He forced himself to remain calm, hoping to mitigate the effects of the misunderstanding. After all, he had nothing to hide.

'First we'll check those crates.' The corporal nodded to one of the soldiers. 'Open 'em up, Bert.' They hesitated when they noticed the horseman riding down the lane towards them. 'Wait a mo... 'ere comes the Cap'n.' The officer pulled his horse to a stop, dismounted and walked towards the group. George was relieved to see that it was his friend, Captain Julian Grant.

'A Captain Grant to see you, Master George.' Jefferson, the Foxleigh butler hovered uncertainly in the breakfast-room doorway. He was reluctant to impose himself on the family while they were partaking on their breakfast.

'It's alright, Jefferson. Captain Grant is most welcome.'

'Very good, Master George.' He gave Julia an apologetic look before retiring to escort their visitor to join them.

'Sorry to intrude, Ma'am... George.' The young captain could barely conceal his excitement as he made his apologies. 'Everything...' he turned towards George, '... went according to plan. The Reverend Darvell is now under arrest for storing contraband.' Julie's gasp made her son turn anxiously towards her.

'Arrest? I... don't understand...' She looked pale and shocked as she waited for Captain Grant's explanation.

'Julian... I think you should join us for breakfast. You can then relate your circumstances leading to the parson's arrest.'

'Yes... yes, do join us.' Julie indicated that their guest should serve himself from the sideboard. Intuition warned her that some conspiracy had been perpetrated by her son and his friend, Captain Grant.

It was the young officer who explained about the anonymous note he had received and also about George's abortive trip to Norwich. 'Unknown to your son, Ma'am, the crates he was carrying contained, not the church artefacts, he thought... but illegal goods. Contraband in fact.'

‘What made you suspect that George was carrying this er... contraband?’ Julie interrupted the captain’s narrative to satisfy her curiosity.

‘The notes, Ma’am.’ He paused to cut a piece of ham and place it in his mouth. For a few moments he chewed pensively, then as if he had clarified the matter in his mind, resumed his story. ‘When George showed me the note he had received from the parson, requesting his help...’ noticing Julie’s puzzled look he elucidated. ‘Help to convey some valuable goods to Norwich Cathedral. Artefacts for the Bishop was the Reverend Darvell’s claim.’

‘It was the parson’s ruse to get me involved...’ George turned to his mother to explain his involvement. ‘In good faith, I helped him load the crates onto my cart, with the intention of delivering them to the cathedral as I passed on my way to market. When I was stopped by the army and the crates opened... we found contraband in all of them.’

‘Why would... Reverend Darvell do such a...’ Julie shook her head in puzzlement, ‘ ... contemptible thing?’ Bewildered by the complexities of it all, she continued to shake her head as she waited for the captain’s explanation.

‘It was...’ his voice contained an angry note, ‘... an attempt by the parson to get George arrested for carrying illegal goods.’ Julie gasped with horror as she realised the implications behind the evil plot. Her son could well have been imprisoned... transported even. The thought induced a numbing shock... for a few minutes she could only stare in stupefying disbelief as the possible consequences penetrated her senses.

‘Thank God... you were there, Julian... otherwise George might have been taken... from me...’ she buried her face in her hands, unable to continue.

‘Yes, Ma’am...’ the young captain nodded grimly, before making further observations. ‘It was seeing George’s note from the parson. I noticed the similarity of the writing to that of the anonymous note that I had received informing me of the smuggling activities. On closer inspection, we realised that not only was the writing the same, but also that the paper was identical. The two pieces of paper... matched perfectly.’

'That could only mean one thing…' George gave his mother a troubled look before continuing, '… the parson had connived to have me apprehended with contraband planted by himself. It was fortunate that Julian was in charge of the operation, otherwise…'

'You could have been incarcerated… even, transported…' Once again a look of horror spread over this mother's face as she realised just how near she had come to losing her son – perhaps forever. Taken from her as his father had been, so many years ago. 'Dear God…' she whispered, '… what would I have done?'

'Darvell was hoping to have me removed, so that he could offer his insidious sympathy to you, mother… and present himself as your only salvation.'

'Never! I would have refused any offer of marriage from that… that wicked man.'

'He'll not bother you again, Ma'am. I've just arrested him. When I return to the rectory we shall be taking him away to await trial at Norwich.'

'Your plan was successful, it would appear, Julian?'

'Aye… it went very smoothly. As a matter of fact we…'

'Plan?' Julie surveyed her two young companion's with a furrowed brow.

'Last night we secretly returned the crates to their original store in the churchyard. At dawn this morning we awoke the parson and explained that as part of our operation against the smugglers we were investigating various leads. When I requested a search of his out-buildings, he was most co-operative. Thinking that the place might be searched, he had cleared the contraband by loading it onto George's cart.'

'How… did you manage to trap him if the place was empty?' Julie's question caused a knowing smile to be exchanged between the young captain and her son.

'Unaware that the crates had been returned, he willingly accompanied me to where the illegal goods were normally stored, pending their distribution. The parson…' Julian paused to sip from his mug, '…nearly fainted with shock when we entered the out-building. There, lined up before us, were the very crates that he had helped George load onto his cart the previous morning. We then had the evidence – and the man.'

'Oh, Julian, what would we have done without your help? Had George been taken from me, I hate to think what might have been my fate.' Anger gradually replaced her sincere emotions as she thought of how the man she trusted had betrayed her. Thankfully he would soon be taken from the village and she would never have to face him again. Aware of his mother's distress, George hurried over to console her.

'I'll wish you goodbye, Ma'am... and thank you for the breakfast.'

'See you shortly, Julian.' George indicated that he would walk across to the rectory, once his mother had become more composed.

Later, as George approached the parson's dwelling, he experienced a feeling of foreboding. Intuition warned him that something was wrong. Had the despicable parson escaped, he wondered. As he entered the rectory he was met by a very worried Julian. He silently took George's hand and pointed to a partly open door.

Concerned at his friend's behaviour, George walked across and pushed the door wider. He remained momentary rooted to the spot at the gruesome sight that met his eyes. Still swinging gently was the body of Robin Darvell. A rope round his neck had been fixed to one of the timbered rafters. Rather than face imprisonment and disgrace and possible transportation... he had hanged himself.

[illegible] that he had helped [illegible]

[illegible]

[illegible]

[illegible] thank you for the [illegible]

[illegible]

[illegible] George [illegible]

[illegible] George [illegible]

Part Four (1829-1830)
The Reunions

CHAPTER THIRTY

A gently breeze stirred the leaves, the only sound in the reverential-like silence. It was as if the trees themselves respected the ground upon which their shadows fell. As if attuned to the prayerful thoughts of the man and two children who stood in respectful silence beside the two freshly marked graves.

Edward, still grieving for Becky after nearly three months, was thinking of that traumatic moment when he and Robert had come upon the scene of Becky and Roger's fatal accident. His thoughts still recoiled from the devastation they found. As first the unbearable desolation had numbed him.

Thankfully, Robert had been there to organise the recovery of the bodies from beneath the wrecked coach and afterwards to encourage him to ascertain why the accident had happened. In a state of shock he had walked beside his friend as they retraced Becky's route, seeking the reason for the carriage being driven onto the verge. Robert's shocked observation had penetrated his numbed senses.

'Look... Edward...' Robert bent low to check the saturated grass verge, '... hoof marks. A couple of riders.' His eyes followed the direction of the prints. 'It appears... that they were riding beside the carriage. At some considerable speed...' As the significance of his observation infiltrated his puzzled senses, Robert's voice had faded into a troubled silence.

Edward vividly remembered the troubled expression on his friend's face as he glanced up to question the riders' presence. 'Who would be riding... beside the carriage...?'

'Bush-rangers!' Edward recalled the burning rage that had pulsed through his body as he confirmed their attendance. Through clenched teeth he had uttered his expectations. 'If we continue our investigation, I don't doubt we shall find further evidence of theses... murderers.' Robert, understanding his friend's anger, nodded silently as he joined in the search for incriminating signs.

Confirmation gradually materialised. Back along the route they came upon the dead bodies of three bandits. Silently, Edward had bent down over the fourth fatality – his faithful old coachman. Beside Ned lay his discharged pistol, confirmation that the body close to him had been his victim. Then Becky, Edward surmised, must have shot the others.

Even in his shocked grief, Edward had experienced silent admiration for the courage of Becky. It was obvious that she must have fought tenaciously to stave off the murderous attackers. The signs of her desperate struggle as she had battled against the odds to reach safety, unfurled before them along the road from Parramatta. Success and safety had been so close. The bush-rangers fiendish action in forcing the carriage off the road had precluded that possibility. Edward remembered how he had surveyed the scene of the attack in shocked disbelief. How could it have... and so near to home? It had been Robert's sympathetic words that had brought him back to reality – and heartache. 'Come, Edward... we must take them home... to Newacres.'

Edward's silent meditation beside the graves of Becky and Roger had manifested the visions of that evening of deep sorrow. It was the gentle touch of his daughter's hand reaching out for his that dispersed his solemn thoughts of finding the lifeless and broken bodies of his loved ones. Beside him, Marian shed silent tears, while a grim-faced Stephen fought to contain his emotions. Edward's deep emotive sigh reflected his anguish as he reached out to place his arms around his children's shoulders.

'Your mother... and Roger... now rest in everlasting peace...' his emotional words were an indication of his suffering, '... but life... has to continue.' They nodded silent agreement as they turned and walked sadly away from the graves. Their carriage was waiting to take them to Sydney. It would be from that port, in two days time, they would sail for England. Only one of them was destined to return.

As their carriage trundled along the road towards Sydney, Edward recalled his conversation with Geoff, as they had discussed details to ensure the continuation of the farm work during his long absence. 'I'll return as soon as possible,' he had confided to his manager. 'It was Becky's wish that we should go, but...' Edward had paused, unable to continue.

'It will be very sad news that you take to her family, Edward. So... distressing for you, old friend.' As they had walked together towards the waiting carriage, Geoff had assured him that Newacres would be taken care of during his absence. 'I promise you'll find it in good shape... if you come back.'

'If?' Edward gave his friend a puzzled glance. 'What makes you think that I might not return?'

'Figure of speech... only.' Geoff, he remembered, had laughed away his words, as he and his family had wished them a pleasant voyage to England. Edward had been unaware of his friend's strong intuition that they would never meet again.

* * * * *

'Oh, Andrew...' Maisie looked up from her tapestry, '... such a dreadful night.' Gale-force winds lashed the rain squalls against the window as she spoke.

'A late autumn storm, my dearest.' As he listened to the howling wind and the rain rattling against the window panes, Andrew said a thankful prayer that he was comfortable and warm in front of a roaring fire. He smiled reassuringly at Maisie as she reacted to a fierce gust of wind that seemed to shake the very foundations of Homefield.

'What was that?' Maisie paused in her work as a loud knocking came from the direction of the front hall.

'Must be something urgent...' Andrew spoke as if to himself. There was a tap on the door and Denison, the new butler, entered with an urgent message. 'Messenger from Highfield farm, Sir Andrew.'

'Who is it, Denison?' Andrew glanced beyond the butler as if expecting Josh to appear.

'A Mr. Tom Gibson. The message appears to be, er... rather urgent, Sir Andrew.'

'Thank you Denison. I'll have a word with Gibson myself.' Andrew exchanged an anxious glance with Maisie before following the butler to the reception room.

'Ev'ning, Sir Andrew.' Tom's face wore a troubled expression. Water dripped from his clothes to form little puddles on the stone floor. 'Reverend Josh sed t'tell yer as how Mistress Alison's baby is on't way an' that Doctor Scott is out on call. He be sorry t'trouble yer on such a night, but wondered if Lady Douglass could help…'

'Hurry back, Gibson, and inform Reverend Kennard that Lady Douglass and myself will be over very shortly.'

'Very good, Sir Andrew. I'll be on me way. Good night t'yer, Sir.' As Andrew walked into the hallway with Tom, he spotted the butler.

'Ah, Denison. Get a message to Lambert. Tell him we shall need the carriage as soon as possible. An urgent trip to Highfield.

Twenty minutes later, Andrew and Maisie struggled against the raging storm to reach the carriage. A worried looking Joe Lambert helped them inside before clambering into his seat. His shouted command to his horses was swept away by the wind. Shaking the reins and cracking the whip above them, encouraged the reluctant animals on their journey. Instinct alerted Joe to his horses agitated responses, especially as they turned onto the road leading to East Wensum. Something was troubling them. They were unusually nervous and Joe was certain it wasn't the atrocious conditions.

Once they were clear of the village, the wind howled across the open fields, buffeting the carriage and tearing down branches from the roadside trees. Trying to avoid the fallen branches in his flickering lights, required all Joe's skills to keep the carriage on the road.

Maisie pressed closer to Andrew in the darkened vehicle as it lurched and bounced under the storm-force winds. 'Oh, Andrew… I'm so glad you came with me.' She rested her head on his shoulder.

'You surely didn't think I'd let you go out alone on a night such as…' he paused to listen against the noise of the storm. There was a loud shattering crash as a tree splintered and began to fall into the road. Joe's shout of urgency to the horses, as he tried to get clear of the falling trunk and branches, caused Andrew and Maisie to stare anxiously out into the darkness.

Next moment there was mayhem as a large splintered branch smashed down onto the rear of the carriage. Andrew was knocked to the floor as the coach-work shattered. Maisie's anguished scream suddenly faded as the carriage disintegrated around them. Helpless and stunned, Andrew found himself trapped by the shattered timber. He called weakly to Maisie above the howling wind, but there was no reply.

Joe picked himself up from the road. Miraculously one of the carriage lights was still glowing feebly. By its flickering light, the coachman beheld an eerie scene. Still dazed and badly bruised, he battled against the driving squalls to reach the wrecked carriage. 'Sir Andrew! Lady Douglass!' His shouts of concern were lost in the banshee-like wailing of the wind.

Peering into the darkness, he could just distinguish the covered part of the smashed coach. His heart sank when he noticed that it was wedged under a large branch of the fallen tree. Joe experienced a moment of shocked sadness as he was certain that no one could survive such an accident. Then, just as he turned away, the thought a muffled shout had come from the shattered coach-work. Joe crawled through the branches until he came to the smashed window of the carriage. Straining to see against the driving rain, he pecred into what remained of the gloomy interior. His hearing must have deceived him as he was certain that his employers could not have survived such a catastrophe.

'Sir Andrew! Your Ladyship!' Joe called to them once again, not expecting any response. Then Andrew's pallid face was staring at him from the smashed window. It caused the coachman a moment of consternation as he wondered briefly it if was Sir Andrew's ghost.

Reality flooded back. 'Are... you badly hurt, Sir Andrew? Is Lady Douglass...' he hesitated, afraid to enquire as to her condition.

'Thankfully... we are both... alive, Lambert. Lady Douglass is however...' he turned a troubled face towards the darkened interior, '... badly hurt.' There was a splintering sound as the branches crushing the carriage settled further down. Inside the darkened vehicle, Andrew grabbed the window edge as he felt the sudden lurch.

'We need help urgently...' Andrew gave his coachman an anxious look. 'It would appear that we are trapped beneath the branches of a fallen tree.' Joe nodded confirmation as he looked into the windswept darkness. He could just distinguish the large branch that had crushed the carriage when the tree had fallen across the road.

'The horses... are they.... Alright?' Andrew raised his voice against the storm.

'Yes. They're very nervous... and entangled... in t'reins...'

'Try and free one... so that you can ride to Highfield... for help. Explain our plight to Reverend Josh. Tell him that we are trapped, but...' Andrew gazed into the darkened wreckage, '... appear to have some shelter from the storm.'

'Very good, Sir Andrew. I'll be as quick as possible. Here, Sir...' Joe removed his cloak, '... for Lady Douglass. It'll keep the worse of the rain off.' Andrew thanked Joe and gratefully accepted the cloak for Maisie.

'Alert the villagers as you... pass through. We shall need... all...'

'Oh... Andrew. I feel... so... so faint...' He felt Maisie's body go still against him in the darkness.

'Quick, Lambert...' Andrew's voice was hoarse with anxiety, '... Lady Douglass... is unconscious.' Frantic with worry, he tried to feel for Maisie's pulse as she lay against him. Was she comatose... or...? Oh, God... no... not Maisie.' Their cramped situation made it impossible to feel her pulse. All he could do in the darkness, was hold Maisie close in his arms and pray.

'Oh, Josh!' Alison clenched her fists as a spasm of pain racked her body. 'I pray that dearest Maisie... will be here soon...' she appealed anxiously to her worried husband.

'It's a terrible night, my love.' Josh's eyes went to the window that rattled under the impact of the raging winds. 'If it is at all possible, rest assured Maisie will make the journey.' He was trying to console his wife as he sat beside her on the bed. Gently he stroked Alison's dampened forehead, deeply concerned at the uncertainty in her eyes.

'Tom has returned from Homefield with the news that Andrew and Maisie are following. They were preparing to leave as he rode away from the hall.' Outside, Josh could hear the incessant roar of the wind and the rain-squalls lashing against the window. He was regretting his impulsive act of sending for his friends on such an alarming night.

As the minutes ticked away and Alison was subjected to another spasm of pain, Josh's apprehension increased. Above the noise of the storm he heard shouts. A commotion of urgency. A knock sounded on the bedroom door. At his invitation, his housekeeper entered with a troubled look on her face.

'Can you come, sir? An urgent message...' Jenny's face was white with shock. 'Very... urgent, sir.' Josh gave Alison a sympathetic look as he rose and followed the distressed housekeeper down the stairs. There he found Holmes, his butler, in agitated conversation with the Homefield coachman.

'Your Reverend...' a bedraggled Joe Lambert pushed past the shocked butler to confront Josh, '... there's bin a... terrible accident. Tree... fell on... carriage. Sir Andrew and Lady Douglass... trapped... badly injured...' Joe was still gasping from his exertions. 'Need help... urgently.'

'Jenny!' Josh turned to his worried housekeeper. 'Look after your mistress... until I return. Say nothing of the accident. We must try not to trouble her at such a delicate time.'

'I'll go to her immediately, sir.' A very anxious Jenny climbed the stairs to comfort her mistress as the birthing pains became more frequent.

As Jenny climbed the stairs, she prayed silently that Doctor Scott would arrive in time, but in this weather she realised that such a possibility was remote. Jenny forced a cheerful smile to her face before entering her mistress's room.

That same prayer had been offered by Josh as he commenced the rescue operations for his friends. On such a terrible night the doctor would have a struggle on his hands to reach Highfield before the baby arrived. Jenny's presence was reassuring as he had confidence that she would be capable of comforting and caring for Alison should any crises arrive.

Josh now concentrated his efforts on the dire situation that had befallen Andrew and Maisie. He hoped that they would be in time to save his brother-in-law and dearest Maisie. What if they were too late ... Josh tried to blot out such a possibility. Nevertheless, with their carriage crushed under a fallen tree, he had to face facts. His silent prayers were offered up for their survival, but he was dreading what situation he might find.

Tom Gibson, aware of the urgency, was already waiting with the carriage as Josh stepped out into the raging storm. 'I've put a couple o'saws an' some ropes inside, sir.' He had to shout to make himself heard against the wind.

'Well done, Tom. Thank you.'

'Mind if I ride back w'yer, reverend?' Josh was surprised to see a shocked and shaking Joe Lambert waiting by his carriage. 'I'd like t'help!'

'Of course... we shall need all the help possible.' He indicated that the Homefield coachman should enter the waiting coach.

'I hope that... Sir Andrew and Lady Douglass are not too badly hurt, sir.' In the light of his lamp, Josh noticed the forlorn expression of the old coachman's face.

'We must pray... that we find the er... situation favourable, Lambert.' Josh was apprehensive, wondering in what circumstances they would find the storm victims. His mind was torn between thoughts of Alison's confinement and those of Andrew and Maisie, trapped and injured in the wrecked carriage. He felt responsible for their plight. His request for Maisie's assistance had been instrumental for both of them being out on the road in such atrocious conditions.

Shrieking winds buffeted the carriage as they sped through East Wensum village. Rain continued to lash against the bodywork and windows in a drumming crescendo. Did the banshee-like wailing of the wind portend a tragedy, Josh wondered, as they battled against the elements to reach the scene of the accident.

Ahead of him in the darkness, the flickering lights of storm lanterns warned Josh of the predicament his relations were in. As his carriage came to a stop beside the fallen tree, he could see the shadowy figures moving in a concerted effort to clear the branches from the remains of the Homefield carriage.

'Dear, God…!' he gasped in shocked disbelief as he surveyed the wreckage in the flickering lamp lights. If Andrew and Maisie have survived such a disaster, it would surely be… a miracle. Josh was expecting the worst as he scrambled among the rescuers to reach the centre of activity, the badly damaged carriage.

As he approached, Josh noticed that one man appeared to be organising the rescue. With his head lowered against the driving rain, he moved nearer to identify the person and also to announce the arrival of additional resources. Having instructed his coachman to hand out the saws and ropes, Josh joined the man who was organising the rescue attempt. Nodding his approval at the progress made, Josh pressed forward, anxious to assess the situation regarding his trapped relations.

He peered in dismay at the smashed coach. A silent prayer filled his thoughts for the unfortunate victims as he was certain that he would not find Andrew and Maisie alive. He turned to the man who continued to shout directions to the rescuers above the howling wind. It was a dangerous operation in the storm, endeavouring to clear away the branches.

Not wanting to distract the man's concentration during this critical activity, Josh remained silent. A momentary loss of attention; a careless slip now, could cause the main branch to collapse fully upon the smashed vehicle. During a brief respite in the rescue work, Josh turned to commend the man for his organisation. 'Leonard!' He was surprised to find that it was the doctor who had been organising the rescue operations.

'Glad… you… made it… Josh.' Lowering his head against the lashing rain, he explained his presence. 'I was on my way… to see Alison… when I came upon the… accident.' Pointing towards the dark shape of the damaged carriage, he shook his head apprehensively.

'How are… Maisie… and Andrew?' A tremor of fear shook Josh's body as he noticed the doctor's disconsolate, rain-soaked features.

'Serious! Very serious, Josh!' In the lantern light his face was grim with anxiety. 'Perhaps you'd like to take charge of the rescue work, while I check on Sir Andrew and Lady Douglass?' Josh nodded a silent acquiescence.

* * * * *

As the first pale light of the dawn broke through the dark, swiftly moving storm clouds, Josh staggered across to where the men were in the act of raising the last splintered branch clear of the carriage. 'Heave!' Urgency was reflected in his strained shout. 'All together now...' he urged, '... heave!'

Aching muscles strained, the ropes creaked as they took the full weight as slowly the branch eased off the wrecked carriage. 'Hold it!' There was a note of relief in Josh's voice. 'Secure the rope to the tree.' He directed the tired and saturated men. As last he was able to relax. 'Good work men. Thank you.' Sighing with relief, he scrambled over to where the young doctor was crouched beside the splintered opening that had been the carriage door.

'How are things...?' his question faded upon his lips. The solemn look on Leonard's face warned him to expect grave news.

'We must get Lady Douglass home... to bed... urgently.' He was already helping a shaken and badly bruised Andrew from the wreckage.

'Th... thank... you... Leonard.' Andrew staggered a few steps, then turned uncertainly with the intention of helping extricate Maisie from the smashed coach-work.

'No, Andrew... you must rest.' Josh eased his brother-in-law clear of the opening, before crawling in to help the doctor ease a semi-conscious Maisie clear of the wrecked coach. Joe Lambert was standing anxiously by with the blankets they had brought from Highfield.

Josh gently wrapped them around Maisie before carrying her to the carriage. Andrew, with the doctor's arms supporting him, staggered silently and weakly behind them.

'Home to Highfield as quick as you can, Tom.' The anxious coachman needed no urging from Josh. He soon had the horses at full stretch with Josh and the doctor inside keeping a concerned eye on the injured Maisie and Andrew.

Maisie's ashen face peeped from the blankets, her eyes sunken and body shaking continuously. Andrew's quiet, appealing look moved from Maisie's pallid features to that of Doctor Scott, who was observing her with troubled eyes. The journey seemed endless as they raced through the clearing dawn that revealed the mayhem of the night's tempestuous winds.

Leonard Scott was praying that nothing would happen to Maisie. Since his arrival to take over from the old Doctor Wallace nearly three years ago, she had extended a sincere hand of friendship to both himself and Agnes, his wife. Very nervous and uncertain, he had come to take up his practice in Aldeburgh. When he had initially presented himself and his wife to the owners of Homefield, they had been greeted warmly and made most welcome by Maisie. Since then, they had been guests at her wedding to Andrew and a bond of friendship had developed between the four of them.

Apprehensively, he felt for Maisie's pulse, only to find it weak and erratic. Trying to hide his concern, he turned and gave her anxious husband a reassuring smile. Andrew had not been deceived, he had seen the worried look on Leonard's face as he had checked Maisie's heartbeats.

Throughout the rescue operations, the young doctor's concentration had been centred on extracting his friends from their wrecked carriage, he had forgotten Alison's imminent confinement. He was now reminded of the situation as he directed the transfer of Maisie from the carriage to a waiting warm bed at Highfield.

As Jenny helped the doctor remove Maisie's damp and crumpled clothing, she informed him that Alison had given birth to a daughter during the night. A safe delivery she assured him. 'Both seem to have survived the ordeal very well, doctor,' she informed him.

'Splendid, Jenny... you did well. Once we have Lady Douglass comfortable and quiet, I'll drop in and check everything is alright...' He paused as he became aware of Maisie's effort to speak. Leaning closer he was able to distinguish the one word... 'Andrew?'

'Jenny! Hurry and fetch Sir Andrew.' Leonard spoke quietly and reassuringly to Maisie, but although her shaking had stopped, he was deeply concerned about her injuries. Thankfully, he had managed to stop the bleeding of her leg wound, but it was the blow to her head, that troubled him most.

Having cleaned the abrasion, Leonard applied a bandage around her head to stanch the bleeding, but she had lost more blood than he would wish for. Intuition warned him that Maisie was at crisis point. Anxiously he waited for Andrew to arrive at his wife's bedside.

As he waited with a heavy heart, Leonard gazed down at the ashen face of the compassionate woman who had befriended him and his family. He had done all that was possible to save her, but the dark shadows and hollowness around Maisie's eyes, caused him to wonder if that had been enough. Just then a grim-faced Andrew entered the bedroom. His shocked glance rested for a few minutes on his wife before he turned with a questioning look towards his friend. Leonard's features remained solemn as he became aware of Andrew's enquiring, almost frantic look across the bed.

'We can but pray, Andrew.' Nodding silent agreement, Andrew lowered his head onto Maisie's hands that rested so cold and unresponsive in his. He said a whispered prayer as tears trickled down his cheeks and splashed onto the hands of his beloved.

Maisie's eyes, dulled with pain, slowly flickered open. Eventually they focused on her husband who was kneeling on the floor beside her bed. 'Andrew... dearest...' he had to strain to hear her whispered words, '... so glad... you're... with me.' A smile lingered around her lips as her eyes gently closed again.

* * * * *

Edward removed a kerchief from his pocket to wipe the perspiration from his brow. It was hot and sultry as the ship's bows sliced through the tropical waters. A light breeze filled the canvas and favoured the ship's progress. As he looked up at the pyramid of sail and heard the rigging creaking under the strain, he was reminded of the months he had served as a press-gang victim in the Navy. He had been a young teenager... so long ago... an age it seemed as he recalled that intolerable period.

Inevitably, his thoughts as he looked out over the glittering ocean returned to the tragedy that had killed Becky and their youngest son, Roger. Becky's words, as she waited to depart for Parramatta on that fateful day, came clearly to Edward's mind. Intuition alerted him to Becky's need to confide in him, yet unusual for Becky, she appeared reluctant to speak the thoughts that were troubling her. The significance of her words became more apparent in the light of the happenings since her death.

Gazing with unseeing eyes across the undulating ocean swell, he had tried to recall every detail, every word that Becky had spoken on that occasion. Their last moments shared before she was taken from him for ever. A sob choked his throat as the vision of Becky at her departure for Parramatta came clearly to mind. She had looked so attractive standing there in her green satin dress and matching bonnet. A picture of radiance and beauty.

'There is something of importance...' she had hesitated as her troubled eyes looked into his, '... an er... confession that I must discuss with you, Edward.' At the time she had one foot on the carriage step and, as she had turned towards him, he remembered the sadness... the uncertainty reflected in her dark eyes. 'Perhaps I should have spoken before of the news that Andrew had conveyed regarding Julie.'

Edward had a feeling that Becky was anxious to inform him of some consequential happening regards his past love. At the time he had been more concerned about Becky's departure as there was a long journey ahead and he wanted her and Roger safely back by early evening. His apprehension was disturbed as Becky tried to explain her reason for not confessing. 'I wanted to tell you, Edward, but... I was unsure about your reactions.' While Becky was speaking, he had been aware of her searching look. It was as if she was watching and waiting for an emotional sign from him as she spoke of Julie.

Hearing her name had momentarily disturbed him. His involuntary reaction had not been lost on Becky. The mention of Julie's name, his one-time betrothed, had stirred him emotionally. Edward had realised from Becky's expression that he had disclosed the compassionate feelings he still retained for the woman he had been cruelly separated from.

'Is it good news you have of... Julie?' He remembered how strange her name had sounded upon his lips as he had enquired about her. Becky's moment of uncertainty had sent a spasm of alarm pulsing through his body. 'She is well? Nothing... amiss I hope...?'

'Julie is in good health, Edward, but...' Anxious for her departure he had suggested that Becky waited until her return before imparting her news.

'You must not delay your departure any longer, my love. To do so will mean you travelling late on the road. Perhaps I should accompany you?'

'No, but thank you, Edward. I shall be alright... there's nothing to worry about.'

'See you this evening then, my dear.' Her smile had been warm and her kiss a promise of love as she had bid him farewell before climbing into the open carriage. He remembered the radiance of her smile and the love in her eyes as she promised to tell him news of Julie over dinner.

Edward's eyes misted with tears as he recalled their last embrace and their kiss... their very last. Tears trickled down his cheeks as swallowing hard he tried to suppress his emotions.

There was a gentle touch on his arm. Becky's vision faded and his reverie disturbed as he turned to find an anxious Marian beside him. Seeing her father's distress, she guessed the reason for his sadness.

'I also share the same heartaches, Pa.'

'Yes, my love... we all do.' Gently he tucker her arm under his as they stood silently gazing back across the billowing ocean. Curious glances from the crew watched their quiet meditation. Rumination's that were about to be shattered.

'Ah! There you are!' Stephen having spent an hour or so with the officers on the bridge, had decided to search out his family to relate his nautical knowledge, gleaned from the experts. Excitedly he had explained how he had helped to steer the ship and been permitted to look through the Captain's spyglass. Glancing eagerly up at the rigging, he declared his intention of climbing to the lower yardarm when the crew next altered sail.

After listening to his son's excited chatter, Edward complemented him on his seamanship and suggested that he might like to make the Navy his career. Stephen frowned in silent contemplation as he gave the matter serious thought.

'Don't think so, Pa. You'll need my help on the farm.' Edward's features remained serious as he nodded agreement. It was then that he decided to enlighten Marian and Stephen as to the true relationship between himself and their mother. Becky had agreed with him, that they should be informed of the situation while on the voyage to England. Now the task would be his alone.

He invited them to sit on the hatches as he had something of great importance to tell them. In great detail he enlightened his two avid listeners as to the circumstances relating to his life before and after his arrival in Australia and the reason for their journey to visit relations they had never seen or been aware of.

Edward began by describing his early teenage months at sea as a press-gang victim. Having got Marian's and especially Stephen's interest, he told of his escape from the Navy when his ship had anchored off Portsmouth. He spoke of his reunion with his sister Maisie and, hearing of his father's drowning at sea when his fishing boat went down in a storm. With their mother already dead, he and his sister were left as orphans.

He continued his narrative by explaining the reason why he and his sister had to make a hurried escape from their father's cottage in Yarmouth. How they made their way to and eventually settled with relations in the village of Foxleigh in Norfolk. 'Your aunt Maisie grew up as a companion to Julie, the daughter of the local squire.' As he paused to momentarily reflect on his sister and Julie, Stephen's question drew his thoughts back to the present.

'What happened to you, Pa?' It was his son's practical mind that motivated the question. Edward gave him an apprehensive look, pleased with the interest his story was generating.

'I helped my uncle in the forge and... did some prize fighting.'

'Prize fighting?' Stephen gasped excitedly as he looked with thrilled expectations towards his father. 'Were you a real prize fighter, Pa?'*

* In Book I The Winds of Destiny

'Yes...' Edward chuckled at his son's astonished look, '... I was East of England champion by the time I was nineteen.' Two pairs of eyes, shining with amazement, watched him closely as his thoughts lingered on the memory at that bout. After a few moments silence, his thoughts drifted back to the present. 'They arrested me...' Edward paused to gaze reflectively at the ruffled water that shimmered brilliantly under a molten sun, '... after the fight.'

'Arrested you? Why'd they arrest you, Pa?' As he explained the episodes leading up to his incarceration and eventual transportation to the penal colony of New South Wales, their eyes widened in astonishment. Dumb-founded, his two children could only stare at him at silent disbelief.

As Edward continued his narrative, his enthralled listeners sat in stunned silence. He noticed the nuances of emotion reflected on their faces as he related his encounter with their Ma and Stephen, her husband on board the Badger. Tears misted their eyes as he explained how in the rescue boat he had promised a dying Stephen that he would care for his young pregnant wife... he hesitated to give them a sympathetic look, '... your Ma.'*

'How... how long were you... and Ma in the boat, Pa?' Marian was showing an increasing interest as Edward continued his story.

'Only three of us remained in the boat when your Uncle Robert came to our rescue. The other occupant, a seaman, was dead, which meant that no other person apart from your Ma was aware that I had taken her husband's identity. That secret was in jeopardy when Andrew, the man responsible for my departure arrived in Sydney. He was searching for information about Edward Payne – my real name.'

He waited for his listeners' reactions. There were none. They remained silent, bemused, as they tried to perceive the implications behind his revelations. 'Andrew came upon my pardon in the Governor's office. The authorities thinking I had been drowned on the Badger, had filed it away and forgotten it – for sixteen years.

'Your Ma and I...' he was speaking once more of the rescue, '... were taken aboard the Cynthia, where your Uncle Robert

* In Book I The Winds of Destiny

and Aunt Elizabeth…' sadness momentarily filled his eyes as he recalled her passing nearly three years previously, '… nursed us both back to health and helped to deliver your Ma of her baby. A daughter… yourself Marian.' He nodded towards her.

Marian gasped in amazement as the implication of her Pa's statement penetrated her thoughts. 'That means I am… an orphan? No one… alone…' Her troubled eyes, the same dark brown as her mother's had a startled look reflected in them. Tears spilled from her eyes and trickled down her cheeks as she struggled to come to terms with her circumstances.

'It seems, Marian…' he moved across and told hold of her hands, '… that I shall always regard you as my daughter – as I have done since your birth. If it is your wish, our relationship will remain unchanged.' Edward watched the changing emotions cross Marian's face as she absorbed his invitation. Consternation… surprise, then sadness gave way to a warm, affectionate smile as her Pa's meaning became clear.

'My wish, pa… is that you will always look upon me as your very own daughter. I would not wish it otherwise. You're the only Pa I've ever known and my dearest wish is that it may continue so.' She rose from the locker to embrace Edward in a compassionate demonstration of her love.

Tenderly he kissed her cheeks, reassuring her that he would always look upon her as his own daughter. 'We shall remain a family for as long as you desire, my love… your Ma would have wished it so.' With a benign look he returned her emotional embrace.

'That, Pa…' she sobbed against his breast, '… will be forever.' Edward kissed the top of her head as he held her close.

Gradually, he became aware of Stephen's serious gaze upon him. His presence had been momentarily forgotten while he had been consoling Marian. Now he must confront Stephen with the true facts of his birth. Inform him that he was born out of wedlock. That he was a bastard child. There was no way that he could mitigate the affect of what would surely be a disturbing announcement.

'Stephen, as your Ma and I wee not married, for reasons you are now aware of, that makes you… a… er…'

'A grateful son, Pa...' Stephen's voice interrupted his declaration, '... and one who will always think of you... and Ma, as wonderful parents.' Edward became aware of the impassioned pride in his son's demeanour. 'What ever the future holds, Pa, I shall always treasure wonderful memories of my childhood. Precious times shared with you and... Ma.' Sadness flickered briefly, like a passing shadow in his eyes.

'Aye, Stephen. Pleasant memories that I also will forever cherish.' Edward sighed deeply as nostalgia overwhelmed him. 'If... only your, Ma...' but he was unable to continue his musing. Any intimate thoughts of Becky still caused him distress... heartache. They had shared so much of life together.

'Our consolation, is still having each other, Pa.' Marian, aware of her father's sadness, reassured him with an affectionate smile.

Edward turned to acknowledge Marian's words of comfort, but the vision before him caused him to stop suddenly in his movement. It was as if he was once again looking into Becky's face. A younger Becky... the young woman he had seen with his sister Maisie... so many years ago it now seemed.

'What... is it, Pa?' Even Marian's frown as she gave him a perplexing look, mirrored her mother's features.

'It's...' Edward hesitated a moment, uncertain about disclosing his thoughts. Marian's uncertain look encouraged him to continue. 'It's just that you're so much like... your Ma, when she was your age.' Silently, he reflected on their likeness before confirming his observations. 'Your voice, your actions and... your friendly and compassionate nature, remind me so much of her. Also...' he gave her a wistful smile, '... you have the same tenacity in the face of adversity.'

'Then I am indeed blessed to have inherited such laudable traits, Pa.'

'Aye...' Edward nodded, '... traits that you are most worthy of, my dear.' Then, feigning consternation, he gave his daughter a serious look. 'Intuition warns me that my most arduous assignment for the future will be shielding you from the amorous approaches of the many suitors who will fall in love with you.'

'Oh, Pa! Now you are teasing me!' Although Edward shared her laughter, he had a premonition that Marian's beauty could well lead to some infatuated encounter. Little could he have imagined the eventual outcome of one such romance.

Chapter Thirty One

'Oh, Andrew! It's such a wonderful feeling.' Maisie's face was flushed with excitement as she expressed her feelings. 'Almost back to... normal.' It was her first time on horseback since her accident. Riding beside Andrew, she experienced an emotional uplift to her spirits as together they took their horses at a gentle canter across the parklands.

Although now fully recovered from the terrifying ordeal of lying trapped and badly injured in her wrecked carriage, the nightmare of those endless hours in the darkness continued to cause Maisie sleepless nights. A traumatic experience that she was endeavouring to forget as she felt the wind in her hair and the warm caress of the late winter sun on her face.

It was now three months since that frightful night when Josh and Leonard had extricated her and Andrew from the wreckage of their carriage. She vaguely remembered her journey to Highfield. For several days she had drifted in and out of consciousness, barely aware of her surroundings. Even the presence of Alison and Josh's new baby daughter, Gail, presented for her to hold, had produced little response. Her reactions at the time had been confused... uncertain.

Throughout those first weeks following the accident, one face, albeit a very worried one, had always been there when a mist-like veil had lifted. Gradually those brief spells of cognisance had lengthened and her faculties had become more lucid. Then had come that unforgettable morning, when Andrew and her son, Jon, along with Josh and his family had all crowded in to wish her the season's greetings. A Christmas Day that she would never forget.

Smiling through her tears, she had asked to be helped into a sitting position. While a relieved Andrew had sat on the bed to support her, Josh had said a short prayer of thanksgiving for Maisie's recovery. Expressions of gratitude for her wellbeing were sincere and unanimous as all present on that joyful occasion endowed her with an affectionate embrace.

From that wonderful morning, her improvement had continued steadily. Eventually, Leonard had given permission for her to return to Homefield. All her staff had assembled to welcome her home on that New Year's Day. Maisie had confided in Andrew that the New Year, 1830, would be a special one for them. Her optimism was soon to be rewarded.

'You're very quiet, Maisie! Is the riding too much for...?'

'Oh, no, Andrew! It's wonderful... just marvellous!' She gave her anxious husband a reassuring smile. 'I was just thinking how fortunate I... both of us are. We could so easily have been killed when the tree crashed down onto our carriage. Our escape was indeed miraculous.'

'We were blessed with good fortune, my dear.' He nodded his affirmation. 'Now, thanks to your full recovery...' he gave her a caring look, '... we shall be leaving for Foxleigh in the morning. I'm looking forward to the last two hunts of the season.' Maisie cast an understanding look in Andrew's direction as he enthused over the exciting prospects of sharing in Foxleigh's last hunts of the season. She smiled as she noticed the sparkle of anticipation in his eyes.

It was late February and the month was still locked in Winter's icy grip. A pale sun was promising a rise in the temperature as the three travellers snuggled under their blankets while the carriage trundled through the frosted countryside. Maisie, glancing through the window, glimpsed the glossy yellow blooms of celandines and a sprinkling of golden flowers on the fiery gorse bushes. A veneer of frost glistened like silver on the roadside vegetation.

Inside the carriage, an anxious Andrew reached over and tucked the travelling rug closer around Maisie's legs. She smiled her appreciation as her eyes met the concerned ones of her husband. His caring and support had been a great encouragement when she had been indisposed, struggling to recover from her accident. His presence these days engendered in her a feeling of love and tranquillity.

'Looking forward to your first meet, Jon?' Andrew's question induced an excited look in his son's eyes.

'Very much so, Father.' It was gratifying to hear his own son addressing him as father. Thankfully, Jon was not aware of the circumstances of his conception. Pray God he never will. Andrew shuddered at such a possibility. Jon, who had been observing his father closely, was perplexed as he briefly glimpsed the look of humiliation in his parent's eyes. A moment of sadness had crossed his father's features.

Some memory of the past had caused him an instant of deep distress. He was sure that his father's anguish was in some way associated with his mother. Whatever had happened between his parents in the past appeared to have been mutually forgiven, as since their marriage the inner sadness that his mother had borne with fortitude had eventually been superseded by a much happier disposition.

A change that had pleased Jon greatly and he was grateful for the man who had precipitated that transition. Apart from the mental changes, Andrew had also lightened the burden of running the estate. Gradually easing the load from his mother's shoulders. Another redeeming feature of his father and one that he greatly appreciated, was the way he always acknowledged him as an equal. He never failed to discuss with him any changes relating to the estate. Changes that were invariably beneficial to Homefield.

Foxleigh gradually came into view through the trees. Its appearance deflected Jon's cogitation's. With an effort he concentrated his mind on their arrival at the Hall. It had been several months since his last visit and now, as he glanced around the estate, he was disturbed.

Even his youthful eyes noticed the faded look of the buildings as their carriage progressed slowly down the badly kept drive. Jon was reminded of the conversation he had recently overhead between his parents when they had received an invitation to visit Foxleigh for the last hunts of the season.

'Oh, Andrew!' He had been aware of his mother's disappointment as she had glanced up from reading the letter just delivered from his Aunt. 'Julie and George are thinking of finishing the hunt. Running it is becoming too great a financial burden for them.' His mother's eyes reflected great sadness as she waited for his father's reaction.

'Of late, I had wondered if the hunt was becoming an unnecessary strain on their resources.' A deep reflective frown had wrinkled his father's eyes as he continued. 'Cousin Julie and George's efforts to keep the estate solvent since my uncle's death, have been a great credit to them both, but...' Silently he gave an uncertain shake of his head.

'Thank goodness Julie never became too involved with that... conniving parson.' Jon detected a note of anger in his mother's voice as she expressed her opinion. 'He had no interest in Julie, only the money and the squireship of Foxleigh.'

'Aye...' his father had paused in the act of helping himself to a piece of cold ham, '... he was an evil man... a scoundrel. Foxleigh was well rid of him.' Jon had noticed on previous occasions how sympathetic he was when discussing Aunt Julie's welfare. He had even mentioned it once to his mother.

After a moments hesitation, she had explained that it stemmed from a regrettable incident that occurred many years ago. 'It had culminated...' sadness and filled her voice as she had continued her explanation, '... in your Aunt Julie's enforced separation from the man she loved. My brother, Edward... George's father.' Further questions on the subject were always thoughtfully answered without any enlightened information being confided to him.

Excited voices brought Jon out of his reverie. They had arrived at their destination, Foxleigh. As Jon followed his mother down from the carriage, he was greeted affectionately by his warm-hearted Aunt Julie. Excitement at their coming had given a flush to her pale face and the smile that welcomed them was radiant with happiness. But the eyes that smile a welcome into his still reflected the sadness in her heart.

'Welcome to Foxleigh, Maisie... Jon and Andrew.' He noticed his Aunt's slight hesitation before his father's name. Had there also been a subtle inflection in her voice? He did notice that their greeting was less effusive than that between his mother and aunt. His father did not seem to notice any lack of cordiality in the greeting as he was very courteous and friendly towards his cousin... Aunt Julie.

Jon listened with interest as they discussed the hunt's future and the estate work in general. Conversation ceased when George entered but was soon resumed after greeting had been exchanged.

It did not take long for the lads to become involved in their own intimate conversation. Although George was the elder by just over three years, the two had always enjoyed each other's companionship. 'I believe you are riding with the hunt tomorrow, Jon? Your first time, if I am not mistaken?'

'Yes! My first time and... thanks for the invitation.' Jon nodded a little apprehensively. 'Truth is...' he gave his cousin a guarded look, '... I'm feeling rather... nervous about it.'

'There's nothing to worry about. I'm sure you'll enjoy it once we set off.' If only I could feel so confident, thought Jon as he gave his companion a furtive glance. There was nothing condescending in George's manner, his words of reassurance were friendly and sincere. 'I'll ride beside you... until you get used to the routine. Then... just try and keep up with the leaders.' Jon was pleased with his older cousin's promised support.

Andrew's help and suggestions, as he accompanied George around the estate, were gratefully appreciated. Prior to the hunt they had ridden together over Foxleigh's land, discussing crop rotation as well as the market prices for the sheep and cattle. Wool prices was a main topic of conversation and, as lambing was in progress, a great deal of speculation was voiced on this annual event.

Julie, aware of Andrew's friendliness towards George and appreciative of his constructive suggestions for the economical growth of the estate, felt her antipathy towards him easing. Andrew's manner these days was impeccable and although she continued to hold him responsible for Edward's transportation, his remorse and genuine humiliation of his earlier misanthropic attitudes, had encouraged a warmer friendliness towards him. She was especially grateful for the way he conferred with George when advocating the need for more economical practices and the introduction of new strains of cattle at Foxleigh.

The mechanised drill for sowing and a small flock of Southdown sheep, raised for their meat and marketable fleece would, she realised, have to wait until their financial situation improved. As for the Herefords, renowned for their beef qualities, there would have to be an improvement in their resources before investments were available for such a project. Nevertheless, Julie was more than grateful for her cousin's interest and advice.

Gradually the resentment, the heartaches he had caused her across the years, were forgiven. It was a very different cousin from the one she had loathed in the past. That detestable person who had indulged in drink and gambling had vanished many years ago. Replaced by a courteous man who had begged for and received her forgiveness for the wrong that had resulted in her betrothed being taken from her so many years ago. Perhaps his… death.

It was a crisp morning. Frost silvered the grass and hedgerows with a veneer of sparkling crystals and caused a thin covering of ice around the shallow edges of the pond by the village green. In a display of glittering brilliance, the early morning sun soon dispersed the sprinkling of frost. A myriad of thawing droplets shimmered with spectrum's of the sunlight. The increasing warmth of the late winter sun was kindling the first growth of spring.

Villagers had gathered early on the common to see their local hunt meet, aware that it was the last of the season. Perhaps the final meeting they would witness. It was common knowledge that Foxleigh, despite stringent financial controls by Mistress Julie and the conscientious endeavours of young Master George, was struggling to survive.

'Oh, Ben…' Nelly gave her elderly husband a worried look, '… I do hope that Mistress Julie and George will not have to dispose of the hunt. They've struggled so hard t'keep it goin'…'

'I'm sure the hunt'll survive, Nell.' Ben, his grey whiskered face sat in a contemplative mood, turned to his younger wife. 'George be a tryer… he'll make it.' Nodded reassuringly as Nelly pressed closer to him in attempt to keep warm.

Her nearness reminded him how fortunate he had been to have her love and support after Sara's death. She had been a good wife to him and had presented him with a fine son, John. A strong lad, who now did most of the forge work.

Thinking of his son drew his eyes involuntarily towards the forge, from whence came the metallic sound of hammer on anvil. John, who had a natural aptitude for blacksmith work, had gradually taken over the running of the forge. Ben had only been too pleased to relinquish the burden onto a willing and stronger pair of shoulders. If only John would forget about prize-fighting. Nell and himself had tried to discourage him, but they had been unsuccessful in their attempts.

'It's in his blood, Nell...' Ben had shrugged resignedly, '... might as well let'm git it out o'his system.' Nell was not deceived, she had glimpsed the proud look in her husband's eyes before he changed the subject.

'They're coming' now... Nell.' A distant barking of hounds reached their ears. Alerted by the familiar sounds of the hunt, the watchers turned their eyes towards the approaching riders and hounds.

George, smart and prominent in his faded scarlet coat, led the hunt on to the common. As Master of the Hunt he would control its activities from the front. Other riders followed him, dressed in black coats and skirts with bowler-like hats.

Ben glanced over the riders as the hunt gathered on the common. He noticed Josh, Andrew and Master Jon who was taking part in his first hunt and a few local gentry. Riders and watchers alike were all saddened by the thought that, not only was this the final meet of the season, but possibly the final one of the Foxleigh Hunt.

George, as became the Master of the Hunt had ensured that all the riders had imbibed of his specially concocted toddy before leaving the Hall. 'A drink to keep out the chill,' he had smilingly encouraged them.

At his command the riders moved off with the hounds, who were accompanied by a couple of assistant, the 'whippers in'. Barking excitedly, the pack spread out as they worked their way across the triangular meadow towards the waterside pastures and the woodland and scrub beyond. The excited cheer of the spectators gradually faded behind them.

Settling into a steady gallop, the hunt moved across the estate's open countryside as the warm sun climbed higher into the azure sky. Thawing conditions made the going a little slippery and dangerous for horses and riders. Julie and Helen remained close together at the rear as the hunt progressed across the late winter landscape.

They had been riding for nearly an hour before the hounds picked up the scent of a fox. As the baying hounds prepared to chase after their prey, George raised his horn to his lips and sounded the 'Tally-Ho!' Suddenly, there was the creak of straining leather as the horses were urged into a fast gallop. Hoof-beats thudded above the rushing air as the steeds raced over the thawing ground in the wake of the hounds. Excited shouts came from the riders as the thrill of the chase sent the adrenaline coursing through their veins.

Julie watched the men as they sped off in full chase. Noticing their general direction, she indicated to Helen that they could catch up by taking a shorter route across the next field. It would bisect the angle and bring them close up with the leaders.

Only one obstacle to overcome, a thick hedge at the far side of the field. Julie was not daunted by its height, she had jumped higher ones on some of her morning gallops. With their approach speed under control, Julie line her horse for a straight jump. Already her heart was racing with anticipation at the thrill of lifting her horse high and smoothly over the hedge.

She was suddenly aware that the area of take off was soft and slippery from the partial thaw. It was too late to make adjustments, as by then she was committed to the jump. Julie watched the horse's fractional loss of impetus at take off. An instinctive feeling warned her that they were not going to jump clear of the hedge.

Despite all her considerable skill as a rider, she was unable to prevent the horse's hooves from catching the top of the hedge. Her mount stumbled badly on landing and rolled partly onto Julie as she endeavoured to get clear. A blackness came crashing painfully down upon her. She lay motionless on the grass as her horse scrambled to its feet and trotted aimlessly away.

Helen's agitated waving eventually attracted the other riders' attentions. Her frantic actions intuitively warned them that there had been a serious accident. George called the hunt off before hastening towards a troubled Helen, who continued to gesticulate frenziedly in their direction.

As George turned his horse to ride towards the group gathered around a fallen rider, he noticed the riderless horse in the adjacent field. Shock-waves pulsed through his trembling body. Fear brought a dryness to his throat as he recognised his mother's horse.

'No. Not mother... please.' He whispered hoarsely as he raced his horse towards the scene of the accident. Before he reached the waiting group he glimpsed his mother lying still upon the ground. He offered a silent prayer that her injuries were not severe, but her stillness warned him to expect the worst.

Sympathetic faces watched his silent approach. Anxious eyes remained upon him as he dismounted and walked towards his mother. Helen and Jon were cradling her head and covering her with coats against the chill wind. 'How... is mother?' A dryness in his throat induced a hoarseness to his words. 'Is... she...?'

'Your mother is unconscious, George.' Helen's worried features betrayed her concern. 'We have sent for Doctor Fenton.' Her words were spoken with forced optimism. She was trying not to distress and already shocked George. He in turn fought back his fears as he knelt down to gaze disconsolately at his mother. If only she wasn't so still... and pallid.

'Mother!' Involuntarily he called her as he reached out to hold her hand. 'Mother...' he called softly once again, '... it's George...' There was no response.

In the deathly hush, he heard the jingle of the bridles as the hoses stamped impatiently. They were restless after their excited gallop and had been suddenly halted. Vapour rose cloud-like from their perspiring bodies to evaporate slowly in the warming air. George was unaware of these familiarities as he waited for some response to his anguished words. He waited in vain.

Suddenly, he felt strong arms offering comfort and support as a sympathetic Josh helped him to his feet. 'We must get your mother home and into bed, George.' He was trying to not show his concern. 'We're ready to carry her now.' George followed his gaze to the gate that four of the hunt members had lifted from its hinges.

Coats were eagerly removed and laid upon the gate for Julie's comfort while being carried to the Hall. It was the sight of his mother's ashen, wax-like face peeping out from under the coats, that induced a shocked numbness. Tremors of distress assailed George's body.

His mother looked so fragile ... so death-like. He choked back the sobs as he walked in a daze beside the make-shift stretcher. Helen walked beside him, trying to bring comfort and reassurance to him as they traversed the route towards the Hall.

'We're almost home, George.' Helen glanced at the forlorn figure beside her. 'It will help your mother's... infirmity once she is tucked up in a warm bed.' He nodded silently, appreciating Helen's attempt to bring comfort. His eyes, however, never strayed from his mother's face. He was deeply concerned for her welfare.

'Thank you... Helen. I pray that mother is not too... seriously injured, but...' his words faded as he became aware of his mother's continued unconscious state.

Maisie, once the entourage had reached the Hall, soon had Julie undressed and into a warm bed. She remained beside her comatose friend until the doctor arrived. 'I would like you to stay, Lady Douglass. I may be glad of your... assistance.' With troubled eyes she watched intently as the doctor examined Julie.

Maisie became aware of his increasing concern as his check continued. It was by this time four hours since Julie's accident and she had yet to regain consciousness. As the doctor looked up, his worried gaze met Maisie's anxious eyes, waiting for a silent look of hope. For a few moments they continued to look into each other's eyes. Eventually, he shook his head slowly... uncertainly.

'I'll have a few words with the others, Lady Douglass.' He nodded towards the door. 'Mistress Julie will need someone beside her... until...'

‘I shall remain with her doctor. Should there be any change… I’ll send word immediately.’

‘Splendid!’ Gathering his bag, the doctor moved silently away from the bed. ‘Splendid!’ he reiterated in a respectful whisper as he turned towards Maisie before leaving. ‘If you’ll excuse me, Lady Douglass?’

‘Down in the reception room, a distraught George anxiously awaited the doctor’s confidence. ‘How… is my mother, Doctor Fenton?’ His voice was shaking with emotion as his eyes sought a sign of optimism on the physician’s grave features.

‘Very ill, George.’ He gave Foxleigh’s young master a troubled look. ‘Very ill indeed. A nasty accident.’

‘Will… my mother…?’ George could not bring himself to ask her expectations.

‘Your mother remains in a coma. We must hope that she regains consciousness soon.’ He looked reflectively at the small group as he hesitated. ‘Until then… there is little more that I can do.’ George murmured his thanks as he accompanied the doctor to the door. ‘You’ll call me if there is… any change.’ After receiving a nodded acknowledgement he concluded. ‘Otherwise, I shall call first thing in the morning.’

Chapter Thirty Two

'A beautiful morning, Pa... but so cold.' Edward turned to find a shivering Marian beside him. Since breakfast, he had been waiting on the upper deck to glimpse the coastline. His first sighting of England for nearly eighteen years. Under full canvas their ship sliced through he choppy waters of the approaches to the English Channel.

'Oh... Pa...' Edward could feel his daughter shivering as she huddled close against him, '... is England... always as cold... as this?' He laughed at Marian's discomfort before assuring her that the country also had its summer weather, but later in the year.

'Next month it will be spring, my dear and the days will be warmer.' Marian's thoughts as she pressed closer to her father were of her home and the lovely days of sunshine that were symptomatic of late February... the end of summer. For a few minutes they stood close together, gazing across the white crested waves at the gulls as they followed their ship with raucous cries.

Suddenly, Edward pointed out a low dark smudge on the grey-misted horizon. 'England!' His eyes searched the distant coastline in a reassuring gesture. 'Yes, England at last, Marian.' She was aware of the catch in his voice as she turned to utter words of comfort, Marian had noticed the tears of sadness in her father's eyes.

'If only Ma and Roger could have shared this moment with us, Pa.' As he lowered his head in silent agreement, she reached for his hand and held it against her cheek as memories of their lost loved ones filled their thoughts.

Stephen joined them as the ship was nearing the harbour entrance. Soon the seamen were out on the yardarm's, furling the canvas as the ship gradually lost way. As it drifted to a position close to the quay, the anchor splashed down into the water. Edward noticed the large number of ships and the lively activities on the harbour front. Portsmouth appeared larger and it certainly looked a much busier port.

Once ashore, Edward arranged for a carriage to take them and their baggage to an inn. On impulse, he first directed the driver towards the Pettersons' old chandlers store.

'It aint there no more, sir.' The old coachman gave Edward a strange look. 'Young Mr Petterson 'as 'is store in town.' He pointed towards the High Street with his whip. 'Want me t'drive yer there?' Having received affirmation, he flicked his whip above the horses and set the carriage moving towards the town.

Edward was impressed at the large store confronting him as their driver came to a stop outside the building. It certainly was an imposing sight. Windows displaying the wares available inside were indicative of the store's nautical trade connections. Asking the driver to wait, Edward then entered the store beneath a sign that informed him that James Patterson and Sons, Ships' Chandlers' were the owners.

His enquiries led him to an office in a corner of the building. An invitation to enter followed his knock on the door. Edward, a smile wrinkling the corner of his eyes, waited for the occupant to look up from the ledger he was checking. Eventually the young man glanced up to give his visitor his full attention. His frown of uncertainty soon gave way to a warm smile of welcome as he hurried across to embrace a friend he had long though dead.

'Edward!' He eased back, holding his caller at arm's length. 'Is it really... you?'

'Aye, it's me alright, Jim.' Edward was warmed by the pleasure his arrival had caused.

'I... that is we... heard that you... were...' He knew from Jim's incredulous stare what news he and his family had received.

'No... it was God's will that I survived.'

'What brings you... home after so many years away, Edward?'

'A short holiday to reassure my family and friends that I am... alive and in excellent health. In passing, I had a yearning to call and see you and your family. How are they?'

'Fine, Edward. Fine! I've had a little success...' Jim indicated the surrounds of his large store.

'A little success!' Edward glanced out of the office window where he could discern half a dozen staff busy at their counters.

'An understatement if ever I heard one.' Jim joined in his friend's laughter. 'Your mother... Emma? They are well I trust?'

'Mother is poorly... frail, but Emma nurses her and attends to her needs. She lives at home and is able to care for mother in her infirmity.'

'Yourself?' Edward gave his companion an enquiring look.

'Married... with two sons. Fred and Thomas.'

'Now you must tell me about yourself, dear friend. The last view mother and I had of you was when the guards were marching you down to the prison transport ship.'

'A long story, Jim...' Edward heaved a heavy sigh at the reminder of that distant memory, '... but I have two of my children outside.'

'Your wife... is she not with you?' Jim sounded surprised.

'Unfortunately, my... er, their mother and my youngest son were killed in a accident a few weeks before we sailed from Sydney.'

'My sincere commiseration's, Edward.' He placed a sympathetic arm around Edward's shoulders as he watched the sorrowful emotions play over his friend's face.

'Why not stay the night with us? I'll fetch mother and Emma over, then you shall tell us of your life in Australia.'

'Your kind offer is accepted, Jim. Our coach does not leave until early on the morrow. We hope to reach Foxleigh Green by Friday.'

'Good!' Jim reached for his hat and coat. 'I shall drive you and your family to my house.'

Very soon they were ensconced in the comfortable surrounds of Jim's large house that he had built on the outskirts of the town. Within the hour, Emma and her mother had arrived. Both were thrilled and excited at the prospect of seeing Edward again. It was with sincere affections that they embraced a friend they had never expected to see again. All were anxiously awaiting the evening to hear abut his life in a land that seemed so very far away.

'... and now, here I am back in England.' Edward brought his narrative to a close. He had covered his activities over the years since he was transported to Australia – as a convict. Not a murmur had come from his spellbound audience.

'My prayers... were answered, Edward.' It was a frail, grey haired Joan Petterson who broke the ensuing silence. 'After your departure, Emma and I prayed each evening for your safety...' She turned towards her blushing daughter for confirmation.

'Indeed we did, Edward.' For a moment he glimpsed in her radiant eyes the love that lay within her soul. Her innermost feelings disturbed him as he looked into her sparkling blue eyes. Emma's naivety, her maidenly existence in caring for her mother did not allow for subtle concealment of emotions. They were revealed to Edward as he glimpsed the love and adoration in her eyes.

'Then I owe you both my undying gratitude.' Edward's gaze as he spoke moved from Emma to the frail, elderly lady beside him. Joan Petterson had also seen the look of love in her daughter's eyes.

'If only...?' but she realised that Emma would never leave her now. It seemed she had resigned herself to remaining a spinster.

According to Edward, he and his family would be sailing back to Australia in three or four months time. Joan hoped that her daughter would have overcome her loving emotions for Edward by then. Edward, however, was destined never to make that return voyage he had planned.

'Good bye, Edward. Don't forget to call on your way back.'

'It will be my pleasure.' He gave Joan an affectionate embrace before expressing his gratitude to Jim and Judy for their hospitality.

'Farewell, Emma!' While his children were saying their goodbyes, Edward embraced Emma and gently kissed her lips. He was emotionally surprised at her sensuous response as their lips momentarily caressed each others. 'I shall look forward to seeing you again... when next we call.'

'I shall be here... whenever you come, Edward.' Neither of them could have foreseen the circumstances, or the outcome of their next meeting.

Edward tried to analyse his emotions, his feelings towards Emma. During his journey to Norwich in the swaying coach, his thoughts dwelt often on the young woman he had said goodbye to. He was still thinking of her as their coach neared its destination. Her blue eyes with their haunting look of love had bewitched him. Stirred him emotionally.

Her close embrace had reminded him of the longing he used to experience when he had held Becky in an affectionate embrace. He must try to forget Emma. He doubted if they would ever meet again. Perhaps that would be for the best as his future now lay in far Australia with his family.

As they approached Norwich, Edward was becoming increasingly apprehensive of what awaited him and his family at Foxleigh Green. He intended to call on his uncle and Nelly at the forge in the hope of learning something of the young woman he was once betrothed to. Who had Julie married, he wondered. Did she still live at Foxleigh Hall with her husband… and family? So much must have happened in eighteen years. She might even be… no, he would not even consider that dreaded possibility.

Across the fields, Edward glimpsed a familiar landmark – Norwich Cathedral. He pointed out this magnificent edifice to his two children as they began the long descent on the city's outskirts. The Cathedral's light stone tower, constructed of stone brought from Caen in Normandy and Barnack in Northamptonshire, was a prominent feature of the skyline as it reached high into the heavens. Fleecy clouds appeared to caress it as they drifted across the Norfolk landscape.

Soon they were clattering over the cobble stones of a city street. 'Whoa… there!' The coachman's shouted command to his horses brought their carriage to a halt. There was much stretching and flexing of cramped limbs after the passengers had climbed down from the coach.

'We shall have to change carriages here,' Edward warned his excited children. Both were fascinated by the hustle and bustle going on around them in the city streets. A cacophony of harsh sounds assaulted ears that were used to vast open spaces and relative silence.

After a short break the three travellers clambered into a small carriage that was to convey them the few miles to Foxleigh Green. Their long journey would soon be over and relatives that Marian and Stephen had only heard of would be greeting them for the first time. Gradually, as they neared their destination, their excitement gave way to a feeling of apprehension.

Despite their Pa's assurance about the warm welcome awaiting them, they continued to experience uncertainty. They were not used to meeting strangers, especially in unfamiliar surroundings. Their father, aware of their concern, reassured them both that they would be greeted with warm affection. He was sure that his Uncle Ben and Nelly, would be thrilled to see them all.

* * * * *

'Julie! Julie!' Maisie called softly to a still pallid face on the pillow. 'Can you hear me?' There was a slight fluttering of eyelids as Julie struggled to respond to Maisie's urging. She was still propped up on pillows, barely able to move.

'Yes... I... can hear... you Maisie,' but her voice was little more than a whisper as she forced the words from between her pale lips. 'Thank you... for... staying... Maisie, dear.' The effort of speaking appeared to have drained her strength. Once again her eyes closed as she lay back on the pillows.

Maisie turned and walked quietly to the window, struggling to stem her flow of tears as she did so. She was aware, from what the doctor had said, that Julie was in agony and that there was little he could do, other than leave laudanum for her. 'If the pain distresses her greatly...' he had advised Maisie, '... administer a dose to ease... her suffering.'

As Maisie gazed across the park, she prayed silently that Becky would arrive soon with some news of her brother. She was sure that whatever information Becky might bring about Edward, she had inferred in her last letter to Josh that her news would be heartening, it would be of some consolation to dearest Julie.

Time was, however, fast running out. Maisie recalled the sorrow in the doctor's eyes as he confided that it was only Julie's willpower that was keeping her alive. Even that must fade eventually. It was a week since the accident and, once consciousness had been regained, Julie had been subjected to excruciating pains.

Through her tear-filled eyes, Maisie watched the approaching carriage. A strange one she noted. Probably a neighbour come to express their concern and sympathy for a person who was loved by all. Julie's pleasant disposition and kindness had overcome the shock and prejudices of her neighbours when it became known that she had conceived a son out of wedlock... a bastard. Over the years their condescending attitudes had turned to admiration and respect as the full facts of her circumstances had become known.

Now, in her hour of need, many prayers were being offered for Mistress Julie's recovery... a miraculous recovery. Maisie turned from the window as she heard Julie's grasp of pain. She felt so helpless as she watched her friend's face grimace in agony as she endeavoured to move her body.

'Let me help you, Julie.' Maisie gently eased her companion of many years into a more comfortable position.

'Thank you... Maisie. You're... so kind.' As her pain abated a benign smile brightened Julie's ashen face. 'I'm... so pleased... that you and Alison... have been able... to stay... with me.'

'Of course we shall stay, Julie dearest.' Maisie forced a reassuring smile to her face. 'We shall remain until... you are fully recovered.' Both patient and nurse intuitively realised that such a possibility would be – a miracle.

'What... of your... families?' Concern was reflected in Julie's faltering voice.

'All is arranged.' Maisie assured her worried friend. 'Andrew and Jon are leaving today and on the morrow, Josh will be returning with Jane and William.'

'I wish... there was... no need... for...' Julie paused as a spasm of pain caused her to screw the bed linen into a ball with her hands. Maisie watched anxiously, wishing it was possible to comfort her dearest friend... to ease her suffering.

Excited voices came from below. A hubbub of conversation as the residents greeted the new arrivals. Maisie strained to identify the voices without success.

‘Sounds as if… we have visitors, Maisie?’

‘Yes. It would appear so. The carriage…’ Maisie glanced out of the window, ‘… that brought our visitors is now leaving.’ Maisie was trying to think, who among Julie’s friends would need to hire a carriage? She was soon to be enlightened.

Suddenly the bedroom door was opened by an excited Alison. Her eyes sparkled with tears of happiness as she hurried across to inform Maisie that her presence was required below.

‘I shall remain with Julie until you return. You must… prepare yourself for a surprise… a shock.’ Conflicting emotions chased across Alison’s face as she urged a startled Maisie to go and meet her visitors.

A thoughtful Maisie descended the stairs. From beyond a half open door she heard a mixture of voices. Subdued talk that faded to silence as a man, speaking in a quiet voice, described how someone was killed in a coach accident.

‘Becky was killed instantly as was our youngest son, Roger.’ The words beat against Maisie’s brains. Becky killed… son…’ She was whispering the words to herself. Realisation dawned… the man must be Becky’s husband. Stephen.

Maisie’s appearance drew all eyes except the visitor’s. He had his back to the door. Aware that his listeners’ eyes were fixed on someone behind him, Edward’s voice faded as he turned to see who had just entered the room. For a brief moment brother and sister faced each other for the first time in eighteen years. As recognition dawned, Maisie’s uncertainty gave way to ecstasy.

‘Edward! Oh, Edward is it really you?’ sobbing with happiness she flung herself into the waiting arms of the brother she had given up as dead. After a few moments, she eased reluctantly from his embrace. She had just remembered Julie, the person that Edward’s presence would also bring so much joy and happiness to. Maisie tried to hide her sadness as she wondered if it would be too late.

‘I must…’ Maisie was preparing to leave the room, ‘… tell Julie.’

‘It’s alright, my dear…’ Andrew assured her, ‘… Alison is already preparing Julie for Edward’s visit.’

'You... are aware of Julie's... condition, Edward?' He nodded silently as he once again embraced the sister he loved. The sister he had never expected to see again. As Maisie's excitement eased, she remembered the news she had overheard about Rebecca.

'Rebecca...' she noticed how her name induced a sad, distant look in her brother's eyes, '... is... is she...?' Maisie was hoping that the information she had listened to through the half-open door related to another person. Edward's sorrow had confirmed her worst fears.

'Becky was killed when bush-rangers forced her carriage off the road... as was our youngest son, Roger. Just three months short of his twelfth birthday.'

'Oh, Edward... how very sad.' She took hold of her brother's arm in a sympathetic act of commiseration. Suddenly her eyes went to his. 'Roger...' her frown deepened as the impact of her brother's words penetrated her excited thoughts, '... was the... son... of you and...' Bewilderment brought her words to a stop.

'Becky...' He smiled at his sister's uncertainty. 'Becky and I had two children of our own and Marian, Stephen's daughter...'

'Stephen... where... what happened...?' Maisie was becoming confused with all the explanations.

'Let me first introduce you to Marian.' As a young lady stepped into view, Maisie had to stifle her gasp of astonishment. It was as if she was seeing Rebecca again. The same friend she had known so many years ago it now seemed. Involuntarily she reached out and held the smiling Marian in a warm and affectionate embrace.

'Oh, Marian! You're so like your mother.'

'Thank you for that wonderful compliment... Aunt Maisie.' Marian kissed her new-found Aunt's cheek, warmed by the sincere friendliness of her Pa's sister.

'And this young man...' Edward drew his sister's eyes towards him, '... is Stephen our... my eldest son.'

'Stephen...' Maisie gave her brother's son a searching look, '... you have the likeness of your father... when he was your age.' Her warm embrace, to the surprised of the young recipient, caused not embarrassment as he had expected, but a joyful emotion. After a few light hearted exchanges, Maisie's thoughts calmed and a puzzled look etched a frown upon her forehead.

'You said that you... and Rebecca...' She gave her brother puzzled stare. 'What of Stephen... is he...?'

'Stephen died on the way out to Australia. He was in the rescue boat that we managed to launch before the Badger went under. Six of us made it to the boat, but Becky and I were the only survivors... just. Later, when we are all together...' Edward looked round at the others, '... I promise that you shall have the full details of my life in that distant country.'

Maisie gave her new-found niece and nephew a benign look. 'I'm so glad that you and Edwa... your father were able to come and visit us. You must come and spend a few days at Homefield before you return.'

'We had planned to stay with Nell and Uncle Ben. I called there first... but when I heard of Julie's accident...' Edward's face was grave as he looked anxiously towards the stairs, '... I came over immediately.

At that moment, Alison came down to inform Edward that Julie was ready to receive him... a gentleman visitor.

'You... you informed Julie that I was waiting...?'

'No, Edward.' She shook her head. 'We wanted your visit to be a... wonderful surprise for her.' Alison's eyes sparkled with excitement at the prospect of Julie and Edward being reunited after so many years apart.

Edward experienced a feeling of remorse as he climbed the stairs. Why, he reprimanded himself, had he not made more positive efforts to find out about Julie, his betrothed? The love he had never really forgotten, despite the many happy years shared with an affectionate and warm hearted Becky. Was it now too late? he wondered. Very soon he would know the answer.

'Please... come in.' The invitation to his knock came from a frail and quiet voice. He paused momentarily in the doorway, his eyes misting with sadness. An uncertain Julie was leaning back on her pillow anxiously watching to see who her visitor was.

Sorrow reached down inside Edward, tearing at his heart as the long years of parting rolled away to reveal a bright vision of a dark-haired Julie – his adolescent sweetheart. Hazel eyes that had once sparkled with love and happiness, were now sombre as they searched his face for signs of recognition. As they looked at each other in silence, Edward noticed the silvery streaks in her hair where it curled over her shoulders. As he took two hesitant steps into the room, the light from the window fell full upon him.

He watched Julie's uncertain frown gradually give way to an incredulous look of happiness. A vision that he was to remember for the remainder of his life. His beloved's face suddenly glowed with ecstasy as her affectionate smile revealed the precious love that still burned for him in her failing body. Her eyes glowed with remembered affections. Remembered dreams.

Julie called his name softly as she held her arms outstretched for Edward's embrace. It was a transient moment of beauty that gave her an angelic appearance. Edward's gentle embrace brought a deep, emotional sigh from the lips he was aching to kiss.

'Edward... my love. I knew... you would... return...' He knelt down beside her bed and placed his arms around her. As he held her close, he tenderly kissed the lips of his old love... his betrothed. Words choked in his throat as he fought to control his heartbreaking emotions.

Julie must have no suspicions of the distressing news he had received from Andrew and Josh. Edward was determined not to reveal that their time together would be but a short one. That heartache must be concealed from dearest Julie.

'Julie, my love... I've come back to remain with you – always.' He whispered his promise as he held her close in his arms.

'My prayers... have been... answered... Edward, dearest.' She turned towards him, her eyes filled with tears. Behind Julie's smile, Edward noticed another emotion... sadness. It was then he realised that his beloved was aware that her life was nearing its end.

'Shall we ask Josh to marry...?' Edward was unable to finish. Words were emotive expressions of his feelings, but now as he tried to speak without disclosing his sorrow, their utterances appeared to choke in his throat. Julie understood his predicament.

'As soon... as I ... am well... enough, Edward.' He leaned closer to hear her words. 'I want... to... be able... to walk beside... you.... down the... aisle.' Her voice faded with the effort of speaking. Her affectionate smile brought only sadness to Edward's aching heart as he realised the implications of her words.

Holding Julie in a close embrace, he kissed her eager lips, experiencing once again the thrill of their sensuous caress. Feelings of ecstasy surged through him as they recalled the love, the longing and the dreams they had planned, but never shared. Their feelings were reminiscent of the waves of passion that had once surged through their beings, before breaking on some euphoric-like shore. Emotional tides that washed across the sands of time in a display of transcendental wonder, before fading to infinity... lost forever.

'May our... marriage...' Edward was gazing into Julie's adoring eyes as he spoke, '... be soon, my dearest.' He noticed how her hazel eyes had the sheen of burnished gold in the reflected sunlight that infiltrated the curtained windows.

'That is also... my wish...' Julie's smile faded as pain caused her to clench her fists in an endeavour to prevent the cry that was waiting to escape. There was a pleading look in her eyes as spasm of pain racked her frail body. Edward, distressed at Julie's suffering, felt so helpless as he witnessed her agony. As the pain eased, he gently wiped the perspiration from her brow and with his fingers tenderly brushed the damp hair from her moist forehead.

'Thank... you... Edward.' Julie's hand reached up and covered his.

'Now you must rest, my love. I shall remain here with you.' Until the end, he promised silently to himself.

As he knelt by the bedside, holding Julie's hand, a knock sounded on the bedroom door. When he noticed her eyes slowly open and a warm smile spread over her face, Edward turned to see who had entered the room.

'Sorry, mother... I didn't realise...' he made as if to retire.

'George!' Julie called his name softly as she invited him to join them. Edward, who had not seen the young man before, was aware of his apprehension as he walked towards the bed. What was puzzling a watching Edward was that he had referred to Julie as mother. Had he heard correctly, he wondered, as his gaze rested on the young man opposite him.

'Edward... like you... to meet, George... my son. Our son!' Julie watched Edward's face as it registered surprise, then disbelief as he looked across the bed into the bewildered eyes of the young man opposite – their son. Both father and son stared in shocked amazement at each other. Momentarily lost for words.

George had heard of his father's unfortunate circumstances from his mother many times. Now he was seeing him in person. He had returned, as his mother had always assured him that he would do so. His eyes held Edward's in a steady, confident gaze as they shook hands across the bed.

'If you will excuse me, mother... father?' He bowed slightly before leaving the room. When he had gone, Edward turned a bemused face towards Julie.

'George... is our son, Julie?' Edward's face was creased with uncertainty as he watched her face light up with a proud, motherly smile.

'Have you... forgotten... that wonderful... morning. In... the cottage...' Julie paused to regain her strength before continuing, '... when... the snow... forced me to... seek shelter?'

'Oh, Julie. I never realised that... that...' Edward shook his head, unable to fully comprehend the situation.

'Maisie... came... with me... on the day... I was hoping to... tell you of... our baby.' She paused as the sorrowful recollection came back to her. 'When... when we... reached the prison... they had... already taken you... away...' Julie's voice faded as excruciating pains once again forced her to steel herself against their presence. Edward felt her vice-like grip on his hands as she endured the agonies.

'The day they escorted me to Portsmouth for transportation?' He had waited with deep anxiety until her spasms of pain had eased before questioning the day of their intended visit.

'Yes.' Julie whispered confirmation as accompanied by a nodding of her head as she became aware of her beloved's arm gently placed around her. Julie's pains were forgotten as she held herself close against Edward, the only man she had ever loved.

She was close in his arms three mornings later as they watched the late winter's sun edge its crimson glow above the trees. Scarlet hues fused into the greyness of the morning sky. A sunrise that portended winds before the bleak winter's day was over.

Edward's sombre thought kept him silent as he gazed across the parkland towards the crimson and golden brilliance of the sunrise. What would happen to the estate when, Julie... his dearest, Julie...?' He tried to force such negative thoughts from his mind.

As if aware of his thoughts, Julie spoke of Foxleigh's future. 'Foxleigh... will be... yours, Edward... after my...'

'Please Julie... we must not think of such...' He stopped as Julie raised her hand. Realising that she had further words for him, he leaned closer to hear her quiet words.

'Promise... you will... take care... of... George... our son... and Foxleigh.' Julie's eyes never moved from Edward's face as she spoke of her request.

'You have my promise, Julie. George and Foxleigh will be taken care of... for always.' Edward had great difficulty in formulating his words as his emotions threatened to overwhelm him.

'Thank... you... Edward dearest. I... love... you... so... very much.' He noticed the angelic smile on her face as she looked into his eyes.

'And I love you also, my dearest Julie.' Gently he embraced her frail body.

'Kiss me, Edward.' Tenderly he pressed his lips to hers as he held her weakening body close against his. A golden shaft of sunlight slanted into the dimness of the room. It's brilliance paled against the radiance of Julie's smile as she looked into Edward's face for the last time.

CHAPTER THIRTY THREE

After a final wave to his children, Marian and George, Edward continued to watch the ship as it sailed down the English Channel, carrying them to a new beginning. He was reflecting on the capricious nature of destiny as he did so. He recalled with sorrow, how fate had reunited Julie and himself, but only in time for him to share the last days of her life as it ebbed agonisingly away.

Thoughts of those anguished hours spent by her bedside induced an emotional heartache. He was remembering Julie, even as he gazed across the sparkling waters towards the distant ship taking his two children away from him. The young newly weds were sailing to a new life in Australia, where the promise of a wonderful future together awaited them. 'May God Bless you both...' he whispered as his thoughts returned to Marian and George's departure.

Would his own life have been different, he wondered? What would have been his reaction had he been aware of Julie's faithfulness... her continuous love for him? She had maintained a devoted vigil for nearly eighteen years, only for fate to deny her the love she had yearned and waited for. A love that she had saved for the only man she had ever desired... himself.

A sob choked in Edward's throat as he recalled the radiance of her smile as she welcomed him home. Once again memories returned of the heartbreaking vigil by her bedside, until she had reached out for his tender embrace – the last one they would ever share. Through misted eyes he gave a last look at the far distant ship taking Marian and George, the son Julie had borne him, to a distant shore where Newacres was to be their new home.

'Please forgive my sentimental emotions, Emma.' Edward turned a melancholy face towards his companion. 'It would appear that destiny of late has seen fit to burden me with the heartache of partings. Everlasting as well as... temporary ones.'

'Apologies are not necessary, Edward... I understand.' Emma turned and put her arm through his as they remembered her own heartache. 'Forgive me, Emma. I had forgotten... your personal loss.' Edward was vexed at his selfishness in not remembering the death of Emma's mother, a few months previously. Reaching across in an involuntary act of sympathy, he took hold of her hand. An action that induced in Emma a stirring of pleasure. Edward noticed the blush on her cheeks as they travelled back to the Pettersons' residence.

Edward was silent. He was sorry that his visit was almost over and that soon he would be saying another farewell. Emma's company had been a joyful one, but now he must face the daunting task of returning to Foxleigh... alone. He had experienced tranquil emotions, sitting beside her and talking of his family's future.

Emma's comforting presence, had help ease the heartache of his children's parting. Their intimate closeness engendered an emotional stirring of affection within his lonely being. A re-awakening of his impassioned feelings that attracted him to the understanding and attractive woman beside him. Her sincerity and pleasantness incited within Edward a feeling of admiration – and love.

'You must miss your mother's company very much, Emma?' Edward experienced the emptiness of the house that had once been filled with the laughter and kindness of the warm-hearted woman who had once lived there.

'Yes...' he was aware of the sadness and loneliness in her voice, '... I miss her greatly, Edward, but...' sorrow filled her eyes, '... many happy memories are my – blessings.' She turned to the man sitting close beside her.

'You must be proud of your children, Edward?' Emma's subtle change of conversation was intended to lighten their sombre mood.

'Yes...' he reflected sadly, '... although Marian is not of my own blood, she has always been as a daughter to me. In many ways she is so very much like her mother... Becky.' He paused as a vision of Becky threatened to overwhelm him with emotional nostalgia. Treasured memories of the happier times shared on their farm back in Australia before... Suddenly aware that Emma was expecting him to continue his narrative, he orientated his thoughts to the present. 'When I brought news of Becky's... death, her brother, Josh, contemplated how best to break the news to his seriously ill parents.'

Edward released a deep sigh before speaking of Marian's visit to Highfield, where she had been the guest of her Uncle Josh and Aunt Alison for a few weeks. 'It was Marian's suggestion that she would like to accompany her uncle Josh when he visited her grandparents to inform them of her mother's death. Josh greatly appreciated her courage and understanding. He was hoping that the presence of Becky's daughter, the grandchild they had never seen, would ease their heartache when the sad news of Rebecca's death was broken to them.

'A distressing situation, Edward.' Emma's words were warm with sympathy.

'Yes...' he nodded, remembering as he did so how very caring and sympathetic Marian had been towards her ailing grandparents, '... but a comforting one as it transpired.' Noticing his companion's puzzled frown, he explained that Becky's mother, in her frail and confused condition, had mistaken Marian for Becky. Josh encouraged Marian to accept the situation and reciprocate the forgiveness as her mother would have wished. Marian's reaction was facilitated by the genuine fondness she had for her grandparents. Josh had expressed his gratefulness for the great comfort she was able to bring them until their end.'

'They are both dead?' Edward nodded a solemn confirmation. 'Within a few weeks of each other.'

'A sad experience for Marian.' Emma's face was lined with sorrow as she remembered her mother's loss.

'Sad indeed, Emma. Fortunately her young heart was soon able to recover, especially when she found solace and love in the company of George... my son. It came as no surprise ...' a smile flickered across his face as he recalled the incident, '... when he asked my permission to marry Marian. A request I willingly granted with my full blessing.'

'Then I took the opportunity of having them together so that plans for their future could be discussed.' Remembrance of that evening induced a moment of heartache, for it reminded him that he would soon be returning to Foxleigh alone. Emma noticed the sorrow in his eyes as he turned towards her. In a spontaneous gesture of sympathy, she reached out and laid her hand upon his.

'When I offered them Newacres, my farm in Australia, as a wedding gift, they were overwhelmed with enthusiasm at the prospect of farming there. Marian was especially excited as she was anxious to return to the familiar surroundings of her home.' A wistful expression lingered on Edward's face as he recalled Marian's warm embrace and smiling face suddenly changing to shocked disbelief as the implication of his statement infiltrated her happy thoughts. She just could not believe that only herself and George would be taking passage to Sydney. When he had promised that he would try and visit them at some future date, Marian's tears had eased.

Aware of Emma's close observation, Edward shook away the memory and spoke of his requirements entrusted to George and Marian. 'I asked that they would also oversee White Gables, my adjoining farm. Fortunately, I had arranged for another of my farms, Greenacres, to be sold during my absence, otherwise an additional burden would have been placed on their young shoulders.

'What of Stephen? I'm surprised that he is not returning to Australia with George and Marian.' Emma noticed a smile hovering around Edward's mouth when she mentioned his son's name.

'Love, Emma dear! Young love!' His smile gave way to a chuckle. 'Stephen has fallen in love with his cousin, Jane. They are to become betrothed on her sixteenth birthday, a mere two months away. He is to stay and run Highfield farm for his future father-in-law. It would have pleased... his mother.' A far away look came to his eyes as he spoke of Becky. 'She once lived at Highfield before sailing with her husband to Australia. So many years ago it now seems.'

Edward heaved a deep sigh and shook his head resignedly, still trying to fully comprehend the astonishing changes that destiny had recently meted out to him. Their implications appeared to have shattered his original arrangements to return to his farm in Australia. Instead, he would be returning to a lonely Foxleigh where memories of dearest Julie remained to remind him of her long, faithful years of waiting for his return. Sadness was still reflected in his eyes as he turned to explain young Stephen's future.

'Now that his parents are dead, Josh is anxious to concentrate on his ecclesiastical duties. After their marriage, Jane and Stephen will live and farm at Highfield. Josh, Alison and their other children are moving into Foxleigh Rectory, the home of Josh's late parents.'

Edward tried to shake off his despondency; his feeling of impending loneliness. Emma's presence helped to pacify his tormented mind, arousing in him emotions of warmth and tranquillity. 'What of your plans, Emma? Will you... remain here?' As Edward gazed into her eyes, he experienced an impassioned stirring as he became aware of his longing for Emma's love.

'I have very little option, Edward.' She shook her head sadly.

'Mother left me the house and its contents to James and myself on the understanding that I continue to live here, while I needed its shelter. So...' she shrugged her shoulders in a gesture of inevitability, '... her I shall continue to live... a lonely spinster.' Edward noticed the disconsolate look on her face as she turned to offer him a passive smile. An acceptance of her lonely fate.

'It need not be so, Emma.' She detected the passionate connotations to his words. Uncertainty was mirrored in her eyes as they sought his. Emma was frowning slightly, unsure of his meaning. Edward's eyes were radiant from his enamoured emotions. A look that was strange to Emma.

'I'm unsure... as to your meaning... Edward.' Her words were little more than a whisper, yet her heart was throbbing from suppressed excitement. She was experiencing the ecstatic feeling of – love. Something wonderful was happening to her. A strange, but wonderful emotion. She became weak from nervousness as she became aware of the love emanating from the man gazing affectionately into her eyes.

'I'm asking you to marry me, Emma. To share Foxleigh with me, my dearest.' Edward permitted an understanding smile to touch his lips as he watched a deep blush spread over his loved one's cheeks. Her colouring complemented the sparkle in her eyes and as Edward looked adoringly into them, he was aware of the joy and love that his proposal had aroused.

'Oh… Edward. Gladly and lovingly I accept your offer of marriage.' Gently and tenderly he held Emma close in his arms as their lips pressed against each others, expressing the love that burned within their aroused bodies. Their kisses flaming with desire, held promises of a precious love that they would soon be able to share.

Edward eased reluctantly from their warm embrace, anxious to discuss their wedding plans before his departure. 'I shall return to Foxleigh and…' he paused to gaze into her radiant eyes as he held her hands in his, '… finish the renovations to the Hall in readiness for – my bride.' Edward's feelings of ecstasy burned with desire as he became conscious of the precious love waiting for him after their wedding. Emma's eyes, radiant with her affectionate longing, promised a joyful future. Momentarily, he glimpsed a change in her eyes, a look of deep concern as her smile faded.

Edward, as if understanding Emma's consternation, reassured her that his need to renovate Foxleigh was for their own future requirements. Quickly he dispelled her uncertainties by explaining Julie's interrelation.

'It was Julie's last wish that I should take care of her beloved Foxleigh and also our son, George. The latter promise has already been honoured. George and Marian now have Newacres and a capital of several hundred guineas. Marian also has a half-share of her grandparents' estate. Her Uncle Josh had insisted that she receive her mother's half share for bringing peace and happiness to her grandparents' final days.

'As for the first promise… Julie, I feel sure, would have approved of the changes in progress at Foxleigh. My intention is…' he moved to the window to observe silently the distant harbour before turning towards Emma again, '… is to bring the estate to its former glory in memory of Julie's love... and faithfulness.'

'A worthwhile ideal, Edward. I shall feel honoured to have the chance of assisting you in such a worthy quest. Between us we shall make Foxleigh a loving monument to a very brave and loyal woman.

Edward, for the first time, felt that his sacrifice in not returning to his farms in Australia would not now be in vain. He was doubly convinced when he experienced the sensuous touch of his future wife's lips upon his.

Foxleigh, would survive and prosper – for many generations to come. Edward was determined to ensure that it did so, for Emma's sake... and Julie's.

The Fateful Years
Epilogue (1842)

Edward's adoring look brought a warm affectionate smile to Emma's radiant features as their carriage trundled down the drive to Homefield Hall. Their silent emotional exchanges manifested a love that remained as impassioned as in their early days of marriage.

Excited chatter shattered their intimate contemplation's as the twins caught a glimpse of the Hall through the trees. Their birth ten years ago had been a blessed event, but because of the strain their parturition had placed on Emma, there had been no more children. Julie, the quieter one of the twins, sat close beside her father, while the more boisterous May was already waving out of the carriage window.

'I can see… Aunty Maisie.' Emma reached out a restraining hand as the excited May, leaning precariously out of the carriage, waved to her waiting relations. 'And…' She stood on tip-toes in an endeavour to lean even further out, '… and Uncle Andrew… and…' Excitement became too much for her, as, joyful with laughter, she fell back onto the seat beside her smiling mother.

'Forgive my imposition, Edward, especially as you have only just arrived, but your sister's orders were most explicit. I was to ensure that you were kept away from the house… for the time being, that is. And as you are no doubt aware…' Andrew gave his brother-in-law a speculative smile, '… no one disobeys… Maisie's order.' Andrew's observation produced a chuckle from both men as they strolled across the park. 'Truth is, Edward, I'm to keep you occupied for abut an hour… So please bear with me.' Edward nodded good-naturedly.

'Do I detect a kind of… conspiracy?' His chuckle turned to laughter as he questioned Andrew, now a special friend as well as a brother-in-law. Despite their deep animosity of the past, both men were now united in a special bond of friendship, engendered by Andrew's dramatic change of character and behaviour.

From a young irresponsible rake, Andrew had matured into a kind and understanding person. As his relationship with Andrew had developed, Edward came to understand why his sister Maisie had found happiness with his compassionate and gentle-hearted brother-in-law.

'Time we returned, Edward!' He was startled as Andrew's words disturbed his brief reverie.

'Yes… of course. I must confess, however, that I am intrigued by these covert operations going on around me.'

'Ah!' Andrew nodded in the direction of the Hall as they approached the entrance. 'No doubt the reason for all these secret actions will soon became obvious.' He invited Edward to precede him into the ballroom. 'The date 20th of September… 1842…' Andrew whispered, '… should give you a clue.' Edward had not time to digest the information as he was already stepping through the door. He came to a sudden stop. For a moment he could only gasp in genuine astonishment.

Sitting around a long table were family and relations. Plates, glasses and silver cutlery sparkled on the table. Down its centre was a beautiful display of flowers, imparting their fragrant smell to the surrounding atmosphere. At a side-table, where meats, cakes and wine were arrayed in a tempting display, servants waited to serve the happy gathering.

'What… on earth… is going on?' Edward was soon enlightened. He had not mentioned his approaching fiftieth birthday, but then his sister Maisie would have no need of its reminder. As birthday greetings were showered upon him by both children and adults, he took his place at the head of the table beside his beloved Emma. Maisie, her eyes full of mischievous laughter, sat beside Andrew, who had just taken the vacant chair between her and their son, Jon. Sitting on Jon's other side was his wife Irene with their two children, Harry and Mary. Opposite his sister's family were Josh and Alison with their teenage children William and Gail. Jane, their eldest daughter, was also there with Stephen and their family… Edward's three grandchildren.

Further down the table Nelly was in the company of her son, John and his wife, Emily. If only his Uncle Ben had lived a few more weeks and been able to celebrate the occasion with Nelly and their family. Edward sighed in a moment of passing sadness.

Seeing Emma's brother, James and his family helped to ease his moment of silent sorrow. He was pleased to see their sons, Fred and Thomas there with their wives and children. A daughter each... the two youngest guests at his celebration. He promised himself to share a few moments with them later.

The five empty chairs brought a lump to his throat. He guessed they were symbolic of his absent family back in Australia. Edward's eyes misted with tears of longing as he thought of Marian and George and their long absence. He had meant to visit them, but time had passed so quickly as he had concentrated on getting Foxleigh back to its former grandeur. Next year, he would make a concerted effort to visit Marian and George and their three children... grandchildren that he had never seen.

Edward took a deep breath to control his emotions. As he did so, he heard scuffled and whispering behind him. Wondering at the interruption, he turned to ascertain its cause. He became transfixed in shocked amazement. For a brief instant, Edward thought that it was Becky standing there smiling at him. Then came realisation as Marian rushed into his open arms to accept his affectionate embrace. He noticed the tears of happiness in her eyes as she kissed him warmly. 'Oh, Pa! It's wonderful to see you again!'

George was also there, waiting patiently to introduce the younger members of their family. All were anxious to greet the man they had herd so many exciting stories about. Marian, still holding her father closely, eased aside so that Edward could welcome George and their children. It was their fist reunion since they had sailed to Australia and Newacres.

Edward was joyful to see them again and all looking so fit and well. It was certainly a wonderful birthday surprise, one that would remain forever in his memory. Especially as he was sharing it with those he loved and cherished. Edward reached for Emma's hand, thankful that the woman he loved was sharing this unforgettable and emotional celebration beside him.

A joyous occasion that reminded him just how fortunate he and also his sister, Maisie, the organiser of his fiftieth birthday celebration, were. It seemed ages since they had fled from their dead parents' cottage as fugitives. Now, he was squire of Foxleigh Hall in the village that Maisie and himself had dragged their cold, hungry and exhausted bodies to on that distant winter's evening.* As for Maisie, she had become Lady Douglass of Homefield Hall, a respected matron in the local community.

Life, however, had not always been so propitious. They had both known heartaches and experienced tragedies over the intervening years. As for the future… who could say? The winds of destiny would make those definitive decisions.

* In Book I The Winds of Destiny

A BRIEF HISTORY OF FENG SHUI

FENG SHUI FOR THE COMMON MAN

FENG SHUI MISCELLANY

THE TIMES OF INDIA

FENG SHUI AND YOU

GITA KAPOOR

Feng Shui and You

First Edition 2008

Published by
Ravi Dhariwal for the proprietors,
Bennett, Coleman & Co. Ltd.,
New Delhi

ISBN : 978-81-89906-23-8

Editorial Team : Soma B Chowdhury, Monali Banerjee

Design : Subhasish Munshi, Balkishan Verma

Printed And Bound By : Paras Offset Pvt. Ltd.

Price : Rs. 295

THE JOURNEY...

How Delhi's greatest joke teller became a Feng Shui Master!

In 2000, when I first started promoting traditional Feng Shui, the most frequently asked questions were "Feng Shui? What's that?" and "Does it work?" All that has since changed. Now many people are aware that a Feng Shui consultancy is not about hanging up symbolic objects. Rather, it is about offering a comprehensive professional service to home or business owners. They now understand that the services range from the calculation of birth data to the physical analysis of residences, charting of energy distribution (Chi flow) and providing solutions and recommendations to bring about better luck and fortune.

For most believers, hanging crystals and activating their relationship corners are deemed as having their place "Feng Shuied"! This is a fallacy as there is a lack of exposure to traditional authentic methods. A lot of "fake practitioners" have been jumping on the bandwagon, eager to promote Feng Shui quickly to a keen audience. To achieve a level of competence as a Feng Shui Master, there is a definite need for more professional training in the traditional classical methods as practised by the Chinese for thousands of years.

The cynical might disregard Feng Shui as a lot of "mumbo-jumbo" or "New Age malarkey"! But everyone knows a house with good "Chi" when they step in through the front door. These houses are the ones that have a charm that makes you want to stay and stay. They are the ones with the pulling power of a lighthouse!

Yet, there are some homes which create feelings of discomfort and can be best described as having "negative energy". Feng Shui assists with suggestions in which one can energize areas of one's home with a positive purpose. Remember, Feng Shui deals with creating a balance. Therefore, in addition to neutralizing negative energy, you can go on to either create or activate the flow of positive energy in your home and pave the way to a better and happier future.

In conclusion, my journey has not yet ended — in fact, it has just begun! As someone who has become so obsessed and passionate about Feng Shui and other Chinese metaphysical sciences like Bazi (Chinese astrology), I-Ching, Mian Xiang (Face Reading), etc, I continue to learn with my Master Joey Yap of the Mastery Academy of Chinese Metaphysics. I hope that one day, I too will be able to achieve some level of the "mastery" he so successfully teaches his eager students around the world during his various ongoing courses each year.

Had it not been for his "generosity" in spreading awareness of this science, perhaps my "journey" and the "journey of million other masters around the globe" would not have begun....

ACKNOWLEDGEMENTS

Dedicated with thanks to my beloved parents Shiela and Sohan Chopra and my wonderful family, for giving me an excellent foundation and enabling me to steer the course of my life.

Thanks to Joey Yap, my Feng Shui Master in Malaysia, for graciously imparting his vast knowledge on metaphysical studies including Feng Shui, Chinese astrology, Face Reading and I-Ching to all his keen students, including me, worldwide. For those interested in these subjects, Joey is the Founder and CEO of the Mastery Academy of Chinese Metaphysics — a global institution for the study of Classical Feng Shui and other Chinese metaphysical subjects.

Thanks to Lillian Too and Grand Master Yap Cheng Hai of Malaysia, who first introduced me to the fascinating world of Feng Shui.

A word of thanks to Sherry Merchant, my mentor, who guides, inspires and supports me at every juncture.

Thank you, Dr Richard TC Frost for your wise counsel and support, and for cheering me on.

My thanks goes out to the *Times of India* team and all the *Delhi Times* editors (particularly Sabina Sehgal Saikia) for giving me a national platform to actively introduce the concept of Feng Shui to readers across the country through my articles, and for their constant support in promoting this science. A word of mention for

Purnima Sharma, Jyothi Prabhakar, Rajiv Rawal and Subbu for publishing my articles on a weekly basis in the Sunday edition of the *Times of India*.

I would like to thank Madhulita Mohanty and Soma B Chowdhury of the Times Group Books for their unflagging hard work, patience and cheerful demeanour in gently "pushing me" to dwell on the subject and meet deadlines to make this book happen.

Finally, thanks to all my wonderful Feng Shui clients who have become close friends. It is their firm faith and trust in my counsel that inspires me to scale even greater heights.

INTRODUCTION TO FENG SHUI

WHAT IS FENG SHUI?

Feng Shui means "Wind and Water" and has been used for thousands of years in China and the Far East as a method for determining the most appropriate locations for a harmonious life. These locations can be the site of a building, the floor plan of a house or just the layout of a room.

WHAT CAN FENG SHUI DO FOR ME?

Feng Shui affects every aspect of our lives and the way it is applied can be both beneficial and detrimental to the way we live and the surrounding environment. Feng Shui is not a religion, although some of its advocates may consider it a part of their religious practice. It is not necessary to follow any religion to understand or practice Feng Shui. Feng Shui is not just a philosophy as it also encompasses many practical tools and techniques. It is not a belief system. Asking someone if they believe Feng Shui is like asking them if they believe in the weather. It is not a question of faith, but a fact of life.

WHAT ARE THE VARIOUS SCHOOLS OF FENG SHUI?

Feng Shui has been around for thousands of years, and over many centuries different schools of Feng Shui have developed. Each school has a slightly different approach to the subject, although the basic principles are the same. The following sections outline the three main schools of Feng Shui:

Form School: This school focuses on landscape contours, along with the shapes of hills and watercourses. It is concerned with the auspicious positioning of buildings and burial sites, which requires that the hills provide protection from the wind (Feng) and there is provision for a good water (Shui) supply without flooding. It can also be considered the ancient Chinese version of surveying. The main concerns within the Form School are finding auspicious landforms called the Tiger and the Dragon. These are found by looking at the contours of the hills surrounding a site and determining whether their layout will bring good luck or bad luck.

Compass School: This style of Feng Shui uses the Eight Trigrams of the I-Ching and relates them to the eight points of the compass. These are laid out to form the eight-sided Pa Kua (often called the Bagua), which is used to interpret the auspicious and inauspicious locations for buildings, house floor plans and room layouts.

Black Hat Sect School: This is a modern version of Feng Shui developed in the USA as a hybrid of Tibetan Buddhism, Taoism and traditional Feng Shui. In this school, a Pa Kua is used, but it is based on the direction of the front door, rather than the compass directions. The house or room is divided into eight sectors, each having a bearing on an aspect of life that might need enhancement.

Whatever school one follows, the underlying principle of Feng Shui is to live in harmony with your environment so that the energy surrounding you works for you rather than against you. After all, why swim against the tide?

TIME & SPACE FENG SHUI OR XUAN KONG FLYING STARS

The most authentic Feng Shui is when a Flying Star analysis of the house or commercial property is done. What many are not aware of is that a premise also has a horoscope based on the year it was "born" (constructed). Based on the facing direction of the house, a Flying Stars Chart — which indicates the kind of energies that are flying in all nine palaces of the house namely N, S, E, W, NW, SW, SE, NE and the Centre — is prepared. It is the combination of these stars which creates the good or bad luck which affects the residents. There are, in all, 81 Flying Star combinations, and one of the amazing aspects of the Flying Star technique is its ability to forecast outcomes based on the interaction or combination of stars.

Flying Star Feng Shui is the system of Chinese Classical Feng Shui that studies how our environment and fortune are affected by various energies, which are changing over Time and Space. In this system, we focus our attention on nine different kinds of energies, identified by the numbers 1 to 9. We also understand that each kind of energy has special properties, some of which will bring prosperity and some that will bring misfortune. These energies are dynamic and moving constantly over time in a fixed pattern. As such, their position and impact at a certain moment of time is predictable. For example, the worst energy is Number 5, which means misfortune and is present in the South location in the current Year of the Rat, ie, 2008. The South location refers to the South of a house, apartment, building, city or country.

Using the Flying Stars Chart, the prosperity and human fortune prospects of any residence or commercial building can be investigated and determined. The nine numbers represent nine stars and signify special combinations of energies that exist. In different periods of time, the star can be either harmful or fortunate. The important question is, when are the stars timely? For example, during Period 7, the Number 7 Red Star was the most timely star. However, in Period 8, the Number 7 Star is unfortunate while the Number 8 Star is the most fortunate star. The combinations of these numbers are studied in the context of good/poor human fortune and good/poor money luck.

There are also different levels of Flying Stars. Besides the year star which affects us for one whole year, like Number 8 in the East during the entire year of 2008, we also have month stars and day stars which will have an influence on our lives for a month or day, respectively. As such, at a certain day in a certain location, three stars are present. If they are all bad stars, then misfortune may happen in such a location on such a day.

How do we read such a chart? The emphasis is more on the pair of numbers on top of each square. They represent two types of energies in each location. The number on the right is called the Water Star and represents money and prosperity. The number on the left is called the Mountain Star and represents human harmony. In Flying Star Feng Shui, time is divided into 20-year cycles. Each cycle carries a number. The current 20-year cycle is called Period 8, so the Number 8 represents the most prosperous energy today. When Period 8 expires on February 3, 2024, the Period 9 energy will take over, and hence Number 9 is also important today as it represents future incoming energy. However, accurate Feng Shui evaluation requires accurate assessment and measurement on site. Without such an opportunity, most of the above analysis can only be based on assumptions that may be totally incorrect.

If we get our Feng Shui right, it can bring great fulfilment. It can help us to harmonize our lives, perform better, achieve more and be more creatively intuitive. When there is harmony in our home and workplace and correct focus in our life, good fortune, growth, longevity and prosperity will naturally follow.

A BRIEF HISTORY OF FENG SHUI

FENG SHUI — MOTHER OF NATURAL SCIENCES

Feng Shui (pronounced Fung Shway) has often been referred to as the Mother of Natural Sciences. It originated in China and is as old as the culture itself. The earliest form of Feng Shui was more concerned with the auspicious orientations of the tombs of the dead rather than the homes of the living. It was believed that a good burial site would bring peace and prosperity to the descendants of the deceased.

Landforms (geomancy) play an important part in Feng Shui. An ideal configuration of a site is called the "armchair" effect. This means, that like an armchair, you have a high back for a secure support, symbolized by the Black Tortoise. To the East of the site is the Green Dragon and to the West, the White Tiger, with the Dragon side slightly higher than the Tiger side. The front, which is the South, is referred to as a "footstool" and is symbolized by the Red Phoenix. In Feng Shui terms, the Phoenix is described as an unobstructed view or a pool of water. Ideally, the water should not be stagnant, move towards or pass the site in a way a Feng Shui Practitioner deems inauspicious.

In Feng Shui, the Lo'pan (Chinese Feng Shui compass) is used to analyse the orientation of a site in relationship to the main door, the bed and the stove. The Lo'pan is an intricate circular object of a simple compass surrounded by movable rings encrypted with Chinese characters. There is a maximum of 36 tiers, with each tier having its own purpose for divination. It is then divided into eight sections or trigrams. The Eight Trigrams are further developed into 64 hexagrams of the I-Ching with the astrological information of the Ten Heavenly Stems, Twelve Earthly Branches, the Five Elements, geological and celestial bodies.

According to the principle of Feng Shui, a geographic site that attracts water is optimal, followed by a site that catches the wind. These two elements affect and shape our environment, which is alive with the hidden force of Chi (energy). Chi is a difficult concept to define. It is often described as vital breath or life energy. It is found in the environment and is carried by the flow of air. Strong winds can disperse Chi and water can retain it. Barriers like mountains, buildings, walls or even furniture can block the movement of Chi.

The ancient Chinese believed that the production, development and alteration of everything in the universe were the result of Yin and Yang interacting with each other. This interaction of Yin and Yang can also be described within the Five Elements. These elements are Wood, Fire, Earth, Metal and Water. They make up the universe, and contain within it colours, shapes, numbers, organs, variables of time and space, seasons, directions, emotions and so on. For example:

METAL/NORTH-WEST & WEST/White, Grey, Gold, Silver/Autumn/Circle/Spicy/Sorrow

WOOD/SOUTH-EAST & EAST/Green, Blue/Spring/Rectangle/Sour/Anger

WATER/NORTH/Black, Dark Blue/Winter/Wavy Lines/Salty/Fear

FIRE/SOUTH/Red/Summer/Triangle/Bitter/Joy

EARTH/NORTH-EAST, SOUTH-WEST & CENTRE/Brown, Yellow/Square/Sweet/Pensiveness

THE FIVE ELEMENTS OF FENG SHUI

In the world of metaphysics, the universe is believed to be made up of five types of matter: Metal, Wood, Water, Fire and Earth. These five types of matter are also referred to as the Five Elements.

Everything surrounding us, whether tangible or intangible, can be classified using any of the Five Elements. From shapes, sounds and colours to a person's attitude, character, body organs, sickness, living environment, family background, relationship with family members, romance, career, wealth and reputation, the list is endless. Everything, yes everything, is solely the product of the magnetic forces that's created when these Five Elements interact.

These Five Elements are very closely related to each other and their relationship can be explained using the Cycle of Birth and Cycle of Destruction.

The basic theory behind the Five Elements, however, can be summed up by three cyclical interactions. The Creative Cycle, the

CYCLE OF BIRTH	CYCLE OF DESTRUCTION
Metal produces Water (when melted).	Metal can cut Wood.
Water can help tree (Wood) to grow.	Water can extinguish Fire.
Wood can help Fire to burn.	Wood can break the ground.
Fire can help to produce dust (Earth).	Fire can melt Metal.
Earth can help mineral (Metal) to form.	Earth can absorb Water.

Destructive Cycle and the little mentioned, Reductive Cycle. The Creative Cycle works in this way: Water nourishes Wood (trees and plants need water to grow); Wood feeds Fire; Fire creates Earth (ash); Earth creates Metal (mined from the earth); Metal creates Water (condensation on the outside of a metal cup).

The Destructive Cycle does not literally mean "to destroy", but rather to restrain through neutralizing, in order to keep each other in check and balance. The cycle is as follows: Wood causes upheaval in Earth; Earth obstructs Water; Water puts out Fire; Fire melts Metal; Metal chops down Wood.

The Reductive Cycle is used as a Feng Shui cure. It corrects the imbalances that are seen in the Destructive Cycle.

WHAT IS FENG SHUI?
— THE CHINESE VIEW OF THE LIVING EARTH

Feng Shui advocates living in harmony with the Earth's environment and energy lines so that a balance is maintained with the forces of nature. It contends that the environment is crowded with powerful, but invisible energy lines, some of which are auspicious, bringing great good fortune, while some are pernicious and hostile, bringing death and the destruction of happiness. Feng Shui offers ways of arranging the home so that these energy lines become harmonious and bring prosperity and harmony, rather than loss and discord.

Feng Shui also instructs us in the clever harnessing of auspicious energy lines, generally referred to as Sheng Chi (the Dragon's cosmic breath), making sure they meander gently through the home and accumulate and settle, thereby bringing good fortune. Feng Shui teaches us to avoid, deflect and dissolve inauspicious energy lines, also known as Sha Chi (the killing breath) caused by

secret poison arrows in the surroundings. One is warned strenuously against sleeping, working, sitting, eating and generally living in places that are hit by these pernicious hostile energy lines.

CLASSICAL FENG SHUI... THE FOUR CELESTIAL ANIMALS

When choosing a property or house to live in, a fundamental tenet of Feng Shui advises you to live with your back to a mountain (Black Turtle) whose hills provide support. So, if your home is backed by something solid and firm like a hill or a building that stimulates the hill, then you will have support all your life. Thus, the first part of Classical Feng Shui involves having the mountain or building behind your house.

The second half of Classical Feng Shui advocates having water in front of your home. This can also mean open space in front of your house, or the Crimson Phoenix whose undulating hills represent opportunity, so that your vision is not hampered and your horizon is visible. If there is also a view of water, it brings auspicious energy to your living area. Moreover, if the river is slow moving and meandering, then good energy has a chance to settle and accumulate before entering your home, thereby allowing you to partake of its essence. Needless to say, the cleaner, fresher and more sparkling the water, the greater the good fortune it will bring.

However, this comes with a warning. Though water in Feng Shui is best associated with good fortune and wealth, for this good fortune to manifest itself, water must activate the appropriate energies, sometimes working in concert with a supporting enhancement in a secondary location. Misfortune may arise when water is placed improperly. Various methods of water placement exist, and while some practices are widely known, others remain closely guarded secrets. Therefore, water should always be placed in the appropriate location only after consultation with a Feng Shui Master or Practitioner.

The third and fourth half of Classical Feng Shui says that on either side of the house, in an armchair formation, one should have hills that bring abundance and prosperity (Green Dragon) and hills that protect (White Tiger). If all four criteria are met, one can safely assume that the house/property has good Feng Shui.

YIN & YANG

According to the Chinese, all things in the universe are either female Yin or male Yang, the dark Yin or the bright Yang. Yin and Yang together make up the wholeness of the universe, which includes Heaven and Earth. Yin and Yang breathe meaning into each other, for without one, the other cannot exist. When there is balance between Yin and Yang, the wholeness of the universe is represented and there is good balance, prosperity, health, well-being, and happiness.

Feng Shui practice always includes a Yin and Yang analysis of room space, land configurations, sunlight and shade, dampness and dryness, bright and pale colours and solids and fluids. Rooms that are too Yin are inauspicious as there is insufficient life energy to bring prosperity. Rooms that are too Yang are said to be damaging because there is too much energy, causing accidents and huge losses. Only rooms or homes with balanced Yin and Yang can be auspicious, and will be made even more auspicious if there is a good balance of Yin and Yang outside.

Yin and Yang are complementary opposites — one cannot exist without the other. Yin/Yang is always relative. What is Yin and Yang in one situation can sometimes be the opposite in another. Yin is dark, Yang is light; Yang is active, Yin is passive; Yang is male, Yin is female; Yin is sinking, Yang is rising. As soon as there's a Yang, there's a Yin. It is instantaneous. When they come together, they merge and try to interpenetrate each other. Yin and Yang should exist naturally in a dynamic state of balance and harmony. Feng Shui adjusts the imbalances that we inadvertently create in our own environment.

HOMES THAT ARE TOO YIN

Houses and buildings built too near graveyards, hospitals, prisons, slaughter houses and police stations are too Yin because such places are associated with the Yin energies of death. The same diagnosis is often pronounced on buildings that are located on land that previously housed these places, making it advisable to research the history of your home. Rooms that never see sunlight, are damp, decorated only in shades of grey and blue, narrow and cramped, always closed and silent, or those which have been occupied for a long time by chronically sick people, have too much Yin energy. They cause sickness and bad luck to the residents. People who stay in rooms that have an excess of Yin energy suffer more than their fair share of misfortune and seem to be shrouded by a cloak of ill luck.

Remedies for a Yin Room

Orient your main door so that it faces away from the Yin structure or the building. Do not have windows that open towards these Yin structures. Paint your door a bright red to signify strong, powerful Yang energy. Make sure your porch is always well lit and keep the light on all the time. Bring in the Yang sunlight by cutting back shady trees. Plant trees with luscious vegetation and grow flowers in the garden. Put garden lights all around the house. Paint your fence a bright, happy colour. Make sure you have a red roof. Introduce Yang objects like boulders, pebbles and stones into the garden.

Repaint the walls with a bright colour like pink, yellow or red. Bring in the light. White walls are very Yang because they are bright. Throw away heavy drapes and curtains and bring sunlight into the room. Use happy colours for your curtains and bright colours for duvets, bed sheets and other soft furnishings. Keep the windows open. If trees are blocking the light from outside, cut them back. Install plenty of lights and keep at least one turned on continuously. Keep the radio or television turned on as sound, life and laughter bring in Yang energy. Have vases of freshly cut flowers in the room. Introduce movement with mobile hangings that move with the gentle motion of the breeze and wind chimes as they symbolize life energy.

HOMES THAT ARE TOO YANG

Buildings that are constantly exposed to bright sunlight or heat of any kind are said to have an excess of Yang energy and bring accidents, disasters and grave misfortune. If you are living too near an electrical transmitter, or you are within view of a large factory or refinery chimneys that belch noxious smoke throughout the day, there is too much Yang energy.

It is advisable to move from such a place, but if you have no choice, then it is necessary, indeed vital, that you combat the excess Yang energy by introducing Yin structures or surrounding yourself with the colours and characteristics of Yin. Water is one of the best cures for too much Yang energy. Creating a small pond of water in the garden will effectively counter the Yang energy.

Remedies for a Yang Room

Paint your door in any shade of blue, as this is a Yin colour. Select muted, cool colours for your interior décor. Avoid too much noise in the house, and never have a red light turned on. Introduce water features like miniature fountains. Hang paintings of lakes and rivers in your home. Maintain a good lawn in your garden. Paint railings and gates black, as this too is a Yin colour.

And finally, remember that a room should have both elements of Yin and Yang but never too much of one or the other. Have music and life in the room, but not all the time. Have peace and quiet in the room, but not to the extent that it becomes lifeless. Opt for a cool décor of blues and greys, but also incorporate a splash of Yang colour which may be represented by a vase of red roses or a painting of a sunrise.

Remember that Feng Shui is a subtle blend of opposite energies that complement each other. What you should always strive for is the harmony of opposites. This is the fundamental guiding principle of Yin and Yang.

EAST *vs.* WEST

Where does one begin? In trying to write about the science of Feng Shui in the context of architecture, I believe the perfect ground for understanding this ancient discipline lies in your backyard and your home, the core of personal well-being and one's family root. How much of our home is deeply rooted in Eastern and Western philosophies architecturally? Is Feng Shui in coexistence with how we live or is design the integral key?

It could be that architecture and Feng Shui may be in direct conflict with one another. But it all must stem from a core idea or concept. Let us begin. Designing a home requires a variety of essential programmes — the entrance, the living room, the bedrooms, the toilets, the dining room and the kitchen. How we place these specific programmes in relation to each other depends on another set of criteria — the site (square footage), cost, material, location and yes, even time.

When I refer to time, I am suggesting the time available to build in retrospect to the changing seasons. Winter seasons tend to halt construction due to freezing soils. Similarly, in the tropics, tropical storms may force a slowdown in building and inadvertently affect budget and unnecessary labour.

Let us now see the basics of Feng Shui and how this fits into the equation.

A clear, open space in front of your entrance with a solid higher ground behind it refers to the Bright Hall and the Black Turtle. This suggests the symbolic nature of opportunity opening out before you and a sturdy foundation to build upon. Architecturally, by creating an open space in front of your home, it creates an opportunity for natural daylight to filter into your home. This gives you a feeling of space and freedom. This main entry area would generally contain your public space, that is, your living room or gallery. The back would typically house the services for the home, kitchen, toilets and servant's quarters due to its secluded nature.

Another rule I found was that the road should never be higher than your bedroom. This is simple enough to understand. Why deal with noise from the traffic and pollution, when the bedroom reflects the epitome of one's private life?

Don't sleep in front of the door. Why deal with someone looking over you when you are asleep?

Place water in the North. This sounds pretty sensible as we can passively cool the home through the use of winds.

Wood to the East? The rising sun comes to mind. Imagine waking up to the breath of fresh air with the warm rays of the sun stroking your every movement. Wood creates the perception of home, the idea of being back to nature.

So technically, we can slowly see that you can connect formal space planning to even the basics of Feng Shui. Therefore, let's investigate the ideals of living a little deeper, and find out how to create a symbiotic relationship that suggests harmony when we combine architecture and the Oriental art of Feng Shui.

A HARMONIOUS ENVIRONMENT

Like it or not, we are sensitive to our surroundings. Our surroundings make us feel and respond to the world in a certain way. These responses affect our health, our career choices, and our marriages, as well as our ability to learn and develop rewarding relationships. According to Feng Shui experts, there are solutions or "cures" for difficulties in these areas, difficulties made worse by our over-stressed, sleep-deprived society. Feng Shui is the Chinese art of creating harmony and balance in the environment. It involves the placement of furnishings in the home or office, the use of property or land, the planting of trees and plants, as well as the use of water and nature to add energy to our lives. Feng Shui, in today's terms, means using our environment in a positive way to create a healthy, prosperous life and avoid the damaging effects of modern technology. By reconnecting with natural elements like water, stones and plants, we can be revitalized by the subtle currents of life force and beauty that flow through the landscape. In this way, we can nourish our human spirit and cherish the natural wonders around us. A home, for instance, should offer its occupants a beneficial connection with the environment if it were near a source of fresh water and protected from harsh winds. This common-sense approach to building occurs in most cultures in the general sense of relating with the earth as sacred space. Feng, Chinese for "wind", refers to moving air. This motion is associated with the cosmic breath or Chi that animates all of nature. Chi is the force that links man and his surroundings and is also known as the human spirit and universal energy. Feng Shui harnesses and enhances environmental Chi, say the experts. This channeling improves the flow of energy in our living and working spaces as well as in our bodies, thus improving our life and destiny. To harmonize the energy flow in landscape and buildings, Feng Shui Practitioners work with three types of Chi: in the earth, in the atmosphere, and in our bodies. This promotes the health and good fortune of the inhabitants. Feng Shui can be thought of as "environmental acupuncture" because it regulates atmospheric and earthly Chi the way acupuncture regulates the flow of Chi in the human body.

FENG SHUI & CHI FLOW

Aches and pains in our body are the physical messages sent by the human body to alert us about the disharmonious flow of Chi (energy). Study this example: Commuters delayed by a train derailment suffer inconvenience. Until the train is repaired at the point of derailment, the coach is unable to either return commuters to the home station or reach its destination.

It is the same with Chi. Until the pressure point is worked on to release the disharmony, the flow of Chi will cause aches and pains. Chi flow should be harmonious. However, when it hits a vulnerable spot, it accumulates at that point and cannot flow as intended, causing a "derailment". We can do well by encouraging the constant flow of healthy Chi in our body. Striving for ultimate health and longevity is the art of being in harmony with nature.

FEELING THE WIND

We tend to understand energies better when we can feel them physically. The wind is one such example. It makes sense to build a wall to stop the cold winds from the North and to live near water which provides transportation as well as enables plants to grow and fish to thrive.

To enjoy good household luck, the focus has always been on finding the physical shapes of the ideal landscape that correspond exactly with that required for a comfortable and safe "cave" in that location. This search for a safe cave goes back to cave dwelling

times. The ideal configuration is one of a supporting hill or higher ground at the rear. The left and right arm of land on either side of this higher land at the rear must look like a basin. In front, the space must be open and fluid. This is also the place where the greatest amount of good Chi accumulates.

In the context of a city, the quality of Chi generated for a city is related to its landscape. A city can have lively and strong Chi because of the orientation of water and mountains around the city. The winding watercourse over an undulating landscape promotes the build-up of Chi, which, in turn, promotes communication and prosperity. The presence of both water and nearby mountains makes them good locations for favourable Chi. This allows buildings to maximize the positive Chi.

CHI: ONE AND THE SAME THING

The notion that Chi is everything and nothing, positive and negative, is much more difficult to grasp. There is no difference between the physical feeling of the wind and Chi itself. It is one and the same thing.

On the climatic level, it is the energy carried by the wind and water. If Chi is wind or air, then wherever air goes, Chi goes. It penetrates through brick and mortar as they are permeous substances. Like germs, Chi can penetrate through certain structures. A room without windows is not necessarily unaffected by Chi. Every building with some sort of entrance, exit and ventilation will allow Chi to penetrate.

Chi is dynamic. Not only can its pace be slowed down or increased, but it can also be changed and manoeuvred. Windows and doors create less obstruction for Chi to flow. They can actually create a new direction for Chi flow — we can manipulate where it comes from and where it flows to by using windows and doors. Remember at all times, we should strive for harmonious Chi flow to create a more balanced environment, either externally or internally.

QUICK FIX FENG SHUI: TIPS TO ACCELERATE YOUR CHI

Clutter: Remove nine unwanted items daily. Do it consistently for ninety days. When you feel better and lighter, increase it to 18. After ninety days, repeat with 27 items and so on until there is no clutter left. Then go back to the basics and remove nine unwanted items daily.

Slow pace of business: Get a bell, go around the premises privately and ring it loudly to invite customers.

Inadequate career advancement: Sit facing your Sheng Chi (success) direction. This is calculated by your Kua number based on your date of birth. The formula for finding your Kua number is provided later on in the book.

Negative energy: Burn incense sticks, walk around and say a prayer to your God depending on your religion, asking for guidance and removal of all negative energy. Prayer is powerful: It works.

Nothing seems to move forward: Be a giver. When things seem to be stagnant, re-examine yourself. Perhaps it is time to engage in volunteer charity work or donate money or unwanted items to charity. Let everything flow.

Need support: Have a wall behind your desk for support. Nothing is stronger than the "mountain" that stands behind you.

Need protection: Hang feathers that you find near the front door.

Need excitement: Carry a big, red purse if you are a woman. If you are a man, carry a red wallet!!

FENG SHUI — WHAT IT IS & WHAT IT IS NOT

Feng Shui is a combination of interior decorating, architecture, town planning and environmental improvement. It places a great deal of emphasis on issues like proper seating, solar orientation, water orientation, the prevailing breeze and proper orientation for usage. Feng Shui is not "New Age" or the latest "fad". Recent archaeological finds show evidence that Feng Shui was practised as long as 10,000 years ago. Feng Shui is not a religion. It is a theory that arose from the Ruist and Taoist philosophies that dominated China for thousands of years. These philosophies propose that man is part of the universe he lives in. Man should respect what Mother Nature bestows on him and act in accordance with Heaven. In fact, they say, what man should do is protect the environment. The philosophies further asserted that man's life path is influenced by Heaven Luck, Earth Luck and Human Luck. In other words, man's life path can be described by three elements: Time, Space and Action. The Time element relates to when a person was born. The Space element relates to the place of birth of a man and the place where he lives (ie, in India, Paris or in the USA). The element of Action relates to what a man does. If a man does the right thing at the right time and right place, he will be fortunate. Otherwise, he will encounter hardships. Earth Luck can be enhanced through Feng Shui by finding a place that is in harmony with nature and is proper to live and work in. This is the art of Feng Shui. Feng Shui works with Chi. Since mass and energy are interchangeable, Chi can be in the form of matter or energy or a combination of the two. Therefore, Chi can be visible, partially visible, invisible or partially invisible. We find this Chi classified into five types by the ancient Chinese: Wood, Fire, Earth, Metal and Water. Simply said, Feng Shui is the study of the distribution of this Chi and the quality of this Chi determined by time, position and location. We can validate this distribution through physics, mathematics, astronomy and geography. This Chi distribution is affected by the surrounding forms as well as the various combinations that are determined through mathematical formulae. As with the introduction of many technologies, Feng Shui was introduced to the West as a very simple system. That system, albeit simple, is also less effective than the long-time or long-term system which we call Time-Space Feng Shui, Conventional Feng Shui or Traditional Feng Shui. It is important to know the difference.

The Time-Space Feng Shui Practitioner will engage in the following tasks:

- Study the surroundings to determine the suitability of location and the shapes of the surrounding mountains, buildings, roads and water features.
- Work with the landscaping so that it enhances the fortunate Chi and suppresses the unfortunate Chi.
- Measure the way the building is sitting and facing.
- Calculate the types and locations of various Chi on the floor plan and survey.
- Design the interior colour and furniture placement to enhance the fortunate Chi and suppress the unfortunate Chi.
- Calculate the Life Gua of each family member of the family to determine the suitability of bedrooms and living areas.
- Work with the interior and exterior of business houses to bring balance and harmony to the work environment, thereby creating more advantageous space for prosperity and health.

With proper Feng Shui, most environments can be optimized for creating what human beings are most interested in: good relationships, good health, prosperity and wealth. Inside those optimized environments, we can further utilize our Heaven Luck and develop our Human Luck with greater facility and ease.

HEAVEN, HUMAN & EARTH LUCK

Human life is affected by three major influences: Heaven, Human and Earth. These three forces have been studied for thousands of years throughout Asia. Natural systems have evolved which reveal their influences in daily life. Chinese astrology, either the Four Pillars of Destiny or the Purple Star Fate calculation, reveal Heaven's influence. Earth's influences are harmonized by Feng Shui, and humanity transforms life with hard work, personal development and Qi-Gong cultivation. Professional life consultants or Feng Shui Masters or Practitioners harmonize these three influences to optimize life.

Feng Shui is the ancient Chinese art of living in harmony with one's environment. It has evolved over thousands of years from a folk art to a sophisticated system containing Asian philosophy, metaphysics, astronomy and universal cosmology. There are many styles of Feng Shui practised throughout the world, some of them generally blending old and new age trends and fads under the umbrella of Feng Shui. One ancient form practised by professional consultants is Xuan Kong or Flying Star Feng Shui. This is based on the principles of the classic Chinese book, *The I-Ching*. Flying Star Feng Shui is the most common form practised throughout Asia and has been relatively unknown until the past few years. It is now growing rapidly in India and in the Western communities including the USA and UK.

Flying Star Feng Shui includes all aspects of traditional Feng Shui, but emphasizes two principles: Time and Space. Time includes specific patterns of Chi related to cycles of time. Space is the directional orientation of a structure and is traditionally determined with a Lo'pan (a Chinese Feng Shui compass). These two aspects separate Flying Star from all other styles of Feng Shui. Time and Space combine to create a dynamic Chi field in a home or in an office. Tools used to evaluate or calculate this Chi field are Yin/Yang, Five Elements and the Eight Trigrams. These principles represent universal cosmology and a language that reveals influences of Chi in a home or in an office. These tools are similar to a CAT scan or MRI as they reveal invisible influences. The information obtained is used to either reduce or harmonize unfavourable influences and optimize favourable influences.

The classic book, *Yi Jing/The I-Ching*, or *Book of Changes* emphasizes a major universal principle. Life consists of perpetual change and to obtain happiness and health, one must learn to harmonize with the changing nature of life. Flying Star Feng Shui is centralized around the changing nature of life. This is the strength of this ancient art and metaphysical science.

FENG PHOOEY — DISPELLING SOME MYTHS

Many people are turning to Feng Shui to maximize their investments in a home. Since this ancient art is so magical and complex, it is easy for uninformed individuals to be scammed. Take time to learn a little about Feng Shui and what you should be wary of.

First, you would want to be comfortable with your Feng Shui adviser. Once you feel you have found a suitable candidate, ask him/her to provide you with a list of references. You would want the names of people the Feng Shui Practitioner has worked with recently, as well as of those who he/she had contact with several months ago. If you only talk to recent clients, they might not have had time to get used to the new arrangement yet, and may not be experiencing any results, either positive or negative. You will be more confident in your decision once you have spoken to several former clients.

Second, make sure you avoid spending any ridiculous amount of money on a room that doesn't really affect you. A practitioner once told a family the bathroom energy was wrong. How often are you going to be in the bathroom? You don't live there! Don't spend Rs.50,000 remodelling a room that does not matter. You should concentrate on areas where you spend most of your time. If you spend eight hours a day in the living room watching Zee Movies, then this room is the important one!

There are usually ways around major remodelling costs. If, for example, you open the door to see a staircase, this is bad Feng Shui. If a practitioner tells you to move the front door, decide if it's really necessary. Perhaps you could just use the back door as your main entrance. Understand the need to make major remodelling changes before handing over the cheque to an interior designer!

Anyone familiar with Feng Shui has probably heard about the power of mirrors and their ability to redirect negative energy and multiply positive energy. This is not true, and any practitioner who insists it is, is incorrect. While mirrors do have a purpose in Feng Shui, redirecting energy is not something they are capable of. Thousands of years ago, mirrors were made of polished brass and, therefore, represented the metal element. Metal elements, not reflections, are capable of making a difference in energy. Modern mirrors contain infinitesimal amount of metal and do not have the same effect as intended.

Try to avoid purchasing too many talismans because they have nothing to do with Feng Shui at all. Feng Shui is very logical. Everything has to make absolute sense or it won't work.

If you decide that you'd rather try Feng Shui yourself, keep in mind the fact that you're dealing with a serious science and that if you don't know what you're doing, you can make your living area incredibly uncomfortable. Just because you bought a book from a bookstore doesn't mean the author knew what she or he was talking about. There are many books out there because they're very easy to write and sell, but a lot of them are filled with illogical things. Trusting in a Feng Shui book is like living your day based on a basic horoscope in the newspaper. How accurate can it possibly be? The only way to get good results is to have a personal Feng Shui reading done by a professional and certified practitioner. Remember the golden rule, though: Before hiring a Feng Shui adviser, make sure you understand a little about it. And remember, Feng Shui cannot remedy a person; it can only bring the best out of what is already there.

FENG SHUI — MAGIC OR SCIENCE?

Feng Shui's methodologies work like Western scientific inquiry. Practitioners observe and record, formulate mathematical models of structures and report findings in both technical and layman's language. Any other sufficiently skilled practitioner can access and assess the work, which is essential to any truly scientific system. A competent Feng Shui Practitioner can track energy potentialities in a structure over a vast span of time if given basic reference points. The initial conditions are critical to calculations. In other words, tell a practitioner the construction date of a structure and its precise orientation and he or she can calculate its energy potential at any point in the past or future. A practitioner can track bifurcation points or nodes in phase space and offer potentialities. That is, a practitioner can take a building's mathematical model and track energy shifts based upon remodelling or other outside interventions like 1-, 20- and 60-year cycles. Feng Shui may not be couched in the same mathematical formulae and terms a physicist or complexity theorist would use, but it is definitely a scientific explanation of what goes on in a structure over time.

Many people question: How do I know if Feng Shui will work for me? Answer: You don't. All you can do is try it and find out. This is a question which is on everyone's minds and lips. However, it is impossible to predict exactly what results you will see from Feng Shui or how long the results will take to manifest. Sometimes, results are dramatic and seen within days or even hours! At other times, it can take weeks or months for the energy to shift. Bear in mind that Feng Shui is a tool, not a magic wand. There are many other factors determining what happens in your life. These include your karma and astrology, and very importantly, your own attitude and actions. If your attitude and expectations are rigid and inflexible, even making powerful changes to the Feng Shui of your home may not result in a noticeable improvement in the situation. This is because you are the critical factor in the equation, and your mental and/or emotional rigidity is interfering with the manifestation of a desired change. Another thing that can happen is that there is a very obvious shift in the situation, but the results of Feng Shui are not exactly what you had in mind. This doesn't mean Feng Shui is not working. It may mean that what you think you want is not what you need, or that your transition will evolve through a series of shifts over a longer period of time. Your issues and priorities can and should change over time. This means that you can come back to Feng Shui again and again to help make your progress easier. If you approach Feng Shui with an attitude of flexibility, an open mind and a sense of adventure, you are well on your way to a successful and rewarding Feng Shui experience. Rigid expectations, fear of the unknown and resistance to change can stop Feng Shui from working, no matter how much time, effort, and money you put into it. So my advice to you is, stop resisting changes. Feng Shui can and will work for you. Trust me.

THE GOLDEN RULE OF FENG SHUI

In Feng Shui, it is your Heaven Luck that is the predominant factor that rules your life. The Feng Shui of your home and workplace can manipulate your Earth Luck. It suppresses — but not eliminates — the negative aspects in your life, and it can enhance positive aspects. For example:

- If your Heaven Luck is good, good Feng Shui can enhance it further.

- If your Heaven Luck is average, good Feng Shui can create the right environment to help you in clear thinking and better decision making.

- If your Heaven Luck is bad, good Feng Shui can lessen the obstacles that you are destined to face.

Then there is the luck of your premises as well. There are some premises that are so badly oriented that they attract very negative energies. The house brings in bad luck in the form of ill health, downfall of businesses and relationships. Sometimes, the misfortune could surface, say, within three years of moving into the premises. One can have a serious illness that could lead to death, separation in marriage or failure in business. For such premises, unless the door can be moved to another direction to bring in auspicious energy, one should move out of the house and find a new place as soon as possible.

If things have been going downhill since you moved into your new premises, it may be due to the orientation of the house. It may also be that you've selected the house during your bad luck period. However, you can always choose to manipulate your Earth Luck to suppress the negativity. In other words, it would be wise to engage professional help. This is where Feng Shui comes in.

VIOLATING NATURAL LAWS

In the philosophy of Feng Shui, everyone has a unique energy that radiates from their body. If the house's energy is not harmonized with a person's energy, it causes the body's internal energy to be scattered. If there is a lack of focused energy, it is easy to be anxious and nervous, to say things one does not mean and to sleep without getting rest. Unable to think and act at one's full potential makes people engage in conflicts, eat the wrong things, do the wrong things and be involved in mishaps.

Feng Shui is about the natural energies of cause and effect. It is a study based on thousands of years of experience and often surpasses the realms of modern science. Those who understand it and know how to use it are able to live more peacefully than those who do not. Those who choose to ignore Feng Shui do not understand that everything is connected. Nor that their misfortune is a society's problem which is a country's burden that prevents the world's progress.

Which is why at the end of my Feng Shui analysis, I always write: *When there is peace in the House, there is peace in the Nation. When there is peace in the Nation, there is peace in the World.*

FENG SHUI — AUTHENTIC, REAL OR QUICK FIX?

Today, Feng Shui has become a term used by many to jump onto the commercial bandwagon of self-help and quick fixes. The exploding interest in Feng Shui has caused confusion between what is authentic or real Feng Shui and what pseudo practitioners pass on as Feng Shui after reading a book or two or attending an afternoon class. Classical Feng Shui or Authentic Feng Shui has its roots in the I-Ching. It is founded on accurate assessment, observations, calculations and formulae derived from a deep understanding of the principles in *The I-Ching*, or *Book of Changes*. Ancient scholars and philosophers of the I-Ching spent years understanding its symbolism and the science and mathematics of the Bagua, the Five Elements, the Nine Flying Stars, the Environment and especially, the aspect of Time. From this, they were able to arrive at formulae used to analyse the environment. Classical Feng Shui is both a science and an art. It is a science because it uses methodical and logical deduction. It is an art because it requires the practitioner to determine which formulae can be used and applied in any given environmental situation. Authentic Feng Shui dates back to the Tang dynasty which lasted for over 2,000 years. More recent schools use the Chinese cultural symbolism and the Eight Life Aspirations (South=Fame, South-west=Romance, North=Career, etc.). Classical schools take the following into consideration: Location, Direction, Forms/Environmental Factors, Time aspect and the Residents. In effect, Classical Feng Shui focuses on the energy coming from the environment itself and on the way it interacts with and affects people living there. These forces of nature can be measured using a Lo'pan (Chinese Feng Shui compass). Once the beneficial energies are determined, they can be harnessed and tapped to promote well-being, prosperity and health. A balanced healthy diet affects the state of one's health, even though we are unaware of the internal processes happening in our body. In the same way, unseen environmental energies affect you, whether you are aware or not. On the other hand, "Pop Feng Shui" espouses the feel-good, psychological effects advocating the placement of objects, good luck items and colours. Classical Feng Shui Practitioners are often under the lineage of an authentic Feng Shui Teacher. They are involved in ongoing studies, research and practical application of the formulae. When a serious practitioner

receives the title of a Feng Shui Master, it is because he or she has achieved results in helping to improve the lives of others over a lifetime. An authentic Feng Shui Practitioner should advise you on the best direction and location to place your doors, stove, bed, etc, so as to tap into the natural energies of your immediate environment. He or she would not recommend a chunk load of products to enhance your luck! There is a misconception that Classical Feng Shui is divided into two schools, Form and Compass. Form and Compass are two techniques employed in all traditional schools. Almost all traditional schools can be classified under two main ideologies or branches: San He (Three Harmony) and San Yuan (Three Cycles). They both use energy or Chi distribution and landform analysis.

WHAT IS A FENG SHUI AUDIT OF A HOME?

A traditional Feng Shui Audit done by a qualified Feng Shui Master would normally consist of the following 11 steps — some of the steps, though, may vary depending on the practice of the Feng Shui Master. In general, they remain almost the same.

- Inspect the front and back of the building in relation to its surroundings. Look for a Dragon Hill in the East and a lower Tiger Hill in the West. It will be most auspicious if the Dragon and Tiger embrace each other. In towns and cities where there are no hills, the Master looks for higher/low buildings/houses on either side of the house that is being audited.

- Use a Lo'pan (Chinese Feng Shui compass) to assess the direction of the main door entrance. To get more accurate results, take the facing direction of the building (stand inside and look outside) and analyse the Flying Stars Chart, which is the horoscope of the house.

- Ask for the age of the building (year of construction) and draw up a Flying Stars Chart based on the period in which it was built (see Period 8 on pg 49). Check with the occupants for any happening or unusual history of the building, for example, suicides and hangings (if applicable).

- Analyse the Flying Stars Chart to determine the prosperity of the building in relation to its physical surroundings and the water and mountain stars. A Flying Stars Chart can either be a 20-year analysis or a yearly analysis chart. A yearly analysis simply means that it is for a particular year in question and will change for the next year and so on.

- Get a copy of the building floor plan from the owner and start inspecting the internal layout of the home.

- Apply the Flying Stars Chart to the floor plan to check for the prosperous Mountain and Water Stars. Determine this in relation to the entrance, open spaces (if any), the living room, dining room, kitchen, bedrooms, toilets, and storerooms. Note down any physical Shas (poison arrows) in any of these locations.

- Check where the bad stars 5 and 2 fall. Hopefully, they fall in the toilet or storeroom. If not, note down which room it falls first for the sake of later analysis.

- Look out of windows to locate any physical Shas.

- Based on the above findings, come up with a plan or suggestion on the best placement of beds and the best layout or arrangement of furniture. If there are any adverse situations, provide advice to neutralize the Sha. Advise the occupants on colours and special interior décor. Make a full Feng Shui Audit Report.

Please note that the above is only a guideline. Feng Shui Home Audits may vary with individual Feng Shui Practitioners. Before engaging a Feng Shui Master, always ask them questions like which Feng Shui technique he/she is using. The best Feng Shui Masters are those who are especially knowledgeable in the Shapes and Form School and the Flying Star Theory, the Four Symbolic Animals and the Five elements — basically the Compass School. There are more, but those listed here are the most important principles in assessing the Feng Shui of a home.

PERIOD 8 FENG SHUI — A NEW ERA FROM 2004–24

The year 2004 had a very special meaning as it was the beginning of a new 20-year cycle in Feng Shui called Period of 8. From February 4, 2004 onwards, we moved from the 20-year cycle of Period 7 to the new 20-year cycle of Period 8. This has resulted in the change of luck of all houses and businesses. Thus, businesses that were unlucky will now do better and houses that had trouble will now become very lucky. Many people have experienced noticeable changes in their lives as a result... have you?

HOW DOES THIS SHIFT OF CHI HAPPEN?

Every building has its own set of inbuilt intrinsic energies. These energies, the Chi or life force of the building, changes from place to place and from time to time. Traditional Feng Shui considers Space and the Time as integral. Using a mathematical formula and a compass to measure the Earth's magnetic field, we can assess the type and personality of the Chi in any building. In short, it is a bit like house astrology. Every building will reveal something about what is happening in a person's life or, in the case of a business, determine the prosperity and longevity of the business.

Combined with the formulae are the forms and shapes of the external and internal environment. For example, a road shaped like a triangle is considered the shape of Fire (one of the Five Elements), or a building with a rounded roof the shape of Metal. These forms will also affect a building.

A house built between 1984 and 2004 is considered a Period 7 house. Depending on which direction the house faces, certain properties of Chi will fly into the house from different directions. These are poetically named the Flying Stars. In Period 7, the Number 7 Red Ruling Star was the most important star for bringing health and wealth to a house. Now that we are in Period 8, the new ruler, known as the Ling Xing is now the Number 8 White Star.

To get the greatest benefit from good Feng Shui, we talk about mountains and water. The ideal site should have a mountain at the back (Yin energy) and water at the front (Yang energy). This is ideal in terms of the forms. Also, the formula should match the forms, giving us a good Mountain Star at the back (for health) and a good Water Star at the front (for wealth). Of course, there's no such thing as perfect Feng Shui but we can certainly try!

HOW TO SELECT GOOD FENG SHUI LOCATIONS

When you go house hunting or even land hunting, you might want to consider the landscape of a place, especially from a Feng Shui perspective. You would do this before you decide to call it home or build an office building or a shopping mall on it, or whatever the building is.

The ancient Feng Shui Masters of China understood that our destiny is enhanced when we live in harmony with nature, thereby tapping into its auspicious influences. Nature is likened to a living organism and its breath pervades everything, thereby giving good and bad vibrations alike. What you want, however, is to ensure that you get the best of this to enhance your life. You should lookout for:

- Gently undulating hilly land
- Places where the air smells good
- Places where winds blow gently
- Places where clean waterways meander slowly
- Places where the surrounding vegetation is lush and green

WHY YOU NEED TO LOOK FOR THESE

In Feng Shui tradition, auspicious locations are usually slightly elevated places where the Green Dragon of the East nestles gently with the White Tiger of the West, with their bodies curving gently towards each other to form a horse shoe or armchair shape. In this way, you are protected from the North winds by a range of hills that symbolize the Black Turtle.

Meanwhile, in the South, the presence of the Vermilion Phoenix enhances a site. When a site faces this wonderful configuration of hills, mountains, moving water and vegetation, then placing one's dwelling here ensures an abundance of good fortune and enormous wealth for the household for many succeeding generations.

FENG SHUI AND THE ENERGY OF GOOD LUCK

Chi is an essential ingredient in the study of Feng Shui. This energy has been described as many things: Cosmic Breath, Life Force, Prana and so on. Yet, Chi is more than that. It is both tangible and intangible and always in a constant state of change. This change is vital to your physical, emotional, mental and spiritual well-being. If there is no change, then Chi is said to be either stagnant or blocked. When Chi in your body is blocked, you may encounter illness, depression or aches and pains. When Chi in your environment is blocked, it is also reflected in your life. You could experience relationship difficulties, problems in business or general bad luck.

Lucky and prosperous energy is known as Sheng Chi. In this state, Chi is flowing and in balance. Sheng Chi brings progress, satisfaction, fertility, happiness and abundance in wealth. In contrast, Sha Chi is known as bad or unlucky energy. If it is imbalanced, it brings problems, obstructions, sickness, setbacks and accidents.

How to avoid Sha Chi: In your environment, this energy can be made up of ugly or unsightly structures, certain road formations or sharp and pointed structures. These formations are said to bring signs of body deformation, bad mental health, body illnesses and bad wealth luck. Therefore, it has become a priority for house seekers to look for areas without ugly external forms. A common poison arrow, T-junction homes are traditionally considered to be unlucky and bring with them misfortune and sometimes, death. This is because the energy brought into the home by the road is very forceful. Houses at T-junctions bring very strong influences to the house. However, if this T-junction is bringing in the prosperous

energy of the current 20-year-period, it could mean that the occupants of the house will prosper very quickly. Occupants must be cautious, however. When the auspicious energy wanes at the end of that Period, they will find that it will just as quickly bring bad luck to the house.

Living next to a graveyard is another common bad formation. Energy from the graveyard is Yin and human beings are Yang. Therefore, it is not to our advantage to live too close to a graveyard. According to the Chinese Five Elements, graveyards are filled with Earth energy. If occupants live surrounded by this energy, they will find that they have missed opportunities or that they can be unreasonable and stubborn.

Characteristics of the home's occupants are said to be affected by the surrounding road formations as well. A Y-shaped road signifies unfaithfulness. Living on the curved side of a bow-shaped road signifies promiscuous women. Roads in the shape of a bent leg signify leg problems and often, there will be someone lame in the house. By planting a hedge or building a wall to block off the view of these roads, you can lessen its degree of destructiveness.

How to identify Sheng Chi locations: When you are living on the embracing side of a river or road, this formation is said to bring lots of auspiciousness and wealth. It is also considered lucky if your home is in the vicinity of winding water. City dwellers will probably not be near real water, so streets and roads are then measured as virtual water. Some roads could be formations that bring glad tidings in the form of recognition or money.

Religious places: It is best NOT to live near religious places. Homes within close proximity to temples, churches and mosques tend to lose their good Sheng Chi or successful energy as these religious places absorb all positive energy from the surroundings. However, if you already have a home near these places, protect your Feng Shui with some cacti in front of your home at the balcony or veranda, but not inside the house.

Roads and Chi: Today, roads serve as conductors of Chi. Steadily-moving traffic on curving roads near our homes is beneficial. Fast traffic and roads pointing at us are not.

Roads: Roads which gently curve and appear to "hug" the house are auspicious Feng Shui. Houses at T-junctions are considered inauspicious since the Chi seems to hurtle towards them. Those living at the junction of such roads are likely to be jumpy. Screeching brakes and even crashes are common at such points. Deflection is needed and a convex mirror or a hedge would help. Mirrors are often used to return the harmful influence back on themselves. Waist-high shrubs and plants on the boundary of the garden as well as plants on the window sill inside the houses will slow down the Chi. An alternative would be to build a porch with the door at the side. If the path to the door faces the road, it would be better to move and curve it.

Flyovers: The visual impact of a flyover in a residential area can be devastating. The fast-moving traffic conducts Chi away from the area and considerably affects the fortunes of those living either at eye level or underneath the flyover. Residents living in houses facing a flyover where the road appears to cut into the apartments

like a knife will feel uncomfortable, while those living in houses under the flyover will feel overwhelmed and apprehensive. For the former, a mirror outside will deflect the problem or coloured glass in the windows facing the road will block the unattractive view while allowing light in. For the latter, lights on the corners of the house will symbolically lift the flyover, but this is not a good house to live in. Residents will feel oppressed and have no energy.

FENG SHUI TIPS FOR BUYING PROPERTY

Here are a few tips you should follow while buying new property.

- The back should be higher than the front. A higher rear means good backing or support. You will have future advancements and your children will prosper. If your back is lower, you'll go "downhill".

- The left (Dragon) side should be higher than the right (Tiger) side. This direction is taken from inside the house, looking out. If the right is slightly higher than the left, you can plant tall trees on the left side to counter the negative effect. A higher right (Tiger) side can cause accidents, illnesses or even death.

- The estate should not be shaped like a knife, chopper or axe. If it does, buy a property on the handle section, not on the blade part.

- If the shape of the estate is irregular, it is problematic not only for the buyers, but also for the developers.

- The back of the property should be equal to or wider than the front. It indicates stability, growth and money bag-like ability to keep wealth.

- The premise should not be "cut" by the curve of a road or a train track.

- The property should not face either an oncoming road or a dead end. The Sha Chi (poison arrow) is very strong and will not be good for the residents. In case it does, put small trees or plants to absorb the Sha Chi.

- A property should not be sandwiched between tall buildings. You and your family will feel oppressed and constricted, short-tempered and narrow-minded.

- A property should not face a narrow space between two buildings on the opposite side. This Sha Chi makes the premise prone to accidents and illnesses.

- A property should not face a tall building or higher ground. The Chi will be blocked and you will feel confronted by obstacles.

THE IMPORTANCE OF USING A GOOD COMPASS

I often get queries from people asking me to tell them ways to determine the facing direction of their house. My standard response always is: "Observing the direction in which the sun rises or sets is not accurate enough!" Hence, I cannot stress enough the importance of using a good compass in the practice of powerful Formula Feng Shui.

The first step in the practice of Formula Feng Shui is to determine your bearings or compass directions, the reading of which needs to be very precise. Second, to get proper bearings, you must learn how to operate a good compass. There are eight main directions, each of which are divided into three sub-directions. For example, the 45 degrees of the East direction are subdivided into 15 degree subsections and are classified into E1, E2 and E3. That makes 24 different directions, of which there are 24 possible recommendations for determining the horoscope of a house. This is the reason why even the most accomplished Feng Shui Master uses a Lo'pan (Chinese Feng Shui compass). Hence, a reliable compass is definitely the most essential Feng Shui tool that no serious practitioner of Feng Shui can do without.

USING THE FENG SHUI COMPASS

If you do not have access to a Feng Shui compass, do not despair. Any ordinary compass can be used to take directions.

- Always stand INSIDE your main front door looking OUTSIDE

towards the main road or garden to determine the FACING of your house. If you happen to live in an apartment, stand INSIDE the main entrance to your apartment building looking OUTWARDS to get your compass bearings.

- Hold the compass level to your naval or mid-abdomen. Rotate the movable dial on the compass so that the N (North) on the dial is aligned with the stationary N on the compass. This now means that the compass needle is pointing to the magnetic North.

- Once you have determined the North direction, look STRAIGHT AHEAD in front of you and read the exact bearing (in degrees) of the direction you are facing. For example, if the reading in front is 80 degrees, then your house faces East 1. If the reading is 280 degrees, then your house faces West 3. If it points to 180, then your house faces South 2.

- Some easy steps to determine the facing direction of your house taken from the main front door are listed below:
  - Take the first reading at your doorstep standing inside, while facing outwards.
  - Then take the second reading one step inside the house, still facing the main door.
  - Last, take the third reading one step outside the house, still facing the main door.

If there is a slight difference in the three readings, you should take an average and deem this to be the direction your main door faces.

If there is a large swing in your compass readings, it is advisable to take a look at the spatial arrangements of furniture and electronic equipment.

Be sure to carry a good compass with you... always!

THE TEN MOST IMPORTANT FENG SHUI DESIGN TIPS

If you wish to design the interior of your house according to Feng Shui design guidelines, there are some major tips that you must bear in mind. To achieve a balanced and harmonious Feng Shui design for any environment, follow these ten tips:

- Feng Shui design should always be done keeping in mind the people living in the house. People's comfort must be a priority.

- Make use of the Five Elements of Feng Shui, namely Water, Wood, Fire, Earth and Metal. An interior designer uses furniture and objects that contain the different elements. These elements should always be in harmonious quantities and according to the Bagua map indications.

- Choose colours according to what they symbolize and represent. Different colours represent different elements and have different symbolism. For example, green is Wood, red is Fire, brown/yellow is Earth, silver is Metal and black is Water.

- Good Feng Shui design does not allow dark spots in it since they do not allow the Chi to flow properly.

- Mirrors should be placed strategically according to the objects you want them to reflect.

- Carefully choose the shapes of the objects and furniture. Different shapes provide different feelings, as well as tend to balance the environment in different ways.

- Couches and chairs should always be placed in a way that allows those who sit on them to easily look at the door.

- According to Feng Shui design guidelines, beds should not be right across the door and should have a wall at one side as a protection.

- Correct Feng Shui design will allow people to feel good and comfortable in that interior without really noticing it has been carefully thought of. It should be natural and balanced, providing comfort to those occupying it.

- Last but not the least, do not overdo and clutter the house with too many items. Remember, balance is the key to great Feng Shui design. Also, most people decorate their homes with instinctive Feng Shui sense. After all, who would like to live in an environment that causes unease?

FINDING THE RIGHT FENG SHUI CONSULTANT

With the increasing popularity of Feng Shui awareness, a number of "so-called Feng Shui Consultants" are trying to jump onto the bandwagon and cash in on this new trend. In fact, there is a lot of "mumbo-jumbo" Feng Shui that's available around the world nowadays.

The scenario is getting pretty grim. Not only are these bogus practitioners promising to change people's destinies immediately, but there are many stores who promise that if you purchase and use their recommended articles, you will become millionaires overnight!

What the unsuspecting public does not know is that these people are only interested in making a quick buck for themselves, and do not really care about authentic Feng Shui. Unfortunately, the number of such "fast-food joints" in Feng Shui is increasing. Also, it does not pay to get advice from a quack. Remember, Feng Shui causes shift in energies, and unless one has a knowledge of Flying Stars, the Wu Xing (Five Elements), Eight Mansion Theory and a number of other theories that involve years of study, it is dangerous to practice. It can ruin people's lives rather than improve their luck.

HOW TO IDENTIFY A PROPER FENG SHUI CONSULTANT

There have been a lot of questions on how to find or identify a good Feng Shui Master. For each able and competent Feng Shui

Master, there are many more who claim to be consultants and masters in this field. You will be surprised to know how many of them just picked up a book and decided to become a Grand Master or — which is worse — have only attended a one-day course or workshop before becoming an "expert" in this field! Certifications really don't matter as a wealth of institutions and courses are readily available but usually cover the thinnest of surfaces for Feng Shui. Before picking a Feng Shui Consultant, it is best to decide the type of consultation you want in your home. You can decide to pick from any of these two categories: New Age Feng Shui and Classical Feng Shui. New Age Feng Shui can involve schools like Intuitive Feng Shui or Black Hat Sect, but don't really tie in to the more authentic schools. Classical Feng Shui would involve Flying Stars, Landscape, Dragon Breath and so on. The following information is for those who prefer to have a Classical Feng Shui consultation done to their home:

Five Elements (Wu Xing) Cycle: Five Elements is the basis of this Chinese science. Ask the Master to explain to you how the Five Elements work together and against each other. Many rulings and remedies come from this age-old cycle. Knowledge of this is necessary and a very basic requirement.

Directions Count: Ask to what extent directions are significant when observing your house. Are all houses and people the same? Each house and person is different. Sitting and facing directions count and will differ from house to house. The members living in the house have their own Kua numbers which will dictate their unique auspicious or inauspicious directions separately. Directions can be good or bad or both.

Knowledge on Remedies: What is the use in identifying what is wrong and not knowing how to properly remedy the situation? Or worse, what is the use if you aggravate the currently bad Feng Shui situation? Knowledge is the key in rectifying bad Feng Shui. Placing a wind chime helps to stimulate the Chi in a given area, but wind chimes will also unknowingly enhance the negative Chi in that area. Know exactly what is afflicting you and how you can solve this problem.

Schools of Feng Shui: The more experienced and knowledgeable in other schools the practitioner is, the better it is. For example, doing a home consultation will incorporate various schools of Feng Shui. Inside the home, they would be using Flying Stars and Eight Mansions Feng Shui. Outside, they would be using Landscape Feng Shui. Although it is virtually impossible for a consultant to know every single school, he or she should at least be specialized in a few schools to incorporate the various factors before making a decision.

Experience: Under traditional rulings, a disciple undergoing training from a Feng Shui Master can do so over many years, and in some cases, the disciple's whole life, until the Feng Shui Master has decided to retire. Just as in hiring a person for any job, experience counts. There are things that no book or amount of listening can teach. Ask about the experience of the practitioner and for any references. Better still, tell them you want to hear of how they faced a complex problem and used the rulings and their own logic to overcome the Feng Shui obstacle.

Explanations and Logic: For each decision made and communicated to you, there will always be logic behind it. There is no such thing as "It is a secret" or "You wouldn't understand". You are paying good money and you are entitled to know why a certain action/remedy/advice is given to you. Feng Shui is a science and its benefits are meant to be shared. A friend of mine put it quite aptly, "If the consultant doesn't want to tell you the 'why', it is probably because he or she is scared that once you know, you're on the same experience or knowledge level as him or her." You could speak to an authentic Feng Shui Master for the whole day, and though you'll know much more than before, you've touched just the tip of the iceberg. Of course, this is not the "be all and end all" in finding a proper consultant. It is a good start. Always remember to ask; the more you ask, the more you know.

To find the right Feng Shui Practitioner that best suits your need, ask the right questions. Follow these tips and you won't go wrong:

- Find out how they learnt Feng Shui. Due to the lack of good Feng Shui courses in India, practitioners may have studied some form of Oriental medicine like Acupuncture, Shiatsu or Chinese herbal medicine. They will often be a member of their appropriate professional association. It is more common now for people with an interior design background to become involved in Feng Shui. Find out how long they have been working as Feng Shui Practitioners and the type of clients they have worked with.

- If you have a preference for a certain style of Feng Shui, ask the type of Feng Shui they practise.

- Find out what is included in the consultation. Are Flying Stars or Nine Star Ki astrology dates for implementing recommendations and/or rituals to change the flow of energy included in your consultation?

- Find out the fees they charge. Some practitioners may ask a fixed fee, others will charge by the hour. Be clear about what this includes. Does the fee cover a written report, travel time, travelling expenses and ongoing advice after the consultation?

- Find out how long the practitioner intends to spend with you. Typical consultations range from one to two hours.

- If you are not quite convinced about the practitioner, ask if you can contact his or her clients for references.
- Last, but not the least, ask to see a certified qualification from a reputed Feng Shui Master or Feng Shui School.

You will get the most out of a consultation if you have trust in and communicate with the practitioner. If you make an appointment by telephone, always talk to the practitioner himself/herself.

WHAT TO EXPECT FROM A CONSULTATION

The first Feng Shui Master, Master Yang Yun Sung (also known as Yang Save the Poor) said that Feng Shui was designed primarily to help people, and money was secondary. That is the most important goal for any ethical Feng Shui Master.

There is no standard Feng Shui consultation style and each practitioner will have his or her own method. This varies from a visit and verbal advice to a visit with a comprehensive written report. Some practitioners carry out rituals to change the flow of energy. It is also possible to have a consultation by post.

A typical Compass School Practitioner will visit the building and meet the occupants to determine the Lo Shu square for right location of certain areas for application: Wealth, health and so on. He will make floor plans, take compass readings and mark them on the plans. He may discuss various options in terms of Feng Shui solutions to get an idea of which changes are realistic. He will find out the dates of birth — of all the occupants to determine the Trigram for their best directions — and the date of moving to the building. This enables him to make up the chart and calculate their success directions. He might ask how their lives have changed since they moved to the building and find out what they want to achieve from their Feng Shui consultation. People (Kua) and Timing (Flying Star) are extremely important to perform an accurate analysis. A house may be very good for you this year, but may be bad for you next year. Further, a house may be suitable for one person but not for another. A Feng Shui Master must be physically present at the building to do an exact calculation by using the Lo'pan (Chinese Feng Shui compass). A few degrees of variation can make the difference between a "good" house and a "bad energy" house. Feng Shui is about creating a peaceful, harmonious balance with your environment to produce vibrant energy. Feng Shui should also be so subtle that it blends in with your personal taste. The Feng Shui Consultant may undertake an internal and external analysis to see if there is any obstruction, negative influence, poison arrows and so on. If appropriate, he may walk around the property and note any important feature, paying attention to the neighbourhood, surrounding buildings and local landscape. Finally, he will ask questions to find out the date the dwelling was built in order to determine the time period, also known as Flying Star. From February 4, 2004, we have entered Period 8, which changes everything that you may have already done!

After the consultation, he will draw out the plans and lay the grid of the eight directions over each floor of the building. He will check to see if there is any water close to the building. Then he will work on solutions and the best dates to implement them. A complete written report and drawings with solutions and dates to implement them should be sent to the clients. Most practitioners are happy to talk over the telephone if any further explanation or help is needed in implementing the recommendations. Personally, I enjoy it when my clients want to know why a certain decision is made. You never know, you might inspire a Feng Shui Master to see a problem in a slightly different and innovative way. Just remember to be polite, and he or she will be more than happy to answer.

A final word of advice: Please do not trust anybody and everybody. By reading books on the subject, you can yourself create balance and harmony in your house. Do not go further until you have found the right practitioner and are satisfied with his or her qualifications.

RED ENVELOPES & THE FENG SHUI TRADITION

According to Feng Shui tradition and culture, Red Envelopes are very symbolic and meaningful. Whenever Red Envelopes are given as a gift, they serve as a wish of prosperity, good luck and happiness to the person who receives them. This symbolism is not only due to the Red Envelope traditions, but also to the colour red, which is a very auspicious symbol of happiness by itself. One way in which Red Envelopes can be used to attract prosperity without receiving them as a gift is by placing two coins in one of them and then placing this on the doorway frame. You can also use this object as a meaningful present to give whenever you wish to send good thoughts, prosperity and happiness to another person. Red Envelopes are also used by Feng Shui Masters in their teaching practices. According to this tradition, whenever a Feng Shui Master transmits information and knowledge to an apprentice, the apprentice must give a Red Envelope back to the Master. This envelope can be empty but according to the most ancient traditions, it should contain coins, small gold ingots or precious gifts. Every time the Feng Shui Master or Feng Shui expert gives a new advice to his trainee, he must receive a Red Envelope as a transaction. The tradition of exchanging advice for Red Envelopes has several reasons and explanations. First of all, it is a way to demonstrate that the apprentice asked for the advice he received and is thankful for it. Besides, this honours the way in which advice and knowledge is transmitted through time and different generations. Whenever a Feng Shui Master conducts an audit of a residential or office premise and transmits information to another person, bad luck may befall the Master for "sharing the secrets of heaven", especially depending on how such knowledge changes the other person's life. In this way, the tradition of transacting Red Envelopes for advice represents protecting the Master from any bad luck that sharing his knowledge can bring him. Thus, this tradition of exchanging Red Envelopes for advice has many different explanations and important foundations that many Feng Shui Masters follow and expect their clients to respect.

FEENG SHUI FOR THE COMMON MAN

USE FENG SHUI TO INCREASE YOUR WEALTH — YOUR KUA NUMBER & YOU

It is believed that our lives are controlled by five factors: Destiny, Luck, Feng Shui, Virtue and Effort. Destiny is based on our karma (the law of cause and effect) and this totals about 40 per cent of our lives. Destiny cannot be changed.

Feng Shui and luck are grouped in the same category. So, basically if you work hard (effort), treat others with respect and kindness (virtue) and have good luck and balanced Feng Shui, your life will be much better. It is only your destiny or fate that remains the same.

So you want to be rich. Who doesn't? Let's face it, most people want to make use of Feng Shui to gain more material possessions. A lot of people seem to believe that implementing Feng Shui in their lives will make them millionaires overnight. In fact, nothing can be further from the truth.

Like everything else, Feng Shui needs time to work. Some people will reap the benefits of Feng Shui in a couple of days or weeks. For some, it might take months or even years. It all depends on your fate, which is destined by your karma.

If you are impatient and seek quick cures, it will work but the effect might not be long-lasting. It is like a packet of two-minute instant noodles — filling for the moment but not good for your health in the long run. Before you spend your hard-earned cash on some mystical "mumbo-jumbo", take some time to try and understand Feng Shui.

The first step involves knowing your Kua number. Try to sleep according to your Sheng Chi direction. For instance, if you have the Kua Number 9, your Sheng Chi direction is East. Position your bed so that your head points to the East direction in your bedroom.

Second, take a good look at your house. Is it near a cemetery or a hospital? Is there a large building in front of it? Is it vulnerable to poison arrows caused by sharp or protruding corners? If so, your chances of amassing wealth may be reduced. If your house is near a building with strong Yin energy (for example, cemetery, hospitals, old and abandoned buildings), leave a light on at all times. Get the Yang energy circulating by playing upbeat music or switching on the television. You can also hang a Pa Kua on the outside of your house, facing the source of the Sha Chi (poison arrow).

The most effective method for making wealth luck last, however, is to use the traditional Xuan Kong Flying Star system to determine a house's natal chart and to find out where the Number 8 Wealth Star is located.

From 2004 onwards, a new energy cycle called Period 8 began for all houses. Thus, to acquire great wealth, one must determine the area in the house where the 8 White Star (Wealth and Prosperity Star) which is the luckiest of all stars, is located. This star brings fortune, nobility, favourable promotion, salary increment, smooth wealth luck, good health and career success.

The Number 9 Star is also the secondary Wealth Star, because the next 20-year period is Period 9, and this makes it a future Wealth and Happiness Star. Indeed, Star 9 brings joyous occasions like childbirth, promotion, marriage luck, favourable investment yields and good support from benefactors and property revenues.

When a good Water Star is activated with the Water element (for example, fountain, aquarium and so on), it brings money luck, wealth, career and material success. However, if a bad Water Star is inadvertently activated in a particular grid by an ad hoc placement of water features, and that particular area is used for conducting business, then one could be facing bankruptcy unless it is properly cured. Therefore, a word of caution: Do not place water features in your house unless advised by a professional practitioner. It is better to be safe than sorry.

KUA NUMBERS & AUSPICIOUS DIRECTIONS

Use the Kua formula to check your best directions and sit facing one of those locations to achieve success, wealth, marriage and health luck. First, determine if you are an East or West group person. Please use the traditional solar calendar using 4 February as the cut-off date. For example, if a child is born on February 2,1988, we take his birth year as 1987 because he's born before 4 February.

If your Kua number is 1, 3, 4 or 9, you belong to the East group. Your favourable directions would be North, South, East and South-east.

If your Kua number is 2, 5, 6, 7 or 8, you belong to the West group. Your favourable directions would be North-east, South-west, West and North-west.

The method for determining the Kua number for Males is as follows: Take 10 minus the sum of the last two digits of the birth year 19XX. For example, a male is born on May 4, 1967. Take 6+7=13. Then add 1+3=4 (when the result is a two-digit number, continue to add until you get a single digit). Now, take 10-4=6. Therefore, his Kua number is 6.

The method for determining the Kua number for Females is as follows: Take the sum of the last two digits of the birth year 19XX and add 5 to it. For example, a female is born on September 2, 1967. Take 6+7=13. Then add 1+3=4 (when the result is a two-digit number, continue to add until you get a single digit). Now, take 4+5=9. Therefore, her Kua number is 9.

Do remember that for Female Kua Number 5, you take it as Kua Number 8. For Male Kua Number 5, you take it as Kua Number 2.

TAPPING YOUR SUCCESS DIRECTIONS

Who doesn't want fame and success? With the help of Feng Shui you can attain this by a simple method of sitting and sleeping in the direction that brings these energies to you. One's personal fame and success orientation can be found based on one's personal Kua number.

You can tap this luck if you sit facing your personal fame and success orientation when you are working at your desk, eating at the dining table and especially when you are attending an important social or professional meeting. When you sleep, your head should be pointing to your personal best direction.

The chart below gives the Kua numbers with the relevant fame and success directions:

YOUR KUA NUMBER	YOUR FAME & SUCCESS ORIENTATION
1	SE for both males & females
2	NE for both males & females
3	S for both males & females
4	N for both males & females
5	NE for males & SW for females
6	W for both males & females
7	NW for both males & females
8	SW for both males & females
9	E for both males & females

There are also many other schools of Feng Shui which can help bring you fame and recognition. These are Flying Star Feng Shui (which depends on the natal chart of your house and the time period in question), Eight Aspirations Feng Shui (which relies on the placement of physical enhancers in your fame corner) and Symbolic Feng Shui (which makes use of Feng Shui ornaments, shapes and designs).

Even if you cannot change the position of your front door, you only need a compass to tap your personal lucky directions. Simple, isn't it?

YOUR KUA AND HEALTH

A person's health luck can be improved by Feng Shui, if done correctly of course. The simplest way to improve a person's health would be to have him or her face what is referred to in Eight Mansions Feng Shui as Tien Yi (the Heavenly Doctor). If you are just recovering from an illness or face frequent health problems, sleep with your head "pointing" to your Tien Yi direction and use this area of your home more often.

For example, I am a Kua Number 9. This means that my Tien Yi is South-east. While sleeping, I should ensure that my head "points" towards the South-east and that I use the South-east sector of my home more.

Those of you who are more familiar with applying the Eight Mansion theories, should also position your stove so that its knobs point in the direction of your Tien Yi.

To calculate your Kua number and look up your Tien Yi direction, refer to the chart below. Your Kua number is calculated using the Chinese lunar calendar. (For those born before 6 or 7 February, you must go back a year. For example, if you were born on February 6, 1959, you would calculate your Kua number using the year 1958).

YOUR KUA NUMBER	1	2	3	4	5*	6	7	8	9
TIEN YI — YOUR HEALTH DIRECTION	E	W	N	S	W NW	NE	SW	NW	SE

FAVOURABLE AND UNFAVOURABLE DIRECTIONS FOR KUA NUMBERS

In Feng Shui, we all have four auspicious and four inauspicious directions based on our Kua number, which, as you have just learnt, is calculated from your date of birth.

When you have determined your auspicious directions, it is important that you remember them. Always try to face one of your most auspicious directions. Each of the eight directions has its own type of luck, good or bad, as they are all based on your Kua number. I advise you to print out the chart or make a copy of it until you are able to remember them. To start your personal Feng Shui journey, use the chart above with the aid of a compass to find your most auspicious corners and locations in your home. By eating, sitting, working and sleeping in your auspicious directions, you will help to increase your luck. If your Kua number is 5, men should use the Kua Number 2 and women the Kua Number 8.

Kua Number Readings: Your Good Directions as per Kua Number

YOUR KUA NUMBER	YOUR AUSPICIOUS LOCATIONS & CORNERS MOST AUSPICIOUS FIRST IN DESCENDING ORDER	YOUR ARE AN EAST OR WEST GROUP PERSON
1	South-east - East - South - North	East
2	North-east - West - North-west - South-west	West
3	South - North - South-east - East	East
4	North - South - East - South-east	East
5	Men: North-east - West - North-west - South-west Women: South-west - North-west - West - North-east	West
6	West - North-east - South-west - North-west	West
7	North-west - South-west - North-east - West	West
8	South-west - North-west - West - North-east	West
9	East - South-east - North - South	East

YOUR 4 AUSPICIOUS DIRECTIONS									
Your Kua Number	1	2	3	4	5*	6	7	8	9
Sheng Chi Your Success Direction	SE	N	S	N	NESW	W	NW	SW	E
Tien Yi Your Health Direction	E	W	N	S	WNW	NE	SW	NW	SE
Nien Yen Your Romance Direction	S	NW	SE	E	NWW	SW	NE	W	N
Fu Wei Your Personal Development Direction	N	SW	E	SE	SWNE	NW	W	NE	S
Your 4 Inauspicious Directions									
Ho Hai Unlucky Direction	W	E	SW	NW	ES	SE	N	S	NE
Wu Lui Kwei Five Ghosts Directions	NE	SE	NW	SW	SEN	E	S	N	W
Lui Sha Six Killings Directions	NW	S	NE	W	SE	N	SE	E	SW
Chueh Ming Total Loss Direction	SW	N	W	NE	NSE	S	E	SE	NW

For the Kua Number 5 the top number is for men & the bottom number is for women

THE NINE BASIC FENG SHUI CURES

There are nine basic Feng Shui cures for achieving the flow of positive energy through a space. These cures are easy to follow and will certainly be helpful in bringing back positive energy. These are as follows:

ELECTRICALLY POWERED OBJECTS

Fountain pumps, TV sets, microwaves, and even computers can encourage positive Chi to flow. If you place your computer so that you face a door while you work, you will operate from a position of strength and control. An electrically powered fountain is also said to promote wealth, a belief born in times when water was essential to the Chinese economy for its role in the growth of rice. One Feng Shui suggestion is to fix leaks immediately to prevent money from being flushed away. Standing water in the bathroom or kitchen can mean a stagnant cash flow. A good practice is to keep toilet seat lids down and cover kitchen drains to conceal the standing water.

MOVING OBJECTS

Interior fountains are also macrocosms of Chi activating water and producing money. Flowing water can be protective because it disperses the killing Chi of design imbalances, some of which include acute room angles, corners that jut into rooms, unused storage spaces or a missing area. Wind and Water, the creative forces of nature that give Feng Shui its name, are brought indoors to encourage profits. Moving air produced by moving water in an indoor fountain captures the essence of Feng Shui.

LIVING OBJECTS

Plants and flowers, either real or artificial, are symbols of life and growth. They breathe new energy into any interior and help circulate what is already there. Plants can boost performance and morale when placed on either side of an entrance because they attract good Chi and bring in money. Fish bowls and aquariums

are also microcosms of the life-giving ocean and evoke nourishing and money-making Chi. A plant placed under an open staircase at home will draw positive energy to the upstairs area.

SOUND

Wind chimes and bells can lure Chi (and customers) in because they produce noise and arouse curiosity. It is good Feng Shui to place a wind chime or bell in dark corners to attract energy. To keep Chi from leaving a room with many doors or windows, add either a wind chime or a bell. The bubbling sound of a small indoor fountain attracts people and introduces a natural background noise.

HEAVY OBJECTS

Stones, statues and other weighty items are used to restrain positive Chi and keep it from leaving a space. Strategically placed in the area of your choice, a heavy object can enhance health, wealth and emotional well-being.

BRIGHT OBJECTS

Crystal balls, lights, candles and mirrors brighten any interior and attract positive energy. Lights can soften a sharply jutting corner, and a crystal hung in the middle of a long corridor can slow down quickly-moving Chi. Mirrors can make a cramped room seem larger. A mirror placed at right angles to the window will bring the view inside. However, a mirror in front of a bed can disturb your sleep.

COLOURS

Red, symbolizing happiness and strength, is the most auspicious colour and is the colour most used in Feng Shui cures. Related colours like purple, pink and plum are also very fortunate. Green promotes growth and tranquility, and blue can be beneficial — or not — depending on the shade (warmer and with a hint of green is best). Brown, tan, yellows and orange harmonize a room with the Earth element.

BAMBOO FLUTES

When hung on a diagonal from the ceiling or on a wall, bamboo flutes symbolize growth, stability and safety. When two flutes, mouth pieces up and tied with red ribbons, are hung on a diagonal from a beam that runs above a stove, desk or bed, then oppressive energy caused by the beam is dispelled.

RIBBONS, FRINGES AND OTHER ITEMS

Since Feng Shui cures evolve and change to address new problems, this category is open to additional ways to increase the flow of positive energy. Ribbons can be tied to doors with knocking knobs. Red tassels can hide and resolve the problem of a slanted beam.

WIND CHIMES, ELEMENTAL CURES & THE SALT WATER CURE

Many people write to me or ask for advice regarding which wind chime to use and their significance in Feng Shui. I have, therefore, decided to specially write on the subject of wind chimes and their use as a potent Feng Shui cure.

There are many types of wind chimes available in the market with different makes and number of rods. Wind chimes can be made of metal, wood and even bamboo. They can have 5, 6, 7, 8 or 24 rods. For metal rods, it doesn't matter whether they are hollow or solid. What matters is that the rods produce a metallic sound, which, in turn, will effectively weaken Sha Chi from malignant stars.

In Flying Stars Feng Shui, wind chimes with metal rods are used to weaken the effects of the malignant stars of 2 Black and 5 Yellow. If you are wondering why, you'll need to know a little bit more about the Five Element Theory. Earth produces Metal and in the process, Earth is weakened. So, in order to weaken Earth Stars like the 2 Black and 5 Yellow, you will need to use Metal — in this case metal wind chimes.

The 2 Black Star causes sickness while the 5 Yellow Star causes accidents and mishaps. So if you are looking to minimize the effects of these two stars, hang a metal rod wind chime in the afflicted areas of your home, office or shop.

Looking to enhance your happiness or perhaps get a promotion? The easiest thing to do is to hang bamboo wind chimes. Locate the Number 9 Star in your home or office and just hang a wind chime made of bamboo in this area! The Number 9 Star is a Fire element Star and the bamboo will fuel this Fire, since Wood produces Fire. So, when the Number 9 Star is empowered with Wood, it is said to result in career changes and a move upwards.

Another popular usage of wind chimes in Feng Shui is to slow fast-flowing Chi caused by T-junctions and long corridors. Fast-flowing Chi is not desirable as it is deemed too aggressive.

Metal cures for Feng Shui Annual Afflictions are an excellent solution when malignant energies like 5 Yellow Star and 2 Black Star decide to take up residence in a key area of your home like your main door or bedroom. These metal cures will weaken the negative energies of these stars, which can often cause bad luck, ill health, mishaps, accidents and in very severe cases, fatal tragedies. Metal is one of the Five Elements that make up the Elemental Theory of Feng Shui. The Productive and Destructive Cycle of the Five Element Theory is a key factor in nearly all Feng Shui applications and formulae. Typically used as a cure or an enhancer in Xuan Kong (Flying Star) Feng Shui, Metal is the cure of choice for many Classical Feng Shui Practitioners. It is used to weaken the effects of the 5 Yellow and 2 Black stars. These are both Earth stars whose energies are weakened by the draining effect the Metal element has on the element of Earth. The 5 Yellow Star has been known to cause mishaps, accidents and in very severe cases, fatal misfortunes. The 2 Black Star is often blamed for illnesses, poor health and a lack of well-being at home. Metal cures like six-rod hollow metal wind chimes and six-coin charms will ensure that the negative energies these stars give off are reduced and its effects are not as powerful.

WATER — THE ESSENCE OF FENG SHUI — AND OTHER ELEMENTAL CURES

Water represents Wealth, Prosperity and Growth in Feng Shui. It is used as an enhancement in Feng Shui, helping with career, health and wealth when positioned properly. Remember not to overdo things, however. In Feng Shui, balance is vital. Go too far and you get the opposite of what you are searching for. A little medicine is good and needed; overdo it and it becomes poison. Similarly, water can be energizing; overdo its use and it becomes an enemy, not a friend!

Water, overdone in bathrooms, kitchens and especially in bedrooms, can be very damaging to the harmony of the environment and therefore, to the A-B-C — awareness, balance, control and calmness.

The key word throughout it all is harmony, the balance of Yin and Yang. The wider application of the terms Yin and Yang further introduces the Five Elements. These Five Elements are moving swirls of energy that are constantly changing. The five activities of Water, Fire, Wood, Metal and Earth are processes in movement and interact. The elements are also connected to the points of the compass by the Chi which is associated with each sector.

To achieve energetic or emotional and decorative balance in your house, one must make sure that all of the five traditional elements are included in your Feng Shui design as given below:

Water: Direction – North
Materials: Glass, Mirrors, Water Features
Colour: Black, Blues

Fire: Direction – South
Materials: Art/Sculpture – Sunrises, Sunflowers, Geometric Abstracts
Colour: Reds

Wood: Direction – East and South-east
Materials: Wood
Colour: Greens & Aquas

Earth: Direction – North-east, South-west and Centre
Materials: Stone (Jewellery), Ceramics, Crystals
Colour: Yellow, Earth tones

Metal: Direction – West and North-west
Materials: Metal (Jewellery)
Colour: Silver, Gold, Copper, Jewel tones

Remember, when you place the elements according to their correct compass direction, you create motivation, creativity, stability and abundance in your life.

THE SALT WATER CURE

According to Feng Shui guidelines, salt water is meant to be very helpful in overcoming diseases and health problems. It can also be used as a prevention to avoid diseases from coming into your house and life. Thus, even if your health is all right, you can still follow a salt water cure to prevent future diseases from coming into your life. Although salt water cures are good for all health problems, there are some specific cases in which its power is particularly potent. These include sore throats and colds. Whenever a person suffers from one of these problems, he/she can overcome them easily by following a salt water cure. If you wish to learn how to do a general salt water cure, you should follow some steps and specific indications. First of all, fill a jar with table salt, sea salt or rock salt. Then place six coins, which should ideally be Chinese coins, over the salt, along with a Re.1 coin. In case of Chinese coins, place them with the characters facing up. After you have placed the salt and coins in the glass jar, fill the jar with water right up to the top. It is important that your jar maintains the combination of one-quarter of water with three-quarters of salt. The next step involves placing the jar in a strategic spot. In order to do this, you should find out which is your personal health Kua number and direction, or the Kua number and direction of the person you wish to help cure. Once you know the specific directions, place the salt water cure jar in that room. In case the person is in bed, you can place the jar near the bed. This cure works like magic, particularly when the 5 Yellow Star of Misfortune or the 2 Black Star of Sickness arrives at your house or bedroom during a particular year. It can actually help prevent ill health, accidents and hospitalization. At best, it absorbs the negativity of your environment and is a very protective remedy in Feng Shui.

CREATING A POWER OFFICE WITH FENG SHUI

More and more people are looking to gain an edge in their working environment. One method that business people are increasingly turning to is Feng Shui. The main reason for this is that Feng Shui promises to create a better career and promote further opportunity and advancement for you by arranging your office environment correctly.

There are some very basic yet potent guidelines in Feng Shui to create an effective office environment which can instantly boost the career quotient of almost any office inhabitant. Although some offices may require more extensive rearrangement to help promote success, most offices only require a few modest changes. Use these suggestions below to create your own Power Office:

- Sit in the power position. This is situated opposite and diagonal from the door or opening to the room. The desk should be here facing the door. Draw more emphasis to this area by creating a focal point with a lamp, artwork, tall plant and so on. This also helps to create a straight line of sight to this area, imbuing even more power and authority. What's more, this corner is also considered the lucky corner of any room, so you definitely want your desk there! If possible, try to use personal Feng Shui by tapping your personal auspicious Kua directions.

- Sit behind a power desk. A power desk is one that is substantially sized and correctly placed. A power desk is never an L-shaped desk (the shape of which is like a cleaver or hatchet and is thought to cut the person sitting at the desk). It also has specific dimensions like 75L X 43W X 33H or 66-70L X 24-27W X 32-33H. Small desks are deemed inauspicious and thwart future growth.

- Sit in a power chair. A good chair is one with a high back and solid armrests. Although the chairs that are designed for the back are very popular right now, their open weave does not provide good symbolic support for the person occupying them.

- Put power behind you. Power includes symbols of mountains and banking and photographs related to business and your

boss. Be sure that your desk does not face your boss' desk. Rather, he or she should be behind you even if he or she is on the other side of the building. This also means you should never sit with a window (no support; unless it is a window with a view to a very prominent business or bank), door (no advancement) or bookshelf (backstabbing) behind you.

- Get power in front of you. Keep the path in front of your desk open and clear. If there are obstructions like chairs, the path to a rise in your career will also be obstructed.

- Activate your desk dragon. Put fresh flowers in the left-hand corner of your desk (as you are sitting at it). You can also place a plant in this corner. This is the Dragon side of your desk and benefits tremendously from the special energy of plants and flowers. Never ever put bonsai plants in your office or your career will be stunted and short-lived. Nor should you decorate your workplace with cacti as your career will be riddled with problems and difficult working relationships.

TEN QUICK TIPS FOR GOOD OFFICE FENG SHUI

- Sit at the farthest corner diagonally opposite the door. You should not sit in the direct path of the door.

- You should have a view of the door so that you are aware of who's coming in and going out.

- Your door should not be at your back or else you'll invite backstabbers.

- Do not have your office door facing a toilet or stairway.

- If your office door faces another, paint a red dot on the door knob of both the doors, so that you see eye-to-eye and avoid confrontation.

- Have an open space in front of you. Do not sit facing a pillar.

- Watch out for poison arrows hitting at you. Move yourself away from the line of the sharp edge facing you or put a tall plant to screen off the pillar or corner from hitting you.

- You should sit with a solid wall behind you to symbolize the support or backing you have in your workplace. If this is not possible, and you are sitting with a window behind you, use solid blinds or curtains.

- Hang a picture of a mountain, tortoise or high-rise building behind you. Do not hang a picture with a water feature behind you.

- Do not have open shelves hitting at you. It is inauspicious as they act like knives cutting at you. You will have body ache, loss of concentration and cause your colleagues to betray you.

FENG SHUI FOR THE BEDROOM

The bed and the bedroom make up a very important area of the home. On an average, you spend one-third of your life in this space. The bed is where you revitalize and heal your body, where you share your most intimate moments with your loved one and your most sacred place of sanctuary. Having the bed and bedroom out of balance can create major problems in your health and can make or break a marriage.

The first thing to look at is the quality or type of bed to use. As far as size goes, the queen-size bed seems to be the best size for the average-sized couple. It is more than adequate in size for two people and still keeps the couple close. The king-size bed has few problems to it. For one, its size alone can create distance for the couple. Secondly, if you look at the box spring of the king-size bed, you will notice it is actually two box springs under the mattress. This creates a natural splitting effect for the parties sleeping on the bed.

Don't worry as there is a special cure for this. Get a form-fitted red sheet and cover the box spring with the sheet. This ties the two box springs together. This red sheet cure for the box spring is also a good cure for any bed. It helps to create more passion in one's relationship and to raise one's Chi if they are weak or lethargic. Any bed smaller than a queen size is too small and will create tension in the relationship by being too claustrophobic.

The bed should always be off the floor, for the floor is where the dirt is. You wouldn't want to be sleeping in the dirt, would you?

To bring more love into your life, use pink linens, as pink is the colour of love. Be careful of peach, for that is the colour of affairs and infidelity. The Chinese call it peach blossom love. So, if you are single and just want to have affairs with lots of people, then peach is your colour. If you want deep connected love, pink is the way.

If your marriage ends, get rid of the marriage bed and the linens, for you do not want to take the old marriage energy into the next relationship. Be careful of buying used beds, for you do not know who slept there or what happened in that previous bed. This goes for antique beds too. You will take on the previous owner's bedroom energy for bad or good.

Do not store anything underneath the bed. The reason for this is when you are sleeping, you go from the conscious world into the unconscious world. When the mind is unconscious, you have no filters on what your mind takes on. Anything in your immediate surrounding can affect you while you are asleep. Be aware of your nightstands and what you have on them. Many people keep those little clock radios and snooze alarms. These devices have electromagnetic fields of up to 2-3ft. This can create health problems and alter sleep patterns. Some modern bedrooms with a plethora of electronic devices give the impression of walking into aeroplane cockpits. These devices will distort energy fields, create health problems and disrupt sleep patterns.

The worst thing for a marriage is having a television set in the bedroom. This will cut down on the couple's sex life. People will watch TV instead of making love.

Be careful of beds and bed frames that have a high metal content, for sometimes they can throw off the natural magnetic fields of the human body. To check for this, take a regular compass and find true North. Now place the compass on the bed. If the compass moves from true North, then you may have to replace the bed or bed frame.

Air mattresses are not recommended as your Chi is floating and not stabilized. Waterbeds are also not recommended as people are sleeping on a great mass of water and that too, stagnant water to boot. This excess of Yin water Chi can weaken the health of a person dramatically. Several cases are known of health problems dealing with kidneys, to the point where the people end up on kidney dialysis. To make matters worse, most waterbeds have a heater attached to warm the water. Hence, the individual who sleeps there is also bombarded with extremely high electrical and electromagnetic fields, which can cause health problems. For the same reason, it is not recommended that you use electric sleeping blankets. With waterbeds, the appropriate cure is to get rid of them altogether.

Mixing energies by keeping a desk in the bedroom can cause problems. It creates confusion so that when you get out of bed you see your desk and you think of work. Conversely, you are at your desk and you see your bed, and you think of sleeping. The energies work at cross purposes with each other. If you must have the same energies in the room like in the case of a studio apartment, try to make clear divisions between the different areas of life, using furniture arrangement, plants, screens and other kinds of partitions.

The positioning of the bed in the bedroom is probably one of the most important aspects to look at in the home. An incorrect bed position can lead a marriage to divorce, keep a single person unmarried or create numerous difficulties in the health of the people sleeping on the bed. So the positioning of the bed should not be taken lightly. There are three primary bed position rules. In bed position 1, as you lie on your bed, you want to be able to see the entryway coming into the bedroom. This creates proper security and allows you to feel comfortable in bed. In bed position 2, you want a solid wall behind the head of the bed. This gives support and foundation to the people sleeping on the bed. In bed position 3, you do not want the bed to be in line or in the pathway of the entryway coming into the bedroom. This is like sleeping in the middle of the road or in the pathway of Chi. Sometimes, you cannot move the bed out of these unfavourable positions, so we can turn to some special cures to help the issues. If you cannot see the door from the bed, place a mirror somewhere in the room, so that as you lie in bed you can see the entryway in the mirror.

If you cannot get the bed out of the pathway of the door, it is advisable that you do something to slow the Chi of the pathway.

You can place a rug perpendicular across that pathway or hang a round-faceted crystal ball from the ceiling in that pathway. If the feet are lined up to the door, it is called the coffin position, meaning the body is lined up to be taken out of the room. With this position, you can do the same as in the previous situation, but you can also place a piece of furniture like a small chest at the end of the bed and a plant or art piece on top of the chest to hold the Chi in the bed.

Odd-shaped rooms: In odd-shaped rooms, the occupants tend to be short-tempered and quarrelsome and may encounter bad luck. Try to make the shape of the room as regular a square or rectangle as possible by placing custom-made cabinets to hide the sharp corners.

Attic bedroom: An attic with sloping ceilings is not suitable as a bedroom. The ceiling should be levelled if possible. This will also hide exposed beams which cause various health issues if one sleeps under them.

Bed facing a toilet: Facing the toilet door when you sleep could affect you. However, due to space constraints, you may have no other choice. Keep the toilet door closed at all times and place a wood element (bamboo chick blinds) between your bed and the toilet to absorb the Sha Chi (negative energy).

Death position: Do not position your bed in the direct path of the door with your legs pointing towards the door. This is often known as the death or coffin position. Shift your bed to another area of your bedroom, away from the direct path of the Chi to minimize health issues and too many dreams which will leave you restless and fatigued. In case you can't re-position your bed, put up a partition or a curtain at the foot of the bed.

Mirrors: Mirrors should never reflect the bed. They cause morning fatigue, restlessness, lethargy and sometimes dreams and nightmares. Install your mirror either in the walk-in dresser or inside the wardrobe door. If you have mirrored doors or walls reflecting your bed, cover them with a cloth before you sleep. It can also cause third-party interference in your marriage which translates to either spouse having an illicit relationship.

Stove behind/above your bed: If your bed is placed with a stove or oven behind or above (if you are living in a double-storey house), you tend to be hot-headed, easily irritated and more prone to fever.

Toilet behind/above your bed: A bed sharing the same wall as the toilet bowl is a no-no. It is bad for your health. The same applies to a toilet above your bed. Dirty waste matters are being flushed over your head.

One important thing that you must remember is that the sleeping position of each occupant is personalized based on their individual birth data. Do not simply paint your room red or pink as some books claim to enhance romance in this way. You can unknowingly activate the quarrelsome or sickness energies in the room.

Remember, your bedroom is for rest, love and sanctuary. Keep it as simple as possible.

FENG SHUI FOR THE BATHROOM

Very few people will take the trouble of applying the principles of Feng Shui in the bathroom or toilet. True, it is not rational to spend a huge amount of money on this area of the home because one does not spend much time in the bathroom or toilet. Nevertheless, the placement of bathrooms and toilets are important because this is where all the cleansing is done. They are the sources of unpleasant odours and disposal of human waste. As mentioned earlier, you do not have to spend lots of money on bathrooms and toilets. The average man spends one-third of his life sleeping and two-thirds on other daily activities like working. Unless you have an obsession with self-cleanliness, you will not spend more time than necessary in that area.

FENG SHUI FOR A BETTER BATHROOM

The bathroom is considered one of the Yin, weak, wet areas of the home or office. When they started building bathrooms in the 1900s inside dwellings, people thought it was the quirkiness of the very rich getting out of hand. They said, "You do not do it in the house, you go outside to do it." The traditional outhouse was the norm until then. Even the bathtub was moved from outside to inside for the weekly baths. In China and Europe, the use of the chamber pot was the norm.

Through modern architecture, the bathroom slowly moved inside the residence. Why is the bathroom considered to be weak?

Because this is a place where you drop your energy, either through bodily waste or through washing your outer body. Everything is leaving the site through the bathroom, through the toilet, the vanity sinks, the bathtub and shower sinks. Since there is so much water in the bathroom, it is considered weak Yin or full of negative energy. Wetness or Yin Chi is the basis of most diseases. It is very important that this energy is overall isolated from the rest of the home or business.

Bathrooms can often be attributed to negative health conditions. To help balance this, try putting the Fire colour of red into the bathroom. One of the most effective ways is to paint the whole inside of the bathroom door red. The next best cure would be a red shower curtain or other strong accents of red. All this red has a neutralizing effect on all the water in the bathroom.

Depending on where the bathroom is situated in the site, it can have a draining effect on a variety of areas in your life like your wealth and health. One of the worst is if the bathroom is visible from the front door entry. The front door is considered the mouth of the site. From here, the food comes in or energy is fed to the house. To see the waste area where the food comes in can create many health issues like problems with elimination, digestion, kidney and bladder issues.

Bathroom location: Wherever the bathroom is located in the site, it is highly advisable to make several adjustments to it so that the positive and vital energy of the home or business is not drained. For one, always make a habit of keeping the bathroom door closed at all times. In this way, the wet Yin energy is not floating around the surrounding area. Also, you will not be able to see inside the bathroom, so your sub-conscious thoughts will not be influenced by waste and cleansing.

Excellent cures: Placing a good-sized mirror on the outside of the door to deflect the positive energy of the rest of the site from going into the bathroom, is an important bathroom cure. This will not work unless the bathroom door is shut. It is also best that when you first walk into the bathroom you see another mirror. This deflects the negative energy back out of the door. It is also best if the toilet is hidden from view upon entering the bathroom. If the toilet is in view as you enter, it is good to hang a round-faceted crystal ball between the entry and the toilet. Again, this helps disperse the Chi coming into the bathroom.

Another excellent cure for the bathroom is to place a small three-inch round mirror and attach it to the ceiling facing down directly over the toilet. According to Feng Shui, it helps to draw the positive Chi up and away from the toilet. Keeping the toilet seat down and the drains closed when not in use also helps leakage of energy.

Keeping the shower curtain drawn and shower door closed also helps the leakage problem. Since the bathroom is considered a wet, Yin energy, it helps to balance the energy with live, healthy, green plants. Aesthetically, it seems that the bathroom is one of the most forgotten areas of the site. Make it a happy place and bring colour and nice art into the surroundings. Bring a sense of warmth into the situation to help balance the wet energy. Never put pictures of living people like family members inside the bathroom. This can drain their energy.

Modern trends: A new trend in home-building today is in the master bedroom. Sometimes, the builders don't even put a door on the master bathroom. So from your bed you quite often have a full view of your bathroom vanity area, sinks included. This is a very negative situation for the health of the people sleeping in that bedroom. Every night, the wet Yin Chi floats around the sleeping area and drains the energy of the people sleeping.

To help this situation, the best remedy would be to actually build a bathroom door. If that cannot be done, try to create some kind of closure, such as a curtain, hanging beads or valances to cover the top of the opening. At the least, hang a round-faceted crystal ball in the entrance to the bathroom to help diffuse the wet, Yin Chi from spreading into the bedroom and to prevent the positive warm Chi of the bedroom from going into the bathroom.

Remember, bathrooms are vital to our cleansing and wastes, but we need to balance the wet energy with the rest of our living space. Last, but not the least, make sure all the plumbing is working correctly. Leaking toilets indicate money leaving the site, and blocked plumbing indicates blocked energy somewhere in the occupant's life.

IS YOUR TOILET HURTING YOUR HEALTH?

Creating a healthy atmosphere in your home is an important part of maintaining your mental and physical health. This may seem like common sense, but just think about your space and how you move in it. For instance, is your space free from obstructions (clutter) that might lead you to trip and bump your head and so on? If you have to adjust yourself to the space (step over something, duck under another thing), then chances are it is making an impact on you mentally and physically. Keeping your home and office clean is another common sense solution to foster good health. This ensures that the energy in your home is smooth and free flowing like a river.

One of the most important elements regarding health is the toilet. It is also one of the biggest areas of concern for Feng Shui. This is because of the very nature of toilets. They carry bodily wastes away, and they are points of contact with germs and diseases. For this reason, it is important to keep them meticulously clean, ensure that the seat and lid is kept down and that the door to the toilet is closed. In a perfect world, toilets should also be enclosed in their own rooms or hidden from view as you enter the room. Feng Shui principles teach that toilets can actually harm your health and well-being if they are situated in the wrong places. Given below is an explanation on how toilets can impact your health — and what you can do about it.

BEDROOMS

Toilets should never share the same wall as a bed. This is very unhealthy. If a bed is against the wall and the toilet is against that same wall on the other side, then move the bed. Likewise, you should never see or hear a toilet or bathroom from your bed. This can lead to respiratory problems.

KITCHENS AND DINING ROOMS

Bathrooms and toilets that are off the kitchen are another health concern. Always keep the door to the toilet closed so that someone in the kitchen cannot see the bathroom, and definitely not the toilet. Even the visual thought of mixing wastes with food is distasteful and can have a negative health impact. If the toilet can be seen from the dining room, this creates another health hazard. Block the view with a curtain or partition of some kind. If a toilet upstairs is over the kitchen or dining room, either try to move the table or discontinue using this bathroom.

FRONT DOORS

Toilets and bathrooms that can be seen from the front door rob the occupants of career opportunities or worse yet put the career you know where: in the toilet. Always close the toilet door and make sure the toilet cannot be seen from the front door.

TOILETS IN THE SOUTH-WEST

Toilets in the South-west portion of the home will give rise to marital troubles or cause someone to remain single for a long time. Again, keep them closed and treat them like you would treat a toilet in the centre of the home (see below).

TOILETS IN THE NORTH-WEST

Toilets in the North-west portion will bring difficulties to the breadwinner of the home. Do something to stimulate the energy. For example, keep a light on in the toilet, or try the suggestions given. Make sure you NEVER put any candles in this bathroom or in the North-west portion of the home. This is a very, very important rule because it can cause a sudden loss for the breadwinner of the family. Therefore, no candles or open flames in the North-west sector.

TOILETS IN THE CENTRE OF THE HOUSE

This is a common problem. Bathrooms in the centre of the house drain vital energy. If you can, paint the room red and place candles in here. You can also decorate with as many red objects as possible to stimulate Fire energy.

WHICH IS THE BEST PLACE TO PUT TOILETS?

Well, for most of us, the toilets are where the builder put them! However, if you are building a home, try to place the bathrooms on the outer walls. Short of that, keep the seats and lids down and the door to the bathroom closed. Try putting a small round mirror (about 4 inches in diameter) above the toilet and one on the door to the toilet. If you can't find a round mirror to put above the toilet (to reflect the bowl), then try putting a mirror over the toilet. Mirrors stimulate energy that the toilets drain. Lastly, don't forget to take out any plants that you have in the toilet. If you have a bathroom with a water closet, plants in the bathing area are OK (still not preferred). However, do not have plants or pictures of flowers next to your toilet.

Hopefully, you've picked up some good tips about the toilets in your home. They are a common source of irritation for many people. Besides their Feng Shui applications, many people debate how they should be left: up or down. The answer is neither. The consideration should be about whether it is "open" or "closed". Still can't convince everyone to close their toilets? Tell them that health experts have found that when a toilet is flushed, the water from the toilet goes into the air and settles on your toothbrushes, countertops and so on, posing a health hazard (yuk!). Good luck with this! Now go put that seat and lid down and close the door. Hurry!

FENG SHUI FOR THE KITCHEN

The kitchen and the stove are considered one of the most important areas in a home. The stove is considered one of the most important items in the house in relationship to wealth and good health.

To start with, the *entire* stove should always be kept immaculately clean and all burners in working condition to enhance maximum prosperity for the household.

Always position your stove to have a clear view of the kitchen door. It should never be seen from the front door of the house. If this is the case, the money of the house is being attacked. Place a screen or partition to hide the stove from the door. Quite often, something heavy like an oven or ventilation hood will hang over the stove and create money problems for the house. Place a small bell or crystal ball from the overhanging item. This will help lift the Chi.

Make sure your stove isn't directly next to the sink or refrigerator as Fire and Water produce steam that is too hot to handle. Relationship problems are created when the stove (fire — male) faces the sink (water — female), and arguments between the sexes follow. Hang a round-faceted crystal ball between the stove and sink to promote harmony. When the stove (fire — male) is next to the refrigerator (water — female), you can again have male/female issues going on. Place a bamboo flute on the side of the refrigerator to promote harmony. This will create a Five Element creative cycle, with Water feeding Wood and Wood feeding Fire.

Many Feng Shui experts recommend placing a mirror behind the stove to double your wealth, promote prosperity and to protect the cook while in front of the stove. Sometimes, the mirror behind the stove can be used to give the cook a view of what is going on behind him/her. While cooking, make sure you can see all the doors so that you aren't startled from behind.

Never have a bathroom coming onto the kitchen. This can create major illnesses for the whole family. It is best not to enter your house from the outside into the kitchen, like coming in from the parking garage. People will have a tendency to put on weight in this location, because their first impression, as they come in, is of food. It is better to use another door.

Never place the stove on a wall that may have a bed on the other side. There is a correlation to brain diseases and tumours with this position. Move the bed. In the kitchen, keep all knives away. Exposed knives can lead to arguments and sharp words. Always keep alcohol spirits away. Exposed alcohol leads to more drinking. Even attractive wine holders add to this problem.

Placing a full bowl of fruit in the kitchen promotes prosperity. Tupperware containers storing grains and legumes also help to promote that feeling of abundance. The kitchen should be airy, bright and happy with its light colours to promote harmony in the household. Placing plants around the sink lessens the loss of water (money) going down the drain. Never leave dishes in the sink. Wash them as soon as you can. Not cleaning up as soon as possible demonstrates a sense of incompleteness and disorganization.

The kitchen affects digestion and your nervous system. If the kitchen is close to the entry of the house, you may be food-oriented. Guests often come to eat, and Chi and wealth could be washed down the sink. It is the place where you create the nurturing food that provides good Chi to yourself and to your family.

Keep your counter tops open and without clutter. Most kitchen items, even those used regularly, can be put away in drawers or cupboards and still be easy to access.

Last, but not the least, never orient the kitchen in the centre of your home. It will deplete surrounding energies and possibly cause bad health.

FENG SHUI FOR CHILDREN'S ROOMS

There are no bad children, only bad behaviour: Our environment affects our behaviour. We know what to expect if we give our kids a lot of sugar or caffeine — they will bounce off the walls. We know what to expect if the temperature in the house is 90 degrees on a summer day — tempers will flare easily. These are normal responses to negative stimulation that most parents know about. But what most parents don't know is that there is negative stimulation in the home that affects their

child's behaviour, health and even their grades. This negative stimulation is invisible. However, it can easily be remedied using a combination of ancient Chinese wisdom and modern day science. Feng Shui is the 4,000-year-old Chinese practice of arranging our living space to be in harmony with the Earth's energy or Chi so that we are in balance with the forces of nature. Applying the practical techniques of Feng Shui to your home will help you take advantage of the good Chi and create a balanced environment. This will help your child grow and develop in a positive way and enhance family harmony.

SLEEPING DIRECTION

We spend the most amount of time in one spot every day in our bed, so the sleeping direction is very important. The goal is to align the child's bed so that the top or crown of the head is pointed towards one of their good Kua directions. Sleeping in the "wisdom" direction will help your child get better grades and improve their attitude about school. The "marriage and family harmony" direction will help decrease fighting and arguing in the household and help your child sleep better. Be sure to use a compass to determine actual compass directions in your home.

EXPOSURE TO EMFS

EMFs or electromagnetic frequencies are harsh energies emitted by electronic devices. They decrease the body's production of melatonin. Melatonin helps prevent sleep problems, moodiness, anger and depression, and also helps the body fight tumours. Arrange furniture so that your child's body is 3–5ft away from TVs, computer monitors, stereos, lamps and other electronic appliances. Never use an electric blanket or waterbed heater and don't let them stare into the microwave waiting for the popcorn! Stay 5ft away while it's on.

WHAT THE CHILD'S EYE SEES

Look at what your child sees every day. A happy family photo visible from the child's bed is comforting to see before they fall asleep and when they awaken. It reminds them they are part of a happy family when they are alone in their room. Posters of kittens, puppies and favourite cartoon characters are non-threatening and comforting for the little ones. Get to know the meaning behind the images in your teenager's room and keep the cool "negatives" to a minimum.

CLUTTER

Cleaning up after a small child is like shovelling the sidewalk while it's snowing. What's the point! But children do need a place to store their stuff to keep clutter under control. If a child's bedroom is also their study room, they won't be able to focus in a lot of clutter. Children should frequently clear out the space under their beds, which tends to become a catch-all for trash and treasures and creates "stuck" energy.

FURNITURE PLACEMENT

The bed should have its headboard against a solid wall. Make sure there is room to walk around each side of the bed. Don't push one side up against the wall. Avoid placing the bed under a window or directly in line with the door. Standing in the doorway, if you can toss a ball straight ahead and hit the bed, energy flowing into the room will also hit the bed. This is not good for the child. Mirrors in the bedroom keep the room "awake" and make it harder to sleep.

COLOUR

Your child's subconscious sleeping habits will let you know whether their room is comfortable or not. If you keep finding your child in bed with you, then their room is not working for them. Avoid using energizing colours like red and other bright colours in the bedroom as they can cause tempers to flare during playtime and result in too much hyperactive energy for the little one to fall asleep at night. Bright colours are good for playrooms but bedrooms need to be more subdued. Blues and light pinks are calming. Greens and skin tones are good.

Creating a comfortable, harmonious bedroom makes for a good night's rest. A good night's rest makes for a refreshed, healthy child.

Special Note: The Fu Wei direction is said to bring luck in education and personal development. It is also referred to as the "Wisdom" direction. It is suggested that schoolchildren and college students sit at their study desks facing their Fu Wei direction and sleep with the top or crown of their heads pointed in their Fu Wei direction to bring in better grades and recognition. To find out your child's Fu Wei/Wisdom direction, see the Kua number chart below. Once you know your child's Kua number, you can find out which direction is his or her wisdom direction. Be sure to use a compass when you are checking your child's current sleeping direction and study desk direction. Using East sunrise/West sunset is not an accurate way to determine compass directions!

Kua Number		Fu Wei or Wisdom Direction
1		North
2		South-west
3		East
4		South-east
5	**Male**	South-west
5	**Female**	North-east
6		North-west
7		West
8		North-east
9		South

FENG SHUI FOR A BABY'S NURSERY

Like the prosperity and health energies present in your habitat, a woman becoming pregnant in a home is considered both an auspicious and happy occasion. The adoption of a child also creates good karma. Often overlooked in most homes, the nursery is an important room to Feng Shui, particularly for first-time mothers. Unlike the Western tradition, Indian tradition considers it unlucky to prepare a baby's room too far in advance. So the new addition to the family usually moves into a space that is newly prepared in the last few weeks before arrival. Hence, designing a nursery according to Feng Shui can ease the newcomer's adjustment from the womb to a room. The first step involves conducting an energy cleansing of the room, ridding it of past energies and creating a "clean slate". Simply air the space out by leaving the windows open on a sunny day. This brings in the Yang energy of the sun, light and fresh air. You can also burn an incense stick in a closed room, remembering to air it out after an hour or two. Ringing bells or clapping are also two other methods of clearing the space. Conduct this cleansing twice: Once before installing new wallpaper or painting the room; and a second time, the day before the new baby arrives. Follow up by tossing a pinch or two of sea salt into all the corners in the room, including closets.

Appropriate colours for a baby or child's room are soft Yin colours that induce serenity and rest. Bright, strong, Yang colours like red and bright yellow are not advisable for a child's room because they stimulate rather than calm down the occupant. Such dynamic colours are great for a play area, but not for a bedroom. Soft, pastel tints like pistachio or mint, turquoise or aqua, greens and blues, with accents of soft buttercup yellow, peach or other complementary colours are preferred. Green represents good health, family life, youth, spring, new beginnings and the element of Wood. Blue, the colour and element of Water generates Wood, so they go well together. Keep the decorations simple. Use light, airy curtains that are white (representing children) or match the wallpaper or paint. Add simple mobiles that move with the room's air currents.

The crib or cot should be located against a wall and not under a window or in direct line with the main entrance into the bedroom. Place your baby in it at night and observe the direction in which he or she is positioned in the morning. Babies tend to intuitively move themselves so that the tops of their heads are pointing towards their most comfortable positions. When you have determined this favourite position, turn the crib or cot to match it.

Soft lighting and classical music or easy listening favourites are perfect for the baby's environment. A live green plant and a slightly open window will stimulate a flow of beneficial Chi energy in the room. As the child grows older, move the plant out of reach.

Water features like aquariums, waterfalls, fountains and waterbeds possess a lot of Yin energy and should NOT be in any bedroom, including the baby's, as they draw wealth away from the family.

Feng Shui is all about living in harmony with nature and the universe. By incorporating the principles of this ancient wisdom into your baby's room, you are providing a peaceful, yet energizing room, as well as bringing it into concordance with the rest of your home.

FENG SHUI FOR FERTILITY

Feng Shui can be used to boost your conception and fertility factor! Some of you may have been married for a while with no luck at babies yet, and some of you may be newly married and just starting out your own household with a baby in mind. You might also still be single but would like to be in the know. I think everyone will benefit from these tips in some way or another. Therefore, do have a good read and enhance your home for auspicious luck in conceiving!

- The Kua of the husband should be tapped first and foremost. Sleep in his Yan Nian (Relationship) direction to enhance fertility and promote spousal well-being as well as increase the intimacy, romance and feelings of affection! If sleeping in his Yan Nian is not feasible, simply re-position your bed to face the direction. Easy!

- Do stay away from decorating your home with fierce pictures of predatory animals in aggressive, dominant poses. These images will fail to nurture and consequently "kill" the warm, fertile ambience you are striving for.

- Dragon symbols are terribly Yang in nature and should only be used outside the bedroom. However, in the case of trying for a baby, a little Yang magic by the bedside may help! An inconspicuous dragon item next to the bed can conjure up the precious Yang energy required to aid conception. Hang either a tassel with a bronze dragon or a small dragon charm next to the bed for this purpose.

- A beaming Buddha statue with children climbing all over him symbolizes the joy of children. It is also said to be able to facilitate the laughter and happiness of your own future children to your home! Display the statue prominently in the East direction of the bedroom.

- Make sure that there is nothing but open space directly outside the front door. Trees, a street or other objects in the immediate vicinity of this door is not good, since this is the main entrance of Chi. Keep this space clean and fresh smelling!

- Elephants are said to be the ultimate symbol of fertility and virility. They can also create auspicious "descendants' Chi" — the very type you need! Place an elephant statue in the West or North-west direction. If you wish for a son, lodge a stone on the back of the statue.

- Cicadas are not just those bugs that make charming night sounds. They are actually a potent symbol of marriage luck and fertility! Couples who are trying to conceive should definitely have an image of the cicada close by in the bedroom.

"WOMB SHUI"

Are our choices for the home driven by a desire for motherly love? Feng Shui asserts that there are natural relationships between objects and spaces in homes and workplaces. If these relationships are properly oriented to enhance the flow of Chi within the space, they can create conditions that bring about optimum health, wealth, love and relationships.

If you visit your local book store, you will discover that there has been a deluge of Feng Shui literature published in the last few years. In addition, Feng Shui Practitioners have proliferated all over the country.

The physical environment has an enormous impact on human emotions, behaviours and relationships. With the wisdom of Feng Shui, one can create a process for designing and redesigning homes so that they become sources of nurture, serenity, harmony and inspiration for those who live in them, thereby radically increasing the potential emotional satisfaction quotient of the home.

This is where "Womb Shui" comes in. The basic idea is that the young of many species, including humans, require a profound bond with their primary nurturer in the first few months of life. This bond is seen by most attachment theorists as an evolutionary strategy for avoiding predators. Fish school to confuse larger fish. Birds flock for the same reason. So do mammals who form herds. Human beings form families, cities, nations, religions and other connections with which they identify. Everyone else is the "other", and untrustworthy.

This theory suggests that this profound connection between mother and child is created in the earliest period of life, perhaps beginning even before birth. In a species that seeks such an attachment, if that bond fails for some reason, the new life will not thrive. In other words, if mummy doesn't love the baby, or the baby perceives that it is not loved, then the baby may die.

What does this have to do with architecture? Well, it has everything to do with it and almost every other human endeavour. If the original attachment between mother and child forms the central emotional context for all human behaviour and colours our interpretation of everything around us, then our emotional architecture, that is, what makes us comfortable, what we see as attractive, what makes us feel special, or important, or secure is at the root of every aspect of accomplishing a home design we will enjoy.

And after all, what is a home but an external model of the womb? Ultimately, what do we all seek in a home? Comfort, security, a sense that we are loved and appreciated and in control of our lives. What do we seek in our décor and home furnishings? Comfort, convenience, self-expression, a sense that we belong and are surrounded by the familiar.

There was a time when we all had peace in our lives. We were warm, protected and completely surrounded by a nurturing environment. Then one day, we lost it all. We were born into a world of harsh light, cold air, loud voices, pain and discomfort. Most of us have been trying to go back "home" ever since.

Sadly, it is a fundamental fact of human life that no matter how hard we try, no matter how successful we become, no matter how much time we spend with a therapist, and no matter how well we come to know ourselves, we can never recover the perfect peace we must have felt floating in embryonic fluid, listening to the murmur of our mother's heartbeat, buffered from the world of travail outside.

I believe there might be a reliable way of leading people towards creating a loving home with Feng Shui design — that represents the deepest and most fulfilling parts of themselves — and architecture that supports their goals and personal growth.

FENG SHUI MISCELLANY

FENG SHUI TIPS FOR WEIGHT LOSS

Obesity is a major health concern all over the world. The ideal diets and exercise regimes change on a weekly basis. Who do we believe? Feng Shui has some simple ideas that can enhance any weight loss programme. Read on!

- Eat your dinner on a black or dark blue plate. The colour of the plate subconsciously diminishes your appetite. Eat dinner meals on dark plates and lunch and breakfast meals on bright colour plates.
- Place a dark tablecloth on the table in the evening. Put it on the table after lunch to curb your appetite for the rest of the day. Restaurants use red tablecloths to stimulate your appetite. (Good trick they have been using for years.)
- Make eating a sacred ritual. Decorate the table with fresh flowers and use the best china for all your meals. Say a prayer of thanks for all the great food that is available to you.
- Do your exercise in bright colours in place of the traditional grey or black jogging suits. The warm colours of the rainbows stimulate activity while the dark colours tire the body.
- Enhance the South area. Place a picture of your face glued to a body type you desire. Place the date of your achievement. Be realistic and safe. Weight loss of 1kg a week is ideal for keeping off the weight and maintaining it.
- Food selection should be varied. Bright colours should dominate the plate and neutral colours should be less than

one-third. There is little Chi value in a plate of pasta compared to a bowl of veggies!

- Place a mirror on the refrigerator to deter you from opening it after certain hours. Do not eat four hours before you go to bed.
- Throw away all food that has little Chi value. Pick up the food and decide if it has positive or negative Chi. Food that clogs and blocks the Chi in the body makes it difficult to do physical activity.
- Clear the home of clutter. Throw away things that are reminders of you gaining weight, for example, the dress from the 80s that you will wear once you lose 20kg. Eliminate items that make you feel tired and unmotivated.
- Make sure the centre of the home is clear of clutter.
- Clean the kitchen of all clutter. The cupboards should not be bulging open with food and kitchen accessories. Keep a bowl of fresh fruit on the counter or table to represent vitality and healthy choices.
- Imagine yourself doing your favourite physical activity and participate in your daydream. Now, make it a part of your daily routine. Rebounding is a great exercise for weight loss and to get the Chi moving and unblocked.
- Front Entrance: What does it say as you enter? Can you see the kitchen or can you see your big comfortable couch calling your name? As you enter the front door, you want to feel energized to make a healthy meal and to do some physical activity. Place red flowers in your view to stimulate the Chi at home.
- Overall Home: What does the home say? Is the home filled with Yin energy? Is it very relaxing and quiet? Infuse some Yang energy to keep you moving. Play Latin dance music to get your feet moving or spray the home with citrus scents. Add a few drops of lemon essential oil in a diffuser with spring water.

Weight loss programmes drain you mentally, physically and emotionally. Use Feng Shui principles to aid in your battle and be victorious with a little help from the unseen world of Chi.

AROMATHERAPY & FENG SHUI

Imagine sitting back on a comfortable lawn chair with the sun shining brightly in the sky. Your whole body relaxes and melts into the chair as you just enjoy the moment. All of a sudden you are awakened from your relaxation because of a lingering smell in the air. The garbage truck has passed through your neighbourhood, leaving the remnants of people's waste in the air. Your moment has been lost with just one whiff!!

Your nose is a very important tool in Feng Shui. The aromas around you can depress, uplift or be neutral to you and your family. The next time you go into your home or a specific room in your house, try this little experiment. Close your eyes and go to the centre of the room and just smell the air. Does the air feel old or stagnant or bright or do you get no sensation at all? Do this for at least a minute and only focus on the smells around you. Our noses are a dynamic sense that will choose the food you eat or the places you visit.

How many times have you walked into a restaurant and eaten a meal way too big as the smell of the food entices you? Your sense of smell is always at work. The art of Feng Shui incorporates aromas to transform a room. Given below is a brief list of the more common aromas and their effect on the average individual. An aroma can invite or turn people away from your home.

FENG SHUI AROMA LIST

Lavender: A relaxing smell that brings calmness to all those around. It is great to have a lavender candle burning during big family functions to keep peace and limit the number of outbursts.

Lemon: An uplifting smell that brings clarity. Great to use when you are studying. Also excellent to give your home a sparkling, clean smell.

Eucalyptus: A good scent to keep colds at bay during the winter season. The smell is invigorating and helps to reduce congestion.

Tea Tree: A great oil to be used as a disinfectant in your mop water. You can also add lemon oil to get that light, clean smell.

Fragrant flowers like gardenias and lilacs are great for stimulating energy.

Aromatherapy is an easy and simple way to bring a missing element into your home. Given below are the more common element aromas that are easy to find and are generally inexpensive.

	Element Aroma List
Wood: Green	Chamomile, Clary Sage, Eucalyptus, Sweet Marjoram
Fire: Spicy	Sweet Basil, Clove, Cinnamon, Black Pepper, Coriander
Earth: Earthy	Sage, Sandalwood, Pine, Frankincense, Cedar
Metal: Citrus	Orange, Lemon, Grapefruit, Tangerine, Citronella, Bergamot
Water	Floral Lavender, Ylang Ylang, Violet, Rose, Geranium

Play with the scents and identify your reactions to the different smells. There is no right or wrong way to incorporate smells into your home. The uplifting smell of lilac may actually depress you because it triggers something from your past. Listen to your intuition and it will guide you.

FENG SHUI & RELIGION

Many people have asked me for ways to reconcile Feng Shui with religion. There are people who know Feng Shui can help, yet hesitate to consult a Feng Shui Master because they are uncertain whether Feng Shui will contradict their faith.

It is important to understand that Feng Shui is *not* a religion. Feng Shui is the recognition or understanding of the laws of nature and of the fact that there are certain patterns of energy. For every force, there is an equal and opposite force. For every cause, there is an effect. This natural phenomenon exists whether you believe in it or not. Feng Shui, in fact, is a science incorporating astronomy, geography, the environment, the magnetic fields and physics. Feng Shui is not a religion or superstition. Modern science has proven it to be a complex mathematical system.

Feng Shui is based on the Taoist philosophy that everything is made of energy or what is called Chi by the Chinese. There is no God in Feng Shui. In Feng Shui, there is an ultimate power or Tai Chi that rules, connects and guides us. This is known as the way or the laws of nature. The energies of nature have a great influence on us. Living in natural settings and nourishing ourselves with natural foods strengthens our bodies. All these things happen regardless of whether you are a Christian, a Buddhist, a Catholic or a Hindu. If there is to be a God in Feng Shui, it would be this power of nature: The source of life. In order to excel, we must respect and understand the ways of nature. When we live by the laws of nature, we can progress and evolve into superior beings. This is the basic purpose of Feng Shui.

In various religions of the world, man has created different names and different images to represent a higher intelligence or divine force. Almost all religions have similar goals — that we are to believe and have hope in a higher energy, a divine source that creates us, rules us, protects us and offers guidance when we have done wrong. Many things that happen in this world do not have an explanation. It is human nature to fear the unknown. We have thus theorized and created our own answers in science and religion. Nonetheless, there are things unexplained by science and religion. Feng Shui offers another perspective to see our world and to deal with, prevent or solve problems we face in our daily lives. Thus, to put doubting minds at rest, I can safely say that Feng Shui is not related to any religion or belief system. It is a scientific discipline based on the analysis of energy. By tapping these energies to live harmoniously with the existing forces, Feng Shui truly works with whatever religion one practises.

FENG SHUI ADVICE FOR GIVING GIFTS

Everyone likes to receive gifts. There are also times when one has to return gifts. According to Feng Shui, there are some gifts that can have the opposite effect than intended and be harmful to the person who receives it, even though it is given with the best intentions. Therefore, it is important that you know these harmful gifts so that you can avoid giving them and unwillingly cause problems.

First of all, you should never give a sharp object as a gift. When giving a sharp object as a gift, you are actually hurting the relationship you have with the person who receives it since the object would cut and damage the bond existing between you and that person. Sharp objects include knives, scissors, swords and so on.

Another object you should never give as a gift is a clock or timepiece of any kind. These objects represent the passage of time and measure the life time that is left. In this way, timepieces symbolize the approach of the end of the life of the person to whom you are giving them. Actually, in Chinese culture, clocks are seen like a representation of death when given as a gift, so avoid choosing this as a present.

Even though red roses are often given as a love symbol, according to Feng Shui, they actually represent quite the contrary. Red roses with long stems and sharp thorns would damage the relationship between you and the person who receives them rather than strengthen it. Pink roses without thorns would be a much better choice. According to Feng Shui, pink roses symbolize love and help to strengthen the bond between you and the person who receives them. Also, giving red and white flowers symbolize death. Avoid giving them as gifts.

The way you present your gifts is also important for Feng Shui. Ideally, you should wrap them in red, since red represents good luck and is a very auspicious colour. Other good colours for wrapping your gifts are orange, yellow, golden and any other bright or cheerful colour which represents a positive wish.

FASHION FENG SHUI

In keeping with the trend of fashion set in motion nowadays, here are some Fashion Feng Shui tips. Basically, Fashion Feng Shui is an innovative, transformational dressing technique inspired by Feng Shui, the ancient Chinese Science of Metaphysics. Based on the premise that you live a happier, healthier and more prosperous existence when your living and working environments are harmonious and balanced, Feng Shui encourages you to visually affirm your intentions in your personal and professional surroundings in order to create them in your life.

Fashion Feng Shui, which considers clothing to be your body's most intimate environment, applies Feng Shui philosophy and principles to personal appearance. Maintaining that what you wear is as influential on your life as your home and business décor, Fashion Feng Shui teaches you to dress with mindfulness and intention so that your clothes express your authenticity and address your deepest desires.

Using the energetic language of nature's Five Elements of Water, Wood, Fire, Earth and Metal to describe physical appearance, preferences and goals, lifestyle and clothing design elements, Fashion Feng Shui elevates what was once a mundane routine to a mindful ritual. Therefore, getting dressed becomes easy, fun and empowering.

THE FIVE ELEMENTAL ARCHETYPES

We are energetic beings. Therefore, Fashion Feng Shui's Five Elemental Archetypes illustrate how nature's Five Elements are represented in the energies of the mind (intentional), spirit (essential), and body (visual). Each Elemental Energy is personified according to his/her archetypal goals, preferences, and appearance.

- Intentional Energy is consciously created. It is the energy attached to what you have "in mind" to be, do and have.

- Essential Energy is unconsciously expressed. It is the energetic lens through which you see the world, the assimilation of your core (driving force), character (emotional nature), and conduct (way of being) — the unique "essence" that is you.

- Visual Energy is physically transmitted. It is the vibrational pattern created by "how you look", influenced by the energies inherent in your physical complexion, ie, dark or fair colour and body shape, and the colours, patterns, textures, fabrics and silhouettes of the clothes you wear.

EVERYTHING IS ALIVE

Chi, the universal life force, animates everyone and everything in our world, giving us a whole new perspective on the people and possessions that surround us. Through the eyes of Fashion Feng Shui, if you consider your surroundings to be alive and talking to you all the time, think about what your clothing is "saying" to people around you and what it reflects about you. Do your clothes speak your truth? Is your wardrobe authentic to who you are? Do your clothes cheer you or jeer you? Does your appearance affirm your goals?

EVERYTHING IS CONNECTED

Everyone and everything is connected by a "worldwide web" of energy. Therefore, your actions and attitudes affect everyone and everything else in the world and vice versa. Through the eyes of Fashion Feng Shui, connect with the people you meet, the places you go to and the pastimes you pursue by mirroring their energy in your appearance. Ponder on the following: Do your clothes reflect your surroundings? Are you dressed appropriately for every interaction and occasion? Is your wardrobe functional? Does it support your desired lifestyle?

EVERYTHING CHANGES

Nature is in a constant state of change. You witness it in the cycle of seasons, the ebbing and flowing of the tides and the waxing and waning of the moon. Change is one thing upon which you can always rely. When you change, you align yourself with the energy of the moment, so should your clothing. Figure out the following: Do your clothes align with the current you? When is the last time you made changes to yourself, your personal style, your living or working environments? Is your wardrobe attuned to the present you? Do you or your clothes require updates?

LIVE WITH WHAT YOU LOVE

The state of your surroundings affects your state of mind. Surround yourself only with your favourite people and possessions. Memories and associations make your wardrobe come alive. Make sure they are all positive ones. Wear only clothes that make your heart sing! Ask yourself: How do your clothes make you feel? Do you love them? Do they return your love? Do some of your clothes drag your energy down (like a ball and chain)? Do some lift it up (like a balloon)? How do you think they affect your life?

PUT SAFETY AND COMFORT FIRST

Avoid filling your environment with "hazardous furnishings", that is, anything that does not contribute to your personal safety and comfort. Small nuisances like uncomfortable clothes, missing buttons, unruly zippers and drooping hems deplete your energy. Do you perform wardrobe audits? Do you regularly identify the garments to keep, sweep or tweak? Are you living with clothes that are not as perfect as you? How does this affect your energy?

ORGANIZE AND EXPRESS YOURSELF

Feng Shui maintains that your environment displays your consciousness and your consciousness creates your environment. Your wardrobe should be in an ideal condition if you expect your life to be so. Ask yourself: Is your wardrobe in a state of disorganization or disrepair? If so, is it a reflection of a like mindset? Or, could it be manifesting the same in your life? Do your clothes display your inner magnificence?

Fashion Feng Shui maintains that, for your personal appearance to be authentic and attractive (literally and figuratively), you must address and integrate your Intentional, Essential and Visual Energies so that you are able to create a Fashion Feng Shui Wardrobe Plan that defines the colours, patterns, textures, fabrics and silhouettes that align with your spirit, affirm your goals and enhance your physical appearance.

When you dress with Fashion Feng Shui, your wardrobe is a holograph of all that you are and all that you wish to be.

COLOURS IN FENG SHUI

Colour plays a very important role in Feng Shui. A house and every room in the house has eight directions: North, South, East, West and North-east, South-west, South-east and North-west. Each of these eight directions has an element and a colour which can be energized to activate the luck of those corners. Depending on the kind of luck one wants to activate, the correct colours can either be painted on the walls of the room or paintings and other objects placed in these corners.

ELEMENT THERAPY WITH COLOURS

Each element is associated with a different colour: Green for Wood, blue or black for Water, red for Fire, white for metal, ochre for Earth. To energize the southern part of your home, for example, one can either paint a wall any shade of red or use red curtains, carpets or paintings.

AUSPICIOUS COLOUR COMBINATIONS

Green/Red: Excellent in the South, good in the East and South-east during winter months.
Red/Yellow: Excellent in the South-west and North-east.
Yellow/Metallic: Excellent in the West and the North-west.
Metallic/Blue: Excellent in the North.
Blue/Green: Excellent in the East and South-east.

INAUSPICIOUS COLOUR COMBINATIONS

Red/Blue or Red/Black: Very bad in the South.
Red/Metallic: Very bad in the West or North-west.
Green/Yellow: Extra harmful in the South-west and North-east.
Yellow/Blue: Very bad in the North.
Green/Metallic: Extra bad in the East and South-east.

To understand the colour combinations, one has to have knowledge of the Productive and Destructive Cycles of Feng Shui.

Productive Cycle of Elements: In the Productive Cycle which creates auspicious colour combinations, the theory is as follows: Water produces Wood produces Fire produces Earth produces Metal produces Water.

Destructive Cycle of Elements: In the Destructive Cycle of elements, Wood exhausts Earth suppresses Water puts out Fire melts Metal cuts Wood.

Colour codes, therefore, have to follow the Productive Cycle of elements to create auspicious and positive energies in a room, house or office.

FISH & ANIMALS — THEIR EFFECT IN FENG SHUI

Fish and various other animals are considered as playing an important role in Feng Shui. A frequently asked question is about fish and their effect in Feng Shui. This is a Feng Shui topic which has often been misunderstood.

FISH AND FENG SHUI

In traditional Chinese Feng Shui, the only recommended solutions are the Five Elements of Wood, Fire, Earth, Metal and Water. The Water element strengthens Wood Chi. Fish have been confused to be a Feng Shui remedy, but this is not true in itself. What it is, is a combination of superstition and misunderstanding.

In Feng Shui, the numbers 6 and 7 are used in the calculations of the trigrams and are representative of metal (6=Chien or hard metal and 7=Tui or soft metal). The Five Element Theory says that Metal strengthens Water. Chinese folklore says that adding six goldfish and one black fish makes the Water stronger. What this is trying to do is to strengthen the Water effect with Metal. Actually, the fish only add decoration to the tank. To really strengthen the Water element, the tank should have the real Metal element with the Water.

Fish do add a couple of things, though. One is beauty and the other is to add circulation to the Water. Further, they are living creatures and bring life to the environment. This is good Feng Shui, but it is not needed in a strict sense for the Water element to be effective. Avoid stagnant water. This becomes a Sha (negative influence) and is not helpful.

Remember, everything in Feng Shui has an explanation. Feng Shui is based on logic and practical application. Moreover, Feng Shui, if properly applied, should appear natural and comfortable, both to people and to fish!

ANIMALS AND FENG SHUI

Animals are sometimes overlooked in the application of Feng Shui. Animals have a life force and each kind of animal has a meaning behind it. It is always good to have a symbol of your personal Chinese birth animal somewhere in your space. This will help to empower your personal archetype.

On a mundane level, your common living animals have different meanings. For instance, dogs are considered guardians. Hence, the use of Fu-dog statues are referred to in Chinese as the "heavenly dogs". Dogs also bring money. Lots of dogs brings lots of money. Fish are also very good for bringing in wealth and good luck. Turtles are symbols of longevity, so by placing one in the North, you can bring on long life and get rid of sickness. Birds also represent wealth and bring opportunities to you. Butterflies represent conjugal love.

Having a symbol or picture of a horse in your office can, at times, be very fortuitous. Horses represent success. They gallop as fast as the wind, speeding you to your destination. When using a horse in your space, it is best to place it between 11am and 1pm, when the Yang energy is at its highest. A group of eight horses is best for acquiring wealth. Placed in the South direction, horses also bring in fame luck.

All animals symbolically mean something and by knowing their meaning, they can have a profound Feng Shui effect in your life. Animals can thus be used as guides and symbols.

Before we became an urban society, humans were more interactive with their surroundings. A hundred years ago, most people lived in a rural setting and had a more direct connection with the animals in the environment.

If you listen to animals, they will talk to you and guide you.

Sometimes, an animal will appear or make something happen in the household that has significant meaning to the Feng Shui consultation. Invariably, when I am on site visits, pets come up to me, and the pet owners are amazed, because they say their pets never come up to strangers. Why is that? The animals have an idea that Feng Shui is going to make their space and lives better too!

Listen to the animals around you. They will guide you and tell you things. They are part of the environment.

PETS ARE GOOD FENG SHUI

A few years ago, a newspaper headline caught my eye. It read "Pet owner dies of shock when his dog was shot at...." I can well believe that. As an animal lover, I think it is extremely bad karma if anyone deliberately harms a creature that cannot really retaliate.

Having pets in the house and nurturing them also makes good Feng Shui sense. When dogs bark and wag their tails happily, they give us lots of exuberant joy. Petting and caring for any animal gives us — and them — great Feng Shui energy as displays of love are always wonderful Feng Shui.

Pets are often looked on as members of the family, and as such, should be considered when you are reviewing the Feng Shui of your home. Every space needs active energy and love, and pets give us both. They also allow us to express our love. This is the most important thing to remember. Their energy and liveliness means we have an active home even when we aren't there, making our homes more

Yang. Dogs, for instance, also provide protective energy for our homes, helping us to feel more secure and safe.

But when are pets not good Feng Shui? There are some instances when the Feng Shui of your home is disturbed by pets. The worst case scenario is when pets are not cared for properly. For example, fish represent success and wealth in Feng Shui. If the fish tank isn't clean and clear and if the water is dirty, then both may elude you.

So, while it is nice to have a pet, the first priority must always be the pet's health, safety and care. If you don't have the proper space or time to care for the pet, then it is better not to have them. Simply put, having animals in poor condition(s) is very bad Feng Shui.

Also, treat your pets kindly. If you have an ill-treated pet like an aggressive dog that barks, jumps on, scares or threatens people as soon as they enter your home, then you have a situation where every time someone comes in, fear comes in with them. Is this the kind of environment you want to live in? If this sounds like your pet(s), then at the very least they should be secured in another room when someone comes to visit. The fear they inspire will create a Yin environment. If this is the situation in your home, then you have a home where your energy is dragging and motivation low.

Feng Shui is all about balance. Use your pets to your advantage with Feng Shui. Simply having a loving pet is good for you. But the pet must also be good for the entire home. The pet should be friendly and clean and not bothersome to your relationships or visitors.

Dogs are wonderful for infusing a home with lively energy. Fish bring success, turtles symbolize longevity and cats are symbols of financial luck (consider lucky cats seen at Asian businesses). Therefore, as hard as it might be, take a long look at your pet situation to make sure that your pets are not harming your Feng Shui but are enhancing your life.

GARDEN FENG SHUI — THE CHI OF EARTH

In Feng Shui, the use of fragrant fresh flowers and lush green plants are often suggested as enhancements for the flow of Chi. Most of us, however, bring flowers into our home, whether from the florists or our own gardens, solely for the purpose of placing them in a vase and then setting them aside.

In the art of Feng Shui placement, we look for the right floral colour to decorate the appropriate sector of the Pa Kua: Red or pink for relationships, blue for wealth, green foliage for health. As we look out of our windows, we study landforms and observe the details of the natural world. Can you see the Dragons in the hills or the comforting Black Tortoise embracing you?

ACTIVATING THE CELESTIAL ANIMALS IN YOUR GARDEN

Activate the Dragon in your garden by creating curved pathways. Incorporate a winding pathway onto the Dragon side of your garden (ie, the left side of your garden, from the inside looking out) or in the East side of your garden. You can make your pathway with pebbles, stones, marble slabs or a small sand path framed on both sides with flowering plants.

By creating a Dragon on the East side of your house, you create extremely auspicious good luck. Therefore, spend some effort on it, especially if you want the flowers to bloom. Usually, the natural fall of plant foliage creates a meandering effect. You do not require much space for this feature.

You can also activate the Tortoise by keeping some live ones in your garden. The North is the sector of the Tortoise. This is even better if the North falls in the back of your house. Keep them in a pond in your garden for support and auspicious good luck.

The rooster can substitute for the Phoenix, but *do not* keep birds in cages. You can, if you wish, keep a rooster as a pet in the South part of your garden. This will activate the Phoenix energy of the sector. Some jungle roosters of the tropics make beautiful pets. But again, on no account should you keep birds in cages. The Chinese believe that nothing brings worse luck than this.

When you find frogs in your garden, let them be. Frogs also bring good luck to the home, so if you find a frog or two in your garden, leave them alone and let them be. If you feel squeamish at the thought of keeping live frogs, you can place brass or ceramic images of frogs in your garden.

LUCKY BAMBOO IN FENG SHUI

Would you like to bring more harmony, success, and passion into your life? Feng Shui is a powerful way to make positive change a reality!

Feng Shui, which literally translates from Chinese into "Wind and Water", is a 4,000-year-old system of analysing and altering the flow of energy in any environment to produce the desired change. The premise behind Feng Shui is that every physical object in our surrounding has an influence on our lives. By altering how energy or Chi flows around and through these surroundings, we can promote happiness, prosperity and good health and feel more energized, positive and passionate about life.

The easiest way to begin, without hiring a trained consultant or totally transforming your home or workplace, is to include some strategically placed elements in your environment. There are numerous objects which have long been recognized as having the ability to enhance the flow of positive Chi. By adding a few simple objects and following some basic Feng Shui placement guidelines, your space will look more attractive, and you will reap the many benefits of a more positive, auspicious energy flow.

Various live plants and objects have been introduced to Feng Shui practice to help enhance positive Chi and counteract the negative Chi and therefore induce luck, fortune and wealth. The most popular live plants and objects are Lucky Bamboo, Money

Plants, Crystals, Coins and other good fortune symbols.

Lucky Bamboo (*dracaena sanderiana*) is a tropical plant from the lily family. Tough, resilient and thriving in very low light, it is the perfect plant for home or office. Lucky Bamboo grows in water like cut flowers, but it will last for years. Care is simple. An inch or two of water, freshened every 15 days should be enough. It is not necessary to feed the Lucky Bamboo. These plants don't need much light or fertilizer. The bamboo adapts to a new environment easily. Low light to bright indirect sunlight suits them well. There is no need to transplant them and put them in soil.

Lucky Bamboo is best purchased when the Chinese New Year is approaching or when you are celebrating a grand business opening. It can be purchased to celebrate the purchase of a new house or just for pure good luck. Lucky Bamboo has the following spiritual meaning:

- Career: Climb up the ladder (advancement)
- Business: Success in business venture (prosperity)
- Health: Harmony and peace in life (longevity)
- Religious: Gracious, honourable and virtuous
- Relationship: Energize your love life
- Feng Shui: Creation of positive energy in your environment

According to Feng Shui principles, Lucky Bamboo is an excellent way to attract positive Chi. For centuries, the Chinese have considered it to be a very lucky and positive symbol. It is said that three stalks attract happiness, five attract wealth, seven result in good health and 21 stalks offer a very powerful all-purpose blessing.

Lucky Bamboo makes for a perfect gift. The ancients say that enhancing another's good fortune will always improve the good fortune of the giver.

CANDLES & FENG SHUI

The basic belief behind Feng Shui is that there are Five Elements, some combinations of which create a Productive Cycle and some a Destructive Cycle. When one of these Five Elements of Water, Wood, Fire, Earth and Metal for the Productive Cycle are combined with an element adjacent to the main element, a Productive Cycle is perpetuated.

The reason being that Water sustains Wood, Wood feeds Fire, ashes create Earth, Earth creates Metal and Metal holds Water. So, if you have a room where Wood is the main element, it would be good Feng Shui to add a Water or Fire element to the room, as Water feeds Wood and Wood feeds Fire. This is where candles would be a nice touch of good Feng Shui.

A look at the Destructive Cycle will show the elements that do not work well together — Water, Fire, Metal, Wood and Earth. We can see that

Water puts out Fire, Fire melts Metal, Metal cuts Wood, Wood clogs Earth, and Earth muddies Water.

Although these elements are generally considered bad Feng Shui combinations, they can be used with an adjacent element in the Destructive Cycle to minimize an overpowering element. For instance, if a room has overpowering metal elements, maybe filled with modern metal furniture, you can minimize it with Wood elements like green leafy plants or Fire elements like red throw pillows, a fireplace or candles.

It is beneficial to bear in mind the Productive and Destructive cycles while decorating. However, for optimum Feng Shui, a room should have an equal balance of all Five Elements, with none being too overpowering. If this isn't the case and there is not one overpowering element, then the Productive Cycle is a good place to start when decorating.

Now that we have a basic understanding of the elements, we can see how to best utilize candles in our decorating. In areas with predominately Metal or Water elements — rooms which have a lot of blue or silver colour or metallic furnishing — a candle would help minimize the overpowering colours and add balance.

If you want to start using Feng Shui in a room with no overpowering elements, you could bring in a candle and a complementary element like a plant or a brown oval rug since that colour and shape are associated with the Earth element.

Candles can be an easy way to bring a natural element into your home and can be a good starting place for implementing Feng Shui design. Not to mention that scented candles are often great Feng Shui because of the mood-enhancing qualities certain scents have. Candles provide a simple start in creating a pleasant ambience and good decorating style.

FENG SHUI YOUR HOME FOR VALENTINE'S DAY!

It is important to create peace and harmony in your life by selecting a home that will nourish your body, mind, heart and spirit.

With life's pace quickening every day, people are looking to escape from the rat race, relax and create a personal home sanctuary for themselves and their family to rejuvenate their body. For life to be revitalizing, it is necessary to have a good flow of life-force energy in your home to welcome your Valentine. First, let us talk about what to do and what not to do with your Valentine.

Did you know that red roses with thorns are not a happy ending sign if you were to give them to your loved ones? The colour red, unless it is used in marriage, represents bleeding. Red roses with thorns are even more undesirable. Thorns represent hardship, so on Valentine's Day, avoid sending your loved ones red roses with thorns unless, of course, you would like to end the relationship! Roses by themselves are not bad; in fact, pink, yellow, peach or cream roses (with thorns removed) are wonderful symbols associated with young love!

Did you know that you could face the right direction and find the right love? When using Feng Shui, you can find your sweetheart by sitting in the right direction. You see, everyone has a personal love (Nien Yen) direction depending on the date they were born. According to the Feng Shui Eight Mansions Formula, each person's personal Nien Yen direction brings them happiness and good luck associated with marriage and matriarchal presence. For men, the Nien Yen direction helps you to attract a good and gentle wife who will bear you many sons and take care of your parents. For women, the Nien Yen direction brings you opportunities to establish yourself as the loved wife of a household and attract a man who will bring you happiness and prosperity through marriage. So, if you've managed to ask someone special out for a dinner date on Valentine's Day, make sure you're sitting and facing your Nien Yen direction on this date to maximize your Feng Shui luck for happiness! Who knows, this person might be the one! If so, do not forget to invite your Feng Shui Master on your wedding date!

Mirror, mirror, on the wall, who is the fairest of them all? Did you know that mirrors in the bedroom are the most effective tools to destroy a relationship? Mirrors in the bedroom are really not advised for any type of relationship, whether you are starting out or reliving a romance, especially if you're pretty serious about this person! Mirrors are often said to reflect a third party in the relationship. Mirrors represent another person always coming in between two people. This often means an extra-marital affair but sometimes, the third person can be anyone like a discouraging relative. Ever heard of "Two's company, three's a crowd!" So, remove your mirrors, hide them or cover them up! Happy Valentine's Day!

FIND YOUR LOVE DIRECTION

If you don't know your love direction, use the table given below for easy reference.

Kua Number	1	2	3	4	5	6	7	8	9
Romance Direction	S	NW	SE	E	NW (Men) W (Women)	SW	NE	W	N

FIFTY-PLUS & STILL SINGLE? DATING TIPS FOR THOSE OVER FIFTY

Time can no longer "ravage" you! With botox, non-invasive face lifts and tummy tucks, one can still look "ravishing" at 50 years.... And if you are still single and searching for dates, given below are some Feng Shui tips to aid you in this process:

- Remove memories of your past love from your bedroom. Give the clothes to charity. Often this is a difficult task, regardless of the circumstances. As you give the garments to charity, imagine the generosity you and your partner are showing towards someone else.

- Then, get rid of all the clothing your ex-love gave you if it brings back moments from the past. You are living in the present and there is no reason to keep returning to the past as you dress each morning.

- Remove all bed linen and, if possible, buy a new bed. Redecorate your room. The old style was for you and your ex-partner. Now is the time to decorate for yourself. Clean everything — under the bed, in each drawer and all the crooks and crannies in the bedroom. Leave no area unturned. After you have cleaned the room, let it "sit" for a couple of hours before you redecorate it. Take a bath during this time to cleanse yourself of the past energies in the room. You want clarity as you decorate your bedroom for the present.

- Remove all photos of your ex-partner from the room. Keep the photos in family albums. You can keep a special photo of someone to remember in the living room. There should be no photo of your love in the bedroom. This is your retreat to cleanse the body and soul. Also, no photos of your grandchildren or kids are allowed in the bedroom. Do you want to always see their faces before you embark on a new relationship?

After the room is cleared of the past, it is time to bring in the future with these Feng Shui cures:

- Decorate your bedroom in soft natural colours like greens and blues. Both colours are healing and green is the other colour of love. Place two decorative pillows on your bed to represent you and your new partner. As you redecorate your bedroom, make it soft and romantic. Fill it with items you love.

- Leave a drawer and some room in the closet empty to allow a new love to enter your life. This does not mean the person will be sharing your bed. It just means you are open to a new relationship and have found room for the person in your heart.

- Indulge in some Love Meditation in the following way:
    - Lie on your bed and close your eyes. Relax all the muscles in your body and just be. As you lie quietly, envision the type of relationship you desire.

    - See yourself on the beach or out shopping with your new partner.

    - Imagine every detail and try to use as many senses as you can.

Each night, do the Love Meditation to bring a partner into your life. Believe it and you will receive it.

WHEN TO DO A FENG SHUI SPACE CLEARING?

Space Clearing is a process that should be followed in order to clean the Chi of an environment if it is bad, or to change it in case it becomes inactive. The way in which Chi flows within a house has a direct influence on the people who live in it. It is, therefore, very important that the Chi of any house or environment is positive and flows with agility.

Whenever the Chi within an environment becomes inactive, it will become reflected on those who live there by making them feel constantly tired, depressed or in a bad mood. This would affect all aspects of the person's life, including his family life, career and health amongst other things.

To avoid the effects of bad or inactive Chi on us, we should do a regular Space Clearing. According to Feng Shui, the first step you should follow while doing a Space Clearing is to actually clean the house as thoroughly as possible. Second, make sure you add the following four elements within the environment you wish to clear: Water; Fire by placing candles or something which symbolizes it; Earth, represented by plants or crystals; and Air, by using incense or music or loud clapping of hands.

There are some specific cases in which a Space Clearing is highly recommended. If you are moving to a new house, it is advisable that you clear the house's Chi to make sure it is new, clean, positive and free of negative factors that the former inhabitants might have left. Also, whenever someone overcomes a health problem, it is recommended that you do a Space Clearing to make sure that the negative Chi which accompanies illness is eliminated.

In cases where people tend to be in conflict or have arguments very often, whether at home, at work or in any other environment, Space Clearing is more often than not, the solution. If, for example, some family members cannot get along well together or have a conflicting relationship, a Space Clearing could be of great help.

For your life to work well, it is vital to have a good flow of clear, vibrant energy in your home and workplace. Feng Shui is a beautifully organized system of knowledge that teaches us ways to enhance this energy flow by improving building design, furniture placement, colour schemes and so on.

Space Clearing is a specialized branch of Feng Shui that works at even deeper levels to cleanse and purify the atmosphere of a building and thus enhance the quality and nature of the energy in the space. Feng Shui always works better and faster when done in conjunction with Space Clearing.

Many people now choose to make Space Clearing a part of their regular building maintenance schedule so that their space is energetically as well as physically clean and clear.

Space Clearing can be used to improve your health, relationships, prosperity and any aspects of your life that feel stuck. It also enhances traditional Feng Shui arts by incorporating Space Clearing purification techniques using sound, especially bells and clapping; and purification through the elements of Earth, Air, Fire and Water.

Who needs to learn Space Clearing and Clutter Clearing? Just about everyone! No matter how much or how little clutter you have, there are always more levels to clutter clearing than you realize, and it is an ongoing process that will continue for the rest of your life. It will inspire you to reach new levels of letting go and to create more joy, confidence, clarity and ease in your life. It is an essential practice for anyone on a spiritual path. Also, there are very few buildings in the world that are so well designed that they don't need regular Space Clearing, and even the most excellent Feng Shui has been found to work better and faster when combined with Space Clearing.

CLEAR THAT CLUTTER RIGHT OUT OF YOUR LIFE!

By now, I'm sure you know very well that Feng Shui is a system of knowledge that teaches us to enhance the flow of good Chi in our homes and offices by improving the design of buildings, the placement of furniture, the colour schemes and so on. What many of us don't know is that Clutter Clearing is also an integral part of Feng Shui. Feng Shui is the art of working with energy, and Space Clearing takes you right to the core of it. It offers a deeper, far more spiritual approach to Feng Shui and is an essential tool for anyone seeking to improve the quality of their life.

WHAT CLEARING OUT MEANS

If your clutter is getting you down and you want to start getting rid of it, you are ready to make changes in your life to bring yourself closer to what you want. Don't underestimate the effects a clear-out can have on you. You may find it painful to get rid of possessions that you have kept for a long, long time and feel that you cannot exist without, even though an inner voice is telling you to let go. To do this, you need to evaluate honestly what is relevant to your life now and in the future.

The effect of Clutter Clearing is remarkable. Clutter Clearing is now recognized as a vital step for anyone seeking to clear out the old frequencies and bring in higher levels of energy to encourage whole new possibilities. Skilled Space Clearing Practitioners have developed the ability to read energy in buildings with their hands.

Everything that ever happens in a space is imprinted on the walls and furniture and then influences those who live or work there ever after. Repetitive or traumatic events are more deeply imprinted and have a correspondingly greater effect. So, if you or the previous occupants have had unhappy relationships, poor health, financial problems or other difficulties, those energies will still be lingering in the building. Therefore, clutter in all its forms — physical, mental, emotional and spiritual — affects you profoundly. You need to clear clutter once you realize how much your junk has been holding you back!

Clutter Clearing is a powerful process that brings startling changes in your life. Don't add crystals and other Feng Shui enhancements until you have tackled your clutter because they will just not work. In cluttered areas of your home, Chi stagnates. Once this stale energy has accumulated, it will grow even more. Junk mail, abandoned craft projects, newspapers waiting for recycling — all these constitute clutter. Clutter also means all those neglected items that you hide in corners, thinking you will make a decision about them later but you never do. Avoiding drastic clear-out can stem from a fear of the future, but once you commit to change, you will move on.

YOUR INNER SOUL

Your home is supposed to mirror your inner self, so mess and inactivity reflect something that is going on inside you. The chaos will also make you feel lethargic and confused about what you want in your life. Once you have emptied your junk hoard, you will feel physically, emotionally and spiritually liberated, and you will have opened the door to wonderful new opportunities.

HOW TO MAKE YOUR HOME A FENG SHUI HAVEN

Invite Joy into your home: When it comes to creating a warm, welcoming home, attention to detail is far more important than budget and space. For instance, have you ever walked into an exquisitely furnished home and yet felt unwelcome? Or entered a modest apartment and never wanted to leave? It is within the walls of a calm home that joy is most easily experienced.

TURN YOUR BEDROOM INTO A COSY SANCTUARY

Turn your bedroom into your ultimate escape. It doesn't take a lot of work or a lot of money, and yes, it'll be worth it. After all, what's better than snuggling in bed (by yourself, or with the one you love)? So, if you don't have a cosy blanket for the chilled air-conditioned room, get one now or put it on your gift list. It's the easiest way to add that "aaah" feeling to your bedroom.

TRY AN ANCIENT SPACE-ENHANCING SECRET

You can create an environment that welcomes health, happiness and love just by moving some furniture and adding a few objects. This will help you to attract and enhance your life energy or Chi according to the arrangement of your space. Start by placing positive elements like plants, candles, wind chimes and soothing colours around your home.

SIMPLE DETAILS MAKE A BIG DIFFERENCE

You don't need a paint job or a furniture makeover to add a sense of light and laughter to your home. You can cheer up your interior with small, inexpensive touches and see big changes! Start by simply clustering candles on a plant stand or draping cosy throws over sofas and chairs.

BRING THE BLOOM INDOORS

Blooming indoor plants bring the beauty and vibrancy of an outdoor garden into your home. Whether you like lavender, jasmine or even flowering plants, these are bound to brighten any room.

CREATE AN INDOOR FOUNTAIN

Water is soothing to the soul especially that musical trickling sound, the constant but quiet movement. So why not soothe yourself and your loved ones with an indoor fountain? It's also great Feng Shui when placed at the front entrance.

PROMOTE HAPPINESS WITH COLOUR

An easy way to transform a room is with a new coat of paint. But which colour matches your mood? Will the yellow in your kitchen soothe guests and keep family members happy? Can the colours violet, blue and green make a small room look bigger? Choose any colour that soothes your nerves and brightens your mood.

BASK IN THE GLOW

Candles are the perfect way to add a warm feeling to your home. An easy alternative is to install a dimmer switch. Candles can create a friendly feeling in the living room, add sparkle to a dinner table and promote romance in the bedroom. Also, everyone looks better by candlelight! Whether it is a cluster of tea lights, a group of candlesticks or a solitary three-wick giant, let the glow of candles fill your rooms and your heart with warmth and light.

CLEANSE YOUR SPACE AND SPIRIT

Treat your spiritual space the same way you treat your home. Keep it clean. Try this simple Space Clearing ritual. All you need are a few incense sticks, a bell and a few loud claps (that's right, hand claps) to clear your home of unwanted negative energy and welcome joy.

TOP TEN WAYS TO BRING BAD VIBES INTO YOUR HOME

Negative energy, also known as bad vibes, can linger in your home without you knowing it. Bad vibes are created by negative experiences that become blocked in the aura of people, animals and things. Before you let someone or something inside your home, remove all the old negative experiences that are connected to them.

INVITING UNFAVOURABLE GUESTS INTO THE HOME

This is the biggest reason why people have negative vibes in their home. Often, we let a family into the home even though they have been unkind to us or our immediate family. To have a home of harmony, you need to meet your family members at restaurants or at other neutral places. In this way, bad energy does not drift into your home and stay for an undisclosed amount of time.

ASHES FROM A DECEASED LOVED ONE

The death of a loved one is very difficult. Often, we want to hold on to their ashes for comfort. Their ashes need to be freed to allow you to begin a new chapter in your life. Also, loved ones stay with us until we are ready to let them go. As difficult as it is, we must let their energy soar. This cannot happen if their ashes are enclosed in a container sitting on your fireplace.

TROPHY ANIMALS

Trophy animals should not be in the home. Yes, the person who killed the animal feels victorious, but the dead animal is stagnant and dead energy.

DRIED FLOWERS

Dried flowers are big business these days. However, they carry negative energy. The flowers are dead and their vital Chi has swirled into the air. Dried flowers are big dust collectors that need to be out of the home.

GIFTS FROM NEGATIVE FAMILY MEMBERS OR FRIENDS

Presents come in all sizes and shapes and we graciously accept all gifts. Only accept gifts given from the heart and donate all other expensive/inexpensive gifts that are not given by the heart.

OTHER PEOPLE'S JUNK

How many times has someone offered to give you their used sofa or some old books? Decline, decline and decline again. Often, we accept other people's junk because we fear not having enough. Sometimes, it is okay to reuse items from friends. However, never accept out of fear of offending them.

PICTURES DEPICTING VIOLENCE

Violence is prevalent in our society. We sell pictures of serial killers, car crashes and other disturbing events. No picture in the home should depict violence. There should be no picture of great wars, violent movies or anything that illustrates negative experiences.

VIOLENT MUSIC

Music can create harmony or chaos at home. Many teenagers will listen to violent music. Violent music is about the sound and not always the words. Before you purchase music, see whether it uplifts, relaxes or makes you feel chaotic and uncomfortable. At home, you want music that will inspire or relax the soul instead of disturbing the equilibrium.

FURNITURE FROM UNKNOWN SOURCE

Furniture is an expensive purchase and is often bought at second-hand stores. Soft furniture like sofas and beds hold the energies of past experiences. Beds should never be used by others as all their issues will begin to become a part of your life.

STOLEN ITEMS

Have you ever bought an item that fell off the back of the truck? As tempting as it may be, it is a wrong thing to do because you save money but at a bad cost. The stolen items give off bad vibes because several people were affected by the item being sold. Only buy items that you know have come from a reputable source.

SPIRAL STAIRCASES, COLUMNS & SKYLIGHTS

Apart from sculptures, paintings, photographs and plants, Feng Shui Practitioners also take into consideration other common design elements which they believe can attract unfavourable Chi if treated incorrectly.

As little kids, we might have found spiral staircases fun and exciting, what with the dizzying feel it gives us as we climb up and go down it. However, expert Feng Shui Practitioners advise that it is best not to have spiral staircases to acquire good Feng Shui for the reason that, in China, spiral staircases symbolize a downward spiral towards death. Some Feng Shui Consultants even see spiral stairways as the worst kind.

WHERE TO PUT SPIRAL STAIRWAYS?

It is especially inauspicious when a spiral staircase is located in the middle of the room. This is because in Feng Shui theory, it creates a vortex which pulls a room's energy down into the death direction. In cases where spiral stairways cannot be done without, one suggestion is to place it in a corner next to a wall to lessen its unfavourable effect on the room's energy. In addition, placing wind chimes at the top and at the bottom of the staircase can also be beneficial.

BLOCKERS OF POSITIVE CHI

As with beams, columns are also seen as blockers of positive Chi in

Feng Shui and are believed to cause quarrels, headaches and insincerity among a house's occupants due to the oppressive and hostile environment it creates.

However, before you knock down that solid and smooth marble column inside your home, know that there are ways to alleviate the detrimental effects it may bring to your home and life. Besides, tearing down that column may even bring about more harmful effects like having a portion of your ceiling or second floor coming down on you! Placing a plant or two in front of a column or near its sharp edges, hanging a soft sculpture from it or placing a bookcase or a mirror in front of or on it are enough to discourage its adverse effects.

SIZE AND PLACEMENT OF SKYLIGHTS

Feng Shui Masters also say that letting light and air in your home is considered advantageous and favourable in Feng Shui. What can be better sources of light and air than windows and skylights? Skylights, however, should be strictly proportional to the room. A skylight that's too big for the room will make the room's energy open to outside forces. Skylights are also discouraged from being placed above a bed as they may cause discomfort to the sleeper by giving the feeling of being exposed. To give home-owners a feeling of safety and security, it is best to use tempered and shatterproof glass for skylights.

THINGS TO WATCH OUT IN FENG SHUI

There are some placements of furniture, objects of daily use and luxury items as well as daily activities that people are usually quite casual about, but which in Feng Shui can be extremely damaging to the residents of the house, and even in the workplace. Do watch out for these:

NEVER HANG YOUR WASHING OUT OVERNIGHT

One Feng Shui taboo is never to leave clothes hanging out overnight. Hanging one's clothes out at night attracts the energies of wandering spirits and encourages them to get attached to the clothes. These clothes, when worn, make the bad energies of these spirits bring bad luck to us.

These are, of course, old wives tales. Nevertheless, Feng Shui Masters also warn against hanging clothes and other washing on the clothesline after dark. But their reasoning has greater appeal for me. They explain this taboo in terms of the unlucky vibes caused by the clothes absorbing the excessive Yin energies at night.

It is for this same reason that Feng Shui Practitioners of the East are often reluctant to hang clothes to dry in dark, windowless rooms.

They prefer to hang clothes out in the open air and during the daylight hours. This allows clothes to absorb the Yang energies of the bright sunlight, thereby imbuing the clothes with life energy rather than lifeless Yin energy.

BE CAREFUL ABOUT BOOKSHELVES

Everyone needs a place to store those books. One of the issues for items like bookshelves is that they are more often than not very tall and heavy. Therefore, it is best not to place bookshelves near beds or work areas. You will feel the weight of the bookcase coming down on you! You will also feel tired and may appear to be carrying the weight of the world on you. Sometimes, headaches and back problems will occur with this positioning.

Never fill your bookshelves completely. This does not allow new information to come to you. Leave some space between your books or place knick-knacks. Place your larger books at the bottom of the shelf and smaller books on top, to give a lighter feeling. Bookshelves should never be directly ahead or behind you. This position can cause confrontation and backstabbing, especially if these shelves are at your workplace. Move the shelves so that they are not in line with your body. This is especially important at work or while you are sleeping.

ART AND ARTEFACTS

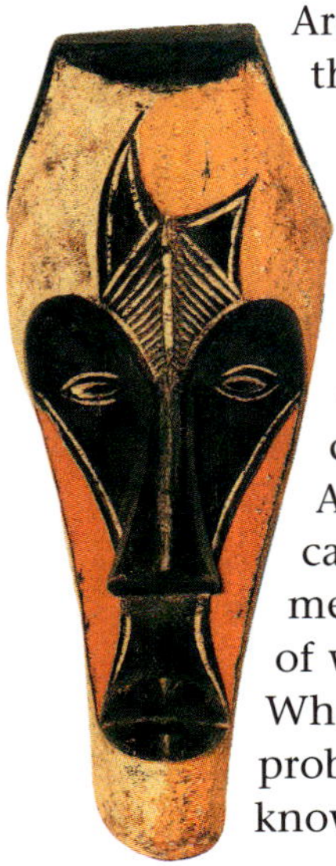

Art is a very subjective matter, or as they say, beauty is in the eye of the beholder. You must enjoy what you see.

Your sub-conscious mind is affected positively and negatively by what you see every day. Strong positive images will lift your Chi while lesser images will bring your Chi down. Art with colour will brighten your life. Modern art, with its unusual designs and forms, can cause confusion in the mind. At worst, it can create schizophrenia. Aboriginal art from cultures like Africa and the Caribbean can also create havoc. In the case of those cultures, always know what the image means. Many times, these pieces will hold strange images of weird fertility rites, warrior initiations and even death. Where it is positioned and how it is seen can create problems for the viewers. Enjoy your art, and like and know what you are looking at.

TELEVISION AND FENG SHUI

The television has become a mainstay in our culture. This item is less than sixty years old and relatively new to Feng Shui. It can be an intrusive and addictive reality for a lot of us. How do we keep this wonderful source of culture and art in balance with our lives?

Keep your TV in a cabinet so it is not so intrusive in the space. To further help that reality, it is good to place the TV in a corner of the room. In this way, it does not become the main function of the room. This is one of the problems of big screen TVs; they simply take over the room because of their large size.

Never put a TV in a bedroom, especially a bedroom that is being shared by a couple. It will have an adverse effect on the love life of the people. Instead of making love, you will end up watching TV! Televisions also radiate certain noxious energies that are not friendly for the sleeping environment. Keep your TV placement in balance, and you will increasingly enjoy the benefits of watching it.

FENG SHUI AND MUSIC

As has been discussed before, everything in your environment can affect your Feng Shui. One thing that can be positive or negative can be music. By adding music to your space, a feeling of relaxation and peace can permeate the space. Music, especially classical, new age and relaxation music, works on the psyche positively. Jazz can, at times, create schizophrenic-like actions, while rock and roll will activate the lower regions of the body and often have a negative effect on sexuality! Music has a tendency to create repetitive actions. Dance music can create happy energies. All music will have an effect on your personal Feng Shui.

Last but not the least: If you want to enjoy good fortune for the next forty years, place all your electronic gadgets (stereos, hi-fi systems, TVs and so on) on the West wall of your living room or family room. The more you play your music or watch TV, the greater will be the energies bringing in good fortune.

KNIFE BLADES AND DANGEROUS EDGES

Are you being hurt by harsh corners? Harsh edges are a Feng Shui trouble spot. Most of the time, these edges are easy to overlook and can hide themselves. Sharp edges and corners can come from doors, square columns, shelves, cabinets and even arrangements of furniture.

In Feng Shui, strong, harsh edges are similar to knife blades, and their energy should be treated that way. Some edges are worse than others, though. Edges that are aimed at the back, such as those from bookshelves behind a desk, or at the neck, from shelves on a wall or open cabinets, are considered especially dangerous.

Look around your home and office to see if there are knife edges aimed at places of importance like your bed, your desk, your dining table, or anywhere you spend a lot of time. Then, consider whether it is worth the risk of exposing yourself to these harsh edges. Most of the time, by a simple rearrangement, you are able to keep the shelf or cabinet without having to do away with it.

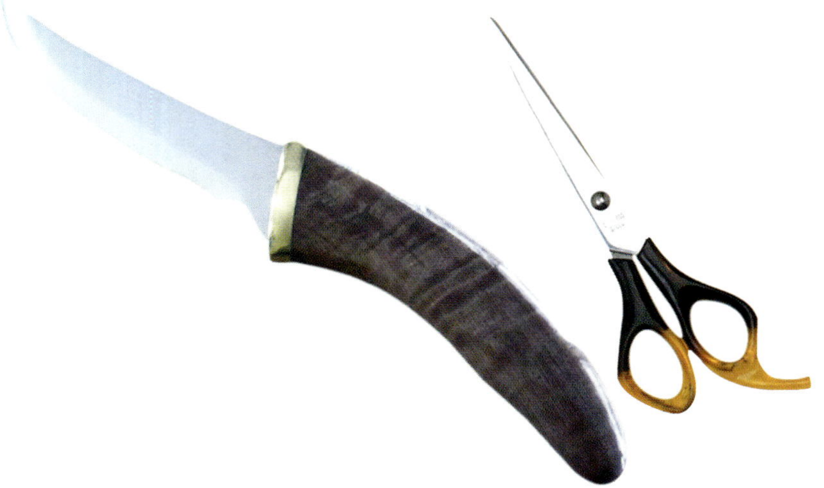

Protective Feng Shui is one of the first steps one must take when looking to improve the Feng Shui of a home or office. Protecting oneself from the dangers of harsh edges should be on your checklist. This ensures that no one is either unprotected or exposed.

Read the suggestions given below for more ideas on handling harmful edges:

Never place shelves overhead: These kinds of shelves can press on the head. If they are simple boards, the sharp edges of the boards can be harmful. Placed either at a desk or against a wall, a sharp edge overhead will make it hard to think clearly or make decisions because of the pressure being exerted. Remove them and place them elsewhere.

Watch out for raised ceilings: These are very popular in home constructions now. If you have one of these over your head while you sleep, it is possible that you feel pressured, have headaches or face difficulty in sleeping. You could even have financial difficulties. Either try to move the bed away from this edge or create a canopy that covers the edge with fabric.

Avoid bookshelf headboards: These have *lots* of sharp edges and are not good for you. Besides muddled thinking, you could also suffer from head ailments ranging from sinuses to poor vision and headaches.

Watch L-shaped arrangements: These kinds of arrangements create the "cleaver" or "hatchet" effect. The long side is the "knife blade". Where do you see these? In L-shaped desk arrangements where the long knife blade is usually your desk! Separate the furniture. Do the same with sofa arrangements as well.

Square columns have harsh edges: Hang a six-rod hollow wind chime in front of the column to lift the energy. You can also place a vine at the bottom to grow around the column or a tall plant, curtain or screen of some kind in front of the column. These columns are very dangerous if they are aimed at your table, your bed, and even worse, at your front door.

Wall shelves create knife blades: Wall shelves, especially those at neck height, act like guillotines. Make sure these are covered and not at your head or neck level, especially if they are located at places where you work or stand a lot like by a stove or sink. Knife blades at the head can create very serious losses.

AVOIDING POISON ARROWS

What is a poison arrow, you may ask. According to Feng Shui Practitioners, a poison arrow represents the ultimate threat to good Feng Shui. Since poison arrows destroy auspicious Chi, you should try to avoid them as best you can.

Poison arrows are easy to identify. Anything sharp, pointed, straight or triangular equals Sha Chi. However, some poison arrows are less obvious. A mailbox, for instance, is a deadly poison arrow. Since it can cause severe headaches, it is best to find a suitable location to place your mailbox in. Otherwise, plant a bush behind it.

Of course, it may not be possible to do anything about poison arrows already aimed at your home. Straight roads and T-junctions are good examples of these. Nevertheless, Feng Shui offers several practical remedies to solve this problem.

Diffuse or disarm the poison arrows in your environment by placing potted plants in the identified deadly areas. In the garden, grow trees with thick foliage to disarm poison arrows.

Another form of poison arrow is your neighbour's triangular roof. If the angle is aimed directly at your front door, use a Pa Kua mirror to deflect this poison arrow. Unfortunately, the effects of this may be harmful to your neighbour. Use this as your last resort.

Avoid sharp pointed buildings, wall corners, furniture or accessories pointed directly at your house, bed or desk. It is reminiscent of a cutting knife edge or a disapproving finger.

The entry of your home or office should be open and inviting. Trim away foliage that may be blocking the path of Chi. Do not block the entry of your home or office in any way.

Landscaping should be manicured regularly so that it does not get overgrown, cover walkways or entries or shadow the house.

After walking in through your front door, it should open into an expansive and "feel good" space, not one that is restrictive in any way or faces a mirror, staircase or an open window.

Mirrors are wonderful for expanding space and direct energy. However, never have them facing the front door. Mirrors can reflect back any good energy entering the house.

It is said in Feng Shui that it is best not to have a larger building next to your structure. Two-storeyed buildings or any building dwarfing its immediate neighbours, deprives the humbler dwelling of Heaven's guardianship. Height is also limited by the belief that good spirits soar through the air at a height of 100ft. If you have a larger building weighing down on your structure, you can place mirrors on the outside of your structure to push the offending energy back.

SEVEN FENG SHUI TIPS FOR WELL-BEING

Who doesn't want to enjoy a happy and joyful life in a pleasant environment? Feng Shui tells you how to improve your emotional and physical health with Feng Shui by following these simple suggestions given below:

REMOVE CLUTTER IN YOUR HOME AND OFFICE

Clutter obstructs the beneficial energy called Chi in your environment, blocking the actualization of the good things you want to achieve in your life. Take a good, hard look at your walls, furniture and accessories. Eliminate half or more of what's there, store it and rotate it from time to time. Dispose ruthlessly in order to allow new things to enter your life.

CREATE A PRIVATE PLACE FOR YOURSELF

It is essential to your well-being to be surrounded by souvenirs, artwork, books, awards, goals, images and mementos that nourish your spirit. Remember that less is more, and change these things as you and your life change. This space can be as small as a favourite corner or chair but is exclusively yours — a place where you can dream your dreams and find peace and serenity.

ENSURE A GOOD NIGHT'S REST

Look around your bedroom with a critical eye to see what might be disturbing your sleep. Eliminate as much electronic equipment as you can because it emanates waves that disturb Chi. Close the bathroom door leading to your room as well as keep the toilet seat covered. Cover up mirrors that activate Yang energy in what should be a Yin environment conducive to rest. Avoid stimulating colours like red and gold, and use instead Yin colours like blues, greens and pastels. Do not place water features or too many live plants or fresh flowers in your bedroom unless specified by a Feng Shui Consultant.

ACTIVATE YOUR RELATIONSHIP AREA

If you are looking to renew or find a new partner for love, romance, companionship and perhaps a permanent commitment, try enhancing the South-west area. In every room of your home, especially your bedroom, examine that direction critically. Is it filled with clutter, a nightstand covered with articles or worse, nothing? Set one or two symbols, usually in pairs, which represent loving relationships in this place: Pink quartz crystals, heart shapes or anything made of Earth materials like porcelain, china, clay, stone and terracotta. Fire elements and symbols like lights and candles will add an extra punch to your efforts, but do not use any Wood or green here.

ADD MORE YANG TO YOUR LIFE

Introduce more light, music, water, air, plants, mirrors, wind chimes, bright colours and flowers into your life. Throw open the drapes and curtains or open up your blinds all the way to literally let the sunshine in. Bring in lots of green houseplants to activate the Yang Chi of joy and happiness.

CREATE AN INTERIOR OR EXTERIOR ENVIRONMENT THAT PROMOTES HEALTH

Fresh, clean, moving water, good air quality, straightforward traffic patterns in your home or office, a balance of dark and light, soft and hard surfaces — all these facilitate the flow of beneficial Chi. If you or other family members often experience illness, accident or calamity, walk around the outside of your house and notice if there are any corners (poison arrows) of buildings pointed directly towards the front entrance of your house or the bedrooms. Block the view with plants if possible or position a small mirror (Bagua) facing the offending corner to send the "killing energy" back to its origin.

BRING IN THE OUTDOOR

Bring the natural world back intc your home and office. Invest in artwork with images of nature as a reminder that there is a world out there. Add lots of indoor plants in the East, South-east and South areas of your home. But shy away from dried flowers, especially in the bedroom. These floral arrangements can wreak havoc on your love and sex life.

THE CHINESE ZODIAC

BAZI — THE FOUR PILLARS OF DESTINY

For the uninitiated, the Four Pillars of Destiny is one of the main Feng Shui techniques used by some of its classical schools to gather useful information regarding people and their relationship with their environment. The Four Pillars of Destiny or Bazi (pronounced Ba-Zhai) is somehow similar to the occidental birth chart or *janampatri* since it provides personal information based on the person's time and place of birth.

This technique allows us to have a birth chart which is based on Four Pillars. These Four Pillars are made of four stems and four branches. Each one of them is based on the person's birth information. The first one of these four main pillars is the Year Pillar, which provides information regarding the person's family background and his relationship with society in general.

The second pillar, that is, the Month Pillar, provides information about the person's childhood and his relationship with his parents. In the third place comes the Day Pillar which lets the person know about his relationship with his spouse as well as with partners. In the fourth place comes the Hour Pillar, which provides information regarding the person's career as well as his relationship with his children.

In this way, the technique of the Four Pillars of Destiny allows its users to gather information about the different aspects of his life. By properly applying and following this method, a person can know more about his relationship with his parents, superiors, children, spouse, siblings, friends and so on. It can also let him learn more about his career and guide him about ways to succeed in his professional life. It also allows us to know the ideal moment for us to do something meaningful in our career or relationships and the skills we should pay greater attention to.

A very important aspect of the Four Pillars of Destiny is that it allows us to learn more about our health and ways to improve it. It can give us information regarding which of our organs are most vulnerable to illnesses, and to which we should pay special attention.

Basically, a Four Pillars Chart is a personal energy blueprint, a map of our own unique Chi. The Four Pillars of Destiny allows us to better understand the potentials and cycles of our lives and ways to enhance our prospects for health and prosperity. It gives us knowledge regarding our possible auspicious/inauspicious time periods, potential health risks and primary personality traits so that we can change ourselves and our environment to have better relationships, health and financial success. Masters of Bazi Four Pillars can advise people regarding ways to prepare for times of abundance and times of challenge.

Along with Feng Shui, which includes the Flying Stars (Xuan Kong), Form School, Eight Mansions and Compass School theories, Four Pillars of Destiny is another important tool in the study and understanding of Chinese metaphysics.

ANIMAL INSTINCTS — THE CHINESE ZODIAC

The Chinese Zodiac is made up of 12 animal signs: Rat, Ox, Tiger, Rabbit, Dragon, Snake, Horse, Goat, Monkey, Rooster, Dog and Pig. They symbolize the 12 Earthly Branches, which, together with the Heavenly Stems, were used to mark the different years in ancient times.

Legend has it that when the Buddha summoned the animals to bid him farewell before he left Earth, only 12 showed up. As a token of his appreciation, he assigned a year to each in the order of its arrival.

The traits commonly associated with each animal sign are given below:

RAT (1912, 1924, 1936, 1948, 1960, 1972, 1984, 1996, 2008)

- Strengths: Generally perceived as joyful, meticulous and good communicators
- Weaknesses: Narrow-minded, suspicious, selfish

OX (1913, 1925, 1937, 1949, 1961, 1973, 1985, 1997, 2009)

- Strengths: Hard-working and determined
- Weaknesses: Bad-tempered, stubborn, forceful and inflexible

TIGER (1914, 1926, 1938, 1950, 1962, 1974, 1986, 1998, 2010)

- Strengths: Courageous, confident, strong in character, ambitious and straightforward
- Weaknesses: Selfish, hasty and temperamental

RABBIT (1915, 1927, 1939, 1951, 1963, 1975, 1987, 1999, 2011)

- Strengths: Gentle and tender by nature, honest, noble, elegant and careful in their thoughts

- Weaknesses: Indecisive, over-cautious, timid

DRAGON (1916, 1928, 1940, 1952, 1964, 1976, 1988, 2000)
- Strengths: Mighty and powerful, strong affinity with luck, courageous
- Weaknesses: Proud, arrogant, bad-tempered, stubborn, selfish, unwilling to take orders

SNAKE (1917, 1929, 1941, 1953, 1965, 1977, 1989, 2001)
- Strengths: Easy-going, smart, kind, humorous
- Weaknesses: Selfish, stingy, revengeful, crude

HORSE (1918, 1930, 1942, 1954, 1966, 1978, 1990, 2002)
- Strengths: Sociable, quick-witted, confident, easy-going, straightforward
- Weaknesses: Talkative, proud, impatient, irritable

GOAT (1919, 1931, 1943, 1955, 1967, 1979, 1991, 2003)
- Strengths: Elegant, artistic, talented, intelligent, loves their families, their luck improves as they grow older
- Weaknesses: Not punctual, irresponsible, pessimistic, clumsy

MONKEY (1920, 1932, 1944, 1956, 1968, 1980, 1992, 2004)
- Strengths: Quick-witted, responsive, intelligent, friendly
- Weaknesses: Mischievous, deceitful, shrewd, impatient

ROOSTER (1921, 1933, 1945, 1957, 1969, 1981, 1993, 2005)
- Strengths: Able to predict the future, smart workers, attentive and likely to score great achievements in life
- Weaknesses: Likes to show off and find faults, proud, selfish

DOG (1922, 1934, 1946, 1958, 1970, 1982, 1994, 2006)
- Strengths: Brave, straightforward, loyal, careful
- Weaknesses: Suspicious, likes to comment on others, forceful, proud, unapproachable

PIG (1923, 1935, 1947, 1959, 1971, 1983, 1995, 2007)
- Strengths: Determined, knowledgeable, persistent, firm
- Weaknesses: Stubborn, insecure, greedy, takes advantage of others

COLOURS OF THE CHINESE ZODIAC

Every animal sign in the Chinese Zodiac has an element, colour, direction, etc. Given below is a table of the lucky/disturbing colours of your sign!

Zodiac Sign	Lucky Colours	Disturbing Colours
Rat	Purple, Mauve, Lilac, Burgundy, Brown, Grey, Green, Cream, Turquoise	Silver, Light Blue, Stark White
Ox	Red, Pink, Dark Blue, Black	Green, Cream, Purple, Lilac, Brown
Tiger	Light Blue, Black, Dark Blue, Stark White, Silver	Grey, Gold, Golden, Yellow, Cream, Green
Rabbit	Purple, Mauve, Lilac, Brown, Turquoise, Grey, Cream, Green, Indigo	Stark White, Silver, Light Blue
Dragon	Gold, Golden, Yellow, Red, Pink, Purple, Brown, Mauve, Lilac, Grey	Turquoise, Dark Blue, Black, Light Blue
Snake	Turquoise, Green, Cream	Red, Pink, Light Blue

Horse	Light Blue, Silver, Stark White	Grey, Mauve, Brown, Purple, Lilac
Sheep	Green, Cream, Purple, Lilac, Brown	Black, Dark Blue, Red, Pink
Monkey	Gold, Golden, Yellow, Grey, Green, Cream	Light Blue, Dark Blue, Black, Turquoise
Rooster	Silver, Stark White, Light Blue	Turquoise, Grey
Dog	Turquoise, Dark Blue, Black	Red, Pink, Yellow, Golden, Gold
Pig	Red, Pink, Light Blue	Green, Cream, Turquoise

THE YEAR OF THE BROWN EARTH RAT, 2008

This Chinese New Year which began on February 7, 2008, is the Year of the Brown Earth Rat and marks the start of a new 12-year cycle of the Chinese Zodiac.

Like the houses of the Western Zodiac, the animals of Chinese astrology are said to influence your luck during the year. Your horoscope for 2008, the Year of the Rat, therefore depends on which animal signifies the year you were born.

It is considered very auspicious to be born in the year of the Earth Rat. Babies born under this sign are intelligent and hard-working. They are intelligent, curious, sociable, and born leaders who do well in any group, but value ties with family and close friends more than social contacts. The Earth influences balance the Rat's Water nature for those born in this year, making them able to control the flights of intellect that often draw the Rat away from a good course. The selfish and calculating aspects of the Rat are toned by the nurturing Earth force. These are leaders to be followed with trust and good partners for a life filled with good fortune. The Rat is clever — sometimes too clever, though. When mixed with the passion and charm of this sign, the Rat can be manipulative as a life partner or business associate. The ability to initiate new ideas and work hard to reach a goal led the Rat to the first place of honour at the side of the Buddha. These are traits that bring success in both business and personal affairs.

Since the Rat year begins a new cycle, remember that decisions made during this year will carry long-term consequences. Do not make changes without careful planning, especially during the beginning of the year.

Here are a few general conclusions from the opinions of the sages:

RAT: 1912, 1924, 1936, 1948, 1960, 1972, 1984, 1996, 2008

The clever Rat has made many ambitious plans that will be put into action this year. Good fortune and good times will surround the Rat in this year of glory. Easy social grace is a gift to those born in this sign, but trusted close friends and family are the centre that the Rat needs to secure prosperity. Beware of the battle of Earth and Water that may confuse the scurrying Rat. This beginning of the year will see the Rat tempted by many flirtatious relationships. Faithfulness and loyalty are difficult with so many admiring glances. Understand the fear of those you care for as you seem to be drawn to many new relationships. Take steps to avoid damage to your true partners. As the year passes, the successful Rat will see more serious relationships bear fruit. Although the Rat is a Water sign, boat cruises are not a good vacation plan. Travelling to exotic lands to explore, meet new people and experience adventure may be the perfect honeymoon.

With the influence of the Earth aspects of this year, promises of commitments become real and those born in this sign may experience the blessings of marriage and of children added to their family. The Rat who cannot focus on success will be misled and find much conflict and many uncomfortable scenes, which are caused by straying from a match that will bring good fortune. When prosperity and love come easily, they may not be treated with respect. The Rat who will succeed is the one who remembers that greed and manipulation may bring quick victories but ultimately strengthen enemies. The cat is ever watchful of the Rat who stole its place. Listen to the guidance of ancestors, loved ones and trusted friends. Beware of the flattery of casual admiration to completely fulfil the promise of extreme good fortune that this year holds.

OX: 1913, 1925, 1937, 1949, 1961, 1973, 1985, 1997

The Year of the Earth Rat brings more good fortune to the steady Ox. The solid back that carried the Rat across the river will be well rewarded. The influence of the Brown Earth Rat means a prosperous and healthy year for the Ox but the influence of Water will make the year interesting. There will be many choices that will lead to success if the Ox remains true to the Earth nature. Do not follow paths that seem to lead to easy success. The wise Ox knows that perseverance brings permanent good fortune. While your hard work will begin to bring rewards in the last half of this year, the real success awaits in the year of the Ox that is coming. Conflicts and confusion can be a problem in the beginning of the year as the Water and Earth elements of the Brown Earth Rat seek balance. Attention to romantic relationships will bring harmony but neglect will bring conflict. Giving tokens of affection will bring great rewards. Do not be obstinate in your business or personal relationships. The last few months will feel the influence of the upcoming sign of the Ox strengthening and lead to full serenity. Wait until then to make those difficult decisions.

TIGER: 1914, 1926, 1938, 1950, 1962, 1974, 1986, 1998

The wild Tiger prospered in the Year of the Dog and the Pig. The Rat year will change the good fortune of the large cat. While not the enemy that the true cat is, there is still some adversity. Both business and personal relationships will be a challenge. You may find many flirtatious moments but they will not lead to serious commitments. You will need to rely on family to move through this confusing time. Happy relationships will suffer from conflict in the early part of the year, but attention to romance and faithfulness will return good fortune. At work, you will also feel these conflicts. You will be more aware of criticism from co-workers and employers. Learn to control your aggressive nature when responding to this and you will find prosperity. Use your abundant energy to turn dreams of success into real plans that will bring rewards as the year ends. Be careful to avoid excesses in work and all things physical, especially in the last half of the year.

RABBIT: 1915, 1927, 1939, 1951, 1963, 1975, 1987, 1999

Many Rabbits will find the Year of the Earth Rat unusually fortunate if they can control the tendency to hop about. The Rat is not normally a harmonious sign for the Rabbit, but this Brown Earth Rat year remembers that both are rodents and does not confuse the Rabbit with the cat. Flirtation, romance and marriage lie in wait for the amorous Rabbit. The conflict will be to find harmony between the three. Take care not to endanger a possible life-long love by continued flirtation. Looking for perfection instead of happiness in love can cause grief. At work, the urge to pick on the shortcomings of co-workers and find dissatisfaction with a good position will cause unhappiness. This may be an auspicious time to make changes in your career path with the Earth influences fuelling new growth for you, but be sure that the change comes from a positive source. Moving towards prosperity will bring a positive cycle. Running from adversity will not. Whether you decide to stay or go, a focus on the positive aspects of your current position will lead to long-term success and good fortune through the upcoming cycle.

DRAGON: 1916, 1928, 1940, 1952, 1964, 1976, 1988, 2000

The Rat is a good friend to the Dragon. The new cycle that starts this year will bring prosperity to the Dragon after what may seem like a long time of struggle. The stream of good fortune that you saw coming your way in a trickle last year will reach fullness this year. Your energy is strong after resting in the Year of the Pig and you will find that difficulties are able to be overcome. You will need energy to keep up with the social whirl coming your way. While much of your focus will be on friendships and love, put some of that energy towards career networking opportunities that will develop this year and will benefit you throughout the next cycle. The conservative nature of this Rat year may give moments of frustration to the Dragon who cannot tame a fiery nature. This is a time to begin ventures that will benefit from the steady nurturing Earth influence, but you will need patience and persistence to see them through to success. The signs are very good for your soulmate to appear. Take care to recognize this most special person or the opportunity may be lost in your busy social life. Home influences are strong, and if you have been dreaming of a major purchase — of a home or for your home — this year is a good time to see the dream fulfilled.

SNAKE: 1917, 1929, 1941, 1953, 1965, 1977, 1989, 2001

This year will find the energetic Rat providing a wonderland of opportunities to the awakening Snake. Show your true self and be honest with those who care about you. This may be difficult for the Snake who is used to keeping tightly coiled, but there will be little need to use your venom to protect yourself this year. Happiness will be abundant in relationships with friends and family as long as you can uncoil. Successful results in businesses, especially new ventures, lie ahead of you. Your ability to take quick, decisive actions and make the right decisions will be a great benefit to your career. This may lead you to some big opportunities that you will be ready to take advantage of. Curb the impulsive to spend unwisely. Earth influences favour conservative spending for the Snake, but with energy flowing so strongly, you may not be able to resist a quick buy that can turn out to be a mistake.

HORSE: 1918, 1930, 1942, 1954, 1966, 1978, 1990, 2002

The Horse is not happy to find the Rat in its barn. Distracted by the energy of the Rat, the Horse will be an easy prey to others. By nature, the Horse listens more to what the heart says, but this year it is the head that will give the best advice. Take comfort in the company of close friends and family and also make sure to exercise, eat well and keep a regular schedule. These will weave a blanket that protects you from the blasts of ill fortune and physical distress that the Rat year can bring. Try not to let your nervousness cause conflicts at home and work. This is not a time to start new ventures or make major decisions. Plans for the future are the way to take advantage of your time. Building knowledge about your career through job training or education will move you ahead without danger. Plan inexpensive, relaxing vacations with friends and family to clear your confusion and find peace.

SHEEP/GOAT: 1919, 1931, 1943, 1955, 1967, 1979, 1991, 2003

The Rat year brings romance for the Sheep that may be true love, but overall, the year will seem less positive than what you may be used to. The year may see unhappiness in romantic relationships. Accepting your part in the disharmony will help to return happiness. In this area, your family may be part of the problem. A trip to a faraway land brings calm back to your love life, but beware of seeming to promise more than you are willing to give. Foolish decisions in the early part of the year can bring ill fortune for this cycle. Seek the advice of family and trusted friends before making hasty decisions about money or career. There are many opportunities but choosing the best path is important. The Rat offers chances for learning and culture. Looking at the past or cultures that are different from your own may lead to knowledge that will bring success in personal and business ventures. Find a group that will offer you the chance to talk about these things. Travel to new places adds to the good fortune and gives you a chance to spend energy in growth instead of following roads that will lead to dead ends.

MONKEY: 1920, 1932, 1944, 1956, 1968, 1980, 1992, 2004

The Monkey who has worked hard will see many rewards in the Year of the Rat. The year may start off slowly, but by the end of March, the full richness of the Rat year will be evident and will continue through the year. The battle of Earth and Water can bring confusion. Tolerance helps you to avoid making enemies by judging friends or co-workers too harshly. Overall, the Rat is a good friend to the Monkey and provides many chances to find good fortune in love and in your career. Take your time to pick the best of these. Avoid the temptation to spend unwisely. This is a year for saving, not spending. The right decisions will see the foundation of a comfortable nest egg building during the rest of the cycle. Enjoy your good fortune.

ROOSTER: 1921, 1933, 1945, 1957, 1969, 1981, 1993, 2005

The Rooster will find many challenges to overcome during the Rat year. Energy is high, but much of it is not positive and there is stress ahead for the Rooster. Quick decisions and emotional outbursts will lead to trouble. Keep a positive attitude and pace yourself. Make a plan for your time and your money, and stick to it. Relationships will be unsteady if the crowing Rooster shows aggression. When that urge appears, step back and use your strong intellect to analyse the problem and create a positive outcome. Matters of money and career will also need this steady approach. The Rat year favours learning and you can overcome many negative aspects at work by seeking training and sharing your knowledge with co-workers. Remember that what you do this year will follow you throughout the cycle, so keep that positive attitude intact and build a foundation for the upswing in your fortunes in the coming years.

DOG: 1910, 1922, 1934, 1946, 1958, 1970, 1982, 1994, 2006

The Dog continues to find good fortune as the Rat opens a new cycle. Family and friends are more important than ever this year, but avoid pressure from this source on business and financial decisions. Relationships that began in the Pig year may be a source of good fortune in this new 12-year cycle. Don't be afraid to let superiors and co-workers see your skills. Accept both the praise and advice that comes to you from this source. Keep your focus as you may find yourself drawn to chasing the Rat, but don't be timid when the time comes to make decisions that will bring change and good fortune.

PIG: 1911, 1923, 1935, 1947, 1959, 1971, 1983, 1995, 2007

The Pig still enjoys the benefits of good fortune as the new cycle begins. The Fire Pig, those born in 1947 and 2007, will be especially fortunate in the Year of the Earth Rat, but anyone born in a Pig year will find the Rat year bringing good fortune. This year promises success in romance and there may be marriage in the year ahead. Finances are no problem for you this year, but be careful of those who would take advantage asking for loans or applying pressure for you to make a major purchase or investment. Steady work will move your career into places you had not expected. Be open to the energy and excitement that this new cycle brings, but conserve your physical strength. There is a Pig tendency to push too hard. There is no need to exhaust yourself in seeking prosperity — especially in the second half of the year.

GLOSSARY

GLOSSARY OF TERMS

Annual Star: In Lo Shu, Magic Square or Flying Stars, the number in the centre is called the Annual Star. In a Flying Stars Chart, the energy or quality of Chi is represented by a number called a star. The Annual Star moves in cycles to a different location each year.

Arrows: Secret Arrows or Poison Arrows symbolize killing energy or bad Feng Shui (pronounced as Fung Shway). The arrows may be sent by structures in the landscape or by furniture placement in the home (such as sharp corners pointing at you or even a T-intersection outside your front door).

Auspicious: A term frequently used in Feng Shui to denote favourable, desirable, and beneficial influences and successful results.

Azure Dragon, also called Green Dragon: A symbolic animal of the Form School and one of the four Landform Guardians. In the ideal cradle or armchair position of the Form School, it refers to rolling hills, trees, or structures that support and protect a building on the left side of the armchair. Before the compass was invented, it was a way to describe the left direction.

Bagua, also Ba Gua, Pa Kua, Pakua: A diagram from *The I-Ching,* Bagua is one of the main tools used to analyse the Feng Shui of any given space. Translated from Chinese, it literally means "eight areas". It has eight external sections and the central one is called the Tai Chi. Each of the eight sections have a trigram name, and references a specific compass direction, number, element, season, colour, various body organs, family member, symbol and aspect of life aspects. The Bagua can be drawn in many different forms and is a tool for most schools of Feng Shui. Simply stated, Bagua is the energy map of any given space that gives you guidance on creating the most harmonious energy flow in your space.

Ba-Gua Mirror: An octagonal mirror that contains the Eight Trigrams, the Ba-Gua Mirror is used by some forms of Feng Shui to deflect negative Chi (for example, poison arrows) and circulate the Chi to prevent it from stagnating. The Ba-Gua Mirror is a powerful Feng Shui cure that is very often misused. First, it should never, ever be used indoors. Second, you will need it only if there is dangerous, sharp, or attacking energy (called Sha Chi) coming towards your house or business. The Ba-Gua Mirror is not a décor element and should not be used as such. The Ba-Gua Mirror comes in both concave and convex forms in either red, green and gold colour designs or yellow, black and red. If you do find yourself in a position to protect your space from potentially dangerous situations, such as the above mentioned Sha Chi (sharp or attacking structures pointed at your building), or bad neighbours, you may choose to use the Ba-Gua Mirror.

Balance (also see Yin/Yang): Feng Shui is about balance and harmony. When we live or work in a good atmosphere, we prosper. When we live or work in a hostile environment, we struggle. Negative and positive energies are in every aspect of our lives. Harnessing these and understanding the role each one plays leads to unification (leading to harmony).

Ba Zhai, also Yigua, Eight House, Eight Mansions, or East/West School: It is the most basic and popular method of determining and regulating Chi in Compass School Feng Shui. First, the sitting and facing directions of a structure are determined. Then the four most auspicious and four least auspicious sections for the space are calculated, each having specific influences on the Chi of a space.

Bazi: Refers to Four Pillars of Destiny, but literally means eight (Chinese) characters.

Beams: Exposed beams can be bad Feng Shui. They represent load-bearing weight and can affect health. Contact a Feng Shui Practitioner for assistance if these are exposed.

Bells: The brass bell is used for clearing, protection and activation. Hang bells from an entrance door to "announce" anyone entering. Their beautiful sounds also deter and distract any bad energy from entering the premises.

Black Tortoise, also Black Turtle: The symbolic animal of Form School is the most important of the four Landform Guardians. In the ideal cradle (or armchair position) of Form School, it refers to hills, mountains, trees or other structures that support and protect a building from behind. In ancient traditions, it was best located in the North. This was based on the climatic conditions of China where the cold winds came from the North. In modern times, it can be located in any direction as long as it provides the supportive back needed for the building. The same principles can be applied inside the building for orienting furnishings (especially orientation of the bed).

Bookshelves: Books that are crammed together create stagnant Chi. Avoid placing bookshelves where corners are directed at anyone. Bookcases should be free of clutter. Exposed shelves without books are symbolic blades and cause Sha energy.

Bright Hall: See Ming Tang.

Cardinal Points: The four primary compass directions: North, South, East, and West.

Celestial Animals: The four celestial animals are the Red Phoenix, Green Dragon, White Tiger and Black Tortoise. Each animal represents a different Earth quality or energy. They also represent landforms.
The front of a building (typically the smallest area of a premises) is

symbolized by the Phoenix. The rear (typically the largest area) is governed by the Tortoise. Standing inside the building facing the front, the Dragon needs to be to the left (and takes up the second largest area of the premises). This leaves the Tiger on the right (second smallest area of the premises). If any of the celestial animals are missing or not in their respective areas, there are negative consequences. Consult a qualified Feng Shui Practitioner.

Certified Feng Shui Practitioner: A Feng Shui Consultant who has achieved a certain level of expertise and/or received a Certificate of Achievement or completion from a Feng Shui school. Please note, while there are exceptional schools, there isn't any national standards as to what qualifies a practitioner and validates their level of expertise. A code of conduct, validation process, continuing education, etc, are all best practices for further development that are undertaken by Feng Shui professionals.

Chi: Dragon's Breath, the life-giving forces of the universe or the Universal Energy in Feng Shui. It is the energy that permeates everything around us. This applies to the energy inside our body, inside the buildings (home or business), as well as outside. Feng Shui concerns itself with the movement and manipulation of Chi with the goal being to create a more positive life experience.

Chi Cultivation: Techniques (like meditation, Qi-Gong and Tai Chi or other rituals such as Acupuncture) and Feng Shui are used to enhance or adjust personal Chi, allowing it to flow smoothly throughout the body.

Chinese Astrology: Refers to a group of divination techniques first used in China, based on astrological (or cosmological) assessments. The most common form assigns a person a zodiac animal based on their natal year as determined by the Chinese lunar calendar. This term also refers to several other methods commonly used in Feng Shui, including Four Pillars of Destiny, Nine Star Ki, Ming Gua, Ba Zhai, Zhi Ping, Purple Star and Flying Stars.

Chinese New Year: When the solar calendar is used, this event happens during the first week of February (typically the 4th or 5th). When the lunar calendar is used, this event happens during January or February and coincides with moon cycles. Determining the start of the New Year is essential in the calculation of several divination techniques used in Feng Shui.

Chueh Ming or Success Din: The severed fate or total loss location. The most inauspicious location in Eight House Feng Shui.

Classic Feng Shui, also called Traditional Feng Shui: The most widely practised category of Feng Shui worldwide. Based on the two original types first used in China, Classic Feng Shui consists of Form School and Compass School principles. Contemporary Classic Feng Shui is related to, and utilizes a variety of modalities that include the directional use of the Bagua, Ming Gua method, Ba Zhai method, Four Pillars, Flying Stars and more.

Controlling Cycle: Also known as Five-elements Controlling Cycle, Dominating Cycle, or some refer to it as the Destructive Cycle (but we don't destroy energy, it just transforms). For example, Metal pierces Wood, Water diminishes Fire.

Corners: Straight lines are foreign to nature, so when two straight lines intersect, this is a powerful manipulation of nature energy. Corners are considered bad Feng Shui as they disrupt healthy Chi flow by sending negative energy. If corners "cut" at people in front of them, this energy needs to be remedied or deflected.

Corridors: Long, straight corridors act as arrows projecting Sha Chi and can symbolize harm or relationships (healthy Chi has nowhere to accumulate). Creating flow by inserting distractions or lights is the remedy (insert distractions or lights).

Cosmic Breath (see also Chi): The motivating life force also called "Cosmic Breath", "Prana" or "Dragon's Breath". It has also been referred to as vital energy, primordial breath, air, breath, and energy. Existing everywhere, it is the term that refers to all forms of energy and its flow. Feng Shui concerns itself with the movement and containment of Chi to create the most beneficial support for a person in their environment.

Crimson Phoenix, also called Red Bird: A symbolic animal from Form School, and one of the four Landform Guardians. In the ideal armchair position of Form School, the Phoenix refers to any low hills, walls, or water features that support and protect the front of a building. It lies in the South compass point and is represented by summer and the colour red.

Crystals: Semi-precious and/or geological stones (such as amethyst or jade) that attract and amplify energy through diffusion of light.

Cure: Some people believe cures are objects, talisman rituals, prayers, actions or intentions used to achieve balance, harmony, and beneficial Chi in a space. Classic Feng Shui, however, only uses the five elements to support, suppress, neutralize or dissipate negative energies (or Sha Chi).

Cycles: There are three cycles used in Feng Shui. 1) The Productive Cycle works clockwise on the element chart. It represents order and balance. Fire produces Earth, Earth produces Metal, Metal produces Water, Water produces Wood, and Wood produces Fire. 2) The Reductive Cycle reduces the power of the dominant phase and is used to minimize negative or dominant Chi. Fire burns Wood, Wood absorbs Water, Water corrodes Metal, Metal moves Earth, and Earth reduces Fire. 3) The Dominating Cycle is exactly that, works by phases, dominating each another. Fire melts Metal, Metal pierces Wood, Wood burdens Earth, Earth blocks Water, and Water diminishes Fire.

Divination: The art or practice that seeks to see or foretell future events or discover hidden knowledge or information by means of intuitive powers, reading omens, and/or use of a tool or interpretation of external objects. Divination is a universal cultural phenomenon that anthropologists have observed as being present in every religion and culture throughout history right up to the present day.

Doors: The size, position and number of doors of a house are important factors in Feng Shui. The front door is especially significant as it is the main point of entry for Chi. It should not be obstructed or too small and should not be positioned to face hostile structures like crosses or/and arrows. Bathroom and toilet doors should remain closed, and doors should not face each other if possible.

Double-Facing: In a Flying Stars Chart, double stars meet in the facing palace. For example, in a cycle-eight structure, both the water eight and mountain eight reside in the facing palace. The energies for this structure are said to be good for wealth but not for health or relationships.

Double-Sitting: In a Flying Stars Chart, double stars meet in the sitting palace. For example, in a cycle-eight structure, both the water eight and mountain eight reside in the sitting palace. The energies for this structure are said to be good for people and health, but not good for money.

Earth Base Star: In a Flying Stars Chart, the energy or quality of Chi indicated by a number representing the birth (closing of the roof) of a structure within a prescribed 20-year time cycle, enclosing the Earth energies of that time period into the structure.

Earthly Branches: 1) Refers to the 12 energies and 12 archetypes, specific divisions in Time and Space offering information about the quality and movement of Chi. The Earthly Branches and the Heavenly Stems are the two primary components of the Four Pillars method and appear as a ring on the Lo'pan compass. 2) The 12 animals of the Asian zodiac.

East/West System: Part of Eight-house Feng Shui. People and buildings are divided into two types, the East Group and the West Group, using the Later Heaven Bagua sequence. See East Life and West Life.

Eight Characters Eight-house Feng Shui, also Eight Mansions (see Four Pillars): Dividing the house into nine sections of the Lo Shu grid determines the four most auspicious and four least auspicious directions and activities for both the person and the building (excluding the centre).

Eight Trigrams: The set of trigrams used to make up the Pa Kua. It is a symbolic representation of the family, time, and seasons. The eight possible combinations of symbols consisting of a combination of three Yin (broken) or Yang (solid) lines. Each trigram is associated with phenomenal aspects of the world expressed as a direction, an element, a number, an organ, a colour, a family member and other life aspects, and makes up the essential components of "Eight House" or "Eight Mansions" Feng Shui. Each trigram is a coded description of a quality of Chi. The Eight Trigrams are an essential component of all Baguas used in Feng Shui and can appear in two different versions: the "Early (Pre) Heaven Sequence" and the "Later Heaven Sequence". When stacked in pairs, hexagrams are formed, creating the 64 combinations of the I-Ching.

Electromagnetic Field (EMF): Whenever electric current (voltage) is running through a wire or a conducting source, an electric field is present in space. Where electric current flow is present, a magnetic field is produced. Over-exposure to excessive electromagnetic fields is harmful to health.

Elements: One of the foundations of Feng Shui theory is rooted in the interaction and balance between the Five Elements, which, in Chinese cosmology are Wood, Fire, Earth, Metal, and Water. Each of these elements governs a specific aspect of life.
Feng Shui is based on the interaction between these Five Elements. Finding a perfect balance for these five through placement is the key to good Feng Shui. Too much of an element can take over another, so be sure not to use too much or too little of an element.

Energy: The practice of Feng Shui concerns itself with the movement and quality of energy or Chi. Creating a healthy and positive flow of energy is said to enhance physical and emotional health and quality of life. The quality of energy is determined by its flow and the frequency of its vibration. By raising that frequency, we improve its quality and beneficial influence.

Facing: The direction that an individual or building faces. This typically represents where the strongest Yang energy is.

Feng Shui: An ancient Chinese practice of living harmoniously with the energy of the surrounding environment. It literally translates to "Wind and Water" and is the study of wind and water in the environment. The practice of Feng Shui is believed to be 6,000 years old. It is the art and science of harmonizing the person with their environment and heavenly influences.

Feng Shui Compass: The Feng Shui compass, also called Lo'pan, is used to access the following: Deeper information about a site or a building, such as the favourable and unfavourable parts and specific areas of the site connected to specific areas of people's lives. From its humble beginnings as a magnetic needle floating in a bowl of water, the Lo'pan evolved into a complex system of rings able to reveal advanced Feng Shui information. In its modern form, it has been translated and colour-coded to simplify its use as a Feng Shui tool. The Lo'pan is part of the rich cultural heritage of Feng Shui. It is also known as Luo-Pan.

Feng Shui Practitioner, also called Feng Shui Consultant: A trained professional who has studied and mastered the principles and practices of Feng Shui. The modern Feng Shui Practitioner is schooled in a variety of modalities hopefully originating in traditional practices. At a minimum, a competent practitioner is a graduate of, or certified by, a reputable school.

Five Elements: The interactive building blocks to life, namely, Water, Wood, Fire, Earth and Metal.

Flying Stars, also called Xuan Kong, a form of Compass School: The astrology of the building. A Flying Stars Chart is the horoscope for the building, describing its energetic condition over time. The Flying Stars method uses the sitting and facing directions of a building and its age (determined by the 20-year cycle in which it was constructed) to create the Flying Stars Chart, a numerological diagram. By studying the number combinations that are revealed in each of the eight sectors of the space, we are able to determine the state of balance and Chi for each. In addition, based on annual and monthly cycles, we can predict when good fortune and less-desirable circumstances are likely to occur. Remedies from the Five Elements (Fire, Wood, Metal, Water, and Wood) are used to balance the energies by reducing inauspicious influences and activating auspicious ones.

Flying Star Theory: A school of Feng Shui that examines the dynamic effect of Time.

Four Pillars: Month, day, year, and time. The year reveals information resulting from genes, health, aptitude and family background. The month reveals information resulting from parents, brothers, sisters, friends and school. The day reveals information resulting from your personality, ambition, appearance, interests, dreams and desires. Time reflects information about one's life: Marriage, family life, career, and successes.

Four Pillars of Destiny, also called Bazi, Zhi Ping: A horoscope derived from an individual's time, date and place of birth. A natal chart consists of four columns or pillars: A year pillar, month pillar, day pillar, and hour pillar. Each pillar contains a combination of animal archetypes and elements that through their interactions and inherent qualities describe the condition of the individual's Chi at birth.

Form School: The oldest method of Feng Shui, it was developed in Southern China several thousand years ago. This method stems from mountainous regions, and is a study of Chi flow through and over the topography (landforms). Its basis is to determine whether the Tortoise, Dragon, Tiger, and Phoenix appear in the terrain and how they interact. Good forms are needed to activate the elemental interaction of Flying Stars.

Fu Dogs: Ancient, mythical creatures that are part-dog and part-lion. A pair of male and female Fu Dogs placed at the entrance to a space act as protective guardians, allowing only benevolent forces to enter.

Fu Wei: The area within a building that controls overall harmony. When in balance, it brings good fortune and peace with a comfortable life. This location protects you against bad fortune.

Green Dragon: A symbolic animal of the Form School and one of the four Landform Guardians. In the ideal cradle or armchair position of the Form School, it refers to rolling hills, trees, or structures that support and protect a building on the left side of the armchair. Before the compass was invented, it was a way to describe the left direction.

Gua, also called Kua: Translates as house or sector. In Compass School, it refers to one of the eight quadrants connected to the eight compass directions. One of the eight outer positions in the Lo Shu square, the Bagua and the Lo'pan compass.

Hexagram: A symbol from *The I-Ching* made up of six solid or dashed lines formed from two trigrams. There are 64 hexagrams in the I-Ching, representing all known combinations of energies or correspondences. They are used to divine a probable course to future events, and read for their philosophical and inspirational insights.

Ho Hai: Represents an area within a building that causes accidents and mishaps such as financial loss or other problems.

Horoscope: A chart that is drawn using the time, location and cosmology aspects of the birth of an individual or building, to be used for the purpose of divination or gaining an understanding of hidden information.

I-Ching: One of the great Chinese philosophical texts, also known as the *Book of Changes*, describing all movements and developments of every event or phenomenon in the universe. It consists of 64 hexagrams based on combinations of the Eight Trigrams. *The I-Ching* has been used for divination and for philosophical guidance for thousands of years and is an important component in the formation of Feng Shui theory.

Inauspicious: Not favourable.

Kua Number: Different people have different energy needs. According to one of the Feng Shui schools called Flying Stars, there are two "energy" groups: East and West group. You will be either one according to your date of birth and gender. The East Group numbers are 1, 3, 4 and 9. The West Group Kua numbers are 2, 6, 7 and 8.

Lui Sha or Geo Ming: The area in a building that brings missed business opportunities, poor health or legal problems. It is a good place for a storage room.

Luo Shu, also called Lu Shu, Loshu, Lo Shu, Luo Shu grid, Magic Square: The foundation of all Feng Shui numerology. It is a three-by-three grid with a sequence of numbers said, in myth, to have been discovered on a giant tortoise shell. It is also called the Magic Square because any three sectors add up to 15 along any diagonal, vertical, or horizontal line.

Ming Gua, also called Ming Kua or Life Gua: A person's destiny trigram with its associated number, element, and life aspects, based on gender and year of birth; an astrological method of divination providing information about a subject, including the four most auspicious directions for the individual.

Ming Tang: Bright hall. The space in front of a site or house/building.

Mountain Star: Expressed as a number denoting the quality of Chi in a sector of a structure. The Mountain Star represents the sitting (rear) direction of a structure in Flying Stars Feng Shui, and is associated with people (health and relationships).

Natal Chart: See Four Pillars of Destiny or Bazi.

Nien Yen: Known as the rich descendant's area. When in balance, it improves family relationships, prevents arguments and solves problems. It is also good for the quality of home life.

Nine Star Ki: A form of divination similar to the Ming Gua method that uses the Eight Trigrams and all related information. It was made popular by the macrobiotic movement in the West. Although it is Japanese in origin, its use was adopted by many of the early Feng Shui Practitioners in the West. It differs from the Ming Gua method in that it uses the same calculations for both male and female subjects.

Palace: Name for each of the nine sections of the Lo Shu square (grid), used to calculate a Flying Stars Chart.

Period: A cycle of Chi, it is the primary requisite for construction of a Flying Stars Chart. This is the beginning process of the Time factor to determine the allocation of Chi throughout the structure. Some schools utilize the move-in date as the essential Time factor. The most widely recognized method is to use the construction date as the determining factor (and more specifically the closing of the roof). Each age or period lasts 20 years and begins on a four-ending year (ie, 1964, 1984).

Poison Arrow: A term that refers to sharp, hostile corners or objects both indoors and outdoors, that which causes an abundance of oppressive energy or Sha Chi to be directed at the inhabitants of a space.

Red Envelope Tradition: In Feng Shui, this refers to an exchange of red envelopes containing some amount of money between a client or student and a Feng Shui Practitioner or Teacher who has been asked for, and has provided, transcendental solutions. This tradition was developed to ritualize, respect and honour the information given, and to acknowledge the exchange of energy between the client and the practitioner. The number of red envelopes given is relative to the significance of the information provided.

San Yuan, also called Great Cycle of 180 Years: Refers to the three cycles of 20 years, each comprising one cycle of 60 years, and is the basis of Flying Stars Feng Shui. A particular Chi is prevalent during each 20-year cycle. These 20-year cycles are based on the cycles of the planets Jupiter and Saturn. Every 20 years they align, causing a major energy shift.

Sheng Chi (Beneficial Energy): Sheng Chi is the bright, refreshing, uplifting energy that is beneficial to your health and well-being. "Sheng" means upward movement energy.

Sha Chi and Si Chi (Harmful and Low Energies): Both Sha Chi and Si Chi come under the category of bad Chi. Sha Chi is also known as "killing" or "attacking" energy. It can be created outside by the sharpness of a structure (man-made or natural) that points to your main door or any of the windows. A house at the end of a T-junction will tend to accumulate Sha Chi because of the strong and constant attacking flow to its main door. Sha Chi can also be created inside the building. For example, a sharp wall angle pointing to your bed or work area will constantly emit attacking energy. In both cases, the proximity is important. The further the attacking element is located from you/your house, the lesser is its influence.
Si Chi is low, decaying energy, the energy that feels lifeless and dying. It can lead to illness and depression for those who are exposed to it for a certain amount of time.

Space Clearing: Refers to any method used to dissipate negative, stagnant, or inauspicious energy in a space, whether residual or current, and to raise the vibratory level, or Chi. Methods include the use of sound, incense, smudging, ritual, dance, pendulum techniques, or simply intention. Space Clearing sometimes refers to the mitigation of ghosts and spirits.

Three Harmonies method, also called San He: A method using the astrological 120 degree relationship to create harmonious relationships. There are sets of three compass positions 120 degrees apart, represented by their corresponding set of three animals of the zodiac that are in harmony with each other. This system is used to determine those with whom a person is astrologically in resonance, or harmony.

Tien Yi: An area within a building known as "Doctor from Heaven". This location cures illness and improves health. When in balance, it is the best location for you when ill.

Water Star: The star represented as a number denoting the quality of Chi that represents the facing direction (front) of a structure in Flying Stars. The Water Star is associated with the energies of money.

White Tiger: A symbolic animal of Form School that sits in the West and is one of the four Landform Guardians. In the ideal cradle or armchair position of Form School, it refers to rolling hills or other support to the right of a home, as well as autumn and the colour white.

Wind Chimes: A common Feng Shui remedy. Considered to create very positive Chi, wind chimes are appropriate in a number of circumstances. Metal chimes are often used where moving metal or strong metal is needed.

Wu Xing: This term has been conveniently translated as Five Elements or Five Phases, or the five types of Chi dominating at different times. Water dominates in winter, Wood in spring, Fire in summer, and Metal in autumn. At the intersection between two seasons, the transitional period is dominated by Earth. Common translations are five agents, five qualities, five properties and five courses.

Yang: The active polarity of the Yin/Yang concept. Yang is symbolized by light, activity, movement, rigidity, strength, and the masculine. It must always be balanced with similarly opposite levels of Yin energy. In the Feng Shui of homes and businesses, slightly Yang conditions are preferred. In the Feng Shui of cemeteries and mortuaries, slightly Yin conditions are preferred.

Yin: The passive polarity of the Yin/Yang. Yin symbolizes darkness, stillness, flexibility, weakness, and the feminine. Yin Chi, or energy, must be balanced in all situations by an appropriate presence of Yang energy.

Yin/Yang Theory in Feng Shui: The Yin/Yang Theory is one of the main theories of Feng Shui. According to it, everything in the universe consists of two opposing, but deeply interconnected forces: Yin (feminine) and Yang (masculine). The movement and interplay of these two forces creates all life around us. A concept from the I-Ching denoting the opposite polarities that came into being when the universe came into manifestation; the Taoist idea that unites all opposites as complementary inseparable forces.

ABOUT THE AUTHOR

Gita Kapoor is a Feng Shui Master who has studied under world famous Feng Shui Grand Masters Lillian Too, Yap Cheng Hai and Joey Yap of Malaysia. A firm believer that education in any science is a continuous process, Gita is engaged in consulting her teachers to acquire further advanced knowledge in the fascinating science of metaphysics and geomancy known as Feng Shui.

Gita started studying Feng Shui from her Grand Masters from July 2000. Till date, she has to her credit certified courses on advanced Feng Shui mastery studies including Xuan Kong (Flying Stars, Chinese Astrology (Bazi, Traditional Yi Jing/I-Ching), including Plum Blossom Numerology, Mian Xiang (Face Reading) and so on.

With the Period of 8 having begun from February 4, 2004, Gita is presently engaged in providing consultancy in existing residential and commercial properties and in the design phase of new buildings and additions. She ensures the well-being of her clients by offering valuable advice on the suitability of purchasing a certain plot of real estate.

Her clients include architects, interior designers, fashion designers, film stars, medical practitioners, entertainers, CEOs, attorneys, restaurateurs, Union ministers, senior bureaucrats, and large industrial houses. They rely on her ability to use Feng Shui to synergize their positive energies and harmonize their lives.

Gita studied at Welham Girls High School, Dehradun. Thereafter, she obtained a Diploma in Business and Office Management. Her work experience spans a large number of corporate companies in India, as well as an Oberoi hotel in Baghdad, Iraq. For the past twenty years, she is employed with The World Bank's office in New Delhi.

Gita Kapoor writes a weekly column on Feng Shui for the Sunday edition of *Delhi Times* and contributes to some other popular magazines. She is widely written about and has appeared on some television shows as well.